TAZIAR'S IN CULLINSBERG. . . .

As Harriman gave this news to Bolverkr, he felt the sorcerer's vengeance-twisted joy as his own.

Good. I've got plans for him and his companions. I want him to watch his girlfriend murdered and his friends hanged. Hurt him. But keep him alive, at least until the day past tomorrow. Bolverkr broke contact.

Fine. Misplaced hatred blazed through the refashioned and tangled tapestry of Harriman's thoughts, sparking ideas far beyond Bolverkr's intentions. Awash in bitterness, Harriman returned his attention to the thief who had brought him the news. "You're certain it's Taziar Medakan?"

"No question," the thief replied.

Taziar's no amateur. If I tell my people to abuse him, Taziar will play them like children. Besides, I'm not accountable for my lackeys' mistakes. Harriman met the thief's questioning gaze with a smile, then tossed a command to his two berserker bodyguards. "Kill Medakan. . . ."

DAW Titles by Mickey Zucker Reichert:

MICKEY ZUCKER REICHERT
THE BIFROST GUARDIANS #4

SHADOW'S REALM

DAW BOOKS, INC.
DONALD A. WOLLHEIM, PUBLISHER

375 Hudson Street, New York, NY 10014

First Printing, May 1990

1 2 3 4 5 6 7 8 9

PRINTED IN THE U.S.A.

For Dwight V. Swain
Who taught so many.
So well.

ACKNOWLEDGMENTS

I would like to thank Dave Hartlage, Sheila Gilbert, Jonathan Matson, Richard Hescox, D. Allan Drummond, Joe Schaumburger, our parents, and SFLIS for their own special contributions.

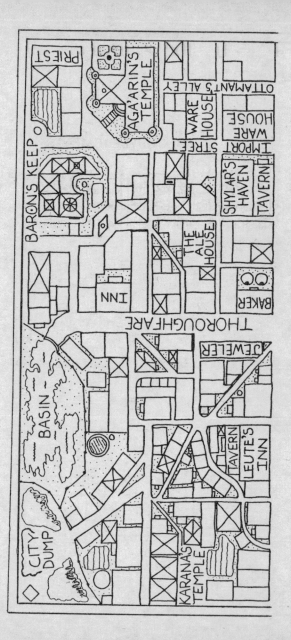

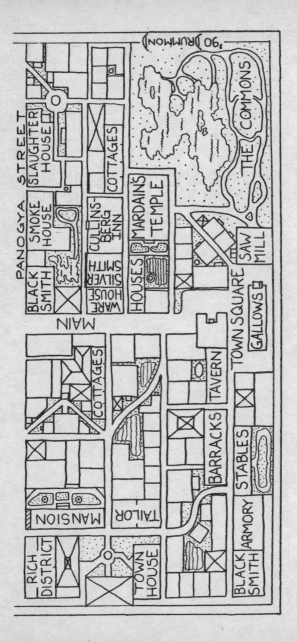

PROLOGUE

The sun rose over the eastern horizon, casting red high-lights across the pastures and grain fields of Wilsberg until the land seemed crusted with rubies. Atop a grassy hillock overlooking the village, the Dragonmage, Bol-verkr, sprawled casually across the doorstep of his man-sion. A breeze ruffled hair white as bleached bone, carrying the mingled smells of clover and new-mown hay. Clouds bunched to towering shapes or drifted to lace in the mid-autumn sky.

Bolverkr stretched, attuned to the familiar noise of the town he had considered home for his last century and a half: the splash of clay pots dipped into the central foun-tain, the playful shrill of children chasing one another through narrow, cobbled lanes, the metallic rattle of pans at the hearth behind him. The latter sound brought a smile to his lips. He twisted his head, peering down the squat hallway of his home to its kitchen. His young wife, Ma-gan, whisked from table to fireplace, black hair swirling around sturdy curves marred by the bulge of a womb heavy with child. She was dark in every way Bolverkr's Norse heritage made him light. *Beautiful. Sensitive to my needs as I am to hers. I picked a good one this time.* Bolverkr chuckled. *Two hundred seventeen years old, and I've finally learned how to select the right woman.*

The throaty low of a cow drew Bolverkr's attention to the southern paddock. A ribby herd of Cullinsbergen cat-tle chewed mouthfuls of alfalfa hay, browsing through the stacks with wide, wet noses. Chickens scurried to peck up dislodged seeds, muddied feathers matted to their breasts. Children, shirking chores, alternately tossed bread crumbs and pebbles to a flock of pullets, giggling whenever the birds flapped and fought over the rocks. From his world on the hill, Bolverkr studied the children's wrinkled homespun and their dirt-streaked faces, aware nearly all of them carried his blood at some near or distant point in their heritage. *Seasons come and go. Cottages crumble and are rebuilt. My grandchildren have spawned grandchildren. And the only constant feature of the farming town of Wilsberg is an old sorcerer named Bolverkr.* Contented by his musings and cheered by the promise of a clear day, Bolverkr eased his back against the doorjamb.

The Chaos-storm struck with crazed and sudden violence. Without warning, the clouds wilted to black, smothering the autumn sky beneath a dark, unnatural curtain of threat. A half-grown calf bellowed in terror. A startled woman flung her jar into the fountain, throwing up her arms in a gesture to ward away evil. The clay smacked the basin stones, shattering into chips that swirled to the muddy bottom. Frightened children fled for shelter. Before Bolverkr could raise his withered frame from the doorway, Northern winds knifed through the town of Wilsberg.

Bolverkr gaped, horror-struck, as the force raged through threadlike walkways, scooped up a handful of children, and hurled their mangled bodies like flotsam on a beach. One crashed into the fountain, slamming a gale-lashed wave of water over the peasant woman. A wall tumbled into wreckage, and the squall tore through Wilsberg like a hungry demon. It shattered cottages to rubble, whirled stone and thatch into a tornado force of wind. The fountain tore free of its foundation; the gale scattered its boulders through homes, fields, and paddocks.

The dragonmark scar on Bolverkr's hand throbbed like a fresh wound. Desperately, he tapped his life energy, twining a shield of magic over a huddled cluster of frightened townsfolk. But his power was a mellow whisper against a raging torrent of Chaos-force. It shattered his ward, claiming sorcery, stone, and life with equal abandon. It swallowed friends, cows, and cobbles, the may-

or's mansion and the basest hovel, leaving a sour trail of twisted corpses and crimson-splashed pebbles.

Bolverkr tossed an urgent command over his shoulder. "Magan, run!" Gritting his teeth until his jaw ached, he delved into the depths of his being, gathering life energy as another man might tap resolve. Holding back just enough to sustain consciousness, he fashioned a transparent, magical barrier of peerless thickness and strength. His spell snapped to existence, penning scores of townsfolk against the base of his hill. The effort cost all but a ragged shred of Bolverkr's stamina. Too weak to stand, he sank to one knee; a dancing curtain of black and white pressed his vision. Sick with frustration, he focused on shadows as panicked men and women bashed into the unseen shield, unaware they were safe from the onrushing winds.

Suddenly, sound thundered, pulsing through the village as if some wrathful god had ripped open the heavens. The gale-force burst through Bolverkr's shield. Once protected, the farmers now became prisoners of the spell. They ran for freedom, only to crash into its encumbering sides. Gusts heaved bodies against the solid remnants of Bolverkr's magic, smashing townsmen into gashed and battered corpses.

Bolverkr staggered to his feet, too weak to curse in outrage. Only one course remained to him, one power left to tap; but he knew it might claim a price equal to the otherworld storm he faced. He felt Magan's touch through the bunched cloth of his tunic. Ignoring his command to flee, she caught his arm, steadying him against the door frame with trembling hands. Raven-hued hair touched his cheek. Magan's abdomen brushed his hip, and he felt the baby's kick. In Bolverkr's mind, there was no longer any question. "Run," he whispered. "Please." He gouged his fingernails against the ledge for support, oblivious to wood slivering painfully into flesh. Head bowed, he fought down the natural barriers that shielded men's minds from the manipulations of sorcerers and began the sequence of mental exercises that would call unbridled Chaos to him.

Bolverkr knew nearly two hundred years had passed since any Dragonrank mage dared to draw power from a Chaos-source other than his own life energy. But, pressed to recklessness, Bolverkr drew the procedure from the cobwebbed depths of memory. His invocation began as a half-forgotten, disjointed mumble of spell words.

And Chaos answered Bolverkr. It seeped into his wasted sinews, restoring vigor and clarity of thought. The method of its summoning returned like remembrance of a lost love. His conjuration grew from a mental glimmer, to a verbal whisper, to a shout. Golden waves of chaos filled him, exultant and suffocating in their richness. Gorged with new power, Bolverkr laughed and raised his hand against the force that blasted grass from the hillside as it raced toward him like a living thing.

The storm, too, seemed to have gained intensity. It howled a song luxuriant with ancient evil, feeding off the same Chaos Bolverkr had mustered. Too late, the Dragon-mage realized the reason, and he shouted his defeat to winds that hurled the cry back into his face. At last, he knew his enemy as a renegade mass of Chaos-force. His rally had accomplished nothing more than luring the tempest to his person and opening his protections to its mercy.

The Chaos-force speared through Bolverkr, cold as Helfrost. He staggered, catching his balance against the door frame as the storm pierced him, seeking the soul-focus of his very being, itself the primal essence of the elements. Fire and ice, wind and wave, earth and sky swirled through his blood, beyond his ability to divine an understanding. It entered every nerve, every thought, every fiber, and seemed to rack Bolverkr's soul apart. It promised ultimate power, the mastery of time and eternity, control of creation and destruction, of life and death. It played him without pity, no more trustworthy than the Northern winds whose form it took. It suffused him with pleasure, drove him to the peak of elation and held him there, tied to a blissful swell of power.

For all its thrill, the tension grew unbearable. Bolverkr felt as fragile as crystal, as if his spirit might shatter from the power which had become his. Ecstasy strengthened to pain. He screamed in agony, and the Chaos-force transformed his cry into a bellow of wild triumph. Sound echoed through the wreckage of Wilsberg. Then Bolverkr exchanged torment for oblivion.

Bolverkr awoke with numbed wits and a pounding headache. From habit, he tapped a trifle of life energy to counteract the pain. The throbbing ceased. His thoughts sharpened to faithful clarity, bringing memory of the previous morning, and realization drove him to his feet. The sun shone high over the ruins of the farm town that had been his home. Straw and boulders littered the ground. Bodies lay, smashed beneath the wreckage, half-buried in mud, or hanging from shattered foundations of stone like the broken puppets of an angered child.

Tears filled Bolverkr's eyes, blurring the carnage to vague patterns of light and dark. Grief dampened his spirit, leaving him feeling awkward and heavy. Faces paraded through his mind: Othomann, the old tailor who had spent more time weaving children's stories than cloth; Sigil, a plain-appearing woman whose gentleness and humor won her more suitors than the town beauties. One by one, Bolverkr pictured the townsfolk, and one by one he mourned them. The shadows slanted toward sunset before he gained the will to move. Only then did he realize he still clutched a piece of his door frame in fingers gone chalky white. Slowly, he turned toward his mansion, heart pounding, deathly afraid of what he might find.

Through water-glazed vision, Bolverkr stared at the rubble of the mansion. Magically warded rock and mortar had crumbled as completely as the mundane constructions of peasant cottages. Half the southern and western walls remained, clinging to a jagged corner of roof. Gray fragments covered the hillock, interspersed with the occasional glimmer of metal coins and gemstones. Only splinters and shards of wood remained of Bolverkr's furniture, much of which he had proudly carved with his own hands.

A pile of rubble blocked Bolverkr's view of the single standing corner. He sidled around it, suddenly confronted by Magan's corpse. She lay in an unnatural pose, mottled white and purple-red. Flying debris had flayed her, chest to abdomen, and blackflies feasted on piled organs. Bolverkr felt as if he had been suddenly plunged in ice water. Horror gripped him. Mesmerized, he shuffled forward. His foot slipped in a smear of blood and flesh, and he stumbled. Flies rose around him in a buzzing crowd. Bolverkr twisted to see what had tripped him. It was another corpse, no larger than his hands and still connected to its mother by a bloodless umbilical cord.

With a frenzied sob, Bolverkr turned and fled. After three running strides, his heel came down on a craggy hunk of granite. His leg bowed sideways. Pain shot through his ankle. He fell, arching to avoid sharp fragments of stone jutting from the grass. Off-balanced, he crashed to the ground and rolled over the side of the hillock.

Bolverkr tumbled. Rock, wood, and bone bruised his skin. He clawed for a grounded rock or plant. Debris loosened by his attempts skidded toward the ground for him to bounce over a second time. Three quarters of the way down the side, his hand looped over a root. It cut into the joints of his fingers. Quickly, he released it, using the moment of stability to turn his crazed fall into a controlled slide. He jarred to a halt, facedown, by a pile of bodies. The air hung heavy with the salt reek of blood and death.

Bolverkr swept to a sitting position. His gaze flicked over the ruins of Wilsberg, and his tears turned from the cold sting of grief to the hot fury of anger. It had taken him fifty years to find the peace of a lifetime. Half a century of peasant distrust had elapsed in misery until one generation passed to the next and the children accepted Bolverkr as a kindly old man, a fixture on the hillock over their village. The term "Dragonrank" meant nothing to them; they were too far removed from the sorcerers' school in Norway to have heard of its existence. *To them, I served as a timeless oddity.* Bolverkr watched blood trickle across his palm, and though it was his own, it seemed to him more like that of the entire town. *So long to create the dream, and so quickly shattered.*

Thoughts raced through Bolverkr's mind, age-old memories of the crimes of his peers. He recalled how Geirmagnus, a man from the future with no magical abilities of his own, had discovered and taught the first Dragonrank mages to channel Chaos-force into spell energy. Then, the sorcerers had called volumes of Chaos from external sources, blithely ignorant of its cost. He remembered how the excess Chaos had massed, taking the dragon-form that gave the Dragonrank sorcerers their name, steadily growing, feeding off the Chaos they summoned for spells more powerful than any known before or since. One such feat gave Bolverkr and his peers the ability to age at a fraction of the rate of normal men. Too late, they realized their mistake. As the chaos-creature grew more powerful, nothing could slay it but the strongest Dragonrank magic. And the calling of Chaos for that magic served only to further strengthen the beast until its presence threatened to disrupt the very balance of the world.

Cruel remembrances fueled Bolverkr's rage. He blinked away the beads of water clinging to his lashes. The mad blur of corpses transformed in his mind to the faces of his ancient friends. He recalled how, in desperation, the mages had forsaken external Chaos sources for their own life energies. The younger sorcerers never learned the techniques of mustering Chaos. Their elders tried to resist marshaling the great volumes of entropy they had used in earlier days; but, having tasted of ultimate power, they slipped back into the old ways. All except Bolverkr. He alone remained true to his promise, and he alone the dragon spared. Singly and in groups, he watched his friends die, clawed to death by the chaos-creature's fury until Geirmagnus trapped it, though he was mortally wounded by Chaos in the struggle. The quest for peace brought Bolverkr to Wilsberg while the pursuit of knowledge drove the younger mages to found the Dragonrank school that Bolverkr had never seen. As generations of sorcerers came and went, he was forgotten or presumed dead.

That storm was no work of nature. Bolverkr's hands clenched to fists, and he stared at the blood striping his knuckles scarlet. Tendrils of Chaos-force probed through the breach he had opened in his mental barriers; where it touched, its power corrupted. Rage boiled up inside the sorcerer, fueled and twisted by the Chaos that had ravaged Wilsberg and, now, found its master. The seam blurred between the meager remnants of Bolverkr's natural life aura and the seeming infinity of Chaos, and it quietly goaded him as if it was the master and he the source of its power. It twisted his thoughts, filling gaps in information, leading to one conclusion: *Someone loosed Chaos against me, and that someone is going to pay!*

Bolverkr leaped to his feet, bruises and aches forgotten. He waded through the wreckage of Wilsberg, the sight of each familiar corpse invoking his ire like physical pain. By the time he reached the town border, Chaos roiled through his veins. A small voice cried out from within him, *Why me? Why me? Why me?* Then, the last vestiges of Bolverkr's grief were crushed, replaced by a blind, howling fury more savage than any he had known. Once a separate entity, the Chaos-force remained, poisoning his life aura, all but merged with it. Chaos promised spell-energy to rival the gods: death, destruction, and vengeances beyond human comprehension. It showed him shattered human skeletons on a shore red with blood, skies dense with tarry smoke, its breath lethal to the men of Midgard.

Not yet fully swayed to Chaos' influence, Bolverkr shuddered at the image, and horror sapped his anger.

Quickly, the Chaos-force amended its simulation, instead showing Bolverkr a clear night speckled with stars. Two men lay chained to a block of granite, their faces twisted by fierce grimaces of evil. Prompted by the Chaos-force, Bolverkr knew these as the men responsible for the destruction of Wilsberg. Understanding whipped him to murderous frenzy. He struggled for a closer look, but the Chaos-force teased him, holding the perception just beyond his vision. Bolverkr shouted in frustration, forgetting, in his rage, that a simple spell could obtain the same information. Instead, he raced without goal into the afternoon, seeking a target for his fury.

Once beyond the borders of the town, Bolverkr ran along a well-traveled forest trail; wheel ruts and boot tracks from the spring thaw dimpled its surface. Branches of oak and maple rattled in a light, autumn breeze, its gentleness a mockery after the tempest that had gutted Wilsberg. Shortly, the creak of timbers and the clop of hooves on packed earth replaced the rasp of air through Bolverkr's lungs. He paused, breathless, as a half-dozen wooden horse carts appeared from around a bend in the pathway. A man marched at the fore of the procession, his chin encased in a crisp, golden beard and his face locked in an expression radiating kindness and demanding trust. The horses appeared gaunt. A layer of grime stained their coats, but their triangular heads remained proudly aloft, ears flicked forward in interest.

Bolverkr knew the commander as Harriman, Wilsberg's only diplomat. He wore briar-scratched leather leggings beneath the blue and white silks that proclaimed his title. Returning from their quarterly trading mission to the baron's city of Cullinsberg, the men aboard the wagons laughed and joked, glad to be nearing their journey's end. The odor of alcohol tinged the air around them.

The Chaos-force seethed within Bolverkr, and he stumbled forward in blind, convulsive rage. Greedily, he seized its power, shaping it to a spell he had not attempted for over a century. Ignorance and lack of practice cost him volumes in energy, but he tapped his new Chaos power with ease.

Harriman's gaze fell across Bolverkr's tousled gray head and harried features. He signaled his men to a sudden stop. The wagons grated to a halt.

Grimly, Bolverkr dredged power through the self-made opening in his mind barriers. Chaos-force coursed through his body, wild as a storm-wracked tide. Driven by a once alien, Chaos-provoked need for destruction, he channeled its essence, calling forth a dragon the size of his ruined mansion. The beast materialized through a rent in the clouds. Sunlight refracted from scales the color of diamonds; yellow eyes glared through the afternoon mists. It struck with all the fury of its summoning. Unfurling leathery wings, it hurtled like an arrow for the wagons.

Harriman and his charges stood, wide-eyed, stunned by the vision of a monster from legend bearing down upon them. One screamed. The sound tore Harriman from his trance. Rushing forward, he drew his sword and thrust for the dragon's chest. It swerved. The blade opened a line of blood between scales. Its foreleg crashed against Harriman's ear. The blow sprawled the nobleman, and the dragon's wings buffeted him to oblivion.

Bolverkr quivered with malicious pleasure, hardened by the Chaos-force whose rage had become his own. A gesture sent the dragon banking with hawklike finesse. A horse reared, whinnying its terror to the graying heavens. Its harness snapped with a jolt, overturning the cart. Richly woven cloth was scattered in the mud, and the odor of spices perfumed the air. Another horse bolted, dragging a wagon that jounced sideways into a copse of trees where it shattered to splinters against tightly-packed trunks. Before the others could react, the dragon renewed its assault. Fire gouted from its jaws. The remaining wagons burst into flame, and the jumbled screams of men and horses wafted to Bolverkr like music. A man staggered from the inferno, his clothes alight, then collapsed after only two steps. At Bolverkr's order, the dragon whirled for another pass.

Again, the dragon swooped, spraying the burning wreckage with flame. Strengthened, the fire leaped skyward, an orange-red tower over the treetops, splattering cinders across a row of maples. A wave of heat curled the hand-shaped leaves. Branches sputtered. Wind streamed acrid smoke, stinging Bolverkr's eyes. The crackle of hungry flames replaced the pained howls of men and beasts. Soon, nothing remained but the diminishing blaze, unrecognizable, charred shapes, and the dragon circling the rubble, awaiting Bolverkr's next command.

Though no less potent, Bolverkr's Chaos-inspired rage became more directed. The identities of the men in his vision, the men responsible for his terrible loss, became as tantalizing as forbidden fruit. He dispelled the dragon with a casual wave. Turning on his heel, he left the fire to burn itself out on the forest trail.

Something stirred at the corner of Bolverkr's vision, and he went still with curiosity. His hard, blue eyes probed the brush, finding nothing unusual. The movement did not recur. Unused to the amount of power he now wielded, Bolverkr approached with the caution of a commoner. Raising a hand, he brushed aside hollow fronds. Stems rattled, parting to reveal Harriman, protected by distance from the dragon's flames. Blood splashed his short-cropped hair. The dust-rimed, blue silk of his tunic rose and fell with each shallow breath. Just beyond his clutched hand, his sword reflected highlights from the dying fire.

Bolverkr scowled. He hooked his fingers beneath Harriman's inert form and flipped the diplomat to his back.

Harriman loosed a low moan of protest, then went still.

Bolverkr's hand curled around Harriman's throat. A pulse drummed steady beats against his thumb, and he paused, uncertain. Despite his bold rampage against the trading party, Bolverkr was a stranger to murder. He explored the firm ridge of cartilage with his fingers, and the wild storm of Chaos eased enough to give him a chance to consider. *Surely I can find a use for a diplomat trusted by the highest leaders of our lands. Wilsberg was Harriman's home, too. No doubt, he will aid my vengeance.* Still influenced by the Chaos-force that had claimed him, Bolverkr did not deliberate over the unlikeliness of their association. Drawing on his new-found power, he wove enchantments over Harriman to dull pain and enrich sleep. Kneeling, he slung the nobleman's limp form over his bony shoulder, using Chaos magic to enhance his own strength and balance. As an afterthought, he retrieved the sword and jammed it, unsheathed, through his own belt.

Harriman's body thumped against Bolverkr's chest and the sword slapped his leg painfully with every step. His journey along the pathway became a taxing hop-step that transformed blood-lust into annoyance and calculation. Plans spun through Bolverkr's mind. Absorbed with his task, he'd nearly reached the edge of the forest before he realized he had no destination. Wilsberg lay ahead, strewn with the bodies of relatives and friends. Carrying Harriman to any other village would invite interference from healers and noblemen, and the woods held no attraction for Bolverkr. He realized he had unconsciously chosen the most appropriate home base. Despite its ghosts, Wilsberg was his town, molded through centuries of effort, and now it would become his fortress. Enemies who could raise a Chaos-force as fierce as the one that had claimed him would need to be studied, their flaws and weaknesses discovered and made to work against them.

The sight of corpses littering the shattered cobbles of Wilsberg's streets set Bolverkr's teeth on edge. Gone was the gentle compassion of Wilsberg's aged Dragonmage; the soft-spoken patriarch who protected the village of his children's children had died with his people. No mercy remained in the heart of this sorcerer forced to view the destruction of the world and loves he had created and nurtured through a century and a half of mistrust. Chaos transformed from intruder to friend; its threats became promises. Their relationship was that of lord and vassal, though a friend who had known Bolverkr in happier times might not have been able to tell which was master and which slave.

Bolverkr shuffled toward the wreckage of his mansion. The familiar features of every dead face became another murder attributed to the men the Chaos-force had revealed in distant images. Bolverkr judged each crime, found every verdict guilty. And he fretted for the time when he might serve as executioner as well.

Once atop the hill, Bolverkr dumped Harriman down

on a dirt floor polished by the unnatural winds. Beyond sight of Magan's corpse, he crouched and traced a triangle on the ground with the point of a jagged rock. Despite the expenditure of massive amounts of his own life energy, Bolverkr's aura still gleamed, nourished by the Chaos. Power surged through him, vibrant as a tiger and every bit as deadly. He channeled a fraction to the shape cut in the soil. Red haze warped its form. Gradually, it muted to a pattern of alternating stripes of green and gray, resolving, at length, into a clear picture of Bolverkr's enemies.

A forest of pine filled the frame, every needle etched in vivid detail. Branches sagged beneath white blankets of snow. Stiff crests of undergrowth poked stubbornly through layers of powder, not quite ready to succumb to autumn gales. Four people tromped across the openings left by dying weeds. One towered over the others. A bitter, Northern wind lashed his white-blond locks into tangles, revealing angular features. Bolverkr stared, uncertain whether to believe what his magics displayed. Pale brows arched over eyes the stormy blue of the ocean. An ovoid face with high cheekbones drew attention from ears tapering to delicate points.

An elf? Have creatures of Faery returned to Midgard? Bolverkr tossed his head and answered his own question. *Not likely. The townsfolk of Wilsberg knew nothing more of elves than they did of sorcerers. If either had become commonplace, rumors would surely have reached us from the North.* Guarded disbelief goaded Bolverkr to take a closer look. The countenance appeared undeniably elven, but their owner paced with the stolid tread of a man. His simple features seemed incongruously careworn, stark contrast to the lighthearted play of elves in Alfheim.

Uncertain what to make of the paradox, Bolverkr turned his attention to the other enemy within the vision of his spell. The elf's only male companion stood a full head shorter. A black snarl of hair fringed pale eyes alive with mischief. Calluses scarred his small hands, positioned on fingerpads rather than the palms the way a warrior's would be. Despite this oddity, both he and the elf wore swords at their hips.

In silence, Bolverkr studied the reflections of enemies brought strangely close by his magic. His concentration grew fanatical, and he stared until his vision blurred. Every detail of appearance and movement etched indelibly upon his memory until hatred drove him to a frenzy. A fit of venomous passion nearly broke the link between Bolverkr and his spell. The scene wavered, like heat haze quivering from darkly-painted stone. He hissed, reclaiming control. The image grew more distinct.

For the first time, Bolverkr turned his attention to the woman at the elf's side. Once focused, he found himself unable to turn away. A heavy robe hugged curves as perfect as an artist's daydream. She sported the fair skin and features of most Scandinavian women. But, where years of labor normally turned them harsh and stout, this woman appeared slim, almost frail. A gust swirled strands of yellow hair around her shoulders. Bolverkr had always preferred the darker, healthier hue of Southerners, but the beauty of this woman held him spellbound.

The elf hooked an arm around the woman's back with casual affection. Bolverkr's hatred rose again, this time with a knifelike, jealous edge. He forced it away. Beyond the conscious portion of his mind, a plan was taking form, a means to cause these enemies the same torment they had inflicted upon him. Though not yet certain of the reason, Bolverkr knew this woman must die. And, with dispassionate efficiency, he rejected his own desire. Only then did he notice the staff she held in a carelessly loose grip. A meticulous artisan had gravel-sanded it smooth as timeworn driftwood. Darkly-stained, it tapered to a wooden replica of a four-toed dragon's claw. A sapphire gleamed between black nails.

Dragonrank. Bolverkr leaned closer until his nose nearly touched his magics. His image reproduced reality with flawless definition. There was no mistaking the gemstone for one of lesser value. Bolverkr had followed the founding of the Dragonrank school closely enough to know the clawstones symbolized rank, the more costly the gem, the more skilled the sorcerer. A sapphire placed this woman just below master. Power even distantly approaching hers was almost singularly rare, but it did not surprise Bolverkr. *Behind any unnatural act of mass murder must stand a Dragonrank mage.*

Despite reckless squanderings of life energy, enough to have killed Bolverkr twice over without the added power of the Chaos-force, the edges of his aura scarcely felt dulled. He studied the woman more carefully. No longer fully absorbed by her beauty, he recognized the fierce glare of a vital, untapped life aura surrounding her. Nearby, a more sallow glow hugged the fourth member of this odd group. Though young and vibrant, her simple attractiveness paled beside her sapphire-rank companion. She stood shorter than any adult Bolverkr had ever seen, slighter even than her dark-haired consort. Her fine features swept into high, dimpled cheeks, and her mane of golden ringlets revealed a Northern heritage. She, too, held a dragonstaff, its ornament a garnet.

Bolverkr hesitated, his next course of action uncertain. Without the advance glimpse the Chaos-force had provided, he could not have centered his location spell on strangers. Even so, he could only visualize a limited range around them. A village sign within the area of his spell might have pinpointed their locale, but it would have been an improbable stroke of luck. Mid-autumn snow suggested Scandinavia. However, endless miles of pine forest covered Norway, far too much for Bolverkr to explore. *And I don't even know their names.*

For several seconds, Bolverkr wrestled with his quandary, the sustained sorcery draining Chaos energy like the endless trickle of water down a gutter spout. His gaze strayed to the wreckage of Wilsberg, and the sight of corpses piled where his own wards had trapped them against the hillock stirred guilt that raged to anger. He knew where to obtain the information he needed. *Somehow, I must enter one of their minds.* He pondered the idea, aware this plan must fail, but goaded by frustration. He knew that nature endowed every man of Midgard's era with mind barriers to protect them from sorcerers' intrusions. Only the minority of humans had enough cognizance of their own barricades to lower them for a dreamreader or mage to interpret nightmares or thought obsessions. *But one of my enemies is not a man.* Bolverkr explored this loophole with eager intent. *I've never heard of any mage breaking into or destroying mind barriers, but I've more power now than anyone before me. Sorcery always works best against other users and conceptions of its art, and the creatures of Faery are products of Dragonrank magic.*

Bolverkr grinned with morbid glee. He could not fathom the effect his attempt might have upon the elf. He had no previous experience to consider. He suspected it might plunge his victim into madness, perhaps kill him. At the very least, it would open his thoughts and memory to cruel manipulation. And the latter possibility caused Bolverkr to smile. He harbored no wish to take his enemies' lives. Not yet. He wanted to return the anguish they had directed upon him, if possible, ten times over.

Bolverkr gathered vitality to him, unable to guess how much energy this spell would require, but certain it would demand more than any other spell he had ever known or used. Supplying too little would cause the spell to fail; too much would cost Bolverkr his life. Once properly cast, the spell would claim as much of the Chaos-force and of Bolverkr's life aura as it needed, draining power too fast for him to control. Like any untried magic, it held the risk of requiring more stamina than he could feed it, of sapping him to an empty, soulless core. But Bolverkr never doubted. The Chaos-force seemed infinite, and its vows of service drove him to impulsive courage.

The location triangle faded as Bolverkr reared to strike. Braced for pain, he smashed into the presumed area of the elf's mental barriers. His attack met no resistance. Alien surprise flowed around him as he skidded through a human tangle of thought processes and crashed into the side of an unwarded brain. The elf's involuntary cry of pain reverberated in his own mind. Bolverkr's confusion mimicked the elf's in perfect detail. *No mind barriers? Thor's blood, no mind barriers!*

Bolverkr actually heard the sorceress' words with the elf. "Allerum, are you well?"

Ideas tumbled through the elf's mind, some leaking through Bolverkr's contact, others fully his own. *Did some god or sorcerer invade my mind again? Or did I burst a goddamned blood vessel?* Bolverkr went still, holding his emotions in check. He watched in fascination as the elf probed his own mind, ungainly and haphazard as a hen in flight. *My enemies are dead, and I've gone paranoid. No need to worry Silme.* The elf shaped his reply. "I'm fine. Just a headache."

No mind barriers. Bolverkr kept the realization to himself, careful not to allow his surprise to slip into the elf's thoughts. Alert to the elf's defenses, he began a cautious exploration of the dense spirals of thought. Only one other person in Bolverkr's experience had lacked the natural, mental protections. Geirmagnus, the man who unlocked the secrets of Dragonrank magic, had come to Midgard from a future without sorcery or the necessity for defenses against it. Bolverkr held his breath. Already, he detected incongruities. The elf's mind was decidedly human and flawed as well. Trailing along thought pathways thick as the deepest strings of a harp, Bolverkr found evidence of tampering. Someone had cut and patched blind loops and inappropriate connections. Others remained, frayed and easily sparked by stress.

With effort, Bolverkr resisted the urge to incite painful memories to torture the elf. Instead, he tiptoed through the intricacies of thought, collecting the information he needed for a full-scale attack. Through the elf's perceptions, Bolverkr learned the identities of his enemies. The elf knew himself as Al Larson, though his companions called him Allerum. The sapphire-rank Dragonmage was Silme, and Larson's love for her rivaled Bolverkr's for his slaughtered wife. The garnet-rank sorceress, Astryd, served as Silme's apprentice. Larson knew his little accomplice by the alias "Shadow." Further probing revealed his true name as Taziar Medakan.

Uncertain of Larson's abilities to police his mind, Bolverkr delved deeper with guarded enthusiasm. He focused on the ideas that brought Larson pleasure. Should Bolverkr accidentally trigger a memory, he hoped Larson would pass it off as fancy, and discovery of the elf's devotions would supply Bolverkr targets for attack. Eagerly, Bolverkr selected a childhood remembrance:

Thirteen years old, Al Larson perched on the ledge of a tiny sailboat beside a girl he knew as his sister. His bare feet dangled into a square-cut hold, and brackish water swirled about his ankles. A triangle of gaily-colored canvas spilled summer winds. The seal-smooth construction of the boat's hull looked like no material Bolverkr had ever seen. The gauzy fabric of Larson's swimsuit and the violently brash colors of the sister's bikini seemed similarly alien.

Suddenly, another craft whipped by Larson's, sail drawn tight to the mast. A middle-aged man with close-cropped yellow hair waved as he passed, and Bolverkr knew him as Larson's father. Behind the father, Larson's younger brother flung sunburned arms into the air with an excitement that caused the boat to rock dangerously. "Slowpokes!" he screamed.

Larson accepted the challenge. He hauled in the sheet, hugging winds into the shortened sail. The boat rocked to leeward as it sprang forward. The tip of the mast scraped the lake, then bounced upward, and icy water surged over the sides. With a short shriek of outrage, Larson's sister thumped to the opposite ledge to balance weight. The line bit into Larson's palms. Using his toes to anchor its knot, he hardened the sail to the mast. His boat caught and inched ahead of his father's, heeling almost parallel to the water. Spray drenched Larson. He laughed at his sister's shrill admonishments to free the winds.

An unexpected gust tapped the slight craft, and its sail brushed the surface of the lake. Quickly, Larson eased the canvas. The sailboat hovered momentarily, then capsized into cedar-colored waters, the sister sputtering, the brother and father laughing until their sides ached.

Bolverkr disengaged from Larson's memory. The scene confirmed his worst suspicions. Like Geirmagnus, Al Larson came from a future time and place. Bolverkr knew Larson's family would have served as the perfect target for his vengeance, but, with ruined hope, he also realized they dwelt beyond the abilities of Dragonrank magic to harm them. He recoiled in dismay and felt Larson grow alarmed in response. Quickly, Bolverkr regained control, masking his emotions with necessary thoroughness. *It's not over yet. There are other things a man grows to love.*

Bolverkr renewed his search with a malice that knew no bounds. He pried information from Larson's mind, discovered deep affection for Silme as well as concern for his other two companions. Bolverkr's efforts also uncovered a pocket of bittersweet grief. He dug for its source to find the remembered image of a samurai named Kensei Gaelinar who had served as a ruthless swordmaster and a friend. Some teachings of this warrior had convinced Larson that a whisper of his mentor's soul still resided in the finely-crafted steel of the Japanese long sword he had taken from the dead man's hands and now wore at his side.

Uncovering no other objects of comparable fondness, Bolverkr turned his attention to Larson's fears and hatreds. These he prodded with meticulous care, not wanting to reveal his presence in a wild induction of rage. He found orange-red explosions of light, noises louder than the nearest thunder, a savage, crimson chaos of future war Larson called Vietnam. Gory corpses with eyes glazed in accusation intermingled freely with the memory of Larson's own mortality. An oddly-shaped parcel of metal chattered like a squirrel grazed by a hunter's arrow as Larson charged enemies with a final, desperate courage. Oblivion followed, a pause of indeterminate length before a rude awakening in a strange elven body and an ancient time.

Larson stiffened. The recognition of an intruder's pres-

ence flowed through his mind, and a conjured mental
wall snapped over the exit. A tentative question followed.
Vidarr? Is that you? Bolverkr froze. When no attack followed, he relaxed. For now, he harbored no desire to
leave; he found the blockade of no significance. After the
consideration of violating biological barriers, a wall
manufactured from substance as ephemeral as thought
seemed a pitiful substitute. Treading more lightly, he
continued his search.

Bolverkr skimmed through Larson's memories, plucking tidbits with the graceful precision of an acrobat. He
found divine allies. These he dismissed, aware gods'
vows would not allow them to meddle in the affairs of
mortals. And among the deities, Bolverkr also discovered
enemies. He watched the elf's sword slice through the
spine of Loki the Trickster, saw Larson hurl the god's
body into the permanent oblivion of Hvergelmir's water-
fall. The corpse toppled through the Helspring, destroyed, as all things, by the magical braid of rivers that
plunged, roaring, from Midgard to Hel. No longer exis-
tent, even in Hel, Loki and the mass of Chaos he controlled were destroyed, tipping the world dangerously
toward Order.

Attempting to restore the balance and free another god
from more than a century in Hel, Larson and Taziar had
traveled to Geirmagnus' ancient estate. Through Larson's
memory, Bolverkr saw the ancient, imprisoned Chaos-
force released, its dragon-form towering to the heavens.
In horror, the sorcerer stared as Larson, Taziar, and Kensei Gaelinar slashed and stabbed at the creature. Bolverkr
saw the Japanese swordmaster dive through razor-honed
wire, killed in a desperate self-sacrifice that incapacitated
the Chaos-creature and bared its head to Larson's sword.
And Larson seized the opening, slaughtering the dragon-
form, apparently unaware that its now unbound Chaos
must seek a living master.

The personal tragedy of this finding burned anger
through Bolverkr. *Your stupidity destroyed me, and you'll
pay with everything you hold dear.* He imagined a teacher's long sword, its shattered pieces strewn across a

meadow stained with Silme's blood. Shards protruded from the scarlet haft Larson clutched to his chest, and his voice loosed the screams of a dying animal. Through the nightmare visions he created, Bolverkr relived his own grief. Yet, despite the temptation, he held his fantasy back from Larson's perception. The Chaos-force and its seemingly limitless power goaded him to recklessness and uncontrolled fury, but it did not make him foolish. Even after a century and a half of peace, he recalled two important rules of a sorcerer's war: never sacrifice surprise, and, when an enemy proves powerful, fight him on familiar territory.

Bolverkr retreated. He turned to the exit from Larson's mind, pleased to see the wall had already faded. Patiently, he waited until it disappeared completely. Stepping out, he immediately attempted to gain access to the minds of Larson's companions. Each effort flung him against natural mind barriers solid as stone. Briefly, he considered. To assault Taziar's mind here would violate both of the battle tenets he had just uncovered from memory. Instead, he slipped back into Larson's thoughts, digging for information about the elf/man's small companion.

Bolverkr's toil exposed a stormy childhood in the city of Cullinsberg. With effort, he dug out revealing shreds of information, most lodged in the deeper, subconscious portion of Larson's mind. Here, Bolverkr uncovered a name. There, he found an incident. In the end, he pieced together a patchwork history of the only son of an honorable and heroic guard captain, a son too slight in build to follow in his father's footsteps. A prime minister's treason against the elder Medakan had cost the captain his life and his honor, turning Taziar's carefree youth into a life of running, hiding, and living on the edges of society. It was this dishonorable stage of Taziar's life that gained him his closest friendships. Bolverkr seized every name he could glean from Taziar's revelations to Larson. And here, too, Bolverkr decided his plan of attack. *If I begin with the little thief's allies in Cullinsberg, I lure my enemies to the south. I have no measure of their true*

*power, but it encompasses at least enough to challenge
gods. Best to start my vengeance with something not currently in their possession.*

Something tugged at Bolverkr's hip. Engrossed in the
mind-link, he slapped at it idly. To his surprise, a sharpened edge sliced his palm. Pain and the warm trickle of
blood hurled him back into his own body on the hill over
Wilsberg. Harriman stood before him, clutching the
sword he had torn free from the belt lying, halved, at
Bolverkr's ankles. The sorcerer rolled more from instinct
than intent. The blade swept the ground, rasping off a
rock shard. Bolverkr managed to work his way to one
knee before Harriman lunged for another attack.

Bolverkr ducked, mouthing spell words with furious
intensity. The blade whistled over his head, and Harriman's foot lanced toward his chest. Desperation made
Bolverkr sloppy. His spell cost him more energy than
necessary. But a shield snapped to life before him. Harriman's boot struck magics as firm and clear as glass.
Impact jarred the nobleman to the ground. Surprise
crossed his features, then they warped to murderous outrage. He sprang to his feet and charged the shielded
Dragonmage.

Harriman's sword crashed against the unseen barrier.
Bolverkr saw pain tighten the diplomat's mouth to a line.
Undeterred, Harriman smashed at the magics again and
again until his strokes became frenzied and undirected.
"Why!" he screamed with every wasted blow.

Bolverkr waited with a stalking cat's patience.

At length, Harriman sheathed his sword, apparently
tired of battering his frustration against a barrier he could
not broach. "Why?" he shouted. His tone implied accusation rather than question.

Bolverkr rose, his sorceries still firmly in place. "Why
what?" he demanded.

Harriman gripped his hilt in a bloodless fist, but did
not waste the effort of drawing the blade again. "Why
did you . . . ?" He trailed off and started again. "Why
would you . . . ?" His broad gesture encompassed the
wreckage of the farming town of Wilsberg.

Suddenly, Harriman's misconception became clear. *By the gods, the fool thinks I destroyed the town.* Bolverkr shook his head in aggravation. "Don't be an idiot, Harriman. I didn't do anything, but I know who did. I need your help . . ."

"No!" Harriman shuffled backward. "You're lying! I saw you laughing when your winged beast attacked me. What have you done with my friends? *Did you kill them, too?*"

"Stop!" Bolverkr hollered in defense. "I attacked you in the same grief-frenzy you just displayed. I apologize for your companions; they died without fair cause. But I want your help against the murderers who slaughtered our kin."

Harriman shrank away. His dark eyes gleamed with disbelief, and behind Harriman's expressionless pall, Bolverkr suspected fear warred with anger. His voice went comfortably soft, soothing without a trace of patronage. "We're not barbarians, Bolverkr. Justice will be done, but it's for the baron of Cullinsberg to decide guilt and punishment. Come with me. I'm certain he'll listen to your story."

Harriman slipped into the role of diplomat with ease, but Bolverkr was too cagey to be taken in by platitudes. He realized his displays of sorcery would work against him. South of the Kattegat, men knew nothing of magic beyond a few mother's stories that sifted to them from Scandinavia. *Common men revile what they cannot understand. No one in Cullinsberg would question my guilt.* "Don't trifle with me, Harriman. Look around you. All our friends have died, massacred by strangers. My wife and child were not spared, but you were. What possible reason could I have for working such evil? If I caused this, why would I slay Magan and leave you alive?"

"I believe you," Harriman said. Though his tone sounded convincing, his sudden change in loyalty did not. "Please. Talk to the baron. He'll believe you, too."

Harriman's deceit angered Bolverkr. "Damn it," he raged. "Listen to what I'm saying! Think, Harriman. I didn't ravage the town. I fought to the last shred of my life to save it.''

Harriman opened his mouth to affirm his sincerity.

But Bolverkr made a curt gesture of dismissal. "Save your sweet deceptions for the baron. I can call dragons from the bowels of the earth and shields from midair. Don't you think I can read your intentions?" Bolverkr glared to emphasize his lie. The mind barriers rendered emotions as impossible to tap as thoughts, but Bolverkr doubted that Harriman knew that fact.

Apparently fooled, Harriman dropped all pretenses. His cheeks flushed scarlet and his expression went hard as chiseled stone. "Of course, I think you killed them. What else could I believe? You're no man; you're some sort of . . . of demon. You were old when my great-grandfather was born. You never caused us any harm before, so we learned to trust you, even love you. But nothing else could have done this." He gestured angrily at the ruins.

Harriman's words stung Bolverkr. In his rage, he forgot that his own insistence had inspired the nobleman to speak against him. "How dare you! I built this village, stone by precious stone. I lent my efforts to every labor, nursed the sick, brought prosperity to an insignificant dot on the landscape." He took a threatening step toward Harriman. "My wife and child lie dead! I'm pledged to avenge myself against their slayers. Are you with me or against me?"

Harriman cowered. He seemed about to speak, then went silent. He started again, and stopped. The inability to act as a negotiator seemed to unman him. Suddenly, he fled.

Caught off-guard by Harriman's unexpected flight, Bolverkr stood motionless for a startled moment. Dropping his shield, he followed the nobleman's course as he bounced and leaped over standing stones and corpses. "Stop!" Bolverkr shouted. "Harriman, stop. Don't force me to use magic." *If he reaches Cullinsberg, he'll turn the barony against me. He'll foil my vengeance!* The realization goaded Bolverkr to prompt action. And, though a more subtle spell might have sufficed, because of his success with Larson, an attack on mental protections came first to Bolverkr's mind. Gathering a spear of Chaos-power, he crashed into Harriman's mind barriers.

Bolverkr's probe met abrupt resistance. For a maddening second, nothing happened. Then Harriman's barrier shattered like an empty eggshell. The nobleman collapsed, face plowing into the dirt. Pain and surprise assailed Bolverkr. His screams matched Harriman's in timing and volume. He floundered in the fog of agony smothering Harriman's thoughts, shocked to inactivity by his own success. The nobleman's shrieks turned solo, but still Bolverkr stared in silent wonder. *How?* "How!" he shouted aloud. He had acted on a Chaos-stimulated impulse. In his centuries of life, he had never heard of anyone powerful enough to break through mind barriers, not even in the days when Dragonmages called on external Chaos sources.

Nonsentient, the Chaos-force did not speak in words. Instead, it drew upon the basest instincts of its master, allowing him to understand. *I wield more power, more Chaos, then any sorcerer or god before me. It's mine to tap freely, restored by the same rest that replenishes my own life aura vitality.* Bolverkr struggled with the concept, at once awed, excited, and frightened by it, irrevocably lusting for the same Chaos power that must ultimately corrupt him with its evil. Pain awoke when he attempted to contemplate the immensity of his newfound strength, and, in self-defense, Bolverkr held his goals to a comprehensible level. *Before I battle my enemies directly, I have to learn to handle my own power, to gain full mastery over this Chaos that has become my own. And I have to draw those enemies to me.*

Bolverkr surveyed the coils of memory composing Harriman's mind, now fully opened to him. Quietly, without further preamble, he set to his task.

CHAPTER 1:

Shadows of Death

Cruel as death, and hungry as the grave.
—James Thomson
The Seasons. Winter

The tavernmaster of Kveldemar hurled wood, glossed with ice, onto the hearth fire. It struck with a hiss, and smoke swirled through the common room, shredded to lace by beer-stained tables. Taziar Medakan blinked, trying to clear the mist from his eyes. His three companions seemed content to sit, sharing wine-loosened conversation, but restlessness drove Taziar until he fidgeted like a child during a priest's belabored liturgy. His darting, blue eyes missed nothing. He watched the tavernmaster whisk across the room, pausing to collect bowls from a recently vacated table. Flipping a dirty rag across its surface, the tavernmaster ducked around the bar with the efficiency of a man accustomed to tending customers alone. Not a single movement was wasted.

Taziar turned his attention to the only other patrons; a giggling couple huddled in the farthest corner, their chairs touching as they shared bowls of ale and silent kisses. Larson launched into a tale about two-man sailboats and a red-water lake, just as the outer door creaked open. Evening light streamed through the gap, glazing the eddying smoke. A middle-aged man stepped across the threshold. Dark-haired and clean-shaven, he seemed a welcome change from Norway's endless sea of blonds. Blinded by the glare, the stranger squinted, sidling around a chair. His soiled, leather tunic scraped against Taziar's seat with a high-pitched sheeting sound. A broadsword

balanced in a scabbard at his waist, its trappings timeworn like a weapon which had been passed down by at
least one generation. Depressions pocked its surface
where jewels had once been set in fine adornment.

Taziar had long ago abandoned petty thievery, but
boredom drove him to accept the challenge. With practiced dexterity, he flicked his fingers into the stranger's
pocket. Rewarded by the frayed tickle of purse strings
and a rush of exhilaration, he pulled his prize free. A
subtle gesture masked the movement of placing it into a
lap fold of his cloak. Taziar's gaze never left his companions. He saw no glimmer of horror or recognition on their
faces, no indication that anyone had observed his heist.
Apparently oblivious, the stranger marched deeper into
the common room and took a seat at a table before the
bar. The tavernmaster wandered over to attend to his new
patron.

Taziar frowned in consideration. The stranger's money
held no interest for him; having developed more than
enough skill to supply necessities for his friends, he had
lost all respect for gold. Only the thrill remained, and
much of his enjoyment would, in this case, come from
devising a clever plan to return the purse to its owner.
Taziar regarded his companions. Larson's words had
passed him, unheard. Patiently, Taziar waited until his
friend finished. Taking a cue from Silme's and Astryd's
laughter, Taziar chuckled and then claimed the conversation. ''Allerum, do you see that man over there?'' He
inclined his head slightly.

Larson nodded without looking. Aside from the engrossed couple, the tavernmaster, and themselves, there
was only one man in the barroom. ''Sure. What about
him?''

Taziar raked a perpetually sliding comma of hair from
his eyes. ''When I was a child, my friends and I used to
play a game where we'd guess how much money some
stranger was carrying.''

''Yeah?'' Larson met Taziar's gaze with mistrust.
''Sounds pretty seedy. What's it got to do with that
man?''

Taziar clasped his hands behind his head. "I'll bet you our bar tab I can guess how much he has within . . ." Unobtrusively, he massaged coins through the fabric of the stranger's purse. Some felt thinner, more defined than Scandinavian monies, unmistakably southern coinage. Having discovered familiar territory, Taziar suppressed a smile. ". . . within three coppers."

Larson's eyes narrowed until his thin brows nearly met. He shot a glance at the stranger. "From here?"

Taziar turned his head as if studying the common room. Ice melted, the hearth fire blazed, now drafting its smoke up the chimney. "Why not? I can see him well enough."

Still, Larson hesitated. Though accustomed to idle barroom boasts, he was also all too familiar with Taziar's love of impossible challenges. "All right," he said at length. "Make it within one copper, and I'll handle every beer between here and Forste-Mar."

Taziar stroked his chin with mock seriousness. "Agreed." He studied the olive-skinned stranger in the firelight. The man ate with methodical disinterest, occasionally pausing to look toward the door. "Hmmm. I'd say . . ." Taziar paused dramatically, defining coins with callused fingertips. "Four gold, seven silver, two copper. And the gold'll be barony ducats."

"Ducats?" Larson's gaze probed Silme and Astryd before settling on Taziar.

"Cullinsberg money." Under the table, Taziar hooked Astryd's ankle conspiratorially with booted toes. "The man looks like a Southerner to me."

Astryd answered Taziar's touch with a questioning hand on his knee.

Larson shrugged. "Very impressive. What do we do now? Ask the man?" He play-acted, catching Taziar's sleeve and yanking repeatedly on the fabric. "Excuse me, Mac. Excuse me. My friend and I have a bet going. You see, he thinks you've got four gold, seven silver, and three copper . . ."

"Two copper," Taziar corrected. "And that won't be necessary." He retrieved the purse and tossed it casually to the tabletop.

Larson made a strangled noise of surprise, masking it with a guileless slam of his hand over the purse that drew every eye in the tavern. Silme clapped a hand to her mouth, transforming a laugh into a snort. Astryd's fingers gouged warningly into Taziar's leg.

Apparently, Larson's crooked arm adequately covered the stranger's property. Within seconds, the tavernmaster and his other patrons returned to their business, but Taziar knew the matter was far from closed. Relishing his companion's consternation, Taziar drained his mug to the dregs.

Larson's voice dropped to a grating whisper. "You ignorant son of a bitch."

"Son of what?" Taziar repeated with mock incredulity. When angered, Larson had an amusing habit of slipping into a language he called English.

"Jerk," Larson muttered, though this word held no more meaning to Taziar than the one before. "You cheated."

"Cheated." Taziar smirked. "You mean there were rules?"

"Damn you!" Larson raised a fist to emphasize his point. He tensed to pound the table. Then, glancing surreptitiously around the barroom, he lowered it gently to his wine bowl instead. "You get insulted when I call you a thief, then you pull something stupid like this! We don't need more trouble than . . ."

Taziar interrupted. "I'm no thief," he insisted.

"Then why did you take this?" Larson lowered his eyes momentarily to indicate the purse still tucked beneath his palm.

"Sport." Taziar shrugged, his single word more question than statement.

"Sport!" Larson's voice rose a full tone. "Let me get this straight. We capture a god in the form of a wolf and battle a dragon the size of Chicag—" He caught himself. "—Norway. As an encore, we face off with a Dragonrank Master holding a bolt action rifle. You're still limping from a bullet wound, for god's sake! Forgive me if you find my life bland, but isn't that enough excitement for you?''

"That was more than a month ago." Taziar's voice sounded soft as a whisper in the wake of Larson's tirade.

Larson passed a long moment in silence before responding. "You're insane, aren't you?"

Taziar grinned wickedly.

The women exchanged glances across the table. Silme's lips twitched into a smile, and she bit her cheeks to hide her amusement.

"You think this is funny, don't you?" Larson's tone made it plain he did not share his companions' glee. "And even you may think it's funny." He jabbed a thumb at Silme who wore an unconvincing expression of bemused denial. "But shortly, that man over there is going to try to pay for his meal. He'll find his money missing; and, if he's half as smart as a chimpanzee, he'll look here first."

"A chimp and Z?" Astryd repeated, but Larson silenced her with an exasperated wave.

"I doubt he's got an attorney. In your lawless world of barbarians, he'll talk with his sword. You're too damned small to bother with." Larson glared at Taziar. "So, I'm going to die because you're crazy. Or perhaps, my dying is your idea of sport. Well, forget it." Larson leaped to his feet. "I'm giving it back."

Before Larson could take a step, Taziar hooked his sleeve with a finger. Mimicking the elf's Bronx accent, he tugged at the fabric, reviving Larson's earlier playacted scenario. "Excuse me, Mac. Excuse me. Your purse just happened to fall out of your pocket. I'd like to return it."

Larson hesitated. "What the hell am I doing?" He retook his seat and jammed the pouch into Taziar's hand. "You're the one who wanted sport. You took it. You put it back."

Taziar rose and bowed with mock servility. "Yes, my lord. At once." He twisted toward the stranger's table, and, despite his facetious reply, he examined the man with more than frivolous interest. The tavern contained too few patrons to hide the antics of one. But the inherent danger of Larson's dare made it even more attractive to Taziar, who had intended nothing different.

A hand tapped Taziar's shoulder. He whirled to face Larson. The elf's features bore an expression of somber concentration. "If you get caught, and he kills you before we can stop him, I just want you to know one thing."

Taziar nodded in acknowledgment, the possibility a particularly unpleasant consequence but one he could not afford to dismiss. "What's that?"

"I told you so."

Taziar snorted. "Jerk," he replied, borrowing Larson's insult. He shook the knotted lock of hair from his eyes and turned back to study the common room. No object passed his scrutiny unnoticed. Two tables, each with four chairs, stood between the stranger's seat and his own, the narrow lane they formed comfortably passable. Beyond the man, a table sat in the opposite corner from the door. Beside it, at a diagonal to the stranger, a cracked, oak table occupied a space beside the one with the engrossed couple near the hearth. Someone had crammed six chairs around the flawed table, though its area was constructed to support only four. The corner of one chair partially blocked the walkway, its legs jammed crookedly against its neighbors.

Taziar feigned a yawn. He stretched luxuriously, splaying callused fingers to work loose a cramp. Not wishing to draw attention by pausing overlong, he trotted farther into the barroom. Skirting the dark-haired stranger, he seized an extra chair from the overcrowded table and spun it toward the couple. His action knocked the misplaced chair further askew. Still standing, he leaned across the back of his seat and spoke to the boy in strident, congenial tones. "Ketil! Ketil Arnsson. I thought it was you." Framing a knowing smile, he tipped his chin subtly toward the girl. "Does your mother know you're here? And what are you doing this far from home?"

Startled, the youth released his partner's hand. "But—but I'm not . . ."

Taziar interrupted before he could finish. "How's the

apprenticeship going? I saw your father yesterday, and he said . . .''

The youth pushed free of his girlfriend. ''Please, sir, my name's Inghram. Kiollsson.''

Taziar continued as if the boy had not spoken. ''He said you'd been spending more time . . .'' He stopped suddenly, as if the boy's words had finally registered and slouched further over the rail for a closer look. ''Inghram?'' he repeated.

''Kiollsson,'' the boy finished.

Taziar straightened, working embarrassment into his voice. ''Oh. I'm sorry. I thought . . . I . . .'' He backstepped. Though the movement appeared awkward, Taziar knew the precise location of every stick of furniture. ''Not Ketil. How did I . . . ?''

Soothingly, the girl spoke in an obvious attempt to help Taziar save face. ''A natural mistake. We don't mind.''

But Taziar acted even more distressed by her comforting. He spun, taking a harried step toward his companions. Carefully executed to appear an accident, his foot hooked the leg of the displaced chair and his thigh struck its seat. The chair toppled, taking Taziar with it. He crashed to the floor, suffering real pain to keep his performance convincing. Momentum slid him and the chair across the polished floor. Gracelessly, he tried to rise. But still entangled in the chair, he lurched toward the stranger, wadding the purse into his fist.

Taziar slammed into the man. Berating his clumsiness with profanity, Taziar used his body to shield his actions from the other patrons. He flicked the pouch into the stranger's pocket. Too late, he realized he had chosen the wrong pocket. But, before he could correct the error, the stranger leaped up, catching Taziar by the wrist and opposite forearm. The purse fumbled, balanced precariously on the edge of the pocket. Taziar stared in horror; his heart rate doubled in an instant.

The stranger's grip tightened. He lowered his head and pulled Taziar to within a hand's breadth of his face, as if memorizing his features. Belted by the odor of onions and ale, Taziar resisted the urge to sneak a look at the teetering pouch of coins. He tried to read the man's intentions, but the blankness of expression did not quite fit the tenseness of the stranger's hold on Taziar. *Allerum, are you blind?* Suddenly, Taziar wished for Silme's and Astryd's abilities to contact Larson through his flawed mind barriers.

"You!" the stranger said, his voice devoid of malice. He used the language of Cullinsberg's barony with an odd mixture of accents. "You?" He blinked in the smoky half-lighting from the hearth. "Is your name Taziar Medakan?"

Taziar all but stopped breathing. Months had passed since he had escaped the tortures of the baron's dungeon, but a thousand gold weight price on his life might prove enough to keep bounty hunters on his trail for eternity. He knew someone would catch up with him eventually, yet he had always expected a direct attack rather than a questioning.

The stranger shifted his weight to the opposite leg. Coins clicked, muffled by linen, though to Taziar they sounded as loud as a drumbeat. "Well?" the man prodded.

Taziar sidled a glance toward his companions. Though too distant to hear words, they watched the exchange with concern. Larson's fingers curled into a fist on the table, his other grip lax against his hilt. Silme's hand rested on his arm, restraining. The bartender feigned disinterest, but his gaze flicked repeatedly to the stranger and his prisoner, awaiting trouble. Though Taziar knew of no other reason why this man should know his name, he answered truthfully in the same tongue. "I'm Taziar. How do you know me?"

The stranger's brown eyes lowered and rose. "You're even smaller than I expected. I have an eleven-year-old daughter bigger than you."

Taziar found the comment annoyingly snide, but familiar with such taunts, he resisted the urge to return a sarcastic comment. "I think I've got my equilibrium now. Could I have my hands back?" He twisted slightly in the man's grasp.

The man seemed surprised. He released Taziar and gestured at a chair across the table. Apparently realizing he had never answered Taziar's first question, he corrected the oversight. "I have a message for you."

"A message?" Taziar ignored the proffered seat. Instead, he caught the toppled chair, positioned it within reach of the stranger and sat. If the opportunity arose, he wanted to flip the purse safely into its pocket.

The stranger sat also, hitching his chair sideways and further from Taziar.

Recognizing an attempt to preserve personal space, Taziar suspected the man was city bred. "Who sent this message?"

"I was told to mention Shylar." The stranger examined Taziar for any sign of reaction.

Taziar gave him none, though the name held more significance than any other the stranger might have spoken. An image rose in Taziar's mind of a matronly woman, a handsome figure still evident beneath sagging skin, dark eyes shrewd and eclipsed by graying curls. She served as madam to Cullinsberg's whorehouse and mother to its beggars and thieves. An uncanny reader of intentions and loyalties, Shylar had recruited pickpockets and street orphans like Taziar, building a faction of the underground that had become not only the most powerful, but peculiarly benevolent as well. Once one of Shylar's favorites, Taziar knew most of his fellows catered to the semi-legitimate vices of men: mind-hazing drugs, women, and gambling. Others acted as spies, scouting the city and its treasures until every corner of Cullinsberg belonged to the underground. Those attracted to politics bought guards and information.

"There's trouble in Cullinsberg," the stranger explained.

"Trouble?" Taziar gripped the edge of the table. "What sort of trouble?"

"Violence in the streets. Merchants robbed to their last ducat, and sometimes beaten and killed. Guards brutalized so badly they've taken to carrying weapons off-duty and using them at the slightest provocation. Daughters dragged away in broad daylight to be sold as slaves in distant ports." No trace of emotion entered the stranger's voice; he relayed information in the matter-of-fact tone of a teacher.

But the words stunned Taziar. He tried to picture his companions assaulting guardsmen in cobbled alleyways, but the image defied his experience. Shylar taught her lessons well. Taziar knew merchants expected to lose a small percentage of wares when they came to the baron's city, but huge profits absorbed the pilferings and encouraged the traders to return. Greedy thefts could only harm trade and, in the long run, destroy the thief's own livelihood. And Shylar's followers would never resort to violence. Taziar spoke, his mouth suddenly dry. "Anything more?"

The stranger shrugged. "I was told to tell you, Taziar Medakan, that the baron's fighting back. His men have infiltrated organized gangs. The guards arrested some of the strongest leaders. They're rotting in the baron's dungeons while he collects a few more before a mass execution on Aga'arin's High Holy Day." The stranger circled his own neck with his fingers, simulating a noose. He made a crude noise, then dropped his head to one side, eyes bulging and tongue dangling from a corner of his mouth.

Taziar scooted backward with a pained noise, the memory of his father's death on the gallows rising hot within him. He recalled the elder Medakan's quietly dignified acceptance of an execution based on betrayal, the convulsing throes of suffocation, and hard, gray eyes still steely after death. Visibly shaken, Taziar gulped down half the stranger's ale before he realized his mistake.

The stranger's face resumed its normal appearance, and he laughed at Taziar's discomfort. "Gruesome, eh, but no worse than they deserve."

Taziar nodded, not trusting himself to speak. He wondered whether the stranger's cruelty had been intentional. Taziar's father had led the baron's guards during the decades of the Barbarian Wars. And anyone in Cullinsberg who didn't know the captain from his years of service would certainly remember his public hanging. Then, too, Taziar's alias as Shadow Climber must have become common information. *He's setting me up for capture.* But something about the situation seemed jarringly amiss. *Only an insider would think to lure me with the name Shylar, but no professional would be stupid enough to send a Cullinsbergen with the message.* Taziar regathered his shattered composure. "You're from Cullinsberg?"

"Me?" The stranger shook his head and spoke with honest casualness. "Many years ago, right about the start of the wars. My father didn't want to make me an orphan, or a soldier when my time came, so we moved away. I spent most of my life in Sverigehavn." He twitched, suddenly appearing uncomfortable. "You probably don't think much of war dodgers, not if you're related to the hero with your same name."

Taziar always prided himself on reading motivations; on the streets, his life depended on it. This man's replies came too effortlessly to be lies, unless they were exceedingly well-rehearsed. His explanations seemed appropriately fluent, his uneasiness heartfelt. He did not stumble over the term "hero," despite the fact that the citizenry had long ago exchanged the word for "traitor." Taziar dismissed the confession with a mild signal of good will. "Not everyone's meant for battle. I was more interested in how you came by the information you just gave me."

"Now that's odd." The stranger reclaimed his mug from Taziar, tracing its rim with a dirty finger. "I'm a dockhand. The ferry, *Amara,* came ashore a few weeks back. An old man approached me, picked me out because of my accent, I guess. He said he'd come on *Amara* from Cullinsberg and asked me to give you that message. I don't know how he knew where I'd find you. Didn't tell me his name, just told me you wouldn't know him and said to mention Shylar. Paid me well enough to make it worth my time finding you."

Taziar studied the stranger more carefully in light of this new information. He noticed a face chapped and windburned from exposure to elements, muscled arms, and hands callused like a laborer's. The last piece of the puzzle slid into place with smooth precision. Though a southerner residing in Sweden was rare, the stranger's story seemed plausible and circumstance supported it. The elderly man could have been any of a hundred street people aided by Taziar's charity; enamored with the thrill rather than the money, Taziar had always freely shared his spoils with hungry beggars. The payment explained why a dockhand carried gold, but a street person from Cullinsberg could only have gathered enough coinage for travel and ferry passage from one source. *Shylar. And if she went to this much expense and trouble to find me, not even knowing whether I'm still alive, she's in serious trouble.*

Taziar frowned, confused as well as concerned. The underground had long ago adopted a complex series of codes for positive identification of authenticity of messages. The stranger's method of delivery defied all correct procedure. *Maybe the signals have changed or Shylar thought I might have forgotten them. Perhaps she was too desperate to waste time with details.* Taziar fidgeted. *Could this be a trap, a trick of the baron's to draw me back to Cullinsberg?* He dismissed the thought from necessity. *If there's any chance Shylar's in trouble, I have to help. I'll just have to be careful.* Another realization jarred Taziar with sudden alarm. "Has the ferry made her last run until spring?"

The stranger bobbed his head in assent. "But she'll winter in the south, so she'll cast off early next week for the return to Calrmar Port."

Taziar laced his fingers on the tabletop, his thoughts distant. *If we leave tonight, we'll still have to travel hard to reach Sverigehavn Port in time. From there, if we push on just as hard, we should make Cullinsberg with a few days to spare before Aga'arin's High Holy Day.* "Could you describe the person who gave you the message?"

The stranger poked a thumb through a knothole in the tabletop. His face crinkled into a mask of consideration. "Tall, thin. He had that withered look of someone who'd weathered plagues that killed his young ones. Had a healthy amount of Norse blood in him, too, by his coloring. But his accent was full barony. In fact, he used that funny speech of the villages south of Cullinsberg.'' The stranger continued, clipping off final syllables with greatly exaggerated precision to demonstrate. ''He migh' o' co' from Souberg or Wilsberg origina'.'' He laughed at his own mimicry. ''Never could figure out how they did that so easily. Always seemed like more effort than it was worth.''

Taziar's answering chuckle was strained. ''Thanks for the information.'' He tossed a pair of Northern gold coins, watched them skitter across the table and clink to a halt against the mug. ''That should cover the drink, too.'' The payment had come from reflex. Abruptly, Taziar realized his mistake. He winced as the stranger reached for his purse to claim the money.

An elbow brushed the precariously balanced pouch. It overbalanced. Ducats and silvers clattered across the polished floor. The barroom went silent, except for the thin rasp of coins rolling on edge, followed by the sputter as they fell flat to the planks.

The stranger remained seated, blinking in silent wonderment. He glanced at Taziar, but addressed no one in particular. ''Odd. Now how do you suppose that happened?''

Taziar rose, suddenly glad the stranger had positioned himself beyond reach while they chatted; it took the blame from him. ''I couldn't begin to guess.'' He trotted back to his own table, leaving the stranger to collect his scattered coins.

Reclaiming his chair, Taziar gathered breath to convince his companions of the necessity of traveling quickly to Cullinsberg. Then, realizing it would take more than a few delicately chosen arguments, he sighed and addressed Larson. ''You know those drinks you owe me?''

Larson nodded.

''Any chance I could have all of them right now?''

Taziar's concern heightened during the week of land and ocean travel that brought them from Norway's icy autumn to the barony of Cullinsberg. He spent many sleepless nights agonizing over a summons he believed had come from Shylar. *What do I know? What skill do I have that Shylar might need desperately enough to send a beggar to find me?* And always, Taziar discovered the same answers. He knew the city streets, but others closer and more recently familiar could supply her with the same information. Though a master thief, Taziar retained enough modesty to believe others with determination could accomplish anything he could. Only two skills seemed uniquely his. As a youth, Taziar had always loved to climb, practicing until his companions bragged, with little exaggeration, that he could scale a straight pane of glass.

Taziar hoped this was the ability Shylar sought, because the other filled him with dread. In the centuries of the barony's dominance, only Taziar had escaped its dungeons, and even he had needed the aid of a barbarian prince. Taziar had paid with seven days in coma and a beating that still striped his body with scars. It was an experience he would not wish even upon enemies, and, despite his love for impossible challenges, he harbored no desire to repeat it. *I doubt my knowledge will serve Shylar, yet I have no choice but to try.*

Two days before Aga'arin's High Holy Day, Taziar Medakan peered forth from between the huddled oaks and hickories of the Kielwald Forest. Across a fire-cleared plain, the chiseled stone walls enclosing the city of Cullinsberg stretched toward the sky, broad, dark, and unwelcoming. A crescent moon peeked above the colored rings of sunset, drawing glittering lines along the spires of the baron's keep in the northern quarter and the four thin towers of Aga'arin's temple to the east. The squat walls hid the remainder of the city, but Taziar knew every building and corner from memory.

Taziar crept closer. From habit, he sifted movement from the stagnant scene of the sleeping city. Sentries paced the flat summit of the walls, their gaits grown lazy in the decade of peace since the Barbarian Wars. Taziar knew their presence was a formality. The city gates stood open, and no one would question the entrance of Taziar and his friends. *Unless the guards recognize me.* The thought made Taziar frown. He turned and started toward the denser center of forest where his companions were camped.

An acrid whiff of fire halted Taziar in mid-stride. It seemed odd someone would choose to set a woodland camp so close to the comforts of a city. Taziar twisted back to face the walls. His blue eyes scanned the tangled copse of trees. Eventually, he discerned a sinuous thread of smoke shimmering between the trunks. Curious, he flitted toward it, his gray cloak and tunic nearly invisible in the evening haze. He pulled his hood over unruly, black hair, hiding his face in shadow.

Half a dozen paces brought Taziar to the edge of a small clearing. A campfire burned in a circle of gathered stones. The reflected light of its flickering flames danced across the trunks of oak defining the borders of the glade. A man slouched over the fire. Though his posture seemed relaxed, his gaze darted along the tree line. He wore a sword at his hip, a quiver across his back, and a strung bow lay within easy reach. Four other men occupied the clearing, in various stages of repose. Each wore a cloak of black, brown or green to protect against the autumn chill. Bunched or crouched against the trees, they appeared like wolves on the edge of sleep, and Taziar suspected the slightest noise would bring them fully awake.

Taziar considered returning to his own camp. He had no reason to believe these people meant Cullinsberg any harm, and the baron's soldiers could certainly handle an army of five men. Still, their presence this near the city seemed too odd for Taziar to pass without investigation. Noiselessly, he inched closer.

As Taziar narrowed the gap, the man before the fire shifted to a crouch. Flames sparked red highlights through a curled tangle of dark hair. The pocked features were familiar to Taziar. He recognized Faldrenk, a friend from his days among the underground. Though not above thievery, Faldrenk had specialized in political intrigue and espionage. Surprised and thrilled to discover an old

ally, Taziar studied the other men in the scattered firelight. With time, he made out the thickly-muscled form
and sallow features of Richmund, a bumbling pickpocket
who scarcely obtained enough copper to feed his vora-
cious appetite. In leaner times, he often joined the baron's guards and always knew which sentries could be
bribed. The other three men were strangers.

Taziar tempered the urge to greet his long-unseen comrades with his knowledge of the changes in Cullinsberg
and the realization that they might be performing a scam
easily ruined by his interference. The evident weaponry
seemed incongruous. Like most of the thieves, gamblers,
and black marketeers of the underground, Faldrenk and
Richmund were relatively harmless, catering to the greed
and illegal vices of men rather than dealing in violence.
Taziar stepped into the clearing. Avoiding names, he
chose his words with care. "Nice night for hunting?"

Every head jerked up. Faldrenk shouted as if in warning. "Taz!" Bow in hand, he leaped to his feet, flicking
an arrow from his quiver to the string. Faldrenk's companions scrambled to their feet.

Taziar's smile wilted. Shocked by his friends' reac-
tions, he went still.

Faldrenk raised his bow and drew. Taziar dodged back
into the forest. The arrow scraped an ancient oak, passed
through the place where Taziar had stood, and grazed a
furrow of flesh from his arm. Pain mobilized him. He
charged through the forest, leaping deadfalls and brush
with a speed born of desperation. He wasted a second
regaining his bearings, aware he needed the aid of his
companions to face this threat. An attack from men who
had once been allies seemed nonsensical, but Taziar did
not waste time pondering. He raced deeper into the forest. Branches tore his cloak. A twig whipped through his
torn sleeve and across his wound, stinging nearly as much
as the arrow.

Taziar careened around an autumn-brown copse of
blackberry and nearly collided with a man, an instinctive
side step all that saved him from impaling himself on the
stranger's sword. The man followed, lunging for Taziar's

chest. Taziar sprang backward, pawing for his own hilt.
His heel mired in a puddle. He fell. The stranger's sword
whisked over his head, then curled back and thrust for
Taziar's neck. Taziar rolled into the wild snarl of brambles. The stranger's blade plowed through mud, splashing
slime and water across the vines.

Taziar floundered free of the encumbering vines, heedless of the thorns that tore welts in his skin. He caught
his swordgrip in both fists and wrenched. Vines snapped,
and the sword lurched gracelessly from its sheath. The
stranger swept for Taziar's head. Taziar spun aside.
"Why?" he managed to ask before the stranger cut to
Taziar's left side. This time, Taziar took the blow on his
sword. The stranger's blade scratched down Taziar's,
locked momentarily on the crossguard. Small and a
scarcely adequate swordsman, Taziar realized, with
alarm, he had little chance against his opponent's superior size and strength.

"Traitor!" the stranger screamed. A sudden push sent
Taziar stumbling backward.

Taziar could hear the crash of his pursuers, growing
closer. He dropped to his haunches, gaining balance with
ease but feigning instability. The stranger pressed his advantage. He stabbed with bold commitment. Taziar
skirted the thrust and dove between closely-spaced
trunks. He hit the ground with head tucked, rolled, and
ran, oblivious to the shouts behind him. His thoughts
swirled past like the endless ranks of oaks. *Everyone's
gone mad! What in Karana's deepest hell is going on?*

Taziar jammed his sword into his sheath as he tore
through underbrush and wove between a copse of pine
trees toward the clearing that sheltered his companions.
The sweet wood odor of a campfire reaffirmed his bearings, the snap of its flames lost beneath the crash of bootfalls. Shouting a warning to his friends, Taziar cut across
a deer path and skittered into the camp, the bandits on
his heels.

Silme stood at the far end of the glade, her manner
alert and her stance characteristically bold. Head low, but
gaze twisted toward the new threat, Astryd muttered spell

words in a furious incantation. Larson charged without question, his swordmaster's katana lit red by flame. Taziar ducked as Larson's sword blocked a strike intended for the Shadow Climber's head. Caught by surprise, the bandit missed his dodge. Larson's hilt crashed into his face, staggering him. The follow-through cut severed the bandit's head.

Taziar dodged past, Faldrenk and his companions in close pursuit. Taziar caught a glimpse of Astryd, abandoning a magical defense foiled by the proximity of battle. He pitched over the fire. Rolling to his feet, he used the moment this maneuver gained him to catch his breath and his balance. Larson thrust for the trailing bandit. The bandit whirled to tend to his own defense, and Richmund came to his aid. Faldrenk and his remaining ally advanced on Taziar from opposite sides of the campfire.

Taziar crouched. Desperate and uncertain, he swept a brand from the blaze and hurled it at Faldrenk's companion. Heat singed Taziar's fingers, the pain delayed by callus, but the bandit cried out in distress. Taziar scuttled backward. Faldrenk's blade missed Taziar's chest by a finger's breadth of air.

"Faldrenk!" Taziar seized his sword hilt as his old friend jabbed sharpened steel for the Climber's abdomen. Taziar lurched sideways, freeing his blade in the same motion. He caught Faldrenk's next sweep on his sword. "Stop! Don't! Faldrenk, we're friends . . ."

Steel chimed beyond the firelight as Larson returned strikes and parries with a ferocity that would have pleased his teacher. Faldrenk slashed. "Adal was your friend, too."

Taziar batted Faldrenk's blade aside, not daring to return the attack. "And that's not changed. Why . . . ?"

Faldrenk bore in, slicing for Taziar in an angry frenzy. Hard-pressed, Taziar gave ground freely. He kept his strokes short, intended only for defense. Sweat-matted hair fell, stinging, into his eyes. From the edge of his vision, he saw Faldrenk's companion closing from around the fire. "Faldrenk, why?"

Faldrenk's voice held a contempt once reserved for

guards who abused peasants in the streets. "Because you're a foul, filthy, shit-stinking traitor." His blade whistled for Taziar's face. "Karana's pit, *treason runs in Medakan blood!*"

The gibe hurt worse than Faldrenk's betrayal. Taziar spun aside, but shock cost him his timing. Faldrenk's blade nicked Taziar's ear, and blood trickled down his collar in a warm stream. The remaining bandit charged into sword range. Taziar abandoned speech as he blocked the stranger's strike with his sword. The force of the blow jarred him to the shoulders. Before he could muster a riposte, the stranger's sword hammered against his again. Impact staggered Taziar. Driven to the edge of the clearing, he felt branches prickle into his back.

Again, Faldrenk lunged, blade sweeping. Taziar leaped backward. Twigs snapped, jabbing into his skin like knives. His spine struck an oak; breath whistled through his teeth. The stranger cut for Taziar's head. Taziar ducked, and the blade bit deeply into the trunk. Taziar seized the opening; he skirted beneath the stranger's arm as the sword came free in a shower of bark.

"Faldrenk, listen . . ." Taziar gasped, nearly breathless. The stranger paid the words no heed. His blade arced toward Taziar. The Climber spun to meet the charge. Their blades crashed together.

Silme's anxious voice rose above the din. "Shadow, behind you!" Astryd screamed a high-pitched, wordless noise.

Taziar spun, slashing to counter Faldrenk's strike. But his friend had gone unnaturally still, sword poised for a blow. Instead of steel, Taziar's blade found flesh. It cleaved beneath Faldrenk's left arm and halfway through his chest. Blood splashed on Taziar and ran along his crossguard, but he noticed only Faldrenk's eyes. The pale orbs revealed fear and shock before they glazed in death. The corpse crumpled, wrenching the sword from Taziar's grip.

Instinctively, Taziar whirled to face his other opponent, dodging to evade an unseen strike. But the stranger, too, had noticed Faldrenk's sudden immobility. Wide-eyed, he backed away from Taziar signing a broad, religious gesture in the air. Once beyond sword range, he turned and ran.

Apparently, Larson's opponents also abandoned their assault; the world went eerily silent. Taziar stared at the lifeless body, once a friend, who had berated him with insults as cruel as murder. The scene glazed to red fog. Unable to discern Faldrenk's features, Taziar knelt. Only then did he recognize the tears in his own eyes. And the realization brought a rush of grief. He placed a hand on the shapeless blur of Faldrenk's corpse, felt life's last warmth fleeing beneath his touch.

Taziar lowered his head. He knew what would come next. In the past, the mere idea of killing had brought memories vivid as reality. Thoughts of his troubled childhood had remained quiescent since the familiar restless attraction to danger had driven him to chase down and slay his father's murderer, and seek adventure in the strange realms north of the Kattegat. Now, back on his home ground, steeped in a friend's blood, Taziar cringed beneath an onslaught of remembrance.

Images battered his conscience like physical blows. He saw his mother's frail form, withered by the accusations against his father. He heard her wine-slurred voice berating her only son with words heavy with reproach and accusation. He recalled how she had trapped him into promising to take her life and forced him to keep that vow, the jagged tear of the knife through flesh, the reek of blood like tide-wrack on a summer beach. Taziar's stomach knotted with cramps. He dropped to his hands and knees, fighting the urge to retch.

A firm hand clamped on Taziar's shoulder and steered him beyond the sight and odor. Larson's tone was soft and nonjudgmental, but liberally tinged with surprise. ''Your first?''

Taziar rubbed his vision clear. He shook his head, not yet trusting himself to speak. Despite heated battles fought at Larson's side against wolves and conjured dragons, Taziar had not killed a man since he slew the traitor in Sweden's forest. ''Third,'' he confessed. He did not elaborate further. ''It's a weakness.''

Larson slapped Taziar's back with comradely force. ''Ha! So you're not perfect after all. If you have to have a flaw, I can't think of one more normal than hating killing men.''

Taziar smiled weakly. ''Thanks.'' As the excitement of combat dissipated, his legs felt as flaccid as rubber. His arm throbbed where the arrow had nicked it, his fingers smarted, and his ear felt hot. Yet, despite pain and fatigue, Taziar dredged up the inner resolve to make a vow. *I'll take my own life before I cause another innocent death. And I'll not allow any other wrongful execution on the baron's gallows.*

Taziar turned his head, noticing for the first time that Astryd stood on shaky feet, her eyes slitted and most of her weight supported by Silme. Alarmed, he ran to her side, ashamed of the time wasted on his own inner turmoil. ''What happened?''

Silme explained with composed practicality. ''She tapped her life energy harder than she should have. She'll be all right.'' She added, her tone harsh with rebuke, ''And she'll learn.''

Taziar caught Astryd to him, relieving Silme of the burden. He knew the spell that weakened Astryd was the one that had frozen Faldrenk, preventing an attack that might otherwise have taken Taziar's life. Sick with guilt and concern, it did not occur to him to wonder why Silme had not aided in the battle.

CHAPTER 2:

Shadows in the City

Beware lest you lose the substance by grasping at the shadow.

—Aesop
The Dog and the Shadow

Sleep eluded Taziar, leaving him awash in pain. He lay on his stomach to avoid aggravating the jabs and scratches in his back. He tucked his arrow-slashed arm against his side; the other rested across Astryd's abdomen, attuned to the exhaustion-deep rise and fall of her every breath. His ear throbbed, and he kept his head turned to the opposite side. But the ache of superficial wounds dulled beneath the anguish and confusion inspired by Faldrenk's betrayal. *He called me traitor. Why? I've not set foot near Cullinsberg in months.* Taziar considered, seeking answers he lacked the knowledge to deduce. *Maybe that's it. Perhaps Shylar needed me, and I wasn't here.* He drummed his fingers in the dirt, ignoring the flaring sting of his burns. *That makes no sense. My friends know I fled with Cullinsberg's army at my heels; how could they hold such a thing against me?*

Aware that Faldrenk would not deem ignorance nor inactivity a crime punishable by death, Taziar abandoned this line of thought. *It wasn't mistaken identity either. Faldrenk called me by name. Something strange is happening, a break in loyalties that touched Faldrenk and Richmund.* Taziar felt his taxed sinews cramp. Having already taken long, careful moments to find a posture that did not incite the pain of his injuries, he resisted the impulse to roll. *But Shylar knows I still care about the*

*underground. Otherwise, she would never have expected
me to answer her summons.* Taziar worked tension from
his muscles in groups. *She knows me too well to suspect
I would act against friends. And she'll have explanations. I have to see her. Until then, I can do nothing.*

Mind eased, Taziar surrendered to the urge to reposition his body. Pain flared, then died to a baseline chorus.
Gradually, Taziar found sleep.

Dawn light washed, copper-pink, across the battlements of Cullinsberg. Huddled within the overlarge folds
of Larson's spare cloak, Taziar felt a shiver of excitement
traverse him. After months in the cold, barbaric lands
north of the Kattegat, returning to the city of his childhood seemed like stepping into another world. He tried
to map the cobbled streets from memory but found gaps
that would require visual cues. The lapses reminded him
of an ancient beggar who knew every street and alleyway
in the city, but, unable to give verbal directions, would
walk an inquirer to his destination.

"What about me?"

Larson's question startled Taziar. Lost in his past, he
had nearly forgotten his companions. "What about you?"

As they neared the gateway and the uniformed guards
before it, Larson kept his voice soft. "I hate to bring up
the subject. I still find it hard to believe myself, but people tell me I'm an elf. In the North, no one seemed to
care much for elves. Am I going to get attacked every
time I step into a crowd?"

"Attacked?" Taziar chuckled. "You're approaching
civilization. Draw steel in the streets and you'll get arrested." Recalling the report of the Sverigehavn dockhand in Kveldemar's tavern, Taziar hoped his description
was still accurate. "Besides, no one in Cullinsberg will
know what an elf is. They'll just assume you're human.
Ugly, but human all the same."

"Gee, thanks." Larson caught Silme's arm and steered
her beyond Taziar's reach. "You little creep."

"Cre-ep?" Astryd repeated, her light singsong adding

a syllable to the English word. "Is that the same as 'jerk'?"

"Exactly," Larson said.

"And its meaning?" Silme showed an expression of genuine interest, but she still fought back a smile.

Larson shot a wicked glance at Taziar. "It's a term of endearment."

"Sure." Taziar worked sarcasm into the word. "Which explains why you're madly in love with that woman . . ." He gestured Silme. ". . . but you've only used the term to refer to me." Adopting a wide-eyed, femininely seductive expression, he grasped Larson's free hand and raised his voice to falsetto. "Sorry, hero, I'm already taken."

Astryd slapped Taziar's back playfully, which, because of the scratches, turned out to be more painful than she had intended. Taziar winced, released Larson, and resumed his normal walk toward the gateway with a final whispered warning. "Avoid my name. If the dockhand told the truth, the baron may have dropped my bounty to concentrate on closer, more formidable enemies. But no need to take a chance."

The four fell silent as they reached the opened, wrought iron gates and a pair of guards dressed in the barony's red-trimmed black linen. Taziar lowered his head, hiding his features beneath the supple creases of his hood. But the guardsmen seemed more interested in his blond companions and the women's oddly-crafted staves. They stared without questioning as Taziar and his companions entered the town.

Despite the early hour, men and women whisked through the main street, rushing to open shops, tend to jobs, or run errands. Merchants pulled night tarps from roadside stands, piling fruit in bins or setting merchandise in neat rows. They worked with the mechanical efficiency of routine. Yet, to Taziar, their manner seemed anything but normal. Mumbled conversations blended to indecipherable din, devoid of the shouted greetings between neighboring sellers who had known one another for years. Stands and merchants older than Taziar had disappeared, replaced by either strangers or glaring stretches of empty space. Others remained. But where women once tended their wares alone, now they shared stalls, hoping to find safety in being part of a group or else they hired men to guard them. Despite laws against it, swords and daggers were boldly displayed. Many of the blades were crusted with dried blood, as if to warn predators that their owners had killed and would do so again if pressed.

Astryd gawked at the bustling crowds and towering buildings. The Dragonrank school required its students to remain on its grounds eleven months of every year, and Astryd had never found time to visit the more civilized lands south of the Kattegat. "So this is Cullinsberg."

Larson watched Astryd's rural antics with wry amusement. "This is the great city you keep bragging about?"

"Sort of," Taziar admitted uncomfortably as he led his companions along the main thoroughfare. Concern leaked into his tone, and his friends went quiet as they followed. Though most of the passersby remained unarmed, they gave one another a wide berth, and Taziar was unable to make eye contact with any of Cullinsberg's citizens. The buildings, at least, seemed unchanged. Rows of stone dwellings and shops lined the streets behind the merchants. Still, something as yet unrecognized bothered Taziar; a piece of city life seemed awry. And, since it was missing rather than out of place, Taziar wandered three blocks before he realized what disturbed him. *Where are the beggars?*

Taziar turned a half-circle in the roadway, gazing across the sewage troughs in search of the ancient crones and lunatics who took sustenance from the discarded peels and cores that usually littered the roadside ditches. The maneuver uncovered neither vagrants nor scraps, but he did notice a scrawny boy dressed only in tattered britches who was huddled on the opposite street corner. The child sat with his head drooped into his lap, his hand outstretched as if from long habit.

Taziar's companions watched him with curiosity.

"Shad—" Silme spoke softly, shortening his alias beyond recognition. "What's the problem? Maybe we can help."

"Is it the child?" Astryd asked, touching Taziar's hand. "We have more than enough money to feed him."

"No!" Taziar answered forcefully. "Something's not quite right. It's subtle, and I don't understand it yet." He spoke low and in Scandinavian, though his companions understood the barony's tongue. Astryd and Silme had learned several languages at the Dragonrank school, and Larson spoke it with the same unnatural ease and accent as he did Old Norse. "I was born and raised here. I've learned the laws of the barony and its streets. This is my river and I know how to stay afloat." Taziar paused, trying to phrase his request without sounding demanding or insulting. "Please. Until I figure out what's bothering me, let me do the swimming. Just follow my lead." Taziar studied the boy. "Wait here." He crossed to the corner, relieved when his friends did not argue or follow.

The boy raised hollow, sunken eyes as Taziar approached. He climbed to skeletal legs and hesitated, as if uncertain whether to run or beg. At length, he stretched scarred fingers toward Taziar. "Please, sir?"

The sight cut pity through Taziar. Impressed by the child's fear, he fixed an unthreatening expression on his face and leaned forward. Unobtrusively, he reached into his pocket, emerging with a fistful of mixed northern coins. "I'm sorry." Taziar edged between the child and the next alleyway, surreptitiously pressing money into the beggar's tiny hand as he shielded the exchange from onlookers. "I have nothing for you today," he lied, gesturing toward Astryd in a matter-of-fact manner. "But my woman insisted I come over and tell you we feel for you, and we'll try to save something for you tomorrow."

The child accepted Taziar's offering into a sweating palm. A sparkle momentarily graced his dull, yellow eyes. Playing along like a seasoned actor, he spoke in a practiced monotone. "Aga'arin bless you, sir." Slowly, he wobbled toward the market square. His gaze fluttered along streets and windows, as if he expected someone to seize his new-found wealth before he could buy a decent meal.

Taziar returned to his companions. Incensed by the beggar's paranoia, he did not take time to properly phrase his question. "Have you ever seen anything like that?"

"No." Anger tinged Astryd's reply. "When did you become stingy? You could have at least given him food."

Taziar laughed, realizing the trick intended to divert thieves had also confused his companions. "I gave him more money than he's seen in his life." A pair of uniformed guards walked by, eyeing the armed and huddled group with suspicion. Taziar waited until they'd passed before elaborating. "I meant the fear. Have you ever met a beggar too scared to beg? Worse, a starving beggar afraid to take money? Who in Karana's darkest hell would rob a beggar?"

"Easy target." Larson shrugged, his expression suddenly hard. "In New York City, the hoods'll rob their own mothers for dope money. There's too many to count how many Vietnamese kids look like that one, and they'll take anything from anyone."

Little of Larson's speech made sense to Taziar. Finding the same perplexed look echoed on Silme's and Astryd's faces, Taziar pressed. "Interesting, Allerum. Now, could you repeat it in some known, human language?"

Larson gathered breath, then clamped his mouth shut and dismissed his own explanation. "Yes, I've seen it before. Leave it at that." He addressed Taziar. "Now, swimmer, what river do we take from here?"

"This way." Tazier chose a familiar alley which he knew would lead nearly to the porch steps of Cullinsberg's inn. Rain barrels stood at irregular intervals; old bones and rag scraps scattered between them. From habit, Taziar assessed the stonework of the closely-packed shops, dwellings, and warehouses hedging the walls of the lane. Moss covered the granite like a woolly blanket, its surface disturbed in slashes where a climber had torn through for hand and toe holds. Taziar glanced at the rooftop. A cloak-hooded gaze met his own briefly, then disappeared into the shadow of a chimney. A careful inspection revealed another small figure in the eaves. A third crouched on a building across the walkway.

Engrossed in his inspection of the rooftops, Taziar never saw the trip-rope that went suddenly taut at his feet. Hemp hissed against his boots, making him stumble forward. A muscled arm enwrapped his throat and whetted steel pricked the skin behind his left ear. A deep voice grated. "Give me your money."

Taziar rolled his eyes to see a blemished, teenaged face. He felt the warmth of the thief's body against his spine, and the realization of a daylight attack against an armed group shocked him beyond speech. It never occurred to Taziar to fear for his life; he knew street orphans and their motivations too well. Instead, he appraised the abilities of his assailant. The youth held Taziar overbalanced backward. The grip was professional. He could strangle Taziar with ease. If threatened, a spinning motion would sprawl Taziar and drag the blade across his throat.

The assessment took Taziar less than a heartbeat. Aware the setup would require one other accomplice to draw the rope straight, Taziar numbered the gang at five. *Whatever happened to peaceful begging and petty theft?* "Fine. I'll give you ten gold. Two for you and each of your friends," he said deliberately, intending to inform his companions as well as appease his assailant.

Taziar felt the bandit's muscles knot beneath his tunic. "No. I want all your money."

Apparently taking his cue from Taziar's calm acceptance of the situation, Larson loosed a loud snort of derision. "Are you swimming now, Shad? Upstream? Downstream? Backstroke?" His taunt echoed between the buildings.

Agitation entered the thief's tone. "Tell your friend to shut up. Now!" Sharp pain touched Taziar's skin. Blood beaded at the tip of the blade, and sweat stung the wound.

Larson's hand fell to his hilt, and he took a menacing step. "Who are you telling to shut up, asshole? I'll cut off your ears and shove them up your nose."

"Calm down." Taziar tried to keep his voice level. He had never seen Larson so hostile, and the thief's greed alarmed him. Ten gold was more than a common laborer might make in a year, and the northern mintage would make it no less valuable. If Taziar had been alone, he would have felt certain that the thug would not harm him; but, challenged by Larson, the youth might be driven to murder. "You're not the one with a knife at your throat." Reminded of what he might have become at the same age, Taziar grew careless of risk. "Friend, you're doing this dumb."

The thief's fingers shivered against the dagger's hilt. He, too, seemed out of his element, unaccustomed to getting lectured by victims. "I'm doing this dumb? Which of us is jabbering on the blade end of the knife? If one of us is stupid, I'm not guessing it's me. Now give me your money and I may not kill you. Everyone else can just drop their purses, turn around, and leave."

Taziar cursed the loose hood that slid over his eyes and made it impossible to meet his assailant's gaze. "Look, friend, you can't have all our money. I offered you some. I'd have given the same to you if you'd asked nicely. Anything more than we're willing to give freely, you'll have to take. You've got four companions. See that man there." He tensed a hand to indicate Larson.

Immediately, the arm clamped tighter around Taziar's neck, neatly closing off his airway.

Taziar fought rising panic. Blackness swam down on him, but even vulnerability could not shake resolve. Given slightly different circumstances, he could have been this teen.

Gradually, the thief's grip relaxed. Taziar gasped gratefully for breath, then forced himself to continue. "If you want to take money from my friend, you'll need at least six more of you. Then, the one survivor can gather the money into a pile and spend it." Taziar measured the thief by his actions, sensed uncertainty beneath forced defiance. "Ten gold could feed you all for a month and more. Are you going to take the ten I offered you, or will you get all your friends slaughtered for the chance to get a few more? I can't compromise. My friends have to eat, too. And you won't live long on the street acting stupid."

"Stop. It's all right." Silme spoke in the rapid, high-pitched manner of a frightened woman, but Taziar knew the sorceress too well not to recognize a performance. She passed her dragonstaff to Larson who accepted it grudgingly in his off hand. "I'll give you my purse. I don't care. Money doesn't mean anything. Just don't hurt him." Reaching into her side pocket, she removed a thin pouch of coins. She approached the thief, flicking her hands in contrived, nervous gestures. "Let him go. You got his ten and mine. That's more than half of it. It's better than the deal he gave you. Just let him go." She pushed her purse at the thief's free hand. "Here. Take it. Take it."

Instinctively, the thief glanced at the purse.

Quick as thought, Silme grasped the youngster's knife hand. Positioning her thumb on his littlest knuckle and her fingers around and over his thumb, she gained the leverage to twist. The blade carved skin from Taziar's cheek. He dodged aside as Silme used her other hand to wrench the dagger from the youth's surprised grasp. A sudden punch beneath his elbow finished him. The thief tumbled, flat on his back, in the street.

A rock sailed from the rooftop.

Larson dropped Silme's staff. His sword met the stone in midair and knocked it aside. He completed his stroke, stopping with the blade against the thief's neck. "One more rock and the next thing in the street's your friend's head."

The gang went still.

Taziar pressed a palm to his gashed face to stop the bleeding. Silme's maneuver had jarred his hood aside, and black hair was plastered to the wound. He watched as Astryd whispered to herself, casting a spell. Hunched behind a rain barrel, the thief's partner suddenly became as immobile as a statue. Taziar knew from the strategies of his own childhood gang that the thief beneath Larson's blade was undoubtedly their leader.

Larson caught the thief by stringy, sand-colored hair and hoisted the youth to his feet. "Bend over."

The thief hesitated, then complied.

Larson raised his katana and yelled to the accomplices on the roof. "One move and your buddy's head comes off." He lowered his voice. "This is how you stop someone in the street, you little jackass."

Taziar stepped around the thief, met eyes dark with hatred. He winced, fearing Larson had taken things too far. Humiliation might force the thief to kill an innocent or a follower to maintain his position as leader. At the least, the youth would have to defy Larson, perhaps at the cost of his own life.

The leader howled. "Idiots! Don't let them get away with this. Throw rocks. Attack! Do something."

"Quiet!" Taziar seized a handful of gold from his pocket, trying to maintain the thief's self-respect by creating an illusion of partial success. "Here's your money." Seeking answers, he dropped the gold at the boy's feet and continued. "This isn't how things work here. I don't care about me. I wasn't in any trouble. I knew you wouldn't hurt me. You were in more danger than I was because there was a good chance the man with the sword would kill the whole damn bunch of you. What, in Karana's hell, is going on here?"

The youth stared, as if noticing Taziar for the first time. "Wait! I know you. You're that filthy Medakan worm. We don't want your blood-tainted money."

Shocked, Taziar searched for a reply.

Larson spoke first. "Uh, could you repeat that for the benefit of the person holding the sword ready to decapitate you?"

"I don't care!" Still hunched, the leader screamed, "I'll die before I'll be humiliated by some traitor."

Larson hollered back, apparently as confused as Taziar. "What's this traitor bullshit?"

The youth refused to elaborate.

Taziar used a soothing tone. "Speak up, friend. Please. Were I you, I'd want to befriend the man holding the sword."

The youth remained stalwartly silent.

Behind the thief, Larson raised a threatening foot.

Afraid for the leader's dignity, Taziar waved Larson off. "Don't kick him."

Larson lowered his foot, but he went on speaking in a voice deep with rage. "What do you mean 'don't'? He put a knife to your throat. I ought to cut his goddamned head off. He's a threat. I can remove a threat in an instant. Want to see?"

"No." Taziar winced, his loyalties suddenly shifted. "Look, Allerum, he's a street orphan. He's got enough problems without you making things worse. I grew up like that, damn it!"

A stone bounced from Astryd's magical shield, unnoticed by anyone but its thrower. Larson relented. "Fine, street scum. Pick up the money and go. Right now!"

The youth did not hesitate. He scooped up the coins and ran. Astryd scarcely found time to dismantle her sorceries before the leader and his smaller companion raced deeper into the alleyway.

Taziar watched the teens' retreating figures. Bleeding stanched, he flicked his hood back over his head and chastised Larson. "Allerum, you can't treat these people like that. He's got enough problems, more than you could ever imagine."

Larson sheathed his sword, breaking the tension, but his expression did not soften. He glared after the gang. "Yeah, well. I've got problems, too. But you don't see me inflicting them on the weak and helpless."

"Weak and helpless?" Silme mouthed, but it was the Shadow Climber who spoke aloud.

"They're just hungry children!" Taziar's hands balled at his sides in frustration as he tried to stifle the flood of memories welling within him: the pain of a week's starvation tearing at his gut; the restless, animal-light naps necessary to protect the few rags he owned. "What's wrong with you? I've never seen you like this." Taziar stared, concerned by Larson's uncharacteristic callousness and aware that his friend's manner had grown more cynical and confident in the month since Kensei Gaelinar's death. It seemed as if Larson felt he needed to fill the void his mentor had left. Yet Larson had never before lost the gentle morality that had driven him to put an elderly stranger's life before his own and had so impressed Taziar at their first meeting. "You've risked your life to protect innocents and children too many times to start hating them now."

"Innocents," Larson repeated forcefully. "And children? Those boys are neither. They get down on their luck, hit a few hard times. Then, instead of trying to better their lives, they take the rest of us down with them." The elf's eyes narrowed, making his face appear even more angular. "Give a kid like that a knife and a little muscle, and he thinks he has the god-given right to prey on people weaker than himself. Anyone with that kind of attitude deserves what he gets when he tries to intimidate some little man and finds out his victim's got a big friend with a howitzer." He slapped a hand to the katana's hilt.

Not all of Larson's speech made sense to Taziar, but the meaning came through despite the strange, English words. The Cullinsbergen pursed his lips, glancing at Silme and Astryd. The women whispered quietly, apparently trying to decide whether to interfere or let the men argue the issue out between themselves. "That's not right. What you saw here today isn't normal."

Larson snorted. "That gang was the most 'normal' thing I've seen since Freyr brought me to your world. For a punk, you're awfully naive."

The insult rolled right past Taziar; he knew Cullinsberg and its streets too well to take offense. But something in Larson's voice made the Climber push aside his anxiety for Shylar and his friends long enough for realization to take its place. Taziar had never heard of or conceived of a city larger than Cullinsberg, yet Larson had once claimed to come from a metropolis called New York, with a population four times that of the entire world. "This is personal, isn't it?"

Larson's frown deepened. "Yeah, you could say that." He nodded, as if to himself. His gaze met Taziar's, but his attention seemed internally focused. "A street gang beat up my grandfather for the thirteen dollars and sixty-seven cents he had in his pocket. That's the rough equivalent of two medium-sized, Northern coppers.''

Taziar closed his lids, his mind gorged with the image of a white-haired elder with swollen eyes and abraded, purple cheeks. Larson's distrust and remembrances of his grandfather's misfortune had become one more obstacle to Taziar's already difficult task. Though he knew it was folly, he tried to explain. "Allerum, you don't understand. I probably put that gang together. All Shylar's people had ways of helping the homeless. Waldmunt paid them handsomely to keep quiet or create alibis. Mandel hired them to know every building and road in Cullinsberg or to study the patterns of changing guards. Shylar just gave freely.'' Taziar scanned the rooftops, making certain the gang youths had departed with their leader. "I shared food and money, too. But, I also taught the younger ones how to survive on the street. I organized them. Alone, a few bad days without food might weaken a child enough to drag misfortune into weeks of starvation, perhaps even death. As part of a group, someone always does well enough to share. And there's companionship. But I never intended them to band together against passersby and threaten lives.''

"You're not thinking about *that* street orphan.'' Larson pointed down the alleyway. "You're thinking about *this* one.'' He tapped Taziar's scalp to indicate childhood memories.

"Exactly.'' Under ordinary circumstances, Taziar would have smiled at how neatly Larson had fallen into his trap; but now, weighed down by concern and confusion, he continued without expression. "And you're thinking about New York. Every issue, every action, every motivation has two sides. These children didn't hurt your grandfather.'' He waved in the general direction the gang had taken. "How can you condemn them until you've seen the streets from their point of view?''

Larson did not let up. "I don't need to know an enemy's life history. When we've got guns pointed at one another, I haven't got time to ask his name before pulling the trigger. You can tell me Cullinsberg gangs are differ-

ent until you're blue in the face, but I know a hood is a
hood. Notice how the scum grabbed the smallest guy in
the group.''

Taziar sighed, cursing the time he was wasting bick-
ering with Larson. *I have a summons to answer. And how
can I hope to defend myself against a charge of betrayal
when I don't even know what I'm accused of doing?*
''Look, Allerum. Cullinsberg isn't New York. You're just
going to have to trust me that what you saw here isn't
normal. My friends are in trouble, and I stand by my
friends.''

''I stand by my friends, too,'' Larson started. ''When
punks threaten them in an alley . . .''

Worried about losing time, Taziar talked over Larson.
''If you continue down this alley, it'll bring you to Cullinsberg's inn. Get some food and take a room on the top
floor. That's the third story. See if you can rent the one
on the south side. I'll meet you there.''

''Meet us?'' Astryd shifted her garnet-tipped staff from
hand to hand, finally goaded to speak. ''Where are you
going?''

Taziar studied the side of a building. The uneven surface of stone would make an easy climb. ''I have to meet
with someone who can explain what's happening.''

Astryd glanced from Larson to Silme, as if wondering
why she seemed to be the only one voicing objections.
''You can't go off alone. You might get killed. Take us
with you.''

Taziar edged toward the wall, amused by Astryd's concern. ''I can't take you with me. If I brought strangers
to the underground's haven, I really would be a traitor.''
The subject of safety turned his thoughts to his companions. ''And if anyone asks for any reason, none of you
knows me.''

''Wait.'' Astryd grounded her dragonstaff. ''Silme and
I can handle room renting. At least let Allerum walk you
part way. He can fight.''

Taziar ignored the backhanded insult to his swords-
manship. In his current mood, Larson would prove worse
than a hindrance.

To Taziar's relief, Larson took his side. "I'll be more trouble to Shadow than I'm worth. He had that situation under control. The boy had no reason to kill him, and they both knew it. Shadow's not threatening. I am. If someone robs Shadow, they'll put a knife to his throat. Someone robs me and Shadow, they'll have to frag us and go through the pieces."

"They'll what?" Astryd rounded on Larson, and Taziar seized the opening to steal a few steps closer to the wall.

"I won't be any protection," Larson clarified. "My presence will mean people have to kill us from a distance to handle us."

Astryd stomped a foot in anger. "You're going with him!"

"I am not going with him," Larson hollered back. "Nobody's going with him. He's safer by himself."

Taziar studied his companions and discovered that only Silme was actually looking at him. He winked conspiratorially and pressed a finger to his lips in a plea for silence.

Silme returned a smile.

"He's not safer by himself!" Astryd challenged Larson. "You can protect him. You're bigger and better with a sword. People are afraid of you. Nobody's afraid of him. He'll get himself killed." Without looking, she gestured at the place where Taziar had been standing.

But Taziar was no longer there. He positioned his fingers and toes in cracks between the wall stones and shinnied to the rooftop. Still, Larson's voice wafted clearly to him.

"Look, I'll settle this. There's one way he can be perfectly fucking safe . . ."

Taziar crept silently across the tiles pausing to assess a parallel thoroughfare.

". . . He can stay the hell here." A restless pause followed, then Larson's voice echoed through the alley. *"Where is he?"*

Harriman paced with the deadly patience of a caged lion. Floorboards creaked beneath heavy bootfalls, betraying his rage to the women in the whorehouse rooms below. Light streamed through the warped, purple glass of the window, striping the desk, and twisting Harriman's shadow into a hulking, animallike shape. "I don't give a damn what you say! I know those little weasels down on the north side are making more money than that. Either you or they are holding out." Harriman stopped, gaze boring into Harti's lean face. He read fear in the smaller man's features, and it pleased him. "You had *damn* well better tell me it's them. If it's you, they're going to be picking the meat off your bones in the street next week!"

Cowed, Harti avoided Harriman's dark eyes, glancing nervously at the other two men in the room. On either side of the door, Harriman's Norse bodyguards, Halden and Skereye, awaited their master's command.

Warped and controlled by an angered mage, Harriman knew no mercy. "So who is it? Who's holding out, you or them?"

"Well." Harti licked his lips with tense hesitation. "Of course, they are, lord. I–I wouldn't hold out on you. I trust . . . I wouldn't. I would never . . ."

"Well, you damn well better never!" Harriman resumed his walk. "Tomorrow, I want double what you brought me here!" He whirled suddenly, jabbing a finger at Harti. "I don't care whether it comes from them. I don't care whether it comes out of your pocket. I don't care if you have to go terrorize some merchant. I don't care what you have to do. Double!"

Harti shrank away.

". . . If you can get it from them, good. That's where it's supposed to come from because I know they've got it. If they're that much smarter than you and strong enough to hold out on you, you better find somebody else to extort. I'm getting double or they'll find your organs scattered through the alleys. Do you understand that?"

Harti's skin went pale as bleached linen. "Yes, please, lord. I've got a wife and six children . . ."

"Widow and orphans." Harriman raised a threatening hand to strike Harti. For an instant, a flaw in Bolverkr's thought-splicing let Harriman's basic nature free. Thoughts jumbled through his mind, liberally sprinkled with confusion. All notions of violence fled him, replaced by guilt, and he turned the movement into a gesture toward the door. Momentarily, he had no idea where he was; then Bolverkr's handiwork regained control. Fury flared anew, and Harriman continued as if he had never paused. "If you stop whining and use some force, maybe you can get money out of those children. Go do it now. Right now! If you don't have that gold in my hands by sundown tomorrow, you're going to be racing the men I'll be paying twice as much in bounty to bring me your head."

Struck by Harriman's inconsistent behavior as well as his irrational anger, Harti backed to the door, caught the knob, and twisted. The portal inched open. Immediately, an anxious voice floated through the crack. "Harriman! I have something to tell you."

Infuriated by personality lapses he could not explain and which might anger Bolverkr and weaken his command, Harriman responded more aggressively than he intended. "What!"

Halfway through the entryway, Harti froze.

Harriman waved Harti away. "You, get the hell out of here and go do what you're supposed to do."

Harriman waited until Harti darted down the hall, then returned to his desk and waited for the speaker to enter the room.

Almost immediately, a portly thief in clean but rumpled silk burst into Harriman's office. Unfastened cuffs flapped at his wrists, and mouse brown hair fringed plump cheeks in harried disarray. "Taz is in town."

Harriman went suddenly still. A long silence followed.

The thief waited, pale eyes interested.

"Who's in town?" Harriman asked carefully, earlier anger forgotten.

"Taziar Medakan. The little worm you told us to wait for. He's in Cullinsberg. Headed this way, too."

Harriman suppressed a smile, holding his expression unreadable instead. Bolverkr had carefully severed from Harriman's mind all memory of the dragon's attack and the hostilities between them. But the Dragonmage had left Harriman's diplomatic skills intact. "Are you sure?

If you're wrong, you're in bigger trouble than the last idiot I was talking to.''

The thief stood his ground. Apparently more accustomed to Harriman's brusque manner than Harti was, he remained unintimidated. "I'm certain. Absolutely reliable sources.''

Harriman needed to be sure. "Would you put your life on it?'' *You realize you are, don't you?*

The thief avoided the question. "It's him. Fits the description. Fits the characteristics. It has to be him. Can't be anyone else.''

Harriman knew the time had come to consult Bolverkr directly. "Stand here. Don't move. I'll be back.'' Rising, Harriman pushed past the thief and his own bodyguards, trotted down the hall to his bedroom, and sat on a hard, wooden chair beside his pallet. Head low, he put mental effort into contacting his master. *Bolverkr?*

For some time, Harriman received no answer. Then a presence slid through his shattered defenses and Bolverkr's thoughts filled the diplomat's mauled mind. *I'm here.*

Taziar's in Cullinsberg.

Harriman felt Bolverkr's vengeance-twisted joy as his own. *Good. I've got plans for him and his companions. I want him to watch his girlfriend murdered and his friends hanged. Hurt him. But keep him alive, at least until the day past tomorrow.* Bolverkr broke contact.

Fine. Misplaced hatred sparked through the refashioned and tangled tapestry of Harriman's thoughts, sparking ideas far beyond Bolverkr's intentions. The sorcerer's meddling had created more than a simple puppet. Though guided, with motivations bent to Bolverkr's will, Harriman had not lost the ability to conspire. Awash in bitterness, he shuffled back to the workroom where the thief stood with obedient forbearance. "You're certain it's Taziar Medakan?''

"No question,'' the thief replied.

Taziar's no amateur. If I tell my people to abuse him, Taziar will play them like children. Besides, I'm not accountable for my lackeys' mistakes. Harriman met the thief's questioning gaze with a smile, then tossed a command to Halden and Skereye. "Kill Medakan.''

CHAPTER 3:

Shadows of the Truth

The treason past, the traitor is no longer needed.
—Pedro Calderon de la Barca
Life Is a Dream

Sunlight gleamed from the crisp, new hoops of rain barrels, slivering rainbows through a nameless alley off Panogya Street onto which the rear entry to Shylar's whorehouse opened. Crouched atop a neighboring warehouse, Taziar studied the walkway. Like most of the less well-traveled thoroughfares, it sported a packed earth floor that mired to mud with every rainstorm. The elements had hammered the black door, chipping away paint to reveal oak maintained in excellent repair.

Despite the closely-packed stonework of the warehouse and an artisan's attention to mortaring chinks, Taziar descended effortlessly into the vacant alleyway. He ducked into the rift between a barrel and the wall, where the shadows of both converged, and hesitated before the familiar doorway. The back entry was reserved for the underground; even they used it only in dire need and with gravest caution. Summoned from a distant land and uncertain of enemies and alliances, Taziar considered his situation urgent enough; but the attack by his former friends outside the city gates made him cautious. *I have to talk to Shylar. I don't dare trust anyone else. No matter how strong the evidence, Shylar knows me too well to consider me an enemy. At the least, she'll give me a chance to explain. And, if there are reasons and answers, she'll know them.*

Shylar's whorehouse had always served as a safe house

and gathering place for Cullinsberg's male citizens, criminals and guards alike. Taziar had never found reason to enter by any means except the front door and once, after his escape from the baron's dungeons, through the emergency, black portal set apart from the regular client areas of the whorehouse. *I hate to break in, but, under the circumstances, Shylar could hardly blame me for being careful.*

Taziar glanced up the wall to the rows of windows lining the second floor. Dark shutters covered many. Others had their shutters flung wide, and filmy curtains in soft pinks and blues rode the autumn breezes. Taziar knew each window opened into a bedroom; the only sleeping quarters in the whorehouse without one belonged to Shylar. Next door, the madam's study did have a window, but it overlooked the crowded main street rather than the alleyway. Taziar frowned. The idea of sneaking into a building in broad daylight, even from a deserted throughway, did not appeal to him; but he dared not waste the hours until night in ignorance.

How much trouble is Shylar in? How long did it take her messenger to find me, and what might that delay have cost her? Taziar shivered. His shoulder jarred the empty water barrel, tipping it precariously. Quickly, Taziar caught it by the base, steadying it and averting the noise that would certainly have drawn guardsmen or curious passersby. He cursed, aware his concern for Shylar was making him sloppy. He knew he would perform better by suppressing the myriad worries and questions that plagued him; he had always managed to do so in the past. But now an image of Shylar's kindly features was rooted in his mind, unable to be dismissed. The darker portions of Taziar's consciousness conjured a nebulous, nameless threat against her, pressing him to a restless panic he had not known since the day he had helplessly watched his father hanged and then taken his mother's life.

Madness pressed Taziar. He rose to his knees, goaded to an action he had not yet planned. It was not his way to act without intense and meticulous research, but the idea of Shylar endangered drove him to do something, anything, no matter how severe the consequences. *The baron's "justice" took my parents from me. No one is going to hurt Shylar without a fight!*

Calm. Calm. Taziar eased back into a crouch, trying to temper need with reason. The inability to picture a specific threat against Shylar gave him pause to think. *Who would want to harm Shylar?* No answers came. She was the one constant feature in a town that had little of permanence to offer its street orphans and beggars. Her position as madam gained her no enemies. She treated her girls like daughters. Well-paid and fed, they came to her as a reasonable alternative to living hand to mouth on the streets. She kept the underground informed, gave shelter and money or jobs to those down on their luck. And, for every guardsman who suspected and felt obligated to report her connection to Cullinsberg's criminal element, three superiors were bribed or loyal clients.

This is getting me nowhere. There's too many things I don't know. I'll just have to talk to Shylar. Having made the decision, Taziar slipped into his calmer, competent routine. He turned to the wall, nestling his fingers into chinks between the stones, and scaled it with the ease of long habit. Drawing himself up to the first unshuttered window, he hesitated. Most of the whorehouse's bedroom business occurred at night, but it was not unusual for the guards on evening shift or night-stalking thieves to bed Shylar's prostitutes during the daylight hours. Quietly, ears tuned for any sounds from within, Taziar peeked through the window.

Pale blue curtains tickled his face. Through fabric gauzy as a veil, Taziar studied the room. A bed lay flush with the wall, covered by a disheveled heap of sheets and blankets. Near its foot, a multidrawered dressing table occupied most of the left-hand wall; a crack wound like a spider's web through a mirror bolted to its surface. Directly across from the window, the door to the hallway stood ajar. Seeing no one in the room, Taziar scrambled inside. Silently, he crept across the floorboards. Pressing his back to the wall that separated the room from the hallway, he listened for footsteps. Hearing none, he peered through the gap.

The unadorned hallway lay empty. Doors on either side led into bedrooms, some shut, some open and some, like the one Taziar peeked out from, ajar. Familiar with the signals, Taziar knew the closed doors indicated active business, the open doors empty rooms ready for use, and the ajar panels tagged dirtied rooms for the cleaning staff. To Taziar's right, the hallway ended in a staircase leading to the lower floor. At the opposite end of the hallway, a pair of plain, oak doors closed off the storage areas. Kept in perpetual darkness, these closets could be used to spy on the bargaining rooms below. Across the hall and to Taziar's left, the doors to Shylar's bedroom and study lay closed. Slipping into the hallway, he crept toward the madam's office.

Taziar had taken only a few steps when a doorknob clicked. A sandal rasped lightly across the wooden floor. Caught between two closed doors, he whirled, tensed for a wild dash back to the bedroom through which he had entered. He found himself facing Varin, a willowy brunette in her twenties. A purple-black bruise circled her left eye, abrasions striped her calves, and several fingers appeared swollen.

Taziar stared, shocked by Varin's wounds. Shylar's rules were strict, protective of her girls almost to a fault. "Varin?" he whispered. Gently, without threat, he shuffled a step toward her.

Varin's mouth gaped. Surprise crossed her features, and she raised whitened knuckles to her lips. Yet Taziar also read a more welcoming expression in her dark eyes, a sparkle of hope. "Taz?" Her voice emerged softer than his own. Her face lapsed into terrified creases. "You've got to get out of here. Go. Go. Quickly." She jerked her head about, as if seeking an escape, and her hands fluttered frantically. "Get away. Go!"

"Varin, please." Concerned for the woman, Taziar ignored the question of his own safety. "Calm down. Just tell me what's going on. Who . . . ?"

Varin's gaze drifted beyond Taziar. Her eyes flared

wide, and she screamed. Fixing her stare directly on the Shadow Climber, she screamed again and again, then whirled and raced toward the staircase.

Taziar's every muscle tightened. He spun to face a burly, dark-haired strong-arm man he knew by sight but not by name. Before the Climber could speak, the larger man lunged for him. Taziar leaped backward, reeling toward the stairs. The man's hands closed on air, and he lurched after Taziar.

Taziar charged down the hallway, not daring to slow long enough to negotiate a corner into one of the rooms. *If I pause to climb through a window, he's got me. Have to get downstairs to the doors.*

The strong-arm man's cry rang through the whorehouse. "It's Taz! The traitor's in the house!" His bootfalls crashed after the fleeing Climber.

Taziar's memory sprang to action, mapping the route through the kitchen to the emergency exit. *The open meeting area's just before the front door. Too many people there. Got to get out the back.* He skidded onto the landing, trying to catch a glimpse of the layout below, prepared to dodge whoever blocked his path to the exit. Below and to his right, a crowd of prostitutes sat bolt upright on gathered couches, benches, and chests. The half dozen men interspersed between them mobilized slowly. Beyond Varin, now nearly down to the lower landing, Taziar saw no one between himself and the door to the kitchen.

The strong-arm man sprang forward, catching a streaming fold of Taziar's cloak.

Yanked suddenly backward, Taziar lost his footing. He twisted. Cloth tore. He pitched into empty air. His shoulder crashed into the hard edge of steps, and momentum flung him, tumbling, down the stairs. Wildly, he flailed for a handhold, but the cloak tangled about his hands, the soft fabric slipping from the wood as if greased. His head struck the banister, ringing. Each step jolted the breath out of him, stamping bruises into his flesh.

Taziar landed, sprawled, at the foot of the flight. Dazed, he staggered to his feet. A wave of rising enemies filled his vision. Cursing the pain, but glad for the seconds his fall had gained him, he burst through the door into the kitchen.

A middle-aged man sat, composed and alone, at the huge dining table across from the cooking fire. At the far side of the room, the exit stood, slightly ajar, and Taziar knew it led into a small food storage room where Shylar screened whoever pounded on the black door, ignoring anyone who did not use one of the assigned, personal codes of the underground. Relief washed over Taziar. If it came to a race, he knew he could beat the stranger to the door. *Once in the entryway, I'm free.* He quickened his pace.

The stranger did not move. An odd smile graced his features, and he made a loud but wordless noise as Taziar caught the doorknob.

Before Taziar could pull it, the door wrenched open violently. For a startled instant, Taziar stared at a leather tunic stretched taut across a muscled chest. He glanced up to fair features so badly scarred that bands of tissue disrupted golden hair in patches. Pale eyes swiveled, unmistakably glazed from the berserker mushrooms some Vikings took to enhance ferocity in battle. Hands large as melons seized Taziar's arms. The Norseman dragged Taziar off his feet and through the doorway, then spun and hurled the Climber into the far wall.

Taziar's shoulder blades crashed into stone. Impact jolted pain along his spine. He heard the door slam shut as he stumbled forward and caught a glimpse of a second Norseman, larger than the first. Then, clenched fists slammed into Taziar's lower chest with the speed of a galloping horse. Something cracked. Pain jabbed Taziar's lungs, and momentum reeled him into the wall. His head smacked granite. His vision blurred and spun, and it required a struggle of will to keep from sinking limply to the floor.

A tottering side step regained Taziar his balance. He raised an arm in defense, his other hand pawing desperately for his sword. The scarred Norseman seized him by the wrists and ripped both arms behind him. Taziar strug-

gled madly, but the larger man pinned him as easily as
an infant. Through a whirling fog of anguish, Taziar
watched the Norseman's partner approach and recognized the same drug-crazed expression on this man's features. "Wait!" he gasped. Doubled fists exploded into
his abraded cheek. Taziar's neck snapped sideways. There
was a sudden flash of brilliant white; blindness descended on him. For a second, he thought he was dead.
Then the huge hands smashed his other cheek, sparking
pain that made him scream.

"My turn." The man holding Taziar used the Scandinavian tongue with selfish eagerness, his grip pinching
cruelly. "You'll kill him before I get a chance." Suddenly, he let go.

Drained of vigor and direction, Taziar collapsed.
Weakly, he struggled to hands and knees, regaining
clouded vision just in time to watch the scarred man's
hand speeding for his face. He lurched backward clumsily. Curled fingers caught a glancing blow across the
bridge of his nose with a blaze of pain. The follow up
from the opposite fist pounded Taziar's lips against his
teeth. Jarred half senseless, he sank to the floor.

"Skereye, enough!" A stranger's voice scarcely penetrated Taziar's mental fog. Through bleary, blood-striped
vision, he examined the man who had been sitting at the
kitchen table and had now entered the room. Dressed in
blue and white silks and leather leggings, he stood with
a quiet dignity that seemed out of place amidst the Norsemen's rabid violence. Despite his commanding manner,
his eyes revealed gentle confusion, as if he had just escaped from a nightmare and had not quite reoriented to
waking reality.

Skereye enwrapped his fingers in Taziar's hair and
hefted the Climber to his feet. The Norseman's gaze
jumped from Taziar to his master and back to Taziar.
Robbed of control by the berserker drug, Skereye buried
a fist in Taziar's stomach. The force sprawled the
Climber. Air rushed from his lungs, leaving him no
breath for a scream. Skereye pressed, hammering wild

punches into Taziar's face until blood splotched his knuckles and Taziar fought for each ragged breath.

Even then, the beating might have continued had the leader not seized Skereye's wrist on a backswing. "I said enough!" He wrenched with a strength out of proportion to his average build.

Skereye stumbled free of his victim, and, with a bellow of outrage, turned on his master. Blood-slicked fists cocked in threat. Skereye's drug-mad gaze locked on his leader, but it was the Norseman who backed down. Skereye lowered his hands with a harsh oath. "You said we could kill him," he accused.

Unable to speak, Taziar raised a hand that shook so intensely he could scarcely control it. He wiped dirt from his eyes, and scarlet rivulets twined between his fingers.

Nonplussed, the silk-clad leader stepped around Skereye, his manner fiercely coiled. "My mind's been changed." Momentarily, he cocked his head, as if listening to something no one else could hear. His expression went strained, and he mumbled so softly Taziar was uncertain whether he heard correctly. "No one deserves to die like this." Then, catching a sleeve, the leader hoisted Taziar to his feet and shoved him into the other bodyguard's arms. "Halden, let him go. Skereye, disobey me again, and you'll know worse than death." Without bothering to clarify his threat, he stormed through the doorway into the whorehouse.

Taziar caught a misty glimpse of curious, female eyes peering through the crack before the leader's snarl sent them scurrying away. The door whacked shut behind him.

Skereye opened the rear entry while Halden hefted Taziar by the hair and a fold of his cloak. Halden tossed a glance over his shoulder, apparently to ascertain that his master had not returned. Satisfied, he hurled Taziar's battered form, headfirst, into the warehouse wall across the thoroughfare.

Taziar's skull slammed against stone. Darkness closed over him, and he crumpled gracelessly to the dirt.

Taziar awoke to a foul liquid that tasted distressingly similar to urine. He choked. The drink burned his windpipe, and sent him into a spasm of coughing. Agony jagged through his chest. He splinted breaths, moving air in a rapid, shallow manner that minimized the pain. The cold edge of a mug touched his mouth. A drop splashed the lacerated skin of his lip, stinging. "No more," he managed hoarsely.

Mercifully, the mug withdrew, and a tentative male voice spoke. "Taz?"

Taziar rubbed crusted blood from his lids. He lay in a narrow alley. Overhanging ledges blocked the midday sun into spindly stripes. Eyes green as a cat's stared back at him from a face a few years younger than his own. Other teens hung back, unwilling to meet Taziar's gaze.

"Taz," the youth repeated with more certainty. He lowered the mug to the street.

The boy's features seemed familiar, but it took Taziar's dazed mind unreasonably long to connect them with a name. He recalled a winter several years past when he had formed a team from a ragged series of street-hardened children. "Ruodger?"

The boy's dirt-smeared cheeks flushed. "They call me 'Rascal' now, Taz." He turned to address someone behind him. "I told you it was him."

A girl crept forward and sneaked a look. Barely twelve, she already matched Taziar in height and breadth.

Dizzily, Taziar worked to a sitting position, back pressed to the wall for support. He knew the girl at once. "Hello, Ida."

"Hi, Taz," she returned shyly. Beyond her, four boys watched with mistrust. He recognized two, a lanky runner known as the Weasel and a portly dropman they called Bag. A child several years shy of his teens twisted a corner of his baggy, tattered shirt. The last was a sandy-haired adolescent with angry, dark eyes and a knife clearly evident at his hip.

Taziar turned his attention to the deep amber drink Rascal had forced upon him. "Did you dredge that stuff from a trough?"

"The alehouse actually." Rascal waved his companions

closer, and they obeyed with obvious reluctance. "A lot of dregs and water, but it's the only stuff we can afford."

Taziar wrinkled his mouth in disgust. "I think I'd rather go without."

Ida nodded silent agreement. She shifted closer. Examining Taziar's punished face, she made a childishly blunt noise of repugnance. Rising, she produced a mangled tankard from a cranny and filled it from a rain barrel. Tearing a rag from the hem of her shift, she soaked it with water and dabbed at Taziar's bruised cheek.

Her touch raised a wave of pain. Taziar winced.

The armed stranger gripped Ida's arm and pulled her from her task. "Quit babyin' the traitor. Stick a knife in 'im, take 'is money, and get the corpse the hell outa our alley."

Rascal slapped the other youth's hand away. "Put your fire out, Slasher. Taz ain't no traitor."

"Is too," Slasher hollered.

"Ain't," Rascal insisted.

Slasher shoved Ida away with a violence that sprawled her onto Taziar. Agony sparked through Taziar's broken ribs, and he loosed an involuntary gasp.

"Harriman says 'e is, and 'e'll 'ave our hearts cut out if'n 'e finds us helpin' Taziar Medakan."

Rascal rose and stepped between Slasher and Taziar. Though slightly taller than the ruffian, he had not yet filled into his adult musculature. "I don't care. Taz ain't a traitor. If it weren't for him, we wouldn't have the group. Early on, we would've starved anyway if he hadn't given us money and facts."

Ida disentangled from Taziar, trying not to hurt him. "You say he's a traitor." She brushed Slasher's arm. "You say he's not." She tapped Rascal's foot with her toes. "Why not just ask him?"

The simple logic of Ida's suggestion stopped Slasher in mid-denial. All eyes turned to Taziar, though no one voiced the question.

The Shadow Climber fought a wave of nausea. "I don't think I betrayed anyone. Maybe you'd better tell me what I'm supposed to have done. And who's this Harriman who would kill children for helping a friend?"

Rascal answered the last question first. "Harriman's head of the underground, of course. Been that way more than a month since Shylar's gone."

Shylar's gone! Horror stole over Taziar. He struggled, aching, to one knee. His vision disappeared, replaced by white swirls and shadows. Weakness washed across his limbs, and he settled back against the wall, head low, until he no longer felt pressed to the edge of unconsciousness. "What do you mean gone? Where did she go?"

Slasher kicked a pebble into the air amid a shower of dirt. The stone bounced from the wall behind Taziar and dropped back to the roadway. "Taz knows.'e's actin'."

"Is not." Rascal glared. "He really doesn't know. Does that look like the face of someone who's lying?"

Obligingly, Slasher studied Taziar. "No," he admitted. "It looks like a face what got kicked by an 'orse."

Weasel and Bag snickered. The waif between them twisted his shirt tighter, stretching it farther out of shape. Ida turned Slasher a disgusted look before replying. "Shylar's arrested."

"No." Taziar shivered, set upon by a strange merger of grief and doubt. Shylar had lived too long among thieves and deception to be taken easily. It was common knowledge that the prostitutes would work for no one else, and the whorehouse would collapse without Shylar to run it. Yet, apparently, miraculously, it had not. "How?" Taziar shook his head, aware this gang of street orphans could not have the political knowledge needed to explain. "Where did this Harriman come from? I can think of half a dozen trustworthy men who served the underground for years. Why would anyone submit to a stranger?"

The youths exchanged uneasy glances. "Half a dozen?" Rascal repeated. "More like eight, Taz. All grabbed by the baron's guards and tossed in the dungeons." Rascal ran down the list with a facility that could only come from repetition. "Waldmunt and Amalric first. Then Mandel, Fridurik, Odwulf, Asril the Procurer, Adal, and Waldhram, in that order. Anyone who could serve as leader was taken even before Shylar."

The Weasel added, "Harriman come along just 'fore

the confusion. Ain't 'fraid ta kill or terrize no one, not even guards. 'e put th'unnerground back together.''

Taziar sat in silent awe, certain he had slipped beyond consciousness and was now mired in nightmare. He rubbed a hand across his face, felt the cold reality of lacerated skin and dried blood. Tears of grief welled in hardened, blue eyes, and he banished them with resolve. Suddenly, the plight of the beggars became clear. The arrests cut them off from Shylar's charity and the money from members of the underground who paid them as witnesses or hired them to aid in scams and thefts. *Starvation must have killed some and driven others to prey upon one another.*

An image came vividly to Taziar's mind, the remembered visage of the dockhand in Kveldemar's tavern, neck twisted in an illusory noose. Dread prickled the skin at the nape of his neck. "What does the baron plan to do with my friends in the dungeons?"

Eternity seemed to pass twice before Rascal responded. "Hanging. Day after tomorrow on Aga'arin's High Holy Day."

"Except Adal," Ida clarified.

Rascal flinched. "Except Adal," he confirmed, and his tone went harsh with rising anger. "A blacksmith found his beaten corpse stuffed in a rain barrel."

Taziar lowered his head, distressed but not surprised. Until his battering at the hands of drug-inspired berserks, he had considered the baron's dungeon guards the most cruelly savage men alive. Grief turned swiftly to rage. He clamped his hand over his sword hilt until his fingers blanched; tension incited his injuries, and he felt light-headed. His awareness wavered, tipped dangerously toward oblivion. "How?" The word emerged as a grating whisper. "How did the baron know who to arrest?"

Strained stillness fell. Every orphan evaded Taziar's gaze, except Rascal. A wild mixture of emotions filled the leader's green eyes, and misery touched his words. "Clearly, some trusted member of the underground betrayed them." He blotted his brow with a grimy sleeve. "Taz, aside from us, no criminal, guard, or beggar harbors any doubt that traitor is you."

"Me?" Startled, Taziar found no time to construct a coherent defense. "That's madness."

"Is it?" Slasher's finger traced the haft of his dagger. "Odd someone informed on ever' leader, 'ceptin' you and th' ones what joined after you left Cullinsberg. Ever' guard questioned, by bribe or threat, has guv your name."

"That's madness," Taziar repeated.

Before he could raise further argument, a long-legged, young woman skittered into the alleyway. "Rascal, Harriman's coming!"

Slasher muttered a string of wicked obscenities. Rascal delegated responsibility with admirable skill. "Ragin, tell the other scouts to stay where they are. Taz, put that hood up. Keep still, and don't say a word. The rest of you, act like normal. Slasher, don't do anything stupid."

Ragin trotted off to obey. The Weasel edged in front of Taziar.

"How can Slasher act normal if he's not doing something stupid?" Ida's quip shattered the brooding strain, and even Slasher snickered.

Moments later, Harriman and his bodyguards entered the alleyway, and the laughter died to nervous coughs. Studying the newcomers from the corner of his vision, Taziar recognized the Norsemen whose malicious pleasure had nearly resulted in his death. Skereye appeared uglier in daylight. Furrows of scar tissue marred his scalp where some sword or axe had cleaved his skull. Thin, white-blond hair veiled his head in a scraggly, nearly invisible layer. A film covered pallid eyes, as if years of the berserker drug had burned him to a soulless shell. Halden, too, appeared marked by battle. One hand sported three fingers. A swirl of flesh replaced a nose once hacked away. But his eyes remained fiercely alert.

A half-step behind the bodyguards, Taziar recognized Harriman as the man who had called his beating to a halt. In Shylar's whorehouse, the new leader of the underground had seemed out of his element. In a rogue-filled alleyway, he appeared even more the piece that jarred. He carried his swarthy frame with a nobleman's dignity, and his trust-inspiring features seemed more suited to a merchant. Only a dangerously fierce gleam in his eyes marred the picture. His gaze traveled over every member of the gang to rest, briefly, on Taziar.

Taziar stiffened. Aware the children's lives would be at stake if Harriman noticed him, Taziar hunched deeper within the folds and hoped the nobleman would not recognize his cloak.

A thin smile etched Harriman's lips and quickly disappeared. Otherwise, he paid Taziar no regard. Brushing aside the towering Norsemen, Harriman approached Rascal. "Only six coppers?"

Rascal swallowed hard. "The rest was food. We had a bad day."

Harriman pressed. "You have more."

Rascal moved his head stiltedly from side to side. Taziar read fear in the youth's demeanor, but his voice remained steady. "I'm sorry, Harriman. Ragin gave you all of it."

Harriman stood unmoving, leaving the children in a silence etched with threat. The unremitting quiet grew nearly unbearable. Suddenly, Harriman whirled to his guards. "Search them. *All* of them."

Taziar jerked backward as if struck. Horror crossed every orphan's face, and Ida hissed in terror. Taziar groped through the creases of his cloak for his sword hilt. He knew he would not last long against the Norsemen; he had barely regained enough strength to stand. But he hoped his interference might give the children a chance to run.

Before Taziar could move, Slasher stepped between Skereye and the remainder of the street gang. "Karana damn you ta hell! Rascal's told you we ain't got more."

Without warning, Skereye jabbed a punch. Slasher threw up an arm in protection. The Norseman's huge fist knocked the youth's guard aside and crashed into the side of his head. Slasher sank to one knee in agony, then scrambled backward to forestall another blow.

Arm cocked, Skereye took a menacing shuffle-step forward. But Harriman caught his wrist. "Enough. Don't hurt the children. They're family."

Harriman's voice and manner revealed genuine concern, but Taziar watched Harriman's eyes and the fleeting upward twitch at one corner of his mouth. By these signs, Taziar recognized a masterful performance. No doubt, Harriman savored the children's discomfort every bit as much as his guards. Abruptly, Taziar realized Harriman had met his gaze. The nobleman gave no indication of recognition, yet the icy lack of reaction failed to soothe. Identified or not, Taziar expected no clues from Harriman. Cursing his helplessness, the Shadow Climber turned his face toward the wall, clasped his hands to his knees, and waited.

"Fine." Harriman used a voice devoid of emotion. "Tomorrow, you'll make up for today. I'll expect a full gold. Whatever you have to do, get it."

Taziar sneaked a peek from beneath his hood. Rascal returned Harriman's stare with no trembling or uncertainty. For a moment, Taziar thought the youth would protest; a full gold would require an extraordinary stroke of luck in addition to the best efforts of every gang member. But Rascal responded with the bland good sense that explained why he, not the tougher but more impulsive Slasher, served as leader. "You'll have it," he said simply.

The matter settled, Harriman nodded. "One thing more. The traitor, Taziar Medakan, is back in town. If you see him, turn him in to me and it'll be worth twenty gold ducats, free and clear." Harriman's gaze roved beyond Rascal to settle, unnervingly, on Taziar. "It's another twenty if you give me the names of anyone who aids him." His voice went soft and dangerous as a serpent's hiss. "Because anyone caught helping him will die." Without another word, he spun on his heel and walked back the way he had come, the Norsemen at his heels. In the ensuing silence, their receding footsteps thundered through the alleyway.

Taziar clambered to his feet, glad to find he could stand without reeling; his mind remained clear.

Rascal seized Taziar's arm with such sudden violence, he nearly knocked the little Climber back to the ground. Though eighteen, three years younger than Taziar, he stood a forearm's length taller. "What's going on here? Harriman recognized you."

"He did not," Ida chimed in to defend Taziar. "If he did, he would have taken Taz."

For once, Slasher remained silent, rubbing his aching cheek.

Taziar winced in sympathy, familiar with the Norsemen's power. "I don't know whether he knew me or not. But if he wanted me, he already had me." Reaching into the pocket of his britches, he emerged with his depleted purse. He dumped the contents into his hand, counting seven gold coins and as many coppers and silvers. He offered the money to Rascal. "Buy horses and traveling rations. All of you, leave town. You're not safe here."

Rascal stared at the assortment of Northern coins without moving. "We can't take all that." He said nothing further, but his tone implied he would refuse to leave Cullinsberg as well.

Taziar pried Rascal's fingers from his sleeve, slapped the coins into the youth's palm, and curled the grip closed. "I owe you that and more. Take it." He released Rascal's hand, stuffing the empty pouch back into his pocket. "Believe me, Rascal. I understand how difficult it is deserting the only home you've ever known." Taziar recalled how his own loyalty to the city of his birth kept him from moving to the farm of an uncle after his parents' deaths. "There's a world outside Cullinsberg. It's a lot less civilized but definitely worth seeing." He broke off there, too familiar with street mentality to lecture. *Sometimes even certain death seems easier to face than the unknown.*

"I'm sorry about what happened, Taz," Rascal said softly, though whether he referred to the incident in the alleyway or his refusal to abandon Cullinsberg was unclear.

"I'm the one who should apologize. I never meant you any trouble." Taziar's hands balled to fists, and, though he addressed himself, he expressed the words aloud. "No more innocent deaths; I can't allow it. The baron's gallows will lie idle if I have to unravel every rope in Cullinsberg with my own hands." He turned to leave amid a tense stillness, the promise a burden that lay, aching, within him. And he had no idea whether he could keep it.

CHAPTER 4:

Shadows of Magic

A man cannot be too careful in the choice of his enemies.

—Oscar Wilde
The Picture of Dorian Gray

Al Larson crouched in the deepest corner of the third-story inn room, his spine pressed to the wall. The last dim glare of the day trickled through the single window, casting a watery sheen over the only piece of furniture. A table stood in the center of the room, carved into lopsided patterns by an unskilled craftsman. Atop it, a pewter pitcher and a stack of wooden bowls stood in stately array. A fire burned in the hearth. Earlier, sunlight through the open window had eclipsed the hearth fire to a flicker of gold and red. Now, the flames cast fluttering patterns on the wall, plainly illuminating Astryd and Silme where they perched on the stacked logs, but knifing Larson's half of the room into shadow.

Larson flicked open his left cuff and glanced at his naked wrist. In the last four months, since the god, Freyr, had torn him from certain death in Vietnam and placed him in the body of an elf, Larson had spent nearly all his nights in evergreen forests. The inn did not seem much different. *It's not as if we'll find mints on our pillows; there aren't any pillows. Sleeping on floorboards and spare clothes can't be much better than sleeping on pine needles and spare clothes. There's the fire, of course. But if I don't shutter the window, it won't provide any more warmth than a campfire in a drafty woods.*

The thought turned Larson's attention to the only win-

dow, cut in the southern wall and directly opposite the
door. From his hunkered position in the southeastern corner, he gleaned a slanted impression of mortared stone
buildings on the other side of the thoroughfare. Ram-
bling, narrow, and discolored by mud, moss, and dying
vines, they reminded Larson of row houses in New York
City, with the graffiti conspicuously absent. From a more
detailed study a few hours earlier, he knew ashes, rotted
vegetables, and broken wood littered the dirt floor. Now,
he heard the crunch of bones as a cat or rat feasted on
the garbage. Every other side of the inn overlooked a
cobbled roadway, and Larson could not fathom why Taziar had suggested this particular room. *Whatever his
reason, it wasn't for the view.*

Astryd tapped the brass-bound base of her staff on the
stacked logs. Metal thumped against wood. "Allerum,
why do you keep staring at the back of your hand? Are
you hurt?"

Self-consciously, Larson rubbed his wrist, unaware that
concern over Taziar's absence had driven him to consult
his nonexistent watch often enough for his companions
to notice. Explaining the conventions of his era always
seemed more trouble than it was worth. Freyr had bridged
time in order to fetch a man from a century without magic
or its accompanying natural mental defenses to serve as
a means of telepathic communication for a god trapped
within the forged steel of a sword. Once, while Silme
attempted to contact the imprisoned god through Larson's mind, a wayward memory had pulled them all into
the deadly light show of the Vietnam war. Since then,
Silme never doubted Larson came from another place and
time. But unfamiliar with faery folk and never having
accessed his thoughts, Astryd and Taziar attributed Larson's peculiarities to the fact that he was an elf.

"Old habit," Larson replied simply, surprised by the
surliness that entered his tone. Though inadvertent, Astryd's curiosity had returned his contemplations to the
one topic he wished to avoid: Taziar's absence. The conversation in Cullinsberg's alley returned in detail, replay-
ing through his mind for what seemed like the twentieth

time. In Vietnam, a competent, reliable companion was forgiven even the most callous insults once the fire action started. Yet Larson could not forget his own unyielding manner, cruel words, and the stricken look on Taziar's face when the Climber found his loyalties torn. *I shouldn't have called those street kids "scum." Shadow's sensitive, and he identifies with them. The punks may be thieves and hoods, but buddies do for each other. I owe it to the little slimeball to watch his back. He'd do the same for me.*

Frustrated by guilt, Larson slammed a fist into his palm. *Astryd was right. I should have gone with Shadow.* He knew his thought was foolish, but it would not be banished. An image filled his mind. As vividly as though it had happened yesterday, he recalled Taziar's wiry frame, clothed in black linen and clinging, naturally as a squirrel, to the "unscalable" wall of the Dragonrank school, returning from an unannounced visit to its "impenetrable" grounds. Again, he glimpsed a flash of steel as Gaelinar, his ronin swordmaster, slashed for Taziar's hands. And, though severely outmatched, Taziar had accepted the challenge, turning Gaelinar's hatred and attempts at murder into a dangerous game of wits. *All it would take is one person to call something impossible, and that jackass, Cullinsbergen friend of mine would go off, half-cocked, to prove he could do it.*

Larson sprang to his feet, his decision made. "I'm going after Shadow. He's in trouble."

"No." Silme's voice scarcely rose above the crackle of flame, but it held the inviolate authority of a general's command. "Allerum, don't be a fool. Shadow knows the city. You don't. If he's in trouble, you're not going to find him. Your leaving can only divide us further and put us all in danger."

Larson could not deny the sense of Silme's logic, yet the thought of waiting in ignorance seemed equally distasteful. "Don't you have some sort of magic that could tell us where he is?"

The women exchanged knowing looks; apparently they had already discussed this possibility. Astryd allowed her staff to slide gently to the floor. "I could cast a location triangle, but it's not in my repertoire. It would cost a lot of life energy for little gain. I'd have to center it on Shadow. We'd get a glimpse of his surroundings, perhaps enough for him to know where he was, but not for people who don't know the city."

Silme elaborated. "If Shadow's fine, we would have wasted Astryd's efforts. If he's in trouble, we won't know where to go, and Astryd won't have enough life force left to cast spells to help him."

Larson lashed out in restless resentment. "Let me get this straight. You can conjure dragons from nothing." He stabbed a gesture at Astryd, then made a similar motion to indicate Silme. "And I've seen you design defenses I couldn't even see that were strong enough to burn a man's hand. Both of you transport instantly from one place to another. And you want me to believe neither of you could make Shadow unrecognizable to the guards or figure out where the hell he is? That makes no sense."

Astryd's brow knotted in surprise. "Why not?"

"Why not?" To Larson, Astryd's confusion seemed ludicrous beyond words. "Because making disguises and finding people seem like they ought to be simple." He raised his voice, waving his arms with the grandeur of a symphony conductor. "Calling dragons and split-second appearances are incredibly dramatic." He dropped his hands to his side. "How come you can do the hard stuff and not the easy stuff?"

Idly, Silme rolled Astryd's staff with her foot. "You're just looking at it the wrong way. Dragonrank magic comes from summoning and shaping the chaos of life energy using mental discipline. By nature, it works best when used for or against users and products of magic." She glanced up to determine whether Larson was following her explanation.

"So?" Larson prompted.

"So," Silme continued. "Large volumes of masterless chaos take dragon form routinely; that's why we're called Dragonrank. Think of calling dragons as summoning the same chaos we need for any spell. How difficult can it be to work that force into its inherent shape? Then, think of a transport escape as moving a user of magic with magic."

"O-kay." Larson spoke carefully, still not certain where Silme was leading, but glad to find a topic other than Taziar. He spun a log from the stack with the upper surface of his boot and sat across from the women.

"But," Silme said. "A disguising spell would require not just moving, but actually changing a human being. Location triangles have to be focused on a person, in this case, one who is not a sorcerer. Understand?"

Larson shrugged, not fully convinced. "And if you cast this location thing to find a sorcerer? It would be easier?"

"Much." Astryd smiled pleasantly. "As long as I knew the sorcerer. If I only had a name and a detailed description, it would cost nearly all my energy. Anything less would prove impossible." She added belatedly, "Yet."

"Yet?" Larson echoed before he found time to consider. Magic made little sense to him. Despite the Connecticut Yankee, Larson doubted a lit match or a predicted eclipse would impress his Dragonrank friends, even if he held enough knowledge of their era to prophesy. One thing appeared certain. *Magic and technology are not the same here.*

Larson did not expect an answer, but Silme gave one. "With enough life force, a Dragonmage could do virtually anything. The problem with creating new spells is that there's no way to know how much energy it'll cost in advance, and no one can have practiced it to divulge shortcuts. Once the spell is cast, it drains as much energy as it needs. If that's more than the caster has, he dies."

Astryd cut in. "You have to realize, Dragonrank mages don't become more powerful by gaining life force. We're born with all the life force we'll ever have. We have to rehearse spells to improve at them. Even though Silme and I are nearly the same age, she discovered her dragonmark much younger. She's had a lot more time to practice and more desperate opportunity."

Larson nodded, having experienced much of that desperate opportunity.

Astryd reclaimed her staff, bracing it against the woodpile. "Magical skill is different than sword skill. You get better by making the physical patterns routine and learning to anticipate enemies. Sorcery is a fully mental discipline. We learn new spells by comparing them with old spells, if possible, and explanations from more experienced mages. Proficiency means using less life energy to cast the same spell. That can only come from mental 'shortcuts,' that is, looking at the techniques in my own unique way."

Larson said nothing, bewildered by Astryd's final disclosure.

Silme attempted to elucidate. "Did you ever have some intellectual problem you needed to solve, but it didn't make any sense no matter how many friends tried to explain it in how many different ways? Then, all of a sudden, you think about it from your own angle and everything becomes instantly clear. You feel stupid and wonder why it used to seem so hard."

Sounds like ninth grade algebra. Only I still feel stupid. Larson shrugged noncommittally. "I guess so." He imagined a cartoon with a mad scientist and a light bulb appearing over the character's head as he composed a wickedly interesting idea.

"Each time one of those personal revelations arises, the spell gets easier . . ." Silme clarified, ". . . for me. But it's hard for me to turn around and teach what made the spell simpler. I can help steer, but eventually Astryd has to find her own shortcuts. Anyway, I can only practice so many spells to this high degree, so I have to limit my repertoire to a fraction of the available spells. Why waste time and energy risking my life to create new ones? Of course, most Dragonranks specialize in those magics most useful to them or the ones they seem to have a natural bent for. Like Astryd's dragon summonings. The larger the repertoire, the less practice time I can give to any particular spell and the more energy it takes to cast."

"It's a trade-off," Astryd added. "It would be as if

Gaelinar taught you sword and bow skills. You could spend all your time practicing footwork and strokes and become a superior swordsman and a mediocre archer. Or you could do the opposite. Then again, you could work on both equally and became reasonably competent in two areas, but you'd probably lose a sword duel against an opponent who put as much time into blade drills as you did into both. Most Dragonrank mages know the basic discipline of a large number of spells, yet they understand only a handful well enough to . . .''

A sudden premonition of danger swept through Larson. He stiffened, interrupting Astryd with a cutting motion of his hand. Rising, he slipped back into the darkened portion of the room and crept to the window.

Abruptly, Taziar's head and fingers appeared over the sill. Wounds marred his familiar features, discolored red-purple from bruises. Concerned about pursuit, Larson caught Taziar's wrists, yanked him through the window, and sprawled him to safety. In the same motion, Larson drew his sword and flattened to the wall beside the opening, waiting.

A moment passed in awkward silence. Taziar clambered painfully to his hands and knees. "Ummm, Allerum. I could have gotten in by myself without you throwing me on the floor."

Cued by Taziar's composure, Larson inched to the window and peered out. The alley lay in a quiet, gray haze, interrupted only by a ragged calico perched on the shattered remains of a crate.

Larson heard movement from his friends behind him. Astryd's horrified question followed. "What happened?"

Larson seized the shutters, pulled them closed, and bolted them against autumn wind and darkness. Turning, he saw that Taziar had taken a seat on the floor before Astryd, his head cradled against her thigh while she tousled blood-matted, black hair with sympathetic concern.

Eyes closed and smiling ever so slightly, Taziar exploited Astryd's pity.

Milking it for all it's worth. Accustomed to boxing,

Larson assessed the damage quickly. He knew most facial bones lay shallow and sharp beneath skin easily damaged on their surfaces. *Broken nose and, from the way he's breathing, snapped a few ribs, too.* "What happened?" he demanded. Urgency made his tone harsh.

Taziar's eyes flared open, the keen blue of his irises contrasting starkly with blotches of scarlet against the whites. Silme and Astryd glanced at Larson in surprise as if to remind him the question had already been asked and far more gently.

Taziar responded vaguely. "I got hit a few times."

Larson squatted, hand braced on the firewood that served as Silme's seat. He dismissed Taziar's reply with an impatient wave. "Obviously. Now I need to know who and why."

Astryd removed Taziar's cloak and tunic, surveying injuries more slowly and carefully than Larson had. Robbed of dignity, Taziar caught her hand before she could strip him fully naked. "Take off anything more and be prepared to enjoy the consequences." He twisted his abraded lips into a leer.

"Shadow!" Astryd reprimanded.

Taziar went appropriately serious. "Honestly, Astryd. You've seen all there is. Anything else would be for fun." He addressed Larson. *"Who* is a pair of berserks working for the new leader of the underground. Having mangled their brains with mushrooms, they now exist only to pound the life from men smaller than themselves." He added beneath his breath, "And not a lot of men are larger." He continued, returning to his normal volume. *"Why* is because someone has convinced the street people I betrayed the underground." He considered briefly. "Which is amazing given it's almost impossible to talk the entire underground into believing anything. And my friends are in trouble. Does that answer your questions?"

"Yes," Larson admitted. "But now I have more. Define 'trouble.' Do your friends owe someone money?"

Astryd ran her hands along Taziar's chest, singing crisp syllables of sorcery while the others talked.

Shortly, the bruises mottling the flesh over Taziar's ribs

faded, and he breathed more comfortably. "My friends are in the baron's dungeons, set to be hanged the day after tomorrow."

Larson winced, recalling Taziar's tales of the prison in the towers of the baron's keep, his vivid descriptions of torture. Taziar had told him most guards hated dungeon duties, but some chose it as a means to satisfy aggression by threatening and battering its prisoners to death. "Uh, Shadow. Just how close are these friends?"

"Close enough that I have to rescue them." Apparently misinterpreting Larson's alarm as reluctance, Taziar turned defensive. "They're thieves and spies and con men. Damn it, I know that! You may not believe me, but they're all harmless and good people nonetheless. I once saw Mandel pay hungry orphans to scout territory he knew by heart. Amalric ran a lottery. He'd collect coppers, remove his share, then award the remainder to a 'random' winner who, somehow, always turned out to be the family most down on its luck." Taziar cringed beneath Astryd's touch. "But no need for you to risk your lives. The three of you go back to Norway. I'll meet you at Kveldemar's tavern."

"Nonsense." Silme's single word left no room for argument.

Still, Larson felt duty-bound to clarify. "What are you, stupid? Of course, we stick together." *Without Shadow's aid, the Chaos-force would have killed me as well as Gaelinar, and the rest of the world with us. I owe him this and much more.* "Besides, we all know the ferry doesn't leave for Norway until spring. Did you expect us to swim the Kattegat?"

Astryd added nothing to the exchange. A light sheen of sweat glazed features drawn with effort. The healing magics had cost her a heavy toll in life energy.

Larson dragged his fingers along the rough surface of bark. "So who are these friends, anyway? Shylar? Adal? Asril?"

Taziar stared. "How did you know?"

Astryd turned her sorceries to repairing Taziar's nose, and the Climber suffixed his query with a gasp of pain.

Larson shrugged. "You told me stories. Occasionally you mentioned names, mostly just in passing. I thought I'd forgotten most of them. They must have registered somewhere, though, because something's dredged those memories back up."

Silme went stiff as a spear shaft. Taziar tilted his head, confronting Larson from between Astryd's fingers. By the alarmed expressions on their faces, Larson could tell they had simultaneously come to a desperate conclusion. He glanced rapidly between them. "What?"

"Allerum." Silme's voice scraped like bare skin against stone. "Have you noticed anyone meddling with your thoughts."

"Meddling? I . . ." Larson trailed off, suddenly uncertain. He recalled a recent rash of mild pressure headaches, but he'd noticed no malicious entity triggering memories to goad or harm him. None of his thoughts felt alien, although he had become dimly aware of the reemergence of seemingly useless recollections in the last month. "I don't believe so. I'm still not used to people mucking around in my brain. I'm not sure I could tell."

"Gods." Taziar made a soft sound of anguish. "I really am the traitor."

They think someone read my mind to get those names. Guilt rose, leaving a sour taste in Larson's mouth. Anger followed swiftly. Since arriving in Old Scandinavia, his thoughts had caused more trouble than any differences in culture. Flashbacks of Vietnam had plagued him unmercifully; his mind lapsed and backtracked at the slightest provocation. His enemies had taken advantage of his weakness, provoking memories of war crimes and dishonor until he teetered on the brink of insanity. Later, they sifted plans from his mind, forcing his companions to leave him ignorant or use him as bait to trap those enemies, a warped cycle of betrayal within betrayal. *But Loki and Bramin are dead, and the world has only a handful of wizards and deities. What are the odds we just happened upon another?* He voiced the thought aloud. "You're suggesting the baron hired a Dragonrank mage to ferret out criminals? Seems extreme and expensive, not to mention farfetched.''

"But remotely possible.'' Taziar's reply emerged muffled beneath Astryd's hands. "More likely, the baron captured one underground leader and beat the information from him. But, in all honesty, that's not a lot more likely. I'd die in agony before I'd intentionally inform against Shylar. And I don't think any of my friends would reveal *every* other peer; at most, the guards could jar loose a name or two.''

Silme spoke with calm practicality. "I think you'll find the informant at the source of the lie. Who's calling you traitor?''

Weakly, Astryd sank to the log pile. Taziar placed a supportive arm around her waist and whispered something soothing which Larson could not hear. In response, Astryd nodded. Having ascertained that Astryd was all right, Taziar addressed Silme from a face vastly improved by Astryd's efforts, but by no means fully healed. "I don't know. I've been told several of the guards named me. I doubt anyone but the baron could get them to agree so consistently.''

"Unless the same person interrogated the guards.'' Silme grasped the situation from the other side. "Then it wouldn't matter what the guards actually said.''

Taziar drew Astryd closer. "That would be the new leader. Harriman. Of course, others in the underground would probably corroborate the story.'' He hesitated, addressing his own thought before it became an issue. "They'd corroborate by questioning other guards, guards paid by the underground . . . specifically, paid by Harriman. And Harriman seemed awfully quick to tell the street gangs I'm a traitor and to put a bounty on me. Odd thing though, he seemed intent on keeping people from talking to me, but he didn't kill me.'' He massaged a faded welt on his cheek. "And if he had wanted to, he sure could have.''

"Methinks Harriman doth insist too much,'' Larson contributed, and even Astryd stared. "Shakespeare, sort of,'' he qualified sheepishly. *My god, now I'm misquoting a man who's not even born* yet. "I just mean if Harriman's making so much effort against you, it's probably to divert suspicion. You're right, he's the stool pigeon." When no one challenged his conclusion or his use of English slang, Larson continued. "Do you think Harriman would interfere with rescuing your friends?"

"No doubt."

"Then our course is clear." Silme reached across the log and took Larson's hand. "One way or another, we have to get rid of Harriman and break Shadow's friends out of prison."

"Oh. Is that all?" Larson tossed his free hand in a gesture of mock assurance. "You make it sound easy. Do you have an 'organized crime boss influencing' spell?"

"Obviously not." Silme ignored the apparent sarcasm. "The mind barriers keep us from altering moods and loyalties as well as thoughts. However, if it was *you* I was trying to manipulate . . ."

Larson interrupted, not wishing to be reminded of his handicap. "You wouldn't have to." Briefly, he leaned his head against her shoulder. "I'm putty in your hands."

Misunderstanding the comment, Taziar gibed. "You're not pretty in anyone's hands."

"You're not particularly pretty right now either," Larson shot back. He rose, attempting to reestablish a semblance of order. "We have a goal, and we have an enemy. Unfortunately, Shadow's the only one who's seen the inside of the prison or knows anything about Harriman." He whirled toward Taziar. "What can you tell us about this Harriman?"

Taziar released Astryd and knotted his hands on his knee. "Not much. I never saw or heard of him before today, but I didn't take much interest in politics either. The street orphans said Harriman used to be a diplomat of some sort from one of the smaller, southern towns. Apparently, some disaster killed everyone in his village, and he blames it on the baron. Harriman came just before the violence started in Cullinsberg." Taziar opened laced fingers. "Not surprising. I'll bet he caused it. He took command of the underground when the leaders got arrested. He had no previous dealings with criminals. He just seemed to appear from nowhere.''

Larson settled back on his haunches. "Just seemed to appear, you say? Like magic? Does he happen to look Norse?''

Taziar leaned against the woodpile and drew his knees to his chest. "Maybe." He considered further. "Not really. He could be a half-breed. Why do you ask?''

Larson shrugged. "Before, you all seemed concerned we might be dealing with a Dragonrank mage. Did Harriman do anything you might consider magic?''

"Not unless you consider dragging a crazed berserk off his victim in mid-punch magic. It's impressive, at least.''

"A good thought though," Silme encouraged Larson. "If Harriman's a sorcerer and of any significant rank, likely either Astryd or I know him. Can you describe him?''

Taziar launched into a detailed description, filled with stiff, golden curls and swarthy features while Silme and Astryd prompted with questions. A half-hour discussion brought no glimmer of recognition. The fire dropped to ash, and Larson restocked the hearth from the stray logs that were not being used as chairs.

Finally, Silme threw up her arms in defeat. "We'll just have to see him ourselves. I hate to use the power, but we have to know what we're up against." She stood, wandering toward the packed clothes and supplies. "Get some sleep. In the morning, Astryd can attempt a location triangle.''

Taziar contested Silme's plan. "Who has time for sleep?''

"You do," Silme insisted. "We're of no use to your friends too tired to think or act quickly.''

"Which is why I can't fathom why you'd want Astryd to cast a spell we know will drain her life energy nearly to nothing." Larson usually avoided decisions involving magic, but strategy would require coordination of all available forces. "And you want her to do it first thing in the morning. She'll be useless the rest of the day.''

"Useless?" Astryd protested feebly.

"What choice do we have?" Ignoring Astryd, Silme

sat amidst the packs. The fire colored her cheeks an angry red. "If Harriman's a sorcerer, we'd better know it. We can let Astryd sleep after the casting."

Something about Silme's explanation jarred Larson. "You have twice Astryd's experience. Can't you pitch this location spell triangle thing tonight before you sleep?" It suddenly occurred to him that more than a month had passed since he had seen Silme cast any spell, even one as simple as a ward. *Of course, things have gone relatively calmly until now. We haven't had much need of magic.* Uninvited to Silme's and Astryd's practices, Larson had no idea how much sorcery they expended. *But Astryd has taken over our nightly protections, too.*

Silme dodged the question. "Good night."

"Wait." Larson refused to let Silme off that easily. "Is something wrong? Did you lose your magic?" Sudden concern drew Larson to Silme's side, and he realized his question must seem foolish. Dragonrank sorcery required only that its caster remain alive. *And well.* Terror gripped him at the thought. "Are you sick?"

"No," Silme replied. "No to all your questions."

Astryd spoke softly. "Better tell them."

Silme hugged her pack to her chest. "No to that, too."

Thoughts swirled through Larson's mind, each worse than the one before. *She's ill. That's it. With all the diseases they had back then . . . back now. And no penicillin. Shit. But can't she cure herself? Cancer. My god, that's it. She's got cancer.* Abruptly racked with nausea, Larson swept Silme into a violent embrace. *I lost her once and spent Gaelinar's life retrieving her. All the forces on heaven and earth would prevent me from doing it again.*

Silme shuddered at the force of Larson's hold. Grim-faced, she fought free. "Allerum, calm down. I'll tell you. It can't possibly be as bad as what you must be thinking." She pressed wrinkles from her cloak with her hands. "I'm going to have a baby."

The announcement struck Larson dumb. *A baby? A baby!* "M-mine?" he stammered stupidly.

Astryd snickered.

The twentieth century, adolescent college freshman

who had been Al Larson reacted first. Panic swept his thoughts clean. "Didn't you . . . couldn't you have *prevented* . . ." Then the combat-trained man returned, and sense seeped back into his numbed brain. *What did I expect her to do? Use the pill?*

Silme accepted Larson's reaction with her usual graceful composure. "Certainly, I could have prevented it. But why would I do that?"

Christ, the last thing we need now is a baby. Larson glanced across the room. The growing expression of terror on Taziar's features soothed him. He watched the Climber train a probing gaze on Astryd, saw her let him sweat before responding. "I don't think we're ready." She added wickedly, "Yet."

A host of emotions were descending on Larson. He knew pride at the accomplishment and shocked self-doubt that a woman of Silme's strength and beauty would choose to carry his child. He knew fear for the unborn baby, for his abilities as a father, unable to control his memories and trained only to fight and kill. The impulse to protect nearly overwhelmed him before he recalled Silme had more than enough capabilities of her own. Confusion touched him. "It's wonderful, of course," he said, not yet ready to contemplate the significance or sincerity of his words. "But what does it have to do with your magic?"

Silme took Larson's palm, tracing calluses with a fingertip. "Spells cost life energy. The baby is an integral part of me; I can't separate its tiny aura from my own. I wouldn't have to drain much to kill it."

Larson closed his grip over Silme's hand. "So you can't cast anything without . . ." He stopped, letting his observation hang.

Silme reached for her staff. "I stored just enough energy for a transport escape." She tapped the sapphire to indicate its location. "That's one of the first spells Dragonrank mages learn. It doesn't take me much life force anymore. Essentially, I have enough to cast a single, simple spell without risk."

Larson hesitated. The urge to keep Silme away from the conflict was strong, but he knew the suggestion would infuriate her. *She'd think I didn't trust her judgment or abilities, both of which are beyond question. But it's my baby, too. I have to say something.* Larson phrased his words delicately. Consequently, they emerged tediously slow. "I . . . love you, Silme. And I'll love the child, too. Don't . . ." He tried to keep from sounding patronizing. "If you must . . ." He gave up, tired of wrestling with parlance.

Silme smiled at his clumsy attempts at speech. "I won't take unnecessary chances. But Shadow needs us all, and even we may not be enough. With or without spells, I'm hardly helpless. I traveled with the greatest warrior in the world for years before you joined us. Do you think he taught me nothing?"

Larson remembered Silme's maneuver against the mugger in the alleyway. When he had happened upon Silme and Kensei Gaelinar as a misplaced stranger in the forests of eleventh century Norway, Silme had rebuffed Larson's initial advance with admirable martial skill. He recalled the sharp sting of Silme's blow and the glib death threat that had followed it. "Gaelinar surrender an opportunity to teach?" He tapped the hilt of the Kensei's katana. "Not a chance in hell."

Despite his casual response, Larson could not dispel the fear that gripped him as tightly as a vise. Concern for Silme allowed him to postpone his many worries and doubts about fatherhood. He knew any lessons Silme had received from Gaelinar had been informal. The focus of her strength lay in magic so advanced as to make her one of the most powerful beings in the universe. *Without it, she might be capable of handling street kids and my romantic advances. But berserks?* Larson glanced at Taziar, the image of bruises and abrasions still vivid in his mind despite Astryd's sorceries. *Shadow's river or not, only one of us has the fighting skills to handle this.* He clutched at the hilt of Gaelinar's katana. *I can't sit back while enemies threaten Silme and Astryd, and Shadow risks his life, alone, on the streets.*

Larson watched his companions prepare for bed, resigned to the fact that, as badly as he needed sleep, it would elude him for much of the night.

The Dragonmage, Bolverkr, had buried his neighbors and loved ones, each in his or her own marked grave, and, for every one of them he'd made a grisly promise of vengeance. Now, perched on the ruins of the fountain in Wilsberg, he frowned as he surveyed his partially-completed fortress. Much of the rubble still remained. But on the hill, at the site of his demolished home, now stood a castle of magnificent proportions. The curtain wall towered, shimmering with the protective magics Chaos had inspired him to create. He alone knew the winding sequence of pathways that would lead a man safely between the clustered spells. Even sorcerers versed in viewing magic would find themselves hard-pressed not to blunder into the jagged arrangement of alarms and wards. No guards would patrol Bolverkr's stronghold; he had no need of armies or mundane defenses. Yet the memory of his dead wife, Magan, staring in awe at the gaudy masonry of the baron of Cullinsberg's keep goaded Bolverkr to decorate his catwalk with magically-crafted gargoyles and crenellated spires.

Bolverkr rose, his tread as hard and unforgiving as it had been ever since the tragedy. His path to the fortress was arrow-straight, and, within a few paces, a boulder blocked his way. The Chaos-force seethed, creeping into the soul focus that was Bolverkr, some mingling inseparably with the gentler chaos of his life aura. Its rage boiled up within him. For an instant, Bolverkr's mind etched Larson's face on the lump of granite that dared stand between him and the world he had built with his own hands and magic. Hungrily, he dredged up the power of Chaos as if it was wholly his own. He shouted a magical syllable, and a stab of his fingers lanced a sun-bright beam of sorceries into the stone.

The boulder shuddered backward. It shattered, flinging fragments in crazed arcs. A chip gashed Bolverkr's arm, and pain dulled Chaos-fueled anger. Confusion wracked him, admitting a pale glimmer of self. *Who am I?* Nameless fear welled up within him, sharpening to panic. The shy, young Dragonmage discovered and trained by Geirmagnus, the years of learning to focus his skills, the decades of gaining peasants' trust all seemed unimportant and distant to Bolverkr. Even his memories of Magan had faded to obscure descriptions of a stranger's life.

Bolverkr's fists clenched. He dropped to his haunches, arms clamped to his chest, calling forth an anger of his own to combat his undirected terror. He threw back his head, howling at the heavens. "Who am I?"

Chaos retreated across the contact, unable to comprehend, but naturally in tune with Bolverkr's need for self-identity. His fear died, replaced by understanding. *It's the Chaos*. Thoughts flashed through his mind in rapid succession, small things deftly underscored by his battle for identity. Again, he became aware of the poisoning that must accompany the near-infinite power Chaos promised. And, as his underlying personality emerged, he realized something else. *I have to jettison some of this Chaos before I become nothing but a vehicle for its power.*

Now Chaos struck back, calmly, insidiously using Bolverkr's own natural, life aura Chaos against him. It probed his weakness, and finding it, incited Bolverkr's need for vengeance, drawing the image of Taziar Medakan, a shattered child curled at Bolverkr's feet and begging for the quiet mercy of death. He saw Al Larson driven to a reckless, destructive madness as ugly and chaotic as the war that spawned him. The Chaos-force sparked Bolverkr to remember that his enemies were far from helpless. The men had bested the same Chaos Bolverkr now possessed; as Dragonrank mages, the women should wield more and different power than their consorts. And Bolverkr came to a conclusion he wrongly believed was his own. *I need the power to destroy my enemies. The Chaos storm came to me because I am the strongest being in existence. I can handle this power. I can shape it to my will. I am the Master!*

And Chaos seeped inward with the patience of eternity.

CHAPTER 5:

Shadows on the Temple Wall

Respect was mingled with surprise,
And the stern joy which warriors feel
In foemen worthy of their steel.
—Sir Walter Scott
The Lady of the Lake

Sadness enfolded Taziar Medakan as he sat, crosslegged, on the bare wood of the inn room floor. His cloak seemed a burden, as if it had trebled in weight during the few troubled hours he'd rested. Heedless of his sleeping companions, sprawled or tucked between packs and blankets, Taziar watched the play of light and shadow on the temple wall across the alleyway. Cold ash filled the hearth. The open window admitted autumn breezes that chilled Taziar to his core.

Taziar had grown familiar with the false dawn; the loyal dance of silver and black on Mardain's church served both as old friend and enemy. He could not recall how many hundred times he had perched on the rotting remains of the apple-seller's abandoned cart in this same alleyway at this same time of the morning watching this same pattern take shape upon the stonework.

A floorboard shifted with a faint creak. Taziar guessed its source without turning. Silme was the lightest sleeper, and the graceful precision of her movements was unmistakable. She approached, knelt at Taziar's side, and, apparently misinterpreting the unshuttered window, whispered. "I hope you're not thinking of running off alone again. You're of no use to your friends dead."

Taziar kept his gaze locked on the wall stones as forms

emerged from the meeting of glare and darkness. He dismissed Silme's words and the subtle threat underlying them. "See that building across the alleyway?"

Silme touched her fingers to the floor for balance. She followed Taziar's stare. "Yes. It's big."

Taziar nodded assent. "Seven stories. Aside from the baron's keep and Aga'arin's temple, both of which are carefully guarded, it's the tallest building in Cullinsberg."

Silme said nothing.

Encouraged by her silence, Taziar went on. "It's Mardain's temple."

"Mardain?"

Taziar remained still as the light shifted, subtly changing the patterns on the wall. "God of life and death." He paused, then added, "Karana is goddess of the same, but Mardain's yonderworld is the stars, and Karana's the pits of hell. After death, Mardain claims the just and honest souls, and Karana gets the rest. Either treats his or her followers well. So long as a person worshiped the right god, he's assured a happy afterlife. Mardain's known for mercy. He forgives the worshipers of Karana whose souls find his star. But if they earn her realm, Karana tortures the followers of Mardain with heat or cold and darkness."

Silme considered several moments before replying. "Sounds like the intelligent thing to do would be to worship Karana. Then you can't lose either way."

"Sure." Taziar remembered the raid on Karana's temple that had resulted in the execution of his young gang companions. Atheism had spared his life; otherwise, he might have been at the temple and died with his friends. "If you're willing to admit to being conniving and untrustworthy. Karana's also the mistress of lies and sinners."

"But . . ." Silme began.

Taziar cut Silme's protestations short as the light assumed its final sequence before the world faded back into the blackness before true dawn. "There. Do you see that?" He pointed across the alleyway.

Silme leaned forward, eyes pinched in question. "What?"

Familiar with the dappled sequences, Taziar discerned them with ease. And, never having shared his discovery, he did not realize how difficult they might prove for a stranger to see. The memory was painful. But, since he had begun, he continued. "Straight ahead. Do you see that shadow?"

Many dark shapes paraded across the masonry. "Yes," Silme said, but whether from actual observation or simple courtesy, Taziar did not know.

"That's the baron's gallows. You can only see it on a clear day when the light hits just so." Grief bore down on Taziar, and he heard his own words as if from a distance and someone else's throat. "I noticed it the morning after they hanged my father." He recalled the restless need the vision had driven through him. "Then, though no one had succeeded before, I tried to climb that wall. At first, I just wanted to get high enough so if I fell, I'd die rather than lie wounded among the garbage. Once there, it seemed silly not to go all the way to the roof. And on top, I discovered another world."

The foredawn dwindled, plunging the thoroughfare into gloom. Finally, Taziar glanced at his companion. Folds and straps from her pack had left impressions on her jaw, and her golden hair was swept into fuzzy disarray. But her cheeks flushed pink beneath eyes bright with interest, and her cloak rumpled tight to a delicate frame. She was one of the few people Taziar knew who looked beautiful even upon awakening. "Another world?" she encouraged softly.

"Quiet. Alone with thoughts and memories and the souls of the dead." He clarified quickly. "I mean the stars, of course. This may sound strange . . ." Suddenly self-conscious, Taziar banished the description. "Forget it."

"Tell me," Silme prodded.

Embarrassed by his reminiscences, Taziar shook his head.

"Come on," she encouraged, her voice honey smooth.

Taziar blushed. "Never mind. It was stupid."

Instantly, Silme's tone turned curt. "Finish your sentence, Shadow, or I'll throw you out the window."

The abrupt change in Silme's manner broke the tension. Taziar laughed. "When you put it that way, how can I refuse your kind request? My first morning on the temple roof, I discovered a star I'd never noticed before. I'm certain it was always there, but, to me, it became my father's soul. It hovers in the sky from the harvest time to the month of long nights." Once his secret was breached, Taziar loosed the tide of memory. "It's small, a pale ghost, a pinprick in the fabric of night. Nothing like my father. He was huge in body and mind, and everything he did, he did in the biggest possible way. Moderating soldiers' disputes, leading the baron's troops, fighting for the barony, even conversation, he did it all in a wild blaze of glory. And only death came in a small way. He was deceived and condemned by the very warriors and citizens who'd loved him."

A rush of sorrow garbled Taziar's words, and he went silent. For the first time in nearly a decade, he felt defenseless and vulnerable. "Shylar and the others are family to me. If Harriman is a sorcerer, if my betrayal results in Shylar's hanging, I couldn't stand it." Taziar lowered his head, but his lapse was momentary. Shortly, his fierce resolve returned, and he felt prepared to face and revise any disaster fate threw at him. Dawn light traced past the window ledge, strengthening his reckless love of danger, and with it came understanding. With his own life at stake, every challenge beckoned. But the excitement of a jailbreak paled to fear when a mistake might cause the death of friends. *And I'm risking Silme, Allerum, their child, and my beloved Astryd for a cause that Allerum, at least, is firmly against.*

This time, Silme guessed Taziar's thoughts with uncanny accuracy. "I know you're concerned for us, too. But we chose to help because we care. If you go off alone, we won't wait around for you. Without your knowledge, I imagine we could get ourselves in more trouble than you could ever lead us into."

Taziar realized Silme spoke the truth. The urge to work alone was strong, but refusing his friends' aid would make his own task more difficult and endanger them as well. "Is mind-reading a Dragonrank skill?"

"A woman's skill, actually," Silme corrected. She smiled. "Shadow, you're just going to have to find some new friends. We know you too well." Silme raised her voice; and, after the exchanged whispers, it sounded like a shout. "Speaking of women, if you'll kick Astryd awake, I'll take care of Allerum."

"I'm up!" Larson said quickly. To demonstrate, he leaped to his feet, scattering blankets and sending the pack he used as a pillow sliding across the planks.

His antics awakened Astryd who groaned. Her eyes flicked open. Finding all her companions awake, she swept to a sitting position, cloak pulled tight against the chill. "No fire?"

"I'll take care of it." Glad for the distraction, Taziar trotted to the woodpile and began arranging logs in the hearth.

Larson pulled on his boots. "I don't suppose we can get room service around here."

Taziar cast a curious glance over his shoulder.

Larson laughed good-naturedly. "I didn't think so." He maneuvered on his boot with a final twist. "I'm going to the kitchen to get breakfast. Any requests?"

Taziar knew the question was polite formality. The fare would depend on the supplies and the inclination of the cook. "Anything not jerked, smoked, or dried for travel." He piled another row of logs, perpendicular to the first.

"Fine choice, sir." Larson assumed a throaty accent Taziar did not recognize. "Anyone else?"

Silme thrust the empty, pewter pitcher into Larson's hand. "More water so we can wash up this morning."

Taziar added a third layer to the stack. "And a brand to get this fire going." He rose, brushing ash from his knees as Larson slipped through the door, pitcher in hand.

Silme slammed the shutters closed and threw the latch.

"Hand me three or four logs." She stretched out her arm for them.

Taziar selected four narrow branches and tucked them beneath his arm. He carried them to where Silme waited on a bare area of floor between the window and the table. One by one, he set the wood on the floor beside her. "What's this for?"

Silme knelt, settling the logs into a crooked rectangle. "Astryd's spell requires a boundary. No need to waste time. Once we know what we're up against, we can make a plan of action." Silme summoned Astryd with a brisk wave. "Besides, if Harriman is a sorcerer, best if he doesn't know we've discovered his secret. And we don't want to give him access to our plot."

Though not spoken directly, Silme's meaning was clear to Taziar. *She wants to take advantage of Allerum's absence. Should Harriman turn out to be a sorcerer, he could dredge any information we give Allerum from his mind.*

Astryd walked to Silme's side. Taziar touched her encouragingly as she passed, and the warmth of that simple gesture sent a shiver of passion through him. Everything about Astryd seemed functional, from her close-cut, golden ringlets to the dancer's grace of her movements and the plain styling of her dress and cloak. And, where Silme's beauty could transform a man into a tongue-tied fool, Astryd had a lithe, homespun quality that made her more real and more desirable to Taziar.

Astryd crouched before the lopsided outline of wood.

Taziar scooted the table closer; the screech of its legs against the floorboards made him wince. Hopping onto its surface, he let his legs dangle, allowing him a bird's eye view of the proceedings.

Silme traced the outline of the rectangle, patting logs securely into place. "Ready?"

Astryd lowered and raised her head once. "I've been considering shortcuts all night."

Silme appeared outwardly calm, but her attempts at delay revealed hidden anxiety. "Any more questions for the man who met Harriman?"

"No." Astryd continued to stare at the rectangle.

Silme glanced questioningly at Taziar who shrugged. The grueling inquiry of the previous night had tapped his memory and powers of observation to their limits.

Astryd closed her eyes. Her lips moved, but no sound emerged. She stirred a finger through the confines of the rectangle. For several moments, nothing happened. Then, white light swirled between the logs on a shimmering background of yellow. Lines of black and gray skipped across the picture. Colors appeared, erratic splashes of amber, red, and brown that melted together and separated into a blurred, featureless man and woman lying close upon a pallet of straw.

Astryd made a high-pitched sound of effort. She sank to her knees, and the image within the rectangle smeared beyond even vague recognition.

Alarmed for Astryd, Taziar gripped the ledge of the table.

"Concentrate," Silme insisted with a casual authority echoing none of Taziar's concern. Her composure eased Taziar's tension, and, apparently Astryd's as well. The picture reformed, strengthened, and became discernible as the stiff-bearded figure of Harriman. Back propped against the wall, he reclined with bed covers drawn halfway up his abdomen. A tangle of golden hair enveloped a well-defined chest. A thickly-muscled neck supported features that might have appeared handsome if not for the unmistakable glaze of madness in his eyes. One arm was draped across the breasts of a slender woman. She lay, wooden with fear, trembling and half-exposed by the turned back blanket.

"That's Harriman," Taziar confirmed. He leaned forward for a better look, holding his balance with his hands on the lip of the table. "That's Galiana with him." Overgenerous to Shylar with his money, Taziar had always found her prostitutes eager to take him to bed.

Despite fatigue, Astryd gave Taziar a sharp look.

Immediately realizing his error, Taziar tried to save face. "I knew a lot of Shylar's girls." He clarified, "I mean I *met* a lot of Shylar's girls." Fearing to offend his

companions, he amended again, "Women." Then, not
wishing to overemphasize the prostitutes' maturity, he
returned to his original description. "Girls." Suddenly
aware his antics were only driving him deeper into trouble, he changed the subject. "That hand at the edge of
the picture. I think it's Skereye's. Can you focus in on
him?"

"Astryd centered the spell on Harriman," Silme explained. "Anyone else in the image is coincidently within
range. To see another, she'd have to recast."

"I don't see an aura." Astryd slouched on the floor,
her hands trembling and her expression strained. "Harriman can't be a sorcerer."

Silme bent forward until her head blocked the patch of
magics from Taziar's view. She gasped in alarm. "Astryd, look again."

Astryd shifted to her hands and knees and tilted her
face closer. Silme's thick cascade of hair distorted her
reply. "There is something there. Fine and almost transparent. He looks awfully alert for someone who's drained
life energy that low."

Silme's words scarcely wafted to Taziar. "We've seen
what we need. Don't waste your energy."

The women sat up, and Astryd dismissed her magics.
The image disappeared immediately, and the polished
wood floor replaced Taziar's glimpse of Harriman's room.

Taziar propped a foot on the table. "What's an aura?"
Engrossed in thought, Silme said nothing.

Astryd's head lolled; her eyes narrowed to haggard
slits. Distracted by Silme's intensity, she answered without emotion. "It's a gross, visual measure of Dragonrank
strength. It looks sort of like a halo of light. The color
and magnitude change depending on fatigue and mental
state." She rolled a bleary gaze. "Mine looks like por-
ridge right now. But Harriman's is worse. The last time
I saw an aura that weak, its master was in a coma."

Silme seized Astryd's arm in a grip so fierce that Astryd snapped to attention despite her exhaustion. "What's
wrong?"

"You didn't recognize that aura?"

Astryd met Silme's intent stare. "No. Should I?"

"You may never have seen it." Silme released Astryd and swept the logs into a pile. "Harriman's not a sorcerer, but he is a product of sorcery. I've seen the spell used before. It requires a Dragonrank mage to kill its victim, body and soul. Then, the corpse can be animated to act as the mage commands, without knowledge, memory, or will. It can only obey simple directions; it can't speak or initiate actions."

The description contradicted Taziar's experience. "Silme?" He cleared his throat, choosing his phrasing to correct rather than confront. "I saw Harriman interact, and speak, too."

"That's impossible." Silme's words implied certainty, but her tone betrayed her doubt.

Taziar persisted. "I watched him extort money from a group of children. He's an expert."

Silme went silent in thought, as if deciding whether to challenge her experience or Taziar's observations. Her chin sank to her chest. Her blue eyes dulled, then went vacant as a corpse's.

"Silme!" Taziar jumped down from the table and skidded to the sorceress' side. "What's wrong?"

Astryd answered in Silme's stead. "She's channeling thought. I have no idea where."

Taziar stepped behind Astryd, massaging her knotted shoulders through the fabric of her cloak. Her muscles quivered, as if from a grueling physical battle. "Is it safe? What about the baby?"

Astryd's voice sounded thin. "Thought extension doesn't cost life energy the way spells do. Just concentration."

"Oh." Taziar accepted the information easily, but his concern for Silme lessened only slightly. Unless she had chosen to contact Larson, she could only have attempted to gain access to Harriman's mind. If so, she had disobeyed her own tenet. *After threatening me not to go off alone, why would she try something like this?*

Suddenly, Taziar found Silme returning his gaze. Her

face was slack, and her fists clenched and loosened repeatedly, as if of their own accord.

Unable to read her emotion, Taziar prodded. "Silme, are you well?"

"Shattered," she replied, her voice strained. "Shattered like winter leaves beneath bootfalls, like a castle door beneath a battering ram." She cleared her throat and addressed Astryd in her normal tone. "I'm supposed to be one of the most powerful mages in existence, second only to the Dragonrank schoolmaster. But what I saw was the result of magic beyond my imagining. Someone smashed a hole through Harriman's mind barriers, accessed his thoughts, then rearranged them to the pattern and purposes he wanted."

"Are you certain?" Astryd's words emerged more like a statement than a question; she had asked from convention rather than disbelief.

"There's a hole, and pieces of the barrier still cling like shards of glass to a window frame. Thought pathways are looped, cut, and tied."

Taziar's hands went still on Astryd's shoulders. "Who?"

Silme ran her hands along her face. "I don't know. I didn't dare to delve too deeply. Surely, the person or thing who damaged Harriman is in frequent contact. If I used anything stronger than a shallow probe, he might have noticed me. At the least, Harriman would have detected my presence and called on his master. Alone and without magic, I couldn't hope to stand against a sorcerer with the power to break through mind barriers." She pressed her palms together, lacing her fingers with enough force to blanch them. Her manner clearly revealed the extent of her fear to Taziar. Even with spells and her companions' aid, Silme obviously harbored no illusions she could win a battle against Harriman's master.

"But I did discover Harriman's basic purposes." Silme stared at her fingers. "He's been instructed to see Shylar and your friends hanged, to destroy the underground, and . . ." She paused, avoiding Taziar's curious stare. ". . . to cause you as much physical and emotional pain as possible."

"Me?" Taziar blinked, stunned.

"Shadow?" Surprise and distress etched Astryd's voice, to be instantly replaced by accusation. "What did you do? Who did you offend who has enough power to do this?"

Taziar considered. His reckless drive to accomplish the impossible might have gained him enemies. But he could only recall two instances where his antics could have angered sorcerers. He had once robbed a jade-rank Dragonmage, but that sorcerer's powers were weaker than Astryd's. He spoke the second circumstance aloud. "I did scale the walls of the Dragonrank school and bypass its protections."

Astryd shook her head. "You didn't steal anything or hurt anyone. Even if the Dragonrank mages wanted to make an example of you, they wouldn't know who you were or where to find you. If they could locate you, even the diamond-rank archmaster would not have the power to destroy mind barriers." She snapped to sudden attentiveness. "Unless . . . Silme, what about a merger?"

Silme dismissed Astryd's suggestion. "It would require every mage at the school to cooperate, an impossible feat in itself." She explained for Taziar's benefit. "It's supposedly possible for Dragonrank mages to combine life force. It's a lot like seventeen artists carving a masterpiece with only one allowed to make the actual cuts and every life hanging on the king's approval of the final project. I've never known any mage willing to entrust his life energy to another. I've been told the magics that ward the Dragonrank school were a result of such a merger. One was slain, drained of life force. Three others fell into coma. Later, two of those died and the third became a babbling idiot. The mage responsible, the one entrusted with channeling life force, eventually killed himself out of guilt."

"Besides," Astryd added. "There are easier ways to kill a man than risking forty-three lives to create a monster. If the Dragonrank mages wanted Taziar, they'd simply kill him or take him back and hang him from the gates."

Taziar stiffened, displeased by the turn of the conversation. "So, whoever Harriman's master is, he wants me to suffer. And we have no idea what we're dealing with."

"Not no idea," Silme's tone went calculating. She stood, rubbing her hands together for warmth. "We know he wants to torture you rather than kill you, or at least before he kills you . . ."

Taziar twined a finger through Astryd's hair. "Thanks for clarifying that."

". . . his delay might work to our advantage. And, we know he or she is intelligent. Notice, he hasn't come after us himself. He sent a pawn. My guess is he found some interesting and frightening things in Allerum's mind, and he's not excited by the prospect of taking us on personally. Ignorant and weakened as we are, I don't think we could stand against him. We need to keep the master away, to reinforce his reluctance by making him even more certain we're powerful. We have to encourage him to send lackeys we can use to assess his abilities."

"Fine." The explanation sounded logical to Taziar. "How do you suggest we do that?"

"By removing Harriman, either by capture or death. It'll get rid of one obstacle to freeing your friends. It'll remove our real enemy's means of keeping watch on you. And it will give us time to organize while Harriman's master decides his next plan of attack."

"I don't know," Taziar started. The idea of killing an innocent pawn repulsed him. But he also realized that Harriman's command of the underground might put his friends, once released, in greater danger from old companions than from the baron's guards. *Besides, Harriman's mind has been ruined. He's no longer truly a man, just a sorcerer's weapon.*

Before Taziar could protest further, the door swung open and Larson appeared in the entryway. He held a loaf of bread tucked beneath his arm, and the pitcher in the same hand. Spilled water slicked his fingers. His other hand balanced a bowl of butter and the flaming brand. Steam rose from the bread, gray-white against Larson's sleeve. The aroma of fresh dough twined through the room.

Silme tensed, casting a warning glance at Astryd and Taziar who went stiff and silent.

Larson caught at the corner of the door with the tip of his boot. "Are you all going to sit there watching me struggle, or will someone give me a hand?"

Leaving Silme to decide what information to share with Larson, Taziar crossed the room and accepted the brand and bowl.

Larson closed the door, shifted the loaf to his hand, and set pitcher and bread on the table. "So, is Harriman a sorcerer?"

Returning to the logs, Taziar placed the bowl on the floor and feigned engrossment in the fire.

"No," Silme replied truthfully.

Larson sighed in relief. "Good. Worrying about some stranger reading my mind, I was beginning to wish you hadn't told me about the baby."

Taziar cringed. The brand tumbled into the hearth, and the Climber felt certain he was not the only one holding his breath.

Larson did not seem to notice the sudden change in his companions' attitudes. He rapped his knuckles on the tabletop. "So what now? We go to the baron, tell him who's causing all the trouble in his city and talk him into letting your buddies out of jail while the guards round up the crime lord and his cronies?"

Just the mention of the baron sent horror crawling through Taziar. "No!" Retrieving the brand, he jabbed it between the lowest layers of kindling. "We take care of the problem ourselves. The baron is a crooked, self-indulgent idiot who thinks loyalty is measured in moments. I'm not going to let my friends take chances with his depraved ideas of justice." Taziar looked up to find every eye fixed on him above expressions of shock at his abrupt and seemingly misplaced hostility. Not wanting to deal with his friends' concern, Taziar returned his attention to the fire.

A brief silence followed. Then Larson spoke in the direct manner he used whenever he felt his otherworld perspective gave him a clearer, more levelheaded grasp on a problem. "Look, Shadow, you're being stupid here. I understand you don't like the baron. That only makes sense, and it really doesn't bother me. But the baron knows this town. We can use him. Hell, you ought to get a perverse joy out of using him. He makes the laws, for god's sake. I mean, he basically runs the town, doesn't he?"

"Yes," Taziar admitted without looking up. "Yes, he does."

"Well, I don't have any great, fond respect for authority, and I've been a victim of politicians myself." A floorboard squeaked as Larson shifted position. "But if something big and bad happened, I'd still go to the police." He clarified. "My world's guard force."

Taziar shrugged, not bothering to respond. As much as Larson claimed to understand, Taziar knew his companion could never know the agony of watching his father publicly hanged, murdered and humiliated by the leader he had served faithfully for a decade. Water glazed Taziar's vision. Angered by his lapse, he fought the tears, smearing ash across his lids with the back of his hand. He lowered his head, not trusting himself to speak.

Larson continued, apparently accepting Taziar's silence as a sign that he was wavering. "The guards see the city from a different side than your friends. We don't have much time. It makes sense to explore every possible source of information."

"No!" Gaining control of his grief, but not his resentment, Taziar whirled to face Larson, still at a crouch. "You don't know Baron Dietrich. I do. Ever since he claimed the title from his father, he's been dependent on advisers. First Aga'arin's temple turned him into a faith-blinded disciple to the point where the church gets a deciding vote in all matters of import. Then, some devious, power-mad worm of a prime minister convinced him to hang his guard captain and torture me to death. Does that sound like a just leader willing to listen to reason?"

"Well," Larson started. As the hearth fire licked to life, a red glow crossed his angular features. "Actually, he sounds pretty easy to manipulate."

"Sure," Taziar shot back. The image of his friends dealing with a petty, unpredictable tyrant off-balanced him. "If you're an Aga'arian priest or a scheming politician. Karana's hell, Harriman's probably already got the baron on his side."

"Well, if he does, don't you think we might want to know that?" Larson snorted viciously, obviously on the verge of anger himself. "Now who's acting stupid because of a personal experience? I don't care how dumb this baron of yours is. He's not going to support some stranger undermining his authority and tearing apart his town."

Silme spoke up, as always the voice of reason. "Shadow, Allerum, listen . . ."

Taziar leaped to his feet, not pausing to let either of his companions speak. His heel cracked against the bowl, sending the butter skidding across his boots, and his unnatural clumsiness only fueled his rage. "I'm upset enough without you babbling about putting yourself in an enemy's hands. I know this town. I know what will work and what won't. No one goes near the baron! Is that clear?"

"I was just going to say . . ." Silme started, but Taziar never let her finish.

"This subject is closed."

"Closed, is it?" Larson shouted.

Taziar glared.

"Very well." Larson spun toward the door. "It's closed. If you want your conniving friends to hang while you drown alone in your own river, it's not my goddamned problem. I need a moment by myself, and I need to take a leak. Do I have your permission, O great and all-knowing god of Cullinsberg?"

Taziar waved Larson off, too enraged to deal with sarcasm and as appreciative of the chance to think without the elf's badgering. *He needs some time by himself to calm down, and so do I.*

Larson stormed through the portal, slamming the panel harder than necessary behind him. The door slapped against its frame, bouncing awkwardly ajar.

Taziar returned to the fire, trying to find direction and solace in the dancing flames. *Allerum's only trying to help.* The Climber would never have believed any cause could drive him to incaution and irrational rage, but the combination of ignorance, helplessness, and concern had done just that.

Silme rose, her manner casual, seeming out of place after Larson's and Taziar's savage display. ''You two stay here. I'm going to talk to Allerum.''

Taziar nodded absently as Silme slipped through the crack. The door clicked closed behind her.

Outside the inn room, Al Larson dropped all pretense of rage. He moved to the end of the hallway at a brisk, stomping walk consistent with the mood he had tried to create, down the staircase, and out the weathered back door into the alley. There, he slowed, pressing his chest to the spongy moss that coated the wall in patches. Not wanting his companions to spot him through the window, he clung to the stone, edging toward the southwest corner of the building. A loam smell filled his nostrils, and dislodged moss clung to his tunic like hair.

Inches from the turn, Larson back-stepped. He patted dirt and clinging plant matter from his clothing before stepping into the morning traffic of Cullinsberg's main street. A pair of elderly women shied from the tall, oddly-featured stranger who appeared suddenly from an alleyway; they skittered to the opposite curb and quickened their pace. Otherwise, the sparse groups of passersby seemed to take little notice of Larson.

Once on the cobbled roadway, Larson paused to get his bearings. Buildings of varying shapes and sizes surrounded him, a miniature panorama of New York City's colossal skyline. To the south, cottages dotted the landscape, gray and faceless, a monotonous series of identical dwellings. Larson turned. Eastward, the towering structures of the inn and Mardain's temple blocked his view; far to the north, a forbidding wall enclosed a structure with several proud, crenellated spires. It reminded Larson of the chipped, wooden rooks of his grandfather's ancient chess set. *That's got to be the baron's castle.* He headed toward it.

Instinctively, Larson adopted the natural protections born city dwellers learn. Though the streets were unfamiliar, he kept his attention fixed straight ahead, never glancing directly to either side nor meeting any person's gaze. He avoided alleys and darkened side streets, favoring the central areas of the main thoroughfares where the crowds tended to cluster. He kept his gait striding and purposeful, trying to indicate to would-be muggers that he had a specific destination and was more than willing to fight to get there.

In truth, the dangerous posture came easily to Larson. His failure to make a point to Taziar that seemed ridiculously obvious annoyed him. As much as he tried to convince himself otherwise, he felt responsible for Taziar's beating. *My unyielding cruelty, my insistence on humiliating street kids whom Shadow identifies with distracted him.* The image of Larson's grandfather rose unbidden, his kindly features swollen around a frown, his eyes moist, as if the city he loved, the one that had welcomed him from war-torn Europe, had betrayed him.

Larson caught himself grinding his teeth, and realized his jaw had begun to ache. He banished the memory, concentrating on keeping his facial muscles loose, forcing his thoughts to other matters. He remembered a day from distant childhood when he was barely five years old. The recollection came in vague and hazy detail, a day with his parents on the beach in Coney Island. High-pitched shrieks and giggles drowned the lazy lap of surf, and the ocean faded to an infinity of fog and water. As before, he heard his mother screaming his two-year-old sister's name again and again, first in question, then in abject panic. He recalled how his father had gone off to search while his mother clutched her son's arm with a grip so tight it pinched, terrified she might lose her other child as well.

Larson's reflection softened his manner. He recalled the husky, uniformed policeman who had returned with his sister, Pam, the child happily licking at an ice cream cone while his mother laughed and cried and wet her pants, too relieved to care who saw. There followed years of lectures on "your friend, the policeman," a concept pounded and etched so deeply that even years of unjust war could not make Larson forget. *Shadow's too much a hero for his own good. He's so afraid of risking any life but his own, he's not thinking straight. He can't go to the baron himself, not with a bounty on his head. But I can. I've finally found something I can do to help, and I'm not going to let Shadow's bias and paranoia take it from me.*

The intensity of Larson's thoughts caused him to drop the city manner he had not needed in the evergreen forests and tiny towns that dotted Norway. Jarred back to reality, he found himself glancing down a narrow, crooked alleyway, a more direct route to the wall-enclosed structure he believed was the baron's keep. For an instant, he hesitated, torn between the desire for safety and a natural urge to shorten his course. Then his sense of fairness prevailed. *I'd like to believe that Shadow uses as much discretion as possible when he's off by himself. I have a wife and a child coming. It's not fair for me to take unnecessary chances.* Responsibility crushed in on Larson, but he forced deep contemplations away. Delay of even a few hours might cost Taziar his friends' lives, and, on the wild streets of Cullinsberg, Larson did not want to get caught daydreaming.

Larson started to turn back toward the main street. Before he could pivot, the sound of footsteps reached his ears, and three men appeared from around a curve in the alleyway. Larson went still. Learned caution immediately set him to assessing the group of people emerging from a side road behind him. He stared at a trio of men, two portly and muscularly robust, the third lean and hard as a special forces ranger. Each wore the black and red uniform of Cullinsberg's guardsmen. Swords hung at their hips, and the thinner one clutched a spear.

Larson smiled in relief. *If the cops just swept through*

there, the alley's probably safe. He remembered Taziar's stories of torture at the hands of the baron's soldiers, but his current thoughts of policemen and their ancient equivalents were positive. *Besides, Shadow was a criminal, a prisoner, and, to their minds, a traitor's son. And Shadow said the cruelest guards take prison duties. These are just normal sentries, pacing a beat.*

Still, Taziar's warnings of corruption and brutality rang clear. Not fully convinced by his own logic, Larson slipped into the alley but kept his attention locked on the guardsmen.

The guards watched Larson, too. Their conversation dropped to silence. But when he passed them, halfway between the main thoroughfare and the bend in the alleyway, they made no hostile gestures. The heaviest of the three nodded in wordless warning or greeting, Larson could not tell which, but no one challenged him.

Not wanting to arouse the guards' suspicions, Larson resisted the urge to glance over his shoulder and watch their progress. He continued onward, trusting his jungle-inspired instincts to alert him to any sudden movements behind him. When nothing untoward happened, Larson relaxed. *Great. Now the little thief's got me jumping at shadows, too.* He groaned at his unintentional pun.

Shortly after the curve, the alleyway ended in another large, cobbled street. Larson stepped out into it, glancing to his right, and the sight of a walled-in structure with four, thin towers froze him in his tracks. *Shit! Is that the baron's castle?* He looked back to the multispired hulk he had been steering toward for the last ten minutes. *Or that?* Frustration sent him into another cycle of teeth grinding, and thoughts rose of his high school girlfriend chastising him for the "male character flaw of driving in random circles in the hope that sometime in the next bazillion years you'll just happen to run into wherever you're trying to go." Larson could not help smiling at the memory. He studied the passing crowds, seeking someone harmless-looking to stop for directions.

While Larson stood in silent indecision, male voices wafted to him from the alleyway. The neighboring buildings muffled their words to echoes, but their tone came through clearly, the mocking, half-shouted taunts of construction workers ogling a pretty woman.

Larson whirled, tensing. *It's none of my business. Let the cops handle it.* Even as the thought surfaced, he knew the guardsmen were the cause, not the solution. The brief realization that Taziar did, indeed, know his city well flashed through Larson's mind, raising an irritation that blazed to anger. His jaw clenched. *Calm. A little teasing never hurt anyone. This is civilization. A real city with real laws. I can't go off half-cocked over nothing.*

The guards' exhortations rose in volume, indecipherable, but goading.

Larson imagined some wide-eyed, teenaged girl who had chosen to walk through the alley, reassured by the presence of the guardsmen, only to have them leer and slobber at her. *Jerks.* He waited, wondering why the woman had not just fled.

Then, the voice of one man rang over the din. "Hey, wench. How'd you like to be stracked by a guard?" He used a crude, local euphemism for sex that Larson had never heard, but its meaning came through clearly enough.

Though soft, the woman's reply cut distinctly above the chaos. "No, thank you," she said simply, and her voice sounded too familiar.

Silme? Larson's heart quickened. *It can't be. Why would she follow me? How could she risk the baby?* Realization tightened his muscles to knots. *She's got no magic!* Outrage cut through him. *If they so much as touch her, I'll rip their goddamned lungs out!* He tensed to charge, delayed by another thought. *Back in the alley with the street gang, Shadow had the situation under control, and I almost turned it into a slaughter. If I go bounding in there like some rabid knight in shining armor, I might get Silme killed.* With caution befitting his combat training, Larson crept toward the bend in the alleyway.

"You don't understand," the same man said, his voice gaining a dangerous edge that made it obvious he no longer considered it a game. "We run this town. We don't have to ask, we take what we want."

Larson's hand crushed down on his sword hilt. He whipped around the curve just in time to see the guards separate and move to the walls, as if to let Silme pass unmolested. As far as he could tell, Silme had done or said nothing to defuse the situation, yet the guards appeared to have decided to let the matter drop. *What the hell?*

Despite the danger, Larson could not help but notice how the morning sun glazed Silme's hair like metallic gold, and her stance as she moved between the guards seemed regal and menacing. She held her dragonstaff in whitened knuckles, with the security of a king's scepter in his own court. Her gaze found Larson, and her frown deepened, warning him not to start trouble where it did not yet exist. But she must have taken some comfort from his presence because her manner relaxed slightly and the blood returned to her fingers.

Larson hesitated, wrestling his anger.

Attentive to Silme and partially turned away from the elf, the guards apparently did not notice Larson waiting deeper in the thoroughfare. Even as she strode past the two portly soldiers, the spear-wielder tossed back a shock of frizzled, dark hair and stepped into the center of the alley, blocking her path. "You might want to stay here where we can protect you from the unsavories out there." He jerked a thumb over his shoulder, blindly indicating Larson.

Silme stopped. Her expression did not change. "I can take care of myself."

Suddenly, the man leaped for Silme. She back-stepped. Catching his hand against her arm, she snapped her staff upward. The brass-bound base slammed into his groin.

The guard pitched forward amid his companions' howls of laughter. His knees buckled. The spear thumped to the dirt. His hands clenched to his genitals, but he managed to keep his feet.

Her pathway still blocked by the guard, Silme waited with patient composure.

That should cool his lust a bit. Larson indulged in a smile, but familiar with violent men who became enraged rather than muddled by pain, he silently edged closer.

Gradually, the injured man straightened. Several more seconds passed before he managed to speak beneath his friends' snickers. When he did, rage deepened his tone. "I was going to make it nice for you. Now I'll pin you down, and we'll all rape you till you scream."

The laughter stopped as if cut. Encouraged by their companion, the other three guards closed in on Silme at once.

Now, nothing could stay Larson. He sprang at the guard's back.

One of the others shouted a warning, but it came too late. Larson grabbed the spearman's right wrist, yanking the arm behind the man's back. His free hand crashed against the base of the guard's skull. Larson pivoted. Drawing up on the arm and shoving down on the head, he whipped the guard off his feet, driving his face into the packed earth roadway.

The guard screamed. Twisting from Larson's grip, he rolled beyond reach. He pawed at his face, blood from abrasions staining his fingers. Luck alone had saved his nose and cheekbones.

The other sentries froze. Larson crouched. Sidestepping the Cullinsbergens with dignified composure, Silme started toward Larson.

But the frizzle-haired guard regained his feet and bullied between them. "You stay out of this, stranger." He jabbed a finger at Larson, keeping his distance and apparently trusting to his companions to guard his back from Silme. "You don't know what you're getting into."

One of us doesn't know. Fury boiled through Larson. His hand fell to his sword, and he kneaded the hilt.

Despite the violence and the guard between them, Silme spoke gently. "Calm down, Allerum. It's not worth it."

Larson settled into a fighting stance, his eyes locked

on the man before him. "I'll calm down when they're all dead."

The guard's hand dropped to his own hilt, and blood smeared the split leather grip. The other two pressed forward, copying their leader's martial gesture.

Silme pressed. "Allerum, we're doing something important. Don't let this get in the way. Let's just leave. It's under control now."

Understanding penetrated Larson's mental fog. *She's not going to stop me from seeing the baron. And, as always, she's right. It's over, and no one got hurt.* He studied the guard's scraped face. *No one important, at least.* The idea of leaving these guards to rape other, less capable women bothered him, but, for now, Taziar's friends had to take precedence. Reluctantly, Larson let his fist fall away from his belt, though his rage would disperse far more slowly. "You're right. Let's go. The baron'll be pissed if I tell him I just had to kill three of his guards . . ." He could not help adding, ". . . because they were *stupid*."

The guards exchanged glances. Their hands still hovered near their hilts, but they did not draw their weapons. "What do you mean, 'talk to the baron?' "

"That's where I was going!" Larson shouted. "You're goddamned lucky I have to see the baron. Otherwise I'd have left you all bleeding in the alley!"

From behind the leader, Silme made a sudden gesture of disapproval.

One of the heavier guards shifted restlessly, his eyes dark with malice. The leaner guard spoke. "What were you going to tell the baron?"

Ignoring Silme's plea for tolerance, Larson snorted. "None of your goddamned business. I'm not going to tell something this important to some jerk who's supposed to be upholding the law but is breaking it instead."

Silme chimed in. "It's urgent. It involves the criminals who are causing problems in the streets."

After the guards' attack on Silme, Larson doubted they would care about crime. But their hands slid away from their sheaths. The sentries exchanged interested, if skeptical glances. Only then, did it dawn on Larson that, regardless of their own brutality, it still fell to the guards to police the streets. Until Harriman inspired the underground, violence was the sole reign of the guard force, and they sublimated their crueler tendencies by intimidating peasants or battering prisoners. As the city turned fiercer, so did the guards. *If we can get the crime element under control, the guards will follow naturally. And it's at least as much in their interest as our own to make the streets safe.*

"Fine." The leader used his handkerchief to staunch the bleeding on his face, his lips twitching into an angry frown. "You want to talk to the baron about that, we'll escort you personally. We'll just make sure nothing happens to you on the way." He smiled wickedly. "Afterward . . ." He glared, meeting Larson's gaze with fiery, green eyes. ". . . you and I are going to have a talk. What just happened here is between us. We'll settle it later."

Larson returned the stare without flinching, and the two stood, unmoving, neither willing to glance away first. "Sounds just fine to me."

In the northern quarter of the city of Cullinsberg, the baron's keep nestled between walls twice the height of a tall man. Standing at the gate with Silme, Larson studied the castle's seven stories of blocked granite, its corner spires rising to the heavens like dragons' tails. In the courtyard, peasants sat in huddled groups while uniformed guards threaded watches between them. A moat slicked with algae reflected the morning light, murky green beneath the lowered drawbridge that jutted from the dark depths of the keep. Two sentries stood before the walkway and rebuffed citizens with words or shoves of their spear shafts. A matching pair of guardsmen met Larson, Silme, and their three guard escort at the open gate.

The larger of the sentries regarded Larson and Silme from beneath a curled mat of blond hair. "Who are you? Do you have an appointment?" He used a condescending tone that denied the possibility. "Does the baron know you?"

Still seething from his confrontation in the alley, Larson found the guard's brusque manner and formality a challenge. He opened his mouth, but before he could speak, one of the robust escorts piped in from behind him.

"It's all right. They're with us."

The sentry regarded the leader of the trio curiously. "Haimfrid?"

The frizzle-haired guard nodded, a single, curt gesture emphasized by the thud of his spear butt against the ground. "They need to talk to Baron Dietrich. We'll take them personally."

The sentries exchanged glances. Apparently, this went against accepted procedure, but Haimfrid must have outranked them because they stepped aside to let Silme, Larson and their accompanying guardsmen through the gate.

Haimfrid led his charges past waiting clusters of townsfolk, across the drawbridge over the moat, and into the mouth of the keep. Braziers lit the hallway in evenly-spaced hemispheres. Though scrubbed clean, the stone walls supported no finery, and Larson suspected that the baron displayed his wealth and artifacts only in places where visiting peasants could not enjoy or steal them. A short distance down the corridor, they came upon an oak door and a hard, wooden bench across from it. "Sit," Haimfrid growled.

The two heavyset guards trotted off to make arrangements.

Larson and Silme sat. Haimfrid stood, stiff as his spear, directly before them. Only his eyes moved, as he studied Silme, taunting Larson with a hungry leer of anticipation.

Silme leaned against her dragonstaff with calm detachment, pretending to take no notice of Haimfrid's stare. Larson chewed at his lip, trying to rein his temper with little success. He latched his fingers onto the edges of the bench, rocking to waste pent-up energy, reminding himself repeatedly that he could never hope to win a battle against guards while in the baron's keep. *Take care of business first. Then I'll rip off the bastard's head.*

Minutes stretched into an hour. Stubbornly refusing to be intimidated, Haimfrid remained standing and gawking long after the position must have grown uncomfortable. Silme dropped into a shallow catnap, and Larson's mood grew progressively uglier. Finally, he leaped to his feet to protest.

At that precise moment, the door edged open, and one of the heavyset guardsmen poked his head through the crack. "Haimfrid?"

"Come with me." Haimfrid beckoned as if no time had elapsed. Walking with the limp of cramped muscles, he led Larson and Silme through the door and into the baron's audience chamber.

A frayed carpet of multicolored squares formed a pathway to the baron's dais. Dressed in a gaudy costume of leather and silk, a finely-etched and jeweled medallion around his throat, the baron perched in a chair carved into the shape of a lion. The maned head topped its back, its mouth opened. Though intended to appear formidable, in Larson's current mood, it looked more as if the creature might swallow the baron's head. The fourteen guards positioned around the courtroom wore red-trimmed black uniforms, but the baron sported gold and silver, the colors of Aga'arin's priests.

As Larson traversed the carpet at Haimfrid's side, it became instantly apparent that the room contained no other exits. During his interminable wait on the bench no one had left by the main doors. *The baron saw no one before us. He made us wait for no good reason.* The realization deepened Larson's rage. *I won't be bullied.*

As if to prove him wrong, Haimfrid slammed the base of his spear into Larson's shin. "That's far enough. Now kneel and kiss the floor."

Pain flared through Larson's ankle. He hissed in fury. "Fuck you. I'm not putting my lips on any floor."

Haimfrid raised his voice so the others in the room could hear. "Insolent fool, you're in the presence of the most high, noble baron of Cullinsberg. What do you mean you won't bow?"

Born and raised in the king's city of Forste-Mar, Silme curtsied with practiced elegance.

Bow? Larson fought the urge to leap bodily upon Haimfrid. "You bastard," he whispered. More accus-

tomed to saluting as a show of respect, he executed a
rigid, clumsy bow.

Haimfrid sneered. "Now do it right, or I'll take this
spear to you." He brandished the weapon in warning.

As the pain in his ankle subsided, Larson dismissed
Haimfrid's threat softly, as if he were nothing more than
a bothersome fly at a picnic. "You go back in the corner
and play with your stick like a nice, little boy and you
won't get hurt."

"Hold." The baron's voice thundered through the
room. "There's time enough for violence if it's necessary. Right now, Haimfrid, you stand off."

Haimfrid couched his spear with obvious reluctance.

Baron Dietrich fondled a paw adorning his handrest.
"You come into my presence. You show an appalling
lack of proper regard. This had better be important."

In an obvious attempt to restore order, Silme broke in
before Larson could gather breath. "You'll have to excuse
him, lord. He comes from another realm where this sort
of circumstance is unusual. He's a bit out of sorts, and the
information we bring is of such great importance I didn't
have time to brief him on all the appropriate courtesy and
decorum someone of your mighty stature deserves."

"Fine. Fine." The baron waved a hand with impatience. "Proceed. If your news is truly important enough
to bring to my attention, I can forgive a lapse of respect
this once."

Silme curtsied again. "As I'm sure you know, the in-
cidence of crime in Cullinsberg has recently increased
and its nature has become more violent."

Forcing himself to remain collected, Larson avoided
Haimfrid's stare.

"Yes, that's so," said the baron. "But we have taken
what we feel to be the appropriate measures and have the
situation under control."

Larson opened his mouth to disagree, but Silme tapped
his other shin with her staff and seized his moment of
surprise to continue. "This is in no way intended to be
disrespectful, lord. The measures taken may eventually
bring crime under control. As yet, they haven't been suc-

cessful. The streets remain unsafe. But we have information regarding a leader of the organized underground who is causing the problems. It might be prudent for you to use the facilities at your disposal to remove this leader, thereby weakening the underground.''

Impressed by Silme's eloquence, Larson awaited the baron's reply with the same quiet eagerness as his soldiers.

''Fine,'' the baron said agreeably. ''I don't believe we still have an organized underground, just a bunch of thugs. But it might prove interesting to question whoever you name. Maybe he does know some useful information. We've already made a sweep of the leaders, but if we missed one, tell us. I'll be grateful, and you'll be handsomely rewarded.''

This is almost too easy. Larson's spirits lifted, and even Haimfrid's persistent glare no longer disturbed him.

''The leader's name is Harriman,'' Silme said.

The baron leaned forward, hands clenched on the lion's paws. ''Who? Repeat that.''

Silme obliged. ''The leader's name is Harriman.''

''Do you have a description of this Harriman?''

Silme repeated the features Taziar had highlighted the previous night. ''Over thirty. Average height but well-muscled. Curly blond hair and beard. Dark, shrewd eyes.''

The baron slumped back into his chair. ''Guards, show them out. I don't want to waste any more time.''

Surprised by the sudden turn of events, Larson shouted. ''Wait! What's going on here? What the hell are you doing?'' As Haimfrid closed in, Larson hollered. ''Idiot!'' He intended the insult for the guard, but the baron took offense.

''Idiot?'' Dietrich screeched in rage, and every soldier tensed. ''Who are you calling idiot, you insignificant peon? Harriman happens to be one of my men, a nobleman in his own right, and not a criminal. You come to me. You make all kinds of demands. You burst into my presence without the proper respect or so much as a vague semblance of courtesy. Then you have the nerve to call me an idiot? Get out of my sight right now or you'll be hanging tomorrow with the rest of the vermin.'' He pounded a fist on the armrest. ''Men, escort them out!''

Larson went rigid. *Baron's court or not, if Haimfrid touches me or Silme, I'll kill him.*

But Haimfrid seemed content to let the court guards do their jobs. He stepped aside as the others pressed in. One reached for Larson's arm. Larson dodged aside, unwilling to lose his freedom of movement. Spears rattled behind him. Concerned for Silme, Larson edged his hand toward the hilt of Gaelinar's katana. Then, realization froze him mid-movement. *If I fight, Silme may get killed. At best, they'd take her prisoner.* Images boiled up within him, of guards like Haimfrid defiling Silme with filthy hands, raping her, beating her, perhaps killing her before the birth of the child she endured their torture to save. *She has that one spell stored. But a transport escape only works on herself, and I don't think she'd leave me.* Hoping to avoid violence, he kept his hands high in a gesture of surrender and moved toward the door. Silme followed.

Haimfrid, his two companions, and a handful of court guards accompanied Larson and Silme from the audience room and down the hallway to the outer door. Then, apparently convinced the pair did not intend to cause any more trouble, one of the guards addressed them stiffly. "Thank you for your interest in the affairs of the barony. We greatly appreciate all assistance that can be given by dedicated citizens such as yourself." The guard paused in his rehearsed monologue, as if noticing Larson's foreign features for the first time. "I'm sure the baron has this under consideration and is currently looking into the matter. Thank you."

"Wait, no." Larson spun to the guards, not daring to believe Taziar had predicted the situation so closely based only on personal prejudice and mistrust. *It doesn't make any sense. An official bribed by a quiet crime lord is one thing. But why would the baron publicly scream about fighting crime while just as vocally supporting the criminals' violent leader?* Larson found himself facing a sneering Haimfrid and four lowering spears.

Silme gave him a warning kick.

"But . . ." Larson started. Then, recognizing the futility of protestation, he finished lamely. "Fine. Okay, fine. Let's go.'' Whirling back toward the courtyard, he seized Silme's arm. "This is insane."

"We can take it from here," Haimfrid said.

Larson heard the rustle of uniforms as the court guards returned to their posts in the baron's audience chamber, leaving Haimfrid and his two companions to escort them from the yard.

In the wake of Larson's failure with the baron, Haimfrid's threats in the alleyway seemed to lose all significance. *Maybe we can talk this damned thing out,* Larson thought, seeing the need to parley, but in no mood to try. He tromped over the drawbridge, footsteps echoing along the moat and shoved through the milling crowds. The same sentries stood aside to let Larson, Silme, and their accompanying guards through the gates in the enclosing walls.

Once in the main street, Larson considered the best arguments to defuse a situation that had grown beyond all proportion.

But Haimfrid prodded Larson's spine with his spear. "All right, hero . . ."

The touch rekindled Larson's rage, but Haimfrid's words sent him over the edge. Kensei Gaelinar had always referred to Larson as "hero," and, from Haimfrid, the taunt mocked not only Larson, but the only man who had ever fully gained his respect.

Oblivious to the depth of his harassment, Haimfrid continued, ". . . you delivered your message. Let's the five of us go for a little walk. We'll take care of you first and save her for dessert."

Larson's control snapped. His vision washed red. "Fine," he screamed. "You want to go someplace. Let's go, right now!" He took two striding steps forward, no destination in mind.

Silme gripped his forearm. "Calm down, Allerum." Her touch radiated concern as well as warning." She addressed Haimfrid. "You're making a big mistake."

One of the two robust guards behind Silme whispered, "Nice, very pretty. This won't be so bad."

Larson shook free of Silme's hand. "They started it. By damn, I'm going to finish it."

Haimfrid laughed. "Go ahead, talk loud. We'll see how loud you scream." He chuckled again. "We'll see how loud *she* screams." He poked Larson a few more times to hurry him away from the baron's keep. "Let's go. Let's go."

Larson whirled to face Haimfrid, glaring, his hands tensed on his hips. The other two guards were giving Silme as much space, though they held no spears.

Haimfrid back-stepped, spear readied.

Shaking his head with contempt, Larson turned to face forward again. He waited only until Haimfrid stepped in and jabbed him one more time. The instant the point touched him, Larson spun. He batted the spear aside with his left hand, pivoted along the shaft, and smashed his right fist into Haimfrid's temple. Haimfrid crumpled without a cry. His spear clattered to the cobbles.

It was a sucker punch, but, accustomed to street fighting, Larson did not trouble himself with ethics. The speed of his strike pooled the blood into his hand until it ached. Ignoring the pain, he sprang between Silme and Haimfrid's startled companions. One reached for his sword hilt, but too slowly. The sword had come only halfway free when Larson snapped a kick that struck the man's fingers. The sword fell back into its sheath.

Larson saw his own anger mirrored on his opponent's face. Again, the fat guard reached for his sword. Quick as thought, Larson knocked the hand away and slapped the ruddy cheeks. The other guard leaped for Silme. Larson hesitated, and his own opponent lunged for his throat. Larson responded naturally. He drove his hands between the guard's arms, back-stepping to draw the guard forward. Seizing a handful of greasy, sand-colored hair, Larson used the guard's momentum to drive his knee into the jowly face. Cartilage crumbled. Blood trickled, warm on Larson's skin, and the man crumpled, moaning, to the cobbles.

Larson looked over in time to see Silme tear the last guard's grip from her sleeve and bar his arm behind him. Larson charged, shoving between them. Before he could raise a fist, Silme hissed a warning from between gritted teeth. "Allerum, hold. Look up. Please, look up now."

Shoving the guard aside, Larson followed the direction of Silme's gaze. A half dozen crossbowmen perched on the curtain wall of the baron's keep, every bow drawn and aimed at Larson.

Silme made a wordless sound of outrage. The sapphire in her staff flared, staining the masonry inky blue. A column of flame sprang to life at the crossbowmen's feet. Flickers of blue and white danced like ghosts through the fire.

Shouts of surprise wafted from the wall top. The crossbowmen scattered. Three loosed bolts that went wild, their metal tips clicking on the cobbles.

Silme grasped Larson's arm. "Run!" She whirled, dragging Larson through the startled crowd and down the stand-lined street.

Muddled by a wash of rising and dispersing emotions, Larson followed without comprehension. Only after they had ducked beyond sight and sound of the baron's keep did he dare to question. "That spell you used. It didn't tap you?"

Silme brushed aside a man hawking jewelry. "I used the sapphire."

Larson pressed. "I thought you only stored a small amount of energy. That spell seemed so powerful."

"A light show." Silme ducked down a side street to avoid a milling crowd. "Harmless. Those flames had no heat. The guards were just too stupid to notice."

Larson frowned, thinking that in the crossbowmen's position, he might make the same assumptions. He studied the roadways to get his bearings. "You followed me from the inn, didn't you?"

Silme nodded.

"Why?"

"I wanted . . ." Silme started. She grinned, the humor striking her even before she spoke the words. "I wanted to keep you out of trouble."

"To keep me out of trouble, huh?" Larson thought about the guard's taunts in the alleyway and how much more easily his audience with the baron could have gone without Haimfrid's interference. "Well, thank God for that."

CHAPTER 6:

Shadowed Alleys

Death is always and under all circumstances a tragedy, for if it is not, then it means that life itself has become one.

—Theodore Roosevelt
Letter

Lantern light gleamed from the upper room of the baron's southern tower. Amidst midmorning sunshine, the glow diffused to pale invisibility; but, from his study in Shylar's whorehouse, Harriman recognized the summons. *Meet now? The old fool.* Harriman slammed his ledger closed, and dust swam through sun rays in a crazy pattern. Not a number in his book was fact; it served only for show and, eventually, for the baron's eyes. The true tallies remained recorded only in Harriman's head.

Slouched near the door of Harriman's workroom, Halden and Skereye had been arguing sword-sharpening techniques since daybreak, their exchange gradually rising in volume and intensity. Harriman interrupted their discussion before it turned to violence. "We need to make another trip to Wilsberg." Without further explanation, he opened the door to the hallway and executed a broad, silent gesture. Skereye abandoned his point with obvious reluctance. Obediently, he trotted off toward the eastern storage chamber to light a lantern in answer to the baron's signal.

Halden flung a whetstone at his companion's retreating back. It bounced from Skereye's thick shoulder and struck the floor with a sharp click. Skereye turned, but Halden pulled the door shut before his companion could retaliate.

Ignoring his guards' antics, Harriman fingered the silks stretched over the back of his chair, gaze focused on the light burning steadily through the baron's window. Shortly, the flare winked out, acknowledging receipt of Harriman's consent. "The old fool," Harriman repeated, this time aloud. Turning, he peeled his plain woolen shirt off over his head and exchanged it for the frayed blue and white silk of his diplomatic uniform. Before Harriman had fully laced his collar, Skereye returned.

Harriman pulled the knots into place and strapped on his sword belt, its buckle and scabbard crusted with diamonds. "Let's go."

Harriman and his Norse entourage wandered past rows of bedrooms. This early, most of the doors lay propped open to indicate vacancy; the few clients would be night thieves, off-duty guardsmen and men of leisure. At the end of the hallway, a staircase led to the meeting and bargaining areas as well as the kitchen, bath, and living quarters that kept this house as much a home as a workplace for the women.

One of Harriman's three privileged officers stood, partway up the stairs, but Harriman made no allowances. He trotted down the steps, flanked by Halden and Skereye. The thief hesitated briefly. With an exaggerated flourish of respect, he gave ground, waiting for Harriman to pass at the base of the stairs.

Harriman acknowledged the sacrifice with a gruff, partial explanation. "We'll return shortly."

The thief nodded once. He made an undulating motion with his fingers to indicate he would see to it things ran smoothly in Harriman's absence, then continued his climb to the upper level.

The staircase ended in an open assembly chamber where seven well-groomed prostitutes reclined on chests, padded benches, or the floor. The instant Harriman appeared, all conversation ceased. Disinterested in the girls' discomfort, he wandered between them to the door. One shrank away from Halden's disfigured, leering face, and Harriman smiled in amusement. He caught the knob, wrenched the door open, and led his bodyguards through the entry hall to the outer door. Unfastening the lock, he pulled the panel ajar, and they emerged into the sunlight. He slammed the door behind them.

Harriman received little attention as he threaded through the thoroughfares of Cullinsberg, but the citizens gawked at his scarred and lumbering bodyguards. He knew that the underground and the street urchins on its fringes would ignore him. It had become common knowledge that Harriman visited the ruins of Wilsberg on occasion or knelt in the forests facing south to mourn family and friends. And, though accepted as truth, the information was spurious, its distribution well-planned. Early on, before he had gained the trust of the underground, he had led their spies to the devastated farm town. Later, as Bolverkr wore himself down constructing his fortress, Harriman steered his curious pursuers into the Kielwald Forest for a phony session of laments and vowed vengeance against Cullinsberg's baron.

The remembrance lasted until Harriman passed through the opened front gates of Cullinsberg. He crossed the fire-cleared plain without a backward glance and guided Halden and Skereye into the forest. Once lost between the trees, he waited. Whenever the baron called a meeting, he stationed one of his most trusted guards on the parapets. If anyone followed Harriman from the city, the sentry would signal by simulating the call of a fox. Harriman frowned at the thought. The majority of these conferences occurred at night or in the early morning when foxes normally prowled the woods. Now, the whirring imitation would sound nearly as suspicious as a shouted warning. But neither noise disturbed the stillness, and Harriman slipped deeper between the trees, certain no one had bothered to trail him.

Sun rays filtered through branches heavy with multi-colored leaves; thick overgrowth trapped the light into a glow, revealing landmarks Harriman knew blind. He traversed the route without even thinking about it, fallen leaves crunching beneath his boots. Behind him, Skereye and Halden crashed like oxen through boughs, scurrying over deadfalls with an ease that belied their bulk. At length, Harriman brushed through a line of towering pines into a clearing blotted gray by overhanging branches. There Baron Dietrich waited, perched upon a stump. The gold medallion of office at his throat contrasted starkly with a tunic and breeks of untooled leather. At either hand, a sword- and spear-armed guard stood, proudly dressed in a uniform of red and black. A scrap of linen hung from one's knee where a briar had torn the fabric, exposing scratched flesh. Though large, the baron's faithful sentries were dwarfed by Harriman's berserks.

Harriman executed a flawless bow of respect. "My lord, you summoned me?" His intended question remained unspoken. *What did you find of such urgency to risk a daylight meeting?*

The baron shifted on the stump. "Two strangers came to my court this morning. They named you as head of the criminals."

Harriman hid exasperation beneath an expression of interest. He spoke soothingly, never losing the tone of deference though he was fully in control of the situation. "Not unexpected, lord. In order to help you destroy the organized underground and bring you the names of their leaders, I necessarily had to win their trust, to make them think I was one of them. We knew this might happen. It's still important that you pretend to see me as Wilsberg's diplomat and dismiss such a suggestion as nonsense."

"I thought I hired you to put an end to the violence." The baron met Harriman's gaze, steely eyes flashing, demanding explanation. "The strangers reminded me that Cullinsberg's streets are still unsafe."

Harriman banished rising anger with professional skill. "Not unexpected either, as you must know, lord." The lies came easily, without a twitch or furtive glance to betray them. "The leaders are in your custody. What you're seeing now is reaction to their capture." His gaze remained locked and steady. "Once the executions have concluded, the violence will die away. Meanwhile, I need to stay to watch for upstart leaders."

The baron fidgeted. Harriman stood, unmoving, aware something as yet unaddressed disturbed Dietrich. The medallion's chain clinked beneath the sough of wind as the baron squirmed. At length, he spoke. "Those strangers. They lacked common courtesy. They badgered my guards into a fight. They insulted me. And . . ."

By the baron's sudden reluctance, Harriman guessed they had come to the root of his discomfort. "And, lord?" he encouraged gently.

"And," Dietrich continued. He leaned forward, his face red in the gloom. "They fought free of three guards, injuring one and humiliating another so badly I had to put him on suspension until he calms down. And if the Norse woman who tried to kill my bowmen with fire isn't a Dragonrank sorceress straight out of fairy tale . . ." He stopped, not bothering to complete the statement, and cast a nervous look at Halden and Skereye.

Harriman resisted the compulsion to swear. He knew Taziar's companions from Bolverkr's descriptions. And, though Bolverkr had never directly told Harriman, the nobleman knew his master planned to destroy Larson as personally and cruelly as he would Taziar. "These strangers you speak of. A willowy, blond man and a beautiful woman with a sapphire-tipped staff?"

Surprise crossed the baron's coarse features. "How did you know?"

So the little thief wants to bring outsiders into our feud. In his annoyance, Harriman conveniently forgot he had done precisely the same thing, and that the quarrel was Bolverkr's, not his own. Instantly, the rules of his game changed. *Anyone who interferes will pay, beginning with those urchins who harbored him.* Harriman regained his composure masterfully and dispatched Baron Dietrich's query without answering it directly. "You'll get no more trouble from them, lord. I'll see to it. And there's something I need to tell you." He met the baron's gaze again. "Taziar Medakan's in town."

The baron's face collapsed into wrinkles, and Harriman attributed his confusion to more than a decade spent working with the guard captain of the same name. Then, the baron's eyes fell to slits and his nostrils flared. "The Shadow Climber?"

Harriman nodded confirmation.

Baron Dietrich drummed his fingers on his breeks, his manner calculating. "That weasel stole an artifact from Aga'arin's temple, escaped my dungeons, and led a faction of my men across the Kattegat *against my orders!*"

Harriman lowered his head and waited.

"Not one of my soldiers made it back, Harriman! Did you know that?"

"Of course, lord," Harriman reminded without offense. In his eighteen years as Wilsberg's diplomat, he had worked well and closely with the baron, cheerfully paying taxes to the last copper and supplying the baron with the best of the traders' crops and wares. Wilsberg's farmers had served their time among the baron's conscription forces in the years of the Barbarian Wars.

The baron went rigid. "I'll send every guard in Cullinsberg after the thief."

Harriman cringed, aware such an arrangement would destroy every trap he and Bolverkr had constructed. "I wish you wouldn't, lord."

The baron went silent, still shaking with anger.

Harriman seized the baron's quiet to continue. "Every criminal in town believes Taziar informed on the leaders. If you arrest him, it'll prove his innocence. The underground will look for another informant, and I'll be exposed as a liar at the least. So will the guards you commanded to name Taziar if questioned. And since nearly all your guards actually believe Taziar *is* the informant, you'll seem like a . . ." Harriman softened the accusation. "Your guards will know you fed them misinformation and wonder why you trusted these men and not them." He indicated the sentries beside the baron. "Criminals are unforgiving by necessity. If your men arrest Taziar, my life and those of several of your guards will become as worthless to the ruffians and assassins on

your streets as Taziar's is now. Believe me, lord. They
can do worse to the Shadow Climber than even your dungeon guards could.'' *And we will.*

"Very well," the baron agreed. "For your sake, I'll
order my sentries to leave Taziar at liberty."

"Thank you, my lord," Harriman said respectfully,
though he never doubted Baron Dietrich would take his
advice. Despite maintaining courtly formality, Harriman
had grasped control of this operation some time ago. *I
may have lost some of that power thanks to Taziar's meddling friends, but I'll get it back.* Harriman harbored no
doubt. *I have some lessons to teach, some warnings to
give, and I'll need to get Taziar back into my custody.*
He smiled wickedly, and, for the first time, a trace of
true emotion slipped through.

Taziar Medakan pitched another log onto the already
well-stocked hearth and watched flames lick around the
cooler bark without catching. The firelight struck red and
gold highlights through hair the color of coal and swept
across fine features ashen with concern. He took a seat
on the dwindling woodpile. Shortly, he grew restless and
chose to sit on the table instead. His back to the fire, he
stared at Astryd, asleep between the packs. An instant
later, he was up again, pacing the length of the inn room.
*I can't believe I let Allerum go off alone, knowing he
wanted to see the baron. What was I thinking?* Taziar
pounded his fist into his palm, aware the problem did not
come from a specific thought, but from no thought at all.
*That headstrong elf can get himself into more trouble eat-
ing breakfast than I did breaking into the Dragonrank
school grounds. I'm just glad Silme was paying more attention to Allerum's intentions than I was.* Now Taziar
frowned, aware more than enough time had passed for
Silme to catch up with Larson, convince him of the foolishness of running off alone, and return with him to the
inn room. *Unless he persuaded her to help him. Gods!
Silme has to know you just don't handle underground
affairs through legal channels.* Taziar cringed, familiar
with Larson's single-mindedness that often transcended

common sense, a trait inspired and nurtured by Kensei
Gaelinar. *Silme might have found it safer and simpler to
give in to Allerum's obsession. But we're wasting valuable time.*

Taziar's ambling brought him to the window over the
alleyway. He stopped, feeling the chill, autumn breezes
on his face, sharp contrast to the warmth of the fire at
his back. From habit, he measured the distance to the
ground, sought miniscule ledges in the featureless stretch
of stonework. *They might need my help. I'll stay out of
sight. How much trouble can I get into just gathering
facts?* Memory of the beating in Shylar's whorehouse that
still left his cheeks and ribs swollen and splotched with
bruises made him wince. His lapse admitted Silme's
warning: ''You're of no use to your friends dead.'' Taziar
wrapped his fingers around the sill. *But I'm even more
useless if they're dead. My one life is worth little compared with their eight. How many others may die for me?*

Taziar had climbed halfway across the window ledge
before he realized it. Astryd rolled in her sleep, and her
movement froze him, dangling from the sill. *What in
Karana's hell is wrong with me? I can't leave Astryd
alone.* He sprang back into the chamber, landing lightly
as a cat on the planking. He crossed to Astryd and
perched on a pack near her head. Idly, he stroked the
soft, blonde locks, pulling free strands that had caught
at the corner of her mouth. Since Larson and Silme had
departed, every position seemed uncomfortable to Taziar, and he found himself unable to sit still. Urgency
spiraled through him, and he fought the impulse to return
to the window.

*Harriman doesn't know where we're staying; other-
wise, he would have found us already. No one will disturb Astryd. Besides, she's hardly helpless.* Taziar
recalled his first encounter with Astryd. He had discovered her locked in a berth aboard the summer ferry. Then,
mistaking him for a captor, she had evaded him faster
than he could think to stop her. Once he managed to
catch her, she had clawed and kicked him like a tiger.
She's slept long enough to restore most of her used en-

ergy, so she'll have magic, too. Taziar kissed Astryd's cheek, felt her settle more snugly beneath her spread cloak. Sliding his sword from its sheath, he placed it near her hand. *You won't need it, but neither will I. I'll feel more comfortable if you keep it.*

Having rationalized leaving, Taziar bounded across the room before he could change his mind again. He paused only long enough to ascertain that the alley stood empty, then lowered his legs through the opening and scrambled to the ground.

Again, Taziar peered the length of the thoroughfare. Satisfied no one had seen him, he turned his attention to the back wall of Mardain's temple. Having grown accustomed to longhouses and simple cottages, the building appeared awesome, taller than any man-made structure in Norway. Taziar accepted the challenge with glee. Recalling the lack of hand and toe holds on the stones that formed the first story, Taziar took a running start. Fingers scraping granite, he sprinted the length of the alleyway, then flung himself at the wall. Momentum took him to the coarse areas of mortar at the second story. From there, he skittered to the roof.

Wind dried beads of sweat from Taziar's forehead as he stared out over the city of Cullinsberg. Shops and dwellings stood in stately rows between the confining square of the city's outer walls. Roads striped, curled, and crisscrossed through the business district, and people traversed the main thoroughfares in crowds. Taziar craned his neck to glance into the alleyway where Rascal's gang had tended his injuries and discussed the changes in the structure of the underground. A lone figure paced the earthen floor. Though distant and at too peculiar an angle to be certain, it looked like a child. Taziar read agitation in the movements.

The muscles of Taziar's chest bunched in worry, and he felt flushed. He found niches in the wall stones and clambered downward, jumping the last story back into the alley. He slunk close to the walls through the dappled shadows of the buildings until he came to a threadlike crossroad. He studied the alley quickly before darting across and into a throughway parallel to the first. Once there, he shinnied up a warehouse. His footfalls made no sound on the roof, and he scrambled to the opposite side. Flattened to the tiles, he peered over the edge.

Far beneath Taziar, Ida scuffed her sandals on the packed dirt floor of the roadway. A dress designed for an adult hung in loose bulges, its hem frayed and filthy. She clutched a tattered cloak tightly over it to protect her from the cold. Her head hung low, and she flung her hand outward on occasion, as if carrying on a conversation with herself.

Taziar examined the pathway; his aerial position accorded him a safe view over the rain barrels and garbage. Finding Ida alone, he descended the wall stones and slipped into the alley beside her. "Ida?"

At the sound of Taziar's voice, Ida jerked her head up. Her limbs went rigid. Tears traced meandering lines through dirt on her cheeks, and her eyes appeared swollen. A crimson bruise marred the soft arc of her jaw.

"Ida?" Cut to the heart, Taziar reached out to comfort her. *What kind of heartless madman would hit a little girl?*

Ida dodged Taziar's embrace, back-stepping until her shoulder touched the wall. Her voice sounded as scratchy as an elderly man's. "Harriman's men trapped Rascal and the others in an old warehouse in Ottamant's Alley."

Taziar cringed, his fear for the children intermingled with his memory of his own arrest in that same alley a few months earlier. "You escaped?"

Ida shook her head, avoiding Taziar's gaze. "They let me go. I'm supposed to tell you . . ." Her breath came in sobs from crying. ". . . they'll kill anyone caught talking to you."

Aware how difficult Ida found her words, Taziar shared her grief. Slowly, without threat, he reached for her again.

Ida shrank away. She blurted, "I don't want anyone else to get hurt." Finally, she met Taziar's stare. "I don't want you to get hurt either."

"Ida, please." Taziar approached. "Rascal and the others . . ."

Ida shuffled backward for every step Taziar took toward her.

Taziar stopped, and Ida stood in miserable, quaking silence. "I'll get them free." Lacking any other way to soothe, Taziar promised without any knowledge of what his vow might entail. "You'll see. I'll release them and get you all safely out of the city."

All color drained from Ida except the angry splotch of the contusion. "Taz. The warehouse . . . Harriman . . ." Sudden panic made her stiffen. Her eyes rolled, revealing the whites like a frightened cart horse. Abruptly, she whirled and ran, the slap of her sandals echoing between the buildings.

For some time, Taziar stood in quiet uncertainty, senses dulled by a heavy barrage of emotion. Grief and guilt weighed heavily upon him, and he knew he had brought disaster to the only Cullinsbergens who dared to trust him. *They're only children.* Taziar wrestled between decisions. *Do I go after Rascal or try to comfort Ida?* The girl's sorrow and fear haunted him, and he made his choice quickly. The sound of her footsteps had already grown faint. Abandoning caution, he chased after her.

Ida had run straight to the alley's end, then turned into a zigzagging branchway. Taziar followed. Aware this lane had no outlet, he was not surprised when her footfalls fell silent. He jogged past rain barrels, skirted a shabby, abandoned cart, and dodged the bones and rotted fruit littering the ground. He saw where one of Ida's footsteps had smashed an ancient apple to brown mush. Ducking around the final corner, Taziar found her slumped between a stack of crates and a pair of barrels. An overhanging ledge hid her in shadow, her form barely discernible in the gloom.

"Ida?" Taziar freed his ankle from a discarded scrap of parchment, approaching slowly so as not to startle her. "Ida?" Concern made Taziar careless. As he moved closer, he noticed that her back was not heaving, though

he would have expected to find her crying. She did not
stir as he reached out and gently grasped her shoulder.

Taziar's touch dislodged Ida, and she fell limply into
his arms. Warm liquid coursed through his fingers. He
cried out in shock and alarm. Catching her chin between
his hands, he met sightless, unblinking eyes; and his grip
glazed blood across her cheek. *Dead. How?* Taziar
wrapped his arms around Ida, cradling her to his chest.
He explored her lower back with his fingers, found the
sticky slit where the knife had penetrated her dress at the
level of a kidney. His grip tightened protectively, and
tears stung his eyes. *Gods, no! She's just a child.* Silently, he rocked her like an infant in a crib.

"Freeze, Medakan *weasel!*" The voice came from directly behind Taziar, accompanied by wild scramblings
amidst the crates.

Taziar's heart missed a beat. Ida's corpse slipped from
his grip, smearing blood the length of his sleeves. He
berated himself with every profanity he could muster. *I
walked into their trap like an ignorant barbarian who
never set foot in a city before and paid with Ida's life
and probably my own.* It occurred to Taziar he might
deserve whatever cruelties these men inflicted on him.
But his survival instinct remained strong, fueled by the
fact that he alone knew about the capture of Rascal's
gang. Driven by the need to help them, he glanced up to
meet the three men who threatened him with swords.

"I'm unarmed," Taziar said, the disclosure intended
to make Harriman's men overconfident rather than as a
plea for mercy. He rose, holding scarlet-slicked hands
away from his empty sword sheath. He backed toward
the wall, and the men closed into a semicircle around
him. They all looked vaguely familiar to Taziar, strong-
arm men and cutthroats from the fringes of the underground.

The one directly before Taziar spoke again. "I said
'freeze,' Taziar. You forget the language?"

Taziar stole a glance at the stonework behind him, not
bothering to reply.

The man continued. "Don't move, and you won't get hurt."

Keep them talking, Taziar reminded himself, aware he had to distract them before he could make a move. "That's not reassuring coming from someone who just knifed a twelve-year-old girl." The words emerged not at all as Taziar had planned. He winced. *That's right, Taz, you idiot. Antagonize the brute with his sword at your chest.*

"We didn't kill her." The man to the right spoke, revealing teeth darkly-stained and rotting. "You did. Murderer!" He spat. "Child killer."

Guilt stabbed through Taziar, sharper than the hovering swords. He back-stepped, feeling cold granite against his spine.

The center man gestured to the companion to his left who turned and started rooting through the crate wood. "Taziar Medakan, you're under arrest."

"Under arrest?" Taziar glanced between the swords, seeking an opening. But the central man took a side step, neatly closing the gap created by his companion's absence. "You can't arrest me. You're criminals, too."

The third ruffian returned. He had sheathed his sword and was clutching a sturdy board of the same length. "Then we'll beat you senseless, drag you to the baron's keep, and leave you on his doorstep as a present." He brandished the plank. "You'll wake up in the dungeon."

I've escaped before. And there might be some advantage to helping my friends from the inside. Taziar banished the thought immediately. *A lot of luck and an inhumanly strong barbarian aided that breakout. If I try something that crazy, I'll need at least Astryd's aid. And thanks to my impulsiveness, my friends have no idea where I am.* He studied the group before him, realizing from their sneers they had no real intention of surrendering him to the baron. *They're lying. Playing me. Probably preparing to take me back to Harriman for another pounding by his berserks.* "What's happened to the underground? We used to take care of each other. We settled differences among ourselves. We never hurt one another, never harmed the children."

The center man snorted. "So the traitor wants to give lectures on loyalty." He inclined his head toward his board-wielding companion. "Take him."

The instant the leader's attention turned, Taziar twisted, leaping for the wall stones. His fingers settled naturally into irregularities, and he scrambled upward. He had nearly reached the level of the ruffians' heads when his blood-wet fingers slipped. He tottered, catching his balance with effort. A hand skimmed the fabric of his pants leg, and he knew the men had him. If that grip closed, they would rip him from the wall and probably beat him in anger and frustration.

Desperate, Taziar sprang backward. Momentum knocked the fingers aside. He sailed over the men's heads, landed awkwardly on a mangled cartwheel, and rolled. He gained his feet as the men whirled toward him. "Get him!" the leader screamed.

Taziar ran. He swerved through the jagged alleyway, the pounding of his pursuers too loud and close for him to pause long enough to get a grip and climb. He charged back into the lane where he had met Ida, sprinted its length, and dodged into a branchway. Uncertain which way to go, he hoped to lose the ruffians in the crowded market streets. He had no goal. He only knew places where he did not dare lead Harriman's lackeys: the inn room that lodged his friends and the warehouse in Ottamant's Alley. *And the back roads are ruled by the underground.*

Taziar careened through the threadlike network of lanes, turned a corner, and slid into the bustling main street. Behind him, the leader's voice rose above the clamor. "Catch him! Murderer! That man killed my daughter!"

Damn! Taziar plunged into the masses, elbowing through tiny gaps, smearing blood across the passersby. A woman screamed. The crowd parted before him, most too afraid to get involved. A hand seized Taziar's cloak, jolting him backward. He slipped to one knee. Pulling

his arms free, he let the fabric slide from his back. The
resistance disappeared, and Taziar lunged forward.
Women skittered, screeching, from his path.

"Murderer! Murderer! He killed someone! He stabbed
a little girl!" The cries emanating from the thugs were
picked up and echoed by the crowd. Blows rained down
on Taziar. He ducked his head, using his arms to shield
his face. No longer certain how close his pursuers were,
he dared not glance back. A foot snagged his ankle,
sprawling him into a tight knot of citizens. They scattered. A boot thumped painfully against his back and
another crashed into his scalp. Dizzy, he staggered to his
feet. Catching a glimpse of the gray mouth of an alley,
he ran for it, no longer concerned about street toughs
and thieves.

Most of the citizens feared the back streets, and the
footfalls and shouts faded to those of half a dozen dogged
pursuers. From the voices, Taziar recognized at least one
of the ruffians among the group. The alley looked unfamiliar, which made Taziar uneasy. He knew the entire
city to some extent, but this side of town least of all, and
he harbored no wish to corner himself in some dead end.
Have to think. Plan my course. Climb? Each breath came
with a burning gasp. Cold, autumn air dried sweat from
his limbs, and he felt simultaneously chilled and over-
heated. *Can't climb here. Enemies too close. Hands
sticky. Buildings too far apart. They'll surround me.* He
raked hair from his eyes, smearing blood across his brow.
*A ruse. Something to gain me time and space, a moment
out of sight.*

Taziar came to a four-way intersection. Recalling a rear
door viewed from one of the alleyways, he chose the left
pathway, grimly knowing it would again lead him to the
main streets. A dozen strides brought him into the market
area, and he plunged into the masses from necessity. Behind him, the leader of the ruffians hollered again.
"Murderer! Catch him! He killed my daughter!"

Taziar counted shops as he ran. He leaped over a foot
intended to trip him and deflected a punch with his elbow. Suddenly, he swerved, swinging wildly. Startled cit-

izens shied from his path, leaving him a lane to the jewelry store. Catching the knob, he sprinted through the doorway. The panel slammed against the wall and bounced closed. A wizened jeweler glanced up from a project. Before a counter covered with tiny gemstones, a patron screamed. Taziar vaulted to the countertop, knocking a colored wash of precious stones to the floor. They scattered, rattling across the granite. The jeweler cursed Taziar with steamy epithets as the Climber sprang to the ground. Unable to gather enough breath for an apology, he struck the back door with his shoulder and emerged into the alley.

Aware his maneuver would only delay his pursuers, Taziar fled. He swung into the first byway, and there discovered a dark crack between buildings scarcely wide enough for the scraggly tomcats that prowled the streets. Skilled in squeezing into tight spaces, Taziar pressed his back to the opening and wriggled inside. Rats scratched and scuttled deeper in behind him. Stonework abraded skin from Taziar's shoulders. He heard the slap of the jeweler's back door followed by a gruff voice. "Which way?"

"This way!" the ruffians' leader called breathlessly. "The other way leads back to the street."

Footsteps pounded toward Taziar. He fought the urge to pant, holding his breath until he thought his lungs would burst. The noises passed, and he gasped gratefully for air. He grasped the edges of the fissure, dragging himself painfully toward the opening. For an instant, he writhed forward. Then he wedged tight, arms straining, the pressure aching through his shoulders. *I'm stuck.* A rat screeched, and Taziar's mind turned the sound into an echoing cry of hunger. He forced down panic. By degrees, he shifted, sucking in a deep breath and exhaling fully before making another attempt at freedom. This time, he edged back into the alley.

Aware his pursuers might return, Taziar took only enough time to wipe the drying blood from his fingers with his shirt. Then, catching handholds in a stone and mud wall, he clambered to the roof. He crept to the opposite side in time to watch the ruffians disappear around the corner of a parallel alleyway. Carefully, he braced his hands on the ledge of a neighboring roof and pulled himself across to it. He slithered down into the roadway they had abandoned and climbed another wall. In this manner, he gradually worked his way toward Cullinsberg's east side and Ottamant's Alley.

Crushed, winded, and alone, Taziar knew he could never hope to save Rascal's gang. *But I have to assess the situation so Astryd, Silme, and Larson have a clear idea of where we're going and what we're against.* He continued toward his goal, springing, climbing, and descending, concentrating on every back street, hidey-hole, and handhold to keep him from the pain of other contemplations. Ida's death, his imprisoned friends, Allerum and Silme facing off with a corrupt baron, Astryd asleep and by herself, he pushed all these thoughts to the back of his mind, not yet able to deal with the grief. Just as after his father's death, the excitement of evading enemies and performing a difficult task channeled aside what he could not face. He threw himself into his task with a fanatical thoroughness.

As Taziar drew closer to Ottamant's Alley, he grew even more absolute in his attention to details. Several blocks from the warehouse, he discovered lone men and women pacing around buildings with an idleness uncharacteristic of citizens or thieves. By establishing patterns and waiting for these guards to turn corners, he avoided them with ease. Closer to the warehouse, he noticed the singles had become groups, their patrols more erratic. With more difficulty, he dodged these, too.

Still two blocks from his goal, Taziar ascended the five stories of the alehouse and studied the layout from above. His vantage allowed him to view three of the warehouse's four sides. Windows were cut into the western and northern walls, with entryways to the north and south. Three men guarded each alleyway around the warehouse, their backs pressed to its walls. Another lay on the roof tiles, watching over the northern side, a crossbow and quiver of quarrels beside him. Acutely aware of the small number of people capable of climbing buildings, Taziar knew the crossbowman would prove quick and agile.

Taziar considered returning to his friends, but he wanted to make certain the children were inside before risking any more lives. A plan took shape in his mind. In the same manner as before, he worked his way to the south side of the alehouse. Locating an alley currently vacant of its guard, he secured a long, narrow board. Pulling off his bloodstained shirt, he wrapped the wood to muffle sound. He hauled the board to the back side of the warehouse across from the one in Ottamant's Alley and cautiously, grip by grip, dragged it to the roof.

Taziar's position gave him a perfect view of the bowman's feet and the three guards in the throughway below. He freed his shirt and tied it to one end of the plank. Secure in the knowledge that people rarely think to look over their heads, Taziar inched the board across the space between his rooftop and the bowman's. The cloth slid soundlessly across tile. He waited, heart pounding. But the man on the rooftop did not turn. Below, the thieves chatted, apparently oblivious to the events directly above their heads.

Taziar continued, the familiar euphoria of fighting against steep odds tainted by the realization that success would require nearly as much luck as skill. Quick efficiency would decrease the chance of a random glance in his direction, so Taziar did not hesitate. He stepped onto the board, felt it sag beneath his weight, and was glad for the slight stature that had served as both blessing and curse in the past. He crossed silently and without incident. The midday sun struck Taziar's shadow immediately beneath him, and he was careful not to let its edge fall near the bowman as he approached.

Reaching the western edge of the warehouse, Taziar flattened to the roof tiles and examined the wall below. The guards pitched stones at pieces of rotting fruit, laughing as a direct hit sent feasting yellow jackets into flight. Halfway between Taziar and the guards, the window lay flat and featureless beneath him. Taking advantage of the thieves' preoccupation, Taziar descended the wall above their heads, balancing speed against the risk of dislodging dirt and vines and thus revealing his location. The alley guards continued their sport as Taziar caught the window ledge and peered inside.

Men filled the room, perched on crates or on the floor, most huddled near the doors. A brief examination of the storage area revealed no sign of the children, and Taziar realized he had been set up. No doubt, the urchins' bodies lay, dismembered, in some back street, labeled with a warning of the consequences of helping Taziar Medakan. Few of the street people could read, but it would only take one man to interpret the writing and spread the news. Taziar froze, half-naked and shivering from cold that pierced deeper than the autumn weather. He watched in horror as a thief's gaze found him. A finger stretched toward the window, accompanied by a shout that mobilized everyone.

Taziar scurried up the granite, catching new handholds as fast as he could loose the ones below. An arrow sailed past his ear as he hurled himself over the ledge to the roof. His head slammed into the crossbowman's face hard enough to set Taziar's skull ringing. Impact knocked him to his side, and he caught a dizzy glimpse of criminals gathering far below him. He reacted instinctively, wrenching himself sideways to change the direction of his momentum. Catching his balance, he charged across the rooftop to the board, realizing as he did that the bowman lay, moaning on the tiles, holding his nose. Taziar raced across the plank, too pained by the children's certain deaths to laugh.

Harriman's men poured into the alleyways, but Taziar had gained distance through his ploy. Dodging, ducking, and climbing, Taziar knew this sector of the city too well to get caught. But despite the excitement of the chase, he was unable to keep the tears from his eyes.

CHAPTER 7:

Ladies of the Shadows

I like not fair terms and a villain's mind.
> —William Shakespeare
> *The Merchant of Venice*

Back in the inn room, Taziar Medakan huddled on the stacked logs, feeling weak and as tattered as an old rag. Everything he had done since arriving in Cullinsberg replayed through his mind in an endless loop of accusation. He had not asked Rascal to drag him, unconscious and bleeding, from the whorehouse alley. Even if Taziar had been coherent enough to warn the children, he had not known the danger. No one could have guessed that Harriman would choose that moment to demand his share of the day's take, nor just how cruel and warped his anger would become. Still, Taziar could not help feeling responsible for the children's deaths. And, after he revealed the information to his friends, the fact that Larson, Silme, and Astryd sat watching him in silent sympathy only strengthened his guilt. Taziar wished just one of his companions would chastise him for running off alone.

Larson crouched in a corner near the window, saying nothing. Astryd sat among the packs, tracing a pattern on the hilt of Taziar's sword. It was Silme who finally broke the silence. "What time of day is the baron planning to hang Shylar and the others?"

Taziar stared at his hands. "Tomorrow sundown, almost certainly. Aga'arin's High Holy Day is the most sacred day of the year. His followers, including the baron, will spend most of daylight on the temple grounds." Taziar looked up, plotting diverting his thoughts from the orphans. "The number of guards on duty won't change. Atheists and worshipers of Mardain will work. But many of the shops will close early or won't open at all, and the streets will be nearly empty." Taziar sat straighter, touched by the first familiar stirrings of excitement that accompanied planning the impossible. "The holiday won't make the escape any simpler, but once we've freed them, we should be able to move through town without much difficulty." Uncomfortable with leaving his friends in prison any longer than necessary, Taziar frowned. "Assuming we wait until tomorrow to release them."

"Which gives us tonight to remove Harriman," Silme spoke gently, but her suggestion inspired a flare of guilt that made Taziar squirm.

"Forget Harriman for now." Taziar's words did not come easily. "We can kill him any time, but my friends could die tomorrow."

Larson looked pensive. "Silme's right, Shadow. Breaking your friends out won't do us any good if we leave an enemy at our backs. Harriman got them thrown in prison once. He can do it again."

Silme continued. "You couldn't talk a gang of frightened children into leaving Cullinsberg. Do you expect Shylar and the others to run away from the only home they know, passively waiting while Harriman destroys the part of city life they created?"

"Of course not." Mercifully, Taziar's remorse and the burden of blame retreated behind this new concern. "At the least, we have to know just how much control Harriman has over the remainder of the underground. We have to define friends and enemies. And that's never an easy thing to do with criminals. When . . ." Taziar avoided the uncertainty implied by the word "if." "When we free the leaders, we have to know who will stand with and who will stand against them. But . . ." He trailed off, licking his lips as he tried to frame the concept distressing him.

Three pairs of eyes confronted Taziar in interested silence, and he met them all in turn. "Harriman knew those children helped me yesterday, but he waited until we raised a hand against him. He killed Rascal and the others only after you went to the baron. I don't think that was coincidence. It was a warning. If we try to kill Harriman and fail, *which of my friends will he destroy next?*''

A hush fell over the room as Astryd, Silme, and Larson considered. Larson spoke first, with the guileless moral insight he had openly displayed before Gaelinar's death had driven him to emulate his swordmaster's gruffer manner. ''This is war, Shadow. In war, innocents die. You can't feel responsible for every sin your enemy commits. The most you can do is limit your own killing to enemies and protect your buddies to the best of your ability. You try. You may fail. Everyone makes mistakes, and, sometimes, the wrong people pay. But there's no excuse for not trying at all.''

Taziar lowered his head. It was against his nature to fear a challenge but it went against all his experience to weigh children's lives in the balance.

Silme returned the conversation to practical matters. ''Who would have the information we need about the underground's loyalties?''

''I'm not certain.'' Taziar wandered through the list of informants in his mind. ''Of course, the people who always knew the most about the goings on in the underground are the ones in prison. I got most of my facts from Shylar.'' Frustrated, he shook his head. The gesture flung hair into his eyes, and he raked it back in place. ''No one will talk to me. They all either hate or fear me, and I won't endanger any more innocents. Certainly, no one will talk to any of you. It took me eight years to gain enough trust to establish the connections I have. You can't accomplish the same thing in a day.'' Another desperate thought pushed through his disillusionment. ''Unless . . .'' he started before he could dismiss the idea as too dangerous.

''Unless what?'' Silme's tone made it clear she would not accept denial or argument. ''Speak up.''

Taziar knew better than to try to hide knowledge from Silme. She had an uncanny ability to read people, and she never brooked nonsense. ''Apparently, Harriman's working out of Shylar's whorehouse. That's not surprising. A lot of information goes through that house, and it's built for meeting and spying. For some reason, men tend to talk to Shylar's girls, and they share disclosures amongst themselves.''

Silme picked up the thread of Taziar's thought. ''And possibly would talk with another girl who joined them.''

Unnerved by the course Silme's mind seemed to be taking, Taziar attempted to redirect the suggestion. ''The girls know and trust Shylar like a mother. Harriman's sly, but I doubt even he could turn them against Shylar. In fact, I can't fathom how the whorehouse is running at all without her. If I could sneak in again and speak with one of the girls . . .''

Larson broke in with a loud snort of disgust. ''Sure, Shadow. You're going to slip past Harriman, his drug-crazed Vikings, forty thieves, guards, and other assorted male citizenry out to kill you so you can talk to a hooker who might just as easily turn you in as talk to you. You'd have about as much chance as a frog on a freeway.''

Larson's last sentence held no meaning for Taziar, but the skepticism came through with expressive distinctness. And having failed once, Taziar could understand his companion's doubt. ''Are you trying to say it's impossible?'' Taziar left his intention unspoken, aware his friends knew that naming a task impossible was to Taziar like dangling raw steak before a guard lion.

Obviously undaunted, Larson rose. ''You're good, Shadow, but not that good. Besides, even if you made it through, you would force Harriman to kill whichever woman you spoke with.''

Silme nodded agreement. ''You're staying if I have to tie you to the door. Harriman may know you, but he's never seen any of us. There's only one logical choice as to who we send for information.'' She looked pointedly at Astryd.

Dread crept through Taziar, a wave of cold foreboding that left him frozen like a carving in ice. ''No,'' he croaked. Then, louder, ''No!'' *I won't blithely deliver the only woman I've ever loved directly into Harriman's hands.*

Astryd responded with calm determination. "It's not your decision, Shadow. It's mine. And I choose to go."

"No!" Taziar sprang to his feet. He measured the distance to the window.

Apparently alert to Taziar's intention, Larson blocked his escape.

"But Harriman will know . . ." Taziar started. He stopped, realizing he was about to reveal information about Harriman's master that Silme had intentionally hidden from Larson. "Silme, I need to talk with you alone." To divert Larson's suspicions, Taziar glanced at Astryd as he spoke.

"Fine." Silme stood, walked to the door, opened it, and gazed into the hallway. "It's clear."

Taziar drew the hood of his spare cloak over his head and followed Silme into the passageway. She closed the door, and he kept his back to the hall so that anyone who passed would not recognize him. "Harriman's master can access Allerum's thoughts. Surely, he knows what we all look like."

"Certainly," Silme agreed. "But Harriman knows only what his master chooses to tell him. That could be nothing. Unlikely, but possible. Even then, it takes time to memorize features well enough to send images. The master wouldn't be able to show Harriman what we look like. That would be like an artist trying to draw a detailed picture of a stranger after only a few brief glimpses. He'd have to give Harriman a verbal description. You gave one of the best I've ever heard when you described Harriman, but I wouldn't have slain the first person on Cullinsberg's streets who fit the description. How would you portray Astryd?"

Taziar shrugged. "Small, short blonde hair, beautiful, female. Carries a staff with a garnet in it."

"Exactly." Silme smiled. "Take away the staff and that fits an eighth of Norway's population."

"Norway's population," Taziar repeated forcefully. "Not Cullinsberg's. Mardain's mercy, Silme, she's got an unmistakable accent. Isn't there something you can do to disguise her?''

Silme leaned against the door to their room. "I suppose. But do you think we have time to shop now? And do you really believe it would matter? New clothes and some makeup isn't going to do much to change a description Harriman only knows from vague reports anyway, other than to draw suspicion if it's noticed.''

"I meant some sort of magical disguise.'' Taziar had never seen any Dragonrank mage change his appearance, even the ugly or elderly ones. But his contact with the rare sorcerers was limited to Silme, Astryd, and the few meetings they led him into, most notably his excursion to the Dragonrank school; and the situation seemed too dangerous not to ask. "Isn't there some way she could make herself look different, even if just to Harriman?''

Silme shook her head. "The mind barriers keep sorcerers from casting anything that works by modifying other people's perceptions or intentions, like dreams or illusions. That's what makes Allerum's lack of mind barriers so dangerous. When he first came here, we couldn't trust anything he saw or heard. His every mood was suspect. Luckily, he learned how to tell when sorcerers tried to manipulate him and even how to fight back a bit.''

Taziar listened carefully. Though quick to revert to English words and a strange, distant morality, Larson doggedly avoided talking about the more serious aspects of his past.

Silme continued, "I might be able to enter Harriman's mind, but not without risking a confrontation with his master.'' She frowned, and fear touched her expression briefly.

Taziar stared. Never before had he seen Silme appear any way except in complete control of a situation.

Silme recovered quickly. "To actually alter Astryd would take phenomenal amounts of magic, certainly more than she has or can afford to waste. Even if she managed it, she'd never get herself back to looking exactly the way she does now.''

Taziar shivered at the thought. It was Astryd he loved,

not her appearance, but he wondered if he could still consider her the same person with unrecognizable features on a face he had come to use as the standard for beauty. *And even if Harriman doesn't recognize her, what if he finds her as attractive as I do?* The image returned, of the nobleman calmly blocking a berserk's punch, tearing Skereye away from his victim like a starved lion from its kill. *Harriman's strong, bold to the point of insanity, and Astryd's never had to physically defend herself against any man larger than me.* "It's too dangerous."

Silme sighed in exasperation, naturally assuming Taziar was still concerned about Harriman identifying Astryd. "She can leave the staff and take another name. This is a huge city. She can't be the only Norse woman in Cullinsberg. Besides, Shadow, everyone in the town would recognize you. Only Harriman might know Astryd. She may even be able to avoid him completely. Harriman may leave the simple chores, like hiring new girls, to his underlings. And you're forgetting the most important thing. If she gets into trouble, Astryd can transport back to us almost instantly. Can you do that?" Her gray eyes probed in question.

Taziar's rebuttal died in his throat. *That's true. As long as Astryd can transport, she's in no danger.* He managed a grimace of acceptance. "You're right, as always. But before she goes, I want to talk to her. I need to describe the layout of the whorehouse, to name some of the people, and give her some directions."

Silme clapped a hand to Taziar's shoulder, too relieved to quibble. "Take all the time you need."

Astryd threaded through the maze of city streets, concentrating on Taziar's complicated series of directions designed, it seemed, to keep her clear of back roads and shadowed alleys. Though still touched by fatigue, nervous energy drove her to shy at every sudden movement. Her edginess drew unwanted attention. The afternoon crowds eyed her with pity, questioning her intelligence or passing whispered comments about the tiny, young woman with no man to protect her from thieves. Under ordinary circumstances, Astryd would have found the citizens' concern amusing, but two days of draining her life energy nearly to nothing had left her more exhausted than a morning nap could overcome. Her aura spread around her, its usual brilliant white sheen dulled by weariness, its edges dark. Anxiety kept her hyperalert; each movement claimed more vitality than normal, fraying the fringes of her aura.

Astryd took slow, deep breaths. Gradually, the rapid hammering of her heart slackened, and she was able to pay closer attention to the shops and landmarks Taziar had detailed. She tried to recall the list of names and descriptions of people she might encounter in Shylar's whorehouse, but it all blended into a verbal lump of colors and shapes; the odd, Cullinsbergen names all sounded alike to her. The realization triggered another burst of stress. She calmed herself using the mental techniques taught in the Dragonrank school.

Astryd turned another corner, and, by means of a rotting signpost, identified her new location as Panogya Street. *Magic or not, I'm the most ill-suited for this task. What does a shipbuilder's daughter know of espionage?* Until Astryd's dragonmark had appeared seven years ago, she had spent a carefree childhood helping her mother and sisters sew clothes and prepare meals or skipping across the timbers her father and brothers used to construct the fishing boats. Every spring, as ice dissolved from the harbors, the thaw turned men restless. Many sailed off, in dragon-prowed ships crafted or patched by her father, to seek war and win treasures in distant lands. They returned, scarred but wealthy, sharing their spoils with a rowdy generosity. But Astryd's father and brothers never joined them. She had come by her slight stature honestly, by breeding, and her menfolk's small hands were unfit for wielding their heavy-bladed axes in wild battles. The most exciting ventures of her town she knew of only distantly and vicariously, from stories leaked thirdhand after drunken boasts in the village tavern.

Spending eleven months of each year at the Dragonrank school, Astryd had learned much of strength, meditation, and magic, but little of human nature. She spent her one month vacations with her family. But the fisher-folk treated her with uncharacteristic reverence. The boys she grew up with had married during her absence, and her relationships with people were as stilted and ungainly as those of a child playing at being an adult.

Astryd's reminiscences brought her to the polished wooden door of Shylar's whorehouse. She wiped sweating palms on her cloak, smoothed the skirts beneath it, and tried, again, to remain composed. Only minimally successful, she hoped the men would attribute her discomfort to the understandable nervousness of a woman requesting employment in a whorehouse. *It may appear appropriate, but it won't help my powers of observation or make my task any easier.* Resigned, Astryd tapped a fist against the door.

Several seconds went by while Astryd feigned engrossment in the panel, avoiding the smug glances of passersby. Then, the door swung open and a male face peered out. "Yes?"

"I'm looking for a job," Astryd said, wishing she sounded less timid.

The man studied Astryd in the afternoon sunlight. Frowning, he gestured her into the entryway. When she stepped through, he closed the door behind her.

"Cooking and cleaning," Astryd clarified. "And running errands."

The man shook his head. "We have someone who cooks, and the girls pitch in with the other jobs. But I'll ask the master." He marched forward. The hallway ended in a door. Pulling it open, he gestured Astryd through it.

Astryd found herself in a huge, open room where women lounged in brightly-colored dresses styled to accentuate the bulges of breasts and thighs. A smaller number of men sat, mixed in with the girls. All discussion ceased as Astryd appeared, and every eye turned toward her. She met their gazes without flinching, making no judgments. Discovering the woman she had seen in her location spell, she smiled.

"Wait here." The man's tone seemed more suited to a threat than a suggestion. He trotted past the base of a staircase and through a door just beyond it.

As the conversations resumed, Astryd turned her attention to the layout of the whorehouse. The walls of the meeting room were painted a soft, baby blue, interrupted by a pair of doors in the farthest corner of the left wall that Taziar had explained led to matched bargaining rooms. The chambers above them remained in perpetual darkness, and knotholes in the floor allowed their occupants to hear and observe any business being conducted in the rooms below. To Astryd's right, the staircase led to the bedrooms, and the door the man had gone through opened onto the kitchen and private rooms of the women who lived here.

Shortly, the kitchen door was wrenched open. The man who had met Astryd emerged first, followed by Harriman and his bodyguards. Harriman was wiping his hands on a rag. His gaze roved up and down Astryd with the intensity of a man purchasing expensive merchandise. His expression never changed, but the movement of his fingers on the cloth slowed and became mechanical.

Astryd shivered. *Does he look at everyone this way? Does he like my appearance? Does he recognize me?* Harriman stepped around the man in front of him and tossed the rag at him. The other man fumbled it, then caught it in a two-handed grip. He sidled out of the way to give Halden and Skereye room to pass.

Astryd looked up at Harriman, studying bland features that appeared more kindly than she'd expected. Taziar's warning rose from memory. *"You're gathering information, Astryd. Don't try anything recklessly heroic. If you get Harriman alone in a position where you can easily kill him and escape, try it. But don't risk your life and destroy your cover for vague possibilities."* The thought of Taziar condemning headstrong courage made her grin.

Apparently thinking Astryd's expression was intended for him, Harriman returned the smile. "Fine. You can start today. Keep the dust off the walls and furnishings and make sure the beds are made. In return, we'll give you room and board. Don't take anything that doesn't belong to you. I'll expect you to run errands for anyone here who asks, but you take your final commands from me. Whatever I say, you do. Understand?''

Astryd nodded. Her glance strayed beyond Harriman to his bodyguards. They towered nearly half again her height; a layer of fat fleshed out their muscles, sacrificing definition for girth. Their scarred features and glazed eyes looked familiar. Astryd had known men addicted to the berserker mushrooms and the blood-frenzy of Viking raids who lived in desperate misery between sessions of pirating. She knew they would prove ferocious and unpredictable warriors, undaunted by pain.

Harriman gestured toward the staircase. "Get to work." He looked beyond Astryd. "Mat-hilde, you come with me. We need to talk." He spun on a heel and trotted up the steps, Halden and Skereye directly behind him.

The woman Harriman had indicated swallowed hard, and several others flinched in sympathy. With a slowness indicating reluctance, Mat-hilde uncrossed her ankles, rose from a stool, and yanked at the clinging fabric of her dress. Astryd read fear in Mat-hilde's eyes, and saw the woman shiver as she climbed the stairs.

Astryd seized the rag from the man's hands and followed, certain of two things. *The exchange won't be pleasant, and I'm going to know why.* She watched as Mat-hilde entered a room. Astryd caught a glimpse of Skereye's back and the corner of a bed before the door slammed shut.

Astryd scurried past rows of bedrooms. The door before the room Harriman had chosen for his conference was closed, but the panel of the next chamber stood ajar. Astryd peeked through the crack into a cramped, pink-walled room with no windows. The bed sheets and coverlet lay rumpled, and a nightstand held a flickering lantern. *Perfect.* Astryd slipped within, pulling the door closed behind her. Aware that the walls would have been built thick enough to block out sounds from neighboring rooms, Astryd tapped her life energy to accentuate her hearing. She pressed an ear to the partition, but Mat-hilde's voice wafted to her as an incomprehensible whisper.

Astryd drew more life force to her, channeling it into her spell. Her aura dimmed, then flared back to blend in tone with the half-lit room.

". . . and Shylar always said we don't have to do anything we don't feel comfortable doing."

Astryd heard the unmistakable sound of a slap, followed by a shrill gasp and a stumbling step. Harriman's voice sounded as loud as a scream. "Shylar's gone, damn it! I'm in charge now, and I say you do whatever the customer wants. Do you understand that?"

Harriman's words pounded Astryd's magically acute hearing, causing pain. She back-stepped, clamping a hand to her ringing ear. Turning, she pressed her other ear to the wall, felt the surface cold against her cheek.

Astryd heard no reply from Mat-hilde. Another slap reverberated through the room and some piece of furniture scraped across the floor. "I asked if you understand."

Mat-hilde's voice held the hesitant, breathy quality of tears withheld. "I . . . understand."

"Good girl." Harriman spoke condescendingly, the way a man might praise a dog. A moment later, the door opened.

Astryd backed away from the wall, furiously pretending to dust. She heard the heightened stomp of footsteps as Harriman and his guards retreated down the hallway and the clomp as they descended the stairs. Quickly, Astryd dismissed her spell, pocketed the rag, and entered the room Harriman had vacated. Mat-hilde perched on the edge of the bed. The corners of her mouth quivered downward as she fought to keep from crying.

Astryd let the door click shut behind her. Without a word, she crossed the chamber, sat beside Mat-hilde, and wrapped her arms around the prostitute's shoulders.

Mat-hilde stiffened, resisting Astryd even as she struggled to contain her tears. Then, apparently reading sincere concern in Astryd's touch, Mat-hilde softened. Her sinews uncoiled, and her tears fell, warm and moist, on

Astryd's neck. Astryd drew Mat-hilde closer; each sob made the sorceress ache with sympathy. Finally Mat-hilde pulled away, and the crying jag died to sniffles.

Astryd hesitated, torn between urgency and the need to take the time to gain Mat-hilde's trust. The thought of taking advantage of Mat-hilde's vulnerability repulsed Astryd, but she saw no other way. "Why do you stay with Harriman if he treats you so badly?"

Mat-hilde looked up sharply. Tears clung to her lashes, but she squinted in suspicion. "Who are you?"

Caught off-guard by Mat-hilde's sudden change in manner, Astryd stammered. "I–I'm a friend of Shylar's."

The creases in Mat-hilde's rounded face deepened. She studied Astryd with the same intensity as Harriman had used downstairs.

Knowing that any simple question would reveal her lie, Astryd amended in the only way that occurred to her. "I'm the friend of a friend, really. I've never actually met Shylar, but we're going to free her." Astryd held her breath, aware all chance of success now depended on Taziar being right about the prostitutes retaining loyalty to Shylar. *And Mat-hilde's use of the madam's name when Harriman confronted her suggests the probability.*

Mat-hilde continued to stare. The hem of her dress had balled up so it now revealed the edges of a gauzy undergarment, but she made no move to straighten it. "You're with Taz Medakan, aren't you?"

Startled by the directness of the question, Astryd answered too quickly. "Who?" She tried to sound confused, but managed only to appear nervous.

"Honey." Mat-hilde brushed moisture from her eyes, revealing irises the color of oak. "If you're not going to trust me, how can you expect me to trust you?"

Aware she was outclassed in affairs of subterfuge, Astryd dropped all pretenses and relied on her instincts. Mat-hilde seemed kindly and forthright. "Yes, I'm with Shadow . . . I mean, Taz." She tensed, waiting for a shout or an attack. When none came, curiosity overcame apprehension. "But how could you possibly know that?"

Mat-hilde smiled. "You live among the underground, you learn to pay attention. Taz came back here and got a greeting he didn't expect." The grin vanished, and she cringed in remembrance. "We all know he escaped the baron's guards by crossing the Kattegat. Then a Norse woman shows up here asking for work at a time when most girls would rather take their chances on the street. When you claimed to be a friend of Shylar's friend, it seemed the only answer."

Astryd frowned, displeased by the ease with which Mat-hilde had targeted her. "I just hope Harriman doesn't put the clues together."

"Men are stupid," Mat-hilde said in a voice that implied she used the phrase with such frequency it had become habit.

"Some," Astryd agreed. "But I can't count on my enemies being the feebleminded ones." Astryd pulled her knees to her chest, watching lantern light flicker through the misty-gray remnants of her life aura. "Don't you believe Taziar is a traitor? No one else we've met seems to have the slightest doubt."

Mat-hilde snorted. "Taziar Medakan a traitor?" She snorted again. "Men are stupid," she repeated in the same tone as before. "Taz has got more morality in him than any ten people together. The men in the underground get so used to constructing evidence and changing circumstance that they fall prey to it if someone does it better than they can. I think it's pride." Mat-hilde straightened, finally tugging her dress back into its proper position. "Besides, men say things and show sides of themselves to women they wouldn't ever let anyone else see. And they brag." Mat-hilde rolled her eyes. "When we girls put enough stories together, we learn a lot. Sure, the evidence against Taz is overwhelming, but there's other things besides evidence to consider. Instead of ten percent, Taz used to donate fifty, sometimes ninety percent of his paid heists to Shylar. Then he'd go out on the streets and hand most of the remainder to street orphans and beggars. Does that sound like the kind of person who would turn traitor?"

"Of course not." Astryd savored her rising excitement. *I've found a friend.* "But I'm biased."

Mat-hilde gave Astryd a knowing look that implied she guessed more than Astryd had revealed. "I don't think you came to listen to me ramble on about men. What do you need?"

"Mostly information. First, you never told me why you're still working for Harriman. Second, I need to know which people are loyal to Harriman and which ones would forsake him if the old leaders returned."

All sadness seemed to have left Mat-hilde's face. Only a fading red mark on her cheek remained as a reminder of the ordeal. "We stayed because Shylar told us to follow Harriman just before they arrested her. We assumed it would be temporary. Shylar's got a lot of connections. As for loyalty . . ." Mat-hilde considered. "Harriman brought those two ugly, blond monsters with him. They follow his every command, and they're always at his side."

"Always?" Astryd prodded.

Mat-hilde loosed a short laugh. "Always," she confirmed. "They eat with him. They sleep in his room. When he goes off to relieve himself . . ." She trailed off.

Astryd crinkled her mouth in disgust. "They go off with him?"

"Always," Mat-hilde confirmed.

Astryd made a mild noise of revulsion. *So much for an easy opportunity to kill Harriman and escape.* "What about the rest of the underground?"

"Harriman pulled in some of the 'fringe guard.' Shylar kept in contact with a few strong-arm men she called on when some rare circumstance required violence. Harriman brought those men to the forefront of the underground. They've got more power and money than they used to, so they'll probably remain loyal to Harriman." Mat-hilde traced a floorboard with her cloth shoe. "There's twelve or fourteen of them. Taz should know who they are. As for the others, they'd be thrilled to abandon Harriman for Shylar and the imprisoned leaders. Careful, though," Mat-hilde warned. "I have no doubt they'll welcome Shylar back, but they still believe Taz informed on her. If they see him, they'll turn him over to Harriman or kill him. And, honey, it's possible even Shylar believes Taziar is the traitor.''

Relief flooded Astryd, despite the fact that she wasn't out of danger yet. *I've got the information I came for, and it was easier than I expected.* "Thanks, Mat-hilde, for your trust and the facts. We'll do all we can to free Shylar and the others, I promise.''

"I'm not certain it's possible," Mat-hilde admitted. "Then again, Taz has done a number of things I didn't think possible." She took Astryd's hand and squeezed encouragingly.

Astryd felt the warm flush of jealousy. Surprised by her own reaction, she tried to override emotion with rationalization. *She knew Shadow for years before I met him. She's a friend; she's not trying to take him from me. We're on the same side.* Astryd returned the handclasp.

Mat-hilde released Astryd. "When do you expect to try this prison break?''

"Tomorrow morning.''

"More specifically?" Mat-hilde pressed.

"I don't know." Interest replaced rivalry. "Why?''

Mat-hilde shook back a mane of dark hair. "Because, if I'm careful, I should be able to send information about the escape to the right people and have them here to help depose Harriman. But he'll get suspicious if I have a large group of people sitting around all day.''

Though short a significant amount of life energy, exhilaration lent Astryd a second wind. *Information and allies. What more could we ask for?* "I need to take what I know back to Taziar and try to find out a time for you." *That means I need the freedom to come and go from here as I please, hopefully without having to resort to magic each time.*

"Go," Mat-hilde encouraged. "Tell Harriman I sent you out for combs and food. He'll believe that, and I'll back it up.''

A sudden knock on the door startled Astryd. A muffled female shout followed. "Mat-hilde?''

"Go on." Mat-hilde indicated the door. "Let them in on your way out. I'll take care of things."

Astryd rose. She pulled the panel open, and was immediately confronted by five prostitutes with worried faces. They stared as she slipped past, then entered the room in response to some gesture from Mat-hilde that Astryd did not see. As she reached the top of the stairwell, the sorceress heard the door snap closed behind her.

Astryd took the steps two at a time. Her mission had turned out more successfully than she'd ever expected. Though dingy and partially spent, her life aura remained strong enough for a few spells at least, more than enough for an emergency transport escape. Still, a sense of foreboding tempered Astryd's joy. In spite of greater numbers, the peaceful members of the underground might not hold out against Harriman and his warriors. The prison break would require a skill even Taziar might not possess, despite the help of a garnet-rank sorceress. And when it was all over, they might still have to face Harriman's master.

Engrossed in thought, Astryd nearly collided with Skereye at the base of the stairs. Startled, she skittered sideways and stumbled over the last step. A hand seized her forearm, steadying her. She glanced up at her benefactor, recognized Harriman's placid features, and a shiver racked her. A burst of surprise nearly caused her to trigger the transport escape, but Astryd held her magics. A spell cast in panic always cost more energy, and the need to break Harriman's grip would have increased the toll on her life force. *Besides, using sorcery now would certainly reveal me and destroy any chance of returning*. Instead, Astryd showed Harriman a weak smile. "Forgive my clumsiness." She tossed a glance around the conference room, noticed six large men with callused hands and scarred faces, and felt even more certain of her decision not to depart with magic. *Something's going on. I think I'd better know what.*

Attentive to the gathered warriors, Astryd missed the nonverbal exchange between Harriman and a stout, greasy man who stood before the door to the entry hall. Harriman's grip tightened, and Astryd twisted back to face him. "What's your name, Missy?"

"Linnea," Astryd replied, choosing the name of one of her sisters for convenience. She trained her gaze on Harriman's hand on her sleeve as an obvious suggestion that he remove his grasp.

To Astryd's surprise, Harriman released her. "Well, Linnea. This is Saerle." He beckoned to the man by the door who trotted forward. "Take him upstairs and do *anything* he asks."

Dread tightened Astryd's throat. She knew better than to protest; that could only earn her Harriman's wrath. *Casting an escape before one man must be safer and less conspicuous than in a crowd.* She maintained her composure. *I may even have enough life energy to evade Saerle and still listen in on Harriman's meeting. So long as I keep enough for a transport, I'm in no danger.*

Astryd studied Saerle. His round face sported a day's growth of beard. A receding semicircle of sand-colored hair revealed a moist forehead, and his green-gray eyes regressed into sockets deep as a skull's. Three bottles of wine swung from between his fingers, the color of the vintage obscured by the thickness of the glass. "Come on," Astryd said. Though revolted by the thought of touching Saerle, she caught his wrist and pattered up the staircase.

Plans swirled through Astryd's mind as they ascended the steps. A natural ability to conjure dragons had biased her repertoire toward summonings. Most of her other spells were basic shields, wards, and defenses against magic, none of which would serve in this situation. But as Saerle and Astryd crested the landing, a distant memory drifted into focus. She recalled her early years as a glass-rank sorceress when she and her peers had spent half the day fashioning wards for the outer walls of the Dragonrank school. Then, boredom had driven her to seek entertainment. By shorting the Dragonrank defenses a few spells each day, she retained enough energy at night to pull pranks on the glass-rank mages who shared her quarters. She recalled a friend sputtering over ale laced with salt and another awakening in the middle of the night, tripping and stumbling over furniture silently re-arranged with magic. The remembrance made her smile. *This might prove the most amusing challenge I've ever faced.* The idea made her laugh aloud. *Amusing challenge? Thor's hammer, now I'm starting to think like Shadow.*

Apparently believing Astryd's pleasure was directed at him, Saerle shuffled all three bottles into his opposite hand. He ran his fingers up her arm, caressing her shoulder briefly before dropping to her breast.

The touch made Astryd's skin crawl. She shivered free, then, realizing her mistake, covered neatly. "Not so eager, handsome. We have all night." It required strength of will not to follow the words with a grunt of abhorrence. She selected an open bedchamber at random and gestured him through the portal.

The room contained a cot with a straw mattress softened with coverlets and fluffed pillows. A tall chair framed of wood stood in the farther corner, pulled away from the wall. Dark green linen stuffed with down stretched over its seat and back. A sturdy end table sat at the opposite side of the bed. Above it, a lantern hung from a ring in the ceiling, its flame flapping light through the windowless confines.

Saerle set the wine bottles on the table. Stepping around the bed to face Astryd, he poised to sit on the edge of the mattress.

Astryd closed the door. She whirled suddenly, causing her skirt to flip partially up her thigh. Having captured Saerle's attention, she invoked her life energy for a spell. Silently, the bed swung around so its side was flush with the wall. "Sit," Astryd purred.

Eyes locked on Astryd, Saerle sat where the bed had stood a moment before. He crashed to the floor, sprawling beside the mattress.

Astryd ran to his side, suppressing a snicker behind an expression of concern. It lacked the sincerity she intended to convey, but Saerle seemed too shocked to no-

tice. His head flicked from side to side as the new location
of the bed registered and he tried to figure out what had
happened. Catching his forearm, Astryd helped him to
his feet. "I know you're eager, handsome, but let's do
this on the bed, shall we?"

Saerle nodded absently. Seizing on his confusion, Astryd unobtrusively used her magic to slide the wine-laden
table out of sight behind the chair.

"How?" Saerle started. He broke off, apparently realizing there was no way to ask the question without appearing insane. His gaze wandered to the site where the
table had stood and froze there. He looked at Astryd,
then suddenly back at the empty space where the table
should have stood.

"Is something wrong?" Astryd reached out, massaging his shoulders seductively. "You feel tense."

"I . . ." Saerle went even more rigid beneath her
touch. "No-o," he said, voice cracking halfway through
the word. He cleared his throat. "I'm fine." He emphasized each syllable, as if to convince himself as well as
Astryd.

"Here, let me help." Astryd sat beside Saerle, her
side touching his. *I hope Shadow appreciates what I'm
doing for him.* She seized the lacing at Saerle's throat and
gently tugged it free. Using two fingers, she loosed the
tie at each eyelet. While his attention focused on her, she
quietly slid the table to the end of the bed, behind him.
Her life aura flickered dangerously, and she knew she
could only afford one more spell if she wanted to save
enough energy for a transport. Catching the hem of
Saerle's shirt, she pulled it over his head and flung it over
her shoulder. At her command, the homespun hovered.

Saerle jerked backward with a startled noise. "My
shirt!"

Astryd stared into Saerle's widened eyes. She wrapped
her fingers around his ribs, trying to draw him closer.

Saerle resisted. "My shirt. Look at my shirt!"

"What's the matter? Did I tear it?" Astryd released
her magics, saw Saerle's gaze fall as she turned. The
fabric lay in a rumpled pile on the floor. "It looks fine

to me." She twisted back to Saerle, clamping her hands to her hips in mock offense. "Are you trying to avoid me?"

Saerle groaned.

"Here." Astryd pushed him to the coverlet. "Have some wine. It'll calm you."

"Wine?" Saerle's voice had fallen to a whisper of its former resonance.

Astryd allowed herself a giggle, and it was only the weakness of having tapped most of her life energy that saved her from breaking into a torrent of laughter. "The wine you brought."

"Where?"

Hiding a grimace, Astryd caressed Saerle's damp forehead. She smothered the urge to wipe oily sweat from her hand. "On the table where you put it, handsome."

Saerle glanced wildly toward the end of the bed, and the sight of the table with its three bottles of wine induced a guttural moan.

"I'll get it," Astryd said helpfully. She leaned across Saerle's prone form, watching the dark glow of her remaining life aura wash across him, making his olive-skinned features appear more ashen. In the flickering light of the lantern, her aura seemed to disappear into the shadows. Frowning, she grabbed the bottles with both hands and dragged them onto the bed. Fumbling the knife she used for eating and odd tasks from her pocket, she jabbed it into a cork and twisted it free. She offered the opened bottle.

Saerle accepted the wine eagerly. Without bothering to sit up, he poured. Liquid sloshed into his mouth, across his naked chest, and trickled into the mattress. He drained a third of the bottle before offering it to Astryd.

Astryd shook her head. "You need it more than I do."

Obligingly, Saerle reclaimed the bottle. Three more gulps emptied it, and Astryd handed him the next. She waited while he drank, her patience thinning. *That meeting could have started already. I can't waste all my time with this idiot.* She clamped a hand to the crotch of his breeks, felt him soft and unresponsive against her palm.

Restlessness made her movement more sudden than intended. Saerle jumped in surprise, the bottle startled from his grip. Purple wine splashed across Astryd, Saerle, and the coverlet, and the bottle thunked to the floor. The room went silent except for the steady trickle of liquid on the planks.

Gracefully, Astryd rescued the remainder of the wine, returning the bottle to Saerle. She raised a hand, making certain he noticed it before replacing it on his genitals. She fondled more carefully, felt the first hint of reaction as the wine relaxed him. Her antics had rattled him, put her fully in control, and Astryd felt reasonably sure he would agree to anything she suggested. "Ever been conquered by a woman?"

Saerle shook his head, whiskers sticky with wine. "No. How does that work?"

Astryd caught interest in Saerle's tone that went beyond sexual desire. *I wonder if he hopes I'll say it involves a third person rearranging the furniture.* "I'll show you." Astryd unbuckled Saerle's belt. Pulling it from around his waist, she looped it around his wrist and lashed it securely to the leg of the cot beneath the mattress.

Saerle finished the last mouthful of wine from the second bottle. "I'm not sure about—"

Astryd cut him off with a finger to his lips. "Relax. Enjoy it." She uncorked the last bottle and pressed it into his free palm. "Drink."

Saerle obeyed while Astryd cut her own sash in two, using the pieces to tie his ankles. She pulled the lacing from his shirt and returned to the bed. Taking the now empty wine bottle from Saerle, she bound his other hand, wincing at what she was about to do. She knelt at the bedside. Softly, she turned his face toward her. "That's not so bad, is it?" Before Saerle could reply, she swung the bottle down, as hard as she could, against his temple.

Saerle went limp instantly, and Astryd hoped he hadn't seen the blow. A sudden thought ground fear through her. *I hope I didn't kill him.* Until that moment, it had never occurred to her that she might have the strength to take a life. She had never killed before, and the idea of doing so as a punishment for seeking paid sexual favors repulsed her. She watched Saerle, and the deep rise and fall of his breathing relieved her conscience.

"Sorry," Astryd whispered. She spread the coverlet over Saerle, carefully hiding his bindings from anyone who might peek into the room. Crossing the room with as little sound as possible, she opened the door a crack. Footsteps filled her ears. She heard a gruff male voice, his words indecipherable, followed by a high-pitched giggle. Then a door slammed and the hallway fell silent.

Astryd slipped from the room. Most of the doors were closed. At the far end of the hall, the storage chamber doors overlooking the bargaining rooms stood ajar. *It must be approaching sundown.* Astryd winced, aware her friends would soon begin to worry about her. *Where would Harriman hold a meeting? Probably not up here, he'll need these rooms for business.*

She edged toward the stairs. At the top, she took a surreptitious glance into the main conference area. Three women and a man sat in discussion. Beyond them, Astryd caught a glimpse of one of Harriman's Norse bodyguards disappearing into a bargaining chamber. The door slammed shut behind him.

Astryd retreated, scarcely daring to believe her luck. Everything was falling into place. She still had enough life energy for a transport, should it become necessary. And Harriman had chosen to hold his assembly in the one place Astryd knew she could observe without being seen. She scrambled to the end of the upstairs hallway, and slipped through the gap into the room above the one the Norseman had entered.

A bar of light from the hallway penetrated a room devoid of furnishings. Astryd stepped into the center where knotholes and cracks between the floorboards gave her a view of activity below. Her aura was nearly lost in the darkness, no brighter than the light leeching through the doorway. Alone, without the nervous enthusiasm of Saerle's challenge, her head buzzed and her limbs felt heavy. She sat, cross-legged, on the paneling, hunched forward for a complete view of the chamber beneath her.

The six grim-faced warriors perched on chairs and stools. Before them, Harriman stood with his arms folded across his chest, flanked by Halden and Skereye. Astryd had to strain to hear his words. "I know . . . location of that . . . traitor . . . Medakan." Every few syllables, his voice fell too low for her to comprehend.

Suddenly alert, Astryd realized the importance of catching every word. A choice confronted her, and she felt too tired to make it. *If I enhance my hearing, I won't have enough energy left for an emergency escape.* The word "murder" wafted clearly to her, and she made her decision. She shaped her magics to listen, feeling dizzy and emptied as the spell wrung vigor from her. She waited until her head stopped spinning, and Harriman's speech became clear.

". . . female, so he has only one fighting friend to help him. A team of women should be able to handle that." Harriman's gaze traveled over each of the men before him. Briefly, he glanced upward.

Astryd went utterly still.

Harriman's eyes never stopped to fully focus, and he continued without a pause or signal to indicate he had seen anything. "Bring him in alive, it's worth a thousand weight in gold. Dead, it's a hundred." He hesitated, allowing time for the mentioned fortunes to register in every mind. "If you don't bring him back, I'd better find out he killed you all. And if he can do that, you've gone softer than my mother."

The warriors met Harriman's statement with grunts of amusement or denial. One cursed Harriman beneath his breath, and his words floated, garbled even to Astryd's heightened hearing.

"I'll get to the plan in a moment," Harriman continued. "But first, I've had a couple too many beers." He made a gesture Astryd could not see, and the men laughed. She watched him open the door, slip through with Halden and Skereye, and close the panel behind them.

Astryd leaned forward with a sigh. Every moment she held the spell cost her life force, but it was still far less than recasting. She waited, not bothering to focus on the warriors' conversations about weaponry. Shortly, she heard the pounding of footfalls on the steps, and terror drove her to her feet. She measured the distance to the door, aware she could never make it back to Saerle in time. *Loki's evil children!* The words seemed as much description as blasphemy. Rummaging through her pockets, she discovered the cleaning rag she had stuffed there. She wrenched it free. The movement flung her knife into the air. Desperately, she grabbed for it, juggled it once, then crammed it back in place. Hurriedly, she went to work dusting a corner as the door creaked fully open.

Astryd whirled, not having to feign her startlement. Harriman and his bodyguards stood in the doorway. The hall lanterns threw their shadows across Astryd. "What are you doing in here?"

"Cleaning," Astryd replied sweetly.

"Cleaning?" Harriman repeated without accusation. "In the dark?"

"There's no lantern in here. And there was enough light from the hall—" Astryd broke off, abruptly realizing her mistake. Taziar had told her the spying rooms were left dark. With the bargaining rooms lit, it accorded a perfect view from the upper room down, but did not allow the people in the lower room to see up between the boards. *But I left the door partway open. Apparently, Harriman saw. I've used my last spell, and now I'm in trouble.* She covered quickly. She reached for the knife in her pocket, closing her hand over the hilt. "The door was ajar. That means I'm supposed to clean it, right?"

"Usually," Harriman agreed. "But right now you're supposed to be with a client."

Astryd hesitated, exhausted. She knew too little of warfare to dream of killing a man with a single stroke of a knife. Even a lucky stab at Harriman would not rescue her from the berserks. "He's asleep. So I went back to work."

"He paid for the night." Harriman's tone betrayed no anger or suspicion. "Asleep or not, you stay with him."

Astryd nodded, not daring to believe she would get off this easily. Once Harriman returned to the meeting, she could still sneak away and warn Taziar, Larson, and Silme. "All right. I didn't know. I'm sorry."

Harriman stepped aside. Astryd wandered around him, tensed for an attack, but he made no movement toward her. Instead, he watched her stagger to Saerle's room.

Astryd released pent up breath in a ragged sigh. Catching the handle, she pulled open the door, unable to recall the panel feeling so heavy before. From the corner of her eye, she glimpsed Harriman's gesture, and his harsh voice followed. "Skereye, stay right by the door and make certain she doesn't leave until morning."

Horror crushed down on Astryd, and she tottered awkwardly into the room. The door crashed shut, leaving her with a comatose client tied to the bed and awash in panic that drained life energy nearly as fast as a spell. *Harriman must know who I am. Why else would he trap me in this room?*

Astryd's life aura faded, its edges invisible, and need alone kept her conscious. Her eyes drooped closed, and rational thoughts scattered or disappeared. *Got to warn Shadow. Enemy trap. Can't go through the door. Window. Window?* Blindly, she stumbled toward the window. She dragged her limbs onward, her mind and movements thick, as if wading through water. After what seemed like an eternity, her hand struck wall. She forced her lids apart and only then realized she was crawling.

Reaching up, Astryd caught the sill. Movement drove her to the edge of oblivion. Curtains fluttered into her face, filmy and clinging. Unwilling to waste a gesture removing them, she peered through. A full story below her, a packed earth alleyway reflected the red rays of sunset in a glow that put her life aura to shame. The black shapes of rain barrels and garbage filled her vision, then spread to engulf her sight in darkness. Astryd collapsed on the whorehouse floor.

CHAPTER 8:

Dim Shadows of Vengeance

The land of darkness and the shadow of death.
—Job 10:21

The last rays of sunlight slipped past the inn room window, leaving the chamber awash in the red glow of the fire. Half-sitting, half-crouched on his pack, Al Larson wondered what it would be like to be a father. The oldest of three children, he tried to recall his siblings' infancies. His sister was scarcely two years younger, and his brother's babyhood faded into a muddled remembrance of wet burps and diapers. *I doubt Silme and I will have plastic bottles and jars of mashed peas.* The thought made Larson smile. He glanced at Silme, perched on the logs by the hearth, eyelids half-closed as she rehearsed some meditative technique too softly for him to hear. The hearth fire accentuated rosy cheeks and unlined features. Hair swept around her shoulders in thick, golden waves. The firelight carved a spindly imitation of perfect curves in a shadow on the floor beside her.

Larson looked away. Memories swept down on him then; though they lacked the nightmarish reality of the flashbacks, they seemed every bit as cruel. He pictured Silme's bumbling, raven-haired apprentice, Brendor, and recalled how he and Silme had planned to raise the boy as a son, until an enemy's magic had turned Brendor into a soulless killing machine. Larson could still feel the pressure and warmth of the boy against him as Brendor wrenched him to the ground with the inhuman strength of the sorcerer who controlled him. The child's grip seemed permanently impressed on Larson's flesh, the knife the boy plunged for his throat a constant in his mind's eye.

Remembrance of Silme's magic tearing apart the body that had once housed Brendor's spirit still brought tears to Larson's eyes, and the image of the child's glazed, blue eyes and blood-splattered features drove him nearly to the madness that had engulfed him at the time. Then the incident had sent him flashing back to Ti Sun, a Vietnamese boy with whom he had shared conversation and chocolate. Now, it came to him in fragments: the hidden grenade in the boy's hand that Larson had not seen, his buddy's gun howling, bullets tearing through the child, one moment so alive, the next as empty as his stained and tattered clothes, the rage that had churned up inside Larson and spurred him to batter his companion in a wild, irrational frenzy.

Larson winced, gritting his teeth against a memory too deeply engraved to keep from sliding into his mind next. Again, he saw Silme, blood trickling from a corner of her mouth, driven to her knees by his blind and misdirected attack, out of time and place. *And all of it because we dared to subject a child to my insanity and our enemies.*

One more boy entered Larson's thoughts, his younger brother, Timmy. Larson had enlisted in the army to ease the hardships on his family after his father's untimely death in an automobile accident with a drunken driver. *Timmy always felt betrayed, that Dad "abandoned" us. Eventually, he'll be old enough to stop blaming Dad for his death. But I promised Timmy we'd always be together, then ran off to a foreign land . . . and died there.* Guilt hammered Larson. When he had left for Vietnam, he was too concerned about grappling with his own mixture of fear and excitement to notice the expression of hostility and grief on Timmy's face. *Then and there, I could have comforted him, put things right. But I didn't. I was too goddamned worried about my own pain.* Only much later did the vision haunt Al Larson. And, by then, there was nothing left to say or do. *The same magical thinking that allows a child to believe his father died to punish him might force Timmy to think his bitterness killed his brother.* Remorse balled in Larson's gut, making him feel ill. *What a burden for a child to have to live with.*

Larson lowered his head. *Barely twenty, one semester of college, a war, and now I have a wife and almost a child.* Panic touched him. He glanced at Silme again, saw a woman more beautiful than any model or actress he could recall. *I'm not even old enough to drink yet. I never got to vote for a president, but I was old enough to die for him.* Larson stared at Silme until his vision blurred and her form went as hazy and unrecognizable as her shadow. Still, the sight of her filled him with joy, and the thought of losing her inspired a wild urge to sweep her into his arms. *I love her more than anything before in my life.* Doubts smothered devotion in a rush. *But I'm not fit to be a father. I'm too young. I'm too inexperienced. And I've lost decency, sanity, and all sense of fairness in a mindless war. What sort of warped morality could I give to a son or daughter? Silme and the baby deserve better than I can offer.*

Seeking a replacement, Larson turned his attention to Taziar. The Climber had been pacing from door to window for the last hour. Now, Larson noticed a change in Taziar's pattern, and curiosity drove self-deprecation and fear from his thoughts. Taziar's course was becoming shorter. He was turning farther from the door and pausing at the window with each pass. And Larson felt fairly certain Taziar had no idea what he was doing. *But I know. Any second now, that little thief is going out the window.*

Feigning indifference, Larson rose and stretched. He watched Taziar stare out the window at the grimy walls across the alleyway for some time before he whirled and started back toward the table. Quickly, Larson crossed the room to the window, not surprised to see Taziar spin back even before the Climber reached the center of the chamber. Casually, Larson placed a hand on each shutter and waited.

Five steps brought Taziar to the window again. He stopped there, palms pressed to the sill, blue eyes focused distantly, seemingly oblivious to Larson's presence. He shifted his grip, leaving a sweaty print on the ledge. Suddenly, he tensed.

Larson slammed the shutters closed. Wood thunked against flesh, and the panels rebounded open. Taziar sprang backward with a startled cry. He nursed the fingers of his left hand, eyes wide and turned on Larson in shocked accusation. "Why did you do that?"

Larson caught the swinging shutters and nudged them closed more gently. "That's 'why the *hell* did I do that?' Don't you people know how to swear?"

Taziar rubbed his pinched fingers. "You *jerk!*" he said in stilted, heavily-accented English. "Why in *Karana's deepest, darkest, frozen pits of hell* would you do something like that?"

Larson resisted the impulse to answer 'sport.' "You were about to climb through that window, weren't you?"

"No!" Taziar responded instantly, then paused in consideration.

"Admit it."

"No," Taziar repeated less forcefully. "But now that you raised the subject, Astryd's been gone far too long."

"I didn't raise the subject, you just did." Larson leaned against the shutters. "But you're right. That's why I'm going after her."

"You?" Taziar and Silme spoke simultaneously, in the same incredulous tone.

"Me?" Larson mimicked. "Yes, me. Of course, me. I am, in fact, the only logical choice. Astryd can transport. If she's not back, it's because someone's holding her. That someone has to be defeated. I may not be the best swordsman in the world, but I'd venture to guess I could beat either of you."

"I can think of other reasons Astryd might not have returned yet," Taziar shot back, his injured hand forgotten. "She may still be gathering information. She could have gotten lost. We can't all go. Someone has to stay here in case she returns. Rescuing her may require stealth and knowledge of the city, so I'm the one to go."

Larson glanced past Taziar, saw Silme shaking her head in disagreement. "I can handle 'stealth,' and I know

Cullinsberg as well as Astryd.'' Though irrelevant, Larson made the latter statement sound as if it held some grand significance. "Besides, even lost, she could still transport. If she's gathering information and you show up, everyone will try to kill you. Plus, they'll know Astryd's with you and try to kill her, too. But no one knows me.''

Taziar tossed a meaningful look at Silme who became suddenly engrossed in the fire.

Lacking the knowledge to make sense of the exchange, Larson dismissed it. "Then it's settled. I go. You stay with Silme.'' Larson hated to use guilt as a tool against Taziar, but he saw no other way to keep the Climber from taking off on his own. "If anything happens to her or my baby while I'm gone, I'm holding you responsible.'' Larson winced, not liking the sound of his own threat. Ignoring Silme's glare, he crossed the room, opened the door, and slipped into the hallway.

The panel clicked closed behind Larson. Through it, he heard Taziar's muffled shout of protest and Silme's curt reply distorted beyond understanding. Larson trotted down the corridor. Soon his companions' voices faded into the obscurity of a dirty passage, its chipped, indigo paint revealing a previous layer of white. Blue flakes crunched beneath Larson's boots, and he trod carefully across boards, warped by water, to the staircase at the farther end. In the center of the steps, the passage of countless feet had worn down its carpet to the planks. But at the corners, the dark brown wool appeared new. Larson passed no one as he shuffled down the three flights into a back room grimier than the halls. A door to his left led to the common room; a wild clamor of voices drifted from beneath it. Choosing the opposite door, he emerged into the alley beneath the chamber window.

The wind felt comfortably cool to Larson after hours sitting idle before the hearth fire. He had grown accustomed to the smoke; the crisp air made his eyes water and the night seemed unusually clear. Around the spires of the baron's keep, he caught a vivid view of stars, like pinholes in black velvet, and picked out the constellation

of Orion. Then his instincts took over. He discarded the
beauty of the night sky as insignificant background. Alert
for movement, he abandoned the alley for a cobbled main
street and delved Taziar's directions to Astryd from his
memory.

The street stood deserted, the shops closed and dark,
the sidewalk stands vacated for the night. The merchants
had hauled away their wares, leaving wooden skeletons
or empty wagons, some protected from the elements with
tarps. Larson moved quickly and smoothly, keeping to
the edges where the walkways met the streets and away
from the yawning darkness of alleys and smaller thoroughfares. A noise snapped through the darkness. Larson flattened against a cart, eyes probing. Across the
road, a gray sheet of canvas fluttered like a ghost in the
breeze. Larson loosed a pent up breath and continued.

Thoughts of survival channeled aside Larson's concerns and self-doubts. His abilities as a father paled before the more urgent matter of Astryd's safety. Lacking
information, he had made no plan, and Kensei Gaelinar's
words emerged from memory, equally as alarming as they
were comforting: "A warrior makes his plans in the instant between sword strokes." But Gaelinar had been capable of split second strategies and instantaneous
wisdom. As much as Larson tried to emulate the Kensei,
he doubted he would ever learn such a skill. *My mind
doesn't work that fast.* But, this time, Larson knew his
life and Astryd's might depend on it.

Larson turned a corner onto another main street and
immediately realized he was no longer alone. Half a
dozen men stood in a cluster. Their breath emerged as
white puffs in the cold. Their conversation wafted indis-
tinctly to Larson. Darkness robbed him of his color vision, making them appear as caricatures in black and
gray. Trained to mistrust groups in towns, Larson backpedaled. Before he could duck back around the turn, he
saw an arm rise and a finger aimed in his direction. Every
head turned toward him.

Something seemed vaguely familiar about the men, but
Larson did not take time to ponder. He dodged around

the corner and broke into a hunched run. The men gave chase. Their footfalls clattered along the empty streets. Larson quickened his pace. Realizing he was on a straightaway, he skittered into an alley, then sprinted around the first narrow branchway. His boot came down on something soft. A screech rent the air. A claw swished across leather, and a cat raced deeper into the shadows. Off-balanced, Larson careened into a rain barrel. Icy water sloshed on his chest and abdomen. He tried to compensate, but the barrel crashed into his hip with bruising force. He fought for equilibrium, lost it, tumbled and rolled. Heavy wood slammed against his foot, followed by the slap as the barrel struck the earthen floor of the alleyway.

Moisture penetrated to Larson's skin. He tensed to rise, found himself staring into a semicircle of drawn spears, and sank back to his knees. Slowly, nonthreateningly, he raised his hands. *Who are these people? What do they want?* Suddenly realizing lifted hands might not serve as a gesture of surrender in this world, he lowered them to his thighs.

"Don't move." The man directly before Larson let his spear sag and hefted a lantern. Light played over the group, revealing an array of male faces and muscled torsos clothed in black and red linen. A seventh man stood behind the others, his face a dark blur. He wore a tunic, breeks, and cloak. He carried no spear, but a sword dangled at his hip.

Uniforms of red and black. Larson relaxed and allowed himself a crooked smile. *Smart move. I just ran from the cops.*

The man with the lantern wore a silver badge on his left breast; apparently he was their leader. "What are you doing out after curfew?"

Curfew? Shadow didn't say anything about a curfew. Larson looked into the leader's round face, met eyes deep brown and demanding. *The curfew probably came as a result of the violence. Shadow wouldn't even know about it.* Larson cleared his throat. "Sorry. I'm a foreigner, and I didn't know about the curfew. A young woman friend went out this afternoon and hasn't returned. I was worried and came looking for her.'' Having spoken the truth, Larson had no difficulty adopting a sincere expression.

Spears bobbed as the guards shifted position. The leader seemed unimpressed. ''What did you take, *thief?*'' His inflection made the last term sound like the most repugnant word in Cullinsberg's language.

''Thief?'' Larson repeated, his tone colored with genuine incredulity. ''Don't be absurd. Do I look like the type who would steal?'' Realizing he very well might, Larson tried another tactic. ''If I was a thief, I wouldn't have lived this long by being inept. You never would have seen me, and you certainly wouldn't have caught me.'' Larson winced. Though unintentional, his comment could be taken as a backhanded insult to the guards' abilities. *And the way things are going today, that's exactly how he's going to take it.*

The leader balanced his spear with the hand he held the lantern in. Light disrupted shadow in crazed arcs. He caught a tighter one-handed grip on the shaft and raised the lantern again. ''If you're not a thief, why did you run?''

Blinded by the glare, Larson blinked. ''I was attacked my first day here. I saw a gang of men in the dark and mistook you for criminals.'' He fidgeted with impatience, and the arc of spears tightened. ''Look, I didn't take anything. You're welcome to search me. Just do it quickly.''

The man standing behind the guards spoke. ''He took something.'' The voice was dry with contempt and familiar to Larson.

The idiot I decked outside the baron's castle. Larson's skin prickled to gooseflesh. He dredged the man's name from memory. *Haimfrid.*

The leader responded without turning. ''What did he take?''

''I don't know.'' Haimfrid shifted closer, and his features became discernible in the light. His dark hair had become even more frizzled, dried blood speckled the

abrasions on his cheek and he sported a day's growth of
beard. The combination gave him the look of a madman.
"I'll think of something." Purposefully, his hand
clamped around his sword hilt.

Larson resisted the instinct to reach for his own
weapon. He already knew he could best Haimfrid in a
fair fight, but the six guards would tip those odds far into
Haimfrid's favor. "Haimfrid, please. What happened before was between you and me. You shouldn't drag your
friends into a personal matter they know nothing about.
I don't have time to fight with you."

"Is this the man . . ." the leader started.

But Haimfrid's attention was fully on Larson. "How
appropriate. The worm's on his knees begging for
mercy."

Anger rose in Larson, hot contrast to the damp chill of
his soaked cloak. He reined his temper in easily, aware
Astryd's safety depended on his dispatching this matter
peacefully and with haste. "If you insist, we'll settle our
differences later. Right now, a woman's life is at stake."

"What a coincidence." Haimfrid's sword jolted from
its sheath with a rasp of metal. "Right now, a man's life
is at stake, too. Get up and draw your weapon!"

It took every bit of self-control for Larson to remain
immobile. "No, Haimfrid. I won't kill without good
cause, and that incident outside the baron's castle is not
good cause." *Threatening Silme was, but I can't afford
to let my temper get me into trouble now.*

Haimfrid made a wild gesture with his sword, and the
spearmen retreated slightly. "Get up!" he screamed.

Larson shook his head. Aware a certain amount of morality must go into the decision to become a guard and
uphold the law, Larson appealed to what little sense of
decency Haimfrid and his companions might harbor.
"I'm not fighting. If you kill me, it's going to have to be
cold-blooded murder." Despite Larson's bold pronouncement, his hand slipped unconsciously toward his
hilt.

Haimfrid's left cheek turned crimson; the right

twitched, lost in shadow. "Just as well. I'll butcher you like the pig you are."

The guards stepped back, closing the circle around Haimfrid and Larson. Haimfrid raised his sword to strike.

Appalled again by the guards' complete lack of respect for life and law, Larson reacted with the instinct of long practice. In a single motion, he wrenched his sword free and slashed for Haimfrid's neck. Surprised, Haimfrid sprang backward. Larson seized the opening to surge to his feet. Haimfrid swept for Larson's chest as Larson continued his maneuver with a downstroke. Haimfrid's blow fell short, but Larson's katana cleaved Haimfrid's scalp. Larson ripped the sword free and finished the pattern. He flicked the blade in a loop that splattered the startled onlookers with blood, then slid it neatly back into its sheath. Haimfrid's corpse flopped to the ground.

The lantern toppled to the dirt, splashing Larson and the guards with glass shards and burning oil. The six spears snapped into battle position in an awkward chaos of ones and twos. Though bothered by the senseless loss of life, Larson prepared to meet this new threat. He kept his hand clamped to his haft. "I'm sorry. He left me no choice. You all saw that it was self-defense. Give me some space, and we can all go in peace."

The points remained, unmoving. Larson drew his sword again, his stance light as he tried to assess all his enemies at once. The sword had scarcely left the sheath when the leader jabbed for Larson's chest. Larson parried, then ducked beneath the opening and spun past. He attempted a parting slash, but his blade skimmed across the linen covering the leader's hamstring. Afraid to turn his back to run, he completed the maneuver with a pivot that brought him around to face the guards. A spear plunged for Larson's abdomen. He deflected it with his sword, caught a glimpse of movement to his left and dodged. A spear tip tore his breeks, slashing a line of skin from his leg. Another guard thrust for him. An awkward lurch back to his left was all that saved Larson. Hard pressed by the three men before him, he was unable to guard his sides. The others slipped by him, hemming him into a circle once more.

Larson took the offensive. He sprang for the leader. A spear pierced the darkness to his left, and he redirected his strike to meet it. Steel crashed against wood. The spear retreated, and another pitched toward him from behind. Larson whirled to meet the attack. A spear butt cracked across the base of his neck. Pain shocked through him, then Larson's world exploded into darkness.

Astryd dreamed of ocean surf. She sprawled, face-down, on the rocks of a beach familiar from her childhood. Waves splashed over her, strangely warm and soothing, the wash revitalizing her where it touched. A seagull shrilled, gliding zigzags through the darkness.

Astryd's hand twitched, banging painfully against wood. She awoke with a suddenness that strained every sinew; her heart hammered in her chest. The shore became a hard, oaken floor, and the noises of the gull dissolved into Saerle's steady snores, each ending with an exhaled whistle. A band of moonlight glazed the planks.

It has to be almost morning. Astryd sprang to her feet. *I've got to get out of here before Harriman comes to check on me.* Her aura blazed around her, restored by the length and depth of her sleep. Despite concern for her companions, Astryd took some satisfaction from the strength of her life energy. *At least one good thing came out of this.* She raised a hand to cast a transport escape when a thought froze her. *Shadow's friends are due to hang tonight. He's going to need all the help I can give him, and a speck of life energy might mean the difference between life and death for all of us. I can't afford to waste it on unnecessary spells.* She studied Saerle one more time. Spread-eagled beneath the bed covers like some warped god's sacrifice, he looked as innocent as a child, and Astryd felt a pang of remorse. *I couldn't possibly have hit him hard enough to keep him out this long; it has to be the wine.* At the time, need had made her too impatient to wait for the alcohol to do its job. Now, she thanked any god who would listen that Saerle had brought it and that she had managed to force it upon him.

Turning her head, Astryd glanced out the window. Wind plucked at a pile of scraps that had once been a child's doll, unable to blow it completely away, but sending the tatters into a wild dance. Placing her fingers on the sill, she brushed aside the curtains and glanced down. A rain barrel sat by the gutter at the corner of the building. Another stood, upended, beneath the window, moss striping the cracks between closely-spaced planks.

The irony was not lost on Astryd. *Now Shadow's got me climbing out windows. What's next? Scaling buildings? Accepting every challenge anyone calls impossible?* Recognizing her contemplations as a delaying tactic, Astryd forced herself to stop thinking and start acting. She clambered onto the windowsill, hunching to keep from banging her head. Though accustomed to ascending riggings and balancing on timbers, slipping through a window was new to her. *At least ropes offer handholds.* She gripped the sill and swung her legs over it. Dangling, she looked down. The barrel lay farther below her than she had guessed it would, and an idea that had seemed so natural before suddenly transformed into a crazed notion. *I should have gone out the front door. Caught by Harriman, I could always transport. If I kill myself, I'm just dead.*

Astryd's grip tightened, and she knew she could still change her mind. But the thought of dealing with Harriman and his berserks sent a shiver of dread through her. *It's not as far down as it seems. Better to just get out as quickly and quietly as I can.* She edged along the sill until the barrel stood immediately beneath her. Whispering a word for luck, she released her hold.

Astryd plummeted, her muscles knotting in anticipation. Her feet struck the barrel with a hollow thud, her bent knees absorbing the impact. For an instant, she basked in triumph. Then the barrel teetered dangerously on one edge. Instinctively, she threw her weight in the other direction to counter, too hard. The barrel overbalanced. Astryd tumbled, headfirst, twisting as she fell.

She landed on her shoulder and rolled. Pain shot through her back, and the barrel slammed against her shin.

For a moment, pain immobilized Astryd. *Too much noise. I have to get out of here.* She staggered to her feet, limping into a side street, down the darkened pathway and into another alley. Youthful voices wafted to her from a cross path, soft but growing louder. She ducked back into the side street, massaging her bruised ankle. And she listened.

For Taziar Medakan, every second of Larson's absence passed like an eternity. Early on, he had tried to converse with Silme, but his thoughts strayed continuously to Astryd and Larson. The need to concentrate on each word stilted his speech, and even simple discussion became a chore. Now they waited in silent contemplation, Silme seated on the stack of logs between the hearth and the door, Taziar on the floor beneath the shuttered window.

Suddenly, Silme snapped to attention with a gasp of horror. "No. By Thor, no!"

Silme's distress drove Taziar to his feet, every muscle coiled for action. "What happened? What's wrong?"

Silme glanced at Taziar. She kept a hand clamped over her mouth, making her reply sound distant. "They got Allerum."

Taziar crossed the room to Silme and grasped her other hand, where it wrapped around her dragonstaff. "Who's got Allerum? How?"

"The guards." Silme's voice was pained.

"The guards? Why would the guards . . . ?" Confusion beat aside urgency, and Taziar dropped to his haunches. "Silme, I don't understand. What happened? How do you know? What can we do to help him?"

"I probed his mind," Silme confessed.

Taziar nodded, careful to pass no judgments on her decision. Tortured by enemies twisting his thoughts and accessing intimate and painful memories, Larson tolerated no intruders in his mind. Taziar knew Silme had long ago promised never to take advantage of Larson's lack of mind barriers; until now, she had respected his privacy. Now, Taziar realized her concern had driven her to forsake her vow, just as his had goaded him to sneak through the window and try to aid Shylar without risking his new friends. "And . . ." he prodded.

"I found nothing. No thoughts, only darkness."

Taziar removed his hand from Silme's clenched knuckles. "Nothing?" The word strangled in his throat. *By the gods, no. He can't be dead. I should never have let him go. I should have protested harder.* "He's not . . . ?" Taziar found himself unable to speak the last word.

"Dead?" Silme finished for him. "No. I dug deeper and found images of men in red and black harassing him with spears. Dead, he would have no memories at all."

The fire felt uncomfortably warm on Taziar's back. The flickering, scarlet glow splashing the walls reminded him of the blood spilled, and a shiver wrung through him. *How many more must die?* "Why would the guards want Allerum?"

Silme flipped her staff so that it rested across her knees. Though understandably pained and concerned, she apparently realized the need to inform Taziar. "One held a grudge from an incident near the baron's keep. According to Allerum's memories, he killed that guard but couldn't fathom why the others allowed the fight nor why they banded against him once the fight was finished." She glanced down to meet Taziar's gaze.

"I can." Taziar rose, reminded of the angry ramblings of an old soldier who had served under his father: "Most of the guards live off the so-called glory of the previous generation. They wear their free uniforms like medals of courage. They hold themselves above their families and display their competence against the helpless: prisoners, beggars, and street orphans." *In the wake of Harriman's violence, the baron has probably given his men free rein to prey on the innocent. No matter the cause, if Allerum killed one, the others would take vengeance against him.* Taziar explained simply. "Harassment is their idea of sport." *What now?* The thoughts that answered his own question seemed foreign and unreal. *They might torture him to death in the streets. More likely, they'll drag him*

*back to the dungeon where they can shackle and control
him.* Taziar kept his thoughts from Silme, but hysteria
edged his voice. "We're wasting time. Do you know
where the incident took place? How long ago?"

"I have no way to judge time. He's unconscious and—"

Something heavy crashed against the door with a groan
of timbers. Taziar scarcely found time to rip his sword
from its sheath before the panel slammed open. Two pairs
of men rushed to the threshold, their drawn swords scattering red highlights through the chamber.

Silme reacted first. Without bothering to stand, she
whipped her staff sideways. Wood cracked against the
leading man's shins. Tripped, he staggered forward. Taziar's harried sword slash tore open the stranger's abdomen. Taziar curled the sword back into a defensive
position.

Caught off-guard by Taziar and Silme's closeness to the
door, the injured man's partner attempted to backpedal.
But momentum from the companions behind him drove
the man onto Taziar's blade. Impact jarred Taziar over
backward. His spine struck the floor with a force that
dashed the breath from his lungs. His head thunked
against wood, and the corpse landed atop him, pinning
him to the planks.

Through the ringing in his ears, Taziar scarcely heard
the door slap closed and the bolt jarred hurriedly into
place. Abandoning his sword, he wriggled from beneath
the dead stranger, blood warm and sticky on his hands
and face. The groans of the gut-slit bandit and the thick
odor of bowel and blood made Taziar's stomach churn.
He tasted bile. Fighting nausea with desperation, he took
in the scene at a dizzy glance. Silme stood with her back
pressed to the door, adding her meager weight to support
the panel that shivered under the force of a battering from
the opposite side. Apparently, the sorceress' quick reflexes had allowed her to latch the door against the last
two assailants. *But for how long?*

Urgency allowed Taziar to gain control of his impulse
to be sick. "Stay there," he whispered. "Don't move."

Scampering across the room, he wrenched open the shutters. In the darkened alley below, two men looked up, returning his stare. Both wore swords, and one clutched a crossbow, a quarrel readied against the string. He recognized them now, strong-arm men on the fringes of the underground. *Harriman's men.* Taziar swore, aware he would have to act quickly. He shot Silme a look intended to reinforce his command, then shouted for the benefit of the men pounding on the door. "Quick! He's going out the window!" He hesitated just long enough to ascertain that the would-be assassins had abandoned their attack on the door. "I'll be back," he reassured Silme and climbed out on the sill.

Beneath him in the alleyway, Taziar heard a wordless shout of recognition. Hurriedly, he hooked his fingers in irregularities in the wall stones and scurried upward. A finger's breadth from his hand, a quarrel glanced off the granite. Reflexively, he jerked away. The sudden movement lost him his toe hold. Dislodged mud chinking pattered to the dirt. Taziar shifted his weight and clung with one hand, pawing blindly for a new grip. Mentally, he counted the moments it would take to reload the crossbow. Then his fingers looped over the edge of the roof. He dragged his body upward, hearing the twang of the bowstring through heightened senses. The arrowhead smacked into hardened mud. He felt no pain, but, as he made a dive to the rooftop, something jolted him so hard he nearly fell. The arrow had pierced his boot, pinning it to the wall but missing his foot with an uncanny stroke of luck. Ripping his leg free of the boot, he rolled to the rooftop.

Once there, Taziar wasted a moment pulling off his other boot while he gazed out over the city. Below him, the men scattered, ready to catch him no matter which wall he chose to descend. To the south, Mardain's temple rose over the inn. To the north, a cobbled roadway gaped between Taziar and a single story dwelling. Some distance beyond it, lantern lights glimmered like stars in the windows of the baron's towers. To the east, Taziar knew he would find another wide street separating him from a cottage. Westward, across a narrower thoroughfare, the roof tiles of the silversmith's combination of shop and home beckoned, one story beneath Taziar. Beyond it, moonlight revealed the irregular stonework of a building roof under repair.

Fearing the strangers might attack Silme if he waited too long, Taziar made his decision quickly. He hurled his boot at the crossbowman in the eastern alley. It struck the ground, a distant miss from its target. But the bowman's shout drew his companions, and Taziar seized the precious seconds this gained him. He sprinted toward the western lip of the rooftop. Doubts poured forth as he reached the edge. The roadway was wider then he had estimated; even a running start might not provide the momentum needed to clear it. For an instant, he imagined himself falling, air hissing through his tunic, until he crashed, broken and bleeding, on the cobbles below. Committed to action, he turned a jump into a reckless dive for the silversmith's roof.

A distant shout wafted from below. Wind whipped the hair back from Taziar's eyes, revealing the ledge silhouetted by starlight. *I'm going to miss that roof by a full arm's length.* The realization upended Taziar's senses, but he clung to life with stubborn determination. The arc of his descent straightened. He slashed crazily through air. The knuckles of his left hand banged painfully against wood. Redirecting instantly, he caught the rim with the fingers of his right hand. He jerked to an abrupt halt, wrenching every tendon in his forearm. Ignoring the shrill ache of his muscles, he clawed his way to the rooftop.

Taziar lay on the tiles, trembling. In spite of bare feet and biting autumn cold, sweat plastered the Climber's tunic to his skin. He climbed to his feet, aware delay would sacrifice the time his maneuver had gained him. He dashed across the rooftop, the tiles chill and coarse against his soles. The shouted exchanges of his pursuers wafted to him, distant, incomprehensible echoes in the night. As Taziar ran, he studied the building ahead. A wind or rainstorm had toppled the chimney near its base, leaving a jagged edging of flagstone. Stone blocks and dirty tiles littered the roadway between it and the silversmith's shop. Boulders stood neatly arrayed on the rooftop in preparation for restoration. Nearby lay stacks of tiles. A ladder angled from the alleyway to the roof, and Taziar could just make out the top of a second ladder on the opposite side.

At the end of the silversmith's roof, Taziar spun and lowered his feet over the side. He wedged his toes into mossy clefts, caught handholds on the ledge, and clambered down the wall with the ease of long practice. Still, his movements seemed clumsy to him. His muscles quivered, and each hold required concentration. He jumped the last half story, careful to avoid the shattered pieces of chimney scattered across the walkway. The footsteps of his pursuers rang through the streets. Taziar forced himself to remain still, sifting and interpreting the sounds. His crazed dive had placed Harriman's men behind him. They rushed toward him from opposite sides of the silversmith's shop.

The instinct to run nearly overpowered Taziar, but he held his ground. *I have to make them think they have me. I can't give them time to think. Otherwise, they'll surround me.* The first pair of ruffians appeared around the corner to Taziar's left. Too restless to wait any longer, Taziar started toward the ladder, feigning the choppy desperation of panic. A contrived limp slowed his escape. Harriman's men rapidly closed in on him. By the time Taziar reached the base of the ladder, they had narrowed the distance to two arms' lengths. *I can't let them get too close, either, or they'll just knock the ladder down with me on it.*

Taziar scurried up the ladder, his quicker reflexes enabling him to regain several steps of his lead. At the top, he whirled, pleased to find that all four of the men had followed him. *Child's play.* Taziar's overtaxed muscles belied his thought. Despite the need for fast action and strategy, his mind groped through a fog of fatigue, and the ache of his injuries could not be ignored. Avoiding the holes and alert for loose tiles, he skittered across the roof to the opposite side. Behind him, the heavier, shod

feet of his pursuers sounded thunderous. Apparently unused to rooftops, the rhythm of their movements was broken and uncertain.

Taziar never hesitated. He caught the top of the ladder,
scrambled halfway down it, then kicked it loose from the
wall. It fell, carrying him in a shallow curve. As he
neared the roadway, he leaped free. He struck the ground,
cobbles jabbing his bare feet, dropped, and rolled. Pain
speared through his legs, and stone bruised his side. The
ladder crashed to the stone behind him.

Taziar sprang to his feet and ran, aware he had turned
the hunt into a race for the remaining ladder. Taziar knew
his jump from the ladder must have seemed madness to
Harriman's men. *A leap from the rooftop would be sure
suicide.* Necessity lent him speed. He circled the building, not daring to waste a second looking up. *They might
shoot quarrels or throw rocks, but I doubt it. They'll be
more concerned with their own escape. They know as
well as I do they're trapped if they don't reach that ladder first.*

Taziar rounded the final corner at a run and hit the
ladder with his shoulder. Momentarily, he met resistance. Then the ladder overbalanced. He heard a short
scream of fright followed by the rapid scramble of fingernails against stone as a man who had started down the
ladder pawed and caught a hold on the ledge. A frustrated blasphemy rebounded through the roadway. Taziar
ducked into a shadowed alley. Angry curses chased him
as he raced through the maze of thoroughfares, but they
soon faded beneath the mingled cries of night birds and
foxes.

When he could no longer hear the men, Taziar paused
to catch his breath. For the first time in days, he allowed
himself a laugh.

The predawn found Bolverkr astride the curtain wall of
his fortress, his legs dangling inches from the glitters of
sorcery as if to challenge his own magic. The constant
construction, the movement of stone and the setting of
complicated defenses had drained his life aura to a wisp

of gray. He felt weak, more tired than he had in years, but it was the comfortable, sated exhaustion that comes of honest labor. Ordinarily, fatigue would have frustrated him, but now he gained a strange satisfaction from the knowledge that even his mass of borrowed Chaos-force had its limits. Secure in the knowledge that Harriman would continue his vengeance, at least against Taziar, Bolverkr rose and headed for the steps cut into the stone.

Thoughts of Harriman made Bolverkr grin. The arrangement had become more convenient than he'd ever hoped, freeing him to build until exhaustion while his enemies tangled with his marionette. Bolverkr's contacts with Al Larson's thoughts confirmed that his enemies were blithely unaware of the master pulling Harriman's strings. *Practical, simple, a fine arrangement.* Bolverkr's smile widened. *Once I've killed Taziar, I'll need to make another puppet for the elf.* Even perilously low on Chaos energy, Bolverkr felt the permanent effects of its poisoning. *Or perhaps Taziar could serve that purpose. Who would know better how to torture Allerum?* The answer came in an instant. *Silme.*

Having reached the steps, Bolverkr hesitated before descending into his partially-enclosed courtyard. He turned, looking out over the wreckage of Wilsberg. Mentally, he replaced each buried corpse, unable to keep from seeing beauty in the natural asymmetry of Chaos' flagrant denial of pattern. Again, he relived the scattered panic of the townsfolk he had loved, watched his protecting magics wall them into a cage of death. Always before, the memory had faded to grief before blossoming into anger. But this time his emotions skipped the pivotal step. Rage warmed him, but it drained life aura, too, and he quickly quelled the mood. *What if I had died with my people?*

It was the first time Bolverkr dared to ask the question, yet the answer came without need for thought. *The Chaos-force would have gone to the next most powerful sorcerer. Silme perhaps? Or some master at the Dragonrank School?* He recalled the blissful agony of Chaos' arrival, the power it promised that he could not have resisted, the transfer that would have killed a lesser man.

I'm of the original Dragonrank. No other mage could have survived it. He imagined the Chaos-force seeking a master, tearing through cities, claiming lives with the unthinking nonchalance of a child picking wildflowers. Every slaughtered servant of Law would weaken the Chaos-force as part of the natural balance. Every Chaos death would strengthen it.

Bolverkr's vision filled with lines of corpses, and a nameless joy welled within him. He raised his head, howling his laughter, and the sight of the turreted towers, built in memoriam to his beloved, jarred him into silence. *Magan.* The image of his sweet, unassuming wife wound a crack through Chaos' control that admitted a ray of the Dragonmage that had once been Bolverkr, a sorcerer who had sought and found the quiet solace and anonymity of a farm town. He recoiled from the same death-visions he had welcomed moments earlier.

I thought I could handle Chaos, but I was wrong. There's too much here for one sorcerer. I have to share it with someone strong enough to wield it. Bolverkr gazed at his citadel. Pictures of Magan made him realize how much he missed her beauty, her calm steadiness and logic and the way she supported him no matter how gloomy or ugly his mood. Then, he remembered his first sight of Silme, the way her radiance had driven him to breathlessness, the lust a single glimpse had raised in him. *Allerum took my woman from me. It's only fair that he should pay with his.*

Chaos seeped slowly back into Bolverkr's wasted sinews as he started down the steps.

CHAPTER 9:

Shadows of Justice

> So long as governments set the example of killing their enemies, private individuals will occasionally kill theirs.
>
> —Elbert Hubbard
> *Contemplations*

By the time Taziar Medakan returned to the inn, dawn was tracing streaks of yellow and pink across the horizon, etching the Cullinsberg skyline dark against the rising sun. The scene was familiar to Taziar; he knew every ledge, angle, and distant spire. But now his concern and fatigue gave the city an alien cast, like the first stirrings of dementia in a loved one or a favorite recipe with an ingredient missing. A week of restless nights followed by a full day of plotting and a run through the roadways had tired him. His thoughts stirred through an encumbering blanket of exhaustion, and he felt certain his movements were equally dulled.

Harriman's master has what he wanted. Anger pierced Taziar's mental haze. *He's got me in pain and torn with guilt, desperate to save my friends from the gallows, and aware I might fail despite my best efforts.* Taziar delved for resolve, shouldering aside fatigue and the heavy burden of mixed and mangled emotions. *Like Silme said, Allerum knows me too well, and through him, so does Harriman's master. I've walked into every trap he's set for me, delivered myself, the children, and Astryd into his hands. He's even forced me to kill.* An image of the corpses in the inn room filled Taziar's mind, but he banished it with rising will. *I'm not going to mourn them. I won't take blame for the deaths of vicious men who lived and, appropriately, died by violence.* Despite his decision, guilt swam down on Taziar, his conscience an accuser too terrible to ignore. *This must be what it's like to be a soldier: killing out of necessity, at first forcing oneself to forget, until each corpse blends into the nameless infinity of murder.*

Taziar poised against the cold granite of the inn wall while he fought a battle inside himself. *Harriman's preying on my weaknesses: my loves and loyalties, the ethics that my father had no right to embrace as a guard captain nor to teach to his only son. Again and again, Harriman has used my emotions as a weapon against me. The only way I can escape Harriman's master is to become someone else.* The idea rankled. The thought of abandoning the tenets he had held since childhood pained Taziar to the core of his being, and the words of his father's underling came unbidden. "You have none of your father's size nor strength, yet you inherited the very things that killed him: his insane sense of morality and his damnable courage." *The time has come to dump the morality and focus on the courage. The urchins are dead; nothing I can do will bring them back. I've killed three times, but men have done worse for baser reasons. If Astryd lives, I'll rescue her; if she's dead, there's nothing I can do for her. I can't be driven to carelessness by sentiment. My cause is to free my friends with as few casualties as possible. Nothing more, nothing less.*

Grimly, Taziar channeled to a single goal, building a wall of determination to hold guilt and sorrow at bay. Weariness retreated, but deep within him, something mourned the price. Taziar started toward the back entry.

A movement froze Taziar in mid-stride. He pressed back into the shadows of the wall as a slight figure flitted toward the door. The first rays of morning sun sparked gold highlights through feathered locks the yellow of new flames. *Astryd?* Joy flooded Taziar, but for the sake of his vow, he crushed passion ruthlessly. Instead, he scanned the dwindling darkness for evidence of someone watching or trailing Astryd. Discovering no one, he caught her arm as she reached out to trip the latch.

Astryd whirled with a gasp of startled rage. Only a reflexive leap backward saved Taziar from an elbow in his gut and a knee in his groin. "It's me," he whispered.

Astryd's expression softened as she recognized Taziar. "Shadow. Thor's justice, it's you." She enwrapped him in an exuberant embrace.

Relief and elation chipped at Taziar's self-erected barriers. Unwilling to abandon the persona thwarting Harriman would require, he hugged Astryd briskly. Pulling the panel open, he found the entry chamber empty; this early, no sound drifted through the cross door from the common room. Gesturing Astryd to the stairs, Taziar yanked the outer door closed. "What happened? Are you well?" He kept his tone businesslike.

Astryd hesitated, struck by Taziar's manner. When she spoke, her voice was frenzied. "I think Allerum's in the dungeon. And Harriman knows you're here. He paid men to capture you!"

Capture? Taziar started up the stairs, taking note of Astryd's choice of words. *So Harriman's not ready to kill me yet. His delay can only work to my advantage.* "Silme and I handled Harriman's men, and we know about Allerum. What detained you? Did Harriman recognize you?"

Astryd followed. "I don't know if Harriman recognized me or not. He gave no indication that he did, but he certainly made things hard for me."

Subtlety is Harriman's style. Taziar kept the thought to himself as he rounded the second story landing and climbed toward the third, cautious and alert for movement.

"I drained my life energy on a lot of small but necessary spells," Astryd continued. "Then Harriman locked me in a room overnight with a client and a guard at the door."

A client? Not wishing to contend with his emotions, Taziar did not request further information and was pleased when Astryd offered none. "How did you get free?"

Astryd's shod footfalls made no more sound on the stairs than Taziar's bare feet. "The same way you would have. Out the window." She smiled up at him, apparently expecting shock or at least a glimmer of curiosity. When Taziar did not question her, she finished in a disappointed mumble. "So here I am, well-rested, untapped, and ready to assist in any way I can."

Resourceful. Astryd's attitude is precisely what we need to defeat Harriman. Taziar did not voice the praise aloud. *Well, I can be resourceful, too.* He crested the steps and headed down the hallway toward their room. "Did you find out anything?"

"I got the information you wanted." Astryd trotted around Taziar, then stopped to stare at the twisted piece of painted black metal that had served as the latch to the inn room door. "Harriman's men?"

Taziar nodded, not bothering to clarify. An explanation would only waste time. "Silme?" he whispered.

Silme's voice wafted through the crack in answer. "It's safe."

Taziar pushed open the door, escorted Astryd through it, and closed it behind them. Apparently, Silme had cleaned up in his absence. She had bolted the shutters against the wind. The corpses were gone. *Out the window,* Taziar surmised, but he did not bother to ask. Silme had stuffed the jumble of traveling gear and blankets back into the packs which lay in a neat stack, ready for travel.

At the sight of Astryd, Silme smiled. She pressed forward, but Taziar interrupted before she could question her friend. "We need to make some fast plans and get out of this inn. First, Astryd, what did you find out?"

Startled by Taziar's brusqueness, Silme abandoned her greeting. Her smile wilted.

Astryd smoothed her skirt with her hands, ignoring Taziar's intent stare. "Harriman's followers include the berserks and twelve to fourteen warriors Mat-hilde claimed you would know." She glanced sharply at Taziar as if to confirm this, but he was deep in thought. "She called them the 'fringe guard.' If I can give her some idea of when we're going to free the leaders, she promised to fill the whorehouse with men who would take their side." She winced, studying Taziar as if to look deep enough into him to understand the change in his usually gentle and caring manner. "Mat-hilde warned, though, that those same men who would help the leaders might kill you."

Taziar ignored Astryd's final statement. Right now, his friends' lives mattered more than his own. "Good. Then we can concentrate on the jailbreak and worry about defeating Harriman afterward." Taziar skirted the women and knelt before his pack. "This is my plan." He emulated Silme's no-nonsense manner, aware his idea would meet with strenuous objections. *Yesterday, I rejected it myself.* "I'll have to get into the prison and work with my friends from the inside."

Silme settled back on the woodpile near the fire. "A breakout from inside the dungeon. Ingenious," she said with a trace of sarcasm. "How do you propose to do such a thing?"

Avoiding Astryd's gaze, Taziar rummaged through his gear. He tried to sound matter-of-fact. "I'll get myself arrested, and—"

"No!" Astryd denied the possibility, achieving the no-nonsense delivery with far more success than Taziar. "The guards might kill you."

"They might," Taziar admitted, keeping his tone level. "But I doubt it. You said Harriman sent those men to capture me. He still wants me alive, for a while at least. Harriman apparently has some influence over the baron on the matter of the underground and its members." Taziar felt leather beneath his fingers and jerked his boots free with a suddenness that sent his spare breeks sliding across the floor. "Besides, there's a mass criminal hanging today. No doubt, the baron would want to make a public example out of the man who robbed Aga'arin's temple and escaped the dungeons. What better way than a hanging on Aga'arin's own High Holy Day?"

"No," Astryd repeated. "What possible good can it do to make you one more person we have to free from the baron's prison?"

Taziar indulged in a smile, pleased Astryd would give him a chance to explain rather than dismissing his plan out of hand. "I've been jailed before. I know the kind of locks the dungeon has and what supplies I'd need to trip them. I can free Shylar and the others from their cells and rally them against the guards. A rope will get us all out the window to safety." He pulled the boots onto his feet, awaiting the inevitable question.

"Rope? A locksmith's tools?" Silme sat and drew her knees to her chest. "After they catch you, the guards will let you keep such things? And I suppose the underground leaders will battle swords and crossbows with their fists."

"I suspect the guards will take everything I have." Taziar recalled his previous arrest. Then, blood loss from an arrow wound had drained him to unconsciousness, and he had no remembrance of being searched. Still, when he had awakened in his cell, he had nothing except his clothes. "But they can't stop Astryd from bringing anything I need."

Surprise creased Astryd's features.

Taziar grasped the opportunity to elaborate. "While I'm getting myself in trouble, the two of you can purchase the tools I'll describe, the longest piece of rope you can find, and as many knives and swords as Astryd can handle. Once I'm imprisoned, Astryd can transport in with supplies." Taziar glanced at his companions in triumph, the comfort of a plausible plan tempered by his new attitude and the growing look of skepticism on Silme's face.

Silme cleared her throat. "It won't work."

The certainty in Silme's voice mangled Taziar's hopes. "Why not?" he challenged her.

"Because Astryd can only transport to a place she's seen before."

The revelation stunned Taziar. "Really?"

"Really," Astryd confirmed.

Taziar recalled an incident that had occurred soon after he'd met Astryd. "But when Mordath held me prisoner on a dinghy, you transported onto it. You couldn't have boarded his boat before."

"No." Astryd shuffled from foot to foot. "But I could

see it from the rail of the ship I was on. I knew exactly where to go. Even so, it was my clumsiest transport since glass-rank. I nearly capsized the boat.''

Still clinging to his idea, Taziar pressed. ''What if I describe the interior of the prison for you? In detail.''

The women shook their heads. ''Not good enough,'' Silme said. ''She'd have to actually see it, with magic at least.''

Silme's clarification raised another possibility. ''A location . . .'' Taziar started.

Astryd kicked at a loose nail in the floorboards. ''A location triangle has to be centered on a familiar person. Background is revealed incidentally. If I centered the spell on Allerum, I could only see the inside of his cell, and my transporting into a locked cage won't help you. If the dungeon is dark, I wouldn't even see that much.''

Sarcasm returned to Silme's voice. ''Despite the practice Astryd's been getting the last few days . . .'' She continued in her normal tone. ''. . . she still expends too much energy casting location triangles. After a location and a transport into the prison, she might not have enough life force to transport back out. She certainly won't have enough to help you and your friends escape.''

It finally occurred to Taziar to question Astryd's knowledge. ''How did you know about Allerum's capture?''

''I heard some children talking about it in an alley. Apparently, a street gang saw the guards' attack and watched them drag their victim off toward the baron's keep. The description fit Allerum. Then I heard Harriman paid the guards well for the victim's sword, and there was no longer any doubt in my mind.''

Silme spoke, her voice painfully calm. ''Shadow, your plan may still work.''

Taziar swung his head toward Silme in expectation; his discussion with Astryd became dim background.

Silme rose. ''Anything Allerum knows, Astryd or I can access. Apparently, the guards dragged Allerum into the dungeon while he was unconscious. Once he wakes up and looks around, Astryd can get her visual image of the prison and transport inside.''

''Perfect.'' Taziar quelled rising excitement. ''Allerum has to wake up eventually. Once I get in, I can tell him the plan. By following his thoughts, you'll know the best time to transport, and it won't even cost a significant amount of life energy.'' Taziar straightened. ''No need to delay any longer. You'll have to carry our packs. The guards will only take them from me. There's another inn at the other end of town run by a woman named Leute. Get a room on the second floor. The north side, if possible. It'll give Silme a place to stay, Astryd a place to transport to, and all of us a place to regroup if something goes wrong.''

Astryd and Silme had gathered up the packs before Taziar finished speaking. Briefly, he described the required locksmith's instruments in layman's terms. ''After you get the supplies, try to find time to give Mat-hilde some idea of when the prison break will happen.'' Taziar tensed, awaiting more criticisms of his plot. When none came, he rose, crossed the room and peered out the window. Dawn light drew familiar shadows on the walls of Mardain's temple, but, mired in his forced emotionlessness, Taziar did not allow himself to study them. Instead, he stared at the alleyway below. Finding it empty, he climbed to the sill. ''Best if you're not seen with me, if possible. We'll be back together soon.'' He did not allow the vaguest trace of doubt to enter his voice, but an image of Astryd's ashen features haunted him as he shinnied down the wall into the alley.

Once solidly on the dirt pathway, concerns, fears, and fatigue closed in on Taziar. He held his worries at bay, turning the thought and energy they might cost him to the matter at hand. Brushing dust from his cloak, he headed from the back street onto the main market roadway leading to Cullinsberg's entrance.

The bang and clatter of opening shops and stands assailed Taziar. Merchants and their apprentices scurried through the city in huddled knots, some guiding cart horses down the cobbled streets. Attentive to their wares,

the merchants seemed to take no notice of Taziar thread-
ing cautiously around them. Unchallenged, he kept to the
sidewalks, moving into the roadway whenever displayed
wares made the walkways impassable. At length, he discovered a guard in the familiar black and red uniform
stationed on the opposite side of the road at the mouth
of an alleyway. He seemed to Taz to be the type who
would respond with reasoning before threat and threat
before violence. He was lean and tall and held a spear in
a lax grip as he watched the flow of traffic through slitted
eyes.

He'll do fine. With exaggerated casualness, Taziar
turned his back to the wall of a butcher's shop and rested
his shoulder blades against the granite. Bending his knee,
he propped a foot against the wall behind him. The position placed him directly across from the guard.

A cart brimming with hearth logs creaked along the
roadway, pulled by a burly chestnut gelding. The topmost
layer of wood rocked with each movement, threatening
to crash to the street at any moment. Taziar waited until
it passed and the lane between him and the guard had
cleared once again. The guard visually followed the
wagon until it rounded a corner. Then his dark gaze
flicked forward. Briefly, the guard inspected Taziar and,
apparently finding nothing of interest, he moved on to a
middle-aged couple ambling toward the Climber.

Taziar assessed the couple. The man sported the heavily callused hands of a smith or builder, and well-muscled
arms completed the picture. A receding line of brown
hair dusted with gray revealed a scalp freckled from exposure to sun. The plump woman at his side wore her
locks swept back into a tight bun. Clothes of unsoiled
linen suggested a comfortable living. Taziar located their
purses by the play of dawn shadow on pocket fabric. He
guessed that the woman carried the bulk of their money
in a recess in her shift, while the left pocket of the man's
tunic held a smaller amount. Taziar suspected they'd chosen the arrangement to confuse thieves, but he doubted
it would succeed against any except a young amateur. *Or
maybe I'm overestimating the average pickpocket.*

Since Taziar sought attention rather than money, he went after the bait. As the couple wandered by, he slipped his fingers into the man's pocket, seized the pouch of coins, and ripped it free. Taziar fumbled it intentionally, catching the bag with a dull clink of coins. Through the fabric, he identified six copper barony ducats before whisking it into the folds of his own cloak. He awaited the woman's scream, the man's bellow of outrage, the guard's shouted command above the irregular clamor of the merchants.

But none of those sounds came. Apparently oblivious, the couple continued down the walkway without so much as a break in stride. Dumbfounded, Taziar turned his attention to the guard. The man chewed a fingernail, stopped, and studied the tattered edge. He picked at it with his thumb, then bit at it again.

Irony struck Taziar a staggering blow. *Aga'arin's almighty ass, I can't be that good.* Stunned by the revelation, Taziar allowed a young man carrying a crate of chickens on his shoulder to pass unmolested. Taziar's hand closed over his spoils. *I have to give this back.* He glanced in the direction the couple had taken, but they had disappeared around a corner. Weighing the time the return would cost him against the couple's affluence, Taziar accepted his new-found money reluctantly. *I'm just going to have to learn to be more inept.* He settled back into his position against the wall.

Within seconds, a young man trotted along the sidewalk, his expression harried. He wore a patched, woolen cloak, sported a blotchy beard, and carried a stand sign tucked beneath his armpit. From a glance, Taziar discovered a pouch of coins in the man's hip pocket. He closed, every movement deliberately awkward. Jamming his hand into the pocket, Taziar meticulously gouged his fingers into the man's pelvic bone before scooping the purse free. It flew in a wild arc, and Taziar caught it with a dexterity that belied his earlier clumsiness. He shoved it into his cloak with the other purse.

The stranger spun with a yell of outrage. "Help! Thief!" The lettered board thunked to the cobbles. He swung a punch at Taziar who dodged easily. The guard rushed toward them from across the street. Locking his gaze on the stranger's hands and seeing that the man intended to grab rather than hit, Taziar suppressed his natural urge to dodge. Thick hands seized the collar of Taziar's cloak and crossed, neatly closing off his windpipe. He gasped and struggled, suddenly wishing he had not made it so simple for the stranger to catch him.

"Stop!" The guard's spear jolted against the stranger's arms. The hands fell away, and Taziar staggered free with a dry rasp of breath. "What's going on here?"

The stranger answered before Taziar could regain enough air to speak. "He stole my money. Guard, that man is a thief."

Taziar cringed, aware most of the baron's guards would seize the opportunity to batter him to unconsciousness.

The guard whirled, his forehead creased. He studied Taziar in the thin light of morning, and his eyebrows arched abruptly in question. His expression went bland as he turned back to face the stranger. "I'm sorry, sir. You've made a mistake. This man took nothing."

Taziar went slack-jawed with surprise, and his victim's face echoed his like a mirror. "He's a thief," the man insisted. "He stole my purse. I demand justice. Are you going to let the little weasel go prey on someone else?"

"I'm sorry," the guard said with finality. "I was standing here, and I didn't see him take anything." He winked at Taziar. "It's your word against his word."

"No, it's not." Desperate, Taziar abandoned subtlety. "I took his purse. I admit it." To demonstrate, he retrieved the pouch and dangled it before the guard.

The stranger's eyes went so wide, the whites showed in a circle around the irises, and he made only a feeble gesture to retrieve his property. As the stranger's fingers touched the strings, Taziar released it. The pouch plummeted to the walkway. A coin bounced free, wound a wobbly course around a cobblestone, and dropped to its side. The guard recovered first. "You've got your money back." He jabbed a finger into the stranger's arm, then waved curtly at Taziar. "You, be on your way, and don't cause any more trouble.'' Using his spear like a walking stick, the guard returned to his post before the alleyway.

Bending, the stranger rescued his money and his sign and continued silently down the sidewalk as if in a trance. Taziar hurried off in the opposite direction, equally confused. The guard's reaction made no sense to him. A decade without war had driven Cullinsberg's soldiers to turn any violent tendencies they might harbor against criminals, orphans, and beggars. Many disdained the justice system, abandoning law for the right price. Taziar shook his head, floored by the idea that he had discovered a guard not only mercifully peaceful, but who disregarded pickpockets without so much as a hint of a bribe. *It was an accident, a bizarre coincidence I'll probably never understand. How hard can it be to find a normal guard?*

Taziar wandered by the stands, noting as he passed that many had not opened because of the holiday. The others would close by midday, and Taziar knew he would need to work fast or lose any chance of getting himself arrested. *Who would have imagined I would find it difficult to get thrown in prison?* He chuckled as he wandered by a barefoot girl in tattered homespun selling flowers. Across the road on the opposite walkway, Taziar saw a guard, eyes glinting from beneath a disorderly mop of hair. One meaty hand prodded an unkempt, young woman who cursed him with oaths vicious as a dockhand's.

Seizing the opportunity, Taziar darted across the street, narrowly missing a trampling by a pair of mules hauling a groaning wagon. The team pulled up reflexively, with the calm indulgence of habit, but the driver's blasphemies paled beneath the girl's coarse profanities.

Oblivious, Taziar skidded across the walkway and caught the guard's forearm. "Wait! She didn't do it. I did."

Startled, the guard and his prisoner stared with perfect expressions of surprise. Gradually, the guard's features lapsed into the same complacent smirk Taziar had seen on the face of the other sentry. "Did what?" the guard challenged.

Taziar tugged at the guard's sleeve. "Whatever she did. What are you arresting her for?"

The guard rolled his tongue around his mouth, then spat on the cobbles. "Freelance prostitution."

I can't get a break. Taziar changed his tactics instantly. "You can't take her in. She's . . . my sister."

The guard glanced from Taziar's fair skin and light eyes to the girl's olive-toned countenance. "Sure." He brushed off Taziar's grip. "Go bother someone else."

"Really. She's my sister." He seized the guard's hand in a grip tight enough to pinch, watched the man's cheeks redden in annoyance. "You're my sister. Aren't you my sister?"

Eager to grasp any chance at freedom, the woman nodded. "I'm his sister." A harsh Western accent made her claim sound even more ludicrous.

The guard made no attempt to free his hand. "Do I look stupid to you? She's not your sister, and I wouldn't let her go if she was your sister."

Taziar met the guard's gaze, followed the pursed lines around the stranger's mouth and read waning tolerance. Carefully, Taziar's hand skittered across the woven linen of the guard's uniform. Discovering a pocket in the lining, Taziar dipped his fingers inside. He was rewarded by the frayed, leather braid of a purse's strings. Seizing it, he pulled it out, released the guard, and slipped the pouch into his own hip pocket. "I'll bribe you to let her go."

The guard kept a firm hold on the prostitute's bony wrists. "How much?"

Taziar groped the contents of the guard's purse. "Four silver."

The guard's grip relaxed. "Fair enough."

Taziar produced the guard's pouch, little finger hooked through the braid.

The guard sucked breath through his teeth. The plump face creased into a mixture of emotions Taziar could not begin to decipher. "You little bastard! That's mine." He reached for it.

Exploiting the guard's consternation, the prostitute

twisted free and ran. The guard lunged for her, missed, and tensed to give chase.

Taziar shot a foot between the guard's ankles. The man crashed to the cobbles as the woman sprinted around a bend in the road and was lost to sight.

The guard scrambled to his feet with the natural grace of a warrior. "Why!" he sputtered. His fists clenched to blanched knots, and his cheeks twitched involuntarily. "What in hell . . . ? Why did you . . . ?" Apparently realizing something more important was at stake, he changed the focus of his verbal attack. "Give me back my purse!"

"No." Glibly calm, Taziar tucked the pouch back beneath his cloak. *This has to be a dream. I know ancient crones on the street who would kill for less cause than this.* "Why should I?"

The guard flushed to the roots of his hair. His fingers slacked and clutched as he fought some internal battle. But when he spoke, his tone sounded almost pleading. "Please. That's two weeks' wages. I've got a wife and three children."

Taziar blinked in astonishment, his sharp retort forgotten in the growing realization that something was terribly wrong. "Aren't you going to arrest me?"

"Were it my decision . . ." The guard's voice remained dangerously flat. ". . . I would stave in your insolent, bloody, little skull." He smiled sweetly, a chilling contrast to his threat. "But the baron has forbidden any of his men to arrest, harm, or even touch you. He says you're working for us. In truth, I liked you better on the other side of the law . . ." He finished from between clenched teeth. ". . . when I could kill you. Fortunately for you, I'd rather starve for two weeks than lose my job."

Taziar went still as death, desperately trying to hide surprise behind a less revealing expression. In silence, he handed the pouch of silver to its owner, adding the six copper ducats from his previous heist in honest apology. When he managed to speak in normal tones, he chose to lie. "The baron asked me to test his men's loyalty to his orders. Forgive my abusive methods, but I wanted to give

you fair trial. You passed, of course, with honors." Taziar
bowed his head in a gesture of respect, turned, and wandered off down the street before the guard could reply.

Taziar waited only until he had passed beyond sight of
the guard before dropping to his haunches beneath the
overhang of the baker's shop. *What now?* The clop of
hooves reverberated from a side street, its rhythm soft in
Taziar's ears. *There's no way Harriman could know I
would try something as crazy as getting myself arrested.
Is there?* Taziar slid to one knee, the thought cold and
heavy within him. *No,* he answered himself cautiously.
*Harriman has other reasons to arrange things so the
guards can't act against me. First, it convinces everyone,
guards, underground, and street people, that I am, in
fact, the informant. Second, the baron cannot interfere
with any plans Harriman might have for me.*

Taziar rose, in awe of Harriman's thoroughness despite
his need to struggle against it. *The stronger the enemy,
the better the fight. If Harriman wants me free, I'll get
myself arrested. And, if the guards won't do it, well,
sometimes a man has to do these things for himself.*

Aware Harriman might still want him prisoner, Taziar
kept to the main thoroughfares where the underground's
spies were less likely to prowl. He traveled northward,
between the puddled shadows of gables and spires.
Through occasional breaks between buildings, Taziar could
see that the edge of the sun had scarcely crested the horizon, touching the eastern skyline with glazed semicircles
of color. Aside from the merchants, the majority of the
townsfolk remained in slumber. Like their baron, most of
Cullinsberg's citizens worshiped Aga'arin. By tradition,
Aga'arin's followers abandoned routine on his High Holy
Day. Instead, they slept until the sessions of prayer which
began at high morning on the temple grounds.

Taziar ignored the scattered merchants, trusting his instincts to protect him while he dug knowledge from
memory. The layout of the baron's keep was common
information, spread throughout the underground as much
from curiosity as necessity. No thief ever attempted to
rob more than the main corridors near the entrance; those

had become appropriately free of grandeur as a result. Since the mansion sported no other inlet, the baron kept his sentries clustered there to prevent any but guards and royalty from penetrating the deeper areas of his keep; there was always enough of the most faithful on duty to prevent a mass bribe. Other routes existed to allow Baron Dietrich and his family an escape in case of emergency, but the underground had discovered that these opened only from the inside and were just as carefully warded.

From rumors in the underground, Taziar had learned that the boulders composing the castle walls had been cut square and polished to shiny smoothness. Between blocks, the builders had layered mortar with an artist's eye for perfection. More than once, friends and strangers had tried to commission the Shadow Climber to obtain items which were in the baron's possession, but Taziar had never found the reasons compelling enough to justify the thefts. The insistence that only the Shadow Climber could scale the castle walls took all challenge from the undertaking; since every member of the underground seemed certain he could succeed, Taziar felt no urge to prove it. He was too busy accomplishing the impossible.

Accompanied only by his own thoughts, Taziar shambled through the streets, uncontested, and soon arrived at the cleared stretch of ground separating the town proper from the wall that enclosed the baron's keep. Tucked into the shadow of a mud-chinked log cottage, Taziar studied the keep from its western side. Lantern light bobbed through windows in the lowest stories, but the upper levels and corner towers remained dark, black arrows silhouetted against the twilit sky.

From remembered description, Taziar located the baron's balcony, which jutted from the fifth floor toward the southern tower. Curtains swirled and flapped in the wind. As they moved, Taziar caught interrupted glimpses of morning's scattered glow sparkling off glasswork. Taziar's position accorded him a flattened view of the southern side of the keep and the seventh story window from which he had escaped the corridor outside the baron's dungeon by plummeting into the moat. *With all my in-*

juries, I would have drowned, too, if Moonbear hadn't pulled me from the water. Taziar grimaced, recalling that the barbarian prince was also responsible for turning his controlled climb down the wall into a crazed fall. *He meant well. Even so, I've no desire to repeat the maneuver nor force it upon anyone else. And I won't have to so long as Astryd brings the rope.*

The other windows remained mysteries to Taziar. As a member of the underground, he had found the floor plan to the baron's keep so readily available it seemed a waste of time, effort, and brain space for him to memorize it. And, though Taziar hated to begin a caper with less than complete knowledge, he doubted he would need to identify the maze of rooms and passageways defining the baron's keep. The object he sought was on the baron's person. *And right now, I can find the baron's person, almost certainly, in the baron's bed.*

More accustomed to working beneath the unrevealing crescent he called the "thieves' moon," Taziar wanted to start while the sun was still low in the sky. Afraid to tarry too long, he crossed the plain and huddled in the block of shadow cast by the keep and its surrounding wall. Once there, he shinnied up the blocked granite of the wall.

Taziar's elevated position accorded him a perfect view of the keep and its courtyard. Young oak and hickory dotted lush grasses tipped with autumn's brown. Carved from stone blocks or twisted from wrought iron, benches were set at the western and eastern sides of the trees to catch the daily shade or sun. The moat spoiled the grandeur of the scene. Its waters shivered in the breezes, an oily black halo near the base of the keep.

Taziar took in the layout at a glance and turned his attention to the sentries who paced through the twilit gloom. Their movements appeared crisp; apparently their shift had just begun. Even so, Taziar found their patterns indecipherable. He had managed to identify two guards who might cross the straight tract he hoped to take to the baron's window, when a scraping sound on the wall startled him. Taziar flattened to the summit, eyes probing the haze. The noises grew louder, transforming to the unmistakable sound of footsteps on granite. A man became visible walking atop the wall, a colorless, dark shape etched against the dawn.

Taziar scuttled over the edge, climbing partway down the wall toward the courtyard. Something sharp jabbed his back. *A spear?* Taziar froze. When no challenge followed, he rolled his eyes, easing his head around until he saw a spreading oak, its branches stretched to the wall, one pressed into his cloak. Taziar loosed a pent up breath which earned him another poke from the limb. The slap of the wall guard's footsteps passed directly overhead then faded as the man's vigil took him beyond Taziar's hearing.

When I watched from town, I didn't even see the sentry on the wall. Gently, Taziar began extracting himself from the hold of the oak. A branch creaked as he moved. He cringed and further slowed his progress. *That's because I couldn't spend all the time I needed to study things. The only way I could have missed him is if there's only one sentry on the wall.* Taziar pulled himself free of a twig. It broke with a faint snap. Suppressing a curse, Taziar gazed into the courtyard. Apparently oblivious, the nearest sentry continued his march. *Stupid place for a tree, this close to the wall.* Taziar guessed it had been planted as a seed or sapling. *Probably no one considered its branches might eventually grow over the walls and provide access to enemies or that its roots might disrupt the structure of the wall.* Looking down, Taziar saw a haphazard pile of sawed off branches and knew he echoed someone else's concerns. Within the week, this tree would sit in pieces, a neatly stacked pile of seasoning hardwood.

The strain of sideways movement tore at the calluses on Taziar's fingers. He finished his descent, toe groping the dirt for a landing place clear of debris. Finding one, he lowered his feet to the ground and turned toward the castle. Again, he examined the sentries, and, this time, their pattern became obvious to him. They paced in overlapping, cloverleaf figures; the arcs had thrown him off track. But now that Taziar had deciphered their motions, he doubted he would have any difficulty pacing his own activity between them. *Simple.* Sudden realization ruined

Taziar's assessment and killed the joy of certain triumph before it even had a chance to rise. *Except for the moat.*

Taziar ducked behind the disarray of branches, hidden from the guards as his thoughts raced. He knew he could swim the brackish waters, but his plan required him to remain dry and only reasonably disheveled. *Somehow, I have to cross over it.* He dug through his pockets while he considered options. *This early, the drawbridge will be up. It's too wide to jump.* Taziar's fingers skipped over crumbs, splinters, and lint. He discovered his utility knife in his right hip pocket along with a striker and a block of flint. The left held only the sailor's sewing needle he had used to rescue Astryd from a locked berth on the ferry boat the day he met her. He had left his other possessions with Silme and Astryd in anticipation of losing everything to the guards. Now he wished he had at least brought his sword.

Stymied, Taziar picked idly at the bark of a tree branch. Thoughts distant, he glanced down at his fingers and suddenly felt stupid. *The logs.* He looked into the courtyard, watching a sentry complete an arc before him. Selecting a timber heavy enough to serve as a bridge, Taziar tugged. Wood shifted with a muffled thunk. Taziar bit his lip, immediately abandoning his efforts. He chose a different log, examining its length to make certain no other branches lay on top of it. He hefted an end. The sweet, cloying odor of wood lice wafted to him, and he realized the log would prove too heavy for him to do anything more than drag it. Unwilling to risk the sound of rustling grass and the ponderous clumsiness the log would lend to his gait, he chose a thinner limb. Uncertain whether it would serve his purposes, he tucked it beneath his arm, timed a sprint between the sentries' routes, and positioned the branch across the surface of the moat.

A breeze ruffled the stagnant waters into white curls. Leaves skittered across the surface like tiny boats, many caught and anchored in a dense layer of algae. Lit by the diffuse glow of lanterns refracted through the windows of the keep, the branch seemed no thicker than Taziar's wrists and fragile as a stem. But the pattern of the guards did not leave him time for hesitation. He stepped onto the wood. It sagged beneath his weight, but it held, and he crossed with nothing worse than damp boots. He eased the limb into the water. The risk of a splash seemed less worrisome than the guards finding his makeshift overpass. If things went according to plan, he would have no need to escape in the same fashion.

The log slid silently into the water and sank, disrupting the slime in a line that marked its passage. Taziar turned his attention to the wall. The sun still had not passed over the keep to light its western side, but dawn light sheened from the glassy surface of stone. Taziar's heart fell into the familiar cadence that welcomed the coming challenge. He savored the natural elation accompanying it. In the depths of his mind, the memory stirred that he had promised to abandon all emotion, but to ignore the excitement inspired by years of addiction to danger seemed as impossible as a thirsty man refusing water or a man spurning sex an instant before the climax.

Taziar never hesitated. He explored the smoothed surfaces with his fingers, and he discovered tiny flaws in the mortaring that another man might dismiss. To Taziar, they were handholds. He wedged small fingertips into the impressions, hauled his feet into a miniscule cleft and reached for another grip.

Taziar climbed with a careless and practiced strength. Attuned to sounds of discovery, he could spare no attention to his climb. Instead, he relied on the same instincts a swordsman taps when a potential killing stroke comes at him faster than thought. Taziar kept his rhythm steady, a continual cycle of hunting crevices, grasping what his trained fingers deemed solid, and hauling his body along the polished surface of stone. He counted stories by windows, their sills like giants' ledges compared with the stone pocks and mortaring imperfections that served as his other holds.

Absorbed in the pattern of movement, Taziar did not notice the baron's balcony until its shadow fell over him. He heaved upward from a toehold, caught a grip on the supporting bars of a railing painted black to protect it from the elements. He examined the outcropping through the striped view the balustrade allowed. A wooden chair overlooked the courtyard, its seat cushioned with pillows, its feet, handrests and back intricately crafted and wound through with gold filigree. Yet, despite the elegance, the legs were chipped and the fabric on the upright showed signs of wear.

A favorite chair, Taziar surmised. *Probably too old for the throne room. Rather than repair it, Baron Dietrich had it placed here where courtiers and visitors would never see it.* The thought ignited anger as swiftly as fire set to dry shavings. *The man blithely executed his guard captain on contrived evidence after more than a decade of meritorious service, yet he remains loyal to a piece of furniture.* The logic defied Taziar and brought all morality under question. *I wanted to smother emotion and vulnerability for a cause. Yet to let Harriman change what I am is little different than letting him kill me. It's Harriman against me and all my sentimental weaknesses and strengths. I'll best him or die in the attempt.* Taziar channeled his concentration back to the balcony, but one idea seeped through before he could banish it. *I hope I have the opportunity to apologize to Astryd.*

Beyond the chair, curtains rippled, revealing a glass door. Through the thick, uneven surface, Taziar caught a warped glimpse of another set of curtains just inside. Soothed by the double barrier, Taziar hooked his arm over the top of the rail and pulled himself to the balcony. Time was running short. He would have to move quickly to catch the baron still asleep. Soundlessly skirting the chair as he crossed the balcony, Taziar grasped the door latch and twisted. It resisted his touch.

Taziar hissed his frustration. A closer study of the handle revealed a keyhole beneath it. The locksmith's tools he had described to Silme and Astryd would have proved useful now, but Taziar did not waste time wishing. Retrieving the sewing needle from his pocket, he slid the tip into the hole. He felt the raspy vibrations as the end eased over the mechanism and the jolt as it fell into the groove. He pinned it in place and turned it, rewarded by the click of the lock opening. Gingerly, he inched the door ajar. Silence met him. He spun the needle again,

heard the answering snap as the mechanism was thrown
back into locked position. Simply shutting the door would
restore it to its former, secure state.

Taziar inched through the crack. Foot wedged in the
doorway, he peered around the curtain. The material was
thick; it lay heavy as sodden wool upon his shoulders.
Once pushed aside, it admitted a roar that shook the door
frame and set Taziar's teeth on edge. He ducked back
behind the fabric, heart pounding, hearing the rush of
exhaled air as he moved. *Snoring.* Taziar gave the realization a moment to register. Then he placed the needle
against the door frame to prop it so it could not close
and lock behind him. Taziar crept around the curtain.

As the curtain dropped back into place, the room fell into
a darkness untainted by sunrise. Taziar stared, standing still
as his eyes adjusted to a deeper gloom than that he had come
from. Soon he could make out a table with widely-splayed,
decorative legs which was right in front of him. A cut-crystal
carafe occupied its center. A pair of clear wine glasses rested
upside down beside it. Relief washed through Taziar as he
recognized the disaster narrowly averted by waiting rather
than blundering sightlessly forward. Directly across the
room, Taziar noted a teak door emblazoned with the baron's
crest, a lion's head with mouth wide open. His ears ringing
with the baron's raucous breaths, Taziar found the symbol
strangely appropriate.

A matched pair of ornately-crafted dressers lined the
walls, the curls of their pattern unrecognizable in the light-
less interior of the baron's chamber. A recess in the wall
held clothing, a blurred collection of silks, brocades and
furs. The baron's bed stood in the direct center of the
room. Four pillars sculpted into the forms of shapely
women supported a canopy. Beneath it, the baron slept
on his side beneath a pile of blankets.

The scene registered instantly. Taziar crossed the room,
his boots sinking soundlessly into a plush carpet. He knelt
at the baron's head. A snore thundered painfully through
his ears, followed by a blast of malodorous breath. Saliva
dribbled through the baron's beard. Beneath the tangle of

hair, the gold medallion of office hung sideways on the sheets, its chain twisted around the baron's neck.

Like a noose, Taziar thought, and only then, thoughts of murder suddenly burned through him. Violence was not his normal reaction to anything, but the cruelties Baron Dietrich's orders had inflicted upon his family went far beyond what any man should have to tolerate. Taziar paused, fingers clenched, jaw tight, mind filled with the frigid whisper of the wind which had stirred his father's dangling corpse, the grim suffocation of his mother's pride, then her own death in a pool of wine and blood and pain. *Damn.* Almost desperately, Taziar dispelled the images, angered by his lapse. *The baron's just a pawn, a figurehead who shouts orders like a king while other men wield his power.* The idea of killing anyone repulsed Taziar; even his hatred and desire for vengeance had not been enough to make him slay the prime minister who had framed his father and goaded the baron into hanging the captain. The need for haste drove Taziar's bitterness aside, and he knew that even had he carried a weapon, he would have had neither the experience nor the coldness to kill the baron. *And it's just as well. I'm not a killer. And the consequences would be dire. If nothing else, the guards would torture my friends viciously to learn the assassin's name.* Taziar shuddered at the memory of his own prison guard inflicted agonies. *Talk about betrayal.*

Turning back to his task, Taziar reached around Baron Dietrich's perfumed curls and undid the chain's clasp. He kept both ends between his fingers, not allowing the slightest tickle of movement against the baron's flesh. The routine was familiar to Taziar; once, on a dare, he had stolen three necklaces and an anklet from a dancing girl. But as he eased the last link free of its owner, the pattern of the baron's breathing changed.

Taziar dove to the floor, jabbing the medallion into his pocket as he moved. He heard the rustle of straw as the baron rolled. The snoring dulled to normal breathing, revealing a deep rumbling previously drowned out by the baron's snores. Taziar rose to all fours and found himself staring into the bared teeth of a huge, black mongrel.

CHAPTER 10:

Dust and Shadows

The jury, passing on the prisoner's life,
May in the sworn twelve have a thief or two
Guiltier than him they try.

—William Shakespeare
Measure for Measure

The baron's snores resumed. Taziar froze, gaze locked on the curled lips and yellowed teeth of the mongrel. He shifted his weight to his feet so slowly that his movement was almost imperceptible. Tearing his stare from the dog, he measured the distance to the table and its fragile burden. A crack of light from beyond the curtain touched the cut-crystal of the carafe, splintering rainbows across the glasses. From the corner of his vision, Taziar saw the mongrel tense to spring.

Taziar dove beneath the table. Snarling, the beast bounded after him. A furry shoulder crashed into a decorative, wooden leg. Taziar sprang free as the table tumbled, then broke into a hunched run. The splash of spilled wine and the chime of splintering glass filled his ears, followed by the dog's surprised yelp. Taziar shouldered open the balcony door. Dashing through, he let the glass panel sweep closed, the click of its locking lost beneath the baron's shout of anger.

Taziar never hesitated. Leaping to the banister, he ran his fingers over the mortaring above his head. Discovering irregularities, he skittered up the final story to the roof. He crouched on the tiles, catching his breath and waiting for his heartbeat to slacken to its normal rate. No sound pursued him. *I don't think the baron saw me.*

Taziar peeked over the ledge, studying the curtains stirring in a gentle current of air. He pulled his head beyond sight of the balcony and the guards in the courtyard. *I left the outer door locked, and Baron Dietrich believes his walls "unscalable." He can't possibly suspect someone slipped in from the outside. Most likely, he'll blame the incident on his dog.* Taziar frowned, his plan gone dangerously awry. *With his attention on the mess and the fact that no items were stolen from the room itself, the baron may not notice his medallion of office is missing.* Taziar crept toward the northern side of the keep, aware any guards in the towers would probably watch over the courtyard rather than the rooftop. *But I can't rely on chance alone. I have to work fast, before word of my theft reaches the dungeon guards.*

Taziar pattered around the northwestern tower, confident that the prison was the last place the sentries would search for a renegade thief. From experience, he knew guards filled the hallways nearest the dungeon, on the south side. So he scooted along the northern edge of the keep, seeking seventh story windows in the polished stretch of wall. Shutters covered the first two he discovered. He found the third open, but voices wafted from it, and his plan required that no one know he had entered through a window.

Taziar continued, rejecting each window with reluctant necessity. He had nearly reached the northeastern corner when a tiny, square opening attracted his attention. It appeared too narrow for even a man of Taziar's size to slip through, but he refused to pass it by without a closer inspection. Clinging to the ledge, he lowered his feet over the side, defying gravity with only the strength of his fingers. His boots scraped stone as he groped for toeholds, found them, and lowered himself to the level of the opening.

A glance across the window revealed an area obscured by darkness. Aware the rising sun would make it easier for anyone inside to see him, Taziar peered over the sill with one eye. The opening admitted only a dim glow of dawn light. The space beyond seemed oddly-shaped, too long and thin for a normal-sized chamber. Taziar's angle did not allow him a glimpse of the floor, but he found no movement or figures to disturb the gloom. He realized he had squeezed through equally tight spaces, the chimney of Aga'arin's temple, for example. But he knew he would pay for such a maneuver with tears in his clothing and skin.

Not wanting to waste time searching for a more suitable entrance, Taziar accepted the challenge. Clinging with his feet and alternate hands, he worked his cloak off his arms and over his back. Freeing the fabric, he tossed it through the opening, tensed for some reaction from inside. When none came, he descended to a position just below the window, seized the sill in both fists, and poked his head and shoulders through the opening.

Taziar's body blocked out what little light normally penetrated into the area beyond the window. He braced his palms on the inner wall, twisting to allow his chest the widest possible angle, from corner to corner. Unyielding stone wedged his shoulders. He wriggled and pushed despite pain, strengthened by the awareness that the harder he struggled, the sooner he would finish. He stuck fast, feet straining against stone. Then his shoulders popped through, abrading flesh beneath the coarse linen of his tunic. He worked one arm through the opening, creating more room for the other.

Taziar probed for the floor with his left hand, felt wooden planks, and steadied his fingers against them. Allowing his weight to fall forward, he dropped his right hand. It slammed against floor sooner than he expected. Surprised, he examined the area with his fingers. To his right, the level rose in increments. *A staircase.* Taziar worked the remainder of his body through the window, hugging the steps to keep from toppling down them. Once inside, he retrieved his cloak, and flung it across his back to hide the dirt and scrapes.

Taziar trotted up the staircase, making no effort to silence his movements. His shoulders throbbed, and the baron's medallion bounced against his hip with every step. His footfalls echoed hollowly.

Two sentries armed with swords met Taziar at the landing. "Halt!" one challenged. "State your name and your business."

Taziar made a gesture of impatience. "I'm Taziar Medakan, loyal citizen and informant to Baron Dietrich." He used the same contrived facts that had worked against his attempts to become arrested to his own advantage now. "The baron sent me to interrogate the prisoner known as Allerum."

The guard who had spoken shook back a mane of sand-colored curls and glanced at his larger companion. "We know nothing of this. Do you carry a writ?"

"No," Taziar admitted boldly. "Baron Dietrich found this matter of such urgency, he didn't waste time writing. Instead, he gave me this to show you." He plucked the medallion from his pocket and displayed it for the guards.

The sentries exchanged startled looks. The taller one cleared his throat. "This is most irregular. I think we should check with the baron."

Taziar adopted an expression of stern annoyance. He placed his hand on his hip, allowing the golden symbol of office to dangle from his fingers. "Very well. The baron found this matter critical enough to hand over his signet, but if you think it's necessary to delay me with your curiosity, it's your necks. I only hope the baron chooses to forgive as easily as I do." He raised his eyebrows, demanding a response.

The smaller guard's gaze followed the ovoid swing of the medallion. "Come with me." He turned and started down the eastern hallway, the keys at his belt clanging as he moved.

Relief flooded through Taziar. Maintaining a regal stance that implied he expected no other reaction, Taziar followed the leading guard. He heard the second guard fall into step behind him but did not bother to turn.

Closed doors of oak broke the wall to Taziar's right at irregular intervals, some emblazoned with the baron's crest. Another corridor halved the path. Ten uniformed guards with swords and bows milled about this crossway, watching Taziar and his escort as they passed. Aside from memorizing their location, Taziar paid them little heed. At length, the eastern corridor ended at a familiar window and a sharp bend to the right. Through the opening, Taziar watched the colors of dawn disperse as the sun crowned the horizon. An image from the past came, unbidden. Again, Taziar crouched on this sill, the hall guards fanned into a semicircle of drawn bows. The remembrance raised sweat on his temples, and a breeze from the window touched him, drying the moisture with chill air.

Taziar banished the memory as the guards led him around the corner and the window disappeared behind him. From here, Taziar knew the corridor led directly to the dungeon.

A trio of guards met Taziar and his guides at the steel-barred outer doorway to the prison. "What's going on?" one asked.

The sentry who had ushered Taziar through the passageways removed the keys from his belt. "Baron wants him to question the new prisoner."

The sentries moved aside to allow their companion to unlock the outer door, nudging one another in silent conspiracy. At length, the same man spoke again. "New one's . . . um . . . 'asleep.' "

The guard's emphasis on the last word speared dread through Taziar, and he hoped the guard used sleep as a euphemism for unconsciousness rather than death. He forced contempt into his voice. "So I wake him up. The weasel's a criminal, not a boarder."

The sentry pushed open the door and gestured Taziar through. "Go on."

Taziar stepped inside, just far enough that the sentries could not close it behind him. Turning, he extended a hand, palm up. "The keys, please."

The guard hesitated, two digits looped protectively through the ring.

Taziar wriggled his fingers, impatiently. He raised the baron's symbol with a curt gesture. "I found my first visit here unpleasant. I'm not going in there without as-

surance I can get back out. If you wish to delay the baron's business . . .''

With a wordless growl of contempt, the sentry dropped
the keys into Taziar's palm. He waited only until Taziar
pocketed the sigil and keys before slamming and locking
the door behind him.

Aware the guards might try to confirm his story and
word of the baron's stolen medallion would reach them
eventually, Taziar trotted down the pathway. Cells lined
the walls; those nearest the outer door lay empty. In the
center stood a row of six cages the size of dog kennels.
A man occupied each of the smaller cells, their faces
blurred by distance.

As Taziar drew closer, he realized two of the larger
cells also held prisoners. One was sitting, though all the
other occupants of the baron's dungeon sprawled on the
granite floor. Taziar approached cautiously, footsteps
making raspy echoes through the tomblike interior. The
prisoners' silence did not surprise him. Noise carried
oddly amidst the metal and stone construction of the baron's dungeon; someone had built it to contain the prisoners' screams and cries, the guards' taunts and curses,
and the brutality of torture.

But when Taziar arrived at the first of the middle row
of cells, he realized none of the prisoners were moving.
He scarcely recognized the man in the closest cage. Fridurik lay on his stomach, face buried in the granite floor
of his cell. Sweat spangled his naked torso. In the past,
if not for a gentle temperament, Fridurik's robust form
would have assured him a warrior's life. Now, tangled
red hair tumbled over his shoulders, brittle from starvation. Taziar saw bony prominences through sagging flesh
mottled with scars and bruises of varying hues.

Taziar knew the pain of every slash. He recalled the
clank of shackles, wrists and ankles rubbed raw from the
steel, the malicious smirk of those guards who dared to
find pleasure in another man's suffering. His stomach
ached in sympathy; and, as he silently paced the cell row,
he felt tears press his vision, a hot mix of sorrow, pity,
and anger. Beside Fridurik, Amalric lay supine with eyes

closed. Excrement stained the remaining tatters of his britches. Even in sleep, he found no peace. He kept his arms tucked defensively across his chest. His breathing remained rapid and uneven, occasionally punctuated by a whimper.

From the next cell, Waldhram's eyes watched Taziar, but they swiveled, dull and lifeless, in gaunt sockets. Taziar returned the stare without expression, awaiting some reaction that would cue him as to how to approach these friends turned prisoners. But Waldhram said nothing. He lay still, giving no sign to indicate he had recognized Taziar. It seemed almost as if his body had died, and his eyes merely followed any movement mechanically.

Taziar shivered, rubbing moisture from his eyes with his fists. *If they've grown weak, I must become strong enough for all of them. I have little enough time to turn them into a fighting force.* The thought seemed ludicrous. Taziar passed Odwulf and Mandel, found them in the same hopeless silence. *Battered, broken, useless.* Taziar shook his head in bleak defeat. *They've been here too long, suffered too much. What chance do I have to rouse them? Do they even know I'm not responsible?*

As if in answer to his unspoken question, a scratchy voice wafted from the final cell. "Did you come to gloat?"

Taziar whirled, met the strange, violet eyes of Asril the Procurer, and found a faint spark of emotion in their depths. Thrilled at this first trace of vitality, Taziar smiled. A moment later, he recognized the gleam in Asril's eyes as hatred and realized his grin of joy must seem unduly cruel. He immediately suppressed it. A glance at the outer cages revealed the last two prisoners as Shylar and Larson. Seeing no other occupied cells, Taziar suspected that Waldmunt had succumbed to the guard's tortures. The sadness that spiraled through Taziar became lost in the mire of his friends' tragedies. Moments passed in aching quiet before Taziar felt compelled to answer Asril's accusation. "I've come to rescue you." He flashed the keys. "You can't really believe I betrayed you."

Taziar turned toward Shylar as he spoke. She sat with her legs folded. Her dress spread in dirty, rumpled waves around her. Aside from the impression of the fabric's weave on one cheekbone, she seemed untouched by the guards' oppression. Still, her wrinkles had deepened. Shylar's gray-tinged curls appeared to have spread; now the white hairs outnumbered the brown. She had aged ten years in the months since Taziar last saw her. Certain she would defend him, Taziar waited. But, though Shylar met his gaze with crisp, dark eyes, she said nothing. In the cell beside her, Larson sprawled in an awkward heap, unmoving.

Taziar started toward Larson, but Asril's challenge jarred his attention back to the violet-eyed thief. "Even the guards know you informed on us. You conniving, little bastard! Admit it, you came to gloat."

Taziar stared, watched anger restore life to Asril's features, and suddenly Shylar's strategy became clear. *All the "proof" in the world wouldn't turn her against me. But she can't afford to league with me while the others truly believe I informed on them. Her silence leaves me free to use any tactic I need.* He bit his lip. Asril's mistrust hurt like physical pain, but he knew he would have to exploit that hatred to rally his friends. "Gloat?" Taziar forced a sneer. "What the hell do I have to gloat over? All I see here are some half-dead, has-been criminals."

Asril's gaze fell to the floor, but Taziar saw interest spark in Mandel's pale eyes. Encouraged, he pressed on, his voice pitched to slander and incite. "People gloat in triumph, but there's no one here worth besting. I have nothing to gloat over, just pieces of jail room furniture cluttering kennels."

Waldhram climbed to the highest crouch the abnormally low ceiling of his cell allowed. "You snake! You have nothing to gain by insulting us. Go away and leave us alone."

"People have left you alone too long," Taziar shot back. He banged a fist against Odwulf's bars, pleased to see Odwulf and Mandel tense in response. "You're all weak. You've degenerated into garbage. Do you think you're the only people ever thrown in the baron's dungeon? I was here! I got free. Am I that much better than you pitiful pack of whining dogs?''

Asril swept to his knees, eyes blazing. "You had help."

"Sure, a lot of help." Taziar downplayed Moonbear's role out of necessity. "I had a big, stupid barbarian who couldn't spell his own name, let alone pronounce mine. And you're hardly by yourself. Look around, Asril. There're eight of you. Are you waiting for your mother to get you out?''

Scarlet swept Asril's cheeks. He made a grab for Taziar through the bars.

Taziar danced aside with a disdainful laugh. "If you had shown that much fire before, you might not be trapped here now.'' Suddenly Amalric rolled over to join the argument. Now, only Fridurik and Larson lay still, and Taziar found himself growing more concerned about the latter with every passing second.

Asril growled. "If I was free, I'd rip your evil head off!''

"You want the opportunity?'' Taziar played through an array of emotions. *I've roused them. Now all I have to do is keep them from killing me before Astryd arrives.* "I'll let you out. All of you.''

"Why?'' Waldhram demanded. He sprang forward, but the passion of fury made him careless. His head smacked the cell roof. He hunched back, the pain apparently fueling his rage. "A hanging this evening isn't soon enough for you? You want us killed by guards instead?''

Taziar hesitated. It was too late to change tactics now without losing the ground he had gained. So far, he had managed to incite without confessing to the crime, without destroying that small shadow of doubt each man must hold within him. The thought of lying to convince his friends he actually did betray them dried Taziar's mouth until he felt incapable of speech. *I can regain their trust but not their lives.* He jabbed a finger at Waldhram, licked his lips, and forced the lie. "Do you really think I got you in here alone? I need to rid myself of my accomplice.

I can help you, and you need my help. Later, we can settle scores. But right now, we need each other." Taziar glanced toward the farthest end of the cell row, noticed Fridurik still had not stirred. *He's the biggest and strongest. We need him most of all.*

Asril's fingers curled around the bars. "Who helped?"

Taziar snickered patronizingly. "Oh, you know. Think. Who had most to gain from your imprisonment? Who's in control of the underground now? You don't need a brain to figure it out." He shrugged in dismissal. "Then again, you got caught, so maybe I do have to explain."

From behind Taziar, Shylar's voice sounded calculating. "Of course. It was Harriman, wasn't it? He made me instruct my girls to serve him. He threatened to kill them all if I didn't obey."

Rage caught Taziar. He knew there must be more to Harriman's trickery, but the gist of the story was there. Self-control vanished and, with it, the glib ease with which he taunted and lied to his friends. *Easy*, Taziar cautioned himself. *Shylar's figured out what I'm doing, and she's playing along with my game.* He spun toward her, fathomed the message in her stance warning him not to ruin her cover. He winked for her alone, the gesture betraying the mockery of his words. "Ah, Shylar. So, you're not quite as stupid as the others."

"Not quite," Shylar returned with venom.

"And on the topic of the girls. Harriman's rule hasn't proved pleasant for them." Taziar addressed his next comment for Fridurik's benefit, aware the shambling red-head felt a strong attachment to the one called Galiana. "He's chosen Galiana as his personal 'favorite.' "

Fridurik stirred.

Encouraged, Taziar continued the lie. "He's with her every night, and the cruelties he's inflicted rival anything I've seen from the guards. I . . ."

The squeak of the outer door resounded through the prison, and six guards filled the entryway.

I've delayed too long. Taziar bounded around the corner, unlocked Larson's cage, and jammed the keys into Shylar's startled grip. "Quick," he whispered. "Free them all. It's too complicated to explain, but if I don't get Allerum up, we're all dead.''

Shylar rushed to obey. Taziar jarred open the cell door, caught Larson by the shoulders and yanked. The elf rolled limply to his opposite side, revealing a dark puddle on the stone floor. Blood crusted a gash in Larson's temple, surrounded by a dark halo of bruise. *Dead? Oh, please, not dead.*

"Get them!" The guard's screamed command rose above the click of opening locks.

"Wake up. Allerum, wake up!" Desperately, Taziar jostled Larson, but the elf lolled, dead weight in his arms.

Impatiently, Astryd waited in Cullinsberg's main street while Silme attempted to access Larson's thoughts for what seemed like the thousandth time. A secreted dagger poked at Astryd's forearm, and she plucked at her sleeve to reposition it. The movement earned her a prod from another blade wrapped against her opposite arm. Astryd swore. She lowered her arms. The fabric of her dress and cloak slid over her wrists, and she shook until the four knives along her arms fell into a comfortable alignment. She let her arms dangle, glad for the respite, but unable to shake a feeling that someone was following them.

I'm thinking irrationally. There're few enough people on the streets, so we ought to notice someone spying on us. The scanty traffic in Cullinsberg's streets pleased Astryd, providing fewer people to stare or giggle at her awkward dances. *Of course, the absence of merchants caused the problem in the first place.* The wares displayed on Aga'arin's holiday consisted almost entirely of necessities: food, firewood, and bottled remedies. Attaining the name of a weaponer had required a bribe, another payment had convinced the man to open his shop, but Silme's and Astryd's desperation doubled his prices. A rope, twelve daggers, and one sword of dubious quality had depleted their resources beyond even the ability to purchase a bag to carry the supplies. The sight of a woman armed with two swords, Taziar's and the purchased one, drew odd looks from the few people they passed. Astryd had hidden the daggers on her person so as not to alarm the guards on Cullinsberg's market thoroughfares.

Silme rose, grim and silent. Without explanation, she hefted the packs. Astryd followed her, not bothering to question; Silme's expression told the story. Larson remained unconscious, and, until he awakened, Astryd was helpless to come to his aid. The discomfort of unseen eyes rose again, but she hid her fears from Silme. *I'm just not used to working under time constraints. Silme's worried enough without my adding imaginary ghosts to her concerns.*

The knives secured to Astryd's legs chafed and itched as she moved, turning her usually graceful walk into an arrhythmic, limping shuffle. Silme's willowy elegance made Astryd appear even more ridiculous, and concern for Larson and Taziar multiplied her discomfort. Though not well-trained or familiar with battle injuries, Astryd surmised that the longer a head injury left a man unconscious, the more potentially fatal it must prove. *When I last saw Shadow, he acted curt and uncaring; Harriman's cruelty may kill the very humanity that attracted me to Shadow.* Astryd ground her teeth at the thought. *And if Allerum doesn't awaken soon, the guards may finish the job.*

Astryd's engrossment in her friends' plight made her careless to her own. She followed Silme past a narrow crossroad, oblivious to its occupants until Harriman's familiar voice confronted her. "There you are, bitch. Who gave you permission to leave for this long?"

Startled, Astryd tensed, and breath hissed raggedly through her nose. Regaining her composure instantly, she turned toward Harriman and found him leaning against the wall at the alley mouth, Larson's katana dangling from a sheath at his hip. Halden and Skereye stood before him; shadows draped their scarred and smirking faces. Astryd considered running, but she knew the slaps and jabs of the daggers would slow her. *And Silme would need to drop the packs and maybe our staves to stay ahead of*

those two monsters. We can handle this peacefully.
"Didn't the girls tell you? I quit."

"Quit?" Harriman stared at Silme as he spoke, eyes
trailing the sorceress' curves with an intensity Astryd
found nauseating. "You can't quit. We have an agreement."

"You haven't paid me yet." It occurred to Astryd that,
unless Harriman killed her, he could do her no harm.
*Once Allerum awakens, I can transport, in Harriman's
presence or not. If Allerum awakens,* she reminded herself with a callous but necessary practicality. *But Harriman could trap Silme. Without magic, she can't
transport.* "Don't bother to pay me for the work I've
done, and I'll consider us even. I appreciate the opportunity to work for you, but I don't feel I can do an adequate job. I quit."

Harriman smiled with calm amusement, attention still
fixed, fanatically, on Silme. "Get them both."

Halden and Skereye sprang forward with alarming
speed. Before Astryd could think of dodging, Skereye's
fingers closed on her forearm. His touch stung her to
anger. She thrust a knee into Skereye's groin, jammed
her hand into his face, and raked. One finger gouged an
eye. "Run!" she screamed to Silme.

Skereye bellowed in rage, and pain drove him into a
murderous frenzy. Rather than the release Astryd expected, his grip clamped tight as a vise. His fist crashed
against her ear. The force of the blow hurled Astryd to
the ground. Dizziness wrung her consciousness to meaningless tatters of reality, and she felt Skereye heft her by
the front of her cloak without understanding the danger
she was in. She heard a slap. Though she knew no further
pain, Astryd cringed. Skereye freed her, and she collapsed to the cobbles, reeling.

Through a curtain of waving patterns, Astryd noticed
the red mark on Skereye's cheek and realized the berserk
had taken the blow she heard. Harriman's reprimand
blurred beneath the ringing in Astryd's ears. "Damn you,
Skereye! Don't hit the girls, or you'll be nursing worse
than bruised privates."

Recalling Mat-hilde's ordeal in the whorehouse, Astryd found Harriman's warning ludicrous. Skereye scowled at his master, fists doubled, and coiled to fight. Light-headed, Astryd struggled to one knee. *Gods, I hope Harriman can control that brute.* Though the thought of praying for Harriman's welfare rankled, Astryd knew if Skereye killed his master, she would become the berserk's next victim. She glanced at Silme, saw her standing, regally dangerous despite Halden's grasp on her arms. Regardless of the awkwardness of Halden's presence, Silme managed to keep the packs balanced on her shoulders, though both dragonstaves lay on the cobbles. That, and the wild disarray of her hair made it clear that she had struggled and lost as well.

Skereye grumbled something unintelligible, seized Astryd's wrist, and hauled her to her feet. He lowered his face to hers. His left eye was tearing from her attack, and a scarlet arc marred the white. He spoke in the Scandinavian tongue, his voice as grating as fingernails scratched across stone. "You little bitch, this isn't over yet. I'll kill you."

Still staggering from Skereye's blow, Astryd managed no reply.

Harriman paid the threat no notice; either he lacked command of the language, or he feigned ignorance. "Take them home." He gestured his guards and their prisoners into the alleyway, stooped to gather the dragonstaves, and followed.

Gradually, Astryd's mind cleared as she traversed deserted back streets. Skereye's tightly-wrapped fingers cut off the circulation to her hands, but she made no mention of the dull throb. She tried to keep her gait as normal as possible, concentrating on the pain in her hands to offset the discomfort of a dozen concealed daggers. Though vindictiveness was not a normal part of Astryd's nature, the vision of all twelve blades buried in Skereye's heart soothed her. The realization that she could summon a dragon and destroy Harriman, the berserks, and a quarter of the city only added to her frustration. *I can't slay innocent townsfolk out of anger, and if I deplete my life*

*energy on vengeance, the guards will kill Shadow and
Allerum.* She sighed, enduring the indignity of Skereye's
harsh tugs as the price of obligatory patience.

The sun had half-crested the horizon when Harriman
and his captives arrived at Shylar's whorehouse. They
passed through the double set of doors in a tense hush.
The early hour and the religious fervor of the holiday left
most of the girls free to lounge and talk. As Harriman
entered the chamber, the hum of conversation died. He
pointed to the stairway. "Take them to my room." He
clarified. "The bedroom. The study has windows. Lock
them in and stand guard. I'll join you shortly." He
handed the dragonstaves to Halden.

Astryd sought Mat-hilde in the crowd, passed over a
myriad of concerned expressions before she discovered
the prostitute's familiar features. Skereye met Astryd's
hesitation with a vicious jab in the spine. "Get moving."

Astryd trotted toward the stairway. Methodically, she
climbed to the landing and into the room Skereye indicated. A moment later, Silme joined her, and the door
clacked closed behind them.

To Astryd's relief, Halden and Skereye waited outside
the chamber. She threw a quick glance at the Spartan
effects of a warrior unused to wealth. The pallet she had
seen in her location spell graced one corner, encompass-
ing a quarter of the room, its covers and pillow crisply
neat. An unadorned, straight-backed chair slanted against
it, and a chest lay at the foot of the bed. A simple table
held a lantern full of fat, its wick alight, its illumination
broad and gray. *A potential weapon,* Astryd noted, but
she realized the two swords and twelve daggers on her
person would serve at least as well. From her personal
link with her rankstone, she knew Harriman had placed
the dragonstaves in a nearby room, but that was the least
of her worries. She had little enough life energy stored
in the garnet stone, and, should it become necessary, she
could retrieve that magic instantly, even from a distance.

"What do we do?" Astryd questioned Silme to discover whether her companion had considered a less formidable plan than her own.

"We have no choice." Silme twisted her head and rolled her eyes in all directions, examining Harriman's chamber in her usual calm manner. "The way Harriman stared, he has no intention of killing me. I can handle myself, but Allerum and Shadow need you."

Silme's composure unnerved Astryd. "The way Harriman stared, he has no intention of ignoring you, either."

Silme met Astryd's gaze. "There's nothing Harriman can do to me worse than allowing Allerum and Shadow to die on the gallows. Now sit there." She stabbed a hand toward the farthest corner. "Keep trying to contact Allerum. Don't stop for anything. If you can't catch him awake, you're just going to have to try to arouse him yourself."

"Arouse him myself?" Astryd repeated, confused. "How?"

"Instead of using a mental probe, you'll have to actually place your presence into his mind. Dig for some sort of sleep-wake trigger, and prod until he responds."

Silme's words shocked Astryd; the task sounded years beyond her abilities. "I've never done anything like that."

Silme shrugged. "Of course, you haven't. How could you? Allerum's the only person I know without mind barriers . . . except Harriman." Silme paused, as if considering her own words. "Since thought intrusions don't cost life energy, you risk nothing other than annoying Allerum." Silme added belatedly, "And one other, more important thing."

Astryd fidgeted, uncomfortable with the prospect. "And that is?"

Silme sat on the chest. "By placing a part of yourself into Allerum's mind, you make yourself vulnerable to any sorcerer who tries the same tactic, also to Allerum's defenses. Once, Vidarr and I entered Allerum's mind, and he accidentally pulled us all into his world, a land of fire and madness." She shivered at the memory of Vietnam. "Apparently, the god, Vidarr, and the great wolf, Fenrir, held an actual battle in Allerum's brain. Just remember, you'll be inside his thoughts, displaced in time, not actually physically with him. You'll need to pull out of his mind before you can transport." Silme leaned closer. "And be careful. If you sense another presence, get out as fast as you can."

Though Silme never specified, Astryd knew the only foreign obstacle she could meet was Harriman's master. *My choosing to stand against a sorcerer of his power would be as absurd as a wounded sparrow challenging a hawk.* She pressed into the indicated corner. "I'll do the best I can." Lowering her head, she thrust her consciousness toward Larson, trusting Silme to keep Harriman and his guards occupied.

Astryd's probe met darkness.

Harriman slipped into his workroom and quietly closed the door behind him, leaning the dragonstaves in the corner by the panel. Dawn light snaked through the misshapen glass of the window, blurring the desktop and a few curled strips of parchment in glare. Harriman extracted a quill pen from the disarray, idly twirling it in loops between his fingers. Knowing better than to further delay the inevitable contact, he sat in the hard, wooden chair, dropped the pen, and drained his consciousness to a single name. *Bolverkr?*

The sorcerer's probe entered Harriman's mind, its touch chilling. *Did you capture him?*

Harriman hesitated, forcing emotion from his surface thoughts with the same ease as he controlled outward expressions. *Taziar?*

Yes.

No, Harriman admitted. *He got away.*

Tangible anger pervaded Bolverkr's silence.

Harriman waited, not allowing the slightest memory or sentiment to come to the fore.

I told you precisely where to find him.

Indeed, lord. And you were right, as always. Harriman stroked, believing his existence was worth less to Bolverkr than the four men Taziar had stranded on the rooftop. *My underlings failed and paid with their lives for the mistake. Next time, I'll catch Taziar myself.*

Next time? Bolverkr's question emerged passionlessly, but Harriman detected guarded hope. *You know where Taziar is?*

Harriman's surprise leaked through his facade. *Lord, I'd hoped to get that information from you.*

Bolverkr's annoyance pounded at Harriman's mind, and the diplomat knew he had struck a sore point. *I've lost my source. Loki's children, you're leader of the underground! Use your own spies. Get every man and child at your command out on those streets and find Taziar Medakan! No excuses. Every moment that little murderer evades us, he could find a way to undo the fate we've designed for him. Force him to watch his friends die. And when that's finished, I want Taziar hanged as well. Do you understand?*

Completely. Harriman picked up on Bolverkr's frustration, and it confused him. Not since the destruction of Wilsberg had any plan of Bolverkr's gone awry. Accustomed to the ever-changing tides of politics, Harriman accepted the unanticipated easily, and the sorcerer's loss of his arrogant self-control appalled him.

Apparently, Bolverkr noticed Harriman's discomfort. Shortly, Harriman felt the heat of Bolverkr's hatred as his own, and it sparked him to the same reckless fury. *Lord, what would you have me do with the women?*

Women? Bolverkr's composure returned in a rush. *What women?*

Taziar's companions. The sorceresses. I have them locked in my bedroom.

Indeed. Bolverkr hesitated, his manner fully calculating. *I doubt you'll be able to hold Astryd long. The one thing all Dragonrank mages learn to do early and well is escape. The other . . .*

Bolverkr's presence trailed away, and only a faint tingle of pleasure alerted Harriman that his master had not yet broken contact. *Lord?* He concentrated on the link so as not to miss Bolverkr's reply.

Bolverkr's words crashed into Harriman's heightened

consciousness. *Force Silme to use her magic. Humiliate her any way you can, and don't quit until she's killed that child.* His message softened. *And Harriman . . .*

Master? Harriman prompted cautiously, unable to recall the last time the sorcerer had called him by name.

. . . have fun doing it. The probe disappeared from Harriman's mind.

Harriman pictured Silme's delicate arcs, firm breasts, and the timeless beauty of her golden features. *I wonder how long it will take to destroy the haughty tilt to her chin, and the fierce gleam in those ice blue eyes?* A smile pinched Harriman's face as he accepted Bolverkr's task with glee.

Gradually, the tug and jostle of Silme freeing hidden daggers became familiar to Astryd, and the smaller sorceress directed her full concentration to Larson's mind. Mired in darkness, she dodged and crawled through loops of thought as chaotic as a bramble copse. Harriman's bedroom disappeared from her awareness; Astryd did not know she still lay, limp and silent, in the corner. She kept her mind focused, all too aware that she could die as easily from another presence in Larson's mind as from a slash of Harriman's sword.

Uncertain how much stress threads of thought could stand, Astryd brushed them aside with a gentle caution. She wondered how much of what she found constituted actual anatomy and how much was her magical perception of memory. As the intensity of her search absorbed her completely, the question faded into the infinity of insignificant facts. Catching sight of a spark of light, she ran to it with the fatal devotion of a moth to a flame. She skidded to a stop before it, felt Larson's annoyance as though it were her own. *If . . .*

The idea sputtered feebly, and died. In frustration, Astryd kicked the pathway that had initiated the thought, watched it flare and grow. *If that sonofabitch doesn't stop shaking me, I'm going to kill him!* Several nearby avenues flashed as confusion pervaded Larson's mind. A survival instinct blossomed. She felt Larson tense and crouch, even before he opened his eyes. Then his lids fluttered, and Astryd caught a close up view of Taziar's worried features. "Allerum! Can you hear me?"

Rows of cages slashed across Larson's vision, and Astryd saw guards with swords rushing toward emaciated, scarred men cowering at the barred doors. Without waiting for Larson to interpret the reality of the dungeon, Astryd withdrew. She found herself back in the corner of Harriman's room.

Harriman's heavy bootfalls sounded in the outside corridor.

Too concerned about the men to consider Silme's plight, Astryd hugged the piled daggers and triggered her escape transport. Golden light erupted in a blinding flash.

When Harriman opened the door, all that remained of Astryd was a rolling pulse of oily smoke.

CHAPTER 11:

Shadows of the Gallows

> Whoever fights monsters should see to it that in the
> process he does not become a monster. And when you
> look long into an abyss, the abyss also looks into you.
> —Friedrich Nietzsche
> *Beyond Good and Evil*

Light exploded in the baron's dungeon, shattering Taziar's vision before he could think to shield his eyes. Larson stiffened, and his sudden movement staggered Taziar into the cell door. Half-blinded, the Climber clawed for support, barking his knuckles on iron clotted with rust. The click of opening locks and the pounding of guards' footfalls gave way to a shocked silence that seemed to amplify Astryd's plea. "Shadow, hurry. Harriman has Silme trapped in the whorehouse!"

Back pressed to the bars and supporting much of Larson's weight, Taziar twisted awkwardly toward the walkway. Through a web of shadowed afterimages, he recognized Astryd. A coil of rope lay slung across her shoulder. Two swords dangled at her side, and she balanced an armload of daggers against her chest. Her beauty seemed so misplaced amidst the filth and gloom of the baron's dungeon, it took Taziar a moment to believe she was real.

Larson's bulk eased off Taziar as the elf came fully awake. Seizing the rope from Astryd, Taziar guided Larson's hand to the swords. "Allerum, keep one and take the other to the redhead." He gestured to the left pathway where Fridurik crouched in the cage closest to the exit and the guards. "Go!"

Accepting the swords, Larson tottered off in the indicated direction.

Sound echoed as sentries and prisoners broke free of the surprise inspired by Astryd's grand entrance. Desperately, Taziar caught Astryd's arm. "Distribute those knives as quickly and quietly as you can. Then transport out and wait. We'll need your help against Harriman far more than we do here." He released her with a mild push toward the prisoners and wished he could spare a second for comforting.

The central pens split the baron's dungeon into two lanes with Larson's cell along the back wall. Shylar had chosen to unlock the doors from the left pathway. Hoping for a clear passage to the outer door, Taziar sprinted to the right. "This way!"

Within three running strides, Asril the Procurer darted alongside Taziar. A quick glance over his shoulder revealed that only Shylar and Mandel had followed them. Apparently, the others had taken the parallel walkway. *Including both swordsmen*, Taziar realized in sudden alarm. He tried to decipher the blur of color and movement through the central cells, obscured by the yellow backwash of Astryd's magical departure. *Thank the gods, at least she got out safely.*

A warning touch from Asril slowed Taziar's reckless pace and brought his attention to a pair of guards with drawn swords blocking the pathway. A third tensed behind them.

Taziar cursed silently as he realized the guards had separated to prevent escape down either pathway. Well within sword range, Taziar and Asril skidded to a halt in front of the guards; Shylar and Mandel backpedaled, avoiding a collision.

The sentry before Asril waved his sword threateningly. "Get back to your cells."

Taziar met the guard's gaze, his hand sliding, unobtrusively, for his own dagger. From the corner of his vision, he realized Asril held a knife, expertly couched against his wrist so the guards could not see it. Taziar's heart raced. *The cage row would have blocked Astryd from the*

*guards' view. Depending on her caution and when these
guards split off from the others, they may not know we
have weapons.* Only then did Taziar recall that Asril was
a street fighter, born to a freelance prostitute barely into
her teens.

Knife still hidden, Asril made a gesture of surrender.
"All right. Don't hurt us." A nervous spring entered his
step, and he shuffled backward with a commitment that
fooled even Taziar. Suddenly, Asril sprang at the guard.
The dagger flashed, then disappeared, buried in the sentry's upper abdomen and angled beneath the breastbone.

The guard gasped in shock and pain. The sword fell
from his hands and crashed to the floor. From the parallel
pathway, steel chimed repeatedly, as if in echo. Asril
shoved the dying guard backward as he ripped his blade
free, but the sentry before Taziar responded more swiftly.
His sword whipped for Asril's head.

No time to draw a weapon! Taziar dove with desperate
courage. His shoulder crashed into the sentry's gut, driving him over backward. The guard twisted as he fell. His
left arm encircled Taziar, wrenching. Taziar struck the
ground sideways, breath dashed from him in a gasp. Recognizing the helplessness of his position, he grabbed
wildly for the guard's sword hilt. His fingers closed over
a fleshy hand. But with superior strength and leverage,
the guard tore free and jammed his elbows into Taziar's
face.

Pain shot through Taziar's nose. The force of the blow
smashed his head against stone, and blood coursed, warm
and salty, on his lips. He saw the sword blade speeding
toward him and knew with grim certainty that he could
not roll in time.

Asril's lithe form sailed over Taziar and plowed into
the guard. Taziar scuttled clear as Asril and the guard
tumbled. This time, Asril landed on top, his arm wrapped
around the sentry's throat. A flick of his wrist drew the
blade of his dagger across the guard's muscled neck.
Blood spurted, splashing Mandel as he darted past Taziar
in pursuit of the third guard who had made a dash for the

outer door amidst the crash and bell of swordplay in the other lane.

Taziar staggered after Mandel. "Stop him!" *We can't let that guard get around the corner to warn the others.* Taziar watched in frustration as the sentry outdistanced the weakened Mandel, sprinted through the outer, barred door, and slammed it behind him. The sentry fumbled with his keys. Jamming one into the hole, he spun it to the locked position then raised his sword and brought it down, hard, against the stem. Metal snapped with the sickening finality of bone. The base of the key clattered to the floor, the remainder wedged in the lock. The guard raced down the passageway.

Mandel hit the door with a force that rattled the steel. Grasping the bars, he shook them viciously. The panel resisted his efforts. Muttering a bitter blasphemy, he snaked an arm through the bars and hurled his dagger at the guard's retreating back.

Taziar cringed, aware only deep urgency could have goaded Mandel to disarm himself. To Taziar's surprise, Mandel's aim was true. He heard the thud of the guard's body striking the floor, followed by the soft and haunting moans of the dying.

When Taziar reached the outer door, he peered through the bars. The guard lay on the floor of the passageway, Mandel's dagger protruding from his lower back. Blood soaked the hem of his uniform, and Taziar guessed the blade had nicked a kidney. Apparently too weak to gather breath for a scream, the guard was inching toward his companions.

A glance down the dungeon's parallel lane revealed the other three guards had fallen to the swordsmen, though only Larson's blade was blooded. Fridurik panted; weeks of torture had taken a toll on his endurance, but Taziar was just glad to see the red-haired giant on his feet.

Shylar stabbed the key into the lock. It sank in only partway despite maneuvering, and she shook her head in defeat. "It won't go."

Mandel copied her gesture, his arm limp between the bars. "I can't get it from the other side either."

Slipping his thinner, more finely crafted knife from his pocket, Taziar knelt before the lock. Before he could insert the tip, a sudden, sharp movement caught his attention. He ducked, scuttling aside as Larson's sword smacked into the door, jolting the metal to its hinges. Larson drew back for another blow.

"Allerum, stop," Taziar hissed.

The sword paused.

"I think I can get us out faster and quieter. Let me try."

Larson nodded once and lowered his sword.

Taziar wiped moisture from his eyes with his forearm, and the red stain it left on his sleeve revealed blood, not sweat, marred his vision. *Not again.* Suddenly it struck Taziar how badly his shattered nose throbbed and his head ached. *The others are hurt worse,* he reminded himself, forcing his concentration to his task. *I have no right to complain.* He eased the tip of the blade into the hole and met the resistance of the broken key trapped in the mechanism. He applied gentle pressure, but in the locked position the key would not budge.

Pain faded before the intensity of Taziar's thoughts. He could hear the prisoners shifting around him, the clink of steel as they gathered swords from the dead guards, and their bleak whispers about the steady progress of the injured sentry in the hallway. Knife point tight to the base of the broken key, Taziar banished the noises around him and twisted the blade in a fabricated silence. He felt the key give ever so slightly. *It's going to work.* Hope flared, tempered by the urgency of time dwindling. He rotated the dagger again, felt the impasse barely budge. *But it's not going to happen fast. Still, it's quicker than Allerum beating on solid steel and a lot less likely to draw the other nine guards.*

As the movement of rotation and slippage became routine, thoughts invaded Taziar's private world. He considered the many lives that now lay in his hands, a list far beyond the ragged band of friends trapped before the prison door. He considered the beggars, the aged, crazed, and orphaned who wandered Cullinsberg's streets through no fault of their own. He would not wish their fate upon anyone, yet there was no one special enough, no one so favored by gods and men that he could not wind up in their position. *Not even the son of the baron's loyal guard captain.* He turned the blade, felt the metal shift. *Perhaps not even the baron himself.*

Taziar's thoughts turned to the women in the whorehouse, loyal to Shylar's final command despite Harriman's brutality. He contemplated the violence and paranoia of the street gangs, inspired by Harriman's greed, and the many innocent merchants who would pay with their lives. *The same citizens who would cheer the hangings of the underground leaders would suffer for their deaths.* Taziar imagined the city devoid of Shylar's charity, Mandel's payoffs and the lotteries Amalric skewed toward families in need of food or shelter. Without fighters like Asril to champion them, the young and the old would succumb to the strong; muggers and assassins would replace children and beggars. Recalling his encounters in the alleyways, Taziar knew Cullinsberg had already changed. *And it's going to get worse unless we stop it.* He wrestled with the jammed key, quickening his pace.

And then there's Allerum. One last picture filled Taziar's mind. He saw Silme, stately and grimly capable. She had spent her childhood protecting her half-human half brother, Bramin, from prejudice and then was forced to devote her youth to hunting him down and killing him. She had rescued innocents from vengeances as cruel and inappropriate as those of Harriman's master, yet her best efforts could not keep Bramin from slaying her parents and siblings. Silme had suffered through too much; nothing seemed to daunt her anymore. Everything she did, she had learned to do with infallible skill and without external emotion. *But deep down, she cares. She dared open herself to the pain loving Allerum might cost her. Quick as she made it, the decision to save the baby rather than Allerum must have torn her apart. And there's only one reason she could have made the choice she did: she believes in me. Silme's more certain I can free Allerum than I am myself, and hers is a trust I won't betray.*

Odwulf's alarm cut through Taziar's self-imposed isolation. "He made it around the corner."

Taziar spun the dagger hard, adding his curses to those of his friends. A click heralded the final movement of the wedged piece of key; though muffled, it came sweet as a shout of triumph to Taziar's ears. He poked, and the metal twig slid to the granite floor with a clang that sounded loud in an abrupt and hopeful hush.

Taziar rose. The sudden rush of blood made his legs throb, and he hobbled painfully aside.

Asril hit the heavy door with his shoulder, and it swung open with a shrill of rusted hinges. "Got to get the guard," the street fighter mumbled as he raced down the hallway brandishing a sentry's long sword.

Taziar and Shylar scrambled after Asril, Larson and Fridurik on their heels. Taziar darted as fast as his awakening legs would allow. Behind him, the footsteps of Amalric, Waldhram, Odwulf, and Mandel wafted to him like drumbeats. His shoulder ached from the weight of the rope, and he wished he had thought to set it on the floor while he worked. Each running step jarred a pins and needles sensation through his thighs. Far ahead, Asril reached the ninety degree turn in the passage and skidded around the corner. Across from the corridor Asril had entered, the long, stone-framed window lay open, silken curtains dancing in the autumn breeze.

Almost there. The scene was too familiar to Taziar. Memory overpowered him, and he felt himself stumbling down this same passageway, fighting for consciousness at the heels of a barbarian prince. Then, guards with swords and crossbows had filled the corridor. *The corridor Asril just entered.* Before Taziar could shout a warning, Asril reappeared.

"Guards!" Asril screamed, sliding to a halt at the window ledge. He glanced through the opening, staring wide-eyed at the seven-story drop to the baron's moat. "Mardain's mercy."

Taziar ripped the coil from his shoulder as he overtook

Asril. He threw only a casual glance at the guards, still some distance down the corridor, and hunted for some object on which to anchor the rope. Finding nothing, he tossed one end through the window and wrapped the other twice around his own middle. Bracing his feet against the wall beneath the window, he sat. "Climb!" he yelled to Shylar. "Fast. And keep everyone together down there. We're going to need all their help to defeat Harriman."

Shylar tossed a meaningful glance of confirmation at Taziar, then obeyed. He felt the tugs as she descended. Taziar gritted his teeth, adding to himself. *And by the gods Shylar, convince them I'm not the traitor.* He looked up to see Asril gawking at the guards. "Go!" Taziar commanded.

"You can't stay there." Asril glanced rapidly from Taziar to the guard-filled corridor behind him. "You're a target."

"Damn it, go!" Frustration and rising anger added volume to Taziar's voice. "Climb down or get the hell out of everyone else's way!" Taziar pulled the rope more securely around him, aware that if the guards killed him, his corpse would still weigh the rope in place to let the others escape.

Sword bared, Larson sprang between Taziar and the guards. Fridurik took a stance at Larson's side. To Taziar's relief, Asril leaped to the windowsill and clambered down the rope. *Good. Shylar will need a fighter like Asril, and at least some of them will make it back to face Harriman.*

Behind Taziar, steel slammed against steel. He did not bother to turn. Any man who could fight through Larson would prove more than a match for Taziar, especially weaponless and tangled in the rope. *But not all of us will survive.* Taziar lowered his head. There was no doubt in his mind that he and Larson would be among the casualties.

Silme stood to face Harriman, her posture projecting dangerous competence. But beneath a calm and imposing exterior, fear coiled in her gut. The feeling seemed alien, from a distant past before the Dragonrank school trained her to a craft few men could stand against. *With magic, I could best him in my sleep. But the handful of tricks I learned from Gaelinar will scarcely delay a soldier who controls a berserk who already overpowered me.*

To Silme's surprise, Harriman seemed unimpressed by Astryd's disappearance. *A sure sign he knows exactly who and what we are.* The thought grated, intensifying her uneasiness until she felt queasy. She took a step back, never losing her quiet dignity and grace.

A smile creased Harriman's handsome features. His dark eyes seemed as flat and emotionless as his expression, but Silme saw madness lurking in their depths. "Well, Silme. I think we're going to become close friends." His voice lingered on the word "close." He approached, regal as a king in his own castle.

He smelled of sword oil, sweat, and perfume. The combination intensified Silme's nausea. Her stomach heaved, and, for a moment, she lost all pretense and sat on the edge of the bed. She regathered her composure, wondering how much of her illness stemmed from the pregnancy. "I think not." Silme managed to keep her voice steady and even added an edge of threat.

Undeterred, Harriman took a seat close behind Silme. Quick as a striking snake, he placed a hand on her head and smoothed the thick, golden waves.

Revulsion turned to rage. Silme caught Harriman's hand before it slid to her breast. She seized it the way Gaelinar had taught her, with her thumb on Harriman's smallest knuckle.

No grimace of pain or surprise flashed across Harriman's face. With a warrior's training, he latched his free hand onto her grip, yanking with a strength that lanced pain through her arm.

It required Silme's full self-control not to gasp. She released his hand, the image of Harriman writhing in magical flames giving substance to her hatred. Still clinging to her hand, he flung her violently to the coverlet. She twisted, clawing for his face with her opposite hand.

Batting the attack aside, Harriman wrenched Silme's trapped arm so suddenly she thought it might break. She rolled back to escape the pain as Harriman pinned her other arm beneath his knee.

Silme felt her bravado slipping. Hot with anger, she was almost overwhelmed by another emotion, one she could not name that scattered her wits and goaded her to fight without direction. "Is it death you seek, Harriman? I can make it cruel." She realized a single gesture and a major expenditure of energy could send him into agonized spasms. Then she could shield or transport away, perhaps create an opening to kill him. The idea of murder soothed Silme, smothering her panic. She fought to free her left hand, but Harriman's knee crushed her wrist.

Harriman laughed, the sound light with calculation and eagerness. "Be cruel, then. I've faced death before, and it doesn't frighten me. I've subdued those two berserks." He said it "bair-sair," the musical, Norse pronunciation sounding out of place amidst his southern accent and clipped, Wilsberg dialect. "I doubt you could do worse, but you're welcome to try."

Silme ignored the taunt, forcing herself to think. *Dare I use magic? Allerum and I could conceive another baby.* The moment of consideration reminded her she still had her utility knife tucked in a pocket of her dress.

Harriman eased the pressure on Silme's hands. "Oh, ach, how cruel." He clutched his throat with his free hand. "How do I bear the anguish?"

Silme knew Harriman mocked her. *He wants me to kill the baby.* She winced, realizing fury had nearly driven her to do exactly what he wanted. Now the idea seemed painfully evil. The child had become real, a solid part of her she had protected through too much already. *Allerum, Taziar, and Astryd might die for this baby. I can suffer through Harriman's indignities for the life of our child.*

Harriman blinked in the silence. When Silme gave him no reply, he shifted, his weight smashing her legs to the coverlet. One-handed, he fumbled with the buckle of his sword belt, unfastened it, and tossed it to the floor.

The weapon flew in a wide arc. Silme recognized the black brocade of its hilt and the slim curve of its sheath. *Gaelinar's katana.* The sword whacked against the floor, leather whisking as it slid across granite. Gaelinar had often claimed a man's sword was an extension of his spirit. She had seen the ronin samurai let wounds gape and bleed while he tended a blade dirtied or nicked in battle. Harriman's casualness dishonored Silme's memory of the greatest swordsman in the world, a single-mindedly loyal bodyguard who had also been a respected friend. Fear retreated, leaving only the blinding rage. She struggled wildly against him.

Harriman jarred a backhanded slap across her cheek and jerked her trapped arm so savagely Silme could not keep from screaming. She went limp, waiting for the pain to subside. Tears filled her eyes, transforming Harriman into a blue-white blur. She felt him paw at her dress, heard the jerk and tear of undergarments, followed by the cold touch of air on her exposed thighs. Unable to contain her terror, she sobbed, then bit her lip. *He may be able to humiliate me, but I won't give him the satisfaction of seeing me cry.*

A single, sharp tug at the ties of Silme's bodice bared her breasts. Harriman's speed shocked her. She twisted her gaze to the knife he clutched, splinters of leather still clinging to the blade. *My knife,* Silme realized. *My last chance to fight him.* Her hands and legs had gone numb beneath him. Bile rose, sour in her throat. He clamped a hand, icy and pinching, to her breast, and her flesh crawled beneath his touch. She met his eyes, soft brown, his expression gentle and incongruous with his actions.

"You're mine, Silme." Harriman stated it as simple fact, as if gloating was not a part of his emotional repertoire. "You belong to me now, and I can do anything I want." As if to prove his claim, he arched against her and reached to unfasten his own garments.

Harriman's words were a challenge. *He believes he owns me, this damaged creature controlled by another sorcerer.* The thought mobilized Silme, and she cursed herself for not considering the option sooner. She gath-

ered and grounded her awareness, burying fear and anger
beneath intensity of will, and thrust her way through the
ruins of Harriman's mind barrier.

Silme's last physical perception was of her body sagging into the straw mattress. Her sense of Harriman's
bedroom, the understanding of pain, Harriman's skin
touching hers all disappeared as she ducked between the
clinging shards of his mental barrier into a world of
thought and memory. The superficial glimpse her probe
had admitted the previous day did not prepare her for the
vast plain of slashed, looped, and knotted pathways, chaotic as tangled harp strings. Harriman's master had made
no attempt to hide his meddling. But no matter how much
time the sorcerer had had to maim and corrupt, Silme
knew his efforts must prove mediocre, at best. In order
to maintain Harriman's abilities as warrior and diplomat,
the experiences that taught him those skills must remain
intact. *The master must have obliterated the connections
between action and emotion.*

Surprise reverberated through Harriman's mind, liberally mixed with confusion and frustration. Silme caught
the name ''Bolverkr'' bright as a signal flare, a desperate
plea for help radiating from Harriman's thoughts.

Silme froze. She harbored no doubt Bolverkr was Harriman's master, a sorcerer whose skill and strength she
could not hope to stand against. *I must find some memory
terrible enough to distract Harriman while I escape. And
I have to work fast!* Silme sprang forward and swam
through the thought pathways, experiencing rapid
glimpses of Harriman's past realities. She found a life
entwined with lies and deception, hidden ideas and expressions. As if from a great distance and through Harriman's perception instead of her own, she felt his body
stiffen. Lust died like a candle snuffed. She heard him
howl, a deep echo in his own ears, heard the click of the
doorknob.

Silme delved faster, hurling aside thoughts and memories like bits of colored string. Recollection sparked and
died, an endless show of fragments. Harriman thudded
against the floor, arms wrapped around his head. Silme

felt him rolling, screaming. Her own cruelty raised guilt. Still she dug, more gently now, seeking a childhood memory Bolverkr might not have bothered to warp. To her surprise, her pang of regret hammered through Harriman's mind, intensified by receptors apparently set by Bolverkr to relay his emotions as if they were Harriman's own.

And Silme found what she sought. She ignited an ancient memory, nurtured and enhanced it like a spark against kindling. Harriman's shrieks stopped abruptly. He waved off the berserks, then sat on the edge of his bed, his face clapped between his palms, and relived the moment with Silme:

Eight years old, Harriman crouched behind a floor-length curtain of velvet and lace, watching naked bodies entwined on the canopied bed at the center of the room. Silme knew the couple as Harriman did, his mother, a maid, smashed beneath the bulk of the duke. As the duke's bastard, Harriman had free run of the keep except for this bedroom. The lure of the forbidden had drawn him here, and now he attributed his mother's moans to violence inflicted upon her by the duke. The scene should have cut him to the heart, but, oddly, it inspired no reaction. Silme separated her mind from Harriman's, discovered the spliced pathways that should have supplied emotion to the scene. Accepting the burden, she forced herself to look upon the incident as a boy concerned for his mother rather than a woman pitying the recollection of a child.

Carefully, Silme added the anguish, rage, and a glimmer of hatred, felt them blossom and Harriman's answering shudder. Linked with his memory, she watched the child that was Harriman dash aside the curtain and run to the bedside. She heard his scream of outrage, felt his tiny fist pound the duke's tautly-muscled back. The duke twisted. A hand lashed out, caught the child a staggering blow across the mouth. The force flung Harriman against the wall. Fighting for breath, hands wet with blood and tears, the child covered his eyes to block out the scene on the bed.

Harriman supplied the memory, Silme the sensation. Magnified by Bolverkr's handiwork, the combination nearly overwhelmed Silme. Tears of rage and pity burned her eyes. She felt Harriman sobbing, too, and released him from the recollection. Quickly, she backtracked, found the remembrances of the berserks battering Taziar, and forced Harriman to confront his actions in the cruel light of his own judgment. Mangled by the passion borrowed from Silme, Harriman shuddered, racked with guilt. Encouraged by her success, Silme shouldered aside mercy, steering Harriman's thoughts to his attack against her.

Suddenly, fingers gouged Silme's shoulder. She gasped and felt her shock flash solidly through Harriman's mind. Whirling, she found herself staring at a tall, thin man dressed in a tunic and hose so neutral gray they seemed to have no color at all. He wore a brown cloak, and, above the collar, Silme met blue eyes as cold as the bitterest, Scandinavian winter. White hair lay sweat-plastered to his forehead. His face was clean-shaven and eternal as mountains. The life aura surrounding him glimmered, as blindingly brilliant as a roomful of high ranking Dragonmages. His stance seemed casual, but it neatly blocked Silme's escape.

Silme knew she confronted Harriman's master yet, oddly, the realization brought no fear. She could not hope to best him; her powers lay so far beneath his, a fight would prove futile. *If he wanted to kill me, he would have done so already.* The awareness released Silme from the need to plot, freed her from all emotion but curiosity, and no pretenses were necessary. "Bolverkr," she said simply, as if well-met over a glass of wine rather than amidst the tatters of a human mind whose owner lay weeping on a granite floor.

"Silme." Bolverkr nodded with careless respect. He continued as if he had come solely to make conversation. "You nearly destroyed my hard work." He flung a gesture at Harriman's mind.

Silme studied Bolverkr's face, unable to guess his age or fathom his intentions. "That was my objective."

"Indeed." He conceded. "And understandable, I suppose."

Silme's gaze followed the lines of Bolverkr's frame. His body obstructed the exit from Harriman's mind too completely for accident. Confused by his pleasantness, she awaited an attack as abrupt and ruthless as the ones perpetrated against Taziar. "I don't suppose you would stand aside and let me leave."

"No need." Bolverkr shrugged narrow shoulders. "You're Dragonrank. A simple transport escape would take you anywhere you wanted to go."

"Not from inside someone else's mind."

Bolverkr shrugged again, this time in concession. "We could go elsewhere. Some place where you could escape with a transport spell."

"Certainly, but at what price?"

"An insignificant expenditure of energy. The life of an unborn child who should never have been conceived. Nothing more."

Bolverkr's game had worn thin and, with it, Silme's patience. "Sorry, it's my baby. I chose to conceive it, and I choose to bear it. That decision doesn't involve you." Annoyance made her bold. "I don't even know you. What possible interest could you have in my baby?"

Bolverkr shifted but left Silme no opening for escape. "That child is as much as anathema as Loki's own. Allowed to live, it might inflict as much evil as its father."

"Evil? Allerum?" Bolverkr's accusation seemed so ridiculous, Silme had to struggle to keep from laughing. She recalled the features that attracted her to Larson: selfless dedication to friends and causes, an unfamiliarity with her world that allowed him to treat her as someone to be loved rather than feared, the ability to cry, and a guileless, solid morality that drove him to defy Gaelinar at the risk of his own life. "That's nonsense, Bolverkr. Allerum acts tough at times. I admit, he's trained to fight, but he wouldn't hurt anyone or anything without good cause."

Bolverkr placed a hand on Silme's shoulder, his touch patronizing. "I didn't question the elf's intentions. You must realize he's an anachronism. He doesn't belong here. Purposeful or not, his presence disrupts the fragile balance of our world. Just like Geirmagnus.''

"Geirmagnus?" Silme repeated, floored by the comparison. "The first Dragonrank Master?" She recalled how Larson had let Taziar describe the men's exploits in the ancient estate of Geirmagnus. At the time, Taziar had mentioned that there was something odd about Larson's knowledge of the ancient Dragonmage's artifacts. but Larson had avoided the subject, passing it off as unimportant. Attributing Larson's reticence to grief for Kensei Gaelinar and reluctance to relive his own near-fatal gunshot wound, Silme had let the matter rest. Now, recalling Larson's tendency to gloss over details of his past that he found too complicated to explain, Silme wished she had pressed him harder for information.

"Geirmagnus wasn't a Dragonrank Master," Bolverkr corrected. "He was the Master of the Dragon Ranks. Doesn't that school of yours teach history? Geirmagnus never had the ability to perform magic. Like Allerum, he came from the future. Geirmagnus used techniques from his era to find potential sorcerers and teach them to channel Chaos. I think he meant well, but he dabbled with the foundations of our world as though they were his personal toys. Because of Geirmagnus, the gods of legend became real and Dragonrank mages can tap power. No doubt, his meddling caused many other changes throughout our world and its past and future history. But forces are made to balance, to keep our world alive; and those forces fought back, Silme. The Chaos Geirmagnus summoned killed him before he could inflict more damage on our world.''

"How could you possibly know all that? The school teaches Geirmagnus' history as well as any man or god has learned it, but he died centuries ago.''

"One hundred eighty-nine years." Bolverkr met Silme's incredulity with an expression so somber, she did not think to doubt him. "I was there.''

"That would make you more than one hundred eighty-nine years old.''

"Two hundred seventeen." Bolverkr patted his chest. "Not bad for a man of my age."

Silme said nothing, the joke lost in a wash of bewilderment. She glanced at the shattered barriers of Harriman's mind and shivered with awe at the amount of chaos Bolverkr must command. The Dragonrank school had taught her that the earliest sorcerers wielded more power than modern mages, and Taziar's story confirmed the speculation. But not even the exaggerations of bards and storytellers had prepared her for the boundless energy of the Dragonmage before her.

Bolverkr cleared his throat. "Is Allerum a sorcerer?"

Silme knew lying would prove fruitless. Bolverkr had already explored Larson's mind, and his question could only serve to test her honestly. "Certainly not."

"Is he strong?"

"Not unusually," Silme admitted.

"Is he skilled with weapons?"

"Yes."

"When he first arrived in our world?"

When I met Allerum, I'm not sure he knew which end of the sword to hold. "No," she said aloud. Not wanting Bolverkr to lose his reluctance to challenge Larson directly, she added, "But Gaelinar . . ."

Bolverkr interrupted. "Yet a man without any special abilities killed a god and a Dragonrank Master, restored life to a sorceress and another god. A god, I might add, the gods themselves could not rescue. Can you explain that?"

Bolverkr's words spurred memories within Silme, a grim mixture of joy and sorrow. The tasks had proven difficult beyond compare. Success had required effort, desperation, gods' aid, threats, and a lot of teamwork. Luck played a large role, and victory had been tainted by the death of friends. Still, Silme was more interested in Bolverkr's theory, so she turned the question back to him. "Clearer purpose and a more focused will." She used the words Gaelinar would have chosen. "But I imagine you have a different explanation."

"Allerum doesn't belong here. Something about misplacement in time makes the natural forces more sensitive to his interference. Silme,'' Bolverkr paused, genuine concern creasing his timeless features. ''Gradually, Allerum will destroy our world. That's why we have to kill him now.''

''You're mad.'' Silme took the offensive. ''And what you propose is madness. I told you before, Allerum would never harm anyone without provocation.''

''No?'' Bolverkr's tone became a perfect blend of grief and triumph, as though he made a solid point at the expense of his own happiness. ''Let me show you.'' With an exaggerated gesture of apology, he grabbed Silme's wrist and pulled her through the exit of Harriman's memory.

A flash of light obscured the maze of Harriman's thoughts. Silme's awareness overturned. Flung back into her body, she barely had time to glimpse Harriman's bedroom before she was wrenched into a vortex of Bolverkr's sorcery. She landed on her back amid a wreckage of stone. Autumn wind swirled, chill through the tatters of her dress. A stomach cramp doubled her up. She rolled, clutching at her abdomen, knees and elbows drawn in tight.

After the deep gloom of Harriman's mind, the ruddy light of sunset seemed bright as day. At length, Silme's vision sharpened and her nausea subsided. But where she expected to find farmers scurrying to finish harvest before nightfall, smoke twining from cooking fires, and goats tramping muddy paddocks, she saw crops uprooted and a shattered jumble of thatch and stone. Corpses were tumbled in awkward piles, terror locked on every upturned face. Grief battered at Silme, and the foreignness of its source frightened her as much as its intensity did. The spell Bolverkr had used to bring her to this location defied all logic. *He drew us out of Harriman's mind to cast it, so we must have transported here. Yet no Dragonmage has ever held the power or knowledge to transport another being.* ''It's a trick,'' she said. ''An illusion.''

''Neither.'' Bolverkr removed his cloak and spread it

across Silme's shoulders. "To make you see something unreal, I would have to access your mind. I would need to do to you what I did to Harriman. I think you know I haven't."

Silme sat up, drawing the cloak over her torn clothing. She winced at the imagined pain of Bolverkr's attack against Harriman. *If Bolverkr holds enough life energy to shatter mind barriers, why couldn't he learn to transport another sorcerer?* Fear clutched at her. *How can I hope to defy a mage with this much power?*

"You're seeing Harriman's last memory of his village and his friends." Bolverkr knelt beside Silme, staring out over the town. His features were etched with pain, but he took the time to answer Silme's unspoken questions. "I created an entrance to this thought so it can be accessed with a transport spell, but, as you can see, I didn't change the memory itself. The sorrow we feel is Harriman's."

The immensity of the tragedy jarred Silme beyond speech. A question came to mind, but Bolverkr answered it before she could put it into words.

"I left Harriman the emotion this scene inspired in order to commit him against the enemies who caused the destruction."

Suddenly, Bolverkr's strategy became clear to Silme. "You want me to believe Allerum and Taziar caused this?"

"Yes." Bolverkr pulled at a fold in his cloak, covering a rip in the fabric of Silme's dress. "But only because it's the truth."

Silme scowled. "You're lying."

"I'm not. And when I explain how they did it, you'll know I'm not."

Silme shrugged. Beneath a noncommittal exterior, she felt ragged with doubt. "Speak, then. But I'll judge for myself."

"I expected nothing else." Bolverkr tipped his face away, and Silme could see the edge of a bitter smile. "Did Allerum and Taziar tell you they killed a manifestation of Chaos?"

"A dragon." Silme felt the queasiness return. "Yes."

"Not just a dragon. The dragon that killed Geirmagnus and nearly all the original Dragonrank mages." Bolverkr seized Silme's hand. "A dragon composed of enough Chaos to balance the resurrection of a god and a sorceress of your power."

Unnerved by the direction Bolverkr's explanation was taking, Silme jerked her hand free. "They told me. What of it?"

Bolverkr accepted her rebuff without comment. His hand hovered, as if uncertain where to go, then it dropped to his knee. "You and I know Chaos is a force, not a being. The only way to destroy chaos is to slay its living host: a man or a god. Dragons are manifestations of raw chaos, not living beings. When Allerum and Taziar killed the dragon, they dispersed that chaos. Dispersed it, Silme, not destroyed it. And the natural bent of such energy, whether of Order or Chaos, is to find itself a master."

Horror swept through Silme, chipping away the confidence she had known since childhood. "You?" Though unnecessary, the question came naturally to Silme's lips. Bolverkr's life aura gave the answer, still so grand as to obscure hers like a shuttered lantern in full sunlight.

"The one man alive since the conception of magic. A logical choice, I think."

Silme doubted Chaos had the ability to reason. *Still, even mindless things seem drawn to survival. Few other hosts could have lived through the transference of that much energy.* She dodged that line of thought, embarrassed curiosity could usurp concern for Larson and Taziar. "Allerum never meant you any harm. He had no idea the Chaos-force would seek you out and no way to know it would kill people. You can't condemn a man for ignorance."

"Why not?" Bolverkr waved his hands in agitation. "The laws do. Imagine if a foreigner killed and robbed a tavernmaster in Cullinsberg. It wouldn't matter to the baron that this was acceptable behavior in the foreigner's kingdom. The murderer would be sentenced and hanged as quickly as any citizen.'' His voice assumed the practical monotone of a lord passing judgment. "The ignorant should not, must not meddle with the fabric of our world. Allerum and Taziar plunge willingly into impossible tasks *without bothering to consider the consequences*. For their crimes, any regime would condemn them to death.''

"No.'' Silme felt as if something had tightened around her chest. "Have you lost all mercy? Allerum and Taziar would never harm innocents on purpose. Even the strictest king would give them another chance.''

"Another chance to destroy the world?'' Bolverkr dismissed Silme's argument, his tone underscoring the ridiculousness of her claim. "Don't let love blind you to reality.''

"Nor should anger and grief blind you!''

Bolverkr's manner went cautious. "Well taken. Neither of us is in a position to judge. However, should we leave the question for our peers, I have no doubt their verdict would be, "Guilty,'' and the execution just. Are you equally certain about your assertion?''

Silme's fingers twined in the fabric of Bolverkr's cloak. She pictured her fellows at the Dragonrank school, recalled the thick aura of arrogance and intolerance that seemed to accompany power. *Bolverkr is right. My peers would condemn Allerum.* A breeze creased the valley between her breasts, and she tugged the cloak impatiently to close the gap between its edges. *And for that, my peers are fools.* Aware she could not convince Bolverkr with this line of reasoning, Silme changed tactics. "Why?''

Bolverkr blinked. He turned his head to meet Silme's gaze. "Didn't I just tell you?''

"I mean,'' Silme started, gaining confidence, "why are you telling me this? I helped to kill Loki. I was the reason Allerum and Taziar fought the dragon.''

"Yes.'' Bolverkr fidgeted.

Sensing his discomfort, Silme plunged ahead. "And?''

Bolerkr folded his fingers together, their skin smooth, elastic, and well preserved despite his age. He hesitated, as if considering options, then sighed, apparently choosing candor. "When I first saw you, I believed I would have to kill you. And I was prepared to do it."

The pronouncement came as no surprise to Silme. Bolverkr's uneasiness gave her the upper hand, and she savored the moment of control. "But something changed that?"

Bolverkr swung around to face Silme directly. Again, he reached for her hand. When Silme shrank from his touch, he did not press the matter further. "People fear what they do not understand. I came to Wilsberg to escape the whispers, the fawning, the isolation. I traveled south to an area where the existence of sorcerers is attributed to legend, to a farm village where even legend might not pierce. I found acceptance. My friendships seemed genuine until necessity forced me to use magic and the townsfolk realized they aged while I did not appear to grow older. They let me stay, whether from familiarity or dread I don't know. And, over time, their grandchildren learned to care as deeply for me as I did for them. But though I fathered many of them and the babies of many others, there was always an awe in their love which kept me distant. They showed the caring of children for a hero rather than the shared love of partners or friends."

Many platitudes came to Silme's mind, but, having no interest in soothing Bolverkr, she kept them to herself. She had a reasonable idea where Bolverkr was heading, and it bothered her. Still, the topic had off-balanced him so she stuck with it rigidly. "You seem to think I have a solution to your problem."

He squirmed with a restlessness that seemed more appropriate to a courting youth than a two-hundred-year-old sorcerer with skills comparable to a god's. "Silme, you're the most powerful woman in existence. You can understand the pain of people staring while they decide whether to run in fear or try to kill you for the fame. You're driven by the same interest, the same need to create, analyze, and experience. I don't frighten you because you know the source of my ability. It makes sense to you. It's concrete and finite, within the realm of your knowledge and experience.'' He added belatedly, ''You're also quite beautiful.''

The compliment was familiar to Silme, the sincerity in Bolverkr's voice less so. She chose the direct approach, hoping to push him further off guard. ''Are you trying to say you've fallen in love with me?''

''Does that surprise you?''

I would think Bolverkr would have learned the difference between romance and childish infatuation. Silme buried the thought beneath the need to win a game whose prize might include the lives of herself, her baby, and her friends. The explanation came to her in a rush. *Everything Bolverkr knows of me comes from Allerum's perceptions, love-smoothed, my shortcomings overlooked or dismissed. Bolverkr believed he gathered information, but he obtained much more. The strength of Allerum's affection influenced him in a way words never could.* Silme realized she had hesitated too long to hide her startlement. ''Of course, I'm surprised. We've never met before.''

''It seems like I've known you for a long time.''

No doubt. Uncertain how to address the comment, Silme said nothing aloud. Bolverkr reached for her hands. This time, in an effort to gain his trust, she let him clench her hands between his long, delicate fingers.

Gradually, a feeling of peace settled over Silme, so comforting she did not recognize it as alien. Her aura seemed to swell, lending her a strength beyond anything she had known before. The still life of Harriman's memory, frozen in time, spread before her, every detail solid as reality. More than just aware of her surroundings, she became a part of them. The ruddy glow of the setting sun bore no relation to the dried and spangled blood of the corpses. It seemed as though the spectrum of color had widened to admit a million shades between the ones she knew.

''Silme.'' Bolverkr's voice seemed a distant distraction. ''I want you to marry me.''

''What?'' Silme stiffened, the word startled from her before she could think. She embraced the heightened sense of awareness, followed every crease of Bolverkr's face to his pale eyes.

Bolverkr's hold tightened. "You can keep the baby. I'll raise it as my own. Only Allerum and Taziar have to die."

No one has to die. Silme glanced beyond the sorcerer to the milk-white aura dwarfing its owner like a soap bubble around a grain of sand. Envy spiraled through her from a source she could not place, and the unfamiliarity of the emotion jolted her back to reality. She tore her hands from Bolverkr's grasp and sprang to her feet. "What did you do to me?"

Bolverkr smiled, indicating his aura with wide sweeps of his arms. "Be calm. I didn't hurt you. Look, there's more than enough life force here for two, and I'm willing to share. I gave you a taste, and already I can tell you want more." He offered his hands. "Here, complete the channel. Open your mind barriers and take as much as you want."

A taste. Chaos. The pleasure Silme had experienced went sour. *The stuff of life, but also the force of destruction.* She knew those who served Chaos, god and man, became whimsical, ruinous, evil. It had always seemed a cruel trick of nature to tie power with spite, to assure that every man endowed with life was also endowed with evil. *This power Bolverkr offers comes from a source external to me. If I can grasp it before it bonds with my own life force, I might be able to tap it without risking the baby.* The whisper of Chaos Bolverkr had shared was gone, leaving Silme with a hunger she could not deny. The Chaos promised a paradise, but she also knew it would claim a price. *If I fail to control it, I will become a slave to it. But without it I have no hope of fighting Bolverkr.* Silme closed her eyes, drawing on inner resolve. Slowly, she knelt and reached for Bolverkr's hands.

CHAPTER 12:

Shadows of Doubt

Our doubts are traitors,
And make us lose the good we oft might win,
By fearing to attempt.

—William Shakespeare
Measure for Measure

Silme folded her legs beneath her, her fingers resting lightly on Bolverkr's outstretched hands despite the crushing tenderness of his grip. Fear and anticipation wound her nerves into tight coils. She wrestled to lower her mind barriers, aware she would need them open to seize the first thin whisper of Chaos that touched her. *Catch it, tap it, and transport.* The words swirled through her mind like a chant. She lowered her head. Hair spilled into her face, and she peered through the golden curtain at the grass spears around her knees. But her mind barriers resisted her efforts; her tension kept them locked closed reflexively.

Frustration heightened every irritation. Silme flung back the obscuring mane of hair, and viciously shook aside each strand tickling her forehead. She became aware of tiny itches over every part of her body, and the inability to claim her hands fueled her annoyance. Again, she struggled against her own defenses, but the more violent the fight, the harder they opposed her.

"Ready?" Bolverkr asked.

"Not yet," Silme snapped back. A light sheen of sweat appeared on her forehead. She called upon the meditation techniques of the Dragonrank, imagining a meadow warmed by summer sun. Stems bowed and rattled in the breeze, while sparrows darted playfully between them.

The scene brought an inner warmth. And while she savored the manufactured peace of her illusion, Chaos stole, unnoticed, through the contact. As Silme built details into the picture, the earliest threads of Chaos seeped in, merged with the substance of her life aura, and magnified her serenity. The weeds muted to the hollow fronds of wheat, tufted with stiff strands of silk and deep, amber seeds. The meadow became a village striped with dirt pathways. Suffused with calm, Silme idly wondered at its immensity. Never before had she achieved such harmony. Pleasure seemed to encompass her, its source lost and lacking a physical center.

The mind barriers. Silme let her imagination lapse, but the bliss remained, strong and comforting within her. Her mental defenses responded, sliding downward a crack. Encouraged, she widened the gap.

Chaos struck with heightened force, collapsing the barrier completely. A rational thought flashed through Silme's mind. *I'm tricked! While I fought my own defenses, Chaos had already bonded.* Then the idea was buried beneath a thunderous avalanche of power. Morality fled before the attack. The imagined scene returned. But, where Silme had constructed waving fields of grain, Chaos showed her the reality of a village in shambles, a wild mix of destruction and death. It twisted revulsion to elation, pity to glee, and laughter rang in Silme's ears.

Savage with anger, Silme's sense of self rose to battle the intruder. But Chaos surrounded her inner being, and her sensibilities fled like shadow before rising flames. Silme saw fires grasping for the heavens, red and golden and glorious. That the blaze ate cities seemed unimportant. They challenged the gods themselves and offered the strength and power of their defiance to Silme.

"No!" Silme's cry seemed to come from elsewhere; it lost meaning before it left her throat. As if from a great abyss, her inner self rebelled, a mouse pinned beneath a lion's paw. It roused memories of Larson wordlessly embracing her while her tears left damp patches on his tunic. But Chaos intervened, stripping emotion as completely as in Harriman's damaged thoughts. Silme gasped, surrendering to the blissful oblivion it offered. Each mighty promise left Silme greedy for the next. Now Chaos no longer needed to come to her; she pursued it. She shuddered. Her grip went murderously tight, and her fingernails burrowed into Bolverkr's flesh.

Bolverkr cried out in pain and surprise. He jerked back instinctively and tore partially free. In the moment of weakness his actions created, Silme's morality launched its attack. *Don't let it have you! Look what it's done to Bolverkr. He claims Allerum and Taziar deserve to die, yet his cruelty goes far beyond simply executing enemies. No amount of power is worth inflicting torture on the guilty or the innocent.*

Chaos responded with a howling whirlwind of fury. It battered Silme's sense of self, pounding it into a darkened corner of awareness. Her sensibilities died to a spark, but that one snippet of consciousness made its final stand. *Got to rid myself of this Chaos long enough to think.* Though crushed and bruised by a force far more powerful than herself, Silme deflected the energy in the only way she knew how. The world clouded to sapphire blue as she channeled all thought to the rankstone clamped between the claws of her dragonstaff.

Designed to store life aura and attuned to Silme, the stone accepted the energy she fed it, brightening as the power gorged it. She felt the gemstone pulse, bloated with Chaos, as her sense of self seeped slowly back into control. *Got to get away from here. How? I can't transport.* She deflected another wave of Chaos.

Power torrented into the stone. Still in Harriman's study, the sapphire quivered, loaded with more energy than its creator had ever intended. Pain engulfed Silme's senses, stretching and pounding from within her, driving her to the rim of unconsciousness. She struggled to retain awareness, unwilling to surrender to Chaos, feeling sanity slip away as darkness crushed in. Another pulse of Chaos ripped through her and crashed into the shuddering facets of the sapphire.

Suddenly, agony splashed Silme's vision in a flash of blinding light. The rankstone exploded, showering fragments through Harriman's study, a blue spray of sapphire chips rattling from the walls and ceiling. Silme screamed, instinctively tearing free of the contact. All sensation fled her, the anguish dulling to an empty ache. She sank to the ground, exhausted, feeling as cold and shattered as her stone. Then, a thought penetrated her muddled senses. *The Chaos I channeled to my rankstone is free, not dead. It has to go somewhere.* Realization mobilized her. *Not somewhere, to someone.* Her vision slid slowly back into focus and Bolverkr's grizzled face, blank with horror, filled her gaze. *Bolverkr, of course! And I'm right in its path!* She floundered to her feet.

Desperately, Bolverkr raised an arm to cast a transport, his other hand groping for Silme.

Slowed by fatigue, Silme felt his fingers close about the torn fabric of her dress. "No!" she screamed. *Chaos will follow Bolverkr. I can't handle the power. If he takes me with him, it'll destroy me and the baby.* She lurched. Cloth tore. She staggered free of his grasp, tripped and sprawled to the dirt.

A storm of Chaos howled toward them.

Bolverkr shouted in frustration and fear. As he transported to the shelter of his fortress, his magic knifed power through Harriman's mind. The Chaos-force blinked out as quickly, trailing a suffocating wake of ozone.

Silme choked. Lungs burning, she clung to her life energy and dove for the only sanctuary she knew.

Al Larson crouched at Taziar's back, his gaze locked on four cocked crossbows. "Fire!" The guard's shout sounded thin as smoke beneath the scrambling of Taziar's friends through the window. The bolts sailed over the heads of five kneeling swordsmen. Larson swung as he dodged. One shaft whisked through the air where his chest had been. His blade deflected the other. The bolt snapped, its pieces clattering along the corridor. Suddenly, Gaelinar's throwing rocks at him during training seemed worth the bruises.

Fridurik gasped in pain. Larson glanced to his left. The redhead clasped a bloody hole in his thigh where one of the bolts had penetrated. As the crossbowmen reloaded, two of the swordsmen charged Larson and Fridurik. Though concerned for his companion, Larson was forced to tend to his own defense. As the guardsman rushed down on him, sword swiping for his neck, Larson dropped to one knee. His upstroke sliced open the sentry's abdomen. He shouldered the man aside in time to see Fridurik lock swords with the guardsman's companion. Fridurik's injury made him clumsy. The guard's knee crashed into the thief's gut. Fridurik doubled over, and the guard struck for his unshielded back.

Larson lunged. His blade sheared through the guard's chest, but the guard's blow landed, too. Both men collapsed, and Larson found himself facing four loaded crossbows alone.

Larson distributed his weight evenly, trying to judge the paths of the bolts in the instant before their release. *Compared with bullets, arrows crawl, and eleventh century bolts move even slower.* Larson gathered solace from the flash of thought. The bolts whipped free. He tensed to dodge. Before he could move, something foreign crashed into his mind with a suddenness that jarred loose a scream. Pained beyond recognition of danger, he caught at his head. The edged steel heads of bolts bit through his left arm and calf, drawing another scream. His sword dropped to the floor.

Larson staggered backward into Taziar. "Allerum!" The Climber broke Larson's fall, though their collision drove him, breathless, to the edge of the window. Dizzied and pain-maddened, Larson could not fathom why Taziar seized him by the hair and jerked him over. The pain of the maneuver seemed a minor annoyance compared with the agony in his skull, and its significance was lost on Larson. But the sensation of falling was not. Wind sang around him as he ripped through air. His composure cracked, his shocked howl vividly betraying fear.

Larson's back hit the moat with a stinging slap. Water smothered him. Dazed and aching, he clawed for the surface. His fingers struck something solid. He grabbed for it, but his frenzied strokes churned it deeper. As the pain in his head died to an ache, sense filtered back into his consciousness. *My god, I'm drowning Shadow.*

Quickly, Larson disentangled from Taziar. His head broke the surface, and he gasped air deep into his lungs. A moment later, Taziar appeared, choking and sputtering, beside him.

"Shit," Larson said. The curse seemed so weak in the wake of near death, that, despite pain, he could not keep himself from laughing in hysteria.

Apparently, Taziar did not find the humor in the scene. He clapped a damp hand over Larson's lips, stifling his laughter. "It's day, and the night sentries will have gone to sleep. But we still have to get by the gate guards." Taziar released his grip and swam toward the far bank with long, steady strokes.

More guards. Larson groaned, following with an ungainly sidestroke that allowed his injured arm and leg to drag. *All this, and it's still not over.* He stared at the wake of blood trailing him through the murky water. His wounds made his limbs ache worse than anything he had known since a college football player put him through a weight training workout in junior high. Then, the ache of tortured muscles had forced him to spend the following morning in bed. He watched Taziar pull himself to shore, shivering as the chill air touched his sodden clothes and skin. *I may not be able to walk, let alone battle through more guards.*

The pain in Larson's head had faded, leaving a foreign presence huddled in a corner of his awareness. It confused him. In the past, when sorcerers and gods had penetrated his thoughts, they had done so without causing him pain. *Except one.* Larson recalled a stroll through a forest in southern Norway when someone or something had entered his thoughts with a violence that left his head throbbing. *Right after it happened, I started recalling sailboating on Cedar Lake, details of the past, and Taziar's stories of Cullinsberg.* Larson reached for the brittle grasses overhanging the bank. *Apparently, the pain comes when the sorcerer breaks in on me at warp speed.* Larson crawled from the water, for the first time sorry his elf form made him impervious to cold. The discomfort might have numbed or, at least, drawn attention from the agony of his crossbow wounds. *Still, despite its desperate entrance, the presence in my mind doesn't appear to be trying to hurt me . . . yet.* It lay unmoving. Larson had discovered he could muster only one form of mental defense against intruders: trapping them in his mind. Quietly, he built a wall around the interloper. *Too much to do now. I'll deal with it later.* Larson ripped strips from the hem of his cloak to serve as bandages.

"Here. Let me do that." Taziar offered his hands to help Larson to his feet. Fearing for his injuries, Larson passed the cloth but waved his friend away. Instead, he clambered to his feet, stiffly guarding the torn, clenched muscles of his arm and calf. With nearly all his weight shifted to the right, he managed to stand.

Taziar knelt. His skilled fingers seemed to fly as he tightened a pressure dressing over the scarlet-smeared hole in Larson's breeks, then rose and tied another on the elf's arm.

The pain of walking proved tolerable if Larson used a pronounced limp. "Now what?" he whispered.

Taziar glanced around hurriedly. "It'll take time for the surviving sentries to get word of our prison break from the tower to the gate guards." He tapped his fingers on his knee as he considered. "I have an idea. Allerum, when you and Silme came to speak with the baron, how many guards stood at the gate?"

Larson considered. "Two. The gates were open, and a lot of people milled around the grounds."

"The holiday will keep the peasants away." Taziar traced some object through the fabric of his hip pocket. "Get everyone together." He pointed vaguely at the trees, benches, and gardens of the baron's courtyard, and Larson noticed the dripping prisoners crouched behind various plants and ornaments. "Lead them behind that clump of bushes." Taziar made an arching motion to indicate a huge copse of grape and berry vines toward the front of the keep. "Quietly," he warned. "When I yell, have everyone run through the gate. Tell them to scatter around the city. We'll meet at the back door of the whorehouse.''

Before Larson could question further, Taziar trotted off, rounding the opposite side of the keep. With a shrug of resignation, Larson approached the hiding prisoners. Locating Shylar, he repeated the plan, and, with her help, herded the others behind the brambles. Through a break in the vines, he watched the guards, standing stiff and solemn before the opened gates. Behind them, the drawbridge overpassed the moat. Larson saw no sign of Taziar, but he knew it would take time for the Climber to cover ground.

Clouds formed a thin, pewter layer over the morning sky, and the day smelled of damp. Larson studied his companions. Of the six survivors, only Shylar and the violet-eyed thief, Asril, appeared alert enough to run. The mad dash from the cells, the descent, and the swim across the moat had taxed the others to the limits of any vitality remaining after the guards' tortures. Most trembled in the breezes, naked or clothed in soaking tatters. Though fully clad in her dress, Shylar kept her arms wrapped to her chest, her lips blue from cold. Odwulf shivered so hard, his teeth chattered.

Without a weapon, Larson felt as bare as his companions. Aside from Shylar, the other five prisoners clutched swords taken from the dead prison sentries, their blades half-raised or dragging in the dirt. Seeing a chance to arm himself, Larson removed his cloak and offered it to Odwulf. ''Here. I'll trade for your sword.''

Odwulf looked at the proffered cloak. Though wet, it would certainly offer more protection than uncovered skin, yet Odwulf did not reach for it.

Attributing the thief's hesitation to mistrust, Larson explained. ''I have to get out of here, too. I'm trained to fight. Harriman's holding my pregnant wife prisoner, and I'm going to get her back.'' Speaking the words aloud roused all the anger the need to escape had suppressed. Larson's pain faded before growing desperation.

Odwulf stared at Larson's face, as if to read the thought beyond the emotion. Wordlessly, he handed Larson his sword. Accepting the cloak, he wrapped it tightly over his bruised and sagging shoulders.

Larson slid the sword into the left side of his belt. He peered through the break in the brush just in time to see Taziar race toward the guards, his shout loud and urgent.

"Guards! Quick!" Taziar slid to a halt several yards from the gate and summoned the sentries with frantic waves. The Climber's disheveled appearance made him look even more desperate. "It's an emergency. Over here. We can't be heard."

The guards did not budge. "What's your problem?" one hollered back.

Taziar jabbed an arm into the air. Sunlight struck gold highlights from an object in his fist. Larson gawked, taking several seconds to recognize the medallion the baron had worn in his courtroom. *Now where the hell did Shadow get that?*

Apparently, others recognized the sigil. "I knew Taz leagued with the baron," Waldhram mumbled.

"Don't be a fool," Asril hissed back. "The Shadow Climber could steal teeth from a guard lion."

"Hush," Shylar insisted.

The guards seemed equally impressed. They shifted and exchanged words too softly for Larson to hear.

Taziar's voice went harsh. "I need you." He made a sharp motion with the medallion, allowing the guards to see it was real. "I command you in the baron's name. Get over here. We haven't time to waste."

Caught up in Taziar's exigency, a guard replied with the same rapid speech. "Wait. We don't understand. We can't leave our posts."

"I don't have time to deal with idiots!" Taziar's tone threatened punishment, and even Larson cringed at the Climber's ferocity. "Your incompetence may cost the baron his life."

Taziar's words mobilized the guards. Hesitantly, they approached him, and Larson had to strain to hear the exchange that followed.

Taziar shoved the sigil into a sentry's hand. "Protect this with your lives. It's more important than any of us.

The ultimate fate of Cullinsberg is at stake. You must deliver it to the baron immediately." Taziar shouted. "Now! Go!" He glanced toward the berry copse, raising his voice still further. "RUN!"

Suddenly realizing Taziar's command was intended as much for him as for the guards, Larson rose. "Run!" he repeated. He hobbled toward the gate, the thieves swiftly outdistancing him.

The walls muffled Taziar's words beyond Larson's ability to decipher them. Unwilling to abandon his friend, Larson pressed his back to the wall and waited for the pain of movement to subside. The thieves had darted off so quickly he had not even seen which directions they had taken. *Without Shadow, I might not even find the whorehouse.*

A moment later, Taziar sprinted through the gate, caught sight of Larson, and ground to a halt beside him. He yanked at Larson's sleeve. "Are you well? Can you walk?"

Larson studied Taziar's small form, thinking his fragile elf frame looked gigantic in comparison. *And if I can't, will you carry me?* Pain made Larson irritable, but he realized with alarm this was not the time for sarcasm. "Come on." Seizing Taziar's arm, he shared the weight of his injured side with the Climber. Together, they managed an awkward lope across the cleared ground and into the town proper.

As Taziar had predicted, Aga'arin's High Holy Day kept the streets empty. Larson felt as if he ran through a crude, western ghost town. Dodging a guard's patrol, they rounded a cottage, sending an old cart horse skittering and bucking like a colt around its pasture. A faltering sprint through Panogya Street frightened a flock of doves into flight, their wing beats thunderous between the buildings. A few steps farther, a stalking cat lashed its tail in anger at their interference. Oblivious, Larson and Taziar skidded around the corner and found that every escaped prisoner had beaten them to the door.

Astryd pushed through the battered leaders of the underground and embraced Taziar. Loosed from the Climber's support, Larson came down hard on his wounded leg. Gasping, he gripped the wall stones, noticing for the first time that blood soaked the bandages.

Astryd explained quickly. "I transported back here to warn Mat-hilde. She called up as many loyal men as she could in such a short time. We think we have enough to fight off any of Harriman's followers who try to get up the stairs." Her tone went apologetic as she addressed Taziar. "It was difficult enough convincing them the prisoners would be freed. We couldn't tell them about you."

"That's all right." Astryd's cloak muffled Taziar's reply. "So long as the leaders don't attack me, I doubt any of the others will."

The sensitive tone of Taziar's words made it clear that he was lying to comfort Astryd, but a more urgent matter pushed aside all of Larson's concern for the Climber. "Silme," he managed through his pain.

"Trapped upstairs." Astryd let go of Taziar. "After two transports, I didn't dare try to confront Harriman and his berserks alone."

Rage snapped Larson's control. The thought of Harriman touching Silme made him crazy with hatred. He ripped the sword from its sheath so abruptly, the leaders skittered from his path. "Let's go!"

"Wait!" Taziar dodged beneath Larson's blade. "You can't take Harriman and his berserks by yourself. You'll need my help, at least. Someone give me a weapon." He reached out a hand.

No one responded.

Larson knew even the leaders still did not trust Taziar. Every second Silme remained in Harriman's hands tore at Larson's sensibilities, and he could not spare the time convincing them of Taziar's innocence might take. "I don't need your help! You fight like a girl." He shoved past. "Get the hell out of my way."

Astryd gave a light rap on the door, and it swung open. Without hesitation, Larson charged through the gap into a sparse crowd of prostitutes and armed men. He raised his sword, prepared to fight anyone who challenged him.

Behind him, Astryd and Shylar warned the crowd. "Stand aside! He's with us!"

To Larson's relief, the people scampered from his path, leaving him a clear trail through another heavy door, across the kitchen, to the stairway. Larson hurtled up the wooden steps to the landing, and only a few scattered footfalls followed him. His hatred for Harriman grew beyond all boundaries. This close, a fortress could not keep him from championing Silme, and outrage inspired adrenaline that masked his pain.

Larson pounded down the hallway. Only one door was closed. Catching the knob, he wrenched and kicked. The panel flew open. Larson caught a glimpse of a single figure, hunched on the bed. Against the walls, on either side of a corner, the berserks crouched. They started to their feet as Larson raced forward and struck with an animal cry of rage.

Larson's blade caught Halden across the ear and cleaved halfway through his head. The berserk fell dead before he realized his danger. Skereye leaped to his feet, catching Larson's sword arm with his left hand. His right slammed into Larson's chin. The berserk's fingernails raked Larson's face, and the force of the blow sprawled him over backward. Still buried in Halden's skull, the sword was wrenched from Larson's grip. Larson crashed to the floor, pain flashing along his spine.

Skereye dove on Larson. A huge arm snaked around Larson's neck. Larson reacted with the training of his high school wrestling coach. *Got to get off my back.* Seizing Skereye's elbow, Larson drew up his knees and dropped his chest. Skereye barrel-rolled over Larson's shoulder. His choke hold twisted free, and Larson spun away.

The fall had reopened Larson's wounds. Blood drenched the bandages, seeping through the frayed arrow holes in his britches and shirt and trickling into his boot. He fought to stand, but his injured leg buckled. He slid back to the ground for another effort as Skereye gained his feet.

Desperate, Larson gritted his teeth, forcing himself beyond pain. His head buzzed as he clambered up. Through blurred vision, he saw Taziar rush Skereye's back, watched in horror as the berserk turned to meet the attack. Skereye hit Taziar's right wrist hard enough to send the dagger skittering across the floorboards. An uppercut caught Taziar in the chin, hurling him into the air. He struck the wall and slid, awkwardly, to the floor. Skereye whirled to face Larson. The berserk's sword whisked free of its sheath as he charged.

Larson cursed. Taziar's offensive had gained Larson the time he needed to stand yet might have cost the little thief his life. Larson wanted to watch for some sign of movement from his friend, but he was forced to tend the more immediate danger of Skereye's sword. The blade whipped for Larson's head. Larson ducked and back-stepped. The stroke whistled over his head, the backcut inches before his face. Dizziness crushed in on Larson, and he realized he needed to change tactics before dodging sword blows drove him to exhaustion.

This time, Skereye slammed a downstroke for Larson's head. Twisting, Larson blocked the sword at its hilt. The impact hammered his left arm to the shoulder, further tearing his wound. Blood ran freely. He screamed in anguish, completing his defense purely from habit. His right fist jolted into Skereye's face.

Pain had sapped Larson's anger, but it fueled Skereye's. His muscled arms shook with fury, and he lunged for Larson with redoubled vigor. Now, Skereye kept his off-hand before him as if to seize Larson and hold him in place for the sword stroke. The first grab fell short. The sword sliced air, gashing the fingers Larson threw up in defense.

Dizzied by blood loss and pain, Larson retreated blindly. He locked his gaze on Skereye's leading hand. Skereye swept forward. Larson caught Skereye's wrist and wrenched it in a drag that spun the berserk toward him. Larson's open right hand slammed Skereye's hilt hard enough to break the berserk's thumb. The sword thumped to the floor.

Larson staggered, too dazed to veer aside. Skereye bellowed in rage. His arms encircled Larson's chest and tensed, crushing. Larson's breath broke, dashed from his lungs. He shuddered, gasping for air, but managed to inhale only a whistling trickle. He felt his consciousness slipping. Panicked, Larson struggled. His fists pounded Skereye's back. His knee slammed into the berserk's groin. But pain only angered Skereye more. His grip tightened convulsively. Ribs snapped, the sound sharp beneath the ringing in Larson's ears. Bone stabbed Larson's lungs. A growing numbness dulled the pain. Unconsciousness beckoned, promising respite from the agony of his injuries, and Larson had to force his thoughts to the fight. *He's got his balance forward now. Use it!* Larson slid his right leg forward, pushing against Skereye, then let his injured leg collapse beneath him.

Skereye's weight and pressure took them both down. Larson had intended to curl and let Skereye roll over his head, but the injuries made Larson clumsy. He landed flat on his back, Skereye atop him. A deep breath filled his lungs but jabbed agony through his chest. Again, Larson worked to his stomach, wrestling mechanically. Skereye clung, driving his fist repeatedly into the back of Larson's head. A sharp twist knocked Skereye to his back and tore Larson from the hold. He staggered to his feet and tensed to run, his only thought for escape.

Skereye sprang to his feet. Larson's retreat gained the berserk the opportunity to scoop his fallen sword from the floor.

"Allerum!" Astryd screamed in warning.

Larson spun as the blade sped for his head. He blocked, catching Skereye's sword hand in both of his own. Aware he could not hope to overpower the berserk, Larson used the leverage of his entire body against Skereye's grip. He stepped to Skereye's side, pivoted with his arms circling over his head, and leaned back toward the berserk. The maneuver whipped the sword to Skereye's back, his arms raised clumsily above his head. And, suddenly, Larson had control of the sword in his left hand, his right still locked to the berserk's wrist. Larson sliced, the blade skimming across Skereye's gut. Larson sprang aside.

Larson naturally passed the hilt to his right hand, certain the blow he'd just dealt was fatal. The incision in Skereye's abdomen gaped open, spilling blood, and pink loops of intestine poked through. Yet, somehow, Skereye remained

standing. He stared at the wound, threw back his head in a
howl that echoed through the hallway, and charged Larson
like an angered bull. Shocked and sickened, Larson scarcely
had time to react. He swung the sword for Skereye's neck.
The blade slashed flesh and through bone, neatly decapitat-
ing Skereye. And this time the berserk collapsed.

It's over. The realization clouded Larson's mind, freeing him from the desperation that had allowed him to
fight beyond his endurance. He sank to the floor beside
the corpse, feeling no pain. Far below him, the battle
between Shylar's faithful masses and Harriman's strong-
arm men faded to indecipherable noise. Larson's body
had gone numb. He could feel Taziar tugging at his calf
as the Climber wrapped another pressure bandage. But
the efforts seemed remote, a distant glimpse of someone
else's leg. *I'm going to die now.* The thought came,
unaccompanied by emotion. Larson closed his eyes, surrendering to an inner peace.

Something shook Larson's shoulders. Serenity fled before a nagging tingle of pain, and the tiny measure of
strength that touched him seemed foreign. He opened his
lids, met Astryd's eyes, the color of faded jeans, her whites
marred by crisscrossing lines of red. "Silme," she said.

The single word lanced concern through Larson. He
rolled to his hands and knees, the movement ripping his
arm from Taziar's grip. Seizing Larson's wrist, Taziar
finished his bandage. "Will he . . ." Taziar started, but
an unseen gesture from Astryd silenced him.

"Silme," Astryd repeated. "Where's Silme?"

Silme. Larson picked up the urgency of Astryd's question. His gaze swung to the bed. Harriman sat, watching
Larson with dull, disinterested eyes. Asril's blade hovered at the nobleman's throat. "Silme." Larson staggered toward Harriman but managed only to sag to his
knees at the bedside, one hand looped over the coverlet.
"Where's Silme?" Though hoarse and tremulous, his
tone conveyed threat.

Harriman blinked in silence. His eyes rolled downward
to stare at Larson.

"Where . . . is . . . Silme?" Larson wanted to hit

Harriman, to beat the answer from him. But he had to satisfy himself with imagining the blow.

Harriman's voice emerged as broken as Larson's own. "Bolverkr has her. Ripped from my mind."

The explanation made no sense to Larson. He let the words swirl through his thoughts, trying to concentrate on each individual syllable.

Astryd pressed. "Bolverkr's your mast . . ." She amended. "A sorcerer?"

Larson guessed that Astryd received some confirmation from Harriman because she abandoned her inquiry and sat, cross-legged, on the floor. Harriman quivered as she searched his thoughts. A moment later, Astryd leaped to her feet. "They're gone from his mind," she said sorrowfully. "Someone used magic. I still find traces of it. Silme could be anywhere."

Larson struggled for awareness. Deep inside, he knew he held an answer, but he could not quite grasp the question. *Sorcerer. Mind. Ripped.* Abruptly, everything fell together. "Astryd. I think I may know where Bolverkr is."

Astryd whirled toward Larson.

Painfully, word by word, Larson described the presence that had assailed his mind in the seventh-story tower of the baron's keep. "I think it's still there."

Gently, Astryd knelt at Larson's side. She stroked his hair, brushing tangled strands from his face. Stripped of sensation, Larson could not feel Astryd's touch nor the caring she intended to convey. "Allerum, I don't think you trapped Bolverkr, but I do believe we may have found Silme. With your permission, I'm going to enter your mind and check."

Anything for Silme. Larson nodded his consent, but Astryd braced her hand against his head to stop the movement.

"I want you to understand what you're agreeing to. It could be a trap, It may not be Silme. If I encounter Bolverkr, he'll certainly kill us both."

Death no longer frightened Larson. "Try."

This time, it was Taziar who looked stricken.

CHAPTER 13:

Shadowed Corners of the Mind

If you love your friends, you must hate the enemies
who seek to destroy them.

—Captain Taziar Medakan, senior

Trusting Asril and Taziar to control Harriman, Astryd
thrust her consciousness into Larson's mind. She entered
a world as gray as tarnished silver. Dull and mostly spent,
her life aura supplied no illumination. Eyes squinted, she
stumbled through patterns of thought, tripped over a stray
loop and crashed into a tangled tapestry of memory. Astryd winced, awaiting the inevitable wild flashes of reaction.

But Larson's mind lay still as a sea becalmed. Astryd
disentangled, glad her clumsiness had not cost him the
pain of sins or fears remembered. Abruptly, she realized
his lack of response could only stem from the severity of
his injuries, and relief gave way to a sorrow that warred
with guilt. *Maybe if I'd used magic in the prison, I might
have spared Allerum some of that beating.* She reviewed
her reasoning, picking her way deeper into Larson's
mind. *Weakened by two transports, I doubt I could have
cast any spell strong enough to influence the fight. And I
was so certain rescuing Silme would require magic, I
didn't dare waste it.*

Astryd caught a glimpse of a faint glow in the distance
and steered toward it. Despite her rationalization, she
still felt responsible for Larson's infirmity. *I tried to heal
him.* The memory surfaced. She had channeled most of
her remaining life energy into a spell to mend his injuries, but that had scarcely gained him the strength to

open his eyes and verbally challenge Harriman. *It wasn't enough. And, now, I'm afraid Allerum is going to die.* A lump filled her throat and tears burned her eyes. She banished them with resolve. *If I'm not careful now, we'll both die.*

As Astryd approached, the illumination assumed the shape of walls, paper thin and translucent, unlike the unyielding steel of natural, mental barriers. The radiance shone from beyond them. Tentatively, Astryd extended a finger and poked Larson's defenses. The substance yielded to her touch, fine as silk, then crumbled to dust. Light blazed through, its source a hovering speck.

Astryd sprang back in surprise. This went beyond the realm of her experience. The shimmering fragment seemed harmless, easily dismissed if not for the overwhelming gloom of Larson's mind. "Silme?" Astryd tried.

"Allerum?" The reply touched Astryd's ears, more like a presence than a sound. Despite the strangeness of its sending, the voice belonged, unmistakably, to Silme.

Astryd exhaled in relief, and only then realized she had been holding her breath. "Astryd," she corrected. "Silme, I don't understand. Are you here or not?"

"It's a probe," Silme explained. "A thought extension of me."

Astryd shook her head to indicate ignorance.

Apparently, Silme misinterpreted Astryd's silence. "Astryd, are you still there?" The odd form of communication relayed Silme's concern as well as her words.

"You can't see me?"

"No. Through a probe I can only read Allerum's current concentration and send or receive mental messages. Nothing more."

Many questions came to Astryd's mind, but she knew most could wait. For now, she needed to know how to bring Silme back to the whorehouse. "You can't leave with me?"

"No." Sorrow touched Silme's reply. "Unlike you, my actual presence is elsewhere. I would need to use a transport escape."

Astryd considered. Realizing Silme could not read her silences, she explained, "I'm thinking." Unable to suppress curiosity, she questioned. "While you were here, why didn't you communicate with Allerum? It would have saved us all grief wondering where to look for you."

"I tried. He walled me in. Usually, he can't detect probes, but I was desperate. I brought all my life energy with me and the baby's. I think I hit Allerum too fast and hard."

"Walled you in?" Astryd stared at the scattered powder remaining from Larson's conjured barriers. "That thing you call a wall fell apart when I touched it."

"A probe has no physical form," Silme reminded.

Larson's mind dimmed as he slipped farther from awareness. *If Allerum dies, I'll lose contact with Silme.* A more desperate thought gripped her. *I'm in his mind. If he dies, I go with him. And Silme, too.* Aware Silme could not know about Larson's injuries, Astryd tried to keep alarm from her voice. "Silme, how do we get to you? Where do we find you?"

Apparently, Astryd's distress trickled through, because Silme's reply betrayed suspicion. "Is something wrong?"

"Yes." Astryd did not want to burden Silme with additional concerns. If nothing else, urgency would increase the cost in life energy of any spell she might need to cast. "You're in trouble, and I want to help. How do we get to you?"

"You can't. Bolverkr created an isolated location in Harriman's memories and transported me to it. I'm displaced in space and time. You can't transport somewhere you've never seen. Even if you could, you would have no way to get me out." The dejection that slipped through Silme's contact unnerved Astryd. She had never known Silme to surrender to a dilemma. "I'll just have to cast a transport of my own."

Raw fear edged Astryd's voice. "That would kill the baby!"

"What choice do I have?" Silme's grief and desperation wafted clearly to Astryd. "I've given this baby every chance I can, but it apparently wasn't meant to be born.

Allerum and I will just have to make another. It might be fun.'' Silme quipped, but the probe betrayed her attempt at humor as false bravado.

Allerum. Terror crushed in on Astryd, and she had to fight for every breath. *By the time Silme returns, that unborn baby may be the only thing left of the man she loves. I can't let her destroy it.* A million possible replies came to Astryd at once, but she forced herself to remain unspeaking until she had full control over her emotions. ''Silme,'' she said with admirable composure, ''we'll find another way.''

''What?'' Silme said with surprise, rather than as a challenge.

Larson's mind went black as he faded into unconsciousness. Astryd stiffened, and desperation jarred loose a memory of her own. The conversation had occurred only a day earlier, but it seemed like months ago. ''Silme, I have an idea! Do you remember when we tried to figure out why a Dragonrank mage would want to kill Taziar, and we talked about spell mergers?''

''Vaguely.'' Silme sounded guarded. ''What are you thinking?''

Astryd was excited now. ''Could you tap my life energy through your probe?''

A pause followed. Though short, it seemed interminable to Astryd. ''Possibly,'' Silme said. ''I've never tried before. You'd have to be at full strength for me to risk it.''

Astryd cringed. The transports and Allerum's healing had tapped her so low she did not hold enough power to transport herself. *But Silme must use less life force than I do for a transport. I have enough for her, I think.*

Silme continued. ''There's no way for me to feel how much life energy you have nor for you to guess how much I might tap. Once I start the spell, it'll claim as much life force as it needs. If I tap you to nothing, you'll die as surely as if you miscalculated yourself.''

Astryd realized that, soon enough, all three of them might die. She had moments to free Silme and less time to make her decision. Urgency made her curt. "I know that."

"Your life is more important to me than any unborn baby. Even my own."

Astryd hesitated. She could not afford to tell Silme about Larson; nervous energy would increase the amount of life force needed for any spell, and Astryd had little enough to spare. *The decision is mine alone.* "I'm at full strength." The lie came with surprising ease. "Tap as much as you need, and come to Harriman's bedroom."

"Astryd . . . ?" Silme started.

"Just do it!" Astryd snapped, aware they could not waste time for platitudes or good-byes. "Please," she softened the command as if in afterthought.

To Astryd's relief, Silme fell silent.

A moment later, Astryd's strength drained from her, and her awareness plunged into nothingness.

Bolverkr awakened pinned beneath the shattered remnants of a fortress turret. Bruises hammered and throbbed through his body. He tensed to shift, but the blocks and chips of stone held him in place. Agony flashed along his spine, and he gritted his teeth against the pain. He sank back into place, his ragged, gray aura flickering over the granite, like a living thing.

Bolverkr had long ago drained his own life force battling the very Chaos that kept feeding him the energy to continue a fight he could never hope to win. The cycle had seemed like endless nightmare to Bolverkr. Unwilling to surrender, he had had no choice but to draw on Chaos to battle Chaos until his citadel toppled into ruin, taking his consciousness and his identity with it. Then, the Chaos-force had done its job, battering the last of Bolverkr's sense of self into oblivion, destroying even the deepest bindings of morality, leaving only a great and ancient intellect to direct its evil.

Now, Bolverkr channeled energy to himself, directing it into a spell that sent boulders sliding down his person and tumbling down the hilltop. Gingerly, aching, he rose to a sitting position, tapping a shred of Chaos to counter the pain of every injury. Chunks of stone, wood, and fabric littered the hilltop. A few jagged columns of wall clung stubbornly to existence, devoid of their protecting magics, the last remains of Bolverkr's mighty fortress.

Not again! No sorrow accompanied Bolverkr's thought, only a savage, crimson fury that sapped life force like a vortex. He sprang to his feet, clutching the remains of the Chaos-force to him, feeling the weakness of it and knowing its vast potential would return only with time and rest. A cry strangled in his throat, and he quenched rage with vengeful promises against the man, elf, and woman who had ruined him. *To attack in anger is simply stupid. I'm too weak to deal with them now. I need to rebuild. Then I'll lure them to me, force them to fight on my home ground.*

Bolverkr took a step forward. A triangular fragment of stone turned beneath his foot, and he staggered into a short stretch of wall that rose to the level of his chest. He grabbed it for support. *I want them dead. And I want them to suffer NOW.* Frustration speared through him, and he embraced the structure as tightly as a father would a crying child. *Patience has won more wars than skill.* Another thought wound a crooked smile across his lips. *There is still one thing I can do without endangering myself.*

Gathering a mental probe, Bolverkr thrust for Harriman's mind.

A brilliant starburst of light snapped open the darkness of Harriman's bedroom. Shocked, Asril the Procurer leaped to his feet, the sword at Harriman's throat fumbling from his grip. Astryd collapsed to the floor. Before Taziar Medakan could identify Silme in the dispersing radiance of her magics, a movement caught his eye. Back in Bolverkr's control, Harriman dove for an object on the floor. Dazzled by the pulse of light, it took Taziar several seconds to recognize Harriman's target.

Gaelinar's sword! Taziar made a wild charge for Harriman. The nobleman dodged, left hand supporting the sheath, right clamped to the hilt. Taziar swept past Harriman. Swearing, the Climber whirled and dove. His out-stretched hands slammed into the diplomat's side as Harriman pulled to free the blade. Drawn crookedly, the katana sheared through the wooden scabbard, taking Harriman's fingers with it.

With a scream of pain and outrage, Harriman caught at his mangled hand. Blood-splashed and nearly as shocked as Harriman, Taziar scarcely sprang out of the way before Asril's sword stabbed through the nobleman's chest. Harriman fell dead without a whimper. The katana bounced to the floor and spun toward the bed, stopping a hand's breadth from Larson's limp fingers.

It's almost as if the sword knew Gaelinar wanted Allerum to wield it. Taziar knew Larson was Harriman's likely target and momentum would logically draw the sword in that direction, but the coincidence still seemed eerie. *Just a few months ago, I would have denied the existence of gods and magic, too.* Taziar stifled the thought, aware he was dwelling on nonsense to avoid the reality of Astryd's collapse. Unable to deny it any longer, Taziar approached Silme where she knelt at Astryd's side.

"She lied to me." Silme's tone went beyond anger toward hysteria.

Clutched by sudden terror, Taziar dared not check life signs for himself. "Silme, is Astryd . . . ?"

"Why would she do something this stupid?" Silme raged, ignoring Taziar's unfinished question. "How could she defy her own teacher? Have I taught her nothing?"

"Silme!" Frantic with concern, Taziar gripped Silme's shoulder in both hands. "No lectures. Just tell me if she's . . ." Words failed him. "If she's . . ."

Astryd rolled to her side with a groan of reluctance, as if awakened from deep sleep after a long and arduous day.

"If she's what?" Silme prodded impatiently.

Joy displaced Taziar's distress in a wild rush. Releasing his hold on Silme, he hunched beside her and gave Astryd's ankle an affectionate squeeze. "Will she be all right?"

"This time," Silme said, and Taziar recognized the

same merciless attention to technique that Gaelinar had always displayed. "Next reckless act of stupidity the Fates might not prove so kind. I'm going to have to take her back to glass-rank lessons."

Taziar smoothed Astryd's rumpled skirt, amused by Silme's anger. "I don't know what Astryd did, and we haven't the time to discuss it yet. But I have no doubt you would have done the same for her." He borrowed Larson's odd mixture of English and Norwegian. "Like one philosopher said, 'Buddies do for each other.'"

Silme's sharp gasp of horror warned Taziar his comment had been callous. He looked up as Silme scrambled to Larson's side, apparently just noticing his limp form half-sprawled across the side of Harriman's bed.

Taziar waited while Silme searched furiously for a pulse. Even from a distance, he could see Larson breathing with the strange, seesaw chest motions his broken ribs allowed. "Silme, did you incapacitate this Bolverkr in some way?"

Silme tucked her hands beneath Larson's armpits and inclined her head toward his legs. "Not exactly. Why?"

Taziar trotted over to help. "Do you think he'll follow you here?" He grasped Larson's ankles.

Together, Taziar and Silme hoisted Larson into Harriman's bed. The elf lolled, unresponsive even to the pain of movement. Silme yanked at the coverlet. Though tears brimmed in her eyes, she kept enough presence to answer Taziar's query completely and without faltering. "Not likely. Right now, he has his own problems to deal with." She jerked the coverlet free of Larson's weight, then spread it neatly over him. "Besides, Bolverkr made a mistake. He opened me a channel to his own power. I tapped it once, and I can do so again." Her gaze never left Larson, and she stroked his arm through the blanket as gently as she would a newborn kitten. "Bolverkr will have to spend some time second-guessing me and plotting strategy. A person as old as he is learns patience. He won't attack a group as dangerous as us in a hurry."

Behind Silme, Asril made a gesture to indicate he was leaving. Reminded of other responsibilities, Taziar stayed

him with a raised hand. "Silme, do whatever you can for
Allerum. He'll need more comforting than I can supply." He smiled, trying to downplay the severity of Larson's condition. "Maybe you can slip into his brain and
remind the *jerk* we need him." Taziar headed toward the
door, and Asril met him halfway. "Asril and I will let
the others downstairs know what's happened here."

Taziar and Asril trotted down the corridor. At the top
of the staircase, an unruly clamor of conversation wafted
to them. Men clogged the base of the stairwell and the
area just inside the front door. The prostitutes clustered
around Shylar on the benches and chairs of the holding
area. Taziar saw no sign of Harriman's strong-arm men,
but splashes of blood on walls and some of the men's
clothing made it clear the matter had been dispatched.
The other rescued prisoners were nowhere in sight; apparently they had gone to some sanctuary to rest and
recover.

The discussions died to a buzz as Taziar and Asril descended. The crowd pressed forward. Taziar paused on
the last step and announced, "Harriman and his berserks
are dead."

Shouts of joy emanated from the women. The men took
the news in silence. Suddenly, a hand seized Taziar's arm
and ripped him from the step. Taziar stumbled into the
masses. Someone gave him a violent shove, and another
set of fingers crushed his opposite forearm. He found
himself staring into a snarl of chest hair through the lacing of a linen shirt and followed the shoulders and neck
up to see Gerwalt, an aging street tough. Hemmed in by
a towering forest of men, Taziar's mind raced as he tried
to devise an escape, aware he might die at the hands of
the very men he had come to help. *Astryd warned me
they all still believe I'm the traitor, but I walked right
into them.* He cringed, recalling how he had even confessed to the crime while mobilizing leaders in the baron's dungeon. *What in Karana's hell was I thinking?*

"Good. Don't let the little worm get away." Gerwalt
ordered. The hold on Taziar's arms tightened, pinning
them behind him.

"Hanging's too good for him," someone shouted.

"You can't possibly really believe I . . ." Taziar started, but he stopped, realizing his words were lost beneath the hubbub.

Shylar leaped to a stool. Her voice cut above the noise. "What are you doing? Let Shadow go! He's—"

Gerwalt interrupted, even more commanding. "Listen, you mother of harlots!"

Angered gasps erupted from the women. Some of the men shifted nervously, and the grip on Taziar eased slightly.

Gerwalt continued inciting. "You've had a soft spot in your heart for this little weasel the whole time. He might have confused you and deceived you, but I'm smart enough to see through his lies. I'm not going to let you let us make the same mistake again." His gesture encompassed everyone in the whorehouse.

Taziar had never seen Shylar so furious. Her fists clutched whitely at the fabric of her dress, and her words confirmed that she had abandoned all restraint. "You stupid, worthless, arrogant bastard!"

Asril sprang from the stairs, brushing aside men like furniture. At Gerwalt's side, he stopped, adopting an indisputable fighting pose, his weight spread evenly, his hand prominent on his sword hilt. He spoke in a low growl, but in the tense hush that fell over the room his threat emerged loud enough. "She may have a soft spot in her heart, but you have one in your brain. I don't know who you think you are. I don't know what authority you mistakenly believe you have, and I don't know how much of Harriman's violent idiocy has worn off on you all. First, no one speaks to Shylar that way. And anyone stupid enough to think Taziar is the informant after all that's happened deserves to be hanged himself. Taz freed us from the dungeon after you left us for dead. And do you know why?"

No one hazarded an answer. The grip on Taziar's arms went warm as sweat leeched through the sleeves.

"He did it to help a friend. Do you really think he'd

risk his life and everything he has to help one friend after informing on the others? Just how stupid are you?''

"Taz has confused you, too." Gerwalt went taut, his hand sliding to his own hilt. "I hate Harriman as much as anyone. I'm loyal to the underground and its leaders. The other leaders told me Taz admitted turning them in, and that he helped Harriman take control."

"Gerwalt, you're an idiot." The crowd fidgeted, the buzz of their exchanges soft beneath Asril's insult. "None of the other leaders really feels that way. Do you see any of them here clamoring for Taziar's blood? The only two prisoners here now are me and Shylar, and both of us are calling you stupid. Consider this a friendly warning. Before I let you do anything to Taziar, I'll slit your ugly throat."

The group thinned as men slipped quietly beyond sword range. Gerwalt went defensive, his tone losing some of its brash confidence. "Asril, why are you bullying me?"

"Because you're dangerous."

"*I'm* dangerous?" Gerwalt glanced about the room, belittling Asril's comment. "Taz is the traitor."

Asril's sword left its sheath, as soundless and quick as a springing cat. "Taz is not a traitor. He's honest and loyal to his friends, exactly the kind of person we need to keep the underground alive. You're swayed by every slick-talking animal with enough connections to back up his lies. You act without knowledge. You're dangerous. If there's any threat to us here, it's you, not him."

Guiltily, the hands fell away from Taziar's arms. Gerwalt's gaze jumped from man to man, seeking support. Apparently finding none, he moved his hands away from his sword to indicate surrender. When Asril lowered his blade, Gerwalt whirled and ran for the door. Mercifully, everyone stood aside and let him leave.

Shylar hopped to the floor, the flush fading from her cheeks, but her voice still tense with annoyance. "Nicely spoken, Asril. You had me worried back there in the prison. You sounded as bad there as this idiot here." She pointed at the door slamming closed behind Gerwalt.

Asril sheathed his weapon mechanically. "Stupidity

strikes the best of us. But the way Taziar and Allerum stuck together convinced me. They were both willing to fight and die for each other. Someone who treats his friends that way doesn't change.'' He slapped Taziar across the back. The force drove the Climber forward a step. ''It took me a while, but I remembered how good a liar Taz was.''

''Thanks,'' Taziar said sarcastically. He stared at Asril, as impressed by the street fighter's loyalty as Asril was by his. ''Just to satisfy my curiosity, tell me. Would you really have killed Gerwalt for me?''

Asril whipped a knife from his pocket and picked idly at his thumbnail. ''I guess we'll never find out.''

EPILOGUE

Shadows blurred and spun through Al Larson's world. He fought for clarity of mind and met sharp, unfocused pain. His thoughts swam through darkness, pinned by the same lead weight that held his body in place. He tried to roll, but his limbs would not respond. His breaths were rapid and shallow against the agony jabbing his lungs.

Gradually, Larson's senses returned. First came touch, and he realized he lay on a bed. *A hospital?* The indecipherable roar of conversation touched his ears, completing the picture. A childhood memory rose, a remote recollection of awakening amid a sea of white coats and strange faces, the odor of chemicals harsh in his nostrils. *Mom? Dad!* Larson attempted to scream, but not even a whisper of sound emerged. A different recollection floated, unanchored through Larson's consciousness, a female voice, thick with grief, speaking words that made no sense to him then or now: "I've done all I can to stabilize him until my life energy returns, but it's not enough. The only thing that can save him now is his own stubborn force of will."

Other memories descended upon Larson now, the smells of excrement, gasoline and death, muzzle flashes and the scream of jets. *The war. My god, I was injured in the war!* Larson remembered a desperate charge into the waiting AK-47s of a Viet Cong patrol. *Jesus Christ! Don't tell me some gung ho surgeon sewed the pieces back together.*

Alarmed by what he might find, Larson gathered enough strength to wrench his eyes open. The pale glow of a lantern blinded him after the dark depths of his unconsciousness; its light revealed a group of people sitting on the floor in a circle as ragged and imperfect as a young child's drawing. Slowly, Larson's vision adjusted, and he identified them. Astryd, Silme, and Shylar kept their backs to him. Taziar's position gave him a sideways view of the bed. Only Asril faced Larson directly. The violet-eyed thief was picking at a splinter in the floorboards, and no one seemed to notice Larson had awakened.

Larson allowed his lids to sink closed, and, finally, Shylar's words became clear to him. ". . . never in any danger from the guards in the prison. You can't believe how much respect my position commands. Harriman may have had the higher ups' ears, but I had their privates. And where men are concerned, the latter is more important."

A wave of polite laughter followed Shylar's pronouncement.

Astryd pressed further. "But if you hold so much power, how did Harriman get you arrested?"

"Even more power and connections. Harriman was the bastard of the duke as well as a competent diplomat. He'd had dealings with the baron for decades, and he learned how to arrange things so people always felt they got the best of any bargain. Once he wrested control of the girls from me, he had everything. But it's not going to happen again. I don't think it could."

Larson recognized Taziar's voice. "What about you, Asril? Shylar's probably safe, but the guards will double patrols looking for you and the others."

Larson opened his eyes in time to see Asril shrug. "It wouldn't be the first time we've gone into hiding." He threw the question back to Taziar. "What about you? Are you staying?" He added hastily. "You know your friends are welcome, too."

Shylar nodded in silent agreement.

Taziar shook his head. "Much as I'd like to, no. We still have a fight to face. Harriman was only a pawn. Our real enemy is a sorcerer willing to destroy people and things to hurt me."

Hopelessness touched Larson. The voices dulled, and darkness clotted his vision.

Asril's reply was shrill. "Are you telling me this person almost got *me* hanged because he was mad at *you.*" He did not wait for affirmation. "Taz, forget what I said about hiding. I'm going to kill the bastard!"

"No." Silme's voice lulled Larson. Pain faded, replaced by a comforting void, and he slowly began to give himself over to the darkness. "Asril, you don't understand. We're not going against some farmer. Bolverkr has power you can't begin to understand. We have no choice except to oppose him, but it may prove impossible . . ."

Taziar glanced toward the bed. Larson let his eyes sag fully closed, but not before he saw the Climber make an abrupt gesture that silenced Silme. "We'd welcome your sword arm, Asril, but we don't need it. Of course, Bolverkr's a challenge. Everything's impossible until someone accomplishes it. They said no one could escape the baron's dungeon, but I've done it. Twice. And I'm just a little thief who *fights like a girl. A jerk. A creep. A swimmer who drowns in his own damned city!*"

Taziar's shout cut through the buzzing in Larson's skull. He anchored his senses on Taziar's words.

Taziar leaped to his feet. "Allerum killed a Dragonrank Master after the finest swordsman in the world failed. As if that wasn't enough, he went on to slay a god in the same afternoon. With Allerum on our side, we can't lose. In fact, Asril, maybe you should join Bolverkr. He's the one who needs help!"

Larson fought aside the numbness clutching at his senses. A whisper of vitality returned, awakening the agony he had tried to escape. But now, Larson savored the pain and the life that accompanied it. He struggled to one elbow, his eyes open and alert. "We'll kick Bolverkr's ass!"

"What?" Taziar asked in confusion. Every gaze spun toward the bed.

Larson managed a shaky smile. "Never mind," he said.

The Fortress of Eternity

ANDREW WHITMORE

AVON BOOKS ◆ NEW YORK

THE FORTRESS OF ETERNITY is an original publication of Avon
Books. This work has never before appeared in book form. This work is
a novel. Any similarity to actual persons or events is purely coincidental.

AVON BOOKS
A division of
The Hearst Corporation
105 Madison Avenue
New York, New York 10016

Copyright © 1990 by Andrew Whitmore
Front cover illustration by Jean Targete
Published by arrangement with the author
Library of Congress Catalog Card Number: 90-93163
ISBN: 0-380-75744-3

First Avon Books Printing: November 1990

AVON TRADEMARK REG. U.S. PAT. OFF. AND IN OTHER COUNTRIES, MARCA
REGISTRADA, HECHO EN U.S.A.

Printed in the U.S.A.

RA   10 9 8 7 6 5 4 3 2 1

BOOK I

Bring me my Bow of burning gold:
Bring me my arrows of desire:
Bring me my Spear: O clouds, unfold!
Bring me my Chariot of fire.

—William Blake

1

CHAPTER ONE

◆

Fortune & Men's Eyes

FOR ONE WHO REMEMBERED Talingmar, with its tall, dreaming spires and crystal minarets, the towers here did not impress. Thin and raddled, they jutted above the shadow-infested streets like the masts of foundering ships, as if a flotilla of baroque galleons had somehow stranded itself on the thick, estuarine mud and been left to rot.

"Julkrease the Golden" a poet had once called it, but he'd either been describing some other city entirely or proven himself an even greater liar than the rest of his profession. Long ago, perhaps, it may indeed have been a pearl of great price—the Jewel on the Western Sea—but centuries of decline had taken a heavy toll, and now it sprawled gracelessly along the river, a mere shadow of its former self. Rust clambered over all the metal; its enamelled facades were cracked and pitted like cheap cosmetics plastered on a corpse, accentuating, rather than disguising, the corruption beneath. Many of the private dwellings (built from crude mud bricks rather than enduring stone) had already capitulated to the relentless advance of time and decay, but their occupants lingered on, eking out an existence as best they could among the ruins. Isaf himself had been forced to take up residence in one such hovel: a dismal flophouse abutting the old Pissing Conduit, full of lice and damp and half-starved rats. It had cost him all the copper

3

he had for a scant week's rent, yet a pig would scarcely
have suffered it. But then again, he was a Jenemun, after
all, and they were generally held in far less regard than
mere swine.

Night fell swiftly here. A few tinsmiths were still hard
at work, squatting wearily over their makeshift forges, but
the streets themselves were all but deserted. The souks and
marketplaces that just a few hours before had seethed with
almost pestilent vitality, now lay still and silent, the tents
and trestles and tattered booths having retired, like their
owners, to await the frantic commerce of another day.

Picking his way through Djinn Alley—that narrow, mud-
choked lanesway snaking around the Slave Market where
the augurs and haruspices plied their trade, rooting out
omens from heaps of smoking entrails or the fall of yarrow
stalks—he was suddenly accosted by an old woman clad in
gaudy velveteen rags and flourishing a pack of greasy playing cards in one hand.

"Read your fortune, master?" she wheezed.

Isaf attempted to brush her aside, but she avoided his
arm, hopping around him like some small, crippled ape and
plucking determinedly at his sleeve. "Only a copper, master!" she pleaded. Close up, her breath stank of aniseed
and decay, like the waft from an open sewer. "Only a
copper!"

"Oh, very well," Isaf told her. Against his better judgement, he allowed the woman to usher him towards a garishly
painted shop-front that stood nearby. It wasn't so much an
act of charity on his part as an admission of kinship—
although Isaf would have been the first to deny it. He'd
acquired any number of burdens over the past thirty years
or so, but self-knowledge certainly wasn't one of them.

The fortune-teller evidently shared her apartments with
at least a dozen others. A young woman huddled just inside
the doorway, suckling a scrawny infant at her breast. Further
on, the hallway was thick with bodies. Anonymous, virtually sexless, they slumped against the walls in identical
attitudes of hopelessness and fatigue. Isaf recognized them
at a glance. Poverty, after all, observed no national boundaries, constituting an independent kingdom in its own right;

a vast, shadowy empire which encompassed every slum and shantytown from Eria to Karling-Tor. They were pathetic creatures, already defeated at birth by a life which they would never even begin to understand. Isaf would have pitied them if he dared. Instead, like so many others, he simply contrived to look the other way.

Still clinging tenaciously to his arm, the old woman led him through a beaded curtain into her sanctum.

It was a depressing place. Her meagre personal effects were scattered among the shadows like funerary offerings in some tiny, long-derelict mausoleum: a simple wooden cot; a few threadbare blankets; some dilapidated wicker chairs; and various pieces of aging bric-a-brac which were presumably of some sentimental value to her. She'd even erected a small shrine in one corner, still faithful, it seemed, to the gods who had so persistently betrayed her. Taken together, the entire collection would scarcely have fetched enough to buy her a pair of shoes, but it was all she had—the harvest, no doubt, of lifetime's incessant toil. Compared to Isaf, though, she was remarkably well-off indeed. All he possessed were the clothes he stood up in and a surfeit of memories, most of which he would gladly have done without.

Ignoring the proffered chair—which looked barely strong enough to support its own weight, let alone his not inconsiderable frame—Isaf squatted down opposite the fortune-teller, who was already sitting cross-legged on the floor, methodically shuffling her cards. A scented candle burnt fitfully between them, presumably for effect as there was still ample light filtering down through the broken rafters overhead.

"All right," he said, taking a single copper coin from his purse and pressing it into her hand. Even this modest payment represented a sizable proportion of his worldly wealth. "Let's get on with it, shall we?"

The woman grinned, revealing a desolation of blackened gums. "You are too generous, master," she observed archly, but asked for nothing more.

Lowering her eyes, she began to rock slowly back and forth, crooning to herself in a language that Isaf had never heard before. Some corrupt northern dialect, perhaps, or nonsense phrases of her own devising. One by one, she peeled off the grubby pasteboard cards and set them down before her.

Isaf had seen such decks before. The crudely executed figures, stripped of whatever meaning they may originally have possessed by centuries of pallid imitation, were a familiar divinatory tool throughout the Four Kingdoms, as well as featuring in numerous antique parlour games. Few took them seriously, least of all the cartomancers themselves, whose success usually depended far more on a keen sense of theatre than the accuracy of their predictions.

She began prosaically enough. The first five cards revealed only that he was a stranger in Julkrease—something which any passing beggar could have told at a glance. "A long road stretches before you," she continued, working her way through the deck so rapidly that Isaf was surprised she could differentiate one card from another, let alone gauge their import. "You shall endure much hardship along the way. But there will be love as well. And unexpected alliances. Appearances may be deceptive—make no precipitate judgements. I see confusion, strife, the revival of ancient enmities. And something else—a betrayal, perhaps. The end is hidden from me. Great changes portend. Whether for good or ill, I cannot say. Whatever happens, you will not return unscathed. A shadow falls across my eyes. Nothing is clear."

By now, only a handful of cards were left unturned. She placed these face down on the floor, then she sat back, as if having suddenly decided to conclude the reading then and there.

"Is that all?" Isaf asked, vaguely disappointed. Compared to the shamans of his lost homeland, whose crazed, ecstatic visions had so terrified him as a child, the woman's performance was almost embarrassingly inept. Drunk on their own urine, bleeding from a hundred self-inflicted wounds, they would thrash and foam and wail like souls in torment whenever Balu and Banu were summoned to pronounce judgement on the tribe. The sacred cow-dung fire; the pounding of rawhide drums; the parched air and high, keening voices: all conspired to instill a belief so piercing and invasive that it amounted to a kind of rape, driving even the proudest warriors to their knees in submission. But that had been a long time ago. He'd grown up since then, and soon come to realise that the Twin Gods revered by his folk were simply crude embodiments of sun and sand. All priests, he'd decided, were fools or worse; all oracles false; all prophecy a vain attempt to impose some order on the chaos of existence. Man's destiny was ruled by his blood, not the heavens, and Isaf would still have been what he was even if the most auspicious star imaginable had presided over his birth—a fact which he, in particular, had ample cause to regret.

"Four cards remain," the woman observed, tapping each of them in turn. "Before proceeding further, however, it is customary for an additional offering to be made, thus disposing the Powers more strongly in one's favour." She smiled shrewdly. "Half an obol should be sufficient, I think."

"From what I've heard so far," Isaf told her, "you've already been paid more handsomely than you deserve. Just tell me what you see. I haven't got all night."

The woman shrugged. "As you wish, master. But I make no promises. Fortune rarely smiles on those who withhold just recompense."

The first card depicted a black-haired horseman. "Here lies the Cataphract," she intoned. "Or Chevalier Mal Fet. Victory follows in his train—and great defeats. Your sword alone will decide the issue." Next came a fortress struck by lightning. Two small figures were suspended amidst the ruins: one dark, one fair; like rival chessmen dislodged from some unseen board. "The Fireflaught covers all. That which was lost shall be regained. Much that is now hidden shall be revealed. Beware of striving too mightily, lest you o'er-reach your grasp." The woman's voice was softer now; a hushed, conspiratorial whisper. As she turned the penultimate card, it dropped still further, so that Isaf could scarcely make out what she said. The grisly portrait, however, required little exposition. "Thanatos," she murmured.

"There is death here, woven through with the rest. Death—
and again death."

Isaf smiled. He'd apparently underestimated the woman,
who was, it seemed, able to play her part most convincingly
indeed when she wanted to. One had to admire, for example,
the skill with which she'd manipulated her deck. The
mounted warrior, of course, was obviously intended to represent Isaf himself. With his ornate broadsword and battle-
scarred countenance, the woman must surely have picked
him for a fighter from the very start, and, like the painted
horseman, he too wore his hair long and loose, so that there
was a faint physical resemblance between them as well. The
Reaper had been an apt, if somewhat uninspired choice; but
with the ruined citadel, the old witch had excelled herself,
although doubtless more by accident than design. Not two
months before, in Folcengard, Isaf's world had indeed tumbled down around him, which merely went to prove how
easy it was for sheer coincidence to masquerade as prophecy. No doubt most of the old woman's patrons were quite
incapable of distinguishing between the two.

Her finale was even more impressive.

No sooner had she turned the last card than a frightful
scream escaped her lips, a sound of such raw, inarticulate
horror that even Isaf's scepticism was momentarily shaken.

"Aiiiieeeee!" she wailed, gazing at the card as if it were
some quintessential nightmare, a distillation of all her most
secret fears. "Oh, see! See! He comes! Moving his slow
thighs! The blood-dimmed tide! An agony of flame!" Hurling the card from her, she slumped forward and lay quite
still, mouthing garbled phrases that Isaf couldn't even hear,
let alone hope to understand.

Exactly what had provoked this outburst remained a mystery. Retrieving the card, Isaf found that it bore no markings
at all, apart from a faint decorative border around the edge,
as if the artist responsible had made a start, then put the
work aside and forgotten about it altogether. The woman
had doubtless shuffled it into her deck by mistake, which
perhaps explained why she'd chosen to end the reading in
so abrupt and bizarre a manner. Even she must have quailed

at the thought of attributing any profound significance to a blank slip of pasteboard.

Reluctant to compromise the integrity of her performance, Isaf left the woman to groan and writhe in peace. As a parting gesture, however, he fished a second coin from his purse and placed it beside the stack of cards. No doubt she would be on her feet soon enough once he'd gone—and cursing him, most likely, for not having paid her more.

It was darker now. Scraps of ragged sunlight splashed across the city like a haemorrhage, staining the towers a deep, unhealthy red, so that they resembled bloody spears raised in futile defiance against the coming night. Off towards the harbour, Isaf could just make out one of the nine great bridges that, according to local legend, dated back to the dawn of time itself, when the Four Great Kings had first cast their mountainous shadows across the world and begun contending among themselves for mastery. More imposing by far than any mortal edifice, it glistened above the tidal reaches like a golden bangle on the wrist of some vast, purulent corpse.

Isaf felt a familiar lethargy settle over him. If nothing else, the fortune-teller's antics had enlivened an otherwise dull evening and helped divert his attention from other, more pressing concerns—but for all that he could still read his own future far more clearly than any deck of cards. Unless he found work soon, the press gangs would have him, and he'd been down that road before.

It was not a particularly pleasant one.

ALONG THE CORNICHE, where empty warehouses bulked against the skyline like the cenotaphs of forgotten kings, Isaf came to a small, unsavoury-looking tavern and, for want of anything better to do, shouldered his way inside.

He'd spent the last few hours blundering about the city like a rat in a maze, frustrated at every turn by the same prejudice, suspicion, and contempt that had haunted him all his life. An attempt to enlist in the duke's household guard had proven a complete fiasco. Upon arriving at the Arsenal, he'd been told, in no uncertain terms, that his services were not required. They were only recruiting pikemen, the ser-

geant-at-arms explained, and applicants were required to
furnish their own cuirass and wicker shield. Why didn't Isaf
try the naval compound instead? There were always plenty
of openings for big strong lads like him, and he'd doubtless
feel more comfortable pulling an oar anyway. A similar
reception had awaited him at the various guildhalls he'd
visited, with none of the merchants being prepared to offer
him anything but the most menial employment. Even the
whoremongers had turned him away. Although they didn't
say as much, it was painfully obvious that he would not be
welcome in their establishments. Perhaps they thought a
Jenemun might be bad for business—although, bearing in
mind the fearsome reputation enjoyed by his people, especially here in the South, they were probably more afraid
he would run amok and slaughter everyone in sight.

Having finally exhausted all other avenues of employment, he was now reduced to hawking his sword from tavern
to tavern in the hope of finding a visiting mercenary company willing to take him on. Failing that, of course, he
could always resort to simple thuggery. Although he preferred, whenever possible, to earn a living by lawful means,
he certainly wasn't above breaking the odd head now and
again when the necessity arose. Besides, if the freemen of
Julkrease wanted to pretend that they were harbouring some
half-feral barbarian in their midst, then he might just as well
act like one. They'd soon discover that having an armed
Jenemun on the loose wasn't quite as amusing as they
thought.

Despite its squalid appearance, the tavern had attracted
a sizable crowd. There were hundreds of such places around
the docks, and to Isaf's jaundiced eye, they reflected the
true nature of the city far more accurately than any number
of lofty towers or ancient monuments. The air reeked of
sweat and stale beer. In the greasy torchlight, he could just
make out a raised platform at the far end of the room, where
scantily clad whores paraded themselves in a bid to arouse
some interest among the hordes of drunken sailors jostling
for space at the gaming tables nearby. Apart from a few
dedicated voluptuaries, however, most of those present
seemed rather more intent on bellowing their disgust at each

unfavourable roll of the dice. Others drank, or brawled, or hurled abuse at those entering and leaving the row of curtained alcoves along one wall which allowed the whores to entertain their clients in some degree of privacy.

The uproar subsided for a moment as Isaf entered. He could sense the weight of eyes upon him, the undercurrent of hostility that rippled through the tavern. Some of the bolder patrons sneered or muttered furtively among themselves, but none dared insult him to his face. One glance at Isaf's burly frame—and the heavy broadsword dangling at his side—was probably sufficient to deter even the most insensate barroom brawler. At any other time, he might have deliberately picked a quarrel with one of them just to salve his wounded pride, but he felt strangely enervated tonight, and rather than risk a possible confrontation, quickly retreated to a table half-hidden in the shadows, squandering his last few coppers on a jug of hot spiced wine.

The pot-boy smiled; the whores smiled; but Isaf did not. When all was said and done, he had precious little to smile about.

His encounter with the fortune-teller had been more unsettling that he cared to admit. Ladoc's face haunted him enough as it was, and he certainly hadn't needed some fool of a woman to remind him of just how much he'd lost beneath Folcengard's adamantine walls. Much to his disgust, he found himself envying the crude camaraderie of those around him. They were stupid, brutish men, but through a mere accident of birth, they possessed something which Isaf could never share, no matter how wise or brave or noble he may have been.

Quite simply, they belonged; whereas he, a stranger even among his own kind, most patently did not.

WHITE POWDER MASKED HER FACE, lending it an oddly sepulchral appearance, so that her more ghoulish clients might have imagined themselves to be embracing some painted corpse, or the ghost of a murdered child. Most men, however, never looked beyond the mass of russet curls draped so artfully about her shoulders, or were so smitten by her sparkling green eyes and winsome smile they spent all their time wondering if they had sufficient copper to enjoy her favours, and whether or not she'd see fit to grant them. Unlike the other whores, she didn't need to bare her breasts or mutter suggestively in men's ears to gain their attention. They desired her for what she was (or what they imagined her to be): not exactly virginal, perhaps, but young, and relatively unsullied, which—as one might expect—made the prospect of defiling her all the more exhilarating. Indeed, she sometimes thought that, without her, Hauba would have been forced to close up shop years ago.

This didn't mean that he necessarily treated her any better than the others. She hadn't had a new gown in months, even though her old one was so threadbare in places that it was all she could do to keep her more valuable commodities tucked safely out of sight. It had been one of her favourites, too. The yellow taffeta clashed violently with her hair, thus contributing to the aura of subtly depraved innocence that her clients found so alluring. One side of the skirt fell open to the thigh, which flashed tantalisingly white as she moved; the other clung tightly about her backside, accentuating the delicate curvature of her hips and thighs. For obvious reasons, she wore nothing whatsoever underneath.

A hand groped there now, its owner so drunk with beer and lust that he appeared to have forgotten just what he'd intended to do with it in the first place. She moved her leg *just so*, and the fellow laughed. She laughed as well, although rather more daintily. It was a delicious sound, as mechanical and soft as camel bells.

The man slipped a silver piece down her bosom, where it lodged, cold and hard, between her breasts. Sometimes she thought that it might just as well have been a knife blade sliding into her heart. Reaching down, she plucked it out and nibbled cautiously at one edge before satisfying herself that the man hadn't tried to cheat her. One got all sorts at Hauba's, most of them rogues. There was a faint clink of metal on metal, then the coin was gone to join perhaps a dozen others in a stout metal chest bolted to the floor of her cubicle. Business was brisk tonight, and she must have already accumulated quite a tidy sum—not that she'd ever see it, of course. By the time Hauba had taken his share, there'd scarcely be enough left over to pay for her room and board, let alone any small luxuries such as perfume, or combs, or a pair of enamelled earrings. Although she'd never actually been branded as a slave (at least not physically), that didn't make her any less dependent on the man, and she had little choice but to accept whatever terms he offered her. No matter how hard life may have seemed in the tavern, it was better than fending for herself on the street, especially since Hauba was hardly likely to surrender his prize attraction without a fight. She'd seen what happened to whores who defied their masters, and didn't care to spend the rest of her days as a cripple, or worse. No, in the end, girls like her had to simply swallow their pride and concentrate on the job at hand. It may not have been pleasant work, but she'd have been hard pressed to find anything better—especially here, in this city of pimps, extortionists, and petty thugs, ruled by a coterie of scheming merchants who cared for nothing outside the sharp-ruled columns of their daily ledgers.

Slowly, she hoisted up the folds of her dress and allowed the besotted sailor to press his weight against her. The distant instrument of her body rocked with him, while her voice obliged with the short, soft gasps that, long ago, might once have bespoken pleasure.

Cayla paid scant attention to the proceedings: it was, after all, hardly a novel experience as far as she was concerned. This one, for example, although somewhat dirtier than most, and smelling like a sack of manure, was virtually indistinguishable from the thousands of others who'd sought a brief spasm of pleasure between her thighs, as if this might somehow compensate for the grinding tedium of their own existence. Poor and drunk and stupid, they thronged to Julkrease by the thousands, like flies to a charnel house. Some she saw here every night. Is this what they came to Julkrease for? To sit and watch their lives burn away like so many guttering candles, growling the same tired obscenities she'd heard countless times before, and to which her unspoken answers were always the same? (*No, not particularly; Yes, as a matter of fact, she had*; and *Perhaps, but it'll cost you a good deal extra.*) If so, she almost pitied them—occasionally, that is, when she had any pity to spare.

"Careful does it," she muttered, as the fellow groped frantically for her breasts. "I'm not a bleeding cow, you know."

Glancing through a chink in the curtain, she noticed a tall, dark-haired figure seated nearby, somewhat apart from the others, and apparently quite unmindful of the whore who circled lasciviously around him. The trouble with Looly, of course, was that she had absolutely no subtlety whatsoever. Did she honestly think that wriggling her back-side like that was going to achieve anything? Next thing you knew, she'd probably try straddling the poor outlander's face! Still, Cayla wouldn't have minded trading places with her just now. The stranger was certainly handsome enough, in a wild, uncouth sort of way, and would have made a pleasant change from Cayla's usual clientele.

After what seemed an eternity of poking and probing and laboured breath, her current partner finally grunted to a climax, unloading his seed like a spray of venom into her aching womb.

About time, she thought, her face betraying a momentary shudder of distaste. *I'll have to bathe for a month to rid myself of the stink*!

She spent a few moments mopping herself down with a towel, then carefully straightened her dress. One of the seams had burst again, and there were large, oily stains on the bodice where the sailor had gripped her. Cursing vehemently, if softly, she waited for him to refasten his trousers, then opened the curtains and stepped outside.

Looly was still hovering about the stranger's table, but, no matter what vulgar stratagems she employed, seemed quite unable to capture his attention. Curious as to what he was doing here, and fascinated by his air of brooding introspection, she drifted slowly towards him, signalling to her colleague that he was already taken. It was a lie, of course, but a working girl had to get by any way she could. In any case, the fellow obviously found Looly's exorbitant cleavage and beefy thighs rather less than appealing—as well he might—and it was about time someone else had the opportunity to display her wares.

Cayla negotiated the crowded drinking-hall with practised ease, discreetly fending off the hand that clutched at her and diverting even the most importunate of suitors with a brief giggle of feigned delight. Her eyes, however, remained fixed on the scowling stranger. She'd seen a Jenemun before, of course. Years ago, when she was still a child, one had been paraded through the streets in chains—the sole survivor of a raiding party that had wreaked havoc on the northeastern frontier before finally being hunted down by a battalion of mercenaries hired expressly for the purpose. His head had adorned the city gate for months. Others appeared on the slave-blocks from time to time, but Cayla had only ever glimpsed them from a distance, and they invariably ended up shackled to an oar on some Julkrean galley, being deemed far too intractable for domestic service. By all accounts, they were a rather bloodthirsty lot, given to roasting their captives over slow fires and inflicting the most hideous atrocities on any woman unfortunate enough to fall into their clutches. Cayla, however, doubted that she had much to fear from this one. Apart from his coarse black hair and hooded eyes, he bore little resemblance to the murderous savage that she'd been led to expect. Indeed, compared to those around him, his manners seemed positively genteel, and, no matter how perverse his appetites, she found it hard to believe that he'd seek to indulge them in the midst of a crowded tavern. Besides, she'd more than fulfilled her quota for the night, and a change, so they said, was almost as good as a holiday.

If the Jenemun welcomed her approach, he did an excellent job of disguising the fact. Not once did Cayla see him so much as glance in her direction.

"He's a hard case, that one," Looly muttered, heading back towards the stage. "Try getting down on your hands and knees. By the look of him, he's probably never had a woman any other way."

"Thanks," Cayla said. "But I doubt that'll be necessary. Now, if you'll excuse me—"

Looly shrugged. "Suit yourself. But I still say you're

wasting your time. They like their women big, these Jenemun. I can't see him going for a scrawny little runt like
you."

Cayla ignored the jibe. Treating Looly's remarks with
the contempt that they deserved, she sidled closer to the
Jenemun, seating herself on a corner of the table and dangling her legs enticingly before him, so that one white thigh
peeked out from the folds of her skirt like moonlight
glimpsed through saffron clouds.

The Jenemun finally looked up. Unlike the other patrons,
he appeared relatively sober, having made little impression
on the wine jug before him. Set deep in his craggy, weather-
beaten face, his eyes were as dark and cold as winter shadows. They seemed to look right through her, as if she wasn't
even there.

She smiled alluringly, but to little obvious effect. Perhaps
Looly's advice hadn't been that wide of the mark after all.

"You are melancholy, my lord," she observed sweetly.
"Is there some way, perhaps, that I might be of assistance?"

The Jenemun's face remained set like stone. "I came
here seeking the solace of wine," he muttered, seemingly
to no one in particular, "not the flesh. As you can see"—
he gestured disdainfully at the jug—" "I have more than
sufficient for my purposes."

Cayla bridled at his tone. She was not accustomed to
being dismissed in so peremptory a fashion. "If I had any
pride, my lord," she said haughtily, "I should hardly choose
to be a harlot. You may save your insults for more respon-
sive ears!"

"Yes," he said quietly, looking directly at her for the
first time. "I might at that." He sounded almost wistful.

She ought to have stalked off then, shoulders squared in
defiance, but she didn't. Instead, she leant closer to him,
head tilted inquisitively to one side. "You're a Jenemun,
aren't you?" she said.

Something like a smile moved within the harsh creases
of his face, but, unused to such subtleties, Cayla saw nothing
but scorn.

"That's right," he said. "A Jenemun."

"From Cariaspa?"

His smile broadened. "Obviously."

Cayla blushed, although only her small ears, dangling with rings, showed it.

"I was born in the Malad-Hras," he said. "Just like the rest of my folk."

She gasped, touching one hand to her lips in a gesture of astonishment and admiration. Even she couldn't have said just how much of it was feigned. "But that is such a frightful place!"

The Jenemun shrugged. "No more so than this city of yours. And certainly far less crowded."

"I've heard of sun that burns the skin black," she told him, eyes widening in their painted frames. "Of sand and wind that flay the flesh from your bones. Is the Malad-Hras really as bad as that?"

"It's a hard land, true—although perhaps not so hard as that." His face relaxed into an almost mischievous grin. "After all, the Jenemun live there, and we are neither black nor fleshless. As you can doubtless see for yourself."

"They must be awfully brave."

"Yes, I suppose they are."

She reached down and fondled the heavy muscles bunched beneath his tunic. "And strong," she asked. "Like you?"

He laughed, the sound swelling from his barrel chest, deep and loud. "And strong," he said. "Though perhaps not all as strong as I."

Without warning, he seized the jug and drained it in a single draught, apparently shrugging off his former ill-humour as one might doff a cloak. Reaching out, he took her by the hand and drew her towards him. She resisted playfully, laughing and chiding him, while at the same time nestling cosily into his lap.

"Tell me," he said, glancing round the tavern for a moment, then smiling once more, "I spend my time in rat-holes like this because they're the only places that will have me. What's your excuse?"

CHAPTER TWO

◆

The Theosophic Assassin

POISED THEATRICALLY in the doorway, his wide-brimmed hat tilted to a rakish angle and adorned with a luxuriant blue feather, he surveyed the tavern's occupants with a mixture of disgust and resignation. For all his dandified ways (the wide, scalloped sleeves, the orange hose, the scarlet tunic, and extravagant pantaloons), he seemed undeterred by the crowd of drunken sailors who glared ferociously up from their gaming-boards as he entered, and the long, two-handed sword slung in baldric across his hefty shoulders suggested that he was more than capable of holding his own in even the roughest company. Stroking his beard meditatively he took a pinch of snuff from a delicately ornamented box, then, arranging his features into an expression of arrogant disdain, strode across to where a black-haired giant and a frail, red-headed whore were laughing and embracing at a corner table.

"Excuse me, sir," he said, clearing his throat noisily.

The giant looked up sharply. "Damn you!" he growled. "Can't you see I'm busy?" He studied the intruder carefully, eyes half-hooded. "Who are you, anyway?"

"I might well ask a similar question," the stranger said. He glanced pointedly at the giant's sword. Wrought from some pale, lustrous metal far brighter than mere silver, the pommel was adorned with complex astrological figures and sundry other motifs, similar to those occasionally found on ancient tombs and obelisks. The exact significance of these inscriptions, of course, was difficult to ascertain—there probably wasn't a man alive who could do so much as hazard a guess as to where it was made. Despite its humble leather scabbard, it was hardly the sort of weapon one expected to find in the possession of an itinerant soldier-of-fortune, which perhaps accounted for the stranger's somewhat rueful smile. "That's a mighty fine blade you've got there," he observed archly.

The Jenemun eyed him with obvious suspicion. "So what?" he snapped. "You planning to try and take it off me?" His hand closed menacingly around the hilt, much to the consternation of his whore, who drew a sharp breath and nuzzled even more closely to him.

"Ah," the stranger said. "I imagine that would be rather foolhardy of me, don't you?" Although there was only the faintest trace of mockery in his voice, his eyes glistened with wry humour, as if he were enjoying some private joke at the Jenemun's expense. "It's just—well, I'd rather expected someone else to be carrying that sword, you see. I had a proposition to put to him, but it seems I'll have to revise my plans a little now, won't I?"

The Jenemun frowned. "I've only had it a short time," he said. "I won it."

"Is that so? Good for you. And how long ago was that, if you don't mind me asking?"

"Four months or so—perhaps half a year. Not that it's any of your business. Now, if you're quite finished—"

"Please, do forgive me. I was merely somewhat surprised to discover the blade in your possession, that's all. You see, the man who bore that sword before you—the one I was expecting—was generally conceded to be the greatest warrior in the world. I'm merely curious to know how you happened to get hold of it."

"This man you speak of, was he from Eredrosia?"

"That's right. His name was Ladoc."

The big Jenemun nodded, his black hair following like a storm. "I know. We served together at Folcengard." He looked down a moment, wringing his hands, then murmured, "You're right—he was the best of us. The best of us all."

Puzzled, the girl turned to him and frowned.

"Then perhaps you might care to explain how you come to be bearing his sword?" the stranger asked.

"Why should I?"

"Because I'd like to know."

"I don't see how it's any of your concern."

"Oh, but it is. Very much so, in fact. I believe you said that you won it?"

"If you must know—I killed him!" The Jenemun's face was troubled. His hands bunched into fists, the muscles in his arms standing out like knots in thick rope.

The dandy nodded. "I see. And precisely how did you manage that?" he asked. "Ladoc was a formidable opponent."

"Does it matter?"

"To me, yes. More than you could possibly imagine."

"Very well then. I challenged him. We fought. He died. It's as simple as that."

The woman stroked his face, but the Jenemun's eyes remained downcast. She glared at the stranger, her own eyes as cold as shattered ice. "Satisfied?"

"Yes," he told her. "As a matter of fact, I am." He turned to the Jenemun once more. "And now, my good man . . ."

"I have a name," the giant growled. His words betrayed a black fury hidden somewhere behind the muted lustre of his eyes.

"Do you indeed? Well, that's quite a coincidence, isn't it?"

"Why?"

"Because I, myself, am equally privileged in this respect. Allow me to introduce myself." The stranger bowed, flourishing his hat before him. "Pagadon Alphen Trevayne," he said. "Entirely at your service." Judging by his tone, he'd apparently expected the name to strike a familiar chord, but neither of their faces betrayed the slightest hint of recognition. Doubtless feeling somewhat foolish, he stood up again almost at once. "And whom, may I ask, do I have the pleasure of addressing?"

"Isaf," the Jenemun told him, albeit grudgingly.

"Cayla," the woman added, blushing furiously. Trevayne grinned at her with such open amusement that she quickly looked away.

"I've got a little job for you, Isaf, my friend," Trevayne said. "I'm sure we're going to get along famously together."

"And who says I'm looking for a job?"

Trevayne laughed. It was a broad and surprisingly honest sound. Reaching inside his doublet, he took out a large purse and flung it down on the table.

Squealing with delight, Cayla seized the purse and peered inside. "Oh, Isaf," she said. "There's a fortune here. I've never seen so much gold!"

"Just what am I supposed to do to earn all this?" Isaf asked.

"A deed worthy of your skill, I think."

"And what might that be?"

"Why, my friend, together we shall slay a god."

A COOL AND GLASSY NIGHT had stolen across the city. Overhead, the heavens were strewn with stars, like ornate necklaces glimmering in a jeweller's window, set against a soft, black velvet sky. The moon hung big-bellied above the river, working its peculiar alchemy on the muddied waters beneath and transforming the sluggish flood into a stream of shivering quicksilver.

Three figures wove their way through the darkness, bound together by the nameless, unspoken dependencies of their kind. Towers soared about them like the heroic dreams of some older, better age, a ghostly light weeping from the stone.

Isaf could at least console himself with the knowledge that he'd finally obtained some manner of employment, although he would have preferred a less melodramatic paymaster. The fellow's name seemed vaguely familiar, although for the life of him Isaf couldn't think where he'd heard it before. He'd spent most of his time in the North,

avoiding the larger mercenary bands where a man was
judged not so much by his skill at arms as by the elegance
of his dress, and thus there was little likelihood of them
having served together in the past. All these Eredrosians
looked more or less the same to him anyway. Even if their
paths had crossed before, he probably still wouldn't have
recognized the face. Then again, it didn't really matter who
the fellow was—he obviously had far more money than
sense, and, with so much gold at stake, Isaf was prepared
to tolerate any amount of posturing and wilful obfuscation.

If his motives for accepting Trevayne's commission were
fairly transparent, the fact that he'd invited Cayla to come
with him was rather less easy to explain, given that he'd
only just met the girl and knew nothing whatsoever about
her. Or perhaps "invite" was the wrong word. He simply
hadn't actively discouraged her from tagging along—which
amounted to much the same thing in the end, as she obviously wasn't about to look a gift horse in the mouth.
Granted, she was a pretty little thing, but there had to be
more to it than that. With the gold Trevayne had offered
him, he could have bought any woman in the city, and she
was, if anything, a trifle scrawny for his tastes. Perhaps he
simply wanted to show Trevayne that he wasn't a complete
outsider, that he possessed friends and acquaintances just
like everyone else. After all, the fellow had apparently taken
it for granted that some kind of bond existed between the
two, and Isaf was reluctant to dispel the illusion. An alternative explanation—that he actually cared for the child and
desired her company—either didn't occur to him, or was
something he steadfastly refused to contemplate.

Cayla too was deep in thought. Trailing a few steps behind
the Jenemun and peering apprehensively into the darkness,
she had no more idea where they might be headed than Isaf
himself. She rarely strayed far from the dockside, which,
for all its filth and grinding poverty, at least rang to the
sound of human voices rather than the mute, vainglorious
echoes of a long-forgotten past. Even whores didn't particularly care to be reminded of the proud heights from which
their people had fallen, and such thoughts were virtually
inevitable here, where deserted thoroughfares gaped around

her like the entrances to so many vast, desecrated tombs. Rats squabbled in the gutters, performing unwitting parodies of those Julkrean merchants who occasionally gathered there by day to reminisce over what they'd once been. Only a dozen or so buildings betrayed any evidence of human habitation, their windows flickering like corpse-lights in a necropolis of starlit towers and silent, shadow-haunted streets.

Repressing a shudder, she wondered what on earth she was doing roaming about the city at this time of night when there was still so much copper to be had back at the tavern for the price of a smile or a toss of her head. The Jenemun's strangeness must have sapped her wits—why else should she give freely what might otherwise be sold at a handsome profit? Hauba, no doubt, would be furious at her for abandoning her post so early in the evening. Although he sometimes allowed girls to leave the premises with their clients, such excursions were usually arranged well in advance, and only after a sizable down payment had been made. To simply walk out like that, as Cayla had done, was tantamount to mutiny, and was bound to invite immediate retribution. Indeed, if she hadn't left in quite such intimidating company, he'd probably have sent a couple of bravos to fetch her back straight away. Not that it made much difference in the long run, of course. He knew she'd have to return sooner or later—and when she did, there'd be ample opportunity for him to exact his revenge. The very least she could expect was a sound thrashing and a few weeks spent servicing galley slaves down at the dockyard. Hauba, however, had little patience with those who rebelled against his authority, and was just as likely to break both her legs and have her crawl around the tavern after customers. All in all, her future seemed rather bleak—unless, of course, the Jenemun could be persuaded to share his newfound wealth. With a few gold coins in her pocket, it wouldn't really matter whether Hauba forgave her or not. For once, she'd be able to go anywhere—and do anything—that she damned well liked.

Speaking of wealth, exactly what was this Trevayne fellow up to anyway? Carrying on about Isaf's sword like that, then spouting some rubbish about killing a god. He must have been out of his mind. After all, who else but a madman would stroll about the place with a king's ransom stuffed inside his shirt? Or perhaps that was just a front. Perhaps he had much more sinister motives for luring them to this desolate quarter of the city. . . . Isaf's enemies had probably hired him to settle some old score. Any moment now, Trevayne's accomplices would leap out and slaughter the pair of them. She glanced around nervously, but saw only starlight and shadows. Very well, perhaps he simply intended to sell them as slaves. The possibilities were endless. He was obviously hatching some kind of plot—you only had to look at him to see that.

In the circumstances, she'd probably have been better off taking her chances with Hauba, but despite everything, a part of her thrilled at the unknown dangers that might lie ahead. When all was said and done, she had precious little to lose. Even if he did take her back, it would only be a temporary stay of execution. As she grew steadily older and less desirable, the flood of customers would slow to a trickle, until the day finally came when she no longer brought in sufficient trade to earn her keep. And then Hauba—or whoever else might be in charge at the time—would simply throw her out. With nothing to show for her years of service except an aching back and various unmentionable diseases, she'd be forced to scratch a living as best she could, peddling her flesh along Goose Lane for half an obol a throw, and picking the occasional pocket, trapped in a self-perpetuating cycle of poverty and despair that would end with her slumped in a gutter somewhere like all the rest, begging alms from passersby who despised her almost as much as she did herself. No matter what happened this evening, it couldn't be half so painful as the knowledge that, barring some kind of miracle, she would almost certainly spend the greater part of her life regretting that she'd ever been born in the first place.

TREVAYNE WOULD DOUBTLESS have found Cayla's bizarre speculations most amusing. At the moment, however, he was still trying to sort out how this latest development might affect his plans, and took care to maintain a discreet distance between himself and the others, so that he failed to notice the excitement, wariness, and resignation that camped like rival armies amidst the chalk-white pallor of her face.

As if matters weren't complicated enough already, now he had some half-witted Jenemun to deal with as well. Not only that, the stupid bastard goes and brings his woman with him as well. A *woman*, for gods'-sake! What were they supposed to do, cart her to Eria and back in a bloody sedan-chair? It was beginning to look as though King Muck wasn't quite as infallible as he made out, which didn't bode well for the remainder of their expedition. If the fool couldn't even get people's names right, Trevayne shuddered to think what sort of problems they might encounter later on.

Still, Isaf seemed a likely enough sort—shoulders on him the size of bloody pork barrels! Ladoc probably never knew what hit him. By all reports, you'd be safer climbing into a bear pit than facing one of these Jenemun butchers in the ring. Hardly better than cannibals, most of them, although this fellow seemed at least marginally civilized: spoke the Common Tongue well enough, and managed to get about without dragging his knuckles on the ground. Must have been quite an intellectual by their standards. Not that it made much difference whether the brute was housetrained or not, just so long as he did as he was told and refrained from poking holes in the wrong people with that pretty sword of his. A little mindless savagery might even come in useful before this business was over.

Trevayne just hoped things would progress a little more smoothly from here on in, that's all. Otherwise, a certain god he knew might finally get tired of waiting —and then they'd really be in trouble.

Damned if we do, he thought bleakly, recalling a promise that had been made to him once; *and doubly damned if we don't. What sort of bloody choice is that?*

Unfortunately, the answer was all too obvious.

The only one you've got, Pagad, my friend. The only one you've got . . . .

* * *

THEY EVENTUALLY ARRIVED at a mouldering, if ostenta-
tious, tower situated near the old ducal palace; a reminder
of those halcyon days when Julkrease had presided over the
greatest maritime empire the world had ever seen. For centuries, its fleets of scarlet-oared galleons had returned to
port each month laden to the gunwales with silver, gold,
precious stones, ambergris, rubber, exotic spices, tobacco,
aromatic woods, birds-of-paradise, marmosets, ornamental
fish, ivory, jade, opals, pearls, onyx, coral, ebony, fragrant
oils, and countless other treasures long-forgotten save in
ancient books and the vaults of foreign kings. Their de-
scendants now supervised an ever-diminishing trade in
blackamoors and cheap baubles plundered from the Strange-
lands, occasionally preying on a lone merchantman bound
for the more prosperous ports of Angar and Sultice-Charr.
Like all those dwelling at the gutter-end of Time, they
refused to accept that the world had past them by, and still
dreamt of old empires and glories that had faded long before
their great grandsires had been born.

Trevayne ushered them through a doorway adorned with
gargoyles and antic nymphs, then up a staircase to a set of
lavish apartments occupying the topmost level of the tower.
From one set of windows, Isaf could see the river coiled
far below him; others looked out across the harbour, grey
and silent beneath its canopy of autumn stars.

A servant fetched them some wine, but Isaf drank only
sparingly, surveying Trevayne sceptically over the rim of
his cup. There were still a number of questions that needed
answering, and he'd never been one to mistake conviviality
for due respect.

"Doubtless you'd like to know a little more about what
is expected of you," Trevayne said, as if reading his
thoughts—which were not, after all, particularly obscure.

His words were directed at Isaf, but it was Cayla who
answered, her eyes aglow with a childish delight. "I would
never have guessed—" she began, then spread her delicate
hands in a gesture of awe. "All this is yours?"

Trevayne smiled condescendingly across at her, having
already seated himself in a comfortable leather armchair,
his sword propped beside him. The others remained stand-

ing: Isaf by the fire; Cayla towards one corner, her garish dress looking somewhat out of place amidst such luxurious surroundings. "I am a man of hidden depths, my child," he told her. "I dare say there are a great many things about me which you would never suspect—but that is scarcely the point I wish to make."

"What is your point, then?" Isaf demanded gruffly.

"Oh, come now, dear fellow." Trevayne changed the direction of his gaze, but the smile remained. "Let's not pretend that you aren't curious as to the precise nature of your employment."

Isaf hesitated, and Cayla seized the opportunity to discreetly turn her back and examine a particularly elaborate item of silverwork on the mantelpiece nearby.

"Ah," Trevayne said. "But perhaps you think me mad? Is that it?"

It was a purely rhetorical question, of course, but Trevayne leant forward and grinned, as if relishing their obvious discomfort.

"Now I have embarrassed you," he said at last. "Please forgive me."

Isaf shifted his feet uneasily. "You spoke of killing a god, did you not?"

"By which you infer that I am in some way bereft of my senses, eh? You may rest assured, however, that I am perfectly sane—or at least as sane as anyone can be in times such as these. But I must confess to a display of undue melodrama when we met in the tavern. Please accept my sincere apologies—I'm afraid I've always had something of a penchant for the dramatic."

Though there was no mistaking the irony in Trevayne's tone, Isaf relaxed perceptibly.

Trevayne took a sip of wine, then pressed home his advantage. His expression hovered somewhere between the bored and the cynical. "Surely you are at least mildly curious about your employer? For instance, wouldn't you like to know who I am?"

"You've told me your name," Isaf replied shortly. "And I've worked for others knowing less. I'd far prefer you just tell me exactly what I'm supposed to do."

Trevayne sighed. "Ah—a man of action, eh? All right, then, we'll get straight down to business, shall we? Do you happen to know anything about the mountains known as Redflas?"

"I've passed that way once or twice in my journeyings," Isaf told him. "Not much to them, is there?"

"Depends where you look. Have you ever had occasion to travel among the mountains themselves?"

"Only the foothills. The rest is barren anyway."

Trevayne grinned. "Not quite. There is one particular mountain known as Eltzen's Crown, which is something of a landmark to those who dwell thereabouts. Or so I've been told. Beneath it stands Hiern Holding, a kind of fortress. There are, I understand, a number of such holdings scattered throughout the mountains. What matters, however, is that Hiern Holding is ruled by a man named Hawk. All I want of you is to go to the Redflas and fetch this Hawk fellow and accompany him to Eria, where I shall meet you."

"That's all?"

"Yes. At least, it's enough for now."

"And what if Hawk decides not to come?"

Trevayne stroked the ginger stubble on his chin. "My dear man," he said, "I'm sure that you can be most persuasive when the mood strikes you. Just make sure that you get him to Eria in one piece, that's all I ask."

"I'll need time to think things over," Isaf told him. "It's a long way to the Redflas—and even further to Eria."

"By all means," Trevayne said indulgently. "Unfortunately, I will be embarking tomorrow on a little errand of my own. One not entirely dissimilar from yours, to tell the truth. Consider the matter at your leisure, but I shouldn't take *too* long over it if I were you. If this thing is to be done, it must be done quickly."

"Why?"

"There are good reasons, my friend. Perhaps, in time, you will be permitted to know some of them. Until then, your time would be better spent concentrating on more practical concerns. Should you accept my offer, you will be paid twenty times the amount I've already given you— assuming, of course, that you deliver Hawk safely to Eria before the winter solstice. I'll make arrangements for your departure before I leave, but let me again stress that time is of the essence. Even a single day's delay might well prove critical in the end.'' For a moment, Trevayne's voice assumed a harsh, even anxious, tone, then he once again relaxed into a smug, supercilious grin. ''And now,'' he said, hoisting himself to his feet, ''I trust you'll accept my hospitality and make full use of the facilities here while you make up that doubtless excellent mind of yours.''

Isaf shrugged. ''I'll stay the night, anyway, if it's all right with you.''

''Why certainly. And what about the little lady here?''

Cayla smiled sleepily, knuckling away the weariness that lurked in the corners of her eyes. She wasn't used to trekking halfway across the city or enduring tortuous conversations. Nevertheless, her voice came soft and slow, like hot butter from a spoon: ''You are too kind, my lord.''

CHAPTER THREE

❖

Night of Swords

SUNLIGHT PIERCED THE ROOM through frosted panes, scattering across the bright mosaic floor. The bed was large, ornate, and empty, its satin sheets bearing only the shadows of sleeping—two quiet ghosts. Outside, they could hear Julkrease stirring. Carts rumbled through the streets amidst a growing clamour of voices, as if some vast engine were being cranked into life once more, weaving souls and substance into the fabric of another day. Here in the tower, however, the sounds seemed strangely distant and scarcely louder than the wind that bore them.

Cayla sat before a gilded mirror, watching her face dissolve in streams of soapy water. Shorn of its cosmetics, her skin felt as bare and raw as a peeled apple, but looked pretty enough in its fashion. One might almost have mistaken her for some governor's daughter, she looked so prim and proper. Perhaps she had been kidnapped as a child by Julkrean pirates and sold into a life of sin, while her father wept bitterly in his far-off eastern prefecture, burning candles of remembrance for her in the local temple.

She stroked her cheek admiringly. How soft it was, how smooth! (Unlike others she could mention.) And that dimple—why, it was positively angelic! Yes, she still did all right by herself, no question of that.

And this place she found herself in now: a veritable palace

by the look of it. Sitting here, surrounded by brocaded curtains and sumptuous woollen rugs, marvelling at the frescoes and tapestries and bright, lacquered walls, it was easy to imagine herself the queen of all she surveyed, instead of a runaway whore. The servants certainly treated her like royalty. For the first time in her life, she could do as she pleased, eating and drinking to her heart's content, without quibbling over the cost or hoisting up her skirts to foot the bill. It was wonderful. If she were dreaming, then she only prayed that she wouldn't inadvertently pinch herself and wake up to the dreary, everyday world she'd left behind. Dreams like this were hard to come by, and infinitely preferable to reality—it would have been a pity to spoil it.

"THAT SUITS YOU BETTER," Isaf said.

Cayla put aside her comb and looked up. "Do you really think so?" she asked, pulling a face. "I feel quite naked like this."

Isaf laughed. "That's when women are at their best," he said. "Besides, you're no great hand as an artist, and the face you paint hardly does justice to the one you're wearing now."

By now she'd grown accustomed to his somewhat affected, almost laboured compliments. At times, he sounded as if he were parroting sentiments he'd read about somewhere rather than experienced for himself. Still, it was the thought that counted. She blushed pleasantly, rewarding him with the small music of her laughter.

"Are you sure?" she teased, rummaging among the jars of powder and scented oil scattered before her. Although Trevayne appeared to live alone, apart from a few servants, he'd obviously entertained numerous women here in the past. Why there were enough cosmetics stowed in this one dresser alone to supply an entire army of courtesans. "Just a little rouge, perhaps?"

"Certainly not," Isaf told her.

She wrinkled her nose in a play of displeasure. "But I look so terribly pale!"

"Nonsense. A few weeks outdoors will cure that, you mark my words."

However unschooled she may have been in other ways, Cayla was no fool and knew better than to let the Jenemun know just how much she wanted to go with him. Experience had taught her that a little coyness now and then was far more effective than simply throwing oneself at a man's feet like some addle-headed strumpet.

"Why, sir," she murmured, "whatever do you have in mind?"

Isaf laughed. "Twenty sacks of gold, for one thing."

"But we scarcely know each other," Cayla protested.

"What does that matter?"

Cayla looked up. "'Well,'' she said shyly, "what happens when you get tired of me?"

Isaf dismissed the suggestion with a crooked smile. "We Jenemun don't tire easily," he replied smoothly. "As you doubtless learned for yourself last night."

"You know what I mean," Cayla said, blushing even more fetchingly than before. "Besides, there's nothing to say you won't toss me aside when someone prettier comes along."

"Ah," Isaf said, "but no one prettier *could* come along." His smile broadened. "Or, if they do, I promise I won't notice them."

"You'd better not," Cayla warned him. "Otherwise I'll scratch her eyes out. And yours, too."

"So it's all settled, then? You'll come?"

Cayla finally relented—or, rather, allowed Isaf to imagine that she had. "If that's what you really want," she said. Smoothing down the silken nightdress that Trevayne had supplied her with the night before, she stood up and kissed him lightly on the cheek. "How could I possibly refuse such a gracious offer?"

"Excellent!" he said. Next thing she knew, he'd seized her by the waist and was whirling her about in his arms.

"Put me down, you great oaf!" she told him, but he merely laughed and tossed her high into the air, so that for a moment, she feared she might fall. Then his strong brown hands closed around her once more. "Stop it!" she squealed. "You're making my head spin."

"I should hope so," Isaf said. Still smiling, he lowered

her gently to the floor, only just managing to avoid a sharp kick aimed at his ankles.

"Now look what you've done," Cayla said, brushing back her hair and straightening her nightdress, which had ridden up to her hips. "What if one of the servants had come in?"

Isaf shrugged. "Judging by the look of this place, I'm sure they've seen plenty of bare backsides in their time. Although never one as charming as yours, of course." He reached for her again, but she skipped lightly back.

"Well, they're not going to see this one," she said primly. "And neither will you, if you keep this up."

She sat down in front of the mirror and resumed combing her hair, watching it gleam like burnished copper in the warm morning sunlight.

"How far is it?" she said at last. "To these mountains Trevayne was talking about?"

"Far enough," Isaf told her. "At least three weeks by boat and another two or so on horseback. You'll get more than your fair share of sun, don't worry about that."

"Boat?" Cayla asked. "What boat? You said the Redflas were in the East, didn't you?"

"That's right. But it's quickest to sail on down to Port Sembaline, and much less tedious than the overland route."

"My geography is so hopelessly vague," Cayla said. She paused a moment, the comb making pleasant rustling sounds in the silence. "When would we be leaving, do you think?"

"Straightaway, I hope," Isaf said. "High tide ought to be around noon. We should have all our gear ready by then."

"So soon?" Cayla tried to choke back her disappointment, but without success.

"I'd rather not stay round here a moment longer than necessary," Isaf said. "Besides, it's a long trip, and Trevayne made it pretty clear that he wanted us to get started as quickly as possible. We have to be in Eria by mid-winter, remember?"

"It just seems a pity to leave all this behind," Cayla said, glancing around the room and reflecting that, even if Trevayne increased their wages a thousandfold, Isaf and she could never have afforded to live like this. "A taste of the high life never did anyone any harm."

Isaf plainly did not agree. He scowled, regarding the ornate furnishings with obvious distaste. "The sooner we're out of here," he said, "the better. I'd have thought you'd feel the same way."

"You dislike Julkrease then?"

Isaf's scowl deepened. "I loathe the place."

Up until last night, Cayla would have been tempted to agree with him. There was, however, nothing even remotely loathsome about her present surroundings, and she felt that Isaf may have been doing the city an injustice. "That's just how it seems to people like us," she said. "The view's always rather bleak when you're sitting in the gutter." She sighed: a wistful sound that quickly gave way to a laugh. "I doubt Trevayne would find the place quite so unpleasant."

"Of course he doesn't," Isaf said, his voice taking on a harsh, abrasive edge. "Which is all the more reason for you to hate him."

Cayla frowned. "Hate him?" she said. "Why on earth should I do that?"

"Because he has all this, while you have nothing," Isaf told her. "Because his life of luxury is purchased at the cost of your own poverty and squalor. Because for every banquet he holds, a hundred beggars starve. Because we, and all those like us, are his slaves—whether we know it or not."

Isaf sounded genuinely outraged, as though he regarded Trevayne's mere existence as some kind of personal affront, and it occurred to Cayla that they probably had far more in common than either of them cared to admit. She'd seen how the others had looked at him in the tavern, the sniggers and thinly veiled contempt that his presence had evoked among them—a similar reception, no doubt, would have awaited any working girl who strayed into one of the more fashionable bistros around Long Walk and Barbican Square. If anything, his plight was even worse than her own. After all, she was simply one of many, and there were certain parts of the city where she could at least pretend to belong, whereas Isaf had no such respite: no matter where he went, he would remain a Jenemun; feared by some, ridiculed by others, despised by all. In the circumstances, it was hardly surprising he should have wanted to lash out at those who, like Trevayne, served as a constant reminder of everything that he could never be.

"It must be hard sometimes," she said. "Being a Jenemun, I mean."

Isaf looked at her sharply, then shrugged. "Yes," he muttered quietly. "Yes, it is."

Cayla smiled. Her nightgown was a delicate affair, all gossamer and lace. With one easy, fluid movement, she slipped it from her shoulders and stood up, allowing it to gather in a puddle of cool black silk at her feet.

"Come here," she told him.

Isaf did so, almost reverently. As his arms closed around her, Cayla found that, for once, she wasn't thinking about how she might profit from the exchange, but of what she had to give. It made a considerable difference—far more of a difference, in fact, than she would ever have thought possible.

Much later, as they snuggled together beneath the soft satin sheet, she rested her head on his shoulder and murmured drowsily:

"Where you come from—the Malad-Hras or whatever it is. Tell me about it."

THE JENEMUN were not so much inhabitants of the Malad-Hras, as victims of it, shaped by the same crude, elemental forces that stripped topsoil from the sun-blasted plateau and heaped it in great aching dunes for as far as the eye could see. They were an austere folk, fanatically loyal to their kin, contemptuous of strangers, leading a largely nomadic existence as they herded scrawny cattle across the wastes, endlessly searching for water and fresh pastures.

Isaf had never really been one of them. Slavers plundered his tribe while he was still a child, so that what he remembered most vividly of those early years were the squat conical huts flaring like torches and the shrieks of his dying kinsmen, as the cool desert night suddenly erupted with blood and fire. Anyone old enough to raise a fist in defiance had been put to the sword, men and women alike. Only a handful were spared. Yoked together like so many yearling calves, Isaf and the other survivors had been carted off to the flesh-markets at Angar, where Jenemun pups fetched high prices on the block. Once domesticated, a Jenemun would gladly die to protect his master, and they made redoubtable soldiers. At the Battle of Helmsmet, thirty Jenemun mercenaries had reputedly held the field against four hundred blackamoors—and some of them, it was said, even lived to tell the tale.

Eventually, after serving half a dozen masters in as many years, he had found his way to Talingmar, once the hub of a mighty empire, now reduced to a cluster of prismatic towers marooned on the shores of a long-vanished inland sea.

It had been centuries since one of the fabled Philosopher-Kings had sat in judgement among the fluted columns and stark, angular shadows of the Hypostyle Hall. The petty warlords who'd replaced them cared little for the past, aping rites and rituals of a bygone age to disguise their own brutal lust for power. They were ruthless men, well-versed in conspiracy and intrigue—none more so than Lord Vellaghar, Chief Custodian of the Ministry of Antiquities (a meaningless title handed down from some ancient bureaucracy which had ceased to function at least a thousand years before), who, while on a visit to the communal barracks, selected Isaf to fill a vacancy in his elite household guard.

Although only fifteen, he already stood a head taller than any of the other guardsmen and was an accomplished enough warrior to have earnt considerable distinction for himself during a skirmish over the order of precedence at a religious festival. At first, Vellaghar seemed a kindly master, and saw to it that Isaf received the sort of education that only Talingmar could provide. Bajaan, Joimel, Ojak, Levantine, Kolon, Palat-Darr; he studied all the great sages of the past. There, in the Great Library, surrounded by the collected works of ten thousand redoubtable scholars, he'd learnt to think and question and observe. He was, in effect, born there. Up until then, he'd been a lump of raw, unfashioned clay, constantly buffeted by events which he didn't even begin to understand, as innocent and malleable, in his way, as a newborn child. The lucid dialectics of dead philosophers turned him into a man.

He learnt that the sun and sky and stars were not, as he'd originally thought, supernal agencies to be placated or defied, but simply parts of a vast celestial machine whose workings, though complex, were no less amenable to logic than any other. He learnt that the daemons and demiurges venerated in shrines and temples and tabernacles throughout the length and breadth of the Four Kingdoms were, on the whole, mere fabrications, and that the true gods (Annukin, Egim, Paymon, Bahumut, Oriens, and the rest), had perished long ago, their deeds now all but forgotten outside the epic pentameters of Zoab's *Annals of the Kings*. He learnt that the world was a far larger place than ever imagined, contiguous in space and durable in time, and that a man's life was what he made of it, rather than a gift, or curse, from above. But, most of all, he learnt how much there was to learn, and how little of it he would ever know.

He studied hard, spending as much time in the library as his duties allowed, and gradually earning the respect of the tutors assigned to him, most of whom had originally regarded his unquenchable thirst for knowledge with a mixture of amusement and disdain.

Why then, he wondered, did Vellaghar and his entourage always laugh whenever he attempted to discuss Joimel's *Twelve Stages of Being* or the import of Galerkin's *Dialogues*? Why was he constantly displayed to all the visiting dignitaries, as if the quotation of extracts from Kolon's *Phenomenology of Human Virtue* were some kind of mindless parlour game?

Did they think him deaf, blind? Or did they simply not think of him at all?

See, there's that young barbarian that Vellaghar's trained to recite philosophy.

Oh, he's awfully good, isn't he? Just listen to him prattling on about the Great Dichotomies—*you'd almost swear that he understood it, wouldn't you?*

It's all a complete farce, if you want my opinion. That bloodthirsty brute of his jabbering on about the fraternity of humankind! Why, he'd slit Vellaghar's throat as soon as look at him if the bastard thought he could get away with it.

And he did.

But he was older then—almost eighteen—and knew full well that he'd never been anything more than an amusing grotesque, a sport of nature whose antics helped Vellaghar while away the idle hours, like some talking parrot or a performing bear. And he realised just why they'd been laughing at him all this time.

The philosophers of Talingmar had been gentle men, preaching a doctrine of tolerance and moderation. Yet all their well-modulated arguments could not still the murderous rage swelling in his heart.

As one of Vellaghar's most trusted servants, Isaf regularly took his turn watching over the Arbiter as he slept, and was thus in the perfect position to revenge himself on the man. Like the other lords of Talingmar, Vellaghar lived in constant fear of assassination (which tended to be by far the most common means of political advancement among Caucus members), and Isaf derived a certain grim amusement from the knowledge that it was this very fear that would help deliver the man into his hands. All he had to do was wait for his next scheduled tour of duty, dispose of his fellow guardsman, then slip inside and cut Vellaghar's throat from ear to ear, just as a Jenemun shaman might slaughter some prize bullock to celebrate the vernal feast. What would happen after that, he neither knew nor cared.

In point of fact, Isaf found himself posted outside Vellaghar's chamber rather sooner than he'd expected. A mysterious illness had swept the barracks—variously attributed to bad wine or an unusually pestilent batch of whores— leaving the palace garrison drastically undermanned. Watches were halved, those unaffected by the plague being forced to work double shifts in place of their bedridden comrades. Isaf almost laughed out loud when, on reporting for duty one evening, he not only found himself detailed to guard the royal apartments that night, but also discovered that the other rostered sentinel (a giant Strangelander by the name of Torak, who might well have posed a formidable obstacle to his plans) had fallen ill less than half an hour before, leaving Isaf to stand watch alone. It was the perfect opportunity: so perfect, in fact, that one might almost have thought that fate itself was a party to the conspiracy against Vellaghar's life.

Around midnight, when the last of the servants and courtesans had finally stumbled to their beds, and the only sound to be heard was the spluttering of oil lamps in the long, pillared hallways that separated Vellaghar's quarters from the remainder of the palace, Isaf set about claiming his vengeance.

The door, of course, was unbolted, otherwise Vellaghar would have been unable to call for help had some enterprising assassin scaled the outside wall or tunnelled into his chamber from below. Moonlight shafted down from high clerestory windows, scattering like shredded silver across the flagstones. Heart thudding inside his chest like a war drum, Isaf silently drew his sword and advanced towards where Vellaghar slept, as pale and unmoving as a cadaver amidst the luxuriant silken bedding of his divan.

Isaf could easily have finished him then and there; a single sword thrust would have been sufficient. But having come this far, it suddenly seemed important that Vellaghar should see the face of his executioner, rather than simply passing into even deeper slumber without ever knowing how, or why, he died.

"Lord Arbiter?" he murmured, edging closer to the bed. "Wake up. It's me, Isaf."

Vellaghar started at the sound. "What is it?" he demanded. "Am I in danger?"

"Yes," Isaf said. He held his sword low, ready to thrust it up through the coverlets should the need arise. "Yes, you are."

"Where are the others then?" Vellaghar said. He sat up, glancing around the chamber with the calm, unhurried gaze of someone who'd survived longer than most in a world where a single dislocated shadow might presage sudden death. "Shouldn't you rouse the guard?"

"That won't be necessary, your eminence," Isaf told him. "I can handle this myself."

Perhaps Vellaghar noticed the gleam of moonlight on naked steel, or perhaps he was simply being cautious: either way, he moved much too late. Even as he made to snatch the jeweled dagger from beneath his pillow, Isaf's hand was already there to pluck it from his grasp.

"There's no point crying out," Isaf said, tossing the knife aside and pressing his sword hard up against the Arbiter's throat. "No one can hear you. And even if they could, you'd be dead long before they got here."

Vellaghar gave an involuntary shudder as the swordblade caressed his neck, but there was no real fear in his eyes, merely a kind of watchfulness, as if he were already sifting through the options available to him. "I don't know what you hope to gain from this," he said, "but however much they're paying you, it's nothing compared to what I can offer." He smiled, though it must have cost him a considerable effort. "Put down your sword, Isaf. We're both reasonable men; I'm sure we can come to an amicable arrangement."

Isaf shrugged. "Perhaps. But you'd still owe me, my lord. Even if you emptied the treasury three times over, you'd still owe me."

"Owe you?" Vellaghar said. "In what way? If I've somehow—"

"You made a fool of me," Isaf snarled, clasping his anger to him like a lover, and revelling in its embrace. "You treated me as if I were so much dirt beneath your feet. And now you have to pay the price."

As he spoke, he edged his sword fractionally closer, until it drew a few pricks of blood from the Arbiter's wizened flesh, and a small, strangled cry from his lips.

"I'll make it up to you!" Vellaghar spluttered. "I swear! I can make you rich beyond your wildest dreams! Power, honours, women—just say the word, and they're yours!" He was weeping now: no longer the proud patriarch who'd commanded whole legions with the merest wave of a hand, but just another frail, grizzled old man pleading for his life.

"Do you want me to beg, is that it? All right, I'll beg. I'll do anything you say! Anything!"

"It's too late," Isaf told him. "You know that as well as I do. Much, much too late." With his free hand, he jerked back Vellaghar's head so that the throat was fully exposed. "I'm sorry," he murmured. "I truly am. But you stole something from me, and this is the only way I can get it back."

He finished it then, with a short, hacking blow such as butchers use. Vellaghar shuddered for a moment, then slumped back onto the blood-drenched couch.

Looking down at Vellaghar's corpse, Isaf felt neither relief nor satisfaction, but merely a kind of emptiness, as though something inside him had died as well. After all, Vellaghar had been like a father to him in many ways—sometimes indulgent, sometimes austere; rewarding or chastising as the occasion warranted—and even though the man had betrayed him in the end, Isaf couldn't help but feel a certain grief at his passing.

"I'm sorry," he murmured again, whether to himself or the ghost of his fallen master, he couldn't really say. Either way, it was nothing less than the truth.

As he turned to leave, he noticed a faint glint of silver on the bloodstained flagstones beside him. On closer examination, he saw that it was the small bronze mirror that, over the years, had become as much a part of Vellaghar's regalia as his turquoise crown or pearl-encrusted staff. He wore it everywhere, suspended on a fine gold chain around his neck, presumably for sentimental reasons rather than as a formal badge of office, since it didn't figure in any of the gigantic relief carvings of previous Arbiters that Isaf had seen along the Avenue of Kings. It looked like the sort of cheap bauble one might pick up at any village market for a handful of coppers, the surface so crudely ground that Isaf could barely make out his face in it at all.

Although, compared to some apartments that he'd visited, Vellaghar's quarters were relatively spartan, Isaf could easily have stuffed his pockets with enough priceless artifacts to set himself up for life. The jewelled dagger alone must have been worth a king's ransom. He had no intention, however, of allowing his act of retribution to degenerate into mere thievery. Nevertheless, he felt that Vellaghar owed him something and the mirror seemed a fitting memento, not of the man he'd slain, but of the one who, in better days, he had very nearly loved. Slipping it into his pocket, he made his way back out into the corridor and down to the stables. None of the guards thought to question his sudden departure, doubtless assuming that he carried some urgent message, perhaps to the Arbiter's country estate, where his consort, it was said, dwelt in permanent exile, safely removed from the complex factional games that raged throughout the city like a clandestine war, so that wives and loved ones were not only hostages to fortunes, but to mortal enemies as well.

Come dawn, Talingmar had dwindled to a mere speck on the horizon. If a price was ever set on his head, he never heard about it. Most likely, the various claimants to Vellaghar's throne had little desire to unmask the real killer, preferring to blame each other for his death in the hope of enhancing their own positions, and thus Isaf was able to cross the border entirely unmolested. From then on, he was a free man—or, rather, enslaved by no one except himself, which, in the end, proved far and away the most onerous captivity of them all.

For the next ten years, he led a nomadic existence, hiring his sword to whoever had need of it. No matter where he went, however, the memory of Vellaghar's treachery festered within him like an open sore. Quick to take offence at any imagined slight, he moved restlessly from one predatory band to the next; a perpetual outsider shunned by his fellow mercenaries, who feared his black rages almost as much as they despised his ability to read and write.

In despair, he'd even tried returning to the Malad-Hras, only to discover at first hand the truth of Bajaan's famous dictum: it was indeed impossible for a man to step into the same river twice. Isaf's cherished boyhood memories bore little semblance to the realities of life among the burning desert waste. His clan had been decimated by war and disease; those who remained seemed little more than savages. He squabbled constantly with the Elders, arguing that their customs were stupid and cruel, their hallowed taboos merely rank superstition. Menstruation, he'd pointed out, could hardly be considered a crime. Nor did it seem reasonable to assume that droughts could be averted by the occasional sacrifice of burnt meat and offal. None of them had even seen their reflection before, and regarded Isaf's mirror (which he too had taken to wearing around his neck, suspended by a simple leather thong rather than Vellaghar's golden chain) with obvious suspicion. The shaman went so far as to claim that a demon lived in it, although whenever Isaf looked, all he saw were his own increasingly exasperated features.

"You do not understand," they told him. And they were right. Even when he did manage to decipher what they were saying, most of it made no sense to him at all.

Bitter and resentful, he eventually left the plateau and enlisted in the ragtag army being mustered to defend Folcengard's mile-high ramparts from a would-be conqueror and his horde of eastern horsemen. It was there he met Ladoc, a dashing young hero who, despite his tender years, had already carved out a reputation as the most accomplished warrior of the age.

Somehow, despite all their differences, the two had become friends. Ladoc was far too sure of his own abilities to resent Isaf's own physical prowess, and seemed quite indifferent to his Jenemun origins. The two soon became inseparable, drinking and roistering to the early hours, sharing confidences, and deriving unreserved enjoyment from each other's company. For the first time in his life, Isaf was truly happy.

And then they quarrelled.

Inevitably, perhaps, it was over a woman. Not one of the gay, big-breasted whores who paraded in the mess-hall each night and auctioned themselves off to the highest bidder (Ladoc and he had enjoyed any number of these, both singly and in tandem, without the slightest shred of jealousy), but a young, waiflike child captured during a sortie against the barbarian supply-train. The men, exultant over their success, had decided to have a little sport with her. Stripping the girl naked, they'd made her crawl about on her hands

and knees, barking like a dog, while they taunted her with
scraps of food. Then they raped her, all twenty of them,
after having first nailed her hands to a doorpost to ensure
her compliance.

Isaf found the child some hours later, torn and bleeding.
She died in his arms.

Having recently been elevated to the rank of company
commander, he had little difficulty in tracing the men involved and seeing to it that they were soundly flogged. The
move proved an unpopular one. There were grumblings of
discontent among the ranks and, within a matter of hours,
rumours had begun to circulate that the child was a Jenemun;
that Isaf had, in fact, been conducting some kind of personal
vendetta rather than simply trying to retain a certain degree
of discipline among the rabble.

As it happened, most of those who'd been flogged belonged to Ladoc's company. By rights, he ought to have
been consulted before any punishment was meted out, although, as officer-of-the-watch at the time, Isaf was quite
entitled to exercise his discretion if he deemed that immediate action was required. The girl's death had enraged him.
He too had once been a frightened, defenceless slave far
from home. Perhaps he'd acted precipitately, but surely no
great harm had been done?

Great harm had been done.

Next morning, Ladoc stormed into Isaf's quarters completely unannounced, his steely grey eyes alight with a fury
that Isaf had never seen before.

"What's the matter?" he asked. "Has something happened?"

Ladoc glared at him. "Who in hell's name do you think
you are?" he demanded.

"What are you talking about?" Isaf said.

Ladoc was almost trembling with rage. "How dare you
have my boys flogged like that! You've made me the laugh-
ingstock of the entire regiment!"

"Don't be ridiculous," Isaf told him. "They deserved
it. You know that as well as I do."

"Why? Just because they wanted to have a bit of fun

with the little slut? From what I heard, she asked for it anyway.''

"For gods'-sake, man, she was just a child!''

"She was a Jenemun, wasn't she? Everyone knows those bitches are in heat from the moment they can walk.''

Isaf felt as if he'd been knifed in the belly. He stared imploringly up at Ladoc, still hoping to forestall the inevitable. "Please," he said, "don't let's argue about it. You're my friend, and—''

"Friend?'' Ladoc roared with laughter. It was a cruel, entirely merciless sound. "How could a Jenemun savage ever be my friend?''

"Ladoc, don't—''

"Oh, stop snivelling, will you!'' Ladoc told him. "You amused me, that's all. I've had pets before, but never one as fawning or faithful as you!''

The raw wound of Isaf's past suddenly burst open once more. A mindless, unreasoning hatred welled up inside him, swamping the fragile ties of friendship and mutual respect which separate man from beast. Almost without realising it, he lashed out and struck Ladoc a stinging blow on the cheek.

Ladoc smiled, fingering the ugly cut where Isaf's gauntlet had opened his flesh to the bone. Blood oozed down his face like slow, red tears. "Now that, my dear fellow, was a mistake," he said coldly. Peeling off one of his own gauntlets, he flung it at Isaf's feet. "Shall we say sundown, then? Perhaps you can persuade one of the camp dogs to act as your second.''

Isaf said nothing.

Still grinning, Ladoc turned and stalked towards the door. He seemed well-pleased with himself, as if he'd somehow tricked Isaf into showing his true colours. And perhaps he had. "I'll see you tonight," he said. "It shouldn't take more than a minute or two." He paused for a moment at the doorway, looking back at Isaf with undisguised contempt. "I think I might send that pelt of yours to the tannery afterwards—it'd make a handsome rug.''

Then he was gone.

That evening, it seemed as if the entire army had assem-

bled to watch the show. The parade ground was a sea of
faces. They pressed hungrily around the roped-off circle
where the combat would take place, jeering and hooting as
Isaf finally appeared to join Ladoc in the ring. Although the
sun hadn't quite set, its failing light was all but lost amidst
a thick bank of clouds heaped above the West Wall. The
courtyard was ablaze with torches, spluttering at the end of
their long staves like fireworks and sending huge, antic
shadows capering across the sand. The supervising captain,
a sinewy young Eredrosian with high-plumed helm and scarlet cloak, read a lengthy list of rules appertaining to the
combat, but Isaf scarcely listened. In the end, it boiled down
to just one thing: *fight or die*. Isaf had known that all his
life.

"Let's get on with it, shall we?" Ladoc said. "I'm going
to carve this Jenemun like a pig on a spit!"

Like Isaf, he was naked to the waist, one hand tied behind
his back to prevent him trying to grapple with his opponent
rather than slaying him outright with his sword. He was a
far smaller man than Isaf, but surprisingly strong, and a
master swordsman, having spent years honing his skills to
a fine edge at the great military academies of Meteora and
Temple Drake, whence only the best and brightest ever
emerged alive. In his hand he held a curious silver blade,
its hilt inscribed with cryptic runes, once rumoured to have
belonged to the legendary Ceer Prince Bunnus, an ancient
hero who'd dared test his mettle against the very gods themselves.

"Begin," the captain said.

And they did.

Ladoc crouched catlike at the edge of the circle, his sword
weaving hypnotically from side to side. "Come on, big
man!" he said. "Show us what you're made of! Piss and
wind, I shouldn't wonder!"

If Ladoc were a cat, Isaf was a bull, his big chest heaving
like bellows. His own sword was common steel and he
wielded it no more daintily than an axe. Each blow, however, would have felled a tree.

He caught Ladoc a glancing blow on the swordarm, drawing groans of dismay from the watching crowd and a thin

trickle of blood from his wrist, but Ladoc scarcely even flinched, immediately unleashing a dazzling assault that sent Isaf stumbling back against the ropes. Twice the silver blade pierced his cumbersome defence—

Once: and a fine spray of blood lay slick across Isaf's belly.

Again: and a foot-long gash opened along his chest.

"Cut the bugger's tripes out!" someone suggested.

There was a ripple of laughter from the crowd. A few of the men started baying like hounds.

"Save us his pizzle, Ladoc! I could use it for a pikestaff!"

Isaf staggered beneath another flurry of blows. Blood seeped from a cut above one eye, half-blinding him, yet he'd not even seen the sword strike home.

Grinning contemptuously, Ladoc lunged forward once more, evading Isaf's clumsy counter-stroke and aiming a mighty blow at his unprotected neck.

By rights, Isaf ought to have died. He'd been outmatched from the very beginning—had Ladoc not wanted to toy with him, he probably wouldn't even have lasted this long. The result had never really been in doubt.

It was only by a miracle that he survived. As Ladoc's blade plunged towards his neck, the clouds suddenly parted, allowing a shaft of brilliant golden light to spear down into the circle, so that, for an instant, the mirror on Isaf's chest blazed amidst the smoke and shadows like an exploding sun. Momentarily blinded, Ladoc threw up one hand to shield his eyes, stumbling as he did so and almost losing his footing completely. As a result, his blow fell wide of the mark, striking Isaf a glancing blow on the shoulder, rather than cleaving him in two. Thrown off balance, Ladoc either let go of his sword or had it wrenched from his grasp. There was a cry of anguish from the ring of spectators as it clattered to the ground some distance away, well beyond Ladoc's reach.

He sagged to one knee, glaring across at his sword as if it had wilfully betrayed him, as if he simply couldn't believe that luck had deprived him of a victory that had always been his for the taking.

Sick with pain, his strength fleeing from him like water

from a broken cup, Isaf raised his own sword and slid it
into Ladoc's exposed neck.

   Almost softly—

"YOU CAN STILL SEE THE SCAR," he told her.

   "Yes," Cayla said, a small frown tugging at her brow.
"I know."

CHAPTER FOUR

---❖---

Embarkations

EARLIER THAT MORNING, Trevayne had woken at the crack
of dawn, peering disconsolately out from his bedroom window as the sun smeared handfuls of pink ashes across the
horizon. Over the past few years, he'd grown accustomed
to sleeping in till almost noon, and resented being required
to forsake his bed at such an ungodly hour. Why, even the
bloody cockerels didn't have to get up this damned early!

Not that he'd slept soundly, of course. If anything, his
nightmares had been worse than ever, and he'd woken
countless times during the night, convinced that a shadowy
figure was prowling about the room, awaiting an opportune
moment to strike. On one occasion, he'd grabbed the dagger
from beneath his pillow and launched himself at an intruder
skulking beside the casement, only to discover that it was
merely a curtain billowing in the wind. But worst of all
were the voices—they reverberated through his skull like
the sound of approaching thunder. Although on waking he
could never recall precisely what they said, he sensed a
vast, malignant intelligence at work, relentlessly plotting
his destruction.

Gazing down at the empty streets below, as yet untouched
by the rising sun, he marvelled at the lengths to which a
man might go to acquire a decent night's rest. From the
look of things, however, no one else around the place ap-

peared to have any great difficulties in this respect. Like a drunken whore, Julkrease was notoriously slow to rouse itself, and most of its inhabitants, no doubt, would keep to their beds for quite some hours yet before finally acknowledging the advent of a new day. A few stalwart souls were already abroad: the guardmen (when they weren't dozing at their posts along the city walls), industrious tavern-owners steeling themselves for another day of beer and bare-faced robbery, the drunken, the despairing, the dispossessed. A cruel wind, fresh from the icy Northern wastes, nosed about the deserted streets like a dog sniffing out bones. The way the cold was gnawing at his insides, Trevayne suspected that it had found some.

It seemed monumentally unjust that he should be freezing his backside off like this while the Jenemun and his piece of fluff were still snug in bed. That's assuming, of course, that they knew what a bed was for. All things considered, he'd probably have been better off putting straw in their room.

Now, if Ladoc hadn't gone and gotten himself killed like that, the entire affair could have been handled quite differently. As it was, Trevayne would be doing the lion's share of the work, while Isaf earnt himself a small fortune simply delivering a bloody letter. There was, however, no alternative. How could he possibly entrust something as important as this to a mere barbarian? If worst came to worst, they might possibly be able to manage without Hawk (whose precise role in the enterprise was somewhat obscure anyway), but this other fellow, so Trevayne had been told, was absolutely indispensable to their mission. It wasn't that he believed for a moment that the Jenemun would reject his offer (his breed were almost as venal as they were blood-thirsty, and not entirely disloyal), he simply couldn't risk having the miserable brute foul everything up on him. No, the shorter and less arduous the trip, the better—that way, at least, the fellow might be able to remember exactly what he was supposed to do.

Resigning himself to the inevitable, Trevayne hurried to his writing desk and scrawled a quick note to the old Hayklut on the *Leviathan* (who, even after all these years, was still good for the odd favour or two), advising him of the sudden change in plans and exhorting the old pirate to treat his employees "with the utmost consideration." Next he moved to a large silver chest, the only key to which was suspended on a chain around his neck, and took out a bag of gold and two rolls of parchments: one old and battered, tied up with a leather thong; the other bound in calf-skin and bearing an ornate seal resembling a stylised octopus. His preparations complete, he tugged impatiently at a bellpull and waited for his manservant to arrive.

Bludsmaugre too must have found the early start somewhat of a shock to his system. He shuffled into the room as if still half asleep, his tunic partly unbuttoned and his hair dishevelled. "Forgive me, sir," he muttered apologetically. "I didn't hear the bell."

This was, of course, manifestly untrue, but Trevayne was content to let it pass. Bludsmaugre had been with him for years, and was one of the few men he actually trusted. He certainly couldn't blame the fellow for sleeping in on a morning like this. "I'll have to be off soon," Trevayne said. "Is my horse ready yet?"

"Very nearly, sir," Bludsmaugre assured him—which probably meant that he hadn't given the matter a moment's thought. Still, Trevayne was confident that he'd have all the necessary preparations finished in time, even if it meant brutalizing a few stable boys in the process. The fellow was marvellously efficient when he had to be.

"Pack plenty of provisions," Trevayne told him. "God knows how long I'll be away."

"Certainly, sir. I'll see to it that everything is in order. You can rely on me."

"Good." Trevayne turned to the collection of odds and ends which he'd assembled on the dresser. "Make sure that our guests are comfortable," he said, "and should the Jenemun decide to embark on this little errand for me, give him these. There's some gold to cover expenses, a map, and a letter of introduction to the captain of the vessel that'll take them to Port Sembaline. Oh, and this parchment here—" Trevayne picked up the tightly bound cylinder and weighed it speculatively in his hand. "I'm told it might prove useful in persuading this Hawk fellow to join our little band. Haven't a clue what it says, of course. After all, I'm just the hired help.'' With a crooked smile, he replaced the parchment and looked up once more. ''Any questions?'' he asked.

''Just one, sir,'' Bludsmaugre said.

''Go on then,'' Trevayne told him. ''Spit it out.''

''Well, sir, what am I to say if anyone should happen to ask after you?''

Trevayne grinned sourly. ''Tell them to look for me in hell,'' he said. ''I understand that's where all the best people are going this year.''

THE GREAT SHIPS shifted uneasily at their moorings, rubbing up against the anchor posts like old, unwanted animals huddled outside an abattoir. Above, leaden clouds hung low on the city, smothering its towers in a heavy mist.

The dockside was already busy, alive with men and horses. Bleary-eyed sailors staggered back to their ships after a night of drinking and whoring, like condemned men making their way to the gallows. Slaves toiled to strip the incoming vessels of their cargo and cram the holds of outgoing merchantmen with tawdry Julkrean goods. Wagons trundled to and fro, wheels rattling across the pailings as they hastened to deliver a consignment of earthenware pots bound for Ishtire or off-load crates of copper mirrors recently arrived from the East.

Isaf had little reason to love the place. After all, it hadn't been that long since his own hands held a Julkrean oar, since he'd felt the sting of oiled whips on his own broad back. Tauru, they'd called him—''The Bull''—and said, laughingly, that they knew just what to do with bulls. He'd almost broken his shackles, thick though they were. Almost. Then they whipped him until he screamed, opening fifty raw wounds for them to scour with salt.

How swiftly the wheel had turned! Now those whips would be working for him: he would speed his way to Port Sembaline on the backs of a hundred screaming slaves, bleeding them of their strength the way Jenemun bled their cattle, because it was all they had to give. The irony of the situation did not escape him. He knew full well that misery and deprivation were the mainsprings of human prosperity, that for every man who enjoyed a moment's ease, a dozen others had to labour until they dropped. He may not have liked being a master, but the only alternative was to be permanently enslaved.

Cayla, of course, had no such misgivings. She'd always found the dockside an enchanting place, full of energy and life, quite unlike the sad, decaying alleys of the city itself. Often of an afternoon, when business was slow, she would steal down here and spend hours watching the ships as they sailed out to sea, their insignia gleaming in the sunlight like vivid, heraldic tattoos. How she'd longed that they might take her with them, away to some strange, exciting shore where she could start her life anew. Although she wasn't sufficiently naive to believe that such places actually existed, at least she tried. It seemed better than nothing.

And now her dreams had finally come true! She gazed intently along the line of ships, wondering which one was theirs. Isaf hadn't said. Not that it really mattered, because they all looked equally grand. To think that, in just a few short hours, they'd be sailing off towards the very ends of the earth. . . . Up till now, the furthest she'd ever been was across the river on a rowboat!

She felt like singing, or shouting, or bursting into tears. Isaf, however, seemed relatively unenthusiastic about the voyage, and she was forced to huddle her joy inside her like a secret fire.

Exactly what her future might hold, she hadn't the faintest idea. There was certainly no way she could return to her old life now, even if she'd wanted to—Isaf had made sure of that. On their way to the docks, Cayla had stopped off at the tavern to collect those belongings which she was reluctant to leave behind, such as the small cameo that had once belonged to her mother and a few other pieces of particular sentimental value. To be quite honest, she'd also wanted to flaunt her new-gained wealth in front of the others, and so much of the unpleasantness that ensued was, she supposed, entirely of her own making.

As expected, Hauba had been in a less than forgiving

mood, threatening to flay Cayla alive for having abandoned
her post the night before and demanding that the Jenemun
make good the losses he'd suffered due to her absence. He
then went on to name a figure that was either grossly inflated
or proof of just how much he'd cheated her over the years—
you could have tumbled the duke's own stepdaughter for
that kind of money, and still taken home a pocketful of
change. Before she'd had a chance to try and reason with
him, Isaf had sprung to her defence, seizing Hauba by the
throat and hurling him roughly to the floor. He'd probably
have throttled the fellow then and there if Cayla hadn't
intervened. Not out of sympathy for him, of course. She
simply didn't relish the prospect of them both winding up
on the wrong end of a hangman's noose.

Even now, it was hard to forget the naked fury in Hauba's
eyes as Isaf escorted her from the tavern. He'd be out for
revenge, nothing surer, both to salve his wounded pride and
to maintain discipline among the other whores, who might
otherwise be tempted to follow Cayla's example. No doubt
he would have made life extremely difficult for them if
they'd remained in the city for any length of time. After
all, there were plenty of hired killers around—from fastid-
ious devotees of the Blue Azalea Cult to the dreaded Brothers of the Rose, whose grossly mutilated victims were fished
from the river with monotonous regularity—and Hauba was
well-connected enough to have at least one of them on their
trail within a matter of hours. She almost wished that Isaf
hadn't been so quick to intercede on her behalf. Life was
hazardous enough without actively looking for trouble, and
she'd always found it safer to avoid such confrontations
wherever possible rather than provoke them. Isaf, however,
apparently thought otherwise. One thing was certain, life
with him would never be dull—she just hoped that he didn't
get the pair of them killed in the process.

Cayla, however, had no intention of dwelling on such
matters right now. This was the day she'd dreamt about all
her life; nothing must spoil it. What did it matter how many
bridges she burned when her future beckoned so enticingly
before her? The important thing was that, by joining Isaf,
she'd finally discovered a means of escaping Julkrease for-

ever. This in itself seemed more than enough reason to love him.

"FOR GODS'-SAKE, man!" the captain snarled. "I thought I told you to clear all the whores off the ship an hour ago! We're almost ready to sail."

The bosun shot a murderous glance at the ill-matched pair behind him. "Begging your pardon, sir," he said. "But the big bloke reckons they got passage booked to Sembalin'."

"That's right," Isaf said, stepping suddenly forward. His words sounded almost like a threat.

The captain took a step back, one hand falling to his sword. His eyes were cold and hard, like chips of dirty ice. "Passage?" he snorted. "What, for a savage and some damn slut I've seen round these docks more times than I've had hot dinners? Don't make me laugh!" He loosened his blade. "Now clear off, before I have both of you tarred and feathered!"

The mate too had begun to draw his sword. He was a short, thick-set fellow, with a face like a chopping block. Someone had once tried to slit his throat, leaving a long, ragged scar across the front of his neck. There were, no doubt, at least a dozen men on board who'd have been only too happy to do the job properly.

It was left to Cayla to try and retrieve the situation. "The letter," she whispered. "Show him the letter."

Still scowling, Isaf plucked the scrap of parchment from his belt and weighed it in his hand. Just to be on the safe side, Cayla quickly snatched it from him and handed it across to the captain.

"I'm sure this will explain everything, my lord," she said, ducking her head obsequiously. "There's just been some kind of misunderstanding, that's all."

"What's this?" the captain said, eyeing the letter dubiously.

"Just read it," Isaf snapped.

"If you would be so kind, my lord." Cayla's conciliatory smile managed to blunt the harsh edge in Isaf's tone. She played her part to perfection—which was hardly surprising, of course. This kind of self-effacing mummery had been her bread and butter for nigh on fifteen years.

Drawing his dagger, the captain broke open the seal and examined the letter with a mixture of impatience and distrust. By the time he'd finished reading it, however, his expression had changed to one of outright astonishment.

"Where'd you get this?" he demanded.

"From a man called Trevayne," Cayla told him. "He wants us to deliver a message for him."

The captain read through the letter once more, then suddenly crumpled it in his fist and flung it angrily away. "Very well," he muttered, glaring morosely across at Isaf before turning at last to the bosun. "Take them to my cabin," he growled. "Until further notice, I'll be dossing down with the crew."

The bosun's mouth gaped open, as if to voice his surprise, but the captain silenced him with a curt wave of the hand. "Get moving, damn you! We haven't got all bloody day!"

The bosun frowned, his butchered face creasing like a leather sack. "Aye, aye, cap'n," he said, glaring across at Isaf and Cayla as if he'd have dearly loved to clap the pair of them in irons on the spot. "Right, you two," he snapped. "Follow me."

CHAPTER FIVE

Pagad's Progress

BRIEFLY NOW.

Eredrosia: Green and flat. Cool days, nights with jaws of ice. Sky like quenched steel. Storm clouds the size of mountains, charcoal and grey. Tall trees—mostly pines and firs. Many animals. Some birds. Few people.

River Thasis: Broad and swift. Plunging down from the mountains like a torrent of liquid glass. Fish the colour of old pennies. Pebbles of quartz veined with gold. Some settlements scattered along the banks—fishing, trading, farming. Bright boats swimming. Foam and bubbles.

Whitewall: Like cliffs of cut glass, or broken marble gravestones. A negative prism, gathering all the colours of land and sky and reducing them to a blinding arctic white, grim and foreboding. About it, lush green pastures. A very blue sky, scattered with high clouds. Sheep browsing among gently sloped foothills. Shepherds conjuring wondrous tunes from bunches of dried reeds. Wolves, lean and hungry, stealing through the shadows like assassins. Snow—like soft, white hammers.

Four weeks he rode.

Here the hills gave way to scarlet sand, crushed beneath

the weight of a huge, arid sky. The sun flared overhead like a cauldron of liquid fire, poisoning the air with heat. Beyond lay the purple haze of far-off mountains, or else the end of the world itself.

Trevayne remained relatively unimpressed. To him, the land was neither a prodigy nor a threat, simply one more obstacle to be overcome before he could finally fulfil his quest and return to other, less harrowing climes. Ten years of semi-retirement had taken a greater toll on him than he'd realised. He'd never been so saddle sore in his life! Some mornings, he could barely stand for the pain in his back and legs, and his arse felt as if he'd been sitting on hot coals for the past four weeks rather than the finest leather that money could buy. It was small wonder that so few travellers ventured out this way. The going was hard in places, and he'd seen some damned queer sights over the last few days, none of them particularly pleasant. But then, what could one expect from a place where even the bloody rocks weren't always quite what they appeared to be?

What infuriated him most was the knowledge that while he was stuck in the middle of some god-forsaken wasteland, sweating his bloody guts out, the Jenemun and his lady friend were doubtless holed up in a nice, comfortable tavern somewhere, having a high old time at his expense. (Well, figuratively speaking, anyway.) According to his calculations, the pair ought to have been nearing the mountains by now—assuming, of course, that they'd seen fit to drag themselves out of bed in time to catch the boat. Bloody layabouts, that's what they were! He'd have liked to see them try and ride from dawn to dusk for the best part of a month. Their bums would probably have dropped off before they got halfway through Eredrosia.

Taking a final sip from his canteen, he urged his horse out across the plain. All too soon, a familiar ache began gnawing at his backside.

Ye gods! he thought sourly. *This damned saddle will be the death of me yet.*

Grudgingly, the landscape receded to allow him passage.

* * *

THE STONE WAS about three feet high, roughly triangular in shape and the colour of dried blood. A small lizard hunched beside it, seeking refuge from the sun in a puddle of shadow. It was the first living thing that Trevayne had seen for days.

Reigning his horse to a stop, he leant down to examine the stone more closely, then tapped it speculatively with one hand.

"I am Arbrigor," the stone announced solemnly.

Trevayne smiled. "Congratulations," he said. "I was wondering if perhaps you might be of some assistance to me."

The stone seemed not to share his own good humour. "Why should I?" it asked peevishly.

By now, Trevayne's gaudy clothes were caked with dust and sweat, and the extravagant plume on his hat had long since wilted like a dead flower. "There's supposed to be a well around here someplace," he said shortly. Weeks of hard riding had worn his patience even thinner than the seat of his pants, and he was in no mood to bandy words with some mindless slab of rock. "Now, where exactly do I find it?"

"How should I know?"

Trevayne sighed. "Look," he said. "I haven't got all day to waste. You folk know everything—or at least that's what I've been told." He pushed back the brim of his hat, eyes narrowing dangerously. "And I've also been told what to do should you refuse to cooperate."

"Your threats don't interest me," the stone said haughtily. "And I have no intention of telling you anything. Now leave me in peace."

Thoroughly exasperated, Trevayne climbed stiffly from his horse and advanced menacingly on the stone. "The well," he demanded. "Where is it?"

The stone retained a sullen silence.

"All right, then," Trevayne muttered darkly. "If that's how you want it."

Taking a deep breath, he grasped hold of the stone and began to lift. The lizard scampered across his boot and disappeared into the endless wastes of sand.

"One last chance," Trevayne grunted, raising the stone a few inches off the ground. It whimpered slightly, but said nothing.

"Suit yourself."

Settling his feet wide apart, Trevayne hoisted the stone to shoulder height.

"You will pay for this!" the stone shrieked. "Your bones will rot in hell for all eternity!"

The stone was heavier than it looked. Trevayne's shoulders were already beginning to knot with cramp and his face was beaded with sweat. Nevertheless, he refused to let it drop. "I'll bear that in mind," he said. "And now, perhaps you'd be so good as to tell me where I might find this bloody well!"

There was no response.

With a mighty effort, Trevayne heaved the stone above his head. "Come on, you bastard!" he snarled. "Out with it!"

The stone screamed, an agonising, inhuman sound, like metal fingers clawing at a sheet of glass.

"Please!" it whimpered. "You cannot know what you do to me!"

"Where is the well?"

"I cannot—"

"The well!"

"In the tallest mountain, there is a gate," the stone told him, "held by two guardians. Beyond the gate there is a tunnel. At the end of the tunnel lies a well. Perhaps that is what you seek."

Hurling the stone away from him, Trevayne sank to his knees, panting for breath. He scarcely had the strength to stand, but somehow managed to stumble across to his horse and haul himself into the saddle.

Looking down at the stone, his lips curled into a malicious grin. "Thank you, my friend," he said. "That's all I wanted to know. Things would have been much easier on both of us if you'd simply kept a civil tongue in your head."

"Laugh while you can, son of flesh," the stone muttered spitefully. "Your fate is already sealed."

"Is that a fact?" Trevayne said.

"Oh, most certainly! You see, I too once sought the well!"

Trevayne spurred his horse on towards the shadowy peaks that massed like thunderheads on the horizon, for once unable to think of any appropriate reply.

HUNCHED BEHIND AN OUTCROP of grey, unsentient rock, Trevayne peered intently at the gateway before him. About ten feet square, it was wrought from some lustrous white metal that he'd never seen before, and stood out from the dark mountainside like the mouth of a grinning skull.

The guardian too was white, his flesh as pale and waxen as a candle. His armour was the colour of ocean foam, his helmet adorned with a plume of milky hair. In one hand he held a spear of bleached wood, its razor-sharp barb honed from a boar tusk fully eight inches long. His other hand hovered warily about the hilt of his sword, which, like his belt and scabbard, was sheathed in snow-white fur. He was certainly an odd looking fellow, and one whom Trevayne suspected he ought to approach cautiously.

Dusting himself down, Trevayne straightened his hat and ambled casually towards the gate.

The guardian seemed thoroughly disinterested in his approach, gazing vacantly out into space like some marbled warrior at the entrance to an ancient tomb. As he drew nearer the gate, however, the guardian stepped slowly forward to bar his passage.

"Hello, there," Trevayne said brightly. "You in charge round here, are you?"

The guardian made no reply. His eyes, scarcely visible through the gleaming metal of his visor, were as hard and bright as diamonds.

"You see," Trevayne continued quickly, "I really do need to get through that gate of yours. And I was wondering if perhaps you'd—"

"None may pass this way," the guardian murmured, his voice as chill and diffuse as a mountain fog.

"Let's not be hasty about this," Trevayne told him. "You see, I've rather pressing business with whoever—or whatever—might lie on the other side, and it would make everything so much easier if you'd simply step aside.''

The guardian stared silently down at him for a moment, then slowly shook his head. "None may pass this way," he repeated. "It is forbidden."

"No one need ever know about it," Trevayne said, "if that's what's worrying you. All I want to do is nick inside a while and talk to someone."

"That cannot be."

"Why not? I'm hardly going to steal the damned thing or anything, now am I?"

"Watch," the guardian said, stepping back from the door and reaching for a small metal lever set in the rock beside it. "I will show you."

As he pulled on the lever, a shutter opened in the centre of the door, allowing Trevayne to see what lay beyond.

"Gods' blood!'' he said, reaching instinctively for his sword. "What in heaven's name is that?"

There, crouching in the shadows, was a hideous, ill-shapen beast roughly the size of a man, covered in shaggy black fur and reeking of decay. It glared savagely up at the open shutter, its lips snarling back to reveal teeth the size of butcher knives.

"That is not for me to say," the guardian told him. "It comes from beyond the mountain."

As he spoke, the beast suddenly flung itself at the door, its claws scrabbling for purchase on the smooth metal. Its eyes, like two polished spheres of ebony, smouldered with rage.

"From the well, perhaps?" Trevayne suggested. He eyed the brute apprehensively. No one had mentioned anything about him having to fight his way past some huge, murderous ape to reach the bloody thing.

"Well?" the guardian said. "What well?"

"That's where the door leads, doesn't it?" Trevayne said. "I mean, that's why you're here aren't you? To guard the well."

"There is nothing beyond the gate save the creature you see," the guard said, closing the shutter once more and resuming his post before the door. "If I were to open the gate, the creature would escape. That is why you cannot pass."

"I see." Trevayne stroked his chin thoughtfully. "Then I don't suppose there's much use me hanging about here, is there? Obviously someone's been having me on. Sorry to have troubled you."

Turning, he started to stroll back towards the stony ravine where he'd tethered his horse. There was something odd going on around here. It seemed best to mull things over for a while rather than try to force the issue. Still, he couldn't resist a brief parting jibe.

"Just one question," he said, flashing the guardian a mischievous smile.

"Yes?"

"Why on earth was the bloody gate put there to begin with?"

The guardian said nothing. Like the ghost of some long-forsaken hero, he stuck steadfastly to his post, as still and patient as a stone.

NIGHTS HERE WERE never pleasant. The land seemed unnaturally silent: there was no rustling of animals in the darkness, no flutter of unseen wings, no dry stridulation of the insects beneath the heavy sand. At times, Trevayne had the eerie feeling that he was trapped in some gigantic painting, that the place was nothing more than a crudely painted backdrop, tricked out with threadbare props and fake perspectives, like the set for some inept provincial pantomime. It was bad enough being plagued by nightmares while he slept without waking up to them as well.

Gnawing at a hunk of stale biscuit (apparently Bludsmaugre's idea of the perfect field ration, since he'd stuffed Trevayne's saddlebags with precious little else), he stared morosely out across the dunes. There was nothing in the least illusory about the rich crop of blisters on his backside or the persistent throbbing in his back. No, despite everything, this place was real, all right, and so too was the question of how he might reach this damned well that he'd been told about. Either the stone had lied to him, or else old white boots hadn't the foggiest idea what he was meant to be guarding. Anything was possible, he supposed, in a madhouse like this. The fellow certainly seemed an odd sort of bastard; hardly human at all, by the look of him—or even alive for that matter. And hadn't the stone said something about *two* guardians? If that were the case, what had happened to the other one?

There seemed nothing for it but to take another look at the gate and see if he couldn't somehow bluff his way through. One way or another, however, this business had to be settled soon. The days were slipping by like sand— and any further delay at this stage could well prove fatal.

Slinging his baldric over one shoulder, he crept stealthily back up the ravine. The piles of ancient rock stooped above him like hunchbacked giants, darker even than the sky. There was no moon, and only a handful of stars shimmered fitfully overhead, so he stood an excellent chance of approaching the gateway entirely unobserved.

At first, he thought that he'd lost his way, as he could find no trace of the gate at all, even though he'd retraced his footsteps as accurately as he could. Only when a stray glimmer of starlight struck the cliff-face did he realise that it was still there; having mysteriously changed color so as to be virtually indistinguishable from the dark stone around it. The guardian seemed to have vanished completely.

As he drew closer, Trevayne glimpsed a shadowy figure lurking near the door, and for a moment he feared that the beast might somehow have escaped and torn the watchman to pieces.

"Who's there?" he demanded, retreating a few paces and groping for his sword. "Show yourself!"

There was a shuffle of footsteps as the figure moved slowly forward.

Trevayne frowned. This entire affair was rapidly getting beyond a joke.

"Good evening," he said, recovering his composure and executing a brief mock-bow. "Got the night shift out already have we?"

Like his diurnal counterpart, the guardian seemed a fairly taciturn sort of chap. He stared silently across at Trevayne, his eyes gleaming like beads of anthracite beneath the dull black metal of his helmet.

"Sorry I'm late," Trevayne said, advancing confidently towards the gate. "Had a few things to do, you see. Just open her up, there's a good fellow. We don't want to drag this out all night, now do we?"

The guardian took a few shuffling steps forward. "None may pass this way," he said, raising his ebon spear menacingly.

"What's wrong?" Trevayne asked. "Didn't the other fellow leave you a message or anything? We sorted it all out this afternoon. I can't imagine why you weren't told about it. Go check with him yourself if you don't believe me."

The guardian, however, seemed quite unmoved. "None may pass this way," he said. "It is forbidden."

Trevayne groaned. "Let's not start all that again," he said. "Just five minutes, eh?"

"That cannot be."

"Come on, be a sport. I'll be in and out like a flash. You won't even notice that I'm there."

"It is forbidden," the guardian said. His voice sounded as cold and hollow as an open grave.

"So you've said." Trevayne felt as if he were trapped in some kind of recurrent nightmare. "But I really don't see what all the fuss is about. Couldn't you just—"

"Watch," the guardian told him. Stepping to one side, he reached for the now-familiar lever concealed in the rocks nearby.

"You can skip the peep show," Trevayne snapped. "I've seen it already."

As the shutters opened, however, he realised that the situation was rather more complicated than he'd originally thought. The beast still hunched murderously in the shadows, but its once coal-black fur was now deathly pale, and its eyes glared balefully up out of the darkness like two saucers of cold white fire.

Trevayne frowned. He didn't like the look of this at all. "How many of those buggers have you got in there, anyway?"

"There is only one Beast," the guardian told him. "It comes from beyond the mountain."

"One?" Trevayne said. "But that's impossible. Unless, of course—" He stopped, a shrewd smile playing on his lips. "Tell me," he said. "Do you stand guard here all the time?"

The guardian nodded. "None may pass this way. It is forbidden."

"Of course. And there's just you, is there? No other guards or anything?"

"Other?" The guardian seemed momentarily confused. "There is no other—there is only the Beast." The statement seemed to reassure him, his voice lapsing once more into a dry, impassive monotone. "Were I to open the gate, the creature would escape. That is why you cannot pass."

Trevayne smirked openly this time.

"Why do you laugh?"

"Forgive me," Trevayne said. "It's just that, for a moment there, you suddenly reminded me of someone else I know."

With a jaunty grin, he turned and sauntered off into the darkness, whistling as he went.

IMPALED ON A NEARBY MOUNTAINTOP, the sun bled rust and cinnabar. Daylight poured across the dark stone like streams of molten wax, drenching the sand in a blaze of crimson fire. Higher up, Trevayne could see fat, pink clouds strewn about the sky, like huge bouquets of roses.

With a weary sigh, he climbed to his feet and tried to work some of the stiffness from his joints. It was, he decided, about time he sorted this nonsense out once and for all. He hadn't come this far to be baulked by a pair of ridiculous painted puppets. No, he'd get through that gate somehow, by hell he would, even if it meant slaughtering the pair of them. There was obviously no point trying to deal rationally with the fellows.

The gateway was still drenched in thick shadows. As dawn trickled down the mountainside towards him, the guardian turned and fitted a key into the door. Twenty yards

away, Trevayne heard a heavy metal bolt snap back, then
the door swung slowly open.

Eyes flaring like corpse-lights, the beast hurled itself
through the opening. It landed on all fours, sniffing the air
and peering cautiously from side to side.

The guardian didn't even so much as glance in its direction. Putting down his spear, he began stripping off his
armour and tossing it negligently towards the doorway.

As each piece clattered to the ground, the beast scurried
after it and began strapping the fragments of metal to its
own monstrous limbs.

Trevayne had seen enough. With a blood-curdling cry,
he grabbed his sword in both hands and launched himself
at the open gateway.

The beast scrambled to one side, clutching fearfully to
its scraps of armour, but the guardian stood his ground, as
if still determined to deny Trevayne passage. Naked to the
waist, his skin shone like polished leather, as black and
supple as the sword he now gripped tightly in his hand.

"None may pass this way!" he croaked hoarsely. "It is
forbidden!"

"Stand aside, or I'll skewer you like a pig!"

The guardian said nothing, his face as blank and expressionless as an unpainted canvas.

"All right, then! If that's how you want it!"

Trevayne lunged forward, heaving his sword towards the
man's unprotected head. The guardian, however, was
quicker than he looked, and evaded the blow quite easily.
His own sword darted out like a sudden shadow, drawing
a prick of blood from Trevayne's thigh.

"Damn!" he snarled. "I'll get you for that, you smug
little bastard!"

He launched a furious attack, sweeping his sword back
and forth like an enormous scythe. The guardian retreated
a step or two, but otherwise treated the whistling blade with
contempt, often allowing it to come within a hairsbreadth
of his face or chest before casually weaving aside.

Glancing over his shoulder, Trevayne saw that the beast
was still strapping on the guardian's discarded armour, apparently oblivious to the fierce battle taking place nearby.

It seemed taller and leaner than before, its brutish snarl replaced by a look of almost human desperation as it struggled to lace the heavy breastplate around its chest.

Trevayne steeled himself for one final assault. Scooping up a handful of sand, he flung it into the guardian's face and sprinted towards the gate. For a moment, he saw the beast shuffling across to intercept him, clad in scraps of particoloured armour, as if splattered with fresh white paint.

Then he was through. Before him lay a narrow tunnel strewn with broken stones. Checking to see that Vellaghar's precious bottle hadn't suffered any irreparable damage, he sheathed his sword and stumbled blindly on into the darkness.

CHAPTER SIX

———◆———

Memento Mori

ISAF AND CAYLA MAINTAINED a somewhat less hectic pace.

Ocean: A smell of brine; the sting of ozone. Drizzle and rain, but no storms. ("Women and ships don't mix," the captain snarled. But no storms.) Nights like buckets of black ice; days scarcely warmer, with a chill wind blustering through the rigging. Sunset turned the sky to bands of glowing metal: steel, tin, brass and gold. (It shone in her hair as well, like copper flames. They stood by a railing, watching the sea burn with light. "You're very beautiful today," Isaf told her, and she smiled.)

Port Sembaline: Another city, but no towers this time. The buildings were low and grey: warehouses, barracks, brothels, and inns. Colour came from the people, from their scarves and jackets and dresses and capes and necklaces and sashes and swords. Many people from many lands: pirates, assassins, and thieves.

Forlunn River: Rustic and quiet; only the crickets in the night were loud. Choked in places with thick bulrushes and clumps of reeds. Birds everywhere, with stilted legs and slender beaks. ("Clumsy beasts," Isaf said. Then they staggered into the air. Cayla clapped her hands with delight. "Angels!" she breathed.) There were no boats.

69

Misibis: Alive with trees and flowers, strange animals lurking among the shadows, and flocks of multicoloured birds. Rain sparkling like sequins on the broad green leaves.

TO THE LEFT WERE rows of jagged peaks, creased with deep shadows, crowned with snow and mist. Far below, Cayla could see the lowlands spread out before her like a rich, variegated tapestry of green and gold, its rivers glistening in the sunlight like bright silver threads.

To be honest, she wondered why anyone in their right mind would want to live up here. The view was pleasant enough, but it had been blowing a gale all day, and the air was bitterly cold. She shivered, bundling the heavy fur cloak more tightly around her. Even the bleakest Julkrean winter was nothing compared to this. Her bones felt like sticks of ice.

Still, she had no regrets. The past four weeks had been an absolute delight, each day as bright and dazzling as a conjuror's scarf, and even this barren, wind-swept mountain had far more to commend it than the life she'd left behind. In any case, Isaf said that they probably wouldn't be here for long, and there was no telling what exotic new sights and sounds might await them in the East. She smiled at the thought, happiness bubbling inside her like a secret, inexhaustible fountain.

Cayla still found it difficult to believe her good fortune. If Isaf hadn't chosen to visit Hauba's tavern that night, and if she hadn't taken the time to seek him out, none of this would ever have happened. It seemed almost unfair in a way. Surely such happiness ought to have been earned, rather than simply stumbled across by accident? Not that she was complaining; anyone stupid enough to start questioning their luck didn't deserve to have any in the first place.

Suddenly, a horn echoed across the mountainside. Shrill and predatory, it clawed at her spine like the howling of a wolf.

"What's that?" she said, glancing nervously around her.

Isaf grinned. He seemed scarcely troubled by the cold at

all, his cloak hanging carelessly from one shoulder. "Mountain folk, most likely," he told her. "I thought they'd have spotted us hours ago."

"What will they do now?"

"Who knows?"

Frowning slightly, Cayla squinted up at the snow-capped summits far above them. At first, she could see nothing but ice and rock. "It's a bleak old place, isn't it?" she murmured. "I shouldn't want to—" All of sudden, something caught her eye. She let out a little squeal of surprise. "Oh, Isaf, look!"

A huge black hawk circled overhead, its wings like slim brush-strokes against the frozen sky.

Isaf glanced at it briefly, then shrugged. "Don't worry," he said, "it won't hurt you. Probably just looking for a bite to eat, that's all."

"I've never seen anything like it," Cayla said. "It's beautiful."

"You'll see plenty more before we're through with this," Isaf told her. "The mountains are full of them."

Cayla pulled a face. "Don't be such a spoilsport," she teased. "I still says it's—"

A second blast of the horn drowned out her words. It seemed much closer this time.

Isaf reigned his horse to a stop and motioned for Cayla to do the same. "Looks like we've got company," he said. "Best see what they want, I suppose."

Cayla drew up close beside him. Peering anxiously out from under her thick fur hood, she looked as pale and vulnerable as a china doll.

"Don't worry," Isaf said, patting her hand reassuringly. "If they meant us any harm, we'd both be dead by now."

Cayla, to her credit, managed a wan smile. "Oh, thanks very much," she said. "That makes me feel much better."

"You there!"

The words, flung down at them like pebbles into a well, might have come from anywhere.

Isaf didn't even bother trying to locate their source. "Greetings!" he said loudly. "I was wondering when you'd finally decide to show yourselves!"

"State your business!" the voice told him, its owner still hidden somewhere among the rocks.

Isaf scowled. "We're looking for Hiern Holding," he said. "Can you tell us where we might find it?"

There was no reply. A blast of icy wind rushed in to fill the sudden silence.

"What's the matter?" Isaf snapped. "Cat got your tongue?"

All at once, a dozen men materialized around them. Tall and lean, their grey eyes slitted against the wind, they stared coldly up at Isaf, as if chiselled from slabs of stone.

Isaf seemed unperturbed by the ring of longbows trained on them. "I have a message for Hawk," he said. "Ever heard of him?"

One of the men stepped forward, easing the tension slightly on his bow. "What sort of message?" he asked.

"Hawk will find that out when he meets me," Isaf growled. "Now, are you going to take us to him, or just stand there gawping all day?"

The man looked round at his companions, then gestured lightly with one hand. Without a word, they melted back into the rocks whence they'd come. Even when Isaf knew where to look, he couldn't see the barest flicker of movement to betray their presence.

"This way," the man said. Sheathing his bow, he darted off along the trail before them, as silent as a shadow.

Cayla and Isaf followed. So quickly did he move, that even their sure-footed highland ponies had difficulty keeping up with him.

"He's like a ghost, isn't he?" Cayla said, eyes round with wonder.

"A goat, you mean," Isaf muttered irritably. "Let's just hope the damn fool knows where he's going, that's all."

Above them, the hawk gave a high-pitched shriek and plunged down towards the mountaintops. Within moments, it was lost from view completely.

As HE MADE HIS WAY through the damp, shadow-haunted corridors of Hiern Holding, Isaf wondered whatever had possessed him to accept an assignment like this in the first place. He was a soldier, not a diplomat. If Hawk choose not to accompany them to Eria, there was precious little that he could do about it. Why hadn't Trevayne sent one of those silver-tongued Julkrean merchants to plead his case? Isaf's own eloquence extended no further than the tip of his sword, and he could hardly have been expected to win Hawk over with blandishments and flowery phrases. What was he supposed to do, take on the entire garrison single-handed and carry the fellow off by sheer force of arms?

Eventually they were ushered into a large, starkly furnished room and told to wait while one of the guardsmen informed Hawk of their arrival. The remaining warriors stationed themselves by the doorway, daggers drawn.

The sound of approaching footsteps drew Isaf's attention to a heavy curtain masking one end of the chamber. As he watched, the hangings slowly parted to reveal a lean, slightly stooped figure clad in buckskins and furs. Had it not been for his unblemished skin and sleek black hair, Isaf might easily have mistaken him for an old man. He moved stiffly, glancing around the room with an air of weary resignation, as though even the smallest movement required considerable effort.

Seating himself at a nearby table, the man raised one gaunt, almost skeletal, hand and beckoned Isaf forward.

"I am Hiern," the man told him. "what is it you wanted to see me about?"

Isaf frowned. "There seems to have been some mistake," he said. "I'm looking for a fellow called Hawk. Do you know where I might find him?"

The man smiled, his thin lips creasing like parchment. "Hawk is dead," he murmured. "You must deal with Hiern now."

"I don't understand." Confused, Isaf took out the letter that Trevayne had given him and turned it over in his hands. They appeared to have traipsed halfway across the world for nothing. In a way, he felt almost relieved. "I'm sorry," he said. "I was told to give Hawk this. Since that's impossible—"

Hiern laughed, a brittle, unpleasant sound. "Impossible?" he said. "Whatever makes you think that it's impossible?'' He fell silent a moment, as if lost in thought, then glared menacingly at Isaf. ''Who are you, anyway?'' he demanded. ''Why have you come here?''

Isaf stepped back, confused by the man's abrupt change of tone. ''My name's Isaf,'' he said. ''And I was sent here to deliver a message. Obviously I've wasted my time—and yours. Now, unless there's anything else you'd like to know, perhaps we ought to be on our way.''

Hiern ignored him. ''And who might you be?'' he asked, looking across at Cayla.

Caught off-guard, she stiffened slightly, then contrived to appear both flattered and humbled by his attention. ''Cayla, my lord,'' she said, curtsying awkwardly in her heavy furs. ''We appreciate you taking the trouble to see us like this.''

''Not at all, *my lady*,'' Hiern said. He seemed genuinely amused. ''We get few visitors here—and certainly never ones as charming as yourself. It has been a pleasure meeting you.''

Cayla blushed. ''You are too kind, my lord.''

''Never that,'' Hiern said quietly. ''No, never that.'' He turned to a pair of guardsmen standing in the doorway. ''Escort the young lady to my mother,'' he told them. ''And see to it that she is made as comfortable as possible. Isaf and I apparently have some business to discuss.''

''What do you mean?'' Isaf snapped. ''I thought you just said—''

''It's all right,'' Cayla said. ''I'd quite enjoy a chance to sit and talk a while.''

''But—''

''I'm sure Hiern knows best.'' Before Isaf could reply, Cayla bowed once more and crossed to the door. Sheathing their daggers, the two guardsmen stood aside to let her pass.

Hiern waited until she had gone, then slumped back in his chair, as if an intolerable burden had suddenly settled on his shoulders. ''And now, my friend,'' he said wearily, ''perhaps you'd care to explain precisely what all this is about.''

''I've told you twice already—I was supposed to deliver a message to Hawk.'' Scowling, Isaf handed him the leather-bound scroll of parchment. "Here," he said. "You can read the damned thing yourself if you like."

Hiern eyed the scroll speculatively, but made no move to open it. "What does it say?"

"How should I know?"

Taking out a small silver knife from his pocket, Hiern carefully broke the seal and unrolled a few inches of parchment. "What have we got here, eh?" he muttered. "Quite a lengthy epistle by the look of it. I wonder who could have—"

Suddenly he stiffened. "Where did you get this?" he said sharply.

"In Julkrease," Isaf told him. "From a man called Trevayne."

Hiern turned the parchment over, examining the seal closely, then continued reading. Every few lines, he paused and stared vacantly into space, mouthing words that Isaf couldn't quite hear.

Finally he looked up. "Tell me," he said. "What were your instructions should Hawk have agreed to this proposal?"

"I was to take him to Eria, where Trevayne would be waiting for us. After that—"

Hiern nodded. "It doesn't matter," he said. "Eria will do for now." Seeing the confusion in Isaf's face, he smiled scornfully. "You fool!" he said. "Hawk is here!" He pointed towards his own chest. "Hiern ate him! Hiern gobbled him up! But he's here—here!"

He roared with laughter, perhaps at the look of sheer incomprehension on Isaf's face, perhaps at some secret jest that he alone could appreciate; then, for no apparent reason, burst into tears.

Even Isaf, who cared little for the suffering of others, couldn't help wondering why.

Why?

(Like poisonous jewels embedded in the aching contours of his skull. Each incident/event/occurrence a stinging barb, crucifying him to his past.)

There!

. . . ONE BY ONE, the cliff-tops came alive with fires. Puddles
of blood-red light split the darkness, flooding over the high
battlements of the holding. Hawk awoke to find a windowful
of brightness splashing across his face. Clambering out of
bed, he slipped on a pair of thick fur buskins and hurried
to the narrow casement that glistened before him as if
drenched with liquid fire.

At first, he thought that the sky had fallen. Cold, gemlike
flames were scattered across the mountains all the way from
Eastwick to Gorgon's Mouth, their light spilling across the
grey, cracked stone like hot metal from a forge.

The stars, however, were still there, faint white pinpricks
above the dark bulk of the Reflas, like tiny candles encased
in ice. These fires were far more wondrous, and far more
terrible, than he'd ever seen before. And yet, they seemed
strangely familiar, as though he looked not outwards but
deep into his own breast, and watched his own lifeblood
blaze like an endless chain of beacons in the night.

When at last Hawk returned to bed, he lay awake for
hours, his head filled with fire and blood and falling stars.

Eventually, he slept . . .

And there!

. . . PANTING, Hawk came to the north wall, clutching his
bow in one hand and a quiver full of slim, dark-fletched
arrows in the other. The previous afternoon, his father had
promised to watch him shoot, and Hawk had already set up
a fresh straw target in the courtyard below. He'd been practising every day for some months now, and could hit the
bull nine times out of ten from fifty paces. He grinned to
himself, imagining how surprised, and proud, his father
would be as one shaft after another flew unerringly towards
its mark. It wasn't often that Hiern could afford to spend
time alone with him—what with the holding to administer
and everything—and Hawk thrilled at the prospect of finally
having a chance to display his skill.

He eventually found his father in one of the ruined gun-towers, dwarfed by the workings of an ancient bombard (far older, so Shembley had told him, than the holding itself, and long since fallen into disrepair) that jutted from its embrasure like a huge accusatory finger toward the ice-capped mountaintops beyond. Although Hawk's footsteps were loud enough to startle a colony of rooks perched nearby, Hiern seemed not to notice him, his entire attention focused upon the plumes of soft white smoke that crowned every peak for as far as the eye could see. Every now and then, one hand strayed to the hilt of his sword and he made as if turn away, but each time the fires drew him back. Had it been anyone else, Hawk might almost have thought he was afraid of something.

For a while, Hawk hid in the shadows, saying nothing. Finally, however, he could restrain himself no longer.

"Father?" he said. "What's happening? Why is everything burning?"

Hiern shook his head. He looked intolerably old and sad. Indeed, it seemed to Hawk that his father aged more rapidly with each passing year. Only a few winters before, his hair had been as dark as Hawk's own: now it glistened in the thin morning sunlight like freshly fallen snow. By comparison, Hawk's mother scarcely appeared to have changed at all, although he recalled her telling him once that she was, in fact, the older of the two.

"I don't know," Hiern muttered. The pain in his voice made Hawk wish that he hadn't spoken at all. "There are stories . . ."

He shrugged, staring out into the distance and wringing his hands. Tercels stooped and soared above them like the banderoles of some phantom army scattered in the wind.

Some time later, it began to rain . . .

And there!

". . . LOOK AT YOU!" his mother chided playfully. "Soaked to the skin, the pair of you! What in heaven's name have you been doing?"

Hiern tried to smile, his lips creasing like stiff leather. "I'm sorry, my dear," he said. "We were looking at the fires. There seem to be even more of them today.''

Hawk saw his mother falter for a moment, then her smile snapped quickly back into place. ''Come and get yourself dry,'' she said. ''You'll catch your death of cold standing around in those wet things of yours. I'll fetch you something warm to drink.''

''Not now,'' Hiern told her. ''I want to have a word with Shembley. Perhaps he can tell me what these damned fires are all about.''

Without waiting for a reply, he turned and strode off down the hallway.

Hawk's mother seemed about to call after him, then bit her lip and looked away. ''Don't just stand there,'' she said to Hawk, motioning him towards the hearth. ''Honestly, sometimes I wonder if you've got any sense at all . . .''

And there!

''. . . IT'S FATHER,'' Hawk told her. ''He seems so tired. Is anything wrong?''

She almost frowned, but caught herself in time and smiled comfortingly instead. ''There's nothing for you to worry about,'' she said, stroking his hair gently. They sat in front of a blazing fire, sipping camomile tea from delicate china cups emblazoned with the curious insignia of their house: a rampant eagle clutching a silver key in its claws. ''It's just that he hasn't had much sleep lately, what with one thing and the other. But he's strong, you know that, and once everything's back to normal—well, he'll be as fit as ever in no time. You mark my words.''

''But what about the fires?'' Hawk asked. ''When I first saw them, I thought they were exciting. I thought they meant that something wonderful was going to happen to us. But that's not what they mean at all, is it? I've seen Father's face when he looks at them. Why do they make him so sad? Does he think they're going to hurt us in some way?''

The smile faded on his mother's lips, and Hawk suddenly hated himself for his weakness, for not being strong enough to keep his fears to himself.

''You're growing up faster than I realised,'' she said at

last. "But you mustn't think less of me when I can't answer your questions. You see, sometimes there just aren't any answers—not even for your father."

Hawk felt a coldness steal through him that no amount of firelight or steaming herbal tea could dispel. "I'm frightened, mother," he said, pressing himself more tightly against her. "What if something bad happens? What if Father—" He could not, dared not, complete the thought.

"Now, now," she murmured, taking him in her arms as she had so many times before. "I'm here, my darling," she murmured gently. "I'll always be here."

Her breath was warm and sweet, like an intimation of spring, and, for both their sakes, Hawk pretended not to notice the tears in her eyes . . .

And there, even brighter than the rest!

. . . THAT NIGHT, his father took him to the High Place.

It was an old place, too; a holy place. No one knew who had hewn this vast subterranean labyrinth whose passageways snaked down to the very heart of Eltzen's Crown, but it had been there long before Hawk's ancestors had raised the first circle of crude stone huts that would eventually become Hiern Holding. One thing alone was certain: it had not been built by men.

The entrance was sealed with a slab of dull, imperishable metal that moved silently aside at the touch of his father's hand. Lighting a torch, he motioned Hawk inside.

Beyond the portal, a narrow staircase descended into the mountainside.

"Come," Hiern said, leading him gently forward. "I want to show you something."

The steps seemed to go on forever. The torch cast a faint pool of light before them; the rest was darkness. Frost glittered on the stones like sprinklings of powdered glass.

Every few yards, they passed a crude wooden platform heaped with bones. It was here that Hawk's grandfather had been entombed, many years before, together with his countless predecessors. Hawk could almost hear their dry, ghostly voices whispering to him, feel the weight of their unseen, unseeing eyes. One day, he and his father would join them: bound, even in death, to the long and fruitless vigil that had consumed their lives.

Eventually, they came to another door, smaller than the first, and flanked by two large stone hawks. Unlike the main gateway, it appeared to have been fashioned by human hands.

Drawing aside the heavy iron bolts, Hiern thrust his shoulder against the door and pushed it open.

They stepped into a small rectangular chamber. At first, Hawk thought it was empty. There were not catafalques or mouldering skulls, no golden death-masks or ornate swords: nothing except a cube of black, translucent rock about the size of a man's head. He felt almost disappointed.

Hiern held up his torch. He looked almost like a corpse himself, his face rendered in a lurid chiaroscuro of firelight and coal-black shadows.

"Look," he said. "Look carefully."

Straining his eyes against the darkness, Hawk peered down at the stone. There seemed to be something buried deep inside.

Something very bright.

Something very silver.

"What is it?" Hawk asked. He felt as if a knife were slowly working its way into his chest.

"The Key," Hiern told him.

As Hawk watched, he felt a wonder so intense that it seemed almost tangible—as if the tiny silver thread were blossoming, not in a block of unliving stone, but within some secret fastness that, until now, he'd never known existed, some hollow chamber buried deep inside him that he had been waiting all his life to fill.

"I see," he cried. "Oh, Father! I see!"

From that moment, his fate was sealed.

"SOME WINE, perhaps?" Hiern asked.

Isaf frowned, but said nothing. He'd given up trying to account for the man's mercurial behaviour. All he wanted was to get this whole ridiculous business over with as quickly as possible. Once they reached Eria, he could collect his gold and let Trevayne sort things out for himself.

"You must be tired after your journey," Hiern continued. Getting to his feet, he crossed to a nearby cupboard and took out a heavy crystal decanter. "Here we are," he said. "Just what we both need, eh? To cement our bargain, I mean."

He filled five wooden goblets and placed them on a tray. "One must be careful not to offend the ghosts," he explained.

"Ghosts?" Isaf said.

"Why, of course," Hiern told him. "Our holding is full of them. The ghosts of the dead—"

Picking up one of the cups, he dropped it casually at his feet.

"The ghosts of the living—"

Another goblet clattered to the floor. Wine streamed across the flagstones like blood.

"And last but not least, the ghosts of those yet to be born."

He hurled a third cup against the wall, then offered the tray to Isaf. "Here," he said. "Now it's our turn. You'll join me, won't you?"

Isaf shrugged. "Why not?"

"And then you must tell me more about this friend of yours. He must be quite a remarkable man."

"He seemed ordinary enough to me."

Hiern sipped quietly at his wine, a wry smile playing across his lips. "We shall see," he murmured. "But I suspect that you may well be in for something of a surprise."

CHAPTER SEVEN

Lair of the Medusa

THE AIR STANK of moisture and age, like an empty tomb. In the distance, Trevayne could hear the sound of water trickling over stone. He shivered—and not entirely from the cold.

Peering intently into the gloom, he edged slowly forward, holding his big sword before him like a divining rod. The well must be around here somewhere; it was simply a matter of finding the damned thing.

Something stirred in the vaulted darkness before him. Far off, he could see two faint lights gleaming among the shadows, a good eighty or ninety feet apart.

Lanterns, perhaps?

The lights blinked, gradually raising themselves up until they hovered above him like a pair of huge, bloated stars.

Not lanterns. Eyes.

Trevayne licked his lips, at last able to make out something of the creature that faced him. It was huge and shapeless, draped across the cavern floor like a beached whale. Its flesh quivered slightly with each intake of breath, like great mounds of isinglass heaped on a beach. Its eyes looked as big as cartwheels.

"ANOTHER ONE?" The words rang in his ears like the tolling of some monstrous bell. "WONDERS NEVER CEASE! AND SO SOON!"

Trevayne fell to his knees, trembling like a child. "Who are you?" he whispered. "What do you what?"

"I AM THE MEDUSA," the creature told him. It seemed almost amused by Trevayne's reaction, as if it were playing some sort of game with him. "I WILL TURN YOU TO STONE."

Somehow, Trevayne forced a bitter smile to his lips. "Is that so?" he said.

"BUT OF COURSE."

The creature shifted its bulk slightly, illuminating another portion of the cavern. Trevayne saw that the floor was littered with piles of creamy white stones, each as smooth as an egg and bigger than a prison cell.

"What are those?" he asked.

"WHY, THEY ARE MY PEARLS," the creature said. Its voice was slightly softer now, almost wistful. "AT LEAST, THAT'S WHAT I CALL THEM."

Trevayne frowned "How do you mean?"

"YOU, PERHAPS, MIGHT CALL THEM LIVES—OR FRAGMENTS OF LIVES."

"Ah," Trevayne said, climbing slowly to his feet. "I think I'm beginning to understand."

"OH, I SHOULDN'T DO THAT," the creature told him. "UNDERSTANDING CAN BE A DANGEROUS THING—VERY DANGEROUS INDEED. IN MY OPINION ONE IS FAR BETTER ADVISED TO SIMPLY TAKE THINGS AS THEY COME."

"Tell me," Trevayne asked. "Have you another name by any chance?"

The creature laughed. "YOU ALWAYS WERE A CLEVER LITTLE FELLOW, WEREN'T YOU, PAGAD TREVAYNE? TOO CLEVER BY HALF, SOME MIGHT SAY."

"You know my name then?"

"I KNOW EVERYBODY'S NAME."

Trevayne grinned. "There are quite a few legends about this place," he said. "Do you know who's supposed to live here?"

"AS YOU SAY, THERE ARE MANY LEGENDS. ONE

OUGHT NOT, I THINK, ATTACH TOO MUCH IMPOR-
TANCE TO SUCH THINGS.''

"Still, some may be more true than others."

"PERHAPS."

"Then tell me your name," Trevayne said. "And we'll
see if the rumours are right."

"I TOLD YOU ALREADY—I AM THE MEDUSA."

"I mean your real name."

The creature's eyes gazed down at him like beacons, then
it laughed once more. "SOME KNOW ME AS TIME," it
said. "I SUPPOSE IT IS AS GOOD A NAME AS ANY."

Trevayne thought a moment, then said. "Those pearls of
yours—are any of them mine?"

"BUT OF COURSE, MY DEAR BOY! OF COURSE!

Trevayne suddenly found himself immersed in a thick,
white fluid that clung to him like molasses, pulling him
down into a darkness so intense as to be indistinguishable
from light.

"Help me!" he screamed. Then the fluid filled his mouth
and he gagged for breath.

There came an answering of thunder.

PAGAD TREVAYNE FOUGHT bravely, as befitted his first commission. A few months before, he'd been just another
dreamy-eyed ploughboy toiling away at the rich Eredrosian
plains. Now all that was behind him. His peasant rags had
been exchanged for motley and silken hose, his spade and
sickle for a bright, two-handed sword. And today, gods'
willing, he would prove himself a man.

As Fjerl's raven banner flapped overhead, he plunged
into the ranks of advancing pikemen with the wild, berserker
fury possessed only by those as yet unschooled in the realities of battle. ("Virgins,'' Fjerl called them. "My pretty
little virgins." But he deployed them in the vanguard all
the same, "to encourage the others.") Arrows showered
down around him, clattering like hailstones against his
breastplate. Others fell, but he did not. At the tender age
of eighteen, he'd honestly believed that he could never die.

It was all over in a matter of minutes. Their line broken,
the Cordarii suddenly turned tail and fled; a broken, dis-

pirited rabble. Some of the Fjerla pursued them, but most fell to looting, scavenging what they could from the piles of corpses heaped across the battlefield. They knew better than to risk their lives in pursuit of a defeated host. Having won the day, they intended to enjoy the fruits of their victory. Only the young and the vainglorious gave chase. Those hungering for a reputation.

It was Trevayne who took the flag. He found the standard-bearer cowering in a ditch—a thin, raw-boned youth scarcely older than himself. The boy's face was white with terror, and it occurred to Trevayne that, had things worked out differently, their roles might very well have been reversed. Since he was vain enough to believe that he'd never ask for quarter, he gave none, slicing open his counterpart's belly the way some northern fisherman might gut a seal. The boy screamed, gazing down in horror as his entrails spilt from the atrocious wound like a coil of bloodstained rope. Sweetbread indeed!

Grinning wolfishly, Trevayne raised the banner high so that all might see. Two scarlet lions fluttered briefly against a field of gold, then, with a howl of triumph, he tore the oriflamme loose and trampled it into the mud.

"Kill the bastards!" he roared, a dark, unruly joy swelling inside him, coursing through his veins like fire. "Kill them all!"

It seemed to him that, for the first time in eighteen years, he was truly alive.

No! It wasn't like that!
COME NOW, HOW COULD IT POSSIBLY HAVE BEEN OTHERWISE?
He'd have done the same to me if he got the chance!
AH, SO IT WAS SELF DEFENCE, WAS IT?
In a way.
VERY WELL, LET'S SEE WHAT YOU MAKE OF THIS, THEN.

THE FARMHOUSE HAD BEEN REDUCED to a burnt-out shell, with only a few small flickers of flame still visible among the ashes. Haycocks smouldered in the fields nearby, filling the air with smoke.

He was with the Cordarii now, older, perhaps a little wiser, with a company of his own. Hands on hips, he watched as his troops rounded up the last of the survivors and put them to the sword. It was a kindness really—with winter coming on, they'd probably have starved to death anyway.

"Right, you lot!" he yelled. "Let's get these bloody carts loaded, shall we? We haven't got all day!"

Leaving them to it, he did a quick circuit of the ruined farmhouse, checking to see that everything was in order. On the far side, he found half a dozen men clustered around the door of a small stone outbuilding.

"What's going on here?" he said.

One of the men turned, his face split with an enormous grin. "Somebody's in there," he drawled, then recognized Trevayne's blue feather and quickly snapped to attention. "We think it might be a woman, sir."

"Well done, boys," Trevayne told them. "I'll take it from here. You'd better go help the others."

The men straggled off, muttering under their breath. No doubt they'd have liked a share of the spoils, but rank had its privileges, and they knew better than to disobey Trevayne's orders. Rumour had it that he'd once flogged a servant to death merely for spilling his soup.

The door was old and rotted. Two blows of Trevayne's big sword, and it splintered like firewood.

Peering inside, he saw a small room stacked with cheeses and baskets of vegetables. The woman was crouched in one corner, half-hidden behind a large pile of turnips.

"Don't be frightened," Trevayne said. "No one's going to hurt you."

The woman shrank further back into the shadows. Her face, though streaked with dirt and tears, was not entirely unappealing, and there seemed more than enough meat on her bones to make quite a tasty little morsel. One day, perhaps, he'd have his pick of the finest courtesans in the land—until then, however, he'd just have to make do with whatever titbits came his way.

"Don't come any closer!" the woman said, brandishing a heavy carving knife at him. Her eyes were wide and wild. "I'll kill you!"

Trevayne grinned, striding confidently towards her. "Why in heaven's name would you want to do something like that?"

"I'm warning you!" The woman gripped the knife in both hands, like some pagan priestess determined to immolate anything that came within reach—or perhaps even herself.

"Now, now," Trevayne chided gently. "There's no need for that. I just wanted to make sure you're all right. There's been a little bit of trouble outside, you see."

The woman frowned.

"Fortunately, we arrived just in the nick of time," Trevayne told her. "Otherwise those brigands would have butchered the lot of you."

"My husband—"

Trevayne smiled reassuringly. "Don't worry, he's fine. Just got a little bump on the head, that's all. He'll be right as rain once he's rested up for a bit. If you come with me, I'll show you where he is."

He moved quickly, taking advantage of the woman's momentary confusion. Who knows, she may actually have believed him.

Lunging forward, he knocked the knife from her grasp and sent it clattering to the floor. It came to rest a foot or so from her outstretched hand—a study in impotence and brute betrayal.

"Now," Trevayne said, licking his lips. "Let's get down to business, shall we?"

The woman screamed, clawing at him like a maddened beast. He hurled her back against the wall, taking out his own dagger and pressing it to her throat.

"That'll do, my sweet," he murmured. "You just stay nice and still, there's a good girl."

With his free hand, he reached down and tore away her skirt, staring approvingly at the soft white thighs beneath.

"Ah," he said. "Very nice. Very nice indeed."

Trevayne pulled her to him. She spat in his face, but he smiled anyway.

"Come on, now," he told her. "Don't be like that. This won't hurt a bit."

But of course he made sure that it did.

STILL WITH US, I SEE? MY, YOU ARE AN OBSTINATE LITTLE SOUL. PERHAPS WE OUGHT TO TRY A SOMEWHAT LARGER DOSE NEXT TIME, EH?

Why are you doing this?

I WOULD HAVE THOUGHT THAT WAS OBVIOUS— TO FREEZE YOUR SOUL TO STONE.

You don't frighten me. I've done nothing that I'm ashamed of.

OH, REALLY?

"WELL, WELL, WELL—if it isn't our old friend, Pagad Trevayne." Fjerl's lips curled unpleasantly above his wine cup, the way a wolf might smile at some newborn lamb that stumbled into its den. "They tell me Cordarii finally gave you your marching orders. That right, pretty boy?"

Trevayne sighed, wondering why, of all the taverns in Julkrease, Fjerl had to choose this one to drink at. They had not, he recalled, parted on the best of terms, and, although a good many years had passed since then, Fjerl had never been the sort to simply forgive and forget. For a moment, Trevayne considered returning to his room—or even, so help him, making a sudden break for the door— but the thought of providing Fjerl with yet another opportunity to laugh at him behind his back was, quite frankly, more than he could bear. Adjusting his hat, he continued on down the stairs, seating himself at a table as far removed from Fjerl and his men as honour would allow, and ordered the pot-boy to bring him a jug of wine.

Fjerl, however, obviously wasn't prepared to let the matter rest. "Hey, Pagad," he said. "I'm talking to you." When Trevayne still failed to answer, he whispered something to his men, then sauntered over and banged his jug down loudly on Trevayne's table. The tavern staff, always a reliable barometer in such matters, had begun to slink off to their various nooks and crannies, obviously of the opinion that there was trouble brewing. Trevayne had a similar premonition himself.

He took another sip of wine, then slowly looked up. Despite the passing years, Fjerl's gaze was as intimidating as ever, and he cursed himself for having left his sword upstairs, suddenly feeling quite naked without it. "Hello, Fjerl," he said wearily. "Is there something I can do for you?"

"Don't get smart with me, Trevayne," Fjerl muttered darkly. His smile, malevolent enough to begin with, was rapidly degenerating into an open snarl. "I asked how come you split with Cordarii? Find himself a new bum-chum, did he?"

"If you mean, have I resigned my commission, the answer is yes." Trevayne took out his silver snuffbox and tossed it negligently in his hand. "Not that it's any of your business."

"Resigned, eh?" Fjerl laughed. "The way I heard it, Cordarii tossed you out on your fat white arse. Not that I'm surprised. Never really had much stomach for the game, did you, Pagad?" He turned to his men, who jostled about their table like a pack of feral dogs, mauling any servant-girl unwise enough to venture near them, and guzzling such prodigious quantities of beer that it was a wonder they could stand at all. "Only ever got himself wounded twice in eight years. Both times in the back!"

Trevayne ignored the chorus of jeers that followed. He had no intention of allowing Fjerl to goad him into a duel, not when the condottiere had a dozen seasoned veterans standing by to take his part, all of them armed and spoiling for a fight. "I can't be held responsible for what you may or may not hear," Trevayne told him. "As it happens, I've decided to strike out on my own. You never know, we might be crossing swords one day soon. That is, unless you're intending to retire, of course."

Fjerl evidently found this hugely amusing. Quaffing down the last of his beer, he threw the jug aside and snatched another from the pot-boy as the poor lad scuttled past on his way back to the taproom. "And just what d'you think you've got to offer as a leader, eh? Personally speaking, I wouldn't trust you to clean out a bloody latrine.''

Trevayne smiled. "Offer?" he said. "I don't know—a certain boyish charm, perhaps? Some employers want a little more for their money than a bunch of half-starved sewer-rats . . . although I don't suppose you've come across very many of those, eh, Fjerl?''

A few of the Fjerla muttered under their breath, but most of them paid no attention whatsoever, apparently too dim-witted to realise they'd been insulted at all. Fjerl motioned for silence with an irritable wave of his hand. "You've really got tickets on yourself, haven't you, Pagad? I'll bet you think your shit don't stink either.''

"I wouldn't really know," Trevayne said breezily, "not having made an extensive study of the subject." He took a pinch of snuff. "Yours obviously does. I can smell it from here.''

For a moment, he thought that Fjerl was going to hit him. Trevayne reached for the dagger tucked inside his doublet, knowing that he stood little chance against such overwhelming odds, but determined to go down fighting. Suddenly, however, the naked fury in Fjerl's face gave way to a sly, calculating smile.

"So," he said. "You think you're as good a man as me, eh?''

Trevayne shrugged. "That's for others to judge. But I'm certainly not a worse one.''

"All right, then." Fjerl threw back his yellow velvet cloak to reveal a huge, double-bladed axe that any headsman would have given his right arm to possess. Trevayne didn't like to think how many lives it must have harvested in its time. "Fancy putting your money where your mouth is, cleverdick?''

"Not particularly." Trevayne poured himself another drink, gratified to note that his hand scarcely shook at all. "At least, not with that mob around." He glanced across at the Fjerla, some of whom were already fingering their knives ominously. The rest milled around one end of the table, where they'd finally managed to bring a pair of serving-wenches to bay, pawing at the girls' clothes like jackals dismembering a corpse. "I'm not a complete idiot, you know. One word from you and those bastards would tear me apart."

Fjerl spat contemptuously. "I don't need their help to deal with *you*. What's the matter, Pagad? Scared you might get hurt?"

"The thought had crossed my mind," Trevayne told him.

"Here," Fjerl said, unslinging his big axe and tossing it to one of his men. "No tricks, see? Just a simple test of skill, that's all."

"What do you suggest? Knucklebones? Mumbudget? I think I've got a deck of cards upstairs somewhere."

"Catch-as-catch-can," Fjerl said. "Three falls to decide the winner." He took a handful of silver coins from his purse. "This says I wipe the floor with you. Care to match it?"

Although Trevayne couldn't help feeling that he'd been comprehensively outmanoeuvred, the prospect of finally paying Fjerl back for all the indignities meted out to him in the past was more than he could resist. This may not have been the perfect time or place for such a confrontation, but it was probably as good as he was ever likely to get. "Why not?" he said. "I'm sure it'll only take a minute or two, anyway." He reached into his own purse. With six months' back pay, and his share of the booty from their last campaign, he had little trouble covering Fjerl's bet. "So long as your bully-boys stick to the rules. I don't want one of them hamstringing me just because I started knocking you around a bit."

Fjerl turned to his men, grinning cagily. "You heard what the man said," he told them. "Keep out of it, all right? This is between Pagad and me." Those Fjerla not still queuing up for their turn at the women yelped and grunted, presumably in agreement. They were Cariaspians for the most part; nasty and brutish, with about as much intellectual refinement as a cartload of turnips—which was one reason why Trevayne had found life among them so unpalatable. With any luck, however, they'd drink themselves into a stupor before the bout was over, thus enabling him to come out of this in one piece.

"Come on, lads," Fjerl continued. "Give us some room. Pretty boy here is going to show us what he's made of."

Fjerla immediately set about overturning tables and demolishing any other stick of furniture they could lay their hands on, apparently for the sheer hell of it. Seizing the chance to escape from their tormentors, two naked servant-wenches fled through the chaos like unusually buxom ghosts being hounded by demons. The innkeeper, a slim, inoffensive fellow who until now had been skulking behind some beer-kegs, voiced a few feeble protests, but was quickly silenced when one of the Fjerla brandished a knife at him and threatened to cut out his tongue. Within moments, a space had been cleared in the centre of the tavern large enough to accommodate an ox and dray.

"Hey, Stickman," Fjerl said, handing both Trevayne's coins, and his own, to the terrified innkeeper. "You can hold the pot. Winner takes all. Understand?"

The fellow nodded, looking down at the coins as if, for the first time in his life, he wished they were somewhere else.

"Let's get on with it, eh?" Fjerl said, stripping off his cloak and jerkin and motioning for Trevayne to do the same. Despite being a little past his prime, he still cut an imposing figure in his black, waist-high boots and silken cummerbund, although his features remained those of the illiterate peasant who'd clawed his way up through the ranks many years before: blunt and oddly lopsided, as if he'd hacked them out himself from a slab of coarse, dark wood. He had a considerable advantage in weight and reach over Trevayne, and was an accomplished street-fighter. By contrast, Trevayne would have to rely almost solely on his speed and wits. At the time, he actually thought that might be enough.

"Whenever you're ready, big man," he said, placing his hat and doublet on one of the few chairs that the Fjerla had left more or less intact. "I hope your friends are sober enough to cart you home afterwards, because you won't be walking anywhere for a while once I'm through with you."

"Dream on it, Trevayne," Fjerl told him, slowly flexing his shoulders, which swelled above his barrel-chest like two chaff-bags stuffed with rocks. "You'll be singing a different tune when I shove your head up your arse.''

Trevayne came at him with a rush, feinting towards Fjerl's neck, then swiftly planting his foot in the man's crotch. Fjerl toppled to his knees like a tree lopped off at the base, gasping for breath. The Fjerla mumbled disconsolately, but held their ground, too shocked or too spineless to intervene.

Trevayne grinned as he prepared to roll his opponent over and complete the throw. ''I think you're getting a bit old for this, Fjerl,'' he crowed. ''Not quite so quick on your pins anymore, eh?''

As he advanced, however, Fjerl suddenly shot out one arm and seized him by the ankles, whipping his feet from under him so that he crashed heavily to the floor. Before he knew what happened, the condottiere had pinned his shoulders. He tried to squirm free, but it was as if a mountain were squatting on his chest.

''One to me, I think,'' Fjerl said. Standing up, he swaggered back towards his men, one who passed him a fresh jug of beer. ''Come on, Pagad! Not throwing in the towel already, are you?''

Trevayne's confusion obviously registered on his face. Fjerl laughed. Reaching down, he pulled a wad of stiffened leather from his codpiece. ''First rule of warfare—always bolster your defences before launching an attack.'' The Fjerla responded with hoots and catcalls, although, to be honest, Trevayne could scarcely hear them for the sound of blood marching through his head. ''You didn't really expect me to fall for a trick like that, did you?'' Fjerl asked him. ''I was a master at this bloody game while you were still sucking on your mother's tit!''

Trevayne staggered to his feet. Judging by the pain in his chest, at least one rib was cracked and the rest badly bruised, but anger smouldered inside him now like a slow fire, making the pain seem remote and inconsequential— simply more fuel for the flames. He waved Fjerl forward. ''At least I had a mother!'' he snarled. ''I hear they found you vomited up in a gutter somewhere!''

''That's the spirit,'' Fjerl said. He emptied the beer jug and belched loudly. ''It's a pity you don't fight as good as you talk, Pagad. There'd be no stopping you.''

Trevayne rushed him again, but this time Fjerl stepped neatly aside, so that he blundered headlong into a crowd of Fjerla standing nearby. He smelt their foetid breath on his face for moment, then they catapulted him back toward the centre of the room, where Fjerl grabbed his arm and twisted it into a hammerlock, until he felt sure it would be wrenched from its socket completely. He lashed out with his free hand, but to little effect. Fjerl simply brushed the blows aside and tightened his grip even further.

"You've got two choices, Pagad," he hissed. "Either concede the fall, or I'll break your bloody arm. What's it going to be, eh?"

Trevayne felt tears welling in his eyes: not of pain so much as fury and impotence; although none the less shameful for that. He could almost hear the sinews tearing in his shoulder, one by one, like halyards snapping in a high wind.

"Aw, leave him alone, Fjerl!" someone shouted. "The poor sod's bawling his eyes out!"

"Well?" Fjerl demanded. "What's it to be?" He twisted again. "First this arm, then the other. And then I start on the legs." By now, he was crooning in Trevayne's ear like a lover. "You want to be a cripple, pretty boy? Eh? You want to crawl out of here on your belly?"

Trevayne shook his head, hating himself for it.

"Then let's hear you beg."

"No!"

"Beg, you little worm!"

"No!"

"Beg!"

Trevayne's entire body was awash with pain. It consumed him, battered him, inundated him: wave after wave. It was an ocean inside him; a furnace devouring his flesh, as vast and pitiless as the sun.

"All right! You win!"

Fjerl chuckled vindictively. "You'll have to speak up, Pagad. I must be going a little deaf in my old age."

"I said you win!" Trevayne spat out the words like a mouthful of poison.

"You mean, you're conceding the fall?"

"Yes, damn you! Whatever you like! Just let me go!" Still the pain increased. *"Please."*

"I still can't hear you, Pagad."

"Please!"

"A bit louder. So old Tanglebones doesn't get confused."

"PLEASE!"

It took some time for Trevayne to realise that Fjerl had let him go. The pain in his shoulder raged on unabated, only the pressure was gone. He stumbled forward, glancing around wildly for his opponent, only to find himself suddenly hoisted up and flung through the air like a sack of straw. He landed heavily on his back, amidst a pile of broken furniture heaped beside the tavern door. Whether or not Fjerl actually bothered to pin his shoulders, he had no idea. His head was still reeling when he heard a familiar chant echo through the tavern, accompanied by a clamour of breaking crockery and stamping feet:

"F-J-E-R-L-A!"

"F-J-E-R-L-A!"

"F-J-E-R-L-A!"

"F-J-E-R-L-A!"

Then Fjerl's own voice cut above the rest, full of exultation and wry contempt: "What did I tell you, lads? Piss in the hand! The stupid bastard never knew what hit him!"

Shivering with rage, Trevayne felt his hand close around something hard and sharp—a discarded knifeblade, perhaps, or a jagged length of pipe—and climbing to his knees, he hurled it at Fjerl with all his strength. The condottiere's scornful laughter suddenly gave way to a howl of anguish. Looking up, Trevayne saw blood streaming from the man's face, saw the Fjerla bare their swords and lunge towards him, no longer a beer-sodden rabble, but as bold and ravenous as wolves.

By then, however, Trevayne was already off and running, scrambling over a heap of rubble and out into the street. As he fled blindly into the night, Fjerl's voice seemed to pursue him through the darkness like a clap of doom:

"I'll get you for this, Trevayne! Just see if I don't! You're dead meat, pretty boy! You hear me? Dead meat!"

Trevayne heard. And he remembered, too. Even now, two decades later, he remembered.

Dead meat.

You bastard!
OHO! A HIT! A PALPABLE HIT!
Leave me alone!
NOW, WHAT SHALL WE TRY NEXT? AH, YES! I THINK I KNOW JUST THE THING. THE COUP-DE-GRACE, AS IT WERE.
What do you mean?
THIS IS ALL FOR THE BEST, BELIEVE ME.
But—
GOOD-BYE, TREVAYNE. IT'S BEEN A PLEASURE TALKING TO YOU. MOST OF MY VISITORS AREN'T HALF SO ENTERTAINING.

THE SCENE WAS only too familiar. For the past ten years, it had haunted him day and night, like murder unrevenged.

He was, perhaps, the most famous mercenary leader of the age. Men flocked to his banner from every corner of the Four Kingdoms, eager to win his favour. They knew full well that the Pagadi were never unemployed.

On occasions, of course, such notoriety had its disadvantages.

"You again, is it?" he said, glancing distastefully at the prostrate figure before him. "What do you want this time?"

The man sat up. With his sharp, pinched face and tiny eyes, he looked more like a large rat than a human being. No one had any idea where he'd come from, but he purported to represent some anonymous eastern monarch keen to engage Trevayne's services. Although the twelve chests of gold which he'd brought as down payment certainly argued his case most eloquently, Trevayne had little liking for the fellow, and was tempted to send him packing then and there.

"Have you given any more thought to my master's offer?" the man asked. "As I've said before, we are eager to conclude this business as soon as possible."

Trevayne shrugged. "That's your problem," he said. "Not mine. And I can't make any decision until you tell me who you're working for. How do I know this isn't some kind of trap?"

"You have my master's word," the ambassador assured him. "Surely that is enough?"

"The word of someone who won't even tell me his name?" Trevayne snorted with disgust. "A fat lot of use that is!"

"All will be revealed in due time. If you will simply accompany me to—"

Trevayne thumped his fist against the arm of his chair. "Now listen to me!" he growled. "I'm not going anywhere until I know your master's name! Do I make myself quite clear?"

"I am not at liberty to discuss the matter further," the ambassador said haughtily. "Either we embark for the East at once or I shall have to take my offer elsewhere."

"Is that a fact?"

"There are plenty of other armies about," the ambassador said smugly. "The Fjerla, for example—"

Trevayne laughed. "You hear that, boys?" he said, looking across at the line of young lieutenants assembled nearby. "Old ratface here thinks we're a pack of no-hopers. He's going to get some *real* men to do the job!" Suddenly, he leant down and grabbed the ambassador by the throat. "For your information," he snapped, "the Fjerla no longer exist. We smashed the bastard two months ago, down at Gethling Vale. He'd be lucky to put two dozen men in the field right now—that's if you could ever find him, of course."

The ambassador wrenched himself free and tottered back, vainly striving to maintain some semblance of dignity. "I can see I'm not welcome here," he muttered stiffly. "If you'll be so kind as to return my gold, I'll trouble you no more."

"Gold?" Trevayne said. "I don't remember any gold." He gestured toward the guards stationed beside him. "Get this fool out of here, will you? He's beginning to try my patience."

Pinning the ambassador's scrawny arms, they started dragging him towards the door. He thrashed about wildly, almost spitting with rage. "You will pay for this!" he hissed. "Oh, how you will pay!"

"What are you going to do?" Trevayne mocked. "Bite me on the leg?"

Somehow, the ambassador wrenched himself free. He glared defiantly up at Trevayne, baring his teeth like a cornered rat. "Laugh while you can, Trevayne! The One Who Waits shall—"

A sword-stroke cut the babbling short. It ended with a wet, gurgling sound, as if his soul were slowly draining from him like water down a pipe.

"He ain't about to give us no more trouble, cap'n," one of Trevayne's lieutenants said, wiping his blade fastidiously on the ambassador's small, huddled corpse. "Must have been off his head, I reckon, talking to you like that."

Next morning, however, he and his fellow officers were informed that Trevayne had suddenly decided to resign from active command, placing Bludsmaugre in charge of the battalion until such time as a successor could be elected from among their own ranks.

He'd left for Eredrosia that very afternoon—and had slept uneasily ever since.

"NOT THAT ONE. You should never have chosen that one."

"YOU ARE NOT STONE!"

"That wasn't very clever, my friend. Not very clever at all."

"I DID NOT—"

Trevayne smiled derisively. "Nice try," he said. "But it looks as if your luck's finally run out. Now, unless you've got any more tricks up your sleeve, I suggest that you stand aside."

"THERE ARE STRANGE POWERS AT WORK HERE," the creature told him, its voice slowly dwindling like the echo of distant thunder. "BEFORE THIS BUSINESS IS OVER, MY FRIEND, YOU MAY WELL WISH THAT I HAD SUCCEEDED."

"Sure," Trevayne said. "It's nice to know that you're so concerned about my welfare."

Suddenly, he was alone. Somewhere close at hand he could hear the splashing of a well.

He headed towards it.

CHAPTER EIGHT

———◆———

Last Rites

"TEA?" the woman asked. "It's one of the few things we still import from the lowlands. A private vice, I'm afraid."

She was old, but still beautiful after a fashion, wrapped in black and sable mink like some precious jade ornament. A silver circlet burnt in her long, white hair, although she looked stately enough without such trappings, just as her delicate features required no cosmetics to enhance their elegance. Cayla, with her cheap paste jewelry and kohl-darkened eyes, felt decidedly tawdry by comparison.

"That would be lovely," Cayla murmured, wondering what polite conversation she might make without (gods forbid!) inadvertently giving offence. Apart from their sex, the two had nothing in common whatsoever. Everything about Hiern's mother marked her out as a woman of breeding and distinction, nurtured from birth like a hothouse flower to take her rightful place among the most exhalted ranks of society; Cayla had never been anything more than a guttersnipe. Hands folded demurely in her lap, she tried to think how a fashionable young debutante would act in a situation like this.

"This is a lovely room, my lady," she said at last.

"Do you think so?" Hiern's mother, having finished pouring the tea, handed Cayla a cup that seemed as small and fragile as an eggshell. "Milk, my dear?" she asked.

"No, thank you."

"How wise." The Lady Hiern paused a moment, blowing steam from her cup, then glanced towards the fireplace, where logs crackled and spluttered in the grate like prime cuts of beef. "At least it's a trifle warmer here," she said. "Not like the rest of the Holding."

"Very pleasant indeed," Cayla said.

A moment's silence.

Then, "Where are you from, my dear?" the Lady Hiern asked.

"A place called Julkrease, ma'am," Cayla told her. "It's a fair way north of here. By the sea."

"Yes, I know." Hiern's mother smiled gently. "We are not completely shut off from the world up here, however much that may appear the case."

Cayla blushed. "Forgive me," she murmured, "I didn't mean—"

"It's quite all right," the woman assured her. "To someone who has grown up on the shores of Ocean, this must seem like the ends of the earth." She sipped quietly at her tea, studying Cayla closely over the rim of her cup. "What brings you to the mountains, anyway?" she said at last. "Travellers seldom venture up this way—particularly now that winter's coming. You must have fairly pressing business here, I'd imagine."

Cayla stirred uncomfortably in her chair. She felt as if Hiern's mother were somehow testing her, probing her defences. Had a man questioned her in such a fashion, she would simply had shrugged the matter off with a giggle or a disarming smile, but the Lady Hiern was not to be dealt with so easily. Like a well-to-do procuress that Cayla had once known, she looked the sort of woman who might be dangerous to cross: all warm and motherly on the surface; as hard as steel inside. Cayla chose her words carefully, trying not to give away any more than was absolutely necessary.

"We were sent here to find a man called Hawk," she said. "But apparently he's dead, so—"

"Dead?" For a moment, the old woman's eyes took on

a cold, almost menacing aspect. Then she smiled. "Whoever told you that?" she asked.

"Why, your son, Hiern. He seemed quite definite about it. You don't think there's been some kind of mistake, do you?"

"Mistake?" The Lady Hiern shook her head. "No, not a mistake—simply a little misunderstanding. In a way, I suppose, my son is right. Hawk no longer exists. But I wouldn't exactly say that he was dead."

Cayla frowned. "I don't understand."

"Hiern *is* Hawk," the old woman explained. "Or was, before his father died. It's an hereditary title, you see. One day, his son will be Hiern, too."

"Oh, I see!" Cayla smiled, then thought of poor Isaf, who was probably still convinced that their mission had been an utter failure. "Oh, dear," she said. "That does make things rather complicated, doesn't it?"

"To outsiders, perhaps," the Lady Hiern said. "If you don't mind me asking, exactly what was it that you wanted to see Hawk about?"

"We have a letter for him, that's all."

"From whom?"

"A man we met in Julkrease. I don't remember his name."

Although the lie came smoothly enough to her lips, Hiern's mother obviously wasn't taken in by it for a moment. "Don't remember?," she said, her tone conveying the softest, most gentle, reproach imaginable. "But surely, to have come all this way—"

"You'd have to ask Isaf," Cayla said quickly, somewhat flustered by the old woman's persistence. "I really don't know much about it at all."

"Isaf? That's your husband, is it?"

Cayla looked away, unable to prevent the blood rushing to her cheeks. "We're just friends," she said quickly, taking a sip of tea, which was still hot enough to scald her tongue.

"I see. Forgive me for prying." Again, the Lady Hiern studied her silently for a time. "You see, it occurred to me that perhaps Hawk had—but, no, I'm just being silly. He would have mentioned something about it before now. Even so . . ."

"Yes, my lady?"

"Well, my dear, Hawk must soon think about finding himself a wife, and, when you mentioned a letter, I thought that—" Hiern's mother smiled. "You must excuse me, child. You know what we mothers are like, always meddling in our sons' affairs. A pretty little thing like you could do better for herself than this draughty pile of rock, I'm sure."

For a moment, Cayla forgot her manners completely, gaping openly at the woman. A whore marry a prince? Well, why not? Stranger things had probably happened. Besides, when you thought about it, wives too were harlots after a fashion, hawking their flesh to the highest bidder in exchange for food and shelter. They just usually managed to drive a somewhat harder bargain, that's all.

"You see," the Lady Hiern explained, "it's customary for Hiern to seek his wife from somewhere outside the Holding. I myself was born in the South, near Porphyry. Our marriage was arranged by a company of lowland bankers. I couldn't help wondering if—"

"Oh, no!" Cayla said, still uncertain whether she was embarassed or amused by the suggestion. "It's nothing like that, believe me. We're simply here to deliver that letter I told you about."

"Of course. I oughtn't to have mentioned it in the first place. I'm just a fond, foolish old woman, that's my trouble. I'm sorry if I offended you."

Cayla smiled. "Not at all." she said. "But I'm surprised to hear that your son isn't married. He seems a fine figure of a man. You must be very proud of him."

"Proud?" The Lady Hiern peered down into her teacup, as if seeking to divine the answer to some complex personal conundrum. "Pride is a luxury we can ill afford at Hiern Holding," she said quietly. "We should all be far better off without it, if you ask me."

Cayla said nothing, a trifle disconcerted by the sudden vehemence in her tone.

"Tell me," the woman said, suddenly leaning forward

and placing one wrinkled hand on Cayla's arm. "How old would you say my son is?"

"Oh, I don't know," Cayla said. She smiled awkwardly. "But he carries himself well, whatever his years. I shouldn't think he'd have much trouble finding himself a wife."

The Lady Hiern laughed, a surprisingly bitter sound. "Nineteen summers!" she said. "Scarcely more than a boy—and just look at him!"

"Nineteen?" Cayla asked. None of this seemed to make any sense whatsoever. The man she'd met had looked at least twice that age. "I don't understand."

"It's killing him. Day by day, piece by piece, it's killing him."

"How do you mean?" Cayla said. "Is your son sick or something?"

The Lady Hiern stared blankly in the distance, eyes misted with tears. She seemed almost to have forgotten that Cayla existed. "First his father," she murmured, "and now Hawk. The price is too high—much, much too high."

"Are you all right?" Cayla asked. She wondered if the woman were having some kind of fit. "Do you want me to call someone?"

"What?" The Lady Hiern stared at her a moment, then smiled, reaching once more for the ornate china teapot. "More tea, dear?" she asked.

"I—" Cayla stifled a frown, then shook her head. "No, thank you," she said. "I've hardly started this one."

EVENING. Ice-cold shadows drenched the walls, gnawing at the stone like streaks of acid. Four figures sat around a heavy oaken table. In the centre, a skull-shaped candle, its fugitive glow dancing across their faces. No sound save the occasional shuffle of feet or the scraping of knives on silver plates. They might have been a convocation of the dead, or mourners huddled inside some bleak, ancestral tomb.

Fortunately, Isaf's appetite was more than equal to the occasion. Refilling his cup, he carved himself a few more slices of meat and heaped them on his plate. So far, Hiern had proven quite a generous host (despite his occasional bouts of moodiness), and the food itself was excellent: venison and wildfowl for the most part, washed down with copious amounts of mead and hot, spiced wine. Come sunrise, they'd be on their way, and until then he was happy to accept any roof over his head, no matter how austere the company. Outside, the sun-devouring wolves of winter stalked unchallenged through the hills, howling and gnashing their teeth. Even Isaf, who was no stranger to hardship, balked at the prospect of sleeping rough on a night like this.

Cayla nibbled at a piece of fruit, occasionally glancing across at Hiern, then looking quickly away, as if both appalled and fascinated by the man. There hadn't been an opportunity for Isaf to learn what had transpired during her conversation with Hiern's mother, but obviously she'd found the meeting unsettling. He reached over and patted her hand reassuringly, eliciting a brief, if troubled, smile. As soon as they'd finished their meal, he'd have to find out exactly what was bothering her.

It wasn't until most of the dishes had been cleared away, save for a few large platters of cheese and sweetmeats, and the servants dismissed, that Hiern seemed willing to break the silence which had closed in around them.

"I've got a surprise for you, Mother," he said, his eyes glistening with almost feverish intensity. "Do you want to know what it is?"

The Lady Hiern did not look up. Pale and unmoving, her face shone in the candlelight as if it, too, were carved from a lump of translucent wax. "If you like," she said.

"Our good friend Isaf here, has asked me to accompany him on a little journey."

"That's nice, dear."

"To Eria."

"Really?"

"I've decided to accept his offer."

"I'm sure you know best, my dear."

Isaf took another sip of wine. He felt as if he were witnessing some esoteric ritual rather than a simple dinnertable conversation between mother and son. The tension between the two was unmistakable. Obviously there was far more to this discussion than met the eye.

"Let's drink a toast, shall we?" Hiern said, grinning like

a death's-head as he raised his heavy pewter mug. "To the future, whatever bitter secrets it may hold for us!"

Gulping down a huge draught of wine, he sat back and smiled, as if he'd won the opening gambit in a contest which Isaf could never hope to understand.

"You must need my son very badly," the Lady Hiern said, turning to Isaf and fixing him with an icy stare, "to have come all this way in search of him."

"I'm just carrying out my instructions," Isaf told her. For some reason, he found the old woman's gaze most discomfiting. "What happens afterwards isn't really any of my concern."

"But it is important that Hiern goes with you?"

"So I've been told."

"According to the letter I received," Hiern said, "it may well have something to do with the Fires."

It showed in the whitening of her tendons; the tiny, almost imperceptible flicker of her eyes. It was something very much like fear.

Hiern shook his head—a gesture so subtle as to be almost imperceptible. His mother opened her mouth, as if to speak, then suddenly looked away.

"I'm sure that our guests must find this conversation tedious," Hiern said. "Why don't you tell us something about yourself, eh, Isaf?"

Isaf shrugged. "There's not much to tell," he said. "At the moment, I'm a messenger. Once we get to Eria, I'll find myself something else to do. There's always plenty of work around for people like me." Which was sheer bravado, of course, considering his recent experience in Julkrease, but Hiern wasn't to know that. Besides, if Trevayne fulfilled his part of the bargain, Isaf would probably never have to work again.

"Ah," Hiern said, licking his lips. "You're a warrior, then?"

"Just a soldier," Isaf told him. He thought of Ladoc, who was the closest thing to a true warrior he'd ever met. "Only a fool fights for glory. The rest of us are trying to make an honest living like everybody else."

"I see. And what of your enchanting lady friend here? She will accompany you?"

Cayla shrank back in her chair, clutching at Isaf's arm. He frowned. "Perhaps," he said. "That's for her to say."

"I see."

For a moment, it seemed that no one had anything further to add. Then the Lady Hiern craned forward, her features bland and impassive once more. "This expedition of yours," she said. "To Eria. When will you will be starting off?"

"In the morning," Hiern told her. "By all indications, we have little time to waste."

"And tonight?" his mother asked.

Hiern frowned. "Tonight certain preparations must be made." His tone was faintly reproachful, as if the subject were not one he wished to discuss in front of a stranger. "You know that as well as I do."

"Yes." The Lady Hiern bowed her head. "Yes, of course."

Isaf decided that he'd had enough. It was as if they were talking in some kind of code, some secret language that took quite commonplace terms and invested them with all manner of bizarre implications. *Fires, preparations*: the words had an ominous, faintly sinister ring, although for the life of him, Isaf hadn't the vaguest idea what they signified. Not for the first time, he wished he'd taken the trouble to read Trevayne's letter for himself.

Getting to his feet, he nodded across at Hiern and stepped back from the table. Cayla followed suit, her arm tucked tightly around his elbow. "We ought to be getting some rest now," he said. "It's been a long day."

Hiern shrugged. "Very well. I'll have someone show you to your chamber."

"Thank you."

"Good night, my lord," Cayla muttered quietly. "My lady."

Both Hiern and his mother, however, seemed engrossed in their own thoughts, and did not reply.

A servant was summoned to escort them from the dining-hall. Pausing momentarily at the doorway, Isaf looked back

to see the pair exchanging heated whispers across the table.
Hiern looked strangely troubled, his face as grey and brittle
as unbleached parchment.

Isaf hurried on, feeling Cayla snuggle against him. "Oh,
Isaf," she murmured, "I can't stand much more of this. I
really can't."

"It's almost over now," he said. "Just get yourself a
good night's sleep, and everything will seem much better
in the morning."

"I'll try." Cayla shivered again. "There's something not
.ight about this place, Isaf. Something Trevayne didn't tell
us about. I can feel it."

Behind them, the skull-candle still flickered and spluttered in the gloom, leering a ghostly smile.

BONE-WEARY THOUGH SHE WAS, Cayla found sleep impossible. She kept turning the day's events over and over
in her head, trying to reconcile what Hiern's mother had
told her with the haunted, almost ghoulish, figure who'd
presided over their meal that night like death at a feast.

On arriving at their quarters—a great stone chamber overlooking the northern battlements, which, judging by its appearance, hadn't been occupied for years—Isaf had wanted
to know all about her conversation with Lady Hiern, but,
having no wish to make a fool of herself by repeating what
seemed like utter nonsense, she'd merely shrugged, maintaining that there wasn't a great deal to tell. They'd drunk
some tea; chatted a little (about nothing in particular); then
the woman had ordered a bath to be drawn so that Cayla
could freshen up for dinner. And that was it. A trifle nerve-
wracking at times, perhaps, since Cayla hadn't been sure
how to behave in front of such a lady, but otherwise pleasant
enough. Certainly a lot better than shivering in some
cramped little tent all evening as she had for the past eight
days or so.

Isaf seemed happy to leave it at that. Not that she'd given
him much of an opportunity to press her further on the
subject, retiring almost immediately and bundling the dusty
bearskin blankets tightly around her. It was getting late,

she'd argued; they could talk about it in the morning, if he
liked. Besides, she was tired.

And so she was. She ached from top to toe after yet
another hard day in the saddle, while the effort required to
disguise her mounting uneasiness had left her mentally
drained as well. Yet here she was, hours later, still wide
awake, still brooding, still pondering mysteries that in the
end defied all comprehension. Hiern couldn't possibly be
as young as his mother claimed. Nineteen summers, indeed!
But why would the woman lie about something like that?
And what exactly was supposed to be killing him? Some
wasting disease, perhaps? That might explain a few things,
she supposed. Then again, a sick man was hardly likely to
suddenly pack up and leave simply because someone handed
him a letter. It just didn't make sense. And so she went
through it

And again.

And again.

(*This is ridiculous*, she told herself. *It's getting me nowhere.*)

And againandagainandagainandagainandagain.

Finally, in desperation, she slipped out of bed and, draping a heavy fur robe around her shoulders, crossed to a
small, rectangular window cut in the north wall, where stars
fluttered like moths against the frost-spangled glass.

Despite the huge blackened logs smouldering nearby, the
room was bitterly cold, and the granite flagstones stung her
feet like blocks of ice until she managed to find a pair of
buskins tucked away in one of the cupboards, snuggling
into them with an almost audible sigh of relief. She moved
as silently as her numbed toes and fingers would allow,
having no wish to face another round of questioning from
Isaf should he wake up. Although he certainly seemed dead
to the world, snoring away as noisily as ever (a sound
already so familiar to her that she wondered how she'd ever
managed to sleep without it), and apparently quite untroubled by thoughts of the melancholy snow queen and her
enigmatic son. Cayla shook her head, wishing that she could
say the same for herself, then returned to the window and

stared thoughtfully out at the night-shrouded mountains beyond.

Moonlight rimed the upper slopes with silver; below, the great stone bulwarks were immersed in darkness, although she could just make out a narrow causeway leading towards the tallest of the peaks, its polished surface sparkling like a mirror.

Then there were the stars: brighter than she'd ever seen before, like a multitude of angels peering down from their stations in the sky. Watching over her, perhaps. At least, that's what her mother had always said, as the two of them gazed heavenwards on those balmy Julkrean evenings when—it being much too hot to sleep indoors—Hauba's rooftop echoed to the sound of girlish laughter and hushed, conspiratorial whispers until the early hours, as if the whole Lupanic Quarter had been transformed into a vast seraglio, and they were pampered courtesans taking the air on one of its many fragrant terraces. *See, my darling? There's nothing to worry about. The angels are watching over us.*

And perhaps they were—although, to be quite honest, Cayla couldn't see what good that did anyone. Their vigilance certainly hadn't prevented Hauba from turning her mother out on the streets once she was of no further use to him, nor lessened Cayla's own anguish a few hours later, when, dragged screaming to his room, she'd been savagely initiated into the mysteries of her profession. Hauba claimed that he was never finished with a woman until he'd enjoyed her three ways, yet, by the time that long night was over, he'd been well-and-truly through with her—several times in fact. The recollection brought with it a wave of anger and disgust. What right had Hauba to treat her like that? And how could the powers governing this world (who had gazed blindly down while she was posed and pummelled and staked and torn, all the while begging, pleading, for him to stop), how could they, those bright and risen angels, possibly have countenanced such a thing?

That initial violation had been re-enacted less brutally in the grubby curtained booths where she'd been entombed for virtually her entire adult life. The faces may have changed, but deep down they were all the same: the drunkards and gamesters, the sailors and guardsmen and the elegant slummers; the toothless old men who ploughed away for what seemed like hours, and the frantic young virgins who came and went in a bewildered rush: to all of them she was simply a toy; a convenient and unobjectionable outlet for their lust.

At least Isaf wasn't like that. He desired her, of course, and thus seemed to assume (as men so often did) that she was no less keen to receive his favours than he was to give them. (Even tonight, when her legs had ached so badly that all she'd really wanted to do was stretch out on the soft tick mattress and rest, he'd gently but insistently had his way with her, as if this were the toll required to ensure his continued patronage and affection.) But at least he treated her like a person, rather than a mere slab of meat—or, if not a person exactly, then certainly something rare and delicate, a gift perhaps, or some unexpected prize, to be coddled and shielded from harm. In fact, he was almost *too* attentive at times. After so many years spent fending for herself, she found it hard to cope with this abrupt change in status, this sudden elevation to a pedestal that existed solely in Isaf's own highly coloured imagination. It was all quite flattering in a way, she supposed, and yet—

Before she could pursue the thought further, she noticed a gaunt, dark-robed figure step out onto the moonlit causeway below. It could have been anybody—one of the night watchmen, most likely, making his rounds—but there was something oddly hesitant about his movements, as if he weren't really sure where he was headed, or what he'd do when he got there. After a dozen paces or so, he turned and gazed back at the fortress, raising his head for a moment so that Cayla felt almost certain that she recognized his face.

"Hiern!" She spoke without thinking, surprised and somewhat disconcerted by what she'd seen. Behind her, she heard Isaf stumble out of bed and start crashing around in the darkness, no doubt trying to find his sword. "It's just me," she told him. "Go back to sleep."

Isaf, however, was already padding across to join her, swaddled in one of the bearskin rugs, his breath billowing around him like smoke. "Is anything wrong?" he asked sleepily. "I thought I heard you cry out."

Cayla smiled, stepping back from the window and meeting him halfway. "I was just feeling a bit restless, that's all, so I decided to stretch my legs for a while. I'm sorry if I woke you."

"That's all right." Cayla couldn't quite make out Isaf's face, but she guessed that he was frowning slightly. "You sure nothing's wrong?"

"I'm fine," she said. "Go back to bed."

"Aren't you coming?" he asked. "You'll freeze to death out here."

"I might stay up a few minutes, I think. My legs are killing me." She leant over and kissed him lightly on the cheek. "Don't worry," she said. "The fire's going. I'll be fine."

"If you're sure—"

"I'll be fine, Isaf. Really."

"Very well." He shrugged, then lumbered back to bed. She heard the frame groan as he climbed in, then the rustle of heavy blankets. "Just remember," he said, "we'll want to make an early start in the morning."

"I won't be long," she promised. "Good night, Isaf."

"Good night."

Cayla crouched by the fire until he was snoring peacefully once more, then tiptoed across to the window, feeling a trifle guilty at having deceived Isaf, if only by omission, and yet rather proud of the way she'd stood her ground. Perhaps now he'd realise that being a woman didn't necessarily make her some kind of invalid, and that she was quite capable of deciding what she wanted to do without any help from him.

Looking down, she saw a tiny silhouette in the distance. Where was he going? she wondered. What could possibly have lured, or driven, him from the holding at such an hour on such a night, without even a torch to guide him? He must have been mad. *Or desperate*, Cayla thought, wiping her frozen breath from the glass so that she could see more clearly. *Desperate enough not to care.*

Although cold and tired and a little afraid, she remained at the window for some time, watching Hiern toil slowly up the causeway—if, in fact, it really had been his face she'd glimpsed earlier, and not simply a trick of the moon-light—winding ever higher, like a spider on some broad silken thread, until the mountainous shadows finally closed around him like a pair of giant wings, and he was lost from view completely.

CHAPTER NINE

◆

Scion of the House of Fire

AFTER ALL HE'D GONE THROUGH to get here, Trevayne had expected something more prepossessing. Pillars of gold, perhaps, or a jewelled serpent spitting fire. But all that lay before him was a ring of old, worn stones, perhaps ten or twelve feet across, perched atop a narrow shelf of rock near the cavern wall. From his vantage point, at least, it looked more like an abandoned cistern than the habitation of demigods.

Ah, well, he thought, mentally revising what he'd been told prior to his departure from Talingmar. At the time, the whole scheme had seemed so utterly implausible that he hadn't really given the matter much thought. Now that he was actually in a position to carry out Vellaghar's instructions, he felt vaguely foolish. Still, Vellaghar seemed to know what he was doing, and having come this far, Trevayne certainly wasn't about to turn back now. *Might as well get on with it, I suppose. Let's just hope this damned place is all that it's cracked up to be. If this ends up being a wild-goose chase, I'll have the bastard's guts for bloody garters. By hell I will!*

Nine steps led up to the lip of the well, each worn smooth as if by centuries of passing feet. After circling around to make sure that were no hidden traps or pitfalls, Trevayne slowly mounted them.

114

One.

Two. (He drew his sword, glancing hastily back over one shoulder. It all seemed far too easy for his liking. What if this were some kind of trap? He was no expert in such matters, but one would have thought that a particularly unpleasant fate was reserved for those who dared disturb the slumbers of the undying dead. *Come on, Trevayne*, he told himself, *let's not look a gift horse in the mouth*. Squaring his shoulders, he continued on.)

Three. (He thought he heard voices whispering in the distance, as if those nightmares that had stalked him so relentlessly for the past ten years were now leaching through the fragile membrane that separates sleep from wakefulness to haunt his daylight hours as well. He paused, straining his ears against the silence, but heard nothing.)

Four. (Again the voices. Louder this time, although he still couldn't quite make out what they were saying. Beads of sweat trickled down his face. He licked his lips and took another step.)

Five. (Like the pounding of a drum . . . Or surf . . . Or the rumble of dry thunder over hills . . . The voices . . . They filled his ears.

Si-x.   ("Help me!"
          "Help me!"
          "Help me!"
          "Help . . ."
          ". . . me!"
          "No, me!"
          "Me!"
          "Me!"
          "Please!"
          "Help me!"
          "I did not . . ."
          "Please!"
          "I beg you!"
          "PLEASE!!!"

Se-v-en. ("No!" Trevayne screamed. He felt lost, disoriented, each step towering before him like a mountainface. *This isn't happening*, he thought desperately, crawling forward on his hands and knees. *I'll wake up in a moment, and they'll be gone.* But the voices would not be denied.

> "Help me!"
>
> "Help me!"
>
> "Help me!"
>
> "Help me!"
>
> "Help me!"
>
> "Help me!"
>
> "I can't!" he screamed again. "Don't you see? I can't!" He was weeping now, his self-possession shattered by the fearsome cacophony raging inside his skull. "There are too many of you! Too many!")

E-i-g-h——t. ("Please . . ."

> "I did not know . . ."
>
> "Could not . . ."
>
> "You must . . ."
>
> "Please . . ."
>
> "Please . . ."
>
> "Help me!"
>
> "Help me!"
>
> "For gods'-sake!" Trevayne groaned. "Leave me be! Just leave me be!"
>
> "What is your pain to us?"
>
> "You, at least, may die . . ."
>
> "Open your veins now . . ."
>
> "Slip a noose around your neck . . ."
>
> "Taste the poisoned cup . . ."
>
> "Seek out a precipice . . ."
>
> "Or the dark, tideless depths . . ."
>
> "And it is over . . ."
>
> "While we linger here . . ."
>
> "Suffering . . ."
>
> "Forever . . ."
>
> And: "Help me!"
>
>   "Help me!"
>
>   "Help me!"
>
>   "Help me!"
>
>   "Help me!"
>
>   "Help me!")

N—

   i——

      n———

         ("It is better to be a worm..."

         "Or a slug..."

         "Or the foulest thing..."

         "That crawls..."

         "Or slithers..."

         "Or hobbles..."

         "Across the earth..."

         "Stinking of corruption..."

         "And decay..."

         "Yet alive..."

         "Rather than the noblest..."

         "Brightest..."

         "Most glorious being..."

         "In all creation..."

         "And dead..."

         "Like us."

         "Help me!"

         "Help me!"

         "Help me!"

         "Help me!"

         "Help me!"

         " N O ! ! ! ! ")

————————e.   (And   Trevayne
looked down into the well, and his tears fell like dead stars
into an endless pit of darkness, and there were faces there,
so many faces, full of fear and horror and confusion and
bitterness and betrayal, and there were hands, all reaching
out towards him like an ocean of drowning sailors, and their
voices swelled to a deafening roar, and pain flared like
lightning from the raw wounds of their eyes, and all of them
called to him, pleading for deliverance, for intercession, for
release:

       "O earth, our mother..."

       "O sky, where sun and moon..."

"Shed light on all in turn . . ."
"See, see how we are wronged!")

But Trevayne was no longer listening. Gritting his teeth,
he stood up and reached inside his jerkin for the slim metal
flask that Vellaghar had given him some months before.
Even now, he found it hard to believe that the Arbiter's
bizarre scheme would work, that one might indeed reach
back through the years and pluck a legendary champion out
of the past like an apple from a bucket, but he unstoppered
the bottle anyway, steeling himself for what was to come.

As he did so, the well suddenly disappeared. Gone too
were the faces and their wild, despairing chorus. It seemed
he'd passed through some unseen gateway into an entirely
different plane of existence—not really a place so much as
a kind of void; an emptiness larger than all creation, and
yet infinitesimally small, so that Trevayne himself had become both centre and circumference of everything he surveyed. Vast, inhuman shapes flickered around him: some
tall and angelic, dark wings unfurled like banners; some
squat and misshapen; others resembling coiled serpents, or
scarabs, or sheets of flame; each one grazing his awareness
for a moment, then vanishing without trace, like shadows
skating across the surface of a mirror. It occurred to Trevayne that this was exactly what they were—ghostly entities
vainly striving to retain some foothold in a world that had
expelled both them and their images countless millennia
before. *You must reach inside yourself, Trevayne*, Vellaghar
had told him. *You must grasp the raw stuff of existence and
shape it to your will*. At the time, this had sounded like
nonsense—the sort of pompous metaphysical waffle Vellaghar often employed in the absence of hard facts—but
now Trevayne understood what he meant: for if the well
and its contents existed anywhere, it was within the aching
vacuity of his own brain; and if he reached down, it was
only into the subliminal darkness underpinning all his
dreams.

Grasping hold of the bottle in both hands, Trevayne tried
to recall the unearthly countenance depicted in Vellaghar's
great brass-bound folio. He pictured a face both ethereal

and faintly barbaric: eyes like veins of yellow ochre; skin like amber; hair disturbed by some unseen wind to a crown of fire about his head. As he refined the image still further, Trevayne noticed that the shadows were no longer swirling madly around him, but had begun to coalesce into a single manlike form whose lineaments precisely mirrored those of the long-dead champion he'd been sent here to reclaim. Concentrating furiously, he slotted more and more features into place—shoulders, arms, chest, hips, thighs, legs, feet—until at last both figures were complete: one immaculately detailed and brimming with life, as only memories can be; the other little more than a vague silhouette, but unmistakably similar.

All right, Trevayne said to himself. *Now let's see what Vellaghar's magic potion can do, eh?*

Upending the bottle, he watched its contents spill into the darkness and gather in a small puddle at his feet. With a shock, he realised that it was blood, warm and rich and red, as if it had just that minute ceased coursing through a living heart. How Vellaghar might have accomplished such a miracle, Trevayne had no idea—nor did he give the matter much thought. He was far more interested in the pool of blood itself, which had begun to trace the contours of his shadowy creation the way rainwater might define some shallow depression that otherwise would have remained quite invisible to the naked eye. Trevayne began to suspect that gods were like that, too: not transcendent beings who sustained the world for their own amusement, but subtle imprints in the texture of time and space which only acquired true shape and substance when fleshed out with belief.

In this case, the process was quite literally taking place before his eyes—fueled, perhaps, not only by his own desires, but those of countless others as well, the untold legions of common folk who still cursed and abjured in the dead god's name, dutifully nailing sprigs of rosemary to their doorposts on Midsummer's Eve in memory of his passing. He saw the blood thicken, saw bones draw themselves out like candles from a tub of wax, saw veins and arteries unravel like coloured threads, then abruptly vanish, as first the muscles and sinews, then the bright, burnished skin, quickly hardened into place.

Within a matter of moments, the transition was complete. Once again, Trevayne stood atop a ring of old, worn stones. Below him, like a corpse on a mortuary slab, lay the fearsome progeny of his dreams: no longer a mere shadow, but the thing itself, puissant, enduring, and alive.

The figure stretched its amber limbs. Eyelids snapped open above twin veins of yellow ochre. A phantom wind teased its hair into a crown of unburning fire.

Trevayne smiled, although his triumph was tempered somewhat by the knowledge that, according to Vellaghar, this had been the easy part. Now that they had their champion, the fun would really begin. Still, nothing ventured, nothing gained—

Tossing the bottle aside, he took a deep breath and slowly stretched out his hand . . .

IT MIGHT HAVE BEEN the chief citadel of Hell itself.

The walls glowed like newly forged iron. There were rivers of flame, steaming vents, fountains of pitch and nitre. Clouds of hot, incandescent gas flared through the darkness like gigantic fireworks. The air was full of sparks and shrieks and the smell of roasting flesh.

Hralik sipped morosely at his wine. Coming back had obviously been a mistake. His years of self-imposed exile had changed him—even more, perhaps, than he was willing to admit. Where once he might have sported with the best of them, now he sat and brooded, shackled to a conscience which he had no right to possess. He'd certainly never courted such an affliction. Nor could he remember exactly where, or how, he'd first become aware of its presence. As far as he could tell, it had taken root quite by accident, the way a seed might fasten itself to some barren outcrop and, against all odds, suddenly blossom into flower. Since his return, however, it had grown increasingly burdensome, shutting him off from his past like a row of prison bars, and forcing him to regard the present with new, somewhat jaundiced, eyes.

It was not a pretty sight.

Beside him, his father lay sprawled across the Topaz Throne, clothed, on this occasion, in folds of soft, billowing flesh. Quaffing down a mug of spiced wine, he grinned as two women and a bull performed some unspeakable act on the stage before them.

"More wine!" he bellowed, clawing at the breast of a naked serving wench who stood nearby. Caught off-balance, she staggered forward, upsetting the wine-flask across his lap.

"You clumsy slut!" his father roared. Seizing hold of the girl's hair, he forced her face down between his thighs. "Now lick it up!"

The girl—a Northerner by the look of her, with wide, brown eyes and a mass of auburn hair—shuddered as he crammed his swollen phallus into her mouth.

Somewhere a man screamed, after being forced to copulate with a fire demon.

Grunting with pleasure, the Flamelord reached over and slapped Hralik on the shoulder. "Well, my son," he said, "how does it feel to be home again, eh?"

Hralik—who felt at home nowhere, and probably never would—merely shrugged and looked away.

"Come now," his father said. "This is supposed to be a celebration. The prodigal son has returned! Surely nothing you found in the Fifth House could ever compare with this!"

Egim smiled. Seated at the Flamelord's left hand, his presence no doubt heralded yet another re-allignment in the bitter internecine war that had been raging now for centuries. At the time of Hralik's departure, Egim and his father had been embroiled in a dispute that had already laid half a continent to waste, and he suspected that the current festivities were as much in the Gnomarch's honour as his own.

"Mortals are not without their uses," Egim observed wryly, nodding toward the serving wench, who, having temporarily slaked the Flamelord's lust, now lay huddled at his feet, coughing and spluttering for breath. "From what I heard, your son grew quite attached to one of them. From Uighur, wasn't she?"

His father shook with laughter. "That's right. The trouble was, she went and died on him! Ought to have known better, of course. Still, there's plenty more where she came from, eh lad?'' He winked lewdly across at Hralik. ''Matter of fact, we got a new batch in from Uighur just the other day— virgins, so I'm told, the lot of them. Bound to be something there that takes your fancy.''

As the Flamelord spoke, Hralik felt a cold, implacable fury descend upon him. He looked up at his father, already mouthing the words that, once spoken, could never be recalled.

''You disgust me,'' he said quietly. ''All of you.''

''What?'' His father turned towards him, eyes burning like twin suns in the blood-red desert of his face. *''What?''*

Servant-girls threw up their hands and fled through the darkness. Even the Gnomarch trembled, his carapace shimmering in the firelight like a beetle's wing.

''WHAT?''

''I find this corruption obscene,'' Hralik said, his voice icy with contempt. ''I think that one such as yourself is hardly fit to rule a sty of pigs, let alone one of the Great Houses. I think—''

''SILENCE!''

Mountains heaved convulsively overhead. Lightning split the sky. Oceans boiled. Stars foundered in their courses.

Such was his father's wrath.

''HOW DARE YOU! MY OWN SON! HOW DARE YOU!''

The Flamelord towered above him like a column of scarlet smoke, awful in his rage. His feet straddled the world.

''HOW DARE YOU!''

A pall of silence had fallen across the room. A thousand faces were turned toward them, locked in the timeless void between one heartbeat and the next. Even the shadows were still.

''I despise you,'' Hralik said.

Then the black beast stirred once more in its immemorial slumber, and all pandemonium broke loose.

Hralik's sword blazed in his hand like a thunderbolt. Plucked from the very furnace of creation—a fragment of the supernal fire that had given birth to man and god alike— it remained the single most potent weapon in existence, the pride of his father's house, able to cleave time and space the way a lesser blade might pierce a silken veil. Were he to unleash its power now, not even the Flamelord could possibly have stood against him.

But he hesitated for just a moment, torn between the hatred he felt for his father and old allegiances that he could neither repudiate nor forget. In that fraction of an instant, while what Hralik had once been wrestled with what he'd become, the Flamelord struck.

And Hralik . . .

(THAT WAS the beginning.

He became a legend in the Fifth House. Driven by fierce, inhuman passions which even he didn't fully understand, he dedicated himself to unseating those mighty Powers which had held the earth in thrall for thrice ten thousand years. He found the human nations weak and disunited, more or less willing pawns in the Great King's endless struggle for supremacy. Within the space of a few generations, he'd forged them into an implacable war-machine, an exquisite and finely-honed instrument of revenge. *Annukin*, they called him: *The Godstalker*. He was their champion; their tempter; their saviour. With him to lead them they were invincible. Surely, at long last, their days of servitude were over.

One by one, the Great Houses toppled into dust, their strongholds sacked, their cisterns poisoned, their towers gutted, their demonic hordes cast back into the yawning gulf of non-being that had spawned them untold aeons before.

First Dragonsea fell, where Bahumut, King of Ships, dwelt in his vast sea-green palace beneath the waves. Heavenspire was next, home to the Sky Lord, Paymon, whose minions had swarmed through the upper airlike flights of vengeful seraphim, or exultations of lark, before perishing with their master in a blaze of lightning and quintessential fire. Egim held out longer than the rest, but in time even he succumbed to the power of Hralik's sword, his labyrinthine fastness reduced to a pile of smoking ruins.

And so it was that, after centuries of unremitting struggle,

Hralik finally turned his eyes towards the East, where there remained one last bastion to be stormed, one final ghost to be exorcised, before a new, and perhaps better, world might somehow raise itself up from the dead ashes of the past.)

PRIDE IN THEIR PORT, defiance in their eye, he watched the lords of humankind array themselves for war.

He saw the Riders of the Moonwind, ten thousand strong, with their milk-white stallions and pale, translucent armour. He saw the savants of Talingmar directing their monstrous engines, each large enough to house a thousand men within its dark iron hull. He saw the steel-clad paladins from Uighur and the horselords from Bowlahoola. He saw the warrior maidens of Udan Adan; the archers of Enthuthon; the columns of tall, grim-faced spearmen from Sithon and Allamanda. They stretched for miles, their standards glistening like nascent stars in the thin, predawn mist.

Some time later, he noticed Ceerbunnus riding up the hillside to join him. From a distance, the Moonrider seemed no less of a prodigy than Hralik himself, as if carved by some inhuman artisan from a block of living jade. Indeed, as Ceerbunnus' mount crested the hillock—to be silhouetted, for a moment, against the louring sky as if lit by a perpetual stroke of lightning—one might easily have thought that both horse and rider were born of something other than mortal flesh.

The illusion, however, was short-lived. Reining up beside Hralik's own great coal-black stallion, Ceerbunnus slipped off her helmet to reveal a delicate face framed by masses of thick tawny hair. Even by human standards, she was remarkably young, yet, despite her tender years, she had already demonstrated a prowess in battle matched only by that of her illustrious namesake, whose sword had helped turn the tide at Ravenskirk over a thousand years before.

"Is that the place?" she asked, looking out across the rocky plain below them: a wasteland as bare and arid as the surface of the moon. At its centre stood a single tower of cold white stone.

Hralik nodded.

"What happens now?"

"We fight," Hralik told her. "Harder than we've ever fought before."

Hralik felt a thrill of anticipation at the thought. The long-awaited reckoning was finally at hand—assuming, of course, that the Flamelord could be lured from his place of power. Despite the vast resources at Hralik's command, he wasn't entirely sure that he could force the gates of Hellmouth should his father decline to meet him on open ground. By the look of things, however, there was no doubt whatsoever about the Fire King's intentions. Huge stormclouds were already darkening the sky, and a hot wind had sprung up from the East, like the blast from an open furnace: harbingers which Hralik recognized only too well.

"Remember what I told you," he said. "No matter what happens, hold your Moonriders back until I give the word. The others will have to weather the initial assault as best they can."

Ceerbunnus nodded, making various small adjustments to her armour, which now glowed more brightly than ever. "So," she murmured. "At last we shall see an end to it, eh?"

"Let us hope so," Hralik said. Raising his sword, he signalled the ranks of spearmen to advance.

And so it began.

The heavens shook with massive hammerblows of thunder. The earth cracked and splintered, unleashing all the old, unnamed terrors of the deep. From Hralik's vantage point, it seemed as if the entire plain was suddenly awash with fire. Where others, however, might have seen only sheets of orange and scarlet flame, he could clearly discern the elementals themselves as they writhed and tumbled through the air like burning leaves caught in the storm front of some immense inferno.

When the two armies clashed, there came a sound such as even Hralik had never heard before—that of ten thousand men screaming in perfect unison as the flesh melted from their bones like wax.

"For pity's-sake!" Ceerbunnus said, her voice barely audible above the tumult. "Call them back, Annukin! They're being roasted alive down there!"

Hralik shook his head. "The elementals can't keep this up for long," he told her. "See, they're beginning to falter already."

Even as he spoke, the sea of flames slowly began to subside. A second wave of spearmen fell, then a third, but still they pressed relentlessly forward, seemingly oblivious to the heat and the smoke and the piles of blackened corpses heaped around them. Their spears were of little use against such adversaries, but some managed to smother the elementals with their shields, while others abandoned their weapons altogether, quenching the fire demons' energies with their own naked flesh. Soon, only a handful of fugitive sparks still smouldered among the dead and dying, like guttering candles strewn across some vast, open-air crematorium.

Hralik smiled. The fire demons had offered far less resistance than he'd anticipated. Apparently their numbers had dwindled over the years, and most of them seemed barely strong enough to sustain their own existence, let alone wreak the sort of havoc he'd witnessed during the War of the Kings, when both they and the world were young. If this was the best that his father could muster, the issue would be settled even more quickly than he'd thought.

When he turned to Ceerbunnus, however, he saw that the Moonrider was glaring at him with a mixture of outrage and disgust. "You don't give a damn about us, do you?" she snarled. "We're nothing more than cannon fodder as far as you're concerned!"

Hralik shrugged. To be honest, the matter seemed quite irrelevant. Compared to him, mortals were no more durable than mayflies, and he couldn't see how it made any difference to them whether they died now or in a few years' time. At least this way their deaths served some purpose—which was more than could be said for most of their kind. "I had to drain the elementals somehow," he said blandly. "Or would you have preferred them to expend their substance on the likes of you and I?"

Ceerbunnus said nothing, gazing mournfully across the corpse-littered plain, and pointedly refusing to meet his eye.

Hralik returned this attention to the battlefield, where,

amidst a sudden eruption of smoke and dust, he saw vague shapes boiling up through the splintered earth.

"Save your hatred for them," he said, watching Ceerbunnus' face darken as the fiery chariots burst into view like earthbound comets, trailing plumes of sparks and incandescent gas. Each was drawn by a pair of coal-black stallions, brothers to Hralik's own, while the faces of their charioteers were equally familiar. Prior to his expulsion from Hellmouth, he'd fought beside them in countless campaigns, shared their wine, participated—not unwillingly—in their orgies and atrocious brutalities. Now he watched with grim satisfaction as his troops closed around them: an inexorable tide of humanity that, although easy prey for the *Annunake*'s swords, seemed destined to triumph eventually through sheer weight of numbers.

By now, almost all of Hralik's forces had been committed to the assault. Horsemen and archers and infantry from a hundred kingdoms swarmed across the plain like ants, whatever cohesion they may originally have possessed quickly giving way to the exigencies of battle, as each man struggled, not so much for victory, but to preserve his own life as best he could. Even the elite guardsmen from Uighur—who fought with such inhuman skill and precision that they seemed more like a single, well-oiled machine than creatures of flesh and blood—had broken ranks, firing their weapons more or less at random, as if no longer able to distinguish friend from foe.

He saw Ceerbunnus finger her sword impatiently. The Moonriders alone were still being held in reserve, and it was easy enough to guess the nature of her thoughts.

Hralik waited until the *Annunake* were fully engaged, then smiled once more.

"All right," he said. "It's our turn now."

There was something like relief in Ceerbunnus' face as she gave the signal for her warriors to attack. Her sword blazed like a streak of summer lightning as she spurred her horse recklessly down the slope.

Hralik followed, his mount darting forward so quickly that he passed Ceerbunnus within half a dozen strides. Behind them, he saw the Moonriders sweep out onto the plain like sequins pouring into a bucket of ash. Together, they might have dealt the *Annunake* a decisive blow, but Hralik's prime objective now was to storm the tower as quickly as possibly, before the Flamelord had time to re-order his defences. He certainly didn't intend to squander his most valuable resource on a battle whose outcome was no longer of the slightest consequence whatsoever. All that mattered now was that he should meet his father face to face and finally exact the vengeance that had been denied him for so long.

Ignoring the carnage around him, he veered towards a break in the milling ranks which one of the Talingmari juggernauts had forged as it maneouvred ponderously across the plain, grinding both men and demigods beneath its massive steel-shod wheels.

Then he was through.

The tower loomed before him: a tall, unburning candle of pure white stone. He roared with triumph, his voice swelling above the clatter of hoofbeats and the Moonriders' own stentorian war cries until it rivalled the very thunder that cracked incessantly overhead.

At that moment, just when victory seemed within their grasp, the ground opened beneath him like a piece of rotten fruit. He reigned back his horse, but much too late, his scream changing to one of anger and impotence as he realised that the Flamelord had been toying with him all along, luring him into a trap from which neither he nor the Moonriders could possibly escape.

He heard the sound of distant laughter; saw Ceerbunnus and the others drowning in blood and fire; felt a cold, implacable darkness tighten around him like a fist, squeezing his soul to dust—

Not one of that glorious company survived. Their deaths, however, were not the same.

Fashioned as they were from mortal flesh, the Moonriders went wherever men go when they die. For Hralik, however, not even death afforded any prospect of release. He went the way of the First Born; the way of hopelessness and old night; the way of the the the well.

At least the children remembered him:

> *Annukin tried*
> *to climb the sky.*
> *He climbed too high*
> *and Annukin died.*

And in Talingmar, landlocked city of the Octopus, there were others who remembered.

Slowly, inexorably, they began to draw their plans.

. . . AND pulled.

Naked, his scarlet hair flickering about him like a torch, he looked like some heroic sculpture cast in gold and amber, only recently plucked from the raging furnace that had given him birth and still glowing with heat of his own creation. In his hand was something that resembled a splinter of frozen fire.

Trevayne smiled. "Lord Annukin, I presume?"

The immortal nodded.

"I've heard a lot about you, my friend. Let's hope you live up to your reputation, eh?" Trevayne paused for a moment, regarding his handiwork with a certain degree of pride. If anything, he'd done his job *too* well: a few subtle changes here and there might well have spared the fellow considerable discomfort.

"Tell me," Trevayne said, "those voices I heard—I don't suppose any of them happened to be yours?"

Annukin seemed not to hear him. He gazed blankly into space, as if surveying some distant prospect invisible to other, less godlike, eyes.

"Ceerbunnus was wrong," he muttered. "There is no end to it."

Together, they descended the nine stone steps and began their long, arduous climb out of darkness into light.

INTERMEZZO

STANDING before an ornate looking-glass, his pale, almost effeminate features sculpted with the same bloodless precision as those on a newly minted coin, he regarded the face in the mirror with surprising equanimity.

It was not his own.

Where the image originated—and why it chose to manifest itself in so bizarre a fashion—he hadn't the slightest idea. Nor were such questions of other than academic interest to him. What mattered was that it seemed drawn to his presence, as if lured from the cold, still centre of the mirror by some oneiric conjuration whose precise nature remained as much a mystery to him as the spectre itself.

Greetings. Although scarcely more than a whisper, the voice swirled around him like the strains of some lush aeolian harp, seeming to emanate from a dozen directions at once. *I trust you are well this morning?*

For a time, when the ghostly visage first appeared, trembling within the glass like a pool of mercurial silver, he'd actually believed that it was the soul of his long-dead father returned to comfort him at last. Though older now, and decidedly less naive, he still felt quite at ease in its presence, and occasionally thought to detect some faint family resemblance between them—the cock of an eyebrow, perhaps, or the sly, faintly mocking smile that hovered so often on its lips. Not that he ever allowed himself to be seduced by such childish fancies; and, as a general rule, he trusted the apparition neither more nor less than he did anyone else—which is to say, not at all.

"Well enough," he said smoothly. "The better for knowing that our plans are apparently progressing quite nicely."

You've had word from your agent then?

The young man nodded. "Yes. A messenger arrived just this afternoon."

And?

"The sleeper has woken."

Ah! The image blurred for a moment, perhaps to conceal the naked triumph in its face. When the focus sharpened again, however, its expression was as bland and insouciant as ever. *What about the others?*

"The matter is in hand. According to my agent's calculations, they should be arriving in Eria any day now."

You have done well, my son, the voice told him. *Very well, indeed.*

"It's a start, anyway," the youth said. "Although I'm still not sure what you hope to achieve. After last time—"

That was a mistake. As I could have told you it would be had you bothered to consult me beforehand. The voice betrayed a sliver of irritation, as if rebuking a wayward child. *This affair needs to be handled with the utmost discretion. Or have you forgotten exactly what is at stake?*

He hadn't, of course. After all, it wasn't mere sentiment that drew him, night after night, to this cold, long-deserted chamber deep within the palace, which none but he had entered for nigh on twenty years. His self-appointed mentor, however, apparently wasn't taking any chances. As he watched, the looking-glass clouded once more, vague shapes taking form within its depths like figures in a waking dream.

He felt as if he were standing on some lofty mountaintop, with the entire world spread-eagled at his feet. If he looked closely enough, he could see the towers and broad-paved thoroughfares of cities far more imposing than Talingmar had ever been, even in its prime. He saw mountain strongholds and thriving ports; lush green pastures and glittering plains; empires so vast and bountiful that, by comparison, the Four Kingdoms seemed no more than a collection of squalid rural hamlets.

All this will soon be ours to command, the voice murmured. *Just as I have foretold. And more besides. Much, much more.*

Again the scene shifted. He gazed now into the heart of an immense darkness, the tideless gulf between the stars where strange new worlds rolled and tumbled through the void like spheres of opalescent glass.

We shall plunder the heavens, you and I. No power in all creation will be sufficient to stand against us. Until then, however, we must bide our time. One false step now, and everything we have laboured so long to achieve might come to nothing. Do you understand?

The young man nodded, his head still reeling with the sheer magnitude of the vision that had been vouchsafed him. Even he, for all his vaulting ambition, had never dreamed of power on such a scale—not until the face had first revealed itself within his father's mirror-haunted chamber. Since then, he'd dreamed of precious little else.

"Yes," he said. "I understand."

Good. Until next time, then.

The mirror slowly cleared, its whirlpool of stars dwindling to a faint, silvery gleam, then winking out of existence entirely. Soon, the gilded frame held nothing but his own pale, imperious reflection.

He lingered there for some time, postponing as long as possible his return to a world that seemed to grow more tiresome and inconsequential with each passing day. Despite having worked hard and long to elevate himself to the highest office in the land, he'd already begun to chafe at the constraints that his position required of him. He was tired of the endless politicking and petty intrigues, the necessity to curry favour among some quarters and distance himself from others, to frustrate the machinations of rival princelings lest they interfere with his own. His thoughts were too large for such tawdry pursuits. What did it matter to him if the price of maize had doubled over the past six months, or if the Supreme Hetera and her eunuchs were conspiring against him in some elegant perfumed boudoir, when all time and space would soon be obedient to his will?

Somewhat reluctantly, he turned and made his way back along the dark, untenanted hallways that wound like a tedious argument through the lower levels of the palace. He walked slowly, having a number of weighty matters to consider before grappling with the dreary bureaucratic minutiae that constituted by far the greater part of his daily routine. Paramount among these was how to dispose of his mysterious benefactor once they had overthrown the last remaining lord of creation and set themselves up in its place. For, despite what his specular associate may have believed, he had no intention of sharing such power with anyone, and, when the dust finally settled, it was upon his shoulders, and his alone, that the mantle of godhood would ultimately descend.

BOOK II

From this the poem springs: that we live in a place
That is not our own and, much more, not ourselves
And hard it is in spite of blazoned days.

—Wallace Stevens

CHAPTER TEN

A Fool & His Gold

ONCE A THRIVING RIVER-PORT, Eria's fortunes had dwindled over the years, until all that remained of its glorious past were a few dilapidated towers, long since abandoned by those merchant-princes who, in days gone by, had held the entire South-East in their thrall.

Having plundered the city as thoroughly as any invading army, its people now eked out a precarious existence among the ruins, like maggots infesting some great stone corpse. Goats clambered over the piles of rubble that had once been temples and libraries and civic halls. Children hunted for mussels along the derelict harbour, where nothing larger than a fishing scow had berthed for more than half a century. The air stank of fish and boiled hides.

Trevayne had never seen such a miserable hole in his life. As he waded through the mud-choked streets, fending off the crowds of beggars that swarmed about him—hawking everything from their own wizened flesh to handfuls of pumpkin seeds—he wondered if this mightn't be an omen of things to come.

Annukin, for his part, remained as aloof and uncomplaining as ever. Wrapped in a heavy woollen cloak, the hood pulled sharply down to obscure his face, he might have been making his way through a quite different city entirely. Once or twice, Trevayne had to glance back over his shoulder to convince himself that the fellow was actually there at all.

This was nothing new, of course. For most of their journey, the demigod had proven about as communicative as a lump of granite. When pressed, he'd simply shrug and turn away, as if Trevayne's questions were of no more consequence than the twittering of a bird. Trevayne couldn't help wishing that he'd been saddled with a slightly less taciturn companion—or one who was at least prepared to acknowledge his existence. The past three weeks had been harrowing enough as it was without Annukin stalking silently beside him like some self-appointed angel of death.

Although, on returning from the well, Trevayne had taken pains to retrace his footsteps as accurately as he could, he saw no evidence of the vast wallowing beast he'd encountered earlier, nor the two metamorphic guardians who'd so strenuously contested his passage just a short time before. Even the gateway had gone, and they were forced to clamber to the surface through a narrow cleft of rock which most definitely hadn't been there when Trevayne arrived.

Outside, the landscape too seemed subtly different. He wasn't sure exactly *what* had changed, as all the major topographical features remained staunchly in place—the dark, brooding mountains, the waste of sand, the overarching sky—but he couldn't shake the feeling that the world he'd returned to was a somewhat distorted replica of the one he'd left behind. In fact, he suspected there might well be just as many exits from the cavern as there were men who entered it, and that none of them led to quite the same place.

To make matters worse, they'd been met by a great black stallion whose statuesque proportions and unnervingly percipient gaze were a match for Annukin's own. Predictably enough, Annukin himself had acted as if it were the most natural thing in the world for a fully harnessed war-horse to suddenly appear just when he had need of one, and mounted the beast without so much as a second glance, leaving Trevayne feeling as if he'd become a pawn in some game devised for the sole purpose of making his life as unpleasant as possible.

And now this. Four days Trevayne had been here, and not a sign of the damned Jenemun anywhere. Probably hidden away someplace, knowing his sort, having a high old time at Trevayne's expense—assuming that the lazy bastard had even bothered to show up at all.

A street urchin plucked at his sleeve, all round, hungry eyes and twisted limbs. Brushing the child angrily aside, he strode off towards the row of battered tenements that lay ahead.

Gods' blood, he thought sourly, *I didn't come two hundred miles to spend my time piss-farting around in a bloody great muck-heap like this*.

LIKE THE OTHER TAVERNS they'd visited (some twenty-five in all, scattered throughout the length and breadth of the city), the *Thricefold Bounty* was a veritable pigsty, its earthen floor littered with fish-heads, dung, and scraps of meat. Behind the counter stood a fat, red-faced man whom Trevayne assumed to be the proprietor, dispensing mugs of watery ale that smelt only marginally less offensive than the contents of an open sewer.

"Nice place, eh?" Trevayne murmured, as he and Annukin pushed their way through the crowd of fishermen gathered inside. A sudden hush fell over the room as they turned to stare at the intruders. Some spat; some sneered; a few even fingered the heavy scaling knives dangling from their belts. "Watch your back," Trevayne said. "The natives seem a little restless tonight." At times like these, it was comforting to know that he had a god on his side.

Eventually, Trevayne managed to reach the counter. Annukin stood slightly to one side, seemingly quite unperturbed by the noisome surroundings. Indeed, to look at him, one might almost have thought that the fellow had drifted off to sleep.

"Ah, hello there," Trevayne said, leaning forward to try and attract the innkeeper's attention. So far, the man had steadfastly ignored them, lounging behind the counter like a sack of offal. "I'm looking for some friends of mine—two men and a woman. Seen them about at all, have you?"

The innkeeper finally looked up. His face, riddled with

blotches and broken veins, reminded Trevayne of an over-inflated balloon. "I see plenty of folks," he said. "Only most of them come in here for a drink, not to ask a lot of daft questions."

Trevayne sighed. "Listen," he said. "I've been on my feet all day. I'm hot. I'm tired. And I want to find my friends. Now, have you seen them or haven't you?"

The innkeeper apparently decided not to push his luck. "What they look like?" he asked.

"One of them's a big, black-haired fellow. A Jenemun. I don't remember much about the girl. Got a nice pair of jugs on her, though."

"Sounds familiar, but I can't quite place 'em." The innkeeper tapped his fingers idly on the bench-top. "The old memory's not what she used to be, I'm afraid."

"Maybe this will help," Trevayne said, scattering a fistful of coins across the counter. "Coming back to you at all, is it?"

The innkeeper licked his lips. "You know," he said. "I think it just might be at that." Pocketing the coins, he turned to walk away.

The other patrons seemed to think this was a great joke. Trevayne, however, was rather less than amused.

Lunging forward, he seized the innkeeper by the throat. "I've just about had a gutful of you," he snarled. "Now start talking!"

A dozen or so fishermen closed menacingly around them. Some had already drawn their knives; others were apparently content to use their fists. The rest of the crowd watched hungrily, like spectators at an execution.

It might have proven a most awkward situation indeed, had not Annukin decided to take a hand. Stepping in behind Trevayne, he suddenly turned and threw back the hood of his cloak.

One look was enough. The fishermen beat a hasty retreat, muttering under their breath and making various cryptic gestures to avert the evil eye. Trevayne almost felt sorry for them. The poor sods probably thought that one of hell's chief ministers had dropped in to pay them a visit.

The innkeeper, for his part, seemed absolutely terrified.

"Please!" he squawked. "I didn't mean no harm! Honest!"

"Let's just get down to business, shall we?" Trevayne said. "Before my associate loses his patience and rips your bloody heart out."

The innkeeper shuddered. "They're here!"

"What?"

"The three you asked about! I let 'em a room last week!"

"Why you—" Trevayne tightened his grip even further. "I ought to wring your scrawny little neck! Where are they now?"

"Upstairs!" the innkeeper told him, frantically gesticulating towards a nearby staircase.

"What room?"

"F-first on your left."

Thrusting the innkeeper aside, Trevayne watched him slump to the floor like a gutted fish. "You just stay right there," he said, "while I go and take a look for myself. And if you're lying to me again—" He did not elaborate. If the need arose, he'd doubtless be able to think of something.

"All right, Annukin," he said. His relief at having finally tracked the others down was mingled with a certain degree of apprehension concerning what now lay ahead. Even so, a slight smile played across his lips as he headed for the stairs. "Let's see what the buggers have to say for themselves, shall we?"

TREVAYNE HAD TO KNOCK three times before eventually getting some response.

He heard frantic whispers inside, followed by the sound of ponderous footsteps.

"I told you to leave us in peace!" someone roared. Either Trevayne had found the right room, or else there was a wounded bear loose in the building.

"Hush, Isaf," a woman said, her voice soft and conciliatory. "There's enough ill-feeling between us already."

The Jenemun, however, turned a deaf ear to her protests. "I've had enough of this!" he snarled, almost wrenching the door from its hinges. His expression, savage enough to begin with, darkened even further when he saw who was waiting outside.

"Oh," he said. "It's you, is it?"

Trevayne smiled. "Good afternoon. You're not an easy man to find, my friend."

Isaf made as if to reply, then apparently noticed Annukin standing to one side. His eyes narrowed. "Who's this?"

"All in good time," Trevayne told him. "Aren't you going to invite us in?"

Still scowling, Isaf drew back to let them pass.

It was a small room, perhaps ten feet square, and certainly far from palatial. The walls were covered with damp, yellow stains, like smears of grease, and the floorboards creaked ominously beneath Trevayne's feet. He could have sworn that a rat scuttled for cover as he stepped inside.

"Good grief," he said. "Couldn't you have found something a trifle less squalid? I mean to say—"

"This is the best we could get," Isaf muttered. "They don't take very kindly to strangers around here."

"So I've noticed." As Trevayne glanced around, he saw Cayla sitting by the window. "Forgive me for bursting in like this, my dear," he said. "But Isaf and I have some rather pressing business to discuss. Not interrupting anything, am I?"

Though clearly unnerved by Annukin's presence, the girl still managed a diffident smile. "Of course not." She paused a moment, then added, as if by way of an afterthought, "We've been looking for you everywhere."

"Is that a fact?" Trevayne's grin broadened. "How very diligent of you both."

"It's your own damned fault, anyway," Isaf said, fixing him with a belligerent stare. "Why didn't you sort something out before we left Julkrease? I asked around, but no one had ever heard of you."

"Yes, yes, all right. Let's just get on with it shall we?"

"Suits me."

"You've got Hawk with you, I trust?"

Isaf nodded towards a makeshift curtain rigged up across one corner of the room. "Over there," he said.

As he spoke, a dark-haired figure appeared from behind

the screen. Dressed all in black, he resembled a lightning-struck tree: thin, gnarled, and subtly menacing. On catching sight of Trevayne, a series of wholly inappropriate expressions flickered across his face, like the shadows of passing birds. He grinned, grimaced, simpered, and scowled, before finally settling his features into a look of casual disdain.

"You are Pagad Trevayne," he said. In no way could it be construed as a question.

Trevayne nodded. "That's right." He cast a sidelong glance at Isaf, who refused to meet his eye. "You got my letter, then?"

The man inclined his head slightly, but offered nothing more.

"Excellent," Trevayne said. To be honest, he suspected that the fellow was a few pennyweights short of the pound, but that was neither here nor there. At least all four of them were finally under the same roof. He turned to Isaf and smiled. "You've done well, my friend."

The Jenemun apparently thought otherwise. "I got your man," he grumbled. "Now where's the gold you promised me?"

"Actually," Trevayne said, "that's one of the things I wanted to talk to you about."

"How do you mean?" Isaf's hand closed menacingly around the hilt of his sword. "Twenty bags you said. Cayla and I both heard you. You going to pay up or not?"

"Look," Trevayne said, "it's a bit crowded in here, don't you think? What say we find ourselves a pleasant little tavern somewhere, eh, and sort everything out there?"

"Very well." Shouldering Trevayne aside, Isaf stalked angrily towards the door. "You coming, Cayla?"

The girl, who'd been studying Annukin with mounting fascination, as if he were some kind of exotic hothouse plant, jumped to her feet and hurried after him.

"I bet that's the quickest they've moved for months," Trevayne muttered caustically. "Hardly the most pleasant travelling companions, I'd imagine." He glanced back over his shoulder. "Eh, Hawk?"

The mountain king stepped slowly forward.

"Call me Hiern," he said.

* * *

EVENTUALLY, after much heated debate (and a certain amount of judicious violence), they managed to obtain a table in one of the old seamen's taverns along the riverside corniche. It wasn't much to look at, with its mouldering frescoes and piles of broken plaster, but at least the beer was drinkable, and the taproom spacious enough to allow some privacy.

"Well?" Isaf demanded. "What's this all about?"

Trevayne poured himself a second cup of wine, then set the pitcher down and slowly wiped his hands, as if deliberately ignoring Isaf's question. Another, even more lengthy pause followed before he even deigned to look up.

"Sorry?" he said. "What was that?"

If it was a confrontation the fellow wanted, Isaf was only too happy to oblige. Reaching forward, he knocked the cup from Trevayne's grasp and sent it spinning across the table.

"Don't mess me about, Trevayne!" he snarled. "You owe us twenty bags of gold! Now hand it over!"

"If you'll sit quietly for a moment," Trevayne told him, "I'll explain everything." He seemed quite unperturbed by Isaf's outburst, almost amused, in fact. "Oh, and by the way," he added, "don't ever, ever, do something like that again—"

Suddenly, there was a knife in his hand.

"—otherwise, my dear boy, I'll cut your bloody tripes out." Trevayne feinted towards Isaf's neck, then smiled dangerously. "Do I make myself perfectly clear?"

The pair would almost certainly have come to blows. Weeks of inactivity had stretched Isaf's patience to the breaking point, and he would have welcomed a chance to wipe the smile from Trevayne's face once and for all. Cayla, however, quickly intervened, seizing hold of his arm and pressing herself against him. "Please!" she said. "Just hear him out! What harm can it do?"

Isaf hesitated a moment, then sank back into his chair. "All right," he muttered. "Go ahead. I'm listening."

"Good lad," Trevayne said. As quickly as it had appeared, the knife was gone, returned to whatever hidden pocket Trevayne had conjured it from.

Hiern, who'd been growing increasingly restless ever since the quarrel began, leant forward and rapped his knuckles loudly on the table.

"If you've got something to tell us, Trevayne," he said haughtily, "I suggest that you get on with it. I didn't come all this way just to watch you two squabble with each other."

"You're quite right," Trevayne said. "We ought to be getting down to business. But first, I'd better introduce my companion here." He gestured theatrically towards the tall, hooded figure beside him. "This, my dear friends, is Annukin."

Cayla pursed her lips and looked away, exhibiting a curious blend of reverence and dismay. Hiern, who'd obviously never heard the name before, retained a sullen silence, seemingly bored with the entire proceedings. Isaf, however, laughed out loud.

"Come on, Trevayne," he said. "You'll have to do better than that. We're a bit old for fairy tales." He snorted derisively. "Annukin, indeed!"

Unlike most people, Isaf had actually ploughed his way through Zoab's monumental saga of the First Age, and knew full well that, had such a being ever existed (which seemed highly unlikely), he'd perished long ago, together with the rest of his kind. Whoever this strange, stilted figure may have been, he was certainly a far cry from the mighty warrior-god whose deeds were recounted in sheaves of epic verse and innumerable folktales.

"I've never been more serious in my life," Trevayne told him. "For gods'-sake, man, you've only got to look at him to realise that he's something more than human."

Although Isaf could see little of the man's face—obscured as it was by the voluminous shadows of his hood—there seemed to be some truth in what Trevayne said. But Isaf was in no mood to concede the point.

"Where'd you find him, then?" he asked snidely. "In a bottle or something?"

Trevayne's face darkened momentarily. He started to say something, but smiled instead, as if determined not to lose his temper. "It doesn't matter where I found him," he said.

"I'll tell you one thing, though, I had to do a hell of a lot more than just deliver a letter."

"Speaking of which"—Hiern stirred impatiently in his chair—"I'd like to know precisely why you sent for me."

"I was just getting to that," Trevayne said. "You see, it's my intention to embark as soon as possible on a journey to the East. And I want you three to come with me."

"And that's all?" Hiern sounded almost disappointed.

Trevayne grinned. "Of course not," he said. "In fact, it's scarcely even the beginning."

"I've had enough of this foolishness," Isaf said irritably. "Just settle up and we'll be on our way."

"Listen," Trevayne snapped. "I realise it's difficult for you to think and breathe at the same time, but just try and use your head for once, will you? After all, I'm hardly likely to go traipsing about the place with a king's ransom packed in my saddlebags, now am I?"

"But you said—"

"I said that you'd be well paid, and so you will. Just stick with me, my friend, and you can have all the gold you want. Whole cartloads of the bloody stuff."

Isaf stared thoughtfully down at his hands. By rights, he ought to have dismissed Trevayne's extravagant claims with the contempt they deserved. After all, talk was cheap, and he'd learnt from bitter experience that the only offers worth taking seriously were those in which hard currency—not vague promises—changed hands. Even so, he was intrigued to discover exactly what Trevayne had in mind.

"This journey," Isaf asked. "Where will it take us?"

"We'll know that when we get there," Trevayne told him, seemingly incapable of giving a straight answer to anything.

"And what happens then?"

"I've told you already, remember? Back in Julkrease. We're going to kill a god."

Isaf looked away. He thought they'd put that particular chimera to rest long ago.

"What do you mean?" Hiern asked.

"I mean a god," Trevayne said. "At least, that's how

you or I would describe him. To Annukin here, he's probably just one of the family.''

Hiern licked his lips, thus lowering himself even further in Isaf's estimation. Ever since leaving his holding, the mountain king's behaviour had, depending on his mood, resembled that of either a dangerous lunatic or a petulant child. Only the knowledge that they would soon be parting company forever had prevented Isaf from strangling the fellow with his bare hands.

"I see," Hiern said. "And he lives somewhere in the East?"

"That's right," Trevayne told him. "In a tower, I believe. So he shouldn't be too hard to find. And then—" He mimed a sword-cut to the throat. "Easy as pie."

Cayla, who actually seemed to be taking some interest in this exchange, suddenly shook her head. "I don't understand," she said, blushing furiously as both Trevayne and Hiern turned sharply towards her. "I mean, if he's a god, like you say, it'd take more than a handful of men to kill him. You'd need an army or something."

Trevayne smiled tolerantly. "That's been tried already, my dear," he said. "Two thousand men. Archers, cavalry, pikemen, the lot."

"And?" Isaf asked, finding himself drawn into the conversation more or less against his will.

"Not one came back."

Cayla paled visibly. Even Hiern's inexplicable enthusiasm seemed to waver slightly, although Isaf suspected that Trevayne was simply making the whole thing up.

"What happened to them?" Hiern asked.

"Your guess is as good as mine." To look at Trevayne's face, one might have thought that the matter was of no consequence to him at all. Isaf, however, thought he saw the man's shoulders stiffen for a moment, as if the question had struck something of a raw nerve. "The poor sods just vanished. The earth might have swallowed them up, for all I know."

"When was this?" Isaf asked him.

"A few years back. As a result, it was decided to try something a little more subtle this time round."

"Subtle?" Isaf laughed bitterly. "You must be off your head, Trevayne. Assuming that there's any truth at all in what you've been telling us—which I seriously doubt—no one in their right mind would send four men to do a job that two thousand couldn't handle!"

"Ah," Trevayne said, "but we have certain advantages over the previous expedition. For one thing, a small party like ours stands a far better chance of evading detection. More importantly, you're the only three men who the god may have some reason to fear."

"What are you talking about?" Isaf demanded. "I can't speak for the others here, but there's nothing special about me. I'm just a common soldier."

"Actually," Trevayne said, "I was thinking more about that fancy skewer of yours."

"You mean this?" Isaf fingered the hilt of his sword, with its aquiline motifs and strange, runic inscriptions. "Take away the decorations, and it's the same as any other blade."

"*No.*" Annukin spoke only the one quiet word, but it was enough. A sudden hush fell over the table as others turned towards him. "Trevayne is right," he said. "The path has been chosen for us. We cannot turn aside."

"There, you see!" Trevayne grinned triumphantly, as if Annukin's pronouncement were some masterly piece of legerdemain on his part. "Straight from the horse's mouth. Now, what's it to be, eh? You with me?"

"This god," Hiern asked. "What is his name?"

Judging by Trevayne's expression, he was beginning to find Hiern's obsessive interest in the matter more than a little irritating. "No one's really sure," he said. "I call him the Waiting God."

"Why?"

"I just do, that's all." A slight note of uneasiness edged into Trevayne's voice. "It's as good a name as any, isn't it?"

"And fires?"

"What do you mean?"

"Fires," Hiern repeated. Though outwardly quite calm, his eyes betrayed a ravenous, almost inhuman hunger, and he gazed at Trevayne with the hot, fixed stare of a true fanatic. "Does he have anything to do with fires?"

Trevayne frowned. "Well, he's occasionally referred to as the Lord of Flames, so I suppose—"

Hiern slumped back in his chair. "I'll go with you, then," he said quietly.

"That's the spirit." Trevayne turned to Isaf. "What about you?"

"We'll go," Cayla said quickly, darting a furtive, almost apologetic, glance at Isaf, then looking down at her hands once more.

Somewhat taken aback, Isaf frowned for a moment, then shrugged negligently. They really had precious little choice in the matter. He'd been less than frugal with the gold that Trevayne had already given him, and most of it was gone. Nor did there seem much chance of him obtaining gainful employment in Eria, where strangers in general—and Jenemun in particular—were afforded the sort of welcome usually reserved for lepers and wild dogs. What troubled him, however, was Cayla's apparent enthusiasm for the venture. He merely hoped that, like him, she was motivated solely by practical concerns rather than delusions of grandeur, as seemed to be the case with both Hiern and Trevayne.

"Well," Trevayne said, "it looks as if your lady friend here has made up her mind. I presume that means you're coming as well?"

"I suppose so," Isaf muttered, a trifle peevishly. "It's either that or starve to death."

"Excellent!" Trevayne slapped his hands on the table, grinning broadly. "We're all set then. I'd say some sort of celebration is in order, wouldn't you?"

The others sat in awkward silence (except Annukin, who was merely silent), as he motioned for the innkeeper to fetch them another jug of ale.

IT WAS LATE AFTERNOON by the time they finally saddled their horses and headed off along the crumbling, mud-soaked thoroughfare that had once linked Eria with its sprawling inland dependencies. A hundred years before,

they might have encountered huge wagons heaped with
grain from the fertile Misibii valley; or desert traders,
with their caravans of ivory, spice, and aromatic wood;
or mule trains from Sirribad, laden with gold and semi-
precious stones. Now, however, the roadway was all but
deserted, save for a few weary fishermen toiling home
from the river with their nets.

Trevayne had wasted no time in making the necessary
preparations for their journey. Within an hour of leaving
the tavern, he'd purchased three pack animals from a rapacious local farrier, and enough dried fish and meal to
last them for months. Somewhere along the line, he even
managed to obtain a fresh suit of motley and a brand
new feather for his hat.

Overhead, clouds the colour of old bruises were rolling
in from the East. Isaf had suggested that they wait until
morning before setting out, but Trevayne wouldn't hear
of it. Perhaps he was afraid that, if given time to think
things over, the others might soon change their minds
about taking part in this lunatic enterprise of his.

Trevayne led the way. He seemed in good humour,
and whistled jauntily as he rode. Annukin followed close
behind, mounted on a majestic black stallion which, together with the blood-red hair now spilling from his
hood, argued the case for his divinity far more persu-
asively than any amount of rhetoric. Next came Hiern,
perched in the saddle of his highland pony like some
equestrian scarecrow: all thin, knotted limbs and flowing
hair. Cayla and Isaf brought up the rear, trailing a good
distance behind the others, as if loath to associate with
such outlandish company.

Soon, it began to rain.

CHAPTER ELEVEN

Brothers in Arms

SOAKED TO THE SKIN, his face numb with cold, and an icy wind cutting through his heavy leather gauntlets like a knife-blade, Isaf hunched his shoulders against the rain and wondered why, in heaven's name, he had ever agreed to Trevayne's ludicrous proposition in the first place.

By now, it was long past nightfall, and the intervening hours had provided Isaf with ample time for reflection, yet he still had no clear understanding of his motives, which, as so often in past, seemed nothing more than a turbid blend of hopelessness, uncertainty, and fatigue. It would have been convenient to pretend that he simply hungered after gold, but this was an evasion. Deep down, he suspected that Trevayne had no intention of paying him anything at all, and may even have been leading the lot of them to their deaths. Though Isaf would never have admitted it, this might well have been the very reason he'd agreed to come along.

What troubled him most, however, was the fifth member of their expedition. If not the legendary hero himself miraculously returned to life, he was certainly a most convincing facsimile. The fellow rode bareheaded now, hair flickering in the wind like a torch, and even the most confirmed sceptic would have found it hard to deny the inhuman beauty of his face. The mere presence of such a creature made Isaf feel distinctly uneasy. Until now, he'd always believed that no matter how objectionable the world might have been, at least it made some vague kind of sense. Annukin, however, seemed living proof this just wasn't the case.

As night progressed, he succeeded in putting these thoughts more or less behind him. Since leaving the city, the road had slowly degenerated into a narrow, rutted track, full of bogs and potholes, so that the horses often sank to their knees in mud the colour of dirty honey. Trees crowded along either side, shuddering like rain-drenched giants with each blast of chill night air. Farther away, Isaf could hear the river Cromis rushing through the darkness on its long, impatient journey to the sea.

"Damn it, Trevayne," he growled. "This is madness."

At first Isaf thought that fellow hadn't heard him; then Trevayne's laughter was blown back with the wind. "What's the matter?" he called. "Not getting cold feet already, are you?"

'We'll freeze to death out here," Isaf replied irritably. "Just how much longer do you expect us to go on?"

"It's not that bad," Trevayne said. All that Isaf could see of him was a vague silhouette, feathers sprouting from his hat like some fantastic, night-blooming plant. "I thought you Jenemun could put up with anything."

"Maybe so. But Cayla can't."

"What do you suggest?"

"Stop. Light a fire."

"What, here?" Trevayne said. A brief stroke of lightning lit his face, revealing an expression that might equally well have been one of amusement or contempt. "You've got to be joking!"

Isaf felt Cayla's hand clutch tightly round his own. "Don't worry about me," she said. "These furs are quite warm, really. I'll be all right."

"That's not the point," Isaf muttered. He raised his voice once more. "For gods'-sake, Trevayne! We're going to have to stop sometime, aren't we?"

"I suppose so."

"Then how do you know we'll find any place better than this?"

This time, Trevayne's laughter was openly insulting. "It could hardly be much worse!"

Fortunately, perhaps, Isaf's reply was lost in the sound of distant thunder.

CAYLA TOO MARVELLED at the increasingly bizarre course her life appeared to be taking. Just a few months before, her horizons had extended no further than the shabby, smoke-stained walls of Hauba's tavern; now, almost without warning, she found herself setting out on a grand adventure, like one of the fearless young heroines of epic romances who'd so fascinated her as a child. Although she trusted Trevayne no better now than at their first meeting, and suspected that he knew far more about this Waiting God than he let on, she didn't doubt for a moment that such beings existed—unlike Isaf, who seemed to regard anything that he couldn't see or touch as superstitious nonsense. Frankly, Cayla would have preferred him to keep such opinions to himself. The gods may have been slow to anger, but no one could expect them to tolerate his blasphemies forever, and Cayla didn't want to be around when the lightning finally began to fall.

Isaf was beginning to try her patience in other respects as well. He'd been more and more ill-tempered of late, picking quarrels where none needed to exist, and often lapsing into fits of depression which Cayla was unable to penetrate. To be fair, Hiern's recent behaviour would have tried the patience of a saint. The fellow had changed markedly since leaving the Redflas. Sometimes arrogant, sometimes petulant, always furtive and aloof, he seemed an even more grotesque figure than the one they'd encountered in his mountain holding a few weeks before. He rarely spoke, except to voice some criticism or complaint, and Cayla, who'd spent half her life among pickpockets and petty thieves, could have sworn that he was hiding something from them—although she hadn't the foggiest idea what it might have been. Just the other day, for example, he'd flown into a terrible rage when, whilst tidying up their room, she dared to shift a sack of his belongings from its allotted place.

And then there was Annukin: Cayla still didn't know what

to make of him. Angels, her mother had once told her, often
found it difficult to tell whether they walked among the
living or the dead. That's how Annukin acted—as if he
were incomparably above and beyond them all, viewing the
world from some alien perspective that they could never
share. He seemed so remote, so self-possessed; yet at the
same time there was a strange air of innocence about him
that Cayla found deeply alluring. She would have liked to
comfort him in some way, to ease the suffering which she'd
glimpsed in his pale, unearthly eyes. It was impossible, of
course. To him, she must have seemed little more than a
walking shadow—if he were aware that she existed at all.

And yet . . .

She brushed the thought aside, concentrating instead on
guiding her horse around a fallen branch that momentarily
blocked their path. No matter what the future might bring,
she was determined to see this thing through. All her life
she'd been buffeted by events, subject to the whims and
directions of others; now, for the first time, she felt free to
choose her own destiny. At least no one could say that she'd
joined the expedition solely because of a blind dependence
on Isaf's company.

In fact, it may very well have been the other way around.

TOWARD MIDNIGHT, where the river slowed momentarily in
its headlong flight to form a shallow lake, they stumbled
across a tiny fishing village half-hidden among the trees.

Had the rain not eased for a time, allowing a few random
shafts of moonlight to trickle through the heavy cloudbank
overhead, they might not have noticed it at all: five or six
small conical huts, each surrounded by a jumble of shells,
fishbones and broken nets, like huge, mud-daubed spiders
hulking in their webs. Although no lamps were burning (the
inhabitants, no doubt, having retired to their beds hours
ago), Trevayne quickly reined to a halt, surveying the village
with obvious delight.

"There!" he said. "I told you we'd find something eventually. Now, let's see if we can't extract a little hospitality
from these folks, eh?"

Motioning for the others to remain behind, he urged his

horse towards the nearest hut. Its door, covered with child-ishly inexact depictions of eels, turtles, and fish, almost threatened to split in two as Trevayne leant over and thumped on it with his fist.

"Oi, you in there!" he shouted. "Open up!"

There was no response.

"Come on! Wakey, wakey!" Trevayne thumped again, even more violently this time. "You've got yourself some visitors!"

For a moment, all was silent, save for the murmur of wind and dripping leaves. He might have been some willful ghost hammering at the entrance to a tomb. Finally, how-ever, he heard footsteps inside, and the door swung slowly open.

"About time," Trevayne muttered. "You bloody deaf, are you?"

The old man blinked and rubbed his eyes. He reminded Trevayne of something you might drag out of a bog: all grey and wrinkled, the flesh hanging dispiritedly from his bones.

"What d'you want?" he grumbled.

"A place to sleep," Trevayne told him. "Some soup, perhaps—or whatever you've got, we're not fussy." He gestured towards the others, who'd assembled a few yards away. "As you can see, it's been a pretty hard day. We'll pay you, of course."

The fisherman stared blankly at him for a moment, then drew back his lips to reveal a mouthful of blackened gums.

"Go to hell," he said.

Before Trevayne could reply, the door slammed shut, as if he were just one more wretched vagabond trying to cadge some food and shelter for the night. It wasn't long, however, before his initial astonishment gave way to a murderous rage.

"Why you arrogant little sod!" he roared. "I'll fix you!" Hauling out his double-handed sword, he prepared to dis-mount.

"Leave him be," Isaf said.

Trevayne turned as if struck. The Jenemun's voice,

though outwardly quite calm, betrayed an anger no less fierce or intractable than his own.

"Trust you to stick up for him," he sneered. "Used to eat at the same bloody trough or something, did you?"

Isaf urged his horse a step or two closer. "It's his decision," he said stiffly. "You can't make him help us."

"Oh, I'll make him all right! Don't you worry about that!"

As Trevayne turned back towards the door, he heard Isaf draw his sword. "I said leave him be, Trevayne. Unless you want to try your luck with me first."

Trevayne's fury was such that he almost felt tempted to oblige. In the queer half-light, however, Isaf looked only marginally less inhuman than Annukin himself. His windswept silhouette bulked against the trees like some huge, barbaric demigod, clutching a sliver of razor-sharp moonlight in his fist.

Scowling, Trevayne sheathed his blade and wrenched his horse around to face the others. "Have it your way, then," he snarled. "Just remember, you were the one who was damned well snivelling about the cold!"

Isaf seemed content to let the matter rest, and promptly returned his own sword to its battered leather scabbard. Perhaps he thought that a dignified silence was the best way to humiliate Trevayne even further.

Until now, Annukin had paid scant attention to the proceedings, seemingly more interested in the remains of a broken earthenware pot scattered at his feet. Suddenly, however, he straightened up, his hair glistening in the darkness like some horrendous wound.

"We must not fight among ourselves," he said distantly. "Our adversary thrives on hatred and mistrust. Do not allow him to use these things against us."

The others looked at him with varying degrees of bewilderment, anxiety, and irritation.

"How do you know all this?" Hiern demanded.

Annukin merely shrugged and returned his attention to the broken pot.

Hiern gazed imploringly across at Trevayne. "Make him say! You've got to make him say!"

"Just shut up, will you?" Trevayne snapped. "None of us can make him do anything. I'd be a fool to try."

Spurring his horse savagely, he headed back towards the eastbound road. At the time, he didn't really give a damn whether anyone else followed him or not.

LATER, huddled in a glade of venerable elms with no fire to sit by and only a sodden blanket to shelter him from the wind, Hiern gathered his retinue of ghosts around him once more. By now their voices were as familiar to him as the beat of his own heart, but he listened anyway. They were the only friends he'd ever known:

—*People like us have a certain responsibility, you see.*

—*Thurgen is gone, sacked by bandits.*

—*Once this holding was a great place, in the days of my father's father.*

—*They used to mine for gold in the Lower Range. Remember the shafts and tunnels down by Gorgon's Mouth?*

—*I've seen the people grow old and bitter, seen their young ones leave, never to return.*

—*We must be better than anyone else. We must be stronger, braver, wiser, nobler, and more pious than the rest. We must be praiseworthy in every single aspect of our lives.*

—*And the holdings too are slowly failing.*

—*Don't you see? There must be something more to all this. Something everyone has forgotten. If only I could . . .*

—*I've watched the holding dwindle with each passing year.*

—*That's what they require of us. And it's our duty to see that we do not fail them.*

—*Now the works are all abandoned.*

—*Perhaps they simply don't care anymore. If so, it means that I have failed them.*

—*They didn't even have enough able-bodied men to mount a guard on the walls.*

—*We are only human, you know. Sometimes they seem to forget that.*

—*Other holders would come here to seek advice, to ask our help, to offer tribute.*

—And now . . . well, you know about that for yourself.

Hiern wondered whether he knew anything at all. At times, he felt little more than a ghost himself, vainly striving to expiate some heinous crime that had been committed centuries before he was born.

One thing, however, was certain: he hadn't come this far to see everything spoilt by some brawling savage or a swaggering buffoon. Annukin was the key. In time, perhaps, he might open the doors of the dead to them, might lay bare all the dark and poisonous secrets of the past. The others, of course, were of no consequence whatsoever. They could tell him nothing.

—Wait, the voices counselled.

—Wait and watch.

That, at least, would be easy enough. He'd been doing it all his life.

CHAPTER TWELVE

◆

Past Masters

THE NEXT WEEK or so passed without major incident, perhaps because there was relatively little for them to quarrel about. The river—and any other settlements it may have sustained—soon disappeared into a steep, thickly wooded ravine, and although the weather remained chill, the worst they had to contend with were a few intermittent showers. Since, with the possible exception of Hiern, they were all well-accustomed to a certain degree of hardship and privation in their daily lives, the necessity for them to sleep rough by the roadside provoked no real grumblings of discontent, and even the unrelieved diet of baked fish and gruel was tolerated without audible complaint.

THEY FORDED THE RIVER at Hydonwall, the site of an ancient, cyclopean causeway that had once helped supply the southern ploughlands with water in times of drought and curb excessive flooding during the spring thaw. Though now in ruins, it still provided the only viable river-crossing this side of the mountains, and was thus a convenient staging-post for those travelling either to or from the eastern steppes.

The nearby village boasted a caravanserai of sorts, where they were able to obtain food and lodgings for the night. Before departing, Trevayne also made sure that he stocked up with enough drinking water to last them throughout the

161

inland leg of their journey. By all accounts, the East was a fearsome place, and he had no intention of perishing from anything as ignominious as mere thirst.

"LOOK!" Hiern said. The anxiety in his voice was such that Trevayne expected to see a horde of blood-crazed savages bearing down at them.

"What is it?" he snapped.

"Fires!" Hiern told him. "Over there!"

For the past ten days, they'd been watching the mountains slowly dwindle behind them: now, as Trevayne peered into the distance, he could just make out a few pinpricks of ruby light away to his left.

"So?" he said.

"Fires," Hiern repeated, more softly this time, as if conjuring some familiar demon out of his own past.

"For gods'-sake," Trevayne said. "Pull yourself together, will you! It's probably just shepherds or something."

"On Eastwick?"

"Damn it, I don't know! But a few bloody bonfires aren't going to hurt us, man!"

Hiern said nothing more, but there was a strange, almost feral hunger in his eyes as he gazed at the far-off mountains, and he did not look away.

SOME DAYS LATER, they entered a wasteland no less desolate than the great Malad-Hras itself, only colder, washed by metallic rains. Dull grey clouds scudded across a sky as raw as hammered iron, and the sun, when it appeared, seemed small and indistinct.

It was the bleakest, most godforsaken place that Trevayne had ever seen. He could well understand how an entire army might have vanished here without a trace: probably starved to death, poor sods. Still, there no point dwelling on the past. He had enough on his mind as it was, simply trying to ensure that their expedition didn't suffer a similar fate.

Unfortunately, Vellaghar's directions had been pitifully vague. East, he'd said. A fat lot of use that was! There was more "East" out here than you could poke a stick at—and, judging by what Trevayne had seen so far, most of it was pretty damned unpleasant. He wondered if he should confer with Annukin, who was supposed to be some kind of bloody expert as far as the Waiting God was concerned. Not that he'd bothered to volunteer any information as yet, so maybe he didn't have a clue where they were headed either. To be quite honest, the fellow looked as though he'd need a map and compass to find own backside.

Talk about the blind leading the blind! Still, according to most theologians, that had always been as good a path to enlightenment as any.

Trevayne grinned at the thought. Perhaps there was hope for him after all.

THE FURTHER THEY PENETRATED into the wasteland, the more sullen and withdrawn Hiern became, trailing silently behind the others like some malignant shadow. Just what threat or revelation the fellow expected to emerge as he stared tirelessly into the distance, Isaf had no idea. All he ever saw was mile upon mile of dry, ashen rock and a few dead trees.

Trevayne, on the other hand, seemed in excellent spirits. With his parti-coloured clothes, facetious grin, and increasingly antic disposition, he cut a clownish figure at times. Even his long-standing animosity towards Isaf began to fade, replaced by a kind of gruff good humour. One night, in fact, as they settled down to their first hot meal in days, having at last scavenged sufficient wood for a fire, Trevayne actually appeared intent on striking up a conversation with him.

"Tell me, Isaf," he said. "Why do you dislike me so much? I mean, we've got quite a bit in common, really, when you come to think it. At least we could try to be civil with each other."

Isaf plucked another charred fish cake from the ashes. "Who says that I dislike you?" he muttered.

"I would have thought it was self-evident."

Isaf shrugged.

"Come on," Trevayne said, leaning forward to warm his hands over the fire. "I'd really like to know."

"You're supposed to be the clever one," Isaf growled. He couldn't help wondering whether the man was baiting him in some way. "Why don't you figure it out for yourself?"

"There, you see?" Trevayne shook his head ruefully. "I can't even ask a simple question without you biting my head off. All right, so we've locked horns on occasion. There's nothing wrong with that. Fellows like us are bound to get a little hotheaded at times. But I've never done you any real harm, have I?"

"It's not what you've done," Isaf told him. "It's what you are."

"Oh, yes? And what's that, exactly?"

"Someone who's grown fat on the labour of others." Isaf looked up, slowly warming to the task. Out here, Trevayne had no army of retainers to back him up, and there were no stocks or whipping posts to salve his wounded pride: for once in his life, he might as well hear the truth. "Someone rich enough to own a fine tower in Julkrease, and arrogant enough to believe that we should be grateful for whatever crumbs he lets slip from his table. Someone who'd let a hundred beggars starve rather than do without silver buttons on his shirt. Someone who can willingly forego luxuries the rest of us will never possess, then wonder why we don't love him for it." He stopped, surprised by his own vehemence. "Satisfied?" he asked.

Trevayne smiled. "So my tower bothers you, does it? And my gold, of course. We mustn't forget the gold." Far from resenting what Isaf had said, he seemed to find the accusations hugely entertaining. "*My* tower, eh! *My* gold!" Suddenly, he howled with laughter, perhaps at the look of sheer bewilderment on Isaf's face.

Although Cayla stared sharply across at him, neither of the others so much as glanced up from their meals. Hunched silently over the fire, they might have been a pair of hierophants making obeisance to some enigmatic deity hidden among the flames.

"I'm sorry," Trevayne said, his face still split with an enormous grin. "Only I'd have thought even you had more bloody sense than that!" He raised his hands in mock despair. "Surely you don't think I'd have tossed so much gold around if it were coming out of my own pocket!"

Isaf scowled. "What do you mean?"

"Gods' blood, man! I'm a humble mercenary, just like yourself. No doubt I've been a mite more successful at it than you—but whatever gold I once had was spent long ago, and there's certainly no fancy tower waiting for me at the end of all this. I'm simply a victim of circumstances, just like yourself."

Isaf suddenly made the connection that had evaded him for so long. "The *Pagadi*!" he said, gazing up at the man with newfound respect. "Of course! You're *the* Pagad Trevayne!" Looking at him now, it was difficult to believe that someone so unremarkable had once been the most famed condottiere of his day.

"Thank heavens for that!" Trevayne said. "For a moment there, I thought you were going to say you'd never heard of me. It's reassuring to know that a few years of semi-retirement haven't destroyed my reputation completely."

Isaf shook his head. "I still don't understand," he said. "If that wasn't your tower back in Julkrease, then where did it come from? The gold, too, for that matter."

"Why, from my employer, the Arbiter of Talingmar himself: Lord Vellaghar."

Two and a half decades of flight, evasion, and corrosive bitterness tightened about Isaf's throat like a hangman's noose. "No," he murmured. "That can't be. Vellaghar is dead."

"What are you talking about?" Trevayne said. "I saw him only a few months back. Certainly looked healthy enough to me."

"Vellaghar is dead, I tell you!" And he was; Isaf had made sure of that. He'd slit Vellaghar's throat from ear to ear, then watched with a mixture of horror and exultation as the man's blood spilt in a great steaming pool on the marbled floor. He couldn't understand what Trevayne was playing at. "He died years ago!"

Trevayne's smile faltered for a moment, then he stroked his chin thoughtfully. "Now that you mention it," he said,

"I believe there was another Vellaghar once. Came to a rather sticky end, by all accounts. In fact, some rumours had it that—" He stopped, eyes widening with surprise. "Well, well," he said. "Seems I'm not the only celebrity around here, eh?"

Isaf looked down, still trying to make some sense of what Trevayne had told him.

"As it happens, my friend," Trevayne continued, "the fellow had a son, also called Vellaghar. And it's his son who rules in Talingmar now."

"The Vellaghar I knew was childless," Isaf said. "You sure you've got the right man?"

Trevayne shrugged. "Apparently the Caucus thinks so, otherwise he wouldn't have been elected Arbiter. When exactly did you . . . I mean, how long's it been since you left Talingmar?"

"Twenty years or so. Why do you ask?"

"Vellaghar's a fairly young lad. Maybe he was still skulking in his mother's belly when you gave his old man the chop."

"How young?" Isaf demanded.

"Early twenties, I'd say," Trevayne told him. "It's never easy to tell with someone like him. He acts as if he's been running the place all his life."

"So you think he might have been born after Vellaghar's death?"

"Seems a likely enough explanation to me."

"How long after?"

Trevayne grinned. "Presumably not more than nine months. Although if his faction were strong enough, he could probably have been sired by a stray dog and still got the job. In Talingmar, preferment mainly depends on whose arse you lick, not the authenticity of your family pedigree."

From what Isaf had seen of the place, Trevayne's cynicism may well have been justified, but that was hardly relevant now. It scarcely mattered how Vellaghar had acquired his position: what concerned Isaf was that he suddenly found himself in the employ of someone who had every reason for wanting to see him strung up at the nearest gallows. "This Vellaghar," he said, "does he know I'm travelling with you?"

"Ah," Trevayne said, "I see your point. To be honest, I really don't know. He certainly didn't mention anything to me about it."

"You haven't told him about me, then?"

"Well, he knows that I've recruited *someone*—that is, I sent him a message to say that all the necessary preparations for our expedition had been made. You see, it was really the sword that he wanted. I don't think he cared very much who—or what—was attached to the other end. I never thought of telling him who was currently in possession of the thing. After all, I'm paid to look after those sort of details. That's what all the gold's for."

"But supposing Vellaghar *did* know about me. What would he do?"

Trevayne pursed his lips a moment, then shrugged. "Not a lot, I shouldn't think."

"Why? I killed his father, didn't I?"

"So? Don't forget, he's gone to an awful lot of trouble to find you—or, at least, the person you turned out to be— so you're obviously of use to him in some way. That's better than being a relative, I can tell you. Vellaghar's a cold-blooded little bastard. Strangle his own grandmother, he would, if it'd help him hold the throne. Besides, if he'd wanted you dead, he would've seen to it years ago. Why wait until now, when he knows full well that your death would jeopardize the entire expedition?"

Although Trevayne seemed to have a point, Isaf still felt uneasy about the whole thing. He knew just how subtle and convoluted the lords of Talingmar could be when it came to matters of honour, and it was entirely possible that Vellaghar had arranged this whole affair for the sole purpose of eliminating his father's assassin in what he considered to be an appropriately aesthetic fashion. Isaf had heard of one case, for example, where a nobleman had devoted more than fifty years to revenging himself on some obscure author who'd dared besmirch his family's name. "I don't know," he said. "If this Vellaghar is anything like the one I knew, he'd be capable of anything. Perhaps I ought to cut my losses and head back to Eria now, before it's too late."

"Nonsense," Trevayne assured him. "The last thing Vellaghar would want to do is spoil his well-laid plans. He's very keen to see the Waiting God dead, believe you me."

Without warning, Hiern thrust his face towards them. In the darkness, he resembled a huge, predatory bird, his cape folded around him like a pair of broken wings. "Why?" he asked.

Having been silent for so long, the others had almost forgotten that he could speak. Trevayne stared at him for moment, then tossed his head and looked away.

"Why what?" he snapped.

"Why should Vellaghar want to kill the Waiting God?"

"He does, that's all." Trevayne seized another piece of fish, his smile having given way to an ill-tempered frown. "All these bloody questions!" he growled. "Can't a man have some damned peace while he finishes his meal?"

"The lords of Talingmar have always been obsessed with the past," Isaf said. "They're forever delving into old tombs and things like that."

"So?" Trevayne crammed half a fish cake into his mouth, perhaps to avoid saying anything more on the subject.

"Perhaps they've learnt to fear it as well." Isaf looked questioningly across at Trevayne. "What do you think?"

"About what?"

"Might Vellaghar have some reason to be afraid of the Waiting God?"

"How the hell should I know?"

There seemed little point in pursuing the matter further. Heaping together another bundle of sticks, Isaf flung them on the fire. There was a brief shower of sparks, then the flames burnt briskly once more.

Beside him Cayla lowered her head and murmured: "No one seems to know much about anything."

EXHAUSTED THOUGH HE WAS, Trevayne found sleep difficult to come by. Somewhere off in the darkness, Isaf and Cayla were engaged in yet another bout of furtive love-making. They were at it constantly: scarcely a night passed when he didn't wake to the sound of their gasps and stifled groans. It was like sleeping next to a cage of bloody hamsters.

Quite frankly, Trevayne couldn't imagine what Cayla saw in the man. She seemed a cut above the usual camp follower (a trifle shop-spoilt, no doubt, but still young enough for her feigned innocence not to appear entirely grotesque), and could surely have done better for herself than some bloodthirsty renegade who didn't even have the sense to realise which side his bread was buttered on. The fellow wasn't exactly in his prime, either. Close to three times her age, by the look of him. If she liked her meat that well-hung, there were any number of fat old merchants back in Julkrease who would've paid well for the privilege of giving her a tumble. All she could ever expect from Isaf was a severe case of shagger's back.

At the moment, however, Trevayne was preoccupied with a far more pressing matter: Hiern had raised a legitimate point. Just why *was* Vellaghar expending so much time and effort trying to engineer the Waiting God's destruction? Their negotiations had always centred around more prosaic aspects of the journey—names, places, dates, and so on— and Trevayne really had no idea what Vellaghar stood to gain from all this. The same went for Annukin. Or even Hiern himself, for that matter. For a fellow no one had ever clapped eyes on, the Waiting God had certainly acquired some fairly powerful enemies.

Trevayne's own motives were straightforward enough— he was frightened. Ever since waking in a distant bivouac to find three ghostly figures stationed at the foot of his bed, he'd realised that the dying ambassador's threats were far from hollow. The creatures had been real enough, no question of that. He'd felt their icy breath on his cheeks as they closed around him, murmuring words that he couldn't quite hear, but which seemed to hold the promise of a most hideous, and implacable, revenge. They might have killed him there and then, he supposed, but apparently the Waiting God was in no great hurry to claim his vengeance. Perhaps he wanted to make Trevayne suffer before he died—in which case, he'd been only too successful.

Trevayne wasn't accustomed to being afraid. Fear had

always been something he'd inspired in others, a means by which to manipulate those weaker than himself, to prove that he, at least, was something more than a slave. Now it was his turn to start at shadows; to people his dreams with phantoms and fiends and dark-faced strangers; to never know whether each new day might prove to be his last; to learn, firsthand, what any fool could have told him: that nothing makes life quite so hard to bear as the prospect of suddenly losing it. Which was why he'd expended a king's ransom trying to hunt down the Waiting God while he still had the strength to do so; and why he'd forged this somewhat unholy alliance with Lord Vellaghar, a man he neither liked nor trusted, but who, for whatever reason, seemed no less anxious to extirpate the god than he himself.

Yes, Trevayne had become well-acquainted with fear over the past few years. He could feel it now, gnawing at his belly like a starved rat.

CHAPTER THIRTEEN

Betrayal

"Isaf?"

He woke slowly, yawning and rubbing his eyes. "What is it?" he said, propping himself up on one elbow as he turned to face her.

Cayla grinned mischievously. "You asleep?" she asked.

"No," he said, stifling another yawn. "Just resting my eyes."

"You were snoring."

"I was not."

"Yes you were."

"I never snore."

"You do so!" she said, running her fingers through the coarse black hair that matted his chest and arms. Only his face was smooth, painstakingly shaved each morning with the aid of the small bronze mirror which dangled from a leather thong around his neck. "Sometimes I wake up at night thinking a horrible great bear is after me!"

Isaf laughed. "Then he'll have to wait his turn, won't he?"

"Don't be so rude," Cayla told him. "Anyway, you've had quite enough for one night." She rolled onto her back and stared up at the sky. Starlight trembled across her face like wisps of silver fire. "Tell me," she said, "if you could

do anything you wanted—anything at all—what would it
be?''

Isaf's hand tightened around her breast. ''I've just done
it,'' he said.

''Oh, for goodness sake,'' she said, breaking free of his
embrace and wrapping the blanket tightly around her. ''Be
serious, will you!''

''Very well.'' Isaf straightened his shoulders and feigned
a ponderous frown. ''Apart from the obvious, I should like
to buy a farm somewhere and build myself a fine house.
I'd breed horses, I think. I've always liked horses. Then
I'd take some copper-haired little minx for my wife, and
father at least a dozen children, just to make sure that she
had plenty to keep her occupied.'' He smiled broadly. ''How
does that sound to you?'' he said. ''Interested?''

Cayla pulled a face. ''In what? Mucking out stables all
day and foaling every spring like the rest of the livestock?
No, thank you!''

''All right then,'' Isaf said. ''What would you do?''

''Oh, I'd want much more than that,'' she told him.
''Much, much more. For a start, I should live in a huge
tower. Like the one Trevayne had, only bigger, and not in
Julkrease either. Talingmar, perhaps. I could be a princess
there, with whole storerooms full of jewellery and beautiful
clothes to chose from. And I'd eat off golden plates, and
have lots and lots of servants to do whatever I wanted. I'd
hold the most splendid dinner parties for my friends, and
marvellous balls that the whole city would attend. And all
the handsome young officers, of course, would want to
dance with me. But I'd just smile at them and say—''

She realised suddenly that Isaf's expression had changed.
He was frowning in earnest now, staring down at her as if
she'd betrayed him in some fashion. Which, of course, she
had.

''I forgot.'' Cayla reached up to stroke his face. It felt
as hard and unforgiving as a gravestone. ''You've been to
Talingmar, haven't you?'' She paused a moment, but the
shadow that had fallen between them needed to be acknowledged, even if, once spoken, it could never be wholly

erased. "Why did you kill Lord Vellaghar?" she asked softly.

Isaf must have guessed what was coming, but he still flinched. Twenty-five years, it seemed, had done little to heal his wound. "It was a long time ago," he said. "There's no point going over it again." Slowly, he shook his head, as if the past were a dream from which he hoped to awaken rather than the gibbet every man builds throughout his lifetime to suffer upon alone. "I was young," he murmured. "I lost my temper. But Vellaghar got what he deserved. After the way he treated me—"

"That's what I don't understand," Cayla said. "What could he have possibly done that was worth killing him for?"

"He made a fool of me!" Isaf growled sullenly. "He treated me as if I was some kind of pet, to be paraded before his guests as an amusing after-dinner entertainment. I had to pay him back. Can't you see that? Otherwise—" He shrugged, his voice dropping to a whisper once more. "Otherwise I might just as well have slit my own damned throat instead."

By rights, she ought to have left it at that. There was nothing to be gained by pressing the matter further. She'd known from the start that Isaf was a killer. Few men weren't, one way or another. That's how the world worked. Women just had to smile and look the other way. For once, however, she found it impossible to hold her tongue. Out here, huddled together in the darkness, surrounded by untold miles of bleak, dry rock, neither of them could pretend to be anything more than what they seemed.

"Men used me all the time," she told him. "I was their plaything, something for them to fondle for a while, to use and then toss aside—but never a person who thinks or feels. *But I never killed anyone, Isaf!*"

"That's different," he said.

Had his tone been less dismissive, Cayla might have forgiven him. A deliberate insult was always far less wounding than genuine contempt. "Why?" she demanded. "Why is it different?"

Isaf seemed startled. Like most men, no doubt, it had

simply never occurred to him that a woman should resent being despised by those who'd made her what she was. "Because you're not a man," he said. "That's why."

"You mean because I'm a whore!"

Isaf's face darkened. He sat up, glaring at her. "That's right!" he said. "A damned whore! But I'm a man—a Jenemun!—and no one treats me like dirt and gets away with it! No one! Honour mightn't mean much to you, but—"

Cayla laughed scornfully. "Honour?" she jeered. "I wouldn't have thought there was anything particularly *honourable* about murdering an old man in his bed."

"What about you?" Isaf snarled. "Spreading your legs for anyone with a handful of coppers in his purse! You proud of that, are you? You proud of being the sort of slut any decent women would spit on?"

By now, Cayla's anger had hardened to a cold, implacable fury. "Do you honestly think you're any better?" she demanded. "I sell what I can to survive, and so do you. At least, my way, no one gets hurt. And at least I don't enjoy what I do." She thrust her face defiantly towards him. "So, who's the whore, eh? Tell me that! Who's the bloody whore?"

Isaf lashed out, striking her full in the face. "Bitch!" he roared. "Filthy, lying bitch!"

She scrambled back, more in horror than alarm.

Isaf held out his hand, perhaps regretting what he'd done, but it was much too late for that.

"You bastard!" she hissed. "I hate you!"

Turning, she hurried off into darkness, determined that he wouldn't have the satisfaction of seeing her cry. Rather than grief or anguish, she felt a strange sense of relief. It was as if some enormous weight had been lifted from her shoulders—a weight that had been pressing down on her for so long that she'd scarcely been aware of its existence. At last she was free. Alone and friendless, perhaps, not really sure where she was going or what would happen when she got there, but free all the same, owing no debt or allegiance to anyone except herself.

Despite the pain, four thick welts on her cheek seemed a small price to pay in return.

ASLEEP, his face resembled the death-mask of some ancient warrior-king: tranquil, imperious, yet faintly barbaric. Untroubled by even the slightest breeze, his hair spilt across the dark stone like a puddle of fresh blood.

Suddenly his eyes snapped open. He didn't blink, or yawn, or betray a single flicker of emotion, but he was awake.

"What do you want?" he asked.

Cayla knelt beside him, lips parted in a coy half-smile. "I thought you might be lonely," she said.

"I see." He regarded her distantly, as if she were rather less substantial than the dreams which her coming had disturbed.

"Don't you ever get lonely, Annukin?" she said, gently drawing the blanket aside and resting one hand on his chest. His skin was hard and smooth, like burnished metal, and curiously hot to the touch. She frowned for a moment, then flashed her most seductive smile. "No one should ever be lonely. Least of all someone as handsome as you."

"What about Isaf?"

"He doesn't own me, you know!" Regretting the sudden shrillness in her voice, she softened it with a giggle. "Besides," she said, "he's only a man."

"And what am I?"

"I'm not really sure."

As he stared silently up at her, she unfastened her cloak, feeling the cool night air prickle against her breasts and thighs. "Show me," she breathed, leaning closer to him, so that a few wayward strands of hair brushed across his face. "Show me."

Annukin reached out and took her by the hand. In comparison to his, it seemed miraculously soft and pale, like milk splashing into a golden bowl. Their eyes met for a moment, then he slowly shook his head.

"Go back to bed," he said. "You'll see things differently in the morning."

Cayla pulled away, clutching her robe tightly around her.

"What's the matter?" she demanded. "Aren't I good enough for you?"

"It's not that." Annukin shook his head again, as if trying to remember, or invent, the appropriate words for what he wanted to say. "I don't know whether Isaf loves you or not," he said. "Right now, you obviously don't think so. But at least he can try—which is far more than I could ever do."

Cayla felt betrayed. Ever since she was a child, she'd been taught the importance of making men desire her. It was the only power she'd ever possessed—was ever allowed to possess—the only means of proving to the world that she actually existed. And now, even this last tiny shred of self-respect had been stolen from her. Clambering to her feet, she glared spitefully at Annukin, hating him for what he'd done.

"You're not a man!" she sneered. "That's the real reason, isn't it? It's not that you won't—you can't!"

Annukin reached for her once more, but she knocked his hand aside. "Leave me alone!" she screamed. "Just leave me alone!"

For the second time that night, she fled into the darkness. She ran blindly, stumbling over unseen rocks and opening an ugly gash along her leg. The pain comforted her in a way. It allowed her to sustain her rage.

Isaf, Annukin, Trevayne, even Hiern: they were all the same. All so smug and superior. Treating her as if she were just so much excess baggage. "Isaf's woman" they called her. But she was more than that—she had to be—and, somehow or another, she'd find a way to prove it.

AT DAWN, Isaf woke to find the camp strangely silent, like a deserted battlefield. Cayla was nowhere to be seen. Glancing around, he noticed that Annukin, too, had gone. Trevayne squatted by the fire, polishing his sword. Further off, Hiern was fastidiously stowing his belongings into a pair of saddlebags, treating each item with the sort of exaggerated respect usually reserved for holy relics, or exquisite instruments of torture. Neither seemed at all concerned that two members of the party had apparently vanished without a trace.

He joined Trevayne beside the fire, racked by an all too familiar sense of guilt and self-reproach. He ought to have gone looking for Cayla at once, rather than lying awake half the night, nursing his wounded pride. Now, of course, it was too late. She might have forgiven him for striking her, but nothing he said or did could possibly make amends for the fact that he hadn't even bothered to find out what had happened to her afterwards.

Trevayne glanced up, a look of sly amusement on his face. "Hello," he said. "You're up bright and early this morning. I haven't even put breakfast on yet."

Isaf ignored the jibe. "I don't suppose you've seen Cayla about, have you?" he asked.

"No, can't say that I have."

"What about Annukin?"

Trevayne shrugged. "What about him?"

"He's not here either."

"So I noticed."

"Well," Isaf said irritably, "where's he gone?"

"Who knows?" Trevayne blew a few flakes of rotten-stone from his sword, then grinned. "Maybe they've run off together," he said. "Although I'll admit that seems unlikely. From the sound of it, they didn't exactly part on the best of terms last night."

"You heard what happened, then?"

"It would have been difficult not to. You certainly clouted the poor bitch hard enough. And she *was* rather vocal about her—disenchantment, shall we say?—with Annukin. It doesn't require a great deal of intelligence to fit the pieces together."

Isaf nodded. "I thought Cayla just wanted to be on her own for a little while," he said. "You know what women are like. But, since she doesn't appear to have come back yet—"

"You think something might have happened to her, eh?"

Isaf nodded again.

"Then Annukin has probably gone looking for her."

"Just looking?" Isaf asked.

Trevayne chuckled, as if savouring some private joke. "Take my word for it," he said, "you've got nothing to worry about on that score. Whatever else Annukin may be, he's certainly no ladies' man."

Isaf might have been slightly more reassured had Trevayne at least made some attempt to disguise his amusement. "I'd better go look for them anyway," he said. "They might be lost or something."

"I don't think that would be a very good idea," Trevayne told him. "This really isn't the sort of place you want to wander about by yourself. Most likely, we'd just end up losing you as well."

Isaf tossed his head impatiently. "Talk sense!" he snapped. "I'm a Jenemun, remember? I was *born* in country like this!"

"Maybe so. But this isn't the Malad-Hras, my friend. You're as much a stranger here as any of us." Trevayne glanced down at his sword, as if admiring its finish, or perhaps simply his own reflection. "Look," he said. "Vellaghar told me that once we got past the mountains, Annukin was to lead us. He didn't explain why, exactly, but my guess is that Annukin has been here before—or at least knows the lie of the land. If that's the case, he stands a much better chance of finding Cayla than you do. He's also far better equipped to look after himself out there. And your girlfriend too for that matter."

Isaf found this last argument less than convincing. Despite his appearance, the only godlike quality that Annukin had demonstrated so far was his sublime indifference to everyone—and everything—around him.

"I don't know about that," Isaf said. "He doesn't look like much to me. Besides, what sort of trouble could they possibly run into around here? The place is as quiet as a bloody graveyard. All they have to worry about is finding their way back to camp—and I can do that as well as anyone."

Trevayne sighed. "Use your head, Isaf. We may have had things easy so far, but our luck can't last forever. I mean, do you honestly expect the Waiting God to sit back and twiddle his thumbs while we string him up by the short and curlies? Sooner or later, my friend, the bastard will try to stop us—and when he does, we need to be ready for him, not chasing around the countryside. That way, we might actually live long enough to realise just how big a pack of fools we've been.''

"What about Annukin?"

"Annukin is something else again."

Isaf fingered the pommel of his sword uncertainly. He was too old for heroics (especially when he hadn't the faintest idea what sort of dangers he might face), and yet, he couldn't help wondering if Cayla mightn't have run away simply to discover whether or not he'd bother coming after her. In that case, his failure to do so would have been an even worse act of betrayal than what had happened the previous night.

"Don't worry," Trevayne said. "Annukin will find her in no time. He's good at that sort of thing."

"I'll give him an hour," Isaf decided. "If he's not back by then—" He left the sentence unfinished, reluctant to make a promise he might not be prepared to keep.

"That's the spirit," Trevayne told him. "In the meantime, why don't you make yourself useful, eh, and sharpen that flashy blade of yours. Unless I'm very much mistaken, you'll be needing it soon."

CHAPTER FOURTEEN

Ruminations of a Lesser God

THEY DROVE her before them like a startled fawn, shouting and waving their hands. Lean, wolfish men, clad in furs and enamelled metal. In her heart, she knew that escape was impossible, that they were simply toying with her, but she ran anyway, terrified of what might happen if she stopped.

All too soon, she felt them closing in for the kill. She tried to quicken her pace, but was tripped from behind, and fell, sprawling face-first across the dry, grey sand. They milled about like a pack of hounds, roaring with laughter and muttering crude obscenities.

"Show us your tits!" one jeered. Another bared his backside to her. "Hey, sweetheart," he crooned. "Kiss my arse!"

She buried her head in her hands, waiting for the pain to begin.

Suddenly there was silence. She glanced up to see that her pursuers had retreated a few steps. At first she couldn't understand what they were waiting for, then she noticed the burly, grey-haired figure standing before her. Unlike the others, he was clearly a stranger to these parts, affecting the yellow velvet cloak and waist-high boots of a Julkrean cavalier. A jagged scar split his face, as if someone had once tried to hack it apart with a meat-axe.

"Well, well," he said. "What have we got here, eh?"

One of the men seized Calya by the hair and hauled her to her feet. "We found her hiding among the rocks," he said. "Thought we might have ourselves a little fun."

The leader raised his eyebrows in mock surprise. "Now, boys," he said. "That's no way to treat a lady. Especially one as lovely as this." Turning to Cayla, he grinned mirthlessly. "You must forgive them, my dear. It gets rather lonely out here, you see. I'm afraid the lads tend to forget their manners at times."

Cayla said nothing. She realised that this too was a game. For all the man's feigned politeness, his voice was edged with a cold malice that frightened her far more than the blatant savagery of his followers.

"Come on," he said. "There's no need to be shy. I just want to ask you a few questions, that's all." He took hold of her face and tilted it up towards him. "For example, what's a pretty little thing like you doing wandering around here by yourself? Especially at this hour of the day. It's all very odd, don't you think?"

Cayla tried to pull away, but without success. The man simply tightened his grip, digging his fingers into her cheek until she cried out with pain.

"Please," she whimpered. "Just leave me alone!"

"Good heavens, child, that's no way to carry on. We're all friends here. And, believe me, someone in your position needs all the friends they can get." The man paused, fondling the huge, double-headed axe he carried slung across one shoulder. "Now then," he said. "Let's get down to business, shall we? I need some information—and one way or another I intend to get it. Do you understand me, Cayla?"

She stared wildly at him, her fear momentarily swamped by a welter of confusion. "Who are you?" she said. "How do you know my name?"

"I'm Fjerl," he told her. "And I know a great deal about you. In fact, it would appear that we share a common acquaintance, you and I." When Cayla didn't reply, he leant slowly forward, teeth bared in a predatory grin. "He calls himself Pagad Trevayne." Fjerl spat out the name as if it were somehow loathsome to him.

"I've never heard of him," Cayla said.

Fjerl laughed. "You're a terrible liar, my sweet. Trevayne's around here somewhere; I can smell it. And you're going to lead me to him. Or else . . ." He produced a razor-sharp stiletto from his belt. "I might have to cut the truth out of you. And we wouldn't want that, now would we?"

Cayla's flesh crawled as he stroked the knife across her cheek.

"Trevayne," he said. "Where do I find Trevayne?"

"I ran away!" Cayla told him. The words hurled themselves desperately from her lips. "It was dark! I couldn't see! I just ran."

Fjerl frowned. "My, my," he said. "You are a silly little girl, aren't you? I'll find out what I want to know eventually—you're just making it harder for yourself, that's all. One thing's certain, there won't be much left for friends to admire once I'm through with you."

"It's true!" she screamed. "Please, you've got to believe me! It's true!"

Fjerl's smile was subtly hungry, less subtly menacing.

"Very well," he sighed. "If that's the way you want it." He motioned two of his men forward. They hastened to obey, grinning and licking their lips. "Let's see what you're made of, eh?"

ANNUKIN CLIMBED SILENTLY up the jumble of broken rocks, his movements deft and precise, like an acrobat practising some astonishing feat of agility for his next performance. Although he'd been running for hours, casting about in ever-widening circles and had covered the last few miles at break-neck speed, he was neither weary nor short of breath. For one such as he, fatigue was no less alien a sensation than camaraderie, or peace of mind. He could easily have maintained a similar pace all day without so much as breaking into a sweat.

It was the voices that had lured him here. He'd been following them for some time, ever since Cayla's first despairing wail had pierced the pre-dawn silence and alerted him to her whereabouts. It had taken this long to make his way around from the other side of the camp and ascertain just where the sounds were coming from. Having listened intently to all that transpired between the girl and her captors, he knew precisely what to expect when he finally breasted the hillock and peered down into the basinlike depression below him.

Fjerl stood out from the others like a wolf among wild dogs. In addition to being a good head taller than any of his followers (whose haggard, emaciated faces and gangling limbs testified to a lifetime of chronic malnutrition), and far more sturdily built, he exuded an air of barely suppressed violence that might have been mistaken for authority.

His entourage, some three dozen strong, had gathered into a ragged circle about him, craning their necks and jostling for a better view of the proceedings. As Annukin watched, two of them stepped forward and seized Cayla's arms. There were hoots and catcalls from the assembled crowd, then an appreciative sigh as Fjerl cut open the girl's robe and bared her to the waist. Another few strokes of the knife and she was naked.

"My, my," Fjerl said. "You are a tasty little thing, aren't you?" He cupped his hand around one of her breasts, the way a lover might, as if marvelling at its perfection. "Why don't you just tell me where your friends are, eh? It'd save us both a lot of trouble."

Cayla seemed not to hear him, her entire attention fixed upon the glittering knife point that hovered within a hair's breadth of her throat.

"All right, my sweet," Fjerl told her. "Have it your way, then." With malicious languor, he lowered his stiletto and carved out a sliver of white, trembling flesh.

Annukin was no stranger to wanton cruelty, and observed Cayla's suffering with a certain degree of detachment. Once or twice he fingered the hilt of his sword, as if tempted to intervene; but in the end he simply lay and watched, constrained by something far more tangible—if less readily defined—than mere indifference.

Fjerl grinned, the scar crumpling with his face. "Your friends, girlie," he snarled. "Where are they?"

Cayla groaned, but seemed incapable of any more coherent response. Pain and fear swirled like sea-mist in her eyes.

It was, even by human standards, a thoroughly inept performance. Any competent torturer would have at least ensured that she remained alert enough to answer his questions. The House of Fire, for example, had boasted artisans so adept at administering pain that they could induce months of the most exquisite agony without so much as bruising their victim's skin. By comparison, Fjerl's methods were both crude and unproductive. Even if Cayla happened to possess the information that he desired, she was no longer in any condition to divulge it.

Not that this seemed to trouble Fjerl at all. Indeed, judging by the look of exultation on his face, he found Cayla's lack of co-operation most gratifying, perhaps because it gave him an excuse to continue his "interrogation," which was really nothing more than a particularly brutal form of rape.

Fjerl grinned hungrily, sliding his knife down towards Cayla's thighs. "Aha!" he said. "I'll bet there's nice meat around here. Eh, boys?"

There was a gale of coarse laughter as he cut again.

And so it continued. For how long, exactly, Annukin couldn't say. His conception of time differed markedly from that of other, lesser beings. Unlike them, he paid scant attention to the endlessly receding tide of years, pausing now and then to examine the spume and spindrift of events washed up at his feet, but seldom discovering anything that warranted close inspection. More often than not, he ignored the present altogether, turning instead to survey the monumental architecture of his past: the mausoleums and pale-white sepulchres of countless gutted dreams; wells of poisoned innocence and the oft-frequented shrines of love betrayed; whole cities of wrath, walled with pride and linked by the broad, enduring thoroughfares of hatred and revenge; temples raised on pillars of hope and fortresses of dark despair; even a few lone outposts of cherished ease, so far off as to be scarcely visible from his present vantage. All fixed, immutable, like exhibits in some huge temporal museum, as accessible to him now as they had been aeons before, when he'd first hewn them from the bare bones of eternity. Rarely did he direct his gaze out to sea, for fear that an immense black beast might surface from the waves and swallow him alive.

In due course, however, even Fjerl began to tire of his sport. Sheathing his knife, he turned and stalked off towards the line of shaggy ponies hobbled nearby. "All right, lads," he growled. "Looks as if we'll have to find the bastards for ourselves. Let's get moving, shall we?"

They did so reluctantly, muttering and dragging their feet, doubtless having hoped to take a more active part in the proceedings.

Annukin waited until the clatter of hoofbeats had retreated well into the distance, then descended to the patch of bright-red sand where Cayla lay, surrounded by scraps of her own butchered flesh, like a freshly slaughtered carcass on the floor of an abattoir. She wasn't quite dead. Even that small kindness had been denied her.

Although, towards the end, Fjerl had seen fit to gouge out her eyes, she appeared to sense Annukin's presence, and made a pathetic mewling sound as he approached. It took some time for him to realise that she was attempting to speak.

"No," she murmured. "No, no, no, no, no . . ."

Annukin regarded her quizzically, perhaps wondering why she should cling so tenaciously to a life that, when all was said and done, endured for the merest flicker of an eye. How could such an ephemeral creature ever appreciate the true splendour and misery of existence, or have any real reason to dread its passing?

Still, he was not entirely devoid of compassion. Drawing his sword, he leant down and stabbed her neatly through the heart. She stiffened for a moment, then slumped face forward in the sand, like a bundle of blood-soaked rags.

"Lamat zabac," he said.

It was a phrase that defied literal translation, variously employed as a curse, a prayer, a lament, or a valediction. Even Annukin wasn't entirely certain which of these corresponded to his precise feelings at the time.

* * *

Isaf's allotted hour had stretched to three before Annukin finally returned. It was Hiern who saw him first,
skating across the plain like a gold and scarlet shadow, his
bare feet padding soundlessly on the heavy sand.

"Isaf!" he shouted. "Over here! Annukin's back!"

Isaf threw down his sword and hurried to join Hiern at
the edge of the camp. The man seemed uncommonly agi-
tated, his face alight with an almost childish enthusiasm.
"There!" he said, gesturing frantically towards the East.
"Near that pile of rocks! Can you see him?"

Peering into the distance, Isaf could just make out a small,
man-like figure advancing towards them. His shoulders
slumped as he realised that Annukin was alone.

"Yes," he said quietly. "I see him."

Trevayne arrived a few moments later. He was still smiling, although with little apparent humour. Perhaps he was
merely relieved that the fellow had made it back in one
piece.

"Here," he said. "You dropped this."

"What?" Isaf glanced down to find Trevayne standing
close behind him. "Oh," he said, taking the proffered sword
and returning it to its sheath. "Thanks."

By now, Annukin had drawn close enough for them to
see his face. As always, it revealed nothing: they might just
as well have tried to divine what had happened by observing
the phases of the moon.

"Any luck?" Trevayne asked.

Annukin failed to reply.

"Well?" Hiern demanded. "Did you find her or not?"

Annukin waited until he was within a few yards of the
others, then stopped, as if noticing them for the first time.
"I found her," he said.

Isaf felt something lurch inside him. "Where is she,
then," he growled. "Why didn't you bring her back?"

"She's dead," Annukin told him.

"What do you mean?" Trevayne said.

Annukin shrugged. "Dead," he repeated. "Some of the
Waiting God's men got hold of her and tried to make her
talk." He shrugged again. "She wouldn't."

Isaf glared savagely at him. "How do you know?" he

said. "How do you know what she told them?"

For the first time, a brief flicker of emotion crossed Annukin's face, as elusive and ill-defined as a figure scrawled in moving sand. He looked at Isaf, then slowly shook his head.

"I'm sorry," he murmured.

"You just watched?"

"There were too many of them, Isaf. Even for me. What else could I do?"

Isaf turned away. There seemed little point blaming Annukin for what had happened. After all, Cayla had meant nothing to him. Isaf was the one who'd failed her, who'd turned his back on her when she needed him the most. Whatever guilt was to be apportioned belonged to him alone.

Striding across the campsite, he mounted his horse and hauled it around to face the others. "All right, Trevayne," he said. "Where do we find this damned tower of yours, eh?"

As he made to ride off, Annukin suddenly stepped forward and raised his hand.

"Isaf—"

"What do you want?"

"I was with Cayla when she died," Annukin told him. "She said that she wanted you to carry on, to make the Waiting God pay for what he's done. And—"

"Well?"

"And that she loved you very much."

Isaf laughed bitterly. "Is that a fact?" he said. "Fat lot of good it did her!"

Then he was gone, hoofbeats ringing like hammer blows on the cold stone.

The others hastened to follow him.

By COMMON, if unspoken, consent, Annukin now assumed *de facto* leadership of the expedition. He set a furious pace, and it was only when both they and their horses were on the verge of dropping from sheer exhaustion that he finally called them to a halt.

Hiern almost welcomed the mind-numbing fatigue that settled on him as he rode. Yet another ghost had joined the train of spectral attendants who dogged his steps. How Cayla, a virtual stranger, had managed to be recruited into this select company, he had no idea, but having clambered aboard, she'd no doubt be with him until the day he died; a plaintive, melancholy sprite, hovering at the very edge of his awareness, like a rebuke or an adjuration.

He'd already offered his condolences to Isaf—much to his own surprise. And Isaf's, too, gauging by the man's reaction. He wondered why Cayla's death had touched him so deeply, opening a hidden vein of sentiment which had been sealed for more years than he cared to recall. Was it because he'd noticed the same anguish in Isaf's face that his mother had displayed many years before, when Shembley and the others dragged his father's shattered corpse from the bottom of Morgen's Gorge?

Perhaps he'd finally realised that he had no monopoly on suffering, and that, no matter how bitter or corrosive his own grief, it was neither more nor less insupportable than any other.

How ironic that he should have had to come so far, and sacrificed so much, only to discover something that even the humblest peasant must have known all his life: that he wasn't the only one who could be hurt, who had been hurt.

It was, he feared, a lesson that none of his predecessors had ever learned.

CHAPTER FIFTEEN

Vengeance

ALTHOUGH TREVAYNE WAS QUITE CONTENT that Annukin should lead the way, he couldn't help wondering precisely where they were going and how long it might take to get there. Rather than proceeding due East, the fellow continually switched direction, sometimes darting off at right angles to their former path, or sweeping around in a long, wide arc, almost threatening to take them back the way they'd come. The logic behind these manoeuvres remained a mystery to Trevayne—assuming, of course, that there was any. Annukin seemed disinclined to offer any explanations.

That evening, after the others had collapsed beneath their blankets like a pair of empty wine sacks, Trevayne decided to try and get a few answers.

Annukin was still awake; Trevayne doubted whether he ever slept at all. Even when his eyes were closed, he remained tense and alert, as if listening to voices that no one else could hear. Now, propped against a nearby stand of rock, he gazed vacantly up at the mass of stars clustered overhead. The cold white light flooded across him like smelted silver, making his face seem even more starkly inhuman than usual. So much so, in fact, that Trevayne began to question the wisdom of intruding on his silence.

"Annukin?" he said.

For a moment, there was no response. Then Annukin

turned towards him. Once again it seemed to Trevayne as if some blood-daubed idol were slowly stirring to life before his eyes.

"Yes?"

"Could you spare a moment? There's something I wanted to ask you."

Annukin sighed. "Very well," he said. It was difficult to say whether his voice was edged with weariness or mere disdain.

Trevayne licked his lips. He'd done pretty well so far. Now came the tricky part. "How's it going, do you think?" he asked. "We making any progress?"

"Some."

"Well, that's good to know, isn't it? How long until we reach the tower?"

"That depends."

Trevayne waited, but the man offered nothing more. "On what?" he prompted.

"We must go deeper yet," Annukin told him. "Much, much deeper."

This seemed a curious choice of phrase, but Trevayne let it pass. Getting a straight answer out of Annukin was like trying to extract water from a stone. He counted himself lucky that the fellow had bothered saying anything at all.

"And these men you saw?" he asked. "The ones who got hold of Cayla. What were they like?"

"Like?" Annukin frowned, as if he'd been asked to describe the precise shading of a butterfly's wing, or the geometry of a snowflake. "Just men," he said. "Mostly short and dark. Dressed in furs." He shrugged. "How can I say what they were like?"

"And their leader?"

"He was different. Taller, and quite thick-set. With a scar running down his face."

Trevayne felt a sudden stab of apprehension. "Did he wear a yellow cloak, by any chance? And big boots?"

Annukin nodded. "That's right. Do you know him?"

"Oh, yes. I know him all right." Trevayne stroked his beard thoughtfully. "Poor Cayla," he said. "He's a nasty piece of work, that one."

Annukin appeared to be fast losing all interest in the conversation. "Scarcely a match for us," he murmured, dismissing the entire matter with a negligent wave of his hand.

Trevayne found it difficult to share the demigod's optimism, which seemed based more on sheer arrogance than a rational appraisal of their position. "We'll find out soon enough," he said. "One thing's for sure, he's not going to let us just waltz up to the tower without a fight. How many men did you say he had with him?"

"About forty."

"Probably just a scouting party. He'll have the rest holed up somewhere in reserve." Fjerl's unexpected appearance complicated things no end. Back in Talingmar, it had all seemed relatively straightforward. They were to find the Waiting God, kill him, then return to a hero's welcome— and more gold than they could poke a stick at. Just like that. Bang, bang, bang. Piss in the hand. And now he suddenly found himself opposed by the one man he'd ever had reason to fear. Fjerl's vengeance was legendary, and of all the mercenary commanders that Trevayne had faced over the years, Fjerl alone had proven his equal. Their last engagement had been a long and bloody affair—and obviously less conclusive than Trevayne had imagined, despite the Pagadi's clear supremacy in numbers and equipment. Now, it seemed, the boot was well and truly on the other foot. "Gods' blood," he muttered. "I thought I'd finished the bastard down at Gethling Vale. What in hell's name are we going to do?"

Annukin, however, wasn't listening. He gazed heavenward once more, like a discarded piece of heroic sculpture, as the stars split their pale, diaphanous libations across his face.

"Thanks a lot," Trevayne said, stalking off to contemplate a future that was growing more uncertain by the minute. "You're a great help, aren't you?"

AND SO THEY COMMENCED THE LAST, most desperate stage of their quest. Time slowed like an expiring clockwork, seizing each day and breaking it on a rack of unrelieved

motion. The landscape was smeared with funereal tones:
dull, leaden clouds; sand the colour of bruised plums; ashen
rocks veined with black; a sky as grey and cheerless as the
ocean under rain. Everything seemed poised, expectant, like
an empty canvas, or a darkened theatre stage.

They were a sombre, dispirited company. Few spoke,
and those who did were seldom answered. Isaf set himself
apart from the others, countering his grief the only way he
knew how—by refusing to acknowledge it. Trevayne was
too busy wrestling with his own presentiments of death and
dissolution to spare any great sympathy for the fellow.

They'd been dogged by misfortune for some days now.
Two of the pack animals had died within hours of each
other, swelling up like parti-coloured balloons after lapping
at a puddle of black, brackish water. The remaining mule
had perished soon after, tumbling into a crevasse that opened
beneath its feet as they traversed a range of low, crumbling
hills. It all happened so suddenly that Trevayne could do
nothing more than stare in horror as the poor creature vanished without a trace, taking with it the lion's share of their
supplies. If that wasn't enough, on breaking open the sole
surviving barrel of salted fish, Trevayne had found it virtually consumed by maggots. Their flour too had spoiled,
the sacks so riddled with weevils that Trevayne had difficulty
scraping together even the most rudimentary of meals. Try
though he may, he found it hard to believe that these in-
cidents were entirely unrelated, that they simply constituted
a run of monstrously bad luck. Surely there was some unseen
hand at work, plotting their destruction. Nor did he have
the slightest doubt to whom that hand belonged.

Gnawing morosely at a piece of rotted fish, he surveyed
the faces around him. Only Annukin's was unmarked by
dejection and fatigue. The fellow ate mechanically, consuming his meagre repast with neither more nor less enthusiasm than he might a suckling pig, or a fatal draught of
hemlock. The others, however, looked decidedly haggard,
like convicted felons awaiting their turn at the gallows. Then
again, Trevayne probably didn't cut a particularly dashing
figure himself.

"Better make the most of it, lads," he told them. "The cupboard's getting rather bare, I'm afraid."

"What do you mean?" Hiern asked. Now that Isaf had usurped his position as chief sulk in the party, the fellow appeared intent on establishing a new career for himself as Trevayne's confidant and self-appointed adviser. So persistent were these overtures that they'd become, if anything, an even greater source of irritation than his former petulance.

Trevayne grinned sourly. "All we've got left is a little flour, and even that won't last much longer. I give us another two or three days at the most, then we'll just have to go without. Unless you want to start carving up the horses."

Although this was tantamount to inscribing the final words on their mutual epitaph, none of the others appeared unduly concerned by his announcement. Even Hiern stared blankly at him, as if unable to see any real cause for alarm. Neither Annukin nor Isaf so much as bothered to look up. Unlike them, however, Trevayne needed more than mere wormwood and gall to sustain his passage from one day to the next.

"Don't you understand?" he said. "We've had it!" Still no response. "We're dead meat, the lot of us!"

Hiern at least had the decency to frown slightly. He glanced down a moment, fingering something beneath his jerkin. "Does it really make any difference?" he said quietly. "In the long run, I mean."

"What *are* you talking about?" Trevayne said. "Of course it makes a bloody difference! I don't much relish the idea of starving to death, do you?"

"We all walk the same road," Hiern murmured, as if reciting some lesson that he'd learnt by heart many years before. "Some amble along, hoping the journey will last forever; some can't wait to see where it might take them; others simply don't care one way or the other. In the end, it all comes down to same thing."

"Oh, very profound," Trevayne said, convinced that the fellow had lost his mind completely. "I'll have to remember that." He turned to Annukin. "What do you think?" he asked. "Any chance of us reaching the tower in the next few days?"

Annukin shrugged. "It depends."

"On what?"

"On how much further there is to go."

Trevayne rolled his eyes in disgust. "That's marvellous, isn't it? Here we are, on the brink of starvation, and you want to play bloody riddles! Maybe Hiern's right. Maybe we should all just lay down and die."

Annukin regarded him with something like amusement. "Don't worry," he said. "We'll be there sooner than you think."

"Let's hope so." Trevayne scraped the last few morsels of fish from his plate, then went to fetch a drink. On doing so, he discovered that their last remaining keg had mysteriously sprung a leak, spewing water across the dark sand like blood from an unstaunched wound.

"You see!" he howled, quickly upending the barrel to prevent it running dry completely. "The bastard's killing us by inches!"

None of the others bothered to help him. Apparently they were content to sicken and die like a mob of neglected sheep. Trevayne, however, had no intention of giving in without a fight. He'd eat dirt if he had to, and drink his own piss, but somehow he'd stay alive long enough to fix the Waiting God once and for all—

Even if it killed him.

ISAF HAD NEVER SEEN SUCH CARNAGE.

They'd been climbing steadily for some time, the land rising before them in a succession of huge, shallow dunes. Now it suddenly dropped away, and they looked down on a flat, narrow plain, about a mile across, that glistened beneath the noonday sun like a sheet of volcanic glass.

There were corpses everywhere.

During his quarter of a century as a professional soldier, Isaf had taken part in countless military engagements, but even the largest of these had seldom involved more than a few hundred men at a time, and most mercenary commanders were pragmatic enough to withdraw their troops from the field before any serious harm was done to either side. This was different. Thousands had perished here, the victims of some horrendous conflagration that had apparently struck without warning, and from which there could have been no possibility of escape. The heaps of blackened bodies seemed to stretch forever, like charred logs piled up on the bed of a gigantic furnace.

"I don't understand," he said. "How could something like this happen? There's nothing to burn out here."

Annukin, who'd been surveying the devastation with detachment, slowly turned towards him. "It was no ordinary fire," he said. "Surely even you must realise that."

"You mean the Waiting God did this?"

"Of course." Annukin glanced once more at the vast crematorium below them. "He must be even weaker than I thought."

"What are you talking about?" Trevayne demanded. His temper had soured markedly over the previous few days, but now his face betrayed an anguish that Isaf had never seen before. "For gods'-sake! Just look at them! The poor bastards never stood a chance."

Annukin shrugged. "They should never have made it this far," he said. "What's more, our adversary was obliged to raise his own hand against them. In days gone by, he'd never even have bothered to acknowledge their existence."

"They were good lads," Trevayne told him. "All of them." He looked down, his voice suddenly dropping to a whisper. "They deserved better than this."

All at once Isaf thought he knew just whose corpses they were, and why Trevayne should have been so distressed to see them.

"That army you told us about," he said. "The one that disappeared. They were Pagadi?"

Trevayne nodded. "Most of them. Vellaghar supplied a few from his household guard. But the rest were mine."

"I see."

"Vellaghar said it was worth a try. How were we to know that something like this would happen?" Trevayne shook his head, as if trying to dislodge some mournful recollection that until now had been securely locked away in the loneliest corridors of his past. It occurred to Isaf that they probably had more in common than either would have cared to admit.

"Two thousand men," he murmured. "Two thousand bloody men."

Annukin silenced them with an imperious wave of his hand. "Listen," he said.

"What is it?" Isaf asked. All he could hear were hooves stirring lazily in the sand.

Annukin cocked his head to one side, then pointed towards the opposing ridge. "Over there," he said.

They listened intently for some time, but still heard nothing.

"You must be imagining things," Trevayne said. He was obviously keen to put the fire-ravaged legions behind him as quickly as possible. Few men could ever have been faced with a more grim, or harrowing, testimonial to the consequences of their folly. "We going to sit round here all day?"

"Wait a minute," Hiern began. "I think—"

Then Isaf heard it, too. A distant rumble, barely audible at first, but growing louder all the time, until it rang in his ears like the sound of waves crashing on a deserted shore.

"Riders," Hiern said. "Lots of them. And coming this way."

Moments later a line of horsemen appeared above the ridge. As their war-cry swelled ever further, Isaf suddenly realised that they were chanting a single word, over and over again:

"F-J-E-R-L-A!"

"F-J-E-R-L-A!"

"F-J-E-R-L-A!"

"F-J-E-R-L-A!"

Trevayne paled visibly. "Come on!" he said, darting an anxious glance over his shoulder. "Let's get going! Those bastards are out for blood!"

"It's too late for that," Annukin told him. "They've already seen us. Besides, they have to be dealt with before we can reach the tower. You said as much yourself."

"Are you mad?" Trevayne squirmed uneasily in his saddle as, with yet another ear-piercing yell, the riders hurled themselves into the black, corpse-strewn plain. "Use your eyes, man! Fjerl must have more than a hundred men with him. He'll tear us to pieces!"

Annukin laughed, a brittle, unpleasant sound as sudden as breaking glass. "I make it only ninety-four," he said. He seemed genuinely unperturbed by the ranks of advancing horsemen. "That's less than two dozen apiece."

Still laughing, he stripped off his cloak and galloped down the slope to meet them, his scarlet hair streaming behind him like a firebrand. For the first time, Isaf caught a glimpse of the brutal, foot-long scar that ran between his thighs, like the sole flaw in an immaculate amber figurine.

Trevayne must have noticed the look of astonishment on Isaf's face. His lips curled in the ghost of a smile. "I told you he wasn't much of one for the ladies. Now you know why."

Isaf gazed almost pityingly at Annukin's retreating form. "How did it happen?" he asked.

"Courtesy of his father," Trevayne said. "At least, that's the story I got from Vellaghar. Apparently Annukin was deemed unworthy of perpetuating the family line."

"What are we waiting for?" Hiern said. Stringing his bow, he stared wildly after Annukin. "At least this way we can take some of the Waiting God's men with us."

Trevayne sighed. "Oh, very well," he said, urging his horse slowly forward. "I suppose there are worse ways to die."

The horsemen were closer now. Sunlight flared from their upraised swords and crude, enamelled armour. Isaf could even make out the faces of those closest to him. His eyes narrowed as he caught sight of the burly grey-haired figure who led the charge. Like Trevayne, the man was a legendary figure among the *condottieri*, although this was the first time that Isaf had actually seen him. He'd disappeared some time ago under mysterious circumstances, and it was generally assumed that one of the man's numerous enemies had finally caught up with him. Even if Fjerl's men hadn't been shrieking out his name, the bright yellow cloak and giant axe would have been more than sufficient for Isaf to realise just who it was he faced.

"That one," he said quietly, "is mine."

Trevayne grinned. "You're welcome to him. Only you'll have to watch yourself—he's a tough old bastard."

Then it began.

By the time he and Trevayne reached the bottom of the slope, Annukin had closed to within a few dozen yards of the Fjerla, apparently still intent on tackling the horde single-handed.

"Wait!" Isaf cried. "You can't fight them by yourself!"

He might have saved his breath. With the Fjerla's war chant still ringing across the plain, Annukin couldn't possibly have heard him.

"FJERLA!" they howled.

"F-J-E-R-L-A!"

"F-J-E-R-L-A!"

"F-J-E-R-L-A!"

"F-J-E-R-L-A!"

As the first wave of riders broke around him, Annukin raised his sword, and the triumphant roar changed to a wail of horror. Isaf saw a dozen men suddenly burst into the flames, like dried leaves heaped onto a bonfire. Still the Fjerla advanced, driven more by sheer momentum than any real desire to close with the demigod now that he'd demonstrated the awesome powers at his command.

"Gods' blood!" Trevayne said. "How I could have used a few like him in the old days!" He seemed to have shrugged off his earlier misgivings, and grinned approvingly as Annukin's sword flared a second time, leaving yet more smouldering corpses in its wake.

Hiern was next to join the fray. Despite his meagre frame he acquitted himself well, stationing himself to one side of Annukin and easily picking off those horsemen who survived the demigod's pitiless assault.

The Fjerla too fought with courage and resolve. Isaf had half-expected them to falter before such an onslaught, but they continued to press forward, if not quite so recklessly as before. Most concentrated on employing their javelins and spears, darting in for the occasional sword-blow whenever Annukin's back was turned, then retiring to a safe distance before he could bring his own blade to bear against them. It was like watching a pack of hunting dogs trying to bring down a lion.

While Annukin was thus engaged, half the remaining

Fjerla wheeled about to bear down on Isaf and Trevayne, who met them with a fury at least the equal of their own.

Until now, Isaf had never tested his silver sword in battle, but it proved a formidable weapon, disembowelling the first horseman who ventured within reach, and slicing the heads from two others as neatly as one might lop apples from a tree. No wonder Ladoc had enjoyed such a spectacular success throughout his brief career. With a sword like this, a man could do anything. Once again Isaf marvelled at the stroke of sheer good fortune that had delivered it into his possession.

Away to his left, he saw Trevayne's horse stumble and fall, as a hastily cast javelin pierced its throat. For a moment he was certain that the man would be cut to pieces, but Trevayne quickly scrambled to his feet and, roaring with laughter, hauled out his big sword.

As the Fjerla swarmed towards him, he hewed away at them like some exuberant woodcutter. When Isaf finally lost sight of the man, he was already knee-deep in corpses, and bellowing for more. It was easy to see why the fellow had been held in such awe by those who'd served under him: pound for pound, he was probably the most ferocious fighter Isaf had ever seen.

And so the melee continued.

Isaf soon lost count of how many men he'd killed. He fought with brutal proficiency, hacking his way through the ranks of horsemen until he found himself momentarily alone. A thick pall of smoke hung over the battlefield, pierced by flashes of raw, demonic light as Annukin continued to reap his terrible harvest among the Fjerla.

Just as Isaf was about to rejoin the fray, he saw a yellow velvet cloak fluttering away to his left. Its owner seemed headed in the opposite direction, but Isaf had no intention of allowing him to pass unchallenged. Spurring his mount forward, he set himself squarely in the rider's path.

"Out of my way!" Fjerl snarled, as Isaf just managed to evade a tremendous blow of his axe. "It's Trevayne I want!"

Isaf said nothing. Hatred was the only thing he had left

to sustain him, and he could ill afford to waste it on mere words.

Fjerl swung his axe once more. "Fool!" he hissed. "Do you think I'm going to let a damned Jenemun stand in my way!"

This time Isaf parried the blow with his sword. He jabbed at Fjerl's throat, but the man twisted aside so that the thrust glanced off his breastplate, gouging away the thick enamel and leaving behind a white, painless wound on metal. Before Isaf could recover, Fjerl lunged forward and trapped his sword-arm in a viselike grip. Caught off-balance, he looked on helplessly as a stiletto plunged towards his vitals.

It was a deft manoeuvre, and one which ought to have proven murderously efficient.

At that precise moment, however, Isaf suddenly felt a sharp burning pain in his chest. He slumped to one side, thinking that Fjerl's blade must already have struck home, but on glancing down saw that his own sword had veered up at a seemingly impossible angle to block the thrust, and was even now burying itself edgewise in the condottiere's face.

With a strangled cry, Fjerl toppled to the ground, his skull sheared almost in two by the force of Isaf's blow. It was, perhaps, a better end than he deserved. No doubt Cayla herself had died far less cleanly.

By this stage, the remaining Fjerla had begun to lose heart, throwing down their weapons and scattering across the plain like a flock of startled gulls. Hiern pursued them for a time, until either he or his quiver was exhausted, but a handful escaped to lick their wounds, doubtless eager to put as much distance as possible between themselves and Annukin.

Sheathing his sword, Isaf gazed sombrely at the desolation around him. Now that the smoke had cleared, it was already hard to distinguish the Fjerla's corpses from those who had perished here years before. All were equally still, equally silent, equally devoid of life. Only the sharp stink of blood served as a reminder that, for some of them, death had clothed itself in honest steel rather than annihilating flame.

He was soon joined by the others. Despite having been wounded in one arm, Hiern seemed almost exultant. Isaf had actually seen him licking the blood from his fingers as he garnered fresh arrows from among the slain.

Annukin, as usual, displayed no emotion whatsoever, although even he hadn't emerged from the battle completely unscathed. Beads of thick yellowish ichor trickled from a wound in his side like jewels spilling from a ruptured urn.

Trevayne was the last to arrive. He'd torn his doublet, and walked with a pronounced limp, but was otherwise unhurt, and strolled jauntily towards them.

"I've been trying to catch myself a horse," he explained. "But they're skittish little brutes. Any of you fancy offering me a lift?"

Since the others paid no heed to the request, Isaf took it upon himself to oblige.

"Here," he said, stretching out his hand. "You can ride with me."

"Thanks." As Trevayne prepared to mount, he noticed Fjerl's lifeless body spread-eagled nearby. "Well, well," he said. "So the bastard finally got what was coming to him, eh?"

Isaf shrugged. Killing Fjerl hadn't changed anything. In his heart, Isaf knew full well that the only meaningful vengeance he could ever exact was against himself. "Hurry up," he murmured. "We've still got a tower to find, remember?"

"All right," Trevayne told him. "I'm coming." He took one last glance at Fjerl, then scrambled up behind Isaf, still grinning broadly. "You know," he said, "I was the one who put that scar on his face." He laughed uproariously. "I've got to hand it to you, old son, you certainly made a better job of it than me."

MORNING BROKE with a storm. Great charcoal clouds blew in from the East, and forked lightning split the sky. Thunder growled ominously overhead, sounding almost articulate at times. Within minutes, Trevayne and his companions were drenched to the skin.

He could well have done without this latest imposition,

even if it meant they wouldn't have to worry about running short of drinking water for a while. Fortunately, however, the cloudbank passed quickly, and dawn at last spread her roseate thighs across the world.

Annukin reigned to a halt, then pointed towards the slowly brightening horizon. ''There,'' he said. ''The tower.''

CHAPTER SIXTEEN

◆

Heroes

THE DAY SURPRISED THEM, like some disreputable fair-ground huckster who succeeds in transmuting lead to gold before a jeering crowd. The sun worked a similar alchemy, imbuing the landscape with a host of bold new colours. The grey, arid plain across which they'd been travelling for most of the night was suddenly veined with indigo and scarlet and jet; boulders glistened with seams of mica and china clay. Even the dunes seemed to glow with their own internal fires, each grain of sand coruscating like a tiny mirror.

It was a heartening prospect. If even this monotonous wasteland could blossom so spectacularly in the sunlight, perhaps they too might derive renewed strength now that the long night was past. Trevayne certainly hoped so. They were going to need all the help they could get during the trials ahead.

Draping his baldric over one shoulder, he carefully preened his battered hat, then slapped it on his head, tilting the brim to a jaunty angle. "Well, lads," he said, "today's the day. Let's see if we can't sort this bastard out once and for all, eh?"

The others said nothing, either engrossed in their own meditations, or else not yet fully recovered from the night's exertions. Trevayne surveyed them critically, the way a portraitist might. After all, this was a rather auspicious

occasion—the dawn, perhaps, of a great new age—not that
anyone would have guessed it. As they prepared to embark
on the final stage of their journey, he and his companions
must have looked more like the survivors of some nameless
disaster than noble paladins bound for death or glory.

Hiern, in particular, seemed anxious to be on his way.
Quickly gathering up his belongings, he leapt into the saddle
and stared impatiently towards the East with an expression
of almost feral anticipation. Isaf remained glum and in-
trospective, doubtless still mourning the loss of his beloved
Cayla—although why the fellow should have grieved so
extravagantly for a girl who, by all indications, he'd known
less than two months, Trevayne had no idea. Personally,
Trevayne had always taken great pains to avoid any strong
emotional attachment to members of the fairer sex, preferring to assuage his appetites in a more businesslike—and
far less harrowing—manner. It was one of the few aspects
of his life which he'd never found the slightest cause to
regret.

At the moment, however, he was far more concerned
about Annukin's condition. The immortal looked paler than
Trevayne had ever seen him, as if the rain had leached some
vital pigment from his skin, and mounted his horse with
difficulty, slumping forward in the saddle and clutching at
his side. His wound had apparently clotted overnight, but
not before he'd lost enough blood to sap even his phenomenal strength. Still, even a maimed demigod was better than
none at all, and so long as he remained fit enough to wield
that sword of his, he would pose a more formidable threat
to the Waiting God than the rest of them put together.

Lacking both fuel and provender, they were deprived the
luxury of a morning meal. Of course, unless the Fjerla had
been eating each other for however long they'd been out
here (which was not entirely beyond the realm of possibility), there had to be a cache of supplies somewhere
nearby, and Trevayne, for one, would have thought that it
was at least worth nosing around a bit before continuing
their journey. Annukin, however, had insisted that they
press on immediately, arguing that even a few hours' delay
would jeopardize the entire expedition. ("The tower is al-

most here," he'd told them. "Unless we seize our opportunity, it might be lost to us forever." Just what he'd meant by this, Trevayne had no idea. Still, if Annukin wanted to pass up the only chance they had of emerging from the wasteland alive, then so be it. Who was he, a mere mortal, to argue with the dictates of a god?)

In any case, food seemed to be the last thing on the others' minds right now. In fact, Trevayne barely had time to clamber up behind Isaf before all three wheeled their mounts and cantered off across the plain, seemingly eager to get this whole business over with as soon as possible.

The tower, which had beckoned so enticingly just a few hours before, now seemed little more than a faint white speck on the horizon. Apparently Trevayne could expect to endure a good deal more discomfort before they finally reached their destination.

After a while he began to notice that although the ground beneath them seemed solid enough, it was actually a vast honeycomb of pits and caverns sealed over by sheets of black, vitreous rock. So thin and translucent was this veneer that at times there seemed to be nothing at all separating them from the yawning chasms below.

Trevayne's initial reaction was to simply shut his eyes and ignore that fact that he and the others appeared to be riding roughshod over a sea of gigantic glass bubbles. When he did at last muster the courage to look down, he saw that many of the caverns were filled with wreckage: the remains, it seemed, of some mighty host that had once passed this way. There were siege towers taller than any Julkrean spire, bristling with strange armaments; there were enormous catapults that must once have launched stones the size of houses; there were rams and mortars and fulminata, any one of which might have levelled a city, and huge engines resembling nothing so much as land-going men-o'-war, with great brazen wheels at least two hundred feet across.

On one occasion Trevayne found himself staring into the face of some long-dead warrior, so miraculously well-preserved that one could still make out the lineaments of pain and horror that death had graven in his face. It took Trevayne some time to realise that the corpse was merely one of many. Below him, a whole mountain of similar carcasses stretched for as far as the eye could see, untold thousands of them. It seemed impossible that the earth could have ever spawned so many men. The thought of destruction on such a scale appalled and terrified him.

"Gods' blood," he gasped. "What the hell happened here, anyway?"

He hadn't realised that Annukin was riding so close to him. The immortal turned, his face pallid and etched with fatigue, lending a strangely human cast to his features. "Like your men," he said, "they pitted themselves against a god. And, like yours, they failed."

"But where did they come from?" he said. He glanced down once more, surveying the ranks of entombed warriors below him. "So many," he whispered. *"So many!"*

"The world was a larger place in those days," Annukin told him. "Talingmar alone ruled an empire of which your own Four Kingdoms constituted only one small province. Even so—" He paused a moment, cocking his head to one side, as if listening to something that Trevayne couldn't hear. "Even so," he muttered, "your ancestors paid a high price for their folly. A very high price indeed. . . ."

Trevayne shook his head wonderingly, only now beginning to appreciate the enormity of the task that had been set them. "And we're supposed to succeed where they failed? Just the four of us?"

Annukin shrugged. "We can try," he said quietly.

THEY HAD GLIMPSED IT, imperfectly, at dawn; now they saw it silhouetted against the gathering darkness, as pure and stark as a votive flame:

"The tower," Annukin said.

They gazed up it at almost reverently—except Trevayne, who merely shifted impatiently on the back of Isaf's horse, massaging his thighs.

"Yes, yes," he grumbled. "I can see that for myself. Let's just get on with it, shall we? My arse is killing me."

Tall and slender, the fortress reared before them like some huge marbled sepulchre, one face stained red by the setting sun. Its shadow, severing the plain like a knife-cut, seemed to stretch for miles.

"What now?" Hiern asked.

"We didn't come all this way just to sit and gawp at the bloody thing," Trevayne told him. "Let's get a move on, shall we? It'll be dark soon."

"Very well," Annukin said. "We had best leave the horses here, I think. They might have trouble keeping their footing further in."

"Suits me," Trevayne said.

Isaf would have preferred to retain his mount, but as it turned out, Annukin was correct. The ground, although smooth enough to begin with, became increasingly treacherous as they approached the tower. With so much rubble about, their horses would have been more of a liability than an asset.

At first Isaf couldn't work out where the debris had come from. A little further on, he noticed that scores of small round shafts had been driven into the plain—apparently by human hands, since there were picks and hammers lying nearby. Crude ladders of wood and hemp snaked down into the darkness, providing access to whatever ancient riches had been interred below.

"Hello," Trevayne said. "What's all this, eh?" He bent to examine one of the shafts, sucking his tooth meditatively. "Now how the deuce did *they* get here?"

Annukin shrugged. "Someone must have dug them," he said. "And recently, by the look of it."

"Yes, I can see that. But who?"

"Men not unlike yourself, I should imagine."

"You mean grave robbers?" Trevayne glanced round hastily. "Here?"

"Why not? Mortals will dare almost anything if there is a profit to be made."

"And the Waiting God let them?" Trevayne snorted with disgust. "Are you trying to tell me that someone who can wipe out whole armies with a wave of his hand is going to sit back and watch while a bunch of fortune-hunters dig for treasure in his own bloody frontyard? Come on, man! Talk sense!"

Annukin's eyes betrayed a flicker of amusement. He glanced up at the tower, fingering the hilt of his sword. "You still don't understand, do you?" he said. "This tower isn't so much a place as a state of mind. Had you ventured here alone, you'd most likely have seen nothing at all."

Trevayne tossed his head irritably. "Spare us the meta-physics, will you? I—"

But Annukin was no longer listening; something in one of the pits had caught his attention. He dropped to his knees and stared intently into the gloom.

"What's the matter?" Isaf asked.

Annukin said nothing—at least nothing audible. Hunched over the shaft, his hair draped across his face like a tattered, bloodstained veil, he seemed to be murmuring something in a language that bore no more resemblance to human speech than the roaring of a fire.

Craning forward, Isaf peered into the shaft himself. Far below lay a figure sheathed in ornate armour that glittered like some jewelled sarcophagus amid the heaps of rubble and broken scaffolding.

By now Trevayne had joined them. He studied the corpse for a few moments, a sly grin playing across his face. "Friend of yours?" he asked.

Annukin looked up with far more emotion than he'd displayed previously. "Immortals have no friends," he said, "merely tools, both willing and otherwise." He glanced into the pit once more, head bowed as if in silent benediction. "Ceerbunnus, here, was perhaps the most finely honed of them all."

Before Trevayne could make some suitably acerbic reply, a sudden tremor rocked the plain, throwing all four of them momentarily off-balance. Hiern fell to one knee, clutching at the ground for support. Even Annukin seemed shaken and confused.

The demigod tried to speak, but his voice was drowned by the roar of splintering rock. The earth buckled and cracked like a sheet of wet plaster, opening a deep trench between themselves and the tower. Great clouds of dust boiled above it, darker than the night.

As Isaf scrambled up, he saw something rise from the shattered plain.

And rise.

And rise.

And keep on rising.

Huge, it reared above them, higher even than the tower, although the greater part of its length must surely have remained coiled in the abyss, thousands of feet below.

"Gods' piss!" Trevayne growled. "What in hell's name is *that*?"

Annukin licked his lips. "Uroboros," he said. "The Stonehammer." He'd drawn his sword but held it tentatively, and there was something very much like fear in his eyes as he gazed up at the great white worm towering above them.

"You mean you've seen this brute before?"

Annukin nodded. "At Earthome, when we sacked the Stone King's place of power." He gazed up at the beast once more, shaking his head. "I don't understand," he muttered. "Uroboros and his kin owed allegiance to the Gnomarch, not the House of Fire."

"That's all very interesting," Trevayne said. "The question is, how do we deal with the bastard?"

"One does not *deal* with Uroboros," Annukin told him. "One flees, and prays that he does not choose to follow."

Hiern apparently had other ideas. Unslinging his bow, he fitted a long, dark-fletched arrow to the string and took aim at the serpent's head. By the time Isaf and the rest had turned towards him, the shaft was already winging towards its mark.

"You fool!" Annukin snapped. "What good do you think that will do?"

Hiern grinned. "I never miss!" he told them, following the arrow's progress with childish delight. "See, I never miss!"

Nor did he—although his shot fell somewhat short, striking Uroboros a good thirty or forty feet further down and vanishing among the folds of slick, translucent flesh.

Isaf wondered what Hiern thought he was playing at. Surely he didn't believe that his arrows could injure the monster. In fact, all he'd done was alert Uroboros to their presence: even now its blunt, featureless head was swivelling towards them.

Hiern, however, refused to concede defeat, and immediately nocked another arrow. As he did, Isaf finally got a good look at the man's face, and realised that it wasn't madness lurking in his eyes, but sheer, unreasoning panic.

He might have continued this futile assault indefinitely, but Trevayne suddenly wrenched the bow from his hands and hurled it aside. "For gods'-sake," he snarled, "do you want to get the lot of us killed? Keep calm, and let's think this thing through. There must be some way of getting a crack at the bugger."

"We should have kept the horses," Hiern said, making a brave but unsuccessful attempt to disguise the terror in his voice. "At least then one of us might have been to able to slip through."

"In a pig's eye we would!" Trevayne told him contemptuously. "You'd be lucky to get a horse within half a mile of something like that." He turned to Annukin. "What happened at this Earthome place?" he asked. "Did you beat it then or not?"

"That was different," Annukin replied. "We had the resources of a dozen empires to hurl against him, and even then we failed to slay him. Do you honestly think that mere swords can achieve what half a million fighting men could not?"

Trevayne smiled. "Mine certainly wouldn't," he said. "But yours might."

"Perhaps." Annukin turned the blade over his hand, weighing its potency against the size and strength of their adversary. "But there is no way I would ever get close enough to use it."

"We'll have to cross that bridge when we come to it," Trevayne said. "I mean, we don't really have much choice, do we? That bastard will nail us pretty soon anyway, so we might as well go down fighting."

Uroboros was certainly much nearer now. Indeed, had Hiern been so inclined, he might easily have emptied his entire quiver into the creature's head as it hunted above them like a compass needle.

Isaf nodded brusquely. "Trevayne's right," he muttered. "We've come too far to turn back now."

"Very well," Annukin said, "I suppose we must prepare to die." He shrugged, as if already feeling the cold hand of mortality settling on his shoulders. "As you say, there is nothing else we can do."

"I'm not so sure about that," Trevayne told him. Despite the overwhelming odds against them, he seemed in remarkably good spirits. Hitching up his belt, he ambled forward a few steps until he was stationed close to Annukin's right hand. "I don't know about the rest of you," he said, "but I've certainly got no intention of waiting until that oversized maggot out there decides to hammer us into the ground like tent pegs. Let's just see what the bastard's made of, eh?" With that, he seized Annukin's sword and sprinted off towards the tower.

Planting his feet squarely apart, he flourished the sword defiantly overhead. Even at a distance, Isaf could see that the hilt was searing his flesh like a burning brand, but Trevayne seemed oblivious to the pain, his face suffused with a kind of reckless joy.

"Come on, you arse-hole!" he roared. "Come and get me!"

Uroboros needed no such encouragement, and was already plummeting towards him. Despite its size, the creature struck so swiftly that none of the others could possibly have gone to Trevayne's assistance even if they'd wanted to.

"Don't be a fool!" Annukin cried, stretching out his hand and taking a few halting steps forward. But it was a token gesture at best, and much, much too late.

Mercifully, Isaf turned away just in time, and so didn't see Trevayne die. Not that he really needed to: the impact alone hurled him through the air like a rag doll tossed aside by some petulant child. As he stood up, shielding his eyes from the dust and shards of flying rock, there was a second, even louder, explosion, and a huge pillar of fire erupted from the abyss, shedding no heat, but brighter while it lasted than a hundred suns.

For a moment, the plain was bathed in light. Each rock and stony outcrop, each pit and declivity, each tiny particle of sand seemed to assume a stark, almost hallucinatory aspect. This was how the world must have looked at the moment of creation, before man had set about cloaking the naked skull of matter with his own fears and fancies and desires.

By persistently ignoring all evidence to the contrary, Isaf had managed to convince himself that Annukin was simply a poseur in fancy dress. Even Uroboros could, with a certain amount of ingenuity, be accommodated by the world-view he'd assembled with such painstaking deliberation over the years. But this was something else altogether: incontrovertible evidence that, not only were there more things in heaven and earth than dreamed of in his philosophy, but that any attempt to understand or explain the world in rational terms was as much an act of faith as the rank superstition he'd so often decried in others.

The light vanished as quickly as it had come, taking with it the last remnants of Isaf's beleaguered self-respect.

Even Annukin seemed awed by what had happened. He gazed silently up at the tower, his eyes blazing with a passion that Isaf had never seen in them before.

"Is it dead, do you think?" Isaf asked him. "Uroboros, I mean. Did Trevayne kill it or not?"

Annukin shrugged. "I don't know," he said. "Uroboros is brother to the great black beast himself. But whether he lives or dies is of little consequence now."

"How do you mean?" Isaf said. "There's still three of us left. And if the way to the tower is open—"

"You don't understand," Annukin said. "Somehow, Trevayne has loosed the quintessential fire, the one weapon that our adversary might have had cause to fear."

None of this made any sense to Isaf at all. "Then that fire we saw, it was in your sword? Is that what you're trying to say?"

"The fire and the sword were one," Annukin told him. "Like ice and water. Now both are gone." He flexed his hands, as if wondering how he'd ever allowed the sword to be torn from his grasp in the first place. "Without it," he murmured, "we can achieve nothing. Nothing at all."

"We still have to try," Isaf told him. "If the Waiting God's power has begun to wane, we might still stand some kind of chance."

As he spoke, however, the trembling began again, and Annukin's reply—if he bothered to make one—was lost in the mounting din.

More thunder.

More dust.

More stone.

Swaying drunkenly, Uroboros lurched into view once more, its monstrous head wreathed in flames. As it soared above them, rising up from the fire-blasted pit like a plume of milk-white steam, the creature slowly began to falter. It shuddered once or twice, as if racked by some fearsome internal spasm, then suddenly shot up even higher than before, thrashing about so violently that Isaf half-expected to see the tower snap in two and come tumbling down around it.

Then it fell. Not smoothly this time, but ravelling itself into huge, flaccid coils, like a discarded length of rope. It seemed an inglorious end for something that, no matter how hideous or destructive, was certainly a more awesome, and far less malevolent, divinity than any of those fashioned in man's own image.

The ground quaked one last time, and then was still. All that remained to mark the great beast's passing was a shroud of thick, grey dust, and a silence so intense that Isaf could almost hear the sweat oozing from his pores.

There was really nothing to say. No words could possibly do justice to what had occurred, and, given the nature of Trevayne's death, neither praise nor lamentation seemed wholly appropriate. Isaf could still see the man standing there as firmly rooted as a tree, gleefully awaiting his own imminent destruction. One could only guess at what might have impelled him to make such a sacrifice, but the single most recognizable emotion in his face had been sheer, unmitigated relief.

After a while, Hiern edged slowly forward. "What was

he?'' he asked, addressing the question to no one in particular.

Surprisingly enough, it was Annukin who answered. By now, the superficial humanity which he'd displayed earlier had evaporated like spittle from hot bricks, and his expression was again as fixed and impassive as a mask. "Who?" he asked.

"Trevayne." Hiern gestured awkwardly towards the shattered plain before them. Compared to Annukin's measured tones, his voice sounded like the rustle of dead leaves in an empty room. "Was he a fool, a hero, or just another madman?"

Annukin considered the matter for a moment, then shrugged. "A little of each, I imagine," he said. "Just like the rest of you." He glanced back up at the tower, stroking the empty scabbard where his sword had been. "We might still have cause to envy him before the day is out. After all, at least he died cleanly enough—which is probably far more than the rest of us can expect."

CHAPTER SEVENTEEN

◆

The Fortress of Eternity

NOTHING COULD FORCE THAT," Isaf muttered bitterly. He kicked the door again, his foot thudding dully against the metal.

It had taken them almost an hour to circumvent the gaping chasm where Uroboros lay, coiled at the foot of a sheer, thousand-foot drop like a puddle of blood and milk. Naturally enough, they'd found no sign of Trevayne at all.

By now, the sun had concluded its ceremonious decline and plunged once more into the vast pit of darkness that lay beyond the world. The door, however, shone with light far brighter than the handful of stars scattered overhead, casting long, distorted shadows across the stone behind them. About eight feet high, and sufficiently broad that three men might enter abreast, it looked obdurate enough to hold fast the gates of hell.

Isaf flung up his hands in exasperation. "You'd need twenty men on a ram to even dent the bloody thing! What can the three of us do?"

Annukin stroked the door gently with his fingers, the way a blind man might fondle a coin to ascertain its worth. "*Argentum regia*," he muttered, as if this somehow explained everything.

"Perhaps if you still had that sword of yours—"

Annukin shook his head. "Not even then," he said. "The

king of metals will not be forced—only cajoled.''

"Are we to be balked by a mere door, then?'' Isaf growled. "After having overcome so much?'' He almost wished that Uroboros had finished them when it had the chance—that way, at least, they'd have been spared this final indignity. Perhaps Trevayne was the lucky one after all, dying in a blaze of glory, whereas they seemed destined to sit here and rot. "There has to be something we can do!''

Suddenly, Hiern stepped forward, tugging at a thin silver chain that hung around his neck. He seemed strangely diffident, like a child who felt compelled to speak but wasn't entirely sure what to say. "I—''

"Oh, for gods'-sake!'' Isaf snapped. "What is it now?''

Reaching inside his jerkin, Hiern pulled on the chain until a small ornament appeared, perhaps two inches long and wrought in the shape of a key. As Hiern cradled the thing lovingly in his palm, Isaf noticed that it glistened with a light virtually indistinguishable from that of the door itself.

"The Key,'' Hiern told them. "I brought it because of the stories my father taught me. *When the Fires come, Hiern must take the Key.* Only they never said where, or why. But now—''

Isaf was more than a little sceptical, but it seemed worth a try. "All right,'' he said. "Give it here.''

Hiern did so, if somewhat reluctantly, flinching visibly as Isaf took it from him, and craning forward so that he might follow Isaf's every move, like a jealous husband who'd momentarily relinquished his wife into the hands of another man.

"Don't worry,'' Isaf told him. "I'm not going to steal the bloody thing.'' Turning, he surveyed the door once more. There was a faint sliver of shadow near one edge that vaguely resembled a lock. For want of anything better to do, he poked the key towards it.

As the two came in contact, there was a sudden flash of light. Isaf leapt back, his fingers throbbing with pain, as if they'd been plunged into an open furnace. He looked down, expecting to see the blackened flesh already peeling from his bones, but his hand was quite unharmed.

"*Gods!*'' he cried. "What happened?''

Annukin shrugged. "Some defensive mechanism, I imagine. To prevent unwanted intrusions by people such as yourself."

Isaf glared ruefully at his hand, which still tingled slightly, although most of the pain had now subsided. "All right," he said. "You have a try then."

"Very well." Annukin glanced up at the door for a moment, then stretched out his hand. "The key," he said. "Where is it?"

Isaf remembered dropping the thing at his feet, but, on looking down, found that it disappeared. "I don't understand," he muttered. "It was here a minute ago."

Then he noticed Hiern's face, and saw the length of silver chain dangling from his fist. "What the hell are you playing at?" he snarled. "We haven't finished with it yet."

Hiern backed away, clutching the key so tightly that even Isaf hesitated to try and take it from him.

"Just hand it over, will you? How else are we supposed to get inside? I mean—"

"It's all right," Annukin said. "Let him do it."

"But—"

"Trevayne brought him here for a purpose. Perhaps this is it."

"Suit yourself." Isaf moved aside, motioning Hiern towards the door. "But I don't see what good it'll do. Trevayne didn't seem to know any more about this place than we do."

Hiern edged slowly forward, like a condemned felon mounting the scaffold.

"Come on," Isaf growled impatiently. "We'll be here all night at this rate."

As Hiern drew closer to the door, his hand began to glow—softly at first, like one of those cheap paper lanterns strung up in peasants' windows to celebrate the Yuletide feast, but waxing brighter with every step, until his bones stood out as sharply as black brush-strokes on a sheet of virgin parchment. He seemed almost unaware of what was happening to him, moving with the slow, deliberate tread of a bride advancing towards the altar, or an assassin closing on his prey. The light swelled even further, crawling along

Hiern's flesh like tongues of unburning fire, until his entire
body was bathed in a radiance so intense that Isaf found
himself forced to look away, lest the mere sight of it strike
him blind.

When he turned back, he saw that the door had disappeared. Head bowed, Hiern stood before the open doorway
like a magician defeated by his own conjuration, still grip-
ping the key in his outstretched hand. Now that its light had
died, it seemed no more wondrous, or refulgent, than any
other piece of antique silverware.

"Who would have thought," he murmured. "I—" Suddenly, he stopped and turned to face the others. Isaf had
never seen such bitterness in a man's eyes before—not even
his own. "For generations, my ancestors and I have devoted
our lives to something that—in the end—only opens a door
after all. Somehow, I'd always imagined there would be
more to it than that."

Annukin appeared to find such sentiments either irrelevant
or totally incomprehensible. "Come," he said, stepping
through the doorway and motioning for the others to follow.
"We still have a great deal to do."

Inside, darkness flooded the tower the way water might
swamp the hold of a sunken ship, full of pale undersea
gloamings and tiny fishlike flickers of movement, so that,
for a moment, Isaf felt as if he were standing on the bed
of some vast, tideless ocean, with a thousand fathoms of
murky shadows poised silently above his head.

From what he could see, this part of the tower was quite
deserted. There was no furniture or other appurtenances, no
colonnades or cabinets or hanging galleries, no tapers or
lamps or candelabra; nothing to indicate that the place had
ever been inhabited at all, by man or god. With its dry stone
floor and air of cultivated disuse, it resembled the interior
of a long-abandoned tomb.

Annukin seemed to have expected something rather different. He hesitated a moment, and it suddenly occurred to
Isaf that the fellow may have been as much a stranger here
as any of them.

The lapse, however, was only temporary. "This way,"
Annukin said, directing them towards a narrow staircase

that spiralled up into the darkness like a complex musical progression or sequential hypotheses in some rigorous theological debate.

They ascended in single file: first Annukin, then Isaf, with Hiern trailing some distance behind, still gazing at the key with a kind of morbid fascination, as if it were a dagger intended for his own breast.

Had he spared a little more thought for his present surroundings, rather than dwelling so obsessively on the past, he might not have evaded certain death by quite so slender a margin.

Both Isaf and Annukin certainly had ample time to take evasive action. They noticed the smell of burning in the air; felt the stairway tremble underfoot; saw something split the darkness above them like a knife-blade plunged through a velvet curtain.

"Watch out!" Annukin said, throwing himself face-down on the steps. Isaf did the same, his back pressed hard against the wall.

Behind them, Hiern continued to mount the stairs, oblivious to everything save the small silver ornament in his hand.

"Get down, you fool!" Isaf yelled, but the man seemed not to hear him. (He couldn't; a thousand ghosts were clamouring inside his skull, and he was duty-bound to listen.) Even when he did look up and see the bolt of blue-white fire descending towards him, he still made no attempt to leap aside, but merely bowed his head, his lips parting in a faint half-smile.

Prompted by some impulse even he couldn't properly define, Isaf launched himself down the staircase, striking Hiern full in the chest and knocking him aside.

There was a hollow, booming sound as the bolt flared above them, close enough for Isaf to feel the skin blistering on his cheek.

Then the darkness returned, seemingly even more intense than before. Once his eyes had re-adjusted to the gloom, Isaf was surprised to discover that, by some miracle, both he and Hiern appeared to have emerged more or less unscathed.

With the danger now past, any concern that Isaf might

have felt for Hiern rapidly disappeared. Climbing to his feet, he glared down at the man with a mixture of anger and contempt.

"What's the matter with you?" he demanded. "You tired of living or something?"

At first, Hiern refused to look up. When he finally did, there was something like hatred in his eyes, as if Isaf had deprived him of the one thing he'd hungered for all his life.

"It's not fair!" he wailed. "I did my best! What more do they want of me?" He clapped his hands across his ears, gazing wildly into the darkness around him, like a man pursued. "Father was right. They expect too much of us—too much!"

Although Isaf found most of this quite unintelligible, the underlying sentiment was familiar enough. "For gods'-sake," he said, "what the hell did you expect? At least you got us into the tower—which was more than Annukin or I could do."

Judging by the look on his face, Hiern had obviously been hoping for something more.

"You don't understand," he murmured. "I thought if I took the Key—like the stories said—everything would be all right. I thought it was what I'd been born to do, that I could finally erase the failure and frustration that had killed my father. But nothing has changed. *Nothing*!"

"Look," Isaf told him. "Any fool can die. I mean, that doesn't make you some sort of hero or anything, you know. Most of the time it's far more painful to live."

Hiern was weeping now. Sprawled across the stairway, he looked so utterly bereft that even Isaf's heart softened for a moment.

"Come on," he said, helping the man to his feet. "There's nothing more you can do here."

Hiern seemed not to hear him. "I did what I could," he said, gazing almost imploringly up at Isaf. "You'll tell them that, won't you? I did my best."

"You did fine," Isaf said. "Just fine. Perhaps you could get a fire going or something, eh? We're probably going to need one by the time all this is over."

"But—"

"Off you go," Isaf said, gently nudging him down the stairway. "It's up to me and Annukin now."

Slowly, Hiern turned and made his solitary way back towards the shadow-drenched chamber below, like a ghost slipping down the unseen interface between one world and the next. Much to his surprise, Isaf found himself wishing the fellow well.

"Hurry up," Annukin said, apparently quite disinterested in the exchange, or what might become of Hiern now that it was over. "We're wasting time."

"All right," Isaf told him. "I'm coming."

He stood there a while longer, watching Hiern gradually vanish into the darkness, then both he and Annukin resumed their wearisome ascent. Behind them, the Key lay where it had fallen—a tiny sliver of brightness on the fire-blackened stone.

THERE IN THE DARKNESS, time and distance seemed little more than abstractions, their relationship to motion becoming increasingly problematical and remote. For all Isaf knew, he may have toiled up the stairs for hours, or aeons, or the merest pulsation of an artery.

As they climbed higher, Isaf noticed a series of small round windows set into the tower wall, each one about the size of a dinner plate, and with such steeply bevelled edges that scarcely any light at all penetrated from outside, which perhaps explained why no trace of them had been visible from the plain below.

Or might have done, at least, had the windows provided a view of anything even remotely resembling the barren waste where Isaf and the others had stood just a short time before.

Instead he found himself looking out across a world half-made, a world still ravaged by the raw, elemental forces that had given it birth. Earth, fire, air, and water, all were melded into a single inchoate mass that seethed and bubbled like a witch's oils. As Isaf peered more closely, he saw four titanic figures coalesce within the tumultuous interplay of light and dark—the masters, it seemed, of a creation as yet untrammelled by the mind of man.

Thoroughly disoriented, he jerked away from the window and looked around, keen to reassure himself that the tower did indeed exist and wasn't simply a figment of his imagination, liable to assume some new, radically different shape at any moment, or vanish altogether in the mere twinkling of an eye. Fortunately, however, his surroundings seemed more or less unchanged. The staircase still wound interminably through the darkness, tracing its helical course between two great pools of shadow, with Annukin poised a half-dozen steps or so above him.

"Is something wrong?" the demigod asked, regarding Isaf with ill-concealed impatience.

"I'm not really sure." Isaf turned back to the window, frowning and shaking his head. "Perhaps you'd better come and see for yourself."

With an almost audible sigh, Annukin padded slowly down the stairway to join him.

"Take a look through there," Isaf said, motioning towards the window. "See what you think."

Annukin obliged, craning forward and putting one eye to the aperture. As he did so, his shoulders suddenly stiffened. He slumped forward for a moment, steadying himself with his hands, then drew away, like someone recoiling from a blow.

"Well?" Isaf asked.

Annukin said nothing. Although his face betrayed little obvious emotion, he seemed diminished, as if part of him had been siphoned out through the portal and lost forever in the raw, amorphous world that lay beyond.

"You saw it, too, didn't you?" Isaf said. "It's not just me. There really is something out there. And you don't know what the hell to make of it either, do you?"

Ignoring the question, Annukin turned and strode silently back up the steps, apparently reluctant to concede that anything untoward had happened at all. But Isaf noticed that the fellow gave each of the subsequent windows a wide berth, keeping to the outermost edge of the stairway and not so much as glancing in their direction.

Isaf, on the other hand, found that the windows exerted a strange fascination, and he was unable to prevent himself from gazing intently through each one to discover what new vistas it might contain.

He quickly realized that the scenes—which, to begin with, at least, seemed a mere heap of jumbled images— were actually arranged in strict chronological sequence, like tableaux in some ongoing pageant stretching back to the very dawn of time, and that what he was witnessing as he hastened, with mounting excitement, from one tiny peep-hole to the next, was nothing less than the history of creation itself.

He saw the swirling vortex of matter gradually coalesce into more recognisable forms. Continents emerged, as if formed by some invisible hand, like great slabs of clay taking shape on a potter's wheel. Mountains and hills appeared, channelling the untamed waters into lakes and rivers and streams. Jungles and woodlands took root; grasslands sprouted on the broad, sweeping plains; hills flowered with wreaths of vines; moist, green valleys teemed with banks of exotic blooms; until it seemed as if the whole vast rotundity of the world were laid out before him: warm, lush and fecund beneath the over-arching vault of sky.

Monstrous beasts arose to dominate the fledgling earth. The oceans teemed with immense virid serpents and sea-shouldering whales. There were other creatures as well, creatures that Isaf had previously thought to be nothing more than extravagant fancies concocted by poets to enliven an otherwise dull tale: Leviathan and his brood, floundering below the waves like huge, waterlogged corpses; tritons and quaking eels and hyaline stags. Dragons filled the air, and giant birds with plumes of fire; while great bronze colossi bestrode the earth, casting down high mountains and trampling whole forests beneath their feet.

Then man strutted fretfully onto the stage, forcing the world to suddenly assume a new, and quite different, aspect. Rather than being intimately woven into the very fabric of existence, the transcendent entities who had previously hovered at the very periphery of Isaf's awareness slowly began to evolve their own distinct shape and substance, like crystals precipitating from solution, as if, in exalting mankind from the dust, they themselves had been subtly debased.

Gradually—over the space of a dozen windows or so—
Isaf watched man's dominion swell to encompass the entire
globe. Cities grew and glittered like puddles of vivacious
jewels. Isaf saw prismatic towers thrust their needle-bright
spires towards the sky, saw nine great gilded bridges span-
ning a mighty watercourse fully twenty miles wide, saw
the cyclopean walls of Folcengard lever themselves, stone
by stone, from the foot of an ancient caldera. He saw the
great causeway at Hydonwall, the gargantuan keelyards of
Sultice-Charr, and a thousand other marvels besides, huge
edifices long since crumbled into dust or buried forever
beneath endlessly shifting seas of sand. Annukin was right.
The world had been a larger place then—much larger, in
fact, than Isaf would ever have dreamed possible.

The next sequence of windows depicted scenes from an
epic conflict that had apparently raged for centuries between
the burgeoning human empires and those immortal powers
who, by this stage, seemed no less deeply immured in the
labyrinth of time and space than the finite, fallible creatures
which they had so casually summoned into being.

If, despite everything that had happened over the previous
few days, Isaf still entertained any lingering doubts as to
Annukin's divine status, they were soon dispelled when he
saw that the champion of the mortal hosts—with his shock
of blood-red hair and fiery sword—was unquestionably the
same man who hovered silently above him now. Whether
commanding a fleet of gilded ships or toiling up the face
of a mountain whose glittering flanks seemed to pierce the
heavens, Annukin provided the sole unifying motif in a
kaleidoscope of mayhem and destruction, blazing in the heat
of battle with his own fierce auroral light. Having witnessed
the power of his sword at first hand, it came as no surprise
to Isaf that even the old gods should have fallen before
Annukin's relentless assault.

From then on, the windows began to offer glimpses of a
more familiar world. Ancient empires degenerated into mere
patchworks of warring states. New cities rose from the
ashes, graceless parodies of the vast metropolises than had
once stood in their place. An endless succession of brigands
and assassins and warrior-kings paraded before his eyes,

each one bearing a slim silver blade whose ornate markings precisely matched those adorning Isaf's own. However disconcerting this may have been—and Isaf felt an almost palpable unease descend upon him as watched triumphant mercenaries saunter along the marbled thoroughfares of Talingmar or two beggars squabbling over a scrap of bread in some wretched Julkrean alley—it was nothing compared to the naked horror that he experienced when, quite without warning, he found himself peering down at the lonely desert campsite where, over thirty years before, his childhood had come to an abrupt and bloody end at the hands of rapacious Angarian slavers.

Isaf took one look, then hurried on, shying away from the remaining windows in case they happened to reveal other, even more harrowing, aspects of his past.

Perhaps because he was no longer concentrating so furiously on the windows themselves, he became aware of a faint ripple of sound behind him, like that of a silken scarf rustling gently in the breeze. At first he ignored it, but the soft, insistent murmur refused to go away, growing steadily louder with each passing moment. However, when he finally glanced back over his shoulder, all he saw was his own shadow mingling imperceptibly with the cavernous darkness below.

"Annukin?" he whispered. "Do you hear anything?"

The demigod turned and looked down at him for a moment. Even at this distance, Isaf could clearly see the faint, rather patronizing smile of his lips.

"Hear what?" he said.

"I don't know," Isaf muttered, feeling vaguely foolish. "But I'd swear that there is someone behind us. You don't suppose it could be Hiern, do you?"

"No," Annukin said. "No, I shouldn't think so."

"But something's there!" Isaf protested. "I can feel it."

"Yes, I know." Annukin sighed, apparently finding the entire discussion either inconsequential or wholly irrelevant. "As I told Trevayne earlier, this tower isn't so much a place as a particular way of seeing things. Perhaps our eyes are simply becoming accustomed to what has, in fact, been following us all along."

Isaf reached out to touch the wall beside him, felt the weight of cold hard stone beneath his feet. "You mean none of this is real at all? We're simply creating it as we go along?"

Annukin shrugged. "Perhaps. Or else it's creating us. I suspect that it may amount to much the same thing in the long run. Either way, we shan't know exactly what is waiting for us at the top of these stairs until we get there."

"Very well," Isaf told him. "Let's get a move on then, shall we? The sooner this whole thing is over and done with, the happier I'll be."

"Somehow, I doubt that," Annukin said, as he turned and climbed slowly on into the darkness. "I doubt that very much."

CHAPTER EIGHTEEN

✦

The Countenance Divine

WHEN AT LAST the stairway came an end, Isaf had been climbing for so long that he stumbled momentarily, his foot instinctively groping for a step that did not exist. Before them lay a circular chamber, no less bare than the echoing vault below, but considerably smaller, and bathed in a faint, pearly phosphorescence. Isaf wondered whether the tower narrowed as it rose, so that they now stood at the very tip of a gigantic obelisk—although it had not appeared so from the outside—or whether this was simply one of many such apartments occupying the upper level. Then again, if, as Annukin maintained, they themselves had somehow conjured the place into existence, it may simply have conformed to a quite different, and far more fluid, geometry than that perceived by the human eye.

"Ah—visitors. How nice."

Isaf could have sworn that the room was empty, but now, as he looked again, he saw a heavy stone table jutting out from the opposing wall. Behind it, toying with a pile of small bronze discs, like someone leafing through a deck of cards, sat the figure who had addressed them.

For a god, he seemed unprepossessing. Dark; finely built; of indeterminate age and origin; he affected the austere white robes of a sacerdote, yet his eyes sparkled with cynical amusement as he waved them closer.

"Come, come," he said. "I can scarcely see you there among the shadows."

Annukin's bewilderment, it seemed, was at least the equal of Isaf's own. He shuffled slowly forward, looking more hesitant and indecisive than Isaf had ever seen him before.

The god laughed. It was so handsome a sound, so bold and infectious, that Isaf almost laughed as well.

But he didn't.

Scowling, he followed Annukin towards the table.

"Are you the Waiting God?" he said. Compared to the laughter that had preceded it, his voice sounded crude and unrefined, as if he were spitting out mouthfuls of gravel.

Isaf watched the thin lips curl in a knowing smile. Viewed close up, the god's features possessed an oddly elusive quality, so that whenever Isaf slackened his concentration, even for a moment, they seemed to merge into a vague, undifferentiated blur, like those of some boyhood acquaintance whose face, once almost as familiar as his own, he could no longer properly recall.

"I may be," the god told him. "And then again, I may not. In the end, it makes no real difference either way. I might just as easily call you Roland, or Lemminkainen, or Ilya-Muromyets—you'd still be what you are." He studied them for a moment, his smile broadening. "No doubt you were expecting something rather more dramatic. Some cloud-compelling deity, perhaps? Or a voluminous master folded in his fires?" He turned towards Annukin, as if savouring some rare joke at his expense. "Sorry to disappoint you."

Annukin shook his head. "But I thought—"

"What did you think, my friend? That I might be your father come again? That your dreams of parricide might be realised at last?"

"My father—"

"Yes?"

"My father—"

"No longer exists."

Annukin stiffened, his face shrivelling like a dying flower around the raw wounds of eyes. "Dead?" he murmured. "Then how . . ."

"Oh, he's not just dead," the god drawled. "Your late, unlamented father has been expunged, as it were, from the very fabric of existence. And not before time, either, if you ask me. He was an anachronism, the decaying remnant of a bygone age. Much the same as yourself, I suppose. Although, unlike you, he no longer retained any significant hold on the human imagination, and was thus relatively easy to dispose of." The god snapped his fingers, a sound that echoed through the heavy silence around them like the crack of a whip. "*Tempus edax rerum*, as the poets say."

"What's he talking about?" Isaf growled. He found the god's bantering tone both irritating and vaguely improper. They'd come to slay a demiurge, not some posturing jackanapes enamoured of his own cleverness.

Annukin ignored him. "But the well," he said. "He should have returned to the well."

"Only if he died, my friend. That's the way it works, isn't it? And, as I said, his fate was rather more comprehensive than that. Indeed, you could search through all eternity and not find a trace of the poor fellow anywhere."

"Who are you?" Annukin demanded. "How did you get here?"

The god made an airy, dismissive gesture with one hand. "We've been through that already," he said. "Names are unimportant. It's *what* I am that matters."

"You are an immortal?"

"Not immortal, my dear boy—*inevitable*. You, of all people, ought to appreciate the difference." The god sighed. "Don't you see? I am that which, by its very nature, defies description. I am Achilles and the tortoise. I am Chuang Tzu's butterfly and Schrödinger's cat. I am as ubiquitous as Feigenbaum numbers, as unfathomable as the Mandelbrot set. I am the shadow of the waxwing; the stranger in the mirror; the worm gnawing at the heart of the rose. I am the dark abyss between thought and act, wherein falls the shadow." He paused, studying Annukin almost pityingly. "I am the myth before myth began—articulate, venerable, and complete."

Isaf shuffled his feet impatiently. "Let's get on with it,"

he said. "We came here to do something, remember? Not talk."

"Ah—yes," the god said, his face brightening once more. "You came to kill me, did you not?"

"That's right," Isaf muttered. Stated so baldly, the whole proposition seemed quite ridiculous.

"You needn't be embarrassed, my friend. I know all about this little expedition of yours. Far more, in fact, than you do yourself. Or even Vellaghar, for that matter. I'm curious to discover, however, what you, in particular, could possibly have expected to achieve by it."

"I was hired to do a job," Isaf said. "And I intend to finish it." Even he was surprised by the lack of conviction in his voice.

"Oh, come now," the god said. "There must be more to it than that. I mean, Annukin here has his reasons—a trifle sordid, perhaps, but certainly compelling enough. And so did the others, after a fashion. Hiern wanted to make amends for his father's failure. Poor old Trevayne was driven by a fairly straightforward—and entirely warranted—fear of the unknown. Lord Vellaghar craved power. But you—"

"I don't need a reason!" Isaf said. Reaching down, he seized the hilt of his sword. "All I need is this!"

"*Bravo!*" the god said, miming applause. "Spoken like a true barbarian!" Suddenly his voice dropped. "Only you're not, are you? Quite the contrary in fact. Indeed, you're standing there now, desperately trying to hate me—because it would all be so much easier then, wouldn't it? There's always revenge, I suppose. That's a convenient excuse for just about anything, isn't it? But revenge for what? After all, I've never done you any harm—at least, not directly. As you can see, I'm a fairly harmless creature—"

"Harmless?" Isaf mustered a rudimentary sneer. "You tried to kill us on the stairway, didn't you?"

The god sighed. "That's one way of looking at things, I suppose. Like most of your kind, however, you tend to confuse causation with coincidence. Take these cards for example—" He indicated the pile of discs before him. "Do they simply predict the future, or do they create it? There is a flash of light. Hiern falls. You assume that the bolt has leapt down to smite him. Viewed from a different perspective, however, the bolt may well have been there all along, with Hiern questing blindly towards it. That being the case, you might just as well accuse a candle of murdering the moth that blunders into its flame.''

Isaf frowned. "What are you talking about?" he said. "Hiern's not dead. I sent him outside just a little while ago.''

"I'm afraid that's impossible," the god told him. "His death is clearly written in the cards." He fingered one of the discs for a moment, then shuffled it neatly back into place. "And what the card fortells must, of necessity, come to pass. Otherwise, why else should they exist?''

"Well, he was alive when I last saw him," Isaf said. "So perhaps you and your bloody cards aren't so clever after all, eh?''

For the first time, the god's face betrayed a shiver of uncertainty. He flipped through the discs once more, apparently deep in thought, then slowly looked up, as if somewhat bemused by what he'd found there. "I fear you may be right," he said. "Which only goes to prove that even I am not entirely omniscient in such matters." He shrugged lightly. "Not that it changes anything, of course. Whether dead or alive, Hiern no longer has any active part to play in this drama of ours—although, I'll admit, it would have been neater had he perished in his allotted place. And kinder, too, I expect. Unless I'm very much mistaken, he shan't have much cause to thank you for what you've done.''

Isaf found the god's soft, measured tones oddly beguiling. "What about Trevayne?" he said, desperately striving to maintain his rage. "And Cayla? I suppose they wanted to die as well, did they?''

"For someone schooled in philosophy," the god said, adopting a wry tone, "you leap to an extraordinary number of conclusions. One should at least try and consider the alternatives, don't you think? Might I not, perhaps, have been incarcerated here by the very Waiting God you and your companions have laboured so strenuously to destroy?

Might not Uroboros just as easily have been my gaoler as
my slave? And might not the stalwart Fjerla have been
posted to keep me in, rather than hold others out? As I said
before, it's purely a matter of perspective.''

"I'm not a complete fool, you know," Isaf said, tossing
his head irritably. "You're just trying to confuse me, that's
all.''

The god chuckled drily. "There's no need," he said.
"You're more than capable of doing that for yourself. Not
that I blame you, of course. It can't be easy, can it? I mean,
there you are, chained hand and foot in a narrow corridor
of time, watching events hurtle endlessly towards you, like
Democritus' atoms tumbling through the void. They coalesce for an instant, buffeting you this way and that; then,
before you can even start to ponder their significance,
they're gone—*poof*!—just like that, disappearing without
a trace into the unfathomable reaches of the past. In the
circumstances, it's only to be expected that you should
become a trifle disoriented on occasions. Why, just look at
your poor friend here—''

Isaf had almost forgotten about Annukin. Head bowed,
his eyes crippled with an all too human anguish and despair,
he gazed down at the blithe, insouciant figure before them
like a penitent waiting to be absolved of some monstrous
crime. He was bleeding badly now, the wound in his side
having opened again (perhaps as a result of their exertions
on the stairway), surrounded by an ever-widening pool of
blood that glittered on the dry, grey flagstones like a sheet
of heraldic stained glass.

"He's gone for good, I'm afraid" the god told him. "Lost
among the memorious architecture of his own brain. Like
so many others, he made the mistake of thinking that just
because he wanted something badly enough, it was certain
to come about. And now that his dreams have been soured,
the poor fellow no longer has anything whatsoever to live
for. It's quite sad really, don't you think? I'm afraid he's
not much use to anyone now, least of all himself." Although
the god's expression remained cool and detached, there was
no mistaking the note of satisfaction in his voice, and it
occurred to Isaf that the fellow may simply have been trying

to delay any possible confrontation until Annukin's strength failed him altogether.

"I've heard enough!" he growled, taking a step closer to the table. Unless he acted soon, the god's relentless sophistry would transfix them both. "It's time we settled this once and for all."

"Quite right," the god said. He put down the disc that he'd been toying with, and folded his hands. "You have something for me, I believe?"

Isaf drew his sword. "Just this."

"Well . . . that, too, I suppose." The god regarded his silver blade with complete indifference. "But I was thinking of something else—something far more important." He motioned towards Isaf's tattered jerkin. "It's in there."

Isaf felt vaguely foolish, as if he were the butt of some elaborate practical joke, or the unwitting dupe lured onstage to assist an illusionist in his cryptic operations. "What the hell are you on about?" he demanded sullenly. "I haven't brought you anything!"

"Oh, but you have, my dear fellow. You have! Otherwise, you wouldn't be here in the first place, now would you? In point of fact, my friend, you are the final link in a chain that stretches back through more centuries that even I care to recall." The god stretched out his hand. "And now," he said, "at long last your destiny is fulfilled. Give me the Numen, Isaf. After all, it's what you were born to do."

"Numen?" The word seemed to echo through Isaf's head like the stroke of a bell. "I've never heard of the bloody thing!"

"That's neither here nor there," the god told him. "What matters is that you have something of mine—something very, very precious to me—and I want it back." Shuffling through his pile of discs, he selected one, apparently at random, and held it up. "Perhaps this will help jog your memory."

Then he turned the disc over—

For all practical purposes, Isaf ceased to exist. That is, he no longer retained any clear conception of his own self; no discrete, unqualified awareness. The sensation was sim-

ilar to that which he'd experienced earlier, on seeing a
fragment of his own past stir to life before his eyes, but a
thousand times more intense, as if he were two different
people occupying wildly disparate points in space and time.
On the one hand, he saw himself attired in the baroque
armour he'd worn twenty-five years before, as a member
of Vellaghar's household guard, spurring his war-horse towards the fray. He gripped his sabre tightly, the blade half-
raised, as if preparing to strike down some unseen enemy,
or recovering from a death-blow that had already been delivered. The other Isaf was clad in bloodstained leather, his
face etched with bewilderment and fatigue, staring uncom-
prehendingly at him through a brazen doorway. Were it not
for the silver sword clutched tightly in his fist, Isaf would
have scarcely believed that they were the same man. Both
seemed equally real, and yet, at the same time, wholly
illusory: like specular images endlessly reflected in a pair
of opposing mirrors.

Somehow he managed to claw his way back into existence. He felt like a shipwrecked mariner scrambling ashore
on some lonely desert island—that island being himself.

Before him, cupped in the god's long, elegant fingers,
lay the portrait of a mounted warrior, virtually identical to
the one that Isaf had seen in Julkrease months before, although then it had been printed on a slip of cheap pasteboard
rather than polished brass. However, unlike the cards he'd
encountered previously, this horseman's countenance was
no mere caricature but a frighteningly accurate reproduction
of Isaf's own.

"I don't understand," he said. "How . . ."

The god smiled indulgently. "Of course you don't understand. That's one of the advantages of being a minor
arcanum. Others aren't quite so fortunate." Placing THE
CATAPHRACT face up on the table, he drew a second
card. "Take THE PRINCEPS, for example."

Very much his father's son, the youth gazed down im-
periously from his octopodal throne. Although there was
little physical resemblance between the two, he'd obviously
inherited a good deal more than the Arbiter's staff and

crown, his eyes glinting with a cold, unimpassioned arrogance that Isaf recognized only too well.

"Oh, you needn't look so surprised. Vellaghar and I are old friends." The god paused for a moment, obviously relishing Isaf's discomfort. "He's watching us, you know, there in his hall of mirrors, no doubt quite appalled at the way events have developed. For a time, he actually imagined himself to be the chessmaster, when all along he was just another pawn in the game. Still, things could be worse, I suppose. At least he's got his health."

More cards followed: THE DEMOGORGON; THE THAUMATURGE; THE JUGGERNAUT; THE CHEMICAL WEDDING; THE MONSTRANCE; THE CELESTIAL FIRE; and a dozen others besides. He saw Annukin chained at the feet of some hideous bat-winged demon; he saw Trevayne dressed in red and yellow motley, grinning at him from behind a trestle strewn with odd theurgic instruments; he saw Fjerla broken beneath the steel-shod wheels of a triumphal car; he saw Cayla gowned in white samite, shyly reciting her nuptial vows; he saw Hiern cradling a silver chalice in his lap; he saw himself as a mere child, wrestling with a playmate beneath the blazing desert sun, each portrayed in such vivid detail that they might have been living faces regarded through some subtle, diminishing lens.

Isaf finally conceded defeat. If he were mad, then his madness was pervasive and absolute, and he could no more hope to extricate himself from its delusions than shatter the chains of nerve and sinew that wedded him to his flesh.

Groping blindly inside his jerkin, he withdrew the tiny mirror that, until now, had always seemed the most trifling and inconsequential of his possessions. In fact, he'd kept it with him all these years more through accident than design, and whatever small sentimental value it may originally have possessed had long since eroded to mere indifference. No doubt, this was the main reason it had survived so long. Had he prized the mirror more highly, or believed for a moment that there was anything in the least remarkable about the thing, he'd have sold it years ago, or else given it away to some chit of girl who happened to take his fancy—

that is, if it hadn't been stolen from him first. Looking down at it now, he saw that the decorative border precisely matched those of the discs arrayed on the table before him.

"Ah!" the god sighed. "At last!" He stretched out his hand, almost quivering with anticipation. "At last I am whole again!"

"It's just a mirror," Isaf said. It was his last line of defence, and a decidedly feeble one. The Waiting God breached it with a single laconic smile.

"Come now," he said, "you know that's not true." Plucking the mirror from Isaf's nerveless fingers, he cradled it lovingly in his hands. "Otherwise, why should I have taken so much trouble to engineer its return? I mean, I'm hardly likely to have brought you all this way for nothing, now am I?"

Isaf shook his head. "Brought me?" he murmured. "But I—"

"Oh, dear me," the god said. "I should have thought it was obvious—even to you." He gestured towards the discs once more. "This, my dear friend, is the crowning moment of your life. You were born to return the Numen—sweating and groaning beneath its weight like an ass bearing gold, never knowing what it was you carried, or where you were headed, but obedient to every prick and spur of the goad. And now, at long last, your journey is at an end. Once we've concluded our business here, you'll be free to trot off and graze on the common along with the rest of the herd."

"But why me?" Isaf asked, numbed by this vision of a grim, mechanistic universe where every human action was shaped by an unseen hand for its own ineluctable purposes; a world stripped bare of such comforting illusions as justice, free will, and the dignity of man. He could almost hear the engines of fate whirring around him, propelling him towards some predetermined end that he neither desired nor understood but was powerless to evade.

The god smiled crookedly. "I have my reasons," he said. "There is, for example, a certain irony in the fact that such a confirmed sceptic as yourself should have been the instrument of my apotheosis. Besides, you're the ones who

insisted on making me a god—it's only to be expected that
I should move in mysterious ways." He gazed at the Numen
for a moment, lost in some meditation. When he looked
up, his face seemed to have assumed a harsher, more sinister
aspect, as if some obscuring veil had suddenly been drawn
aside. "And now," he said, "there remains only one last
task for you to perform. After that you can spend what
remains of your life trying to convince yourself that none
of this ever happened at all."

Isaf frowned. "Task?" he said.

"Oh, something eminently suited to your talents, I should
think," the god told him. "It merely occurred to me that,
while you're here, we might just as well kill two birds with
one stone, so to speak." Still clutching the Numen in his
right hand, he leant forward and selected the card known
as THANATOS, with its grisly reaper amid a field of
corpses. "In a way, it's the very thing you came here to
do in the first place."

Isaf looked down at his sword. "I came to destroy you,"
he muttered quietly.

The god laughed. "Yes, well, that wasn't *quite* what I
had in mind—but you're certainly on the right track." With
the exaggerated delicacy of a headsman composing his victim on the block, he placed the card squarely across THE
DEMOGORGON. "After all, I'm not the only god here,
you know." He glanced towards Annukin, who had now
slumped to his knees, apparently oblivious to what was
taking place around him. "There's your nemesis, my friend.
Kill him, and we can both be free."

Isaf shrank back, appalled. "You must be mad! I've no
quarrel with Annukin."

"But of course you have, my dear fellow. After all, he
let Cayla die, didn't he? Surely that demands some sort of
retribution?"

"It wasn't his fault," Isaf murmured, a pathetic denial
that convinced no one, least of all himself. "You're lying!"

"Am I?" The god held out his hand, revealing the bright,
burnished surface of the Numen. "Here," he said. "See
for yourself."

The mirror seemed to tremble a moment, like a bowl of

quicksilver, then grew strangely opaque. Shadows swirled and writhed within a deeper darkness—analogous, perhaps, to the primal chaos from which all matter had originally descended; the vast, noumenal abyss which, according to some philosophers, constituted the only true reality. As Isaf watched, a familiar landscape took shape before him: no bigger than the palm of his hand, yet possessing all the emotive resonance and preternatural clarity of a waking dream.

He saw a group of figures milling about on a rocky plain, surrounded by hillocks of dry, grey stone. Then the focus shifted slightly, revealing Cayla's pale, terror-stricken face.

Try though he might, Isaf found it impossible to look away. Like a bear chained to the stake, he looked on helplessly as the scene proceeded towards its inevitable conclusion.

Naked, her arms empurpled with bruises, Cayla stared vacantly into space. Fjerl towered above her, a stiletto winking menacingly in his hand. Then the knife plunged down. Isaf could almost feel the sudden stab of pain as it sliced down through her breast, hear the agonized scream as she slumped forward, smell the blood pouring from her ruined flesh. Worst of all, however, was the knowledge that her suffering had only just begun.

"No!" he howled—less a roar of defiance than the cry of some wounded animal. "*No!*"

Now Annukin's face swam into view. Lounging atop a nearby hillock, he was observing the proceedings with a kind of indolent detachment, as if Cayla's death meant nothing to him. To look at his face, one might have thought he was some idle schoolboy watching a spider slowly devour its prey.

"There was nothing he could do," Isaf groaned, but even as he spoke, the scene shifted yet again. He saw Annukin mounted now on his great black stallion, the Fjerla breaking around him like surf around a rock. Calmly, dispassionately, he slaughtered them by the score, his sword a roaring tunnel of flame consuming everything it touched. In the flickering light, both horse and rider were imbued with the heroic grandeur of a statue. No mortal foe, however numerous, could possibly have stood against them.

"He let her die." The words seemed to echo down to Isaf from an immense distance. "Don't you understand? *He let her die!*"

Before Isaf could respond, the mirror suddenly cleared, and he found himself gazing numbly at his own anguished reflection.

"Kill him!" the god said. "Make him pay for what he did!"

"But why?" Isaf murmured. "He had no cause to hate her. Why should he just stand back and let something like that happen?" It was a foolish question, of course, because whys and wherefores weren't important anymore—it was simply a matter of whether he had sufficient strength to disregard the thousand generations of barbarism coursing through his veins, the shrill, ancestral voices that exhorted him to uphold their procrustean laws.

"Who knows?" the god told him. "He may simply have been afraid of allowing himself to care for anyone except himself. He loved a mortal girl once, so I understand, until death stole her from him. Perhaps he was loath to make the same mistake again. Personally, I favour a rather less romantic explanation. After all, he knew full well that you were beginning to have some doubts about the expedition, and, by orchestrating your lady friend's death, he ensured that you had a compelling reason to see the journey through. Fjerl may have wielded the knife, but it was Annukin here who killed her, just as surely as if he'd cut the poor child down with own hand."

There was no denying the god's cold, insidious logic, and Isaf gradually felt his resolve begin to weaken. After all, he was no stranger to vengeance; most of his life had been governed by this single, brutal imperative, this crude approximation of justice that demanded recompense for every injury, no matter how slight, and which allowed a man no other means of affirming his own worth than by constantly subjugating others. Yet still he resisted.

Glancing down at Annukin, he slowly shook his head. "It looks to me as if he's paid a high enough price already.

My killing him isn't going to achieve anything.''

"Fool!" the god hissed. "Don't you see? Unless he dies by the sword—Ceerbunnus' sword—he'll simply return to the well. And then all our efforts will have been in vain!" For a moment his mask slipped, allowing Isaf a glimpse of the grinning death's-head that lay beneath. And yet, at the same time, he realised that this too was a mask, and that the god's true face was the Numen itself, eternally mirroring the very creation which it had somehow brought into being. *"Kill him!* And together we shall refashion the world in a different image!"

Isaf felt the silver blade shift in his hand as it had done at least twice before—although on both occasions he'd steadfastly refused to acknowledge the fact. A mere spectator now, he watched the sword raise itself above his head in preparation for a murderous, double-handed blow that neither man nor god could resist.

"No," Isaf groaned. He tried to hurl the sword aside, but its hilt seemed welded to his flesh. "I won't do it!"

"Oh, but you will, my friend," the god assured him. "The choice is no longer yours to make."

Slowly at first, but gathering speed as it went, the sword toppled relentlessly towards its mark.

Still Isaf struggled to hold it back, to be the master rather than the slave. But it was like trying to restrain a thunderbolt.

Then the sword struck home.

Drained of all hope and strength, Isaf looked down to see what he had done.

There before him, slumped across the stone table like a discarded suit of clothes, the Waiting God grinned triumphantly at him from the wreckage of his butchered face. Rather than blood, a dark, malignant radiance pulsed from the frightful wound that Isaf's sword had carved through his flesh. Fanning out all directions, it cut great swathes through the walls and ceiling, the pale stone dissolving before it like banks of morning mist.

"I knew you wouldn't fail me!" he cried, somehow forming the words without recourse to tongue and lips. "At last I shall take my rightful place in the world, free of the mind-forged manacles that have bound me for so long! Free of all your metaphysics and tiresome observances; the blind tyranny of existence! No longer huddled within the interstices of creation, but eternal, unbounded—FREE!''

By this time, only a few ragged scraps of flesh remained. The god's voice swelled to fill the entire chamber, trumpeting through the heavy air like an anthem, brimming with exultation and a wild, insuperable joy.

"FREE!'' he sang. ''AFTER AN ETERNITY IN CHAINS! *FREE*!''

The tower shuddered. Half the opposing wall had already evaporated like frost in the noonday sun, so that Isaf found himself staring blindly into the night. Sections of roofing tumbled around him like giant snowflakes, melting as they fell.

Casting aside the remnants of his sword (now little more than a blackened stump, the hilt crumbling in his hand like a fistful of ashes), he took hold of Annukin's shoulder and tried to help the fellow to his feet.

"Come on,'' he said. ''Let's get out of here before the damned place falls in on us.''

Annukin shrugged him off. "Let me be.''

The air was thick with falling stone. A section of floor gave way within inches of Isaf's foot. "Don't you understand?'' he said. ''It's over! We've done all we can! Why throw away your life for nothing?''

There was no reply.

"For pity's-sake!'' Isaf said as the tower writhed once more. ''Aren't two deaths enough for you?''

Annukin finally looked up, his face no longer even vaguely reminiscent of a man's. "The Waiting God was right,'' he murmured. ''My time has past. I no longer belong here.''

"But—''

"Just let me be!''

More debris showered down around them. The uppermost portions of the tower had now vanished completely, revealing a broad expanse of open sky. Night sprawled across the heavens like a corpse, stricken with leprous stars. Glancing anxiously over his shoulder, Isaf saw the entire stairway quiver for a moment like water glass.

"Get up, damn you!" Isaf said. "You're coming with me whether you like it or not."

Annukin remained slumped on the flagstones, either unable, or unwilling, to reply.

"All right, you bastard!" Isaf snarled. "Suit yourself!"

Draping the demigod over one shoulder, he turned and fled through the mounting chaos, arms windmilling madly as he struggled to retain his balance. More slabs of masonry started to give way beneath him, but he somehow managed to reach the stairway before it collapsed altogether and, with an inarticulate cry, plunged headlong into the roiling sea of shadows below.

EPILOGUE

AGAINST ALL ODDS, they made it out alive.

Behind them the tower evaporated like a half-forgotten dream. Shafts of cold black light streamed from the deliquescent stone, snuffing out the stars and plunging Isaf into a darkness scarcely less impenetrable than that residing within his own soul.

He staggered blindly on until weariness and despair finally brought him to his knees. It seemed futile to struggle further. Their horses, no doubt, had fled long ago, and without adequate provisions, there was little hope of him negotiating the barren wasteland that stretched, unseen, for a hundred miles in every direction. Even if he did survive, who could say what fresh torments the future might hold in store for him? Perhaps Annukin had been right after all—perhaps it was better to die rather than endure a life purchased only at the cost of unrelieved misery and countless petty betrayals. The platitudes which he'd mouthed so blithely on the stairway returned to mock him. *Any fool can die: it's far more painful to live*. How presumptuous he'd been, how insufferably smug and condescending. It was a wonder the fellow hadn't laughed in his face.

How long he knelt there, cradling Annukin gently in his arms, Isaf had no idea. Eventually, however, he was roused by the sound of approaching footsteps, and looked up to see Hiern striding through the darkness towards him, a makeshift torch spluttering fitfully in one hand.

"Isaf?" Hiern hesitated a moment, then lurched forward once more, legs pumping furiously beneath the tattered black shadow of his cloak. "Isaf!" he cried. "I've been looking everywhere—I thought—" Catching sight of Annukin, he skittered to a halt, gazing down at the fallen demigod with such unabashed concern that Isaf found it hard to believe he was the same man who just a short time before had stalked his own destruction with all the persistence of a trained assassin. He seemed younger somehow, his wide, brown eyes filled with an uncharacteristic innocence and compassion.

"Is he all right?" Hiern asked.

Isaf shrugged. Annukin's flesh had never been anything more than a disguise, a gilded carapace which revealed little of the arcane spirit housed within it. Looking at him now, there was no way of telling whether he was dead or simply asleep—if, indeed, there existed any valid distinction between the two as far as he was concerned. Blood still trickled from his wounded side, but otherwise he displayed no sign of life whatsoever. A strange, cloying scent pervaded the air around him, like the smell of rotting flowers. "I think he wants to die," Isaf said. "Only he doesn't know how."

"Come on," Hiern told him. "I managed to get a fire going. Perhaps he'll be more comfortable there."

"Comfortable?" Even by Hiern's standards, it seemed a remarkably foolish thing to say. "What that hell has *that* got to do with anything?" Isaf shook his head. "For gods'-sake, man, don't you understand? The poor sod's finished—and so are we!"

"Still—" Hiern shifted his feet uneasily, looking so utterly forlorn that Isaf immediately regretted his outburst.

"Oh, very well." Hauling himself up, he took hold of Annukin's shoulders, motioning for Hiern to help him. "Here," he said. "Give us a hand."

With Annukin slung between them, they shuffled off into the gloom, headed towards the far side of the tower. At first, the going was comparatively easy. Although Hiern's torch provided no more light than a single guttering candle, they could still see well enough to avoid tripping over each other's feet. After a while, however, the terrain grew steadily more rugged and uneven. Piles of loose, crumbling earth reared up to block their path, and on numerous occasions Isaf found it all but impossible to retain his footing as he clambered over the many shallow embankments that criss-crossed this section of the plain.

"Watch your step," Hiern told him, which Isaf considered rather superfluous—he'd been doing precious little else for the past quarter of an hour. "Whoever dug those other shafts has been at work around here as well. They're not always easy to see in the dark."

This too proved something of an understatement. Time and again, Isaf only just managed to avoid plummeting to his death as a series of huge, gaping pits opened in the rock before him. He counted scores of them, scattered among the debris like so many plundered graves. Recalling the entombed warriors that Isaf had seen on his way to the tower, he suspected that may have been exactly what they were.

Just when Isaf was beginning to think that Hiern must have lost his bearings completely and was leading them around in circles, he noticed a faint, ruddy glow in the distance.

"Almost there," Hiern said, gesturing awkwardly with one elbow. "It's just the other side of this hillock."

Isaf, who could see nothing between themselves and the fire except a mass of undifferentiated shadows, retained a weary silence. Either Hiern's eyes were sharper than his, or else the fellow was simply making things up—either way, Isaf had little choice but to continue as he'd begun, stumbling blindly along in the other's wake. After all, it wasn't as if he had anywhere else to go. Readjusting his grip on Annukin's shoulders, he trudged on, content to have at last been provided with a firm direction in which to proceed.

After toiling through the darkness for what seemed like hours, they finally arrived at a small clearing, roughly el-liptical in shape and surrounded by heaps of rubble and volcanic slag. Apparently the treasure hunters had considered this a highly propitious site for their excavations. At least a dozen shafts had been opened in the floor of the clearing, some no bigger than a barrel-head, others wide enough to have accommodated Uroboros itself. Beside one of these pits lay the remains of Hiern's fire, now little more than a handful of smoking embers. What light it did produce seemed to augment rather than dispel the starless void around them, so that Isaf felt as if he were entering some stark, torchlit chamber buried deep beneath the earth: some crypt that had been waiting for him all his life, and from which he lacked both the ability and the resolve to ever escape.

Isaf wondered if perhaps the three of them were dead already, only they just hadn't noticed it yet.

"All right," Hiern said, gingerly poking his way towards the fire. "Just set him down for a moment while I stoke up the fire."

Isaf helped deposit Annukin on a patch of sandy ground close to the shaft, then sat back on his haunches while Hiern collected some pieces of dry, splintered timber that lay nearby and tossed them onto the fire. They ignited almost immediately, sending plumes of dense black smoke coiling up into the night.

"There!" Hiern said, gazing approvingly at his handiwork. "That's better, isn't it?"

Isaf shrugged. "I suppose so."

Hiern squatted down beside him, like a thin and strangely avid shadow. "Well?" he asked. "What do we do now?"

"Do?" Isaf stared glumly into the fire. "I don't know. Just sit back and see what the morning brings, I suppose."

"At least there's plenty of water around here," Hiern told him, indicating the yawning shaft beside them. Now that the darkness had receded somewhat, Isaf could see a wooden ladder jutting up above one edge. "That ought to keep us going for a while."

Isaf shrugged. "Maybe so, but I still don't much fancy our chances of making it out of here alive."

Hiern's newfound enthusiasm, however, was not so easily dampened. "You never know," he said. "Something might turn up. Once it's light, we can start looking for the horses.

I don't suppose they can have strayed too far in a place like this.''

Isaf said nothing. He felt tired and hungry, aching in every sinew and terrified of the dreams that might come when he finally slept. Silence closed in around them like a deadening shroud until, it seemed, Hiern could restrain himself no longer. He hunched forward, his fingers knotted awkwardly in his lap.

"What happened, anyway?" he asked diffidently. "In the tower, I mean. Did you find what you were looking for or not?"

Although Hiern's tone seemed quite congenial, Isaf realised only too well where the conversation was headed, and gazed steadfastly at the fire, half-afraid of the hunger he might see in the man's eyes if he looked up. "Oh, yes," he muttered. "We found him all right."

"And?"

To be honest, Isaf scarcely knew himself. His encounter with the Waiting God had already begun to assume a hazy, unreal quality, as if it were something he'd read about, or been told, years before, rather than actually experienced for himself. He recalled the basic sequence of events clearly enough, but was unable to place them in any logical context, so that he felt like a child trying to assemble the pieces of some complicated puzzle whose proper configuration he neither recognized nor understood. Nevertheless, he felt obliged to say something. Surely Hiern deserved at least that much.

Haltingly Isaf described the bizarre encounter that had taken place atop the tower. Only towards the end did he stray significantly from the truth—or what he perceived to be the truth—having no intention of sharing Cayla's death-agony with anyone. Nor did he particularly care to dissect the complex interplay of hatred, compassion, understanding, and revenge that had led him to spare one god and slay another: perhaps for fear that he still might find some cause to regret his decision.

What Hiern made of all this, he had no idea. Even to his own ears, it sounded patently ridiculous, a clumsy fabrication that bore little or no resemblance to what had actually transpired. The fellow, however, listened as if spellbound, constantly nodding his head and interrupting from time to time to clarify some point that, as far as Isaf was concerned, seemed no more or less baffling than any of the others: *How had the Waiting God known their names? What had he looked like? Why should Annukin have expected to find his father in the tower? What was so special about Isaf's mirror? Why couldn't the Waiting God kill Annukin himself? Why did the tower suddenly fall apart?* He evaded these questions as best he could. Little that he'd seen or heard in the tower made any sense at all, and almost none of it bore thinking about too closely.

Hiern had no such reservations.

"So we did it," he murmured. If there was any satisfaction in his voice, it had been purchased at so great a cost as to be indistinguishable from grief. "He's dead."

Before Isaf could reply, the memory of his last, despairing confrontation with the Waiting God struck him like an actual blow, brushing aside his meagre defences and reminding him (as if he needed any reminder) just how hollow their victory had been. For a moment, the two stood face to face once more, Isaf's sword arcing down between them like a thunderbolt. He heard the god's gleeful laughter as the blade struck home, saw the darkness stream from his shattered corpse, spearing out through the tower and casting a pall of shadow across the stars like some vast, predatory bird enfolding the earth in its wings.

"No," he said quietly. "No, I don't think so."

Hiern's shoulders slumped. "Then it was all for nothing. Everything we went through to get here, everything we suffered along the way—*for nothing!*"

"We did our best," Isaf told him. It was scant consolation, but better than none at all. "And, in any case, he's gone. I don't know where, exactly. Or how. But he's gone. At least that's something."

"Yes, but—" Hiern stopped, suddenly directing his gaze to a patch of sky somewhere above Isaf's left shoulder. "Isaf," he said. "Isaf, look!"

Turning, Isaf noticed a faint glimmer of silver in the East. At first he thought the stars were coming out; then the light began to swell, casting a cold, baleful luminescence across the plain.

"What is it?" Hiern asked. "What's happening?"

Isaf dared not answer, dared not put into words what both of them, in their hearts, already knew: that the world they had helped bring into being was finally acquiring its presiding spirit, and that nothing—*nothing*—would ever be the same again.

Annukin must have sensed it, too. He shuddered in his sleep, clenching his hands as if he could feel something indefinitely precious slipping from his grasp. Not life, or strength, or hope—all of which, no doubt, he would have relinquished without a qualm—but rather, perhaps, the subtle weft of dreams, common to man and god alike, that made such lives and dreams possible in the first place.

We are all outcasts now, Isaf thought. *Every last one of us. And we always will be.*

Suddenly he felt tears coursing down his cheeks. He wept for Cayla, for Trevayne, for Annukin, for Hiern, for a steel-eyed swordsman and a slaughtered king, for everyone, everywhere—both long-dead and as yet unborn—who, like him, were doomed to be bound and broken on the agonising rack of being.

When he next looked up, the light had begun to swell even further, lifting itself above the horizon like the ravaged, pockmarked face of some ancient torturer peering down at his victims from the top of an oubliette.

There was a bad moon on the rise.

Australian science fiction writer ANDREW WHITMORE
was born in Melbourne and early on developed an interest
in science and ancient history. While still an undergraduate,
he attended the first Australian science fiction writing work-
shop, which was run in conjunction with the Melbourne
World Science Fiction Convention, and hosted by Ursula
K. LeGuin.

Since earning his B.A. in Literature and Ancient History
from Monash University, Mr. Whitmore has won the William Atheling Award for best Australian science fiction criticism and the Ditmar Award for best Australian short fiction.
Currently he resides in a small town in western Victoria
with his wife and two daughters. *The Fortress of Eternity*
is his first novel.